PRAISE FOR *BOOK OF NUMBERS*

"This is an astounding undertaking. In *Book of Numbers* the wizardly Joshua Cohen relocates the line between tragedy and comedy. His lurid and high-achieving characters create and suffer the Internet—which is now tightening around us all. I don't know of any other work like this one." —Norman Rush

"Joshua Cohen's *Book of Numbers* is a lot of things—a disquisition on and aping of the Internet, a dissection of friendship and romance in the Digital Age, and a doppelgänger tale—but for me it's most poignant as an elegy for the written word, and as a rebuke to its decline."

—Joshua Ferris, author of *To Rise Again at a Decent Hour*

"Joshua Cohen is one of the most intelligent, witty, and moving writers we have, and *Book of Numbers* is his most magnificent and ambitious book. This novel illuminates the mysterious and near-invisible landscape of right now."

—Rivka Galchen, author of *American Innovations*

"There once was a time Before Computers—a second B.C.—that we're now using our computers to delete: a time before e-mail, msgs, apps, and urls, when privacy wasn't a setting and attachments were to people, when search meant finding something in the real world, and being connected meant you weren't alone. These are some of the things I was reminded of while reading Joshua Cohen's brilliant *Book of Numbers*, the single best novel yet written about what it means to remain human in the Internet Era." —Adam Ross

PRAISE FOR JOSHUA COHEN

"To sum this up in Web terms, he'll make you want to be an angel investor in his stuff. What's a book but a public offering? You'll want to be in on the ground floor." —Dwight Garner, *The New York Times*

"Intelligent, lyrical, prosaic, theoretical, pragmatic, funny, serious . . . [Cohen's] best prose does everything at once." —*The New Yorker*

"Cohen, a key member of the United States' under- 40 writers' club (along with Nell Freudenberger and Jonathan Safran Foer), is a rare talent who makes highbrow writing fun and accessible." —*Marie Claire*

"In Mr. Cohen's hands, a meme is a matter of life and death, because he goes from the reality we all know—the link, the click—to the one we tend to forget: the human. . . . Mr. Cohen is ambitious. He is mapping terra incognita."

—*The New York Observer*

"Like [David Foster] Wallace, Cohen is clearly concerned with the depersonalizing effects of technology, broken people doing depraved things, and how the two intersect in tragic (and, sometimes, hilarious) ways." —*The Boston Globe*

ALSO BY JOSHUA COHEN

Four New Messages

Witz

A Heaven of Others

Cadenza for the Schneidermann Violin Concerto

BOOK OF NUMBERS

0011100000101111001100100011011100111111100100000000110010001110000011111100100000001110100011101110110111100100000011001000110000101111001011100110010000011001100100000011000100110010101100110011011110111001001100101001000000110010101101110011001000010000001101111011001100010000000101001001100001011011010110
[illegible]

0100BOOK0OF0NU
MBERS1001101A
11NOVEL101JOSH
UA10COHEN1111
HARVILL011SECKER
0110LONDON0110

1 3 5 7 9 10 8 6 4 2

Harvill Secker, an imprint of Vintage,
20 Vauxhall Bridge Road,
London SW1V 2SA

Harvill Secker is part of the Penguin Random House group of companies
whose addresses can be found at global.penguinrandomhouse.com.

First published in the UK by Harvill Secker in 2015
Published in the United States by Random House in 2015

www.vintage-books.co.uk

A CIP catalogue record for this book is available from the British Library

ISBN 9781846558658

Printed and bound by Clays Ltd, St Ives plc

Book design by Simon M. Sullivan

CONTENT

1

But as for you, your carcases, they shall fall in this wilderness. And your children shall wander in the wilderness forty years, and bear your whoredoms, until your carcases be wasted in the wilderness. After the number of days in which ye searched the land, even forty days, each day for a year, shall ye bear your iniquities, even forty years, and ye shall know my breach of promise.

—NUMBERS 14:32–34, KING JAMES VERSION

And your corpses you will fall in this desert. And your children will be of shepherds in the desert 40 years and will support your prostitution/adultery until the perfection/destruction of your corpses in the desert. In the number of days you searched the land 40 days the day to the year the day to the year you will support your poverty/violation 40 years and you will know my opposition/pretext.

—NUMBERS 14:32–34, TRANSLATION BY TETRANS.TETRATION.COM/#HEBREW/ENGLISH

8/27? 28? TWO DAYS BEFORE END OF RAMADAN

If you're reading this on a screen, fuck off. I'll only talk if I'm gripped with both hands.

Paper of pulp, covers of board and cloth, the thread from threadstuff or—what are bindings made of? hair and plant fibers, glue from boiled horsehooves?

The paperback was compromise enough. And that's what I've become: paper spine, paper limbs, brain of cheapo crumpled paper, the final type that publishers used before surrendering to the touch displays, that bad thin four-times-deinked recycled crap, 100% acidfree postconsumer waste.

I have very few books with me here—*Hitler's Secretary: A Firsthand Account, Benjamin Franklin: An American Life,* whatever was on the sales table at Foyles on Charing Cross Road, and in the langues anglais section of the FNAC on the Rue de Rennes—books I'm using as models, paragons of what to avoid.

I'm writing a memoir, of course—half bio, half autobio, it feels—I'm writing the memoir of a man not me.

It begins in a resort, a suite.

I'm holed up here, blackout shades downed, drowned in loud media, all to keep from having to deal with yet another country outside the window.

If I'd kept the eyemask and earplugs from the jet, I wouldn't even have to describe this, there's nothing worse than description: hotel room prose. No, characterization is worse. No, dialogue is. Suffice it to say that these pillows are each the size of the bed I used to share in NY. Anyway this isn't quite a hotel. It's a cemetery for people both deceased and on vacation, who still check in daily with work.

As for yours truly, I've been sitting with my laptop atop a pillow on my lap to keep those wireless hotspot waveparticles from reaching my genitals and frying my sperm, searching up—with my employer's technology—myself, and Rach.

My wife, my ex, my "x2b."

\

Living by the check, by the log—living remotely, capitalhopping, skipping borders, jumping timezones, yet always with that equatorial chain of blinking beeping messages to maintain, what Principal calls "the conversation"—it gets lonely.

For the both of us.

Making tours of the local offices, or just of overpriced museums to live in. Claridge's, Hôtel de Crillon. Meeting with British staff to discuss removing the UK Only option from the homepage. Meeting French staff to discuss the .fr launch of Autotet. Granting angel audiences to the CEOs of Yalp and Ilinx. Being pitched, but not catching, a new parkour exergame and a betting app for fantasy rugby.

This was micromanaging, microminimanaging. Nondelegation, demotion (voluntary), absorption of duties (insourcing), dirtytasking. All of them at once. In the lexicon of the prevailing techsperanto.

This was Principal spun like a boson just trying to keep it, keep everything, together.

At least until Europe was behind us and we could stay ensuite, he could stay seated, in interviews with me. Between the naps, interviewing for me.

You call the person you're writing "the principal" and mine is basically the internet, the web—that's how he's positioned, that's how he's converged: the man who helped to invent the thing, rather the man who helped it to invent us, in the process shredding the hell out of the paper I've dedicated my life to. Though don't for a moment assume he regards it as, what? ironic or wry? that now, at our mutual attainment of 40 (his birthday just behind him, mine just ahead), he's feeling the urge to put his life down in writing, into writing on paper.

He has no time for irony or wryness. He has time for only himself.

\

cant wait 4 wknd, Rach updates.

margaritas tonite #maryslaw

ever time i type divorce i type deforce (still trying 2 serve papers)

read that my weights the same as hers—feelingood til the reveal: shes 2 inches taller—ewwww!!

"She" who was two inches taller was a model, and though Rach's in advertising I never expected her to be just as public, to enjoy such projections.

To be sure, she enjoys them anonymously.

My last stretch in NY I'd been searching "Rachava Cohen-Binder," finding the purest professionalism—her profile at her agency's site—searching "Rachava Binder," getting inundated with comments she'd left on a piece of mine ("Journalism Criticizing the Web, Popular on the Web," *The New York Times*). It was only in Palo Alto that I searched "Rachav Binder" and "Rach Binder," got an undousable flame of her defense of an article of mine critical of the Mormon Church's databasing of Holocaust victims in order to speed their posthumous conversions ("Net Costs," *The Atlantic*), and finally it was either in London or Paris, I forget, because I was trashed, that I, on a trashy whim, searched "Teva Café Detroit MI," but the results suggested I'd meant "*Tevazu* Café Detroit MI"—cyber chastisement for having incorrectly spelled the place where I'd proposed with ring on bended knee.

One site—and one site alone—had made that same spelling mistake, though, and when I clicked through I found others even graver:

a-bintel-b was a blog, hosted by a platform developed by my employer, which is more famous for having developed the search engine—the one everyone uses to find everyone else, movie times, how to fix my TV tutorials, is this herpes? how much does Gisele Bündchen weigh?

Though her accounts lack facts—and Majuscules, and punctuation—

I haven't been able to stop reading, can't stop reminding myself that what I read was written in my, in our, apartment. Between the walls, which have been redone a univeige, a cosmic latte shade—the floors have similarly been buffed of my traces.

I wasn't ready to get reacquainted with the old young flirty Rach. Not on this blog, which she began in the summer, just after we severed, and especially not while I was estranged abroad, in London, Paris, Dubai as of this morning—if it's Sunday it must be Dubai—with Principal negotiating the dunespace for a datacenter.

Apparently.

\

Remember that old joke, let's set it in an airport, at the security checkpoint, when a guard asks to inspect a bag, opens the bag, and removes from it a suspicious book.

"What's it about?" he asks.

And the passenger answers, "About 500 pages!!!!"

Contracted as of two weeks ago, due in four months. Simultaneous hardcover release in six languages, 100,000 announced first printing (US), my name nowhere on it, in a sense.

As of now all I have is its title, which is also the name of its author, which is also the name of his ghost.

Me, my own.

Though my contract with Principal has a confidentiality clause—beyond that, a clause that forbids my mentioning our confidentiality clause, another barring me from disclosing that, and yet another barring me from going online, I assume for life—I can't help myself (Rach and I might still have a thing or two in common):

I, Joshua Cohen, am writing the memoir of the Joshua Cohen I'm always mistaken for—the incorrect JC, the error msg J. The man whose business has ruined my business, whose pleasure has ruined my pleasure, whose name has obliviated my own.

Disambiguation:

Did you mean *Joshua Cohen*? The genius, googolionaire, Founder and CEO of Tetration.com, as of now—datestamped 8/27, timecoded 22:12

Central European Summer Time—hits #1 through #324 for "Joshua Cohen" on Tetration.com.

Or *Joshua Cohen*? The failed novelist, poet, husband and son, pro journalist, speechwriter and ghostwriter, as of now—datestamped 8/28, timecoded 00:14 Gulf Standard Time—hit #325 "my" highest ranking on Tetration.com.

#325 mentions my first book—the book I'm writing this book, my last, to forget. The book that everyone but me already buried. Also I'm trying to earn better money, this time, at the expense of identity. Rach, my support, had been keeping me in both.

But it was only after my session with Principal today—two Joshes just joshing around in the Emirates—that I decided to write this.

Coming back from Principal's orchidaceous suite to my own chandeliered crèmefest of an accommodation, alive with talk and perked on caffeines, I realized that the only record of my one life would be this record of another's. That as the wrong JC it was up to me and only me to tell them to stop—to tell Rach to stop searching for her husband (I'm here), to tell my mother to stop searching for her son (I'm here), to send my regrets to you both and remember you, Dad—I'm hoping to get together, all on the same page.

://

10 years ago this September, 10 Arab Muslims hijacked two airplanes and flew them into the Twin Towers of my Life & Book. My book was destroyed—my life has never recovered.

And so it was, the End before the beginning: two jets fueled with total strangers, terrorists—two of whom were Emirati—bombing my career, bombing me personally. And now let me debunk all the conspiracies: George W. Bush didn't have the towers taken down with controlled demolitions, the FAA didn't take its satellites offline to let the jets fly over NY airspace unimpeded, the Israeli government didn't withhold intel about what was going to happen (all just to have a pretext for another Gulf War), and as for the theory that no Jews died or were even harmed in the attacks—what am I? what was this?

That day was my final page, my last word, ellipses . . . ellipses . . . period—closing the covers on all my writing, all my rewriting, all my investments of all the money my father had left me and my mother had loaned me in travel, computer equipment/support, translation help, and research materials (Moms never let me repay my loans).

I'd worried for months, fretted for years, checked thesauri and dictionaries for other verbs I could do, I'd paced. I couldn't sleep or wake, fantasized best, worst, and average case scenarios. Working on a book had been like being pregnant, or like planning an invasion of Poland. To write it I'd taken a parttime job in a bookstore, I'd taken off from my parttime job in the bookstore, I'd lived cheaply in Ridgewood and avoided my friends, I'd been avoided by friends, procrastinated by spending noons at the Battery squatting alone on a boulder across from a beautiful young paleskinned blackhaired mother rocking a stroller back and forth with a fetish boot while she read a book I pretended was mine, hoping that her baby stayed sleeping forever or at least until I'd finished the thing its mother was reading—I'd been finishing it forever—I'd just finished it, I'd just finished and handed it in.

I handed it to my agent, Aaron, who read it and loved it and handed it to my editor, Finnity, who read it and if he didn't love it at least accepted it and cut a check the size of a page—which he posted to Aar who took his percentage before he posted the remainder to me—before he, Finnity, scheduled the publication for "the holidays" (Christmas), which in the publishing industry means scheduled for a season before "the holidays" (Christmas), to be set out front in the fall at whatever non-chain bookstores were at the time being replaced by chain bookstores about to be replaced by your preferred online retailer. The book, my book, to be stuffed into a stocking hanging so close to the fire that it would burn before anyone had the chance to read it, which was, essentially, what happened.

Finnity, then, edited—it wasn't the book yet, just a manuscript—handed, manhandled it, back to me. The edits had to be argued about, debated. I was incensed, I recensed, reedited in a manner that reoriginated my intentions, then when it was all recompleted and done again and my prose and so my sanity intact I passed the ms. back to Finnity who sent it to production (Rod?), who turned it into proofs he sent to Finnity who printed and sent them to me, who recorrected them again, subtracting a word here, adding a chapter there, before returning them to Finnity who sent them to a copyeditor (Henr*y*?), who copyedited and/or proofread them (Henr*i*?), then sent them to production (Rod?), who after inputting the changes had galleys printed and bound with the cover art (photograph of a synagogue outside Chełm converted into a granary, 1941, Anonymous, © United States Holocaust Museum), the jacket/frontflap copy I wrote myself, not to mention the bio, which I wrote myself too, and the publicity photo for the backflap (© I. Raúl Lindsay), which I posed for, hands in frontpockets moody, within a tenebrous archway of the Manhattan Bridge. All that, including the blurbs obtained from Elie Wiesel and Dr. Ruth Westheimer, being sent out to the critics four months before date of publication (by Kimi! my publicist!), four months commonly considered enough time for critics to read it or not and prose their own hatreds, meaning that galleys, softcover, were posted in spring, mine delivered around the middle of May—tripping over that package left in my vestibule by a courier either lazy or trusting—though I held a finished copy only in mid-August—after I insisted on nitpicking through the text once again in the hopes of hyphen-removal—when Aar sent to Ridgewood two paramedics who stripped off their uniforms to practice CPR on each other, then gave me a defibrillatory lapdance and a deckled hardcover.

Every September the city has that nervy crisp air, that new season briskness: new films in the theaters where after a season of explosions serious black and white actors have sex against the odds and subplot of a crumbling apartheid regime, the new concert season led by exciting new conductors with wild floppy hair and big capped teeth premiering new repertoire featuring the debuts of exciting new soloists of obscure nationalities (an Ashkenazi/Bangladeshi pianist accompanying a fiery redheaded Indonesian violinist in *Fiddler on the Hurūf*), new galleries with new exhibitions of unwieldy mixedmedia installations (*Climate Change Up:* a cloud seeded with ballot chad), new choreography on new themes (*La danse des tranches, ou pas de derivatives*), new plays on and off Broadway featuring TV actresses seeking stage cred to relaunch careers playing characters dying of AIDS or dyslexia.

September's also the time of new books coming out, of publication parties held at new lounges, new venues. Which was why on that free-floating Monday after Labor Day, with the city returned to itself rested and tanned, my publisher gathered my friends, frenemies, writers, in the type of emerging neighborhood that magazines and newspapers were always underpaying them to christen.

Understand, on my first visits to NY the Village had just been split between East and West. SoHo went, so there had to be NoHo. When I first moved to the city the realestate pricks were scamming the editors into helping reconfigure the outerboroughs too, turning Brooklyn, flipping Queens, for zilch in return, only the displacement of minorities despite their majority. At the time of my party, Silicon Alley had just been projected along Broadway, in glassed steel atop the Flatiron—each new shadow of each new tower being foreshadowed initially in language (sarcastic language).

Call this, then, as I called it, TriPackFast: the four block triangle north of the Meatpacking District but south of the barred lots for Edison Park-Fast. Or Teneldea: the grim gray area beginning where 10th Avenue switches from southbound to northbound traffic and ending where the elevated rail viaduct crosses that avenue just past the NY offices of the Drug Enforcement Administration.

A pier, jutting midway between where the Lusitania departed and the Titanic never arrived, where steamers and schooners had anchored to unload the old riches of the Old World like gold and silver and copper slaves, before wealth turned from tangible goods and favorable tradewinds to a matter of clicking buttons—where the newest warehouses were filled with "cultural capital"—where "money," which was still silver in French (*argent*) and gold in German (*Geld*), had become a gentrified abstraction.

A purposefully unreconstructed but rebranded wreckage harbored on the Hudson—the interior resembled a ruin, a rusted halfgutted rectilinear spanse. Hangaresque, manufacturingesque. Previously a drydock, formerly a ropery. Had it just been built, it would've been a marvel—the type of modern design that architects and engineers torment themselves over, the natural course of things achieved by falling apart: foundation issues, an irresolvable roof, problems with the electric and plumbing.

A table was set, laid with midpriced wine to be poured not into plastic cups but glass glasses, that's how intensely my publisher was investing in me, offering red and white and, blushing, trays of stinky chèvres and goudas, muensters, gruyères, a dozen varieties of crackers, veggie stix 'n' dip, sexual clusters of muscats, sultanas, ruby grapes without seed, selections of meze with pita.

A trio performed klezmer, or rehearsed it, a screechy avantklez that didn't distinguish between rehearsal and performance: a trumpeter, bass, drums, soloing always in that order.

Copies of the book were piled into pyramids? ziggurats? but ziggs are goyish, the pyramids are for the Jews.

The press began arriving, all my future peers, my colleagues. The newspaper people, the dailies, a half hour fashionable. The magazine people, the weeklies, the monthlies, an hour. Aaron's joke: the longer the leadtime, the later they showed. A cymbal tsked. The bass followed a note and stayed with it, not a note so much as a low throb, as if it were the guest of honor everybody felt they had to notice but nobody much liked to be stuck with, just the excuse for all the busyness swirling—that guest was me, terrified.

I was uncomfortably complimented in my suit, the suit that'd needed shoes, the shoes that'd needed socks, belt, shirt, tie—the only thing I'd already owned was the underwear.

The mic was taken from the trumpeter, tapped. Wine courtesy of Pequot Vintners, beer from Masholu, please join me in thanking our generous sponsors—that was Kimi!

Everyone applauded, drowning her introduction of Finnity.

My book was called "a migrant story," "a quintessential American tale"—inheritance of loss, bequest of suffering transmitted genetically, the people of the book, after millennia of literacy, interpretation, commentary, the book of the people of the book, at the end of the shelf of the century.

Finnity, all prepped, Harvard vowels and Yale degree, tweedly, leatherpatched not just at elbow but also at shoulder—he would've worn patches on his knees, on his khakis. He mispronounced *tzedakah,* "said ache a," misused *tshuvah,* "a concern for Israel in the guise of a tissueba," mentioned the Intifadas, all zealotry being inherently suicidal, democratic pluralisms, Zionisms plural, concluded by saying in conclusion twice, "It's the testimony of two generations," everyone nodded, "a witness to one America under or over God, with or without God," and everyone nodded again and clapped.

It was his honor, publishing me.

I dragged up to the front like a greenhorn with a trunk and Finnity went to hug or kiss and I went to shake his hand.

I gave a speech—and the speech was my Acknowledgments (the book itself didn't have any). I had a lot of people to thank. My mother, for one, who fled Poland, for giving me the money to travel to Poland, only so I could write a book about her life. (I left the inheritance from my father out of it—spent.)

I thanked my Tante Idit and Onkel Menashe, whom I visited and interviewed in Israel, and my cousin Tzila, who drove me directly from a Tel Aviv club to a shabby Breslov minyan in Jerusalem so I could interrogate a former block commander who'd been interrogated before by better, the obscurer relations, honorary inlaws, and strangers who'd responded to my letters from Kraków, Warsaw, Vienna, Graz, Prague, Bratislava, the good people of Los Angeles, and of Texas, Florida, and Maine (survivors), the faculties of Harvard, Yale, and Columbia, and the stern lady clerks of the Polish State Archives, who helped me sift cadastral registries, deportation manifests, and Zyklon B inventories, who not only confirmed Moms's memories—the color of a hat ribbon or shoelace, the flavor of the cream between favorite wafers—but who gave them flesh and future too—the location of Gruntig's butcher stand (by the mikvah, on what became the corner of Walecznych and Proletariuszy Streets), the fate of schoolfriend Sara (Cuba, aneurysm)—assisting with the granular details: how many grams of bread my uncles were allotted in what camp on what dates, how many liters of soup were allotted per prisoner per week/month in what camp vs. the amount on average delivered. How my grandparents last embraced in Zgody Square, Kraków ghetto, 10/28/42, 10:00.

Appreciated—and when I was finished everyone stormed to congratulate me, shake my hand, and Caleb nodded, from a huddle of girls, and Aaron nodded too, gesturing for a smoke above a scrim of critics, reviewers. Someone congratulated me by hugging and kissing and someone said, "Introduce me to your mother." But Moms wasn't in attendance, she hadn't been invited. "She wouldn't have enjoyed it—this isn't exactly her crowd."

I leaned between brass poles, velvet suspended into satisfied smiles. Aar sparked a joint and we smoked it and the air was gassy and my suit was wool and Cal filed out with the girls.

We stumbled down 10th in celebration, or observance—in memoriam—afterparties bearing the same relationship to parties as the afterlife to life. Straggling to get cash, to get cigs and a handle of vodka, to decipher the Spanish on a wall shrine to a child shot or stabbed, to do chinups on new condo construction scaffolding.

Gansevoort Street: everything smelled like meat and disinfectant. The bouncer was a big black warty dyke bound in leather and chains, checking IDs, grabbing wrists so as to break them, to stamp the back of the hand and someone said, "This is like the Holocaust," and someone said, "The Holocaust wasn't airconditioned neither."

Behind the bar were crushed photographs of the uniformed: cops, firefighters, Catholic schoolgirls. Businesscards between the slats, as if phone fax email were all that held the walls together, all that fused the landfilled island.

The bartender served Cal and me our sodas and we took them to a banquette in the back to mix in the vodka while Aar ordered a whiskey or scotch and while it was being fixed wound his watch and left a bill atop a napkin and left.

Someone had the hiccups, someone slipped on sawdust.

Kimi! publicized by the banquette:

"The deal is the publisher's picking up the tab for beers and wines," and Cal said, "Why didn't you say so?" and Kimi! said, "How many do you need?" and Cal counted how many girls we were sitting with and said, "We need six of both," and Kimi! snorted and Cal stood to go with her, but instead they went to the bathroom.

I had to go to the bathroom too. But all of college was crammed into the stall, Columbia University class of 1992, with a guy whose philosophy essays I used to write, now become an iBanker, let's call him P. Sachs, or Philip S., sitting not on the seat but up on the tank, with the copy of my book I'd autographed for him on his lap—"To P.S., with affect(at)ion" rolling a $100 bill, tapping out the lines to dust the dustjacket, offering Cal and Kimi! bumps off the blurbs, offering me.

"Cocaine's gotten better since the Citigroup merger."

A knock, a peremptory bouncer's fist, and the door's opened to another bar, yet another—but which bars we, despite half of us being journalists, wouldn't recollect: that dive across the street, diving into the street and lying splayed between the lanes. Straight shots by twos, picklebacks. Well bourbons chasing pabsts. Beating on the jukebox for swallowing our quarters. "This jukebox swallows more than your mother." "Swallows more than The Factchecker."

The Factchecker changed by the party, the season. Any fuckable female publishing professional could be The Factchecker—if it could be proven that she was between the ages of 18 and 26, and that she had fucked precisely zero people since arriving in NY.

Last call was called, and Kimi! went up to tab bourbon doubles for us and for herself a gin and tonic and Cal and I drank ours and even hers and shared a cig between us and my mouth tasted like nickels, like dimes, and my gums needed a haircut.

The lights went up, the jukebox down, I hurled a cueball at the dartboard—Finnity had left with The Factchecker, Cal asked, "Anyone want to come back to my place?"

We still had vodka in the bag, two girls in each cab, two cabs taxiing to the Bowery, to the apartment Cal's parents, half Jewish and full Connecticut stockbrokers each, had bought for him. I was in the back and he was in the back and Kimi! was between us (The Factchecker's roommate was up front), and I asked if anyone had talked to Aar but Kimi! was already calling him though she must've been calling his office, because he didn't have a phone on his person, this was before everybody had phones on their persons.

Aar was waiting outside Cal's building, wrapping his silk scarf around a Russian or Ukrainian or close enough gift—a present to himself shivering in only a frilly cocktail waitress shirt and a drink umbrella skirt and a nametag. Cal poked with the keys, Aar poked his Slav from behind with a handle of rye, and we all crowded into the elevator, stopped on every floor, Kimi! and Missy having plunged into pressing all the buttons.

I'd lit a cig on the street and was still smoking in the elevator and the cig I was smoking was menthol.

Missy, being The Factchecker's roomie, whining to Kimi! and me about her job as a temp receptionist, and "Why can't I get a job at an agency?" and "Can you I'm begging you introduce me to Aar?" as Cal scoured around stuffing tightywhities into drawers, as Aar and his Masha? Natasha? he'd picked up from hostessing the restaurant of the Jersey City Ramada, the same place I'm sure he'd picked up the rye, set about mixing Manhattans.

Cal tidying the shelves, rearranging and flipping what he must've considered the respectable reads, the larger and wider reads, the complement of Brontës, the Prousts, the Tolstoys, centrally and spine out, exchanging the livingroom's Flags of the Confederacy poster for the kitchen's canvas of abstract slashes by a dissentient Union Square Lithuanian, fussing with the stereo, putting on some hiphop, some rap, clearing away the motivational improve your vocab lectures he worked out to. I left Kimi! and Missy to help him move the treadmill to the bedroom, left him trying to fold the treadmill into the closet at the buzzing, went to the door and buzzed them in: a dozen people, a 12-pack, dangling in the hall, dangling like keys passed from the fire escape to the acquainted, from the acquainted to the strangers they'd invited, assisterati and receptionistas arriving, schedulers and reschedulers early and late, marketing and distribution cultureworkers I didn't know and who didn't know me but we, this was our business, pretended. More pot and coke, which, as P.S. said again, had gotten better since the Citigroup merger. Tequila in the sink, martinis in the shower. Ash in both and in energy drinkables. Masha or Nastya was asking if we had any games and after Cal realized she didn't mean Monopoly mentioned that his neighbor was a firstperson fanatic—not the literary gambit, the gaming—and suddenly six fists were knocking at Tim's door demanding to borrow his system, and Tim, calculus teacher at Stuyvesant, answered the door red and tousled senseless, and hauled into Cal's his system and even connected it to Cal's TV with the bigger screen and bigger speakers, the night blooding the morning as P.S. and some random hair-curtained-in-the-middle guy tested each other in mortal combat avatared as laser-tusked elephants and wild ligers with rocketlaunching claws, as Aar left with his Slav who had to get back to Staten Island by her cousins' curfew, as Tim's girlfriend who had the flu trundled over in a balloonpocked blanket and scowled and sneezed and coughed and left taking Tim but not his system with her, as some random hair-curtained-in-the-middle guy left with his decentbodied girlfriend, as Cal grinded Missy and took her into the bedroom, as I fumbled with Kimi! and got a burp, which sent her to the bathroom to vomit, which sent Missy to the bathroom to help her, and P.S. kept playing with himself, and in the hall Missy was into hooking up with Kimi! but not Kimi! with Missy, P.S. suggested they call The Factchecker to confirm whether and which sex acts she was perpetrating on Finnity, Missy and Kimi! left, P.S. left with them, and after opening the fiercely bulbed fridge to find expired mustard and ketchup sweating, just sweating, I suggested calling for delivery, but the good place was closed and we were just a block outside the bad place's delivery zone, and the freezer wasn't just out of ice but out of cold from being left open, and there was a cushion wet on the floor in the hall, and there was sleep without dreaming.

I was woken—lumped in the contents of a dumped jar of vitamins—by Kimi!'s phone, which she'd left behind. Cal picked it up, and Kimi! yelled at him and he yelled at me to find the remote, but all I was finding was a jar and vitamins.

Then Kimi!'s phone went dead and Cal was gone.

My mouth tasted like tobacco and mucus and lipgloss, absinthe (strangely), marijuana, coke bronchitis.

I had an ache in the back of my head, and was deciding whether to vomit. The screen was still showing the game, 1 Player, 2 Players, New, Resume, and on the way to the window I stopped to resume the function for the time, but the screen just filled with smoke, the sky with smoke, and in the weeks to come, the months to come, into 2002 when the paperback release was canceled and beyond, my book received all of two reviews, both positive.

Or one positive with reservations.

\

Miriam Szlay. Still to this day, I'm not sure whether she made it to the party. Either I didn't notice her, or she was too reluctant to have sought me out, because she was kind. Or else, she might have skipped it—that's how kind she was, or how much she hated my susceptibility to praise, or how much she hated paying for a sitter.

I never asked.

Miriam. Her bookstore was a messy swamp on the groundfloor of a lowrise down on Whitehall Street—literature cornered, condescended to, by the high finance surrounding. Before, it'd been a booklet store, I guess, selling staplebound investment prospectuses and ratings reports contrived by a Hungarian Jew who'd dodged the war, and bought Judaica with every dollar he earned—kabbalistic texts that if they didn't predict commodity flux at least intrigued in their streetside display. At his passing he left the property and all its effects and debts to his children—Miriam, and her older and only brother—who broadened the inventory to include fiction and nonfiction of general interest to the Financial District's lunch rush, which as a businessplan was still bleak.

Miriam—who kept her age vague, halfway between my own and my mother's—was the one who ran the shop and hired me: straight out of Columbia, straight out of Jersey, a bridge & tunnel struggler with a humanities diploma between my legs but not enough arm to reach the Zohar. She was inflexible with what she paid me an hour ($8 or its equivalent in poetry), but was flexible with hours. She respected my time to write, knew that I wasn't going to be a clerk all my life (just throughout my 20s), knew that a writer's training only began, didn't end, with alphabetical order. Another lesson: "subject" and "genre" are distinctions necessary for shelving a book, but necessarily ruinous distinctions for writing a book deserving of shelving.

Miriam was my first reader—my second was her brother, who became my agent. Aaron signed me on her word alone—a demand, not a recommendation—and helped me clarify my projects. A memoir (I hadn't lived enough), a study of the Israeli-Palestinian conflict (I had no credentials), a novel about the Jersey Shore (no story), a collection of linked short stories about the Jersey Shore (no linkages), a long poem conflating the Inquisitions and Crusades (not commercial). Then one fall day in 1996 Aar came back brutalized from Budapest, cabbing from JFK to Whitehall to drop a check with his sister (the shop would never be profitable). His trip had been coital, not cliental, but out of solicitousness he talked only profitability, Mauthausen, Dachau, family history. That was the moment to mention my mother.

My mother was my book, he agreed, and he met me monthly after work, weekly after I left work to finish a draft, to discuss it—how to recreate dialogue, how to limit perspective—still always meeting at the register, where I'd give my regards to Miriam, and him a check to Miriam, then rewarding ourselves at a café up the block. Not a café but a caffè—as the former could be French, and the latter could only be Italian. Aar taught, I learned: how to tie a Windsor and arrange a handkerchief, how a tie and handkerchief must coordinate but never match, which chef who cooked at Florent also subbed at which Greek diner owned by his brother only on alternate Thursdays, who really did the cooking—Mexicans. Actually Guatemalans, Salvadorans. A Manhattan should be made with rye, not bourbon. Doormen should be tipped. Aar—quaffing a caffè corretto and marbling the table with stray embers from his cig, when smoking was still permitted—knew everything: stocks and bonds and realestate, Freud and Reich, the fate of the vowels in Yiddish orthography, and the Russian E and И conjugations. When was the cheapest day to fly (Tuesdays), when was the cheapest day to get gas (Tuesdays), where to get a tallis (Orchard Street), where to get tefillin repaired (Grand Street), who to deal with at the NYPD, the FDNY, the Port Authority, the Office of Emergency Management, how to have a funeral without a body, how to have a burial without a plot.

9/11/2001, Miriam was bagladying up Church Street to an allergist's appointment. She must've heard the first plane, or seen the second. The South Tower 2, the North Tower 1, collapsing their tridentate metal. Their final defiance of the sky was as twin pillars of fire and smoke.

Sometime, then—in some hungover midst I can't point to, because to make room for the coverage every channel banished the clock—a seething splitscreen showed the Bowery, the street just below me, and it was like a dramatization of that Liberty sonnet, "your huddled masses yearning to breathe free," "the wretched refuse of your teeming shore": the old homeless alongside the newly homeless and others dressed that way by ash, none of them white, but not black either, rather gray, and rabid, being held at bay by a news crew with lashes of camera and mic. I spilled Cal's mouthwash and spilled myself downstairs, leaving the TV on, and thinking a minty, asinine muddle, about this girl from last night who said she lived on Maiden Lane like she was inviting me there anytime that wasn't last night, her date she was carrying who said he was too blitzed to make it to Inwood, and thinking about my book, and Miriam, and Aar, and how vicious it'd be to get all voxpop man on the street interviewed, and be both outside and inside at once.

But downstairs the crew was gone, or it never was there—so I went onto Houston and through the park, beyond. Chinatown beyond. Chinatown was the edge of triage. A firetruck with Jersey plates, wreathed by squadcars, sped, then crept toward the cloud. A man, lips bandaged to match his bowtie, offered a prayer to a parkingmeter. A bleeding woman in a spandex unitard knelt by a hydrant counting out the contents of her pouch, reminding herself of who she was from her swipecard ID. A bullhorn yelled for calm in barrio Cantonese, or Mandarin. The wind of the crossstreets was the tail of a rat, swatting, slapping. Fights over waterbottles. Fights over phones.

Survivors were still staggering, north against traffic but then with traffic too, gridlocked strangers desperate for a bridge, or a river to hiss in, their heads scorched bald into sirens, the stains on their suits the faces of friends. With no shoes or one shoe and some still holding their briefcases. Which had always been just something to hold. A death's democracy of C-level execs and custodians, blind, deaf, concussed, uniformly tattered in charred skin cut with glass, slit by flitting discs, diskettes, and paper, envelopes seared to feet and hands—they struggled as if to open themselves, to open and read one another before they fell, and the rising tide of a black airborne ocean towed them in.

"If you can write about the Holocaust," Miriam once told me, "you can write about anything"—but then she left this life and left it to me to interpret her.

A molar was found in the spring, in that grange between Liberty & Cedar, and was interred beneath her bevel at Union Field.

Aar dealt with insurance, got custody of Achsa—Miriam's daughter, Ethiopian, adopted, then eight. He moved her up to the Upper East Side, built her a junglegym in his office. His neighbors complained, and then Achsa complained she was too old for it. He fitted the room with geodes, lava eggs, mineral and crystal concretions, instead.

The bookstore still stood—preserved by its historical foundations from the damage of scrapers. But Aar couldn't keep it up. It wasn't the customer scarcity or rehab cost, it was Miriam. The only loss he couldn't take. He put the Judaica in the gable, garnished the best of the rest and sold it, donated the remainder to prisons, and sold the bookstore itself, to a bank. For an unstaffed ATM vestibule lit and heated and airconditioned, simultaneously, perpetually.

He kept the topfloor, though, Miriam's apartment, tugged off the coverlets that'd been shrouding its mirrors since shiva, moved his correspondence cabinet there, moved his contract binders there—fitted his postal scale between her microwave and spicerack—the entirety of his agency. He kept everything of hers—the bed, dresser, creaky antiques, coffinwood, the clothes, the face products. Took her antianxieties and antidepressants and when he finished them, got prescriptions of his own. Meal replacement opiates—he'd chew them.

The only stuff he moved was Achsa's, in whose old room he set up his rolltop and ergo swiveler. Computer and phone to accept offers, reject offers, monitor the air quality tests. He had different women working as assistants—Erica, and Erica W., and Lisabeth—junior agents in the kitchen, preparing my royalty statements, my rounding error earnings against advance. But on their days off and at nights he'd have his other girls over, his Slavs—helping them through their ESL and TOEFL exams, writing their LaGuardia Community College applications, fucking them, fucking them only in the stairwell, the hall, where Miriam's scent didn't linger—as insomniac corpses came and went for cash below, on a floor once filled with rare gallery catalogs and quartet partitur, just a ceaseless withdrawing, depositing, fluoresced, blown hot and cold.

Caleb, however—that September made him. He'd done better at history, I'd done better at English, he'd become a journalist directly out of Columbia, with bylines in the *Times*, and I'd become a bookstore clerk, but published first—a book.

Then I fell behind.

What destroyed me, created him—Cal—the sirens were his calling. After filing features on Unemployment (because he was happy with his employment), and The Gay Movement (because he was happy being straight), he put himself on the deathbeat, jihad coverage. He left the Bowery and never came back. He was down at the site round the clock, digging as the searchers dug, as the finders sifted, but for facts. Every job has its hackwork, promotions from horror to glamour. Not to my credit, but that's how it felt at the time.

He tracked a hijacker's route through the Emirates, Egypt, Germany—to Venice, Florida, where he proved himself going through the records of a flight school, turning up associates the FBI had missed, or the CIA had rendered. At a DC madrassa he got a tip about Al Qaeda funding passing through a Saudi charity and pursued it, cashed out on the frontpage above the fold. His next dateline was Afghanistan. He went to war. Combat clarified his style. He had few contacts, no bodyarmor. But when his letter from Kabul prophesied the Taliban insurgency, *The New Yorker* put him on staff. It's difficult for me to admit. Difficult not to ironize. I was jealous of him, envious of risk. The troop embeds, the voluntary abductions, hooded with a hessian sandbag and cuffed, just to tape a goaty madman's babble. He was advantaging, pressing, doing and being important, careering through mountain passes in humvees with Congress.

Cal returned to the States having changed—in the only way soldiers ever change, besides becoming suicidal. He was clipped, brusque, and disciplined—his cynicism justified, his anger channeled. He brought me back a karakul hat, and for the rest of his fandom a .doc, an ms. A pyre of pages about heritage loss, the Buddha idols the mullahs razed. About treasurehunting, profiteering (Cal's the expert). About the lithium cartels, the pipelines for oil and poppies (Aar told him to mention poppies).

Cal certainly had other offers for representation, but went with Aar on my advice. The book sold for six figures, and got a six figure option, for TV or film, in development, still. I edited the thing, before it was edited, went through the text twice as a favor. But I'll type the title only if he pays me. Because he didn't use my title. Which the publisher loathed. 22 months on the bestseller list: "as coruscating and cacophonous as battle itself" (*The New York Times,* review by a former member of the Joint Chiefs of Staff), "as if written off the top of his head, and from the bottom of his heart [. . .] anguished, effortless, and already indispensable" (*New York,* review by Melissa Muccalla—Missy from my bookparty). The Pulitzer, last year—at least he was nominated.

My famous friend Cal, not recognized in any café or caffè famous but recognized in one or two cafés or caffès and the reading room of the 42nd Street library famous—writerly anti-nonfamous. I've never liked Cal's writing, but I've always liked him—the both of them like family. He's been living in Iowa, teaching on fellowship. All of Iowa must be campuses and crops.

"And I've been working on the next book," according to his email. This time it's fiction, a novel. Aar hasn't read a word yet. Cal won't let it go until it's finished. "And I've been thinking a lot about you and your situation and how you can't be pessimistic about it because life can change in a snap, especially given your talent," according to his email. Don't I know it, my hero, my flatterer.

\

Caleb was off warring and I was stuck, ground zero. Which for me was never lower smoldering Manhattan, but Ridgewood. Metropolitan Avenue. Out past the trendoid and into the cheap, always in the midst of transition, enridged. Blocksized barbedwired disbanded factories. Plants where the bubbles were blown into seltzer and lunchmeats were sliced. My building was an industrial slabiform, not redeveloped but converted, in gross violation of the informal zoning code of prudence. Used to be a printing facility, the only relic of which was a letterpress, a hulking handpress decaying screwy out in the central courtyard, exposed to the weather, too heavy to move. From time to time I'd stumble on a letter, wedged between the cobbles.

The unit itself was a storage facility 20 × 20, not certified for even a moment of frenetic pacing let alone habitation, and with a rabid radiator the resident antisemite, but without a window, I had to take from the rear dumpsters a bolt of billiard baize for a doorstop, for ventilation. Sawhorses supporting a desk of doublepaned wired glass. International Office Supply wood swiveler, the least comfortable chair of the Depression. Banker's lamp. Bent shelves of galleys, from when I reviewed, of my own galleys from when I'd be the reviewee. My mother's potted cups, one for caffeine, the other an ashtray. In a corner my airbed and bicycle, in another the pump for both. Brooklyn by my left leg, Queens by my right, hands between them, an intimate borough. At least there was a door. At least there was a lock.

My apartment, my office—I had nothing to do but practice my autograph. I didn't. I sat, I lay, pumped, adjusted the angle of recline.

I was the only NYer not allowed to be sad, once it came out what I was sad about, the bathroom was common and down the hall, all my sustenance was from the deli.

I bought a turkey sandwich, cheese curls, frosted donuts, lotto scratchers, Cossack vodka I'd drink without ice, from the spare change trough emptied and unwashed, Camel Lights I'd smoke out in the hall through the bars of the airshaft, smoking so hard as to crack a rib.

That's what I bought—representatively, each day—but also exactly, precisely, the day I spent the last of my advance. Summer 2002.

No further monies would be earned from my book—from all that labor. My advance was now behind me.

I tried to write something else—tried some stories (Hasidic tales recast), translations (from the Hebrew). But nothing—I was wasted, blocked, cramped blank by my "mogigraphia," "graphospasms." Translation: spending all my time online, blotted in a cell glutted with paper. I became a cursor, a caret, a button pressed and pressing—refreshing reactions to Cal's work.

Then, with the anniversary approaching, the *Times* got in touch. An editor emailed to ask if I'd write an "article," a "piece," about my luck. For the Sunday Styles section. I opened and closed her email for weeks, for months after the close of that summer, until rent was due, utilities too, and then I answered. I didn't just write back in the affirmative, I wrote the thing itself, which was shocking. After being so incapable, so incapable of wording, to spew out what I spewed—all bodytext, no attachments—I was shocked.

Because I sent it out and received an immediate rejection. I wasn't timely anymore. But I could still read between the lines. My tone had been too charged, my rhetoric too raging.

The editor, however, either pitying or gracious, passed me along to the Sunday Book Review, which offered me its font (Imperial)—if I could contain myself, be selfless, mature. My initial assignment was a book about the events—not as they affected me, but as they affected everyone (else).

Though I've since forgotten everything about the book—its title, its author, but that's only because they're online—I do recall the work: being mortified by it, and enjoying it. Enjoying my mortification. The clippings collected. My precocious ghosts, paper creased yellow. "Edifice Rex." "Rubble Entendre."

I became a legit critic, one of the clerisy, the tribe that had ignored me—and it was all because I'd been ignored that I was fair, accurate, pretentious. I always went after the feinschmecker stuff. Wolpe at Carnegie Hall (centennial of his birth), Whistler at the Frick (centennial of his death). *The Atlantic, The Nation*. Though my assignments were usually kept to Jewish books, to be defined as books not just about Jews but by them. *The Holocaust Industry: Reflections on the Exploitation of Jewish*

Suffering, American Judaism: A History—for *The New Republic* a novel called *The Oracle* or *The Oracle's Wife* set entirely in Christian New Amsterdam but written by a woman called Krauss—I wrote Edward Saïd's obituary for *Harper's*.

I explained, explicated, expounded—Mr. Pronunciamento, a taste arbiteur and approviste, dispensing consensus, and expensing it too: on new frontiers in race and the genetics of intelligence (Rabbi Moshe Teitelbaum and heterozygote fitness), on new challenges to linguistics (connectionist vs. Chomskyan), circumcision and STDs ("Cut Men, Not Budget"), manufacturing jobs shipped overseas and other, related, proxies for torture ("Contracting Abroad: Black Boxes and Black Sites"). All for casual readers who specialized in nothing but despecialization, familiarity. They didn't want to know it, they just wanted to know about it. Culture justified by cultural calendaring: the times and addresses and price.

But then, a break.

A site was about to launch—a bright blue text/bright white background site that if it wasn't defunct would be ridiculous now, but it wasn't then—in NY urls were still being typed and discussed with their wwws. It was amply backed by old media, amply staffed by new media, and was to be given away for free—its publication was its publicity—www.itseemedimportantatthetime.com, believe me.

They emailed with a Q: Would I like to interview Joshua Cohen?

My A: Why not?

But not this type of Q&A—instead, a profile, though they wanted only 2,000 words. They had infinite room, eternal room, margins beyond any binding or mind, and yet: they wanted only 2,000 words (still, @ $1/word).

It was a gimmick—everything is, and if it isn't, that's its gimmick—and yet, I accepted, I had to, I had to meet myself.

Joshua Cohen—Principal, but not yet mine—would be in NY for only a minimized window. I was instructed to meet him at Tetration's HQ, at some strange time, some psychoanalyst's 10 or so intersessionary minutes before or after the hour. In the lobby, in a waterfront fringe of Chelsea being rezoned for lobbies. They'd just gone public, at $80/share, for a market capitalization in excess of $22B.

My first reaction was, this was a railshed of reshunted freight that coincidentally included office furniture—Tetration was still moving in. I entered as the gratis vendingmachines were being installed, empty, gratis but empty. They'd purchased the railshed before Cohen had even toured it, apparently. This would be a first for us both.

The meet & greeter's badge wasn't brass but a brasscolored sticker on his vneck, below which were black slacker jeans, holstered taser. He smirked at my license, summoned an elongated attenuated marfanoid flunky to take me up, but instead of elevators or escalators or stairs, we took the ladders, rope ladders, rigging. An obstacle course of rainbow-banded enmeshments. We scuttled past androids fumbling to hook up their workstations, arraying plushtoys, wire/string disentanglement puzzles, tangrams, rubikses, möbiuses, slinkies.

The conference room was massive and vacant and carpet interrupted by tapemarks. The flunky left and rolled back with a chair and positioned its casters over the tapemarks and to keep the chair from rolling away chocked the casters with lunchboxsized laptops, left finally.

The ceiling panels were black and white, a chessboard defying gravity with magnetized pieces in an opening gambit of ♘f3 d5, g3 ♝g4, b3 ♞d7, ♗b2 e6. The wallpaper, a cohelixing of the DNA of Tetration's founders, a physical model of their alliance—or, just design.

Portals, portholes, had a vista over a plaza whose rubberized T tiles were proof of the four color map theorem, and stacked cargo containers and bollards being retrofit for a children's playground. The pier of my bookparty was just beyond, but which it was, I wasn't sure, as all the piers were becoming trussed in steel or repurposed into monocoques of electrochromic smartglass, available for weddings, and bar and bat mitzvot.

Our fleshtime: Principal entered, and the one chair was for him because he sat in it and I was still standing but all was otherwise similar between us.

"How's it treating you, NY?" I said.

"Banging, slamming," yawning.

"Not tubular?"

"Whatever the thing to say is, write it."

"I take it you don't have a great opinion of the press?"

"The same questions are always asked: Power color? HTML White,

#FFFFFF. Favorite food? Antioxidants. Favorite drink? Yuen yeung, kefir, feni lassi, kombucha. Preferred way to relax? Going around NY lying to journalists about ever having time to relax. They have become unavoidable. The questions, the answers, the journalists. But it is not the lying we hate. We hate anything unavoidable."

"We? Meaning you or Tetration itself?"

"No difference. We are the business and the business is us. Selfsame. Our mission is our mission."

"Which is?"

"The end of search—"

"—the beginning of find: yes, I got the memo. Change the world. Be the change. Tetrate the world in your image."

"If the moguls of the old generation talked that way, it was only to the media. But the moguls of the new generation talk that way to themselves. We, though, are from the middle. Unable to deceive or be deceived."

In the script of this, a pause would have to be indicated.

"I want to get serious for a moment," I said. "It's 2004, four years after everything burst, and I want to know what you're thinking. Is this reinvestment we're getting back in NY just another bubble rising? Why does Silicon Valley even need a Silicon Alley—isn't bicoastalism or whatever just the analog economy?"

Principal blinked, openshut mouth, nosebreathed.

"You—what attracted us to NY was you, was access. Also the tax breaks, utility incentives. Multiple offices are the analog economy, but the office itself is a dead economy. Its only function might be social, though whatever benefits result when employees compete in person are doubled in costs when employees fuck, get pregnant, infect everyone with viruses, sending everyone home on leave and fucking with the deliverables."

"Do the people who work for you know your feelings on this? If not, how do you think they'd react?"

"Do not ask us—ask NY. This office will be tasked with Adverks sales, personnel ops/recruitment, policy/advocacy, media relations. Divisions requiring minimal intelligence. Minimal skill. Not techs but recs. Rectards. Lusers. Loser users. Ad people. All staff will be hired locally."

"You realize this is for publication—you're sure you want to go on the record?"

"We want the scalp of the head of the team responsible for this wallpaper."

I had a scoop, then, as Principal kept scooping himself deeper—and deeper—digging into his users, his backers, anyone who happened to get on the wrong side of his pronoun: that firstperson plural deployed without contraction (not "all that bullshit we got for having Dutch auctioned the offering, we could've thrown it in their faces but didn't," rather "*we could have* thrown it in their faces *but did not*").

"The investors lacked confidence in Tetration or in the market?"

"Confidence is liability packaged as like asset, and asset packaged as like liability. Only we were sure how it would play, going public."

"I missed out on it totally—what was your stake, again?"

"Nobody noticed that the 14,142,135 shares we equitized ourselves was a reference to √2."

"What?"

"The square root of 2: 1.414213562373—stop us when you have had enough."

"I will."

"095048801688724209698078569671875376—stop us whenever—where were we?"

"5376?"

"7187537694?"

"If I dial that, I'm calling your aunt in the Bronx?"

"We do not have an aunt in the Bronx."

"What about the name?"

"The name of what?"

"Joshua Cohen."

"We invented that too?"

"Not at all, too unoriginal. That's why they have me writing this, you realize? I'm trying to work in something about the future of identity, something about names linking, or mislinking. Two Joshua Cohens becoming one, or becoming you, how it makes us feel?"

"We have the same name?"

"That wasn't mentioned?"

"No."

"No?"

Pause for a blush: "Dumb—it makes us feel dumb."

"Dumb because you have me beat in the rankings? Or dumb because you hadn't been privy to what we've been sharing?"

But he'd gone dumb like mute. Dumb like no comment.

"I mean, we even resemble each other? The nose?"

Principal pinched his nose. Rigidified.

I leaned against a wall, between magicmarker scribbles labeling imminent workstation emplacement: "A unit," "B unit." The dictaphone clicked, time to flip.

Remember that? the dictaphone?

I went back to Ridgewood and typed it all up, doubled my 2000 word limit but figured with this material they'd have to accommodate: how he hadn't wanted to meet, but had been compelled, how I hadn't wanted to meet, but had been compelled. I demarcated our respective pressures: his partners and shareholders, my rent and ConEd.

I delineated the effect of Principal's affect, the texture of his flatness, how he'd left a better impression on the chair, how the chair had left a better impression on the carpet, and concluded like the session had concluded with an account and analysis of the one thing that'd converted his format, from .autism to .rage—his ignorance.

Anything he missed didn't exist for him, and whoever pointed it out to him was destroyed. The reader was supposed to be that person—standing around, like I'd stood around, gaping at the chutzpah.

I emailed it in—jcomphen@aol.com, back then. The site was pleased. But then Tetration got in touch and requested quote approval. The site, without consultation, agreed. Then Tetration requested nonpublication. They were expecting doublefisted puffycheeked blowjob hagiography. I was expecting to be protected. But no.

The writeup was killed, it was murderized. The only commission of mine ever dead, stopped at .doc.

The site paid me half fee, and then another envelope arrived in the mail containing a copy of my book, with an inscription on the flyleaf, "great read!!" and an impostor's signature, "Joshua Cohen." The bookmark was a blank check likewise signed, made payable to me from Tetration, which I filled in and cashed for $1.41—proud of my selflessness, proud of my ignorance—all endeavor is the square root of two.

\

Nothing of mine has appeared since "in print"—rather it has, just anonymously, polyonymously, under every appellation but my own. I spent mid to late 2004 through early to mid 2006 responding to job listings online, falsifying résumés to get a job falsifying résumés, fabricating degrees to get a job fabricating papers for degrees, undergrad and grad, becoming a technical writer, a medical and legal writer, an expatriate American lit term paper writer, a doctoral dissertation on the theological corollaries to the Bakhtinian Dialogue writer: Buber, Levinas, Derrida, references to Nishida tossed in at no additional cost.

I edited the demented terrorism at the Super Bowl screenplay of a former referee living on unspecified disability in Westchester. I turned the halitotic ramblings of a strange shawled cat lady in Glen Cove into a children's book about a dog detective. I wrote capsule descriptions of hotels and motels in cities I'd never visited, posted fake consumer reviews of New England B&Bs I wasn't able to afford but still, two thumbs up, four and a half stars more convincing than five, A– more conniving than +, "the deskclerk, Caleb, was just wonderfully polite and accommodating." Or else I posted as "Cal," dropping his name to assert that the B&Bs were closer to attractions, or farther from garbage dumps, more amenitized, or less pest infested, than otherwise claimed, while for rating car rental businesses I trended toward black, posting with interpolations of the names of dead presidents, "Washington Roosevelt," and for spas and pampering ranches I tended dickless as a "Jane"—Dear John, Sincerely, Doe.

I wrote catalog copy: "Don this classic tartan wool driving cap and suddenly you're transported to the greenest backroad in County Donegal. You stop to let a shepherd get his flock across—is he wearing the same Royal Stewart as you?"

"The time is yours and the weather is balmy. You settle into the Arawak Hammock. You don't notice the mesh—it's handwoven, not knotted, using the highest-grade cotton twill—you don't notice the staves—they're handcrafted seasoned oak, providing maximum stability, and preventing bunching and coiling. You just notice: the waves. You sway along with the tide. Have you ever been so comfortable? (Mount and chains incl.) (4' W × 6 ½' L, 16 lbs)."

I responded to an ad posted by a MetLife jr. manager seeking a speechwriter for a banquet honoring a sr. manager on his retirement, and when the superior told the inferior he'd enjoyed the speech, the inferior told the superior he'd had a professional write it and the superior congratulated the inferior on his honesty, emailed for my email, and commissioned a toast for his granddaughter's baptism.

Menu tweaks came in cycles, booms and busts, from fancying up to fancying down, from overselling the Continental to underselling the American, both culinarily and linguistically. If it wasn't mille-feuille, it was a millennial reduction of simple proteins, grains, and greens. The NY Landmarks Conservancy was giving some medal to someone, a donor who lived in a landmark no doubt, and wanted to get a second opinion, wanted a clause or two trimmed to fit the citation. Then there was that spate of unusually tricky translations from the Hebrew, everything from subtitling a documentary about the Jenin refugee camp ("Why was the UN factfinding mission denied entrance? was it because after the Israelis massacred the women and children, they still had to massacre the evidence?"), to a promotional brochure for Ben Anak Defense Systems' Dual-Mission Counter-Rocket, -Artillery and -Mortar Midrange Defense System ("Shield the skies from foreign threats, now and tomorrow, day and night, all weather").

I responded to an ad posted by an ad agency, which was ridiculous—how boring, brief, the ad was, yet how clumsily cumbrously phrased, it was, misspellt? mis-punctuated!

It sought a copywriter, with special experience in the tourism sector. I wrote a letter, telling the truth: I'm the author of (I forget what number of) fake reviews for travel sites, which have generated (I forget what sum) in revenue—to be sure, I made up the number, and made up the sum, but only because I'd lost track when I tried to count all my postings, and when I called the coordinator of the compliment firm to ask after the revenue generated she answered that under no circumstances would I be paid by the click and hung up on me and never hired me again and I have to admit, being paid by the click had never occurred to me.

I wrote up Anguilla, an island—a BOT, or British Overseas Territory—I'd never been to, whose tourism board was eager to promote it as a vacation destination. The salient point was that it had survived hurricanes with its tax shelters intact. The board was so generous they flew the agency over, the agency was so generous they gave my ticket to an intern. They returned and described, provided photos. Big money tourism requires big history. The expense of recreation justified by indigenous settlement (native dwellings to visit), colonial presence (churches), frigatebirds, barracudas, whose narratives I plagiarized from nononline sources, for an account that appeared in two periodicals I once wrote for, inside the promotional box.

That job got me recommended for another, and that for another, more—it feels like I'm giving a testimonial for myself. I consulted on brandings, renamings (what to call a convertible child safety seat/pram for the Latino, rather Latina 18–40 demographic? what to call a cunt of a Hispanic boss who claimed my "Buggé" as her own?).

I never accepted offers to stay on, never worked at an agency on more than one account.

Once I showed up to the same building, the same floor, but to a different agency—in the neighborhood's last tunnelward sewer to have resisted redevelopment, Hell's Kitchenette. My boss this time, the sr. creative to my jr., was—I'll sell her:

Imagine taking home this beautiful young paleskinned blackhaired late-model Jewess. Into fitness, healthy living. Raised good in better Yonkers. Mother a Hebrew School teacher, which means for her a traditional education. Father a chief risk officer for an energy provider in the Midwest. They're not in touch, but still he makes his payments. Imagine getting to know this girl, a recently promoted sr. creative who'll stay jr. by a decade forever. Think of the investment opportunity. NYU grad, very oral.

Read the smallprint: too tall for me. Fit, healthy: orthorexia, multiple gym memberships. Jewish means "babycrazy." Maternally bonded.

Daddy issues. CV relative to youth indicates a stop at nothing ambition. Potential for growth is immaturity. Oral means "communications major."

Still, I was 35, 36, and life was tighter than the plaids and jeans I still wore from college.

The time for redress had come—bachelors buy on impulse.

If it's too bad to be true—it's worse, it's Rach. Contrary to her blog we didn't wait until "[my] stint was finished." Even when I was still working under her, I was atop her. Contrary too, I hadn't been pleading to be kept on when she, "putting career before [her] heart," refused me. "i made the choice 2 fire a colleague but hire a boyfriend"—please. "U&I," as she refers to the agency, is "Y&B"—clever. The Y I never met, but the B stands for Bernoff, feely in the office. He spanked Rach once, promoted her again. Account management. Rach always omits the spanking. We went to Italy and Greece on her new salary, and for a business thing to amorous Detroit, where I proposed at that shisha and arak joint she's forgotten. I didn't have a diamond, that's true, but her "he gave me his fathers dud pinkie ring" is bullshit. That was Dad's wedding band. Moms has never worn one (jewelry, confinement, makes her nervous).

Rach encouraged me to write again, but encouragement has always been best expressed in joint accounts. We were married at City Hall, 2008. "he wouldnt even let me have a wedding, or rabbi"—but it was more like her mother wanted Rach's childhood rabbi and my mother wanted my childhood rabbi and I was more interested in peace than in shattering circles under a chuppah. "he refused to have a party because i wasnt smart enough for his friends and he didnt have any friends left anyway"—but she can't have it both ways, or can.

"he refused to have a honeymoon," but we'd just put a payment down, or Rach had just put a payment down, and we were owned by a mortgage, on a two bedroom on 92nd & Broadway. "when my father had business in the city he wouldnt meet him," but who's the "he" and who's the "him"? and wasn't Rach the one who'd nixed it, ultimately with some mad insane passive-aggressive, codependent gambit, something like how we both have to stay home waiting for when the new dishwasher's delivered?

"he never wanted a kid." Didn't I try not just to want one but to have one? “before we tried 4 a kid we were never unhappy.” Now you’re speaking for me too, like Principal, in plural?

“he hated therapy.” But didn’t I go? “and couldnt be faithful.” To whom?

“he was never writing,” “hell never write again.”

Not like you I wasn’t, not like you I won’t.

“but this is all just too rushed and emotionul,” “im trying to serve him papers but cant track him down and trying to benefit the doubt if i cant im just gonna have to shame with embarasment.”

Please, Rach—humiliate me with your pettiness, your money mania, your body/mind volatilities, your typos.

“2 put down everything,” “all. of. it.”

://

I couldn't complain, or have been more unemployed, insured, or domesticated—even a jaunt to the postoffice could feel like a fulltime job.

Between 9/11 and 2009, Aar and I had drifted, and the drift was my fault and then it was his and I was a failure and he a success and I spent more time mentally recording what I took to be his snubs and negs than I did manually recording any serious writing—I spent so much time imagining blame and resentment that if I'd laid it out all plain on the page, it would've been another book, another scuppered friendship.

But now, by having gotten married, it was as if I'd become—acceptable. Not socially—because Aar had never cared for niceties and still did his share of uglybumping with the underprivileged and Green Cardless—but psychologically, maybe, I'd become psychologically tamed.

I wasn't this demonstrably disgruntled troll anymore, living under an overpass in the ghetto woods and pawing at an aimless compass—I'd become an equal, an adult, equally unhappy but undramatic in adulthood—I was trying to salvage something of myself, and maybe if this more stable, more functional blame and resentment lasted, something literary would be makeable too. This, at least, was one explanation, and though it was harsh, the other explanation was harsher: laziness, on both our parts. I'd drifted out of my boroughed burrow and into Manhattan, settling just across the park, which became our adjoining backyard: west side, east side, Aar and I were neighbors. We could be close now in every sense, we could have our rapprochement—all relationships are cheats of convenience, but NYers are cruel enough to neglect a bond due only to trackwork on the L.

I'd say he got in touch first, he'd say I got in touch first, anyway we were meeting—I was hauling across the park from West 92nd, once a month, every two weeks, whenever he didn't have to get to the agency, whenever he didn't have a lunch, to meet him at a diner. Past the mansions and into slummy deli territory—inconvenience must be treated as ritual, ceremony.

The diner was a kitsch joint of a bygone pantophagy, all unwiped formica and unctuous linoleums, leaks rusting into a bucket used for pickling. We always ordered the same from the same smack casualty waitress who never remembered the order, so we always had to order, Aar ordered: the smoked fishes for him, the poached eggs for me, and we'd split, but with the roles reversed—with 15% going to the writer, 85% to the agent, who though he talked faster ate faster too.

Aar avoided talking about my writing, even avoided mentioning books by authors still alive and in this language—rather his topics were: sex, Achsa, aging, Miriam, and he'd vary them in the manner of the menu: Miriam, aging, Achsa, sex—aging, Miriam, sex, Achsa—bagel with creamcheese, bagel with egg and cheese, bagel with creamcheese and lox. Not that my own fixations were any more fixable, or more palatable: Rach and I had fought and I'd left, Rach and I had fought and she'd left, we'd fought and she'd thrown a jug (Moms's), we'd fought and she'd thrown a mug (Moms's).

Absolutely, a refill. Pulp.

\

Caleb—he was never mentioned either. Not what he was doing, not that Aar and I were both in touch with him and knew we were both in touch and knew what he was doing.

Cal, he'd be able to write it. He'd be able to avoid all these redundancies, these doublings. This summary, synopsis. What in all the matinee movies and noon TV I took in was communicated by montage—time passing, elapsion: lie, sit, stand, sit, lie, drag to individual therapy, to couples therapy, sleep on the loveseat in the hall, wake up on the airmat in Ridgewood—today's writing, especially Cal's, is too impatient for.

"What are you doing with yourself?" Aar asked me, just before last Passover.

Any question might be the forbidden question, and any answer might expose present weakness, the latest changeable bandage for the writing wound (the not writing wound).

"Nothing, nothing," I said. "First seder by Rach's mother's, my Ramses-in-law, second in Jersey, chometz and matzah."

"I meant, what are you doing still married?"

What could I say? I could have told him—that I'd wanted to marry (I had wanted to), or that I'd loved her (I had)?

I, like my father before me, had been a wandering Aramean, seeking refuge in a distant land in the hopes of surviving the coming drought, the coming famine, only to become enslaved in that land, forced to make mud bricks and arrange them into pyramids for my own tomb? Not even—for the tomb of the man I used to be?

All men are Arameans, whoever they are, and we commemorate our enslavement to our female taskmasters and their mothers—our mothers—not just two nights a year, but daily. L'chaim.

Basically, though, the answer to his question was my book. Our book. That was the reason I married. That was the reason I was still married.

Why I got and stayed together with Rach wasn't the book's nonexistence unto itself, but rather was within that nonexistence, was covered by it: the generations broken, the family broken, to be repaired like a dropped pot or snarled ark of reeds, that unshakeable Jew belief in continuity, narrative, plot, in plopping myself in creaky unreclinable chairs around tables of prickly leaves to commiserate through recitation: flight into Egypt, plagues, flight out of Egypt, desert and plagues—a travail so repeated without manumission that it becomes its own travail, and so the tradition is earned.

But instead of explaining all that, I said, "I'm treating life like a book—like I'm the hero of my own life."

"A book you're living, not writing?" Aar had never been so direct.

I'm not sure it's good writing to say what my reaction was—it was bad.

I don't want to continue with that meeting—but then neither do I want to have to prose just one of our regular meetings: who'd you fuck, who do you want to fuck, Achsa's college application essay he wanted my read on (How I Dealt With My Grief), remember that guy who tried to sell Miriam his father's library comprised entirely of a single book the father had published about how to make rocks talk on Wall Street—the father had bought enough copies to make it a bestseller and put him on the lecture circuit, when he died his son found pallets of the stuff, books still wrapped, in a vault registered to the father in Secaucus. Or that other guy who'd tried to sell some other inherited junk: a raft of detectives, Westerns, that tatty crap by two nobodies named Thoreau and Emerson (first editions).

Or the way Miriam would pick her nose and silently fart at the register or if the fart refused to be silent how she'd slam the register drawer.

The scarves she always wore.

Let this meeting be as cryptic—as representative/nonrepresentative—as the Arameans, a people that never had a land of their own but still managed to leave behind their language—the only thing they left behind, their language. Aramaic. *Ha lachma anya.* This is the bread of affliction. *Eli Eli lama shavaktani?* Father, Father, why didn't Christ quote the Psalms in Hebrew—was he that inept, or does excruciation always call for the vernacular?

Aar would pay, and would say as he said every time: "I never gave you anything for your funeral."

He'd pay in cash—"My condolences on your continued nuptials," and I'd slap down Rach's card, and he'd put his hand atop mine and hold it, palm on palm on Visa and say, as if conspiring, as if pledging undying service, "Cash only."

Always has been. Always will be.

Then I'd walk him to Lexington—leave him by the 4 train, or the M102 bus, and walk quickly, quickly, toward the museums, and don't turn around, don't judge him for never waiting or descending, rather striding to the curb to flag down a ride.

\

That was the last we'd intersected before the spring—I'll have to check the contract: 4/29/2011. I'd been sleeping—how to put this? where? I could say it was a time apart thing suggested by Dr. Meany, I could say I'd been sent back to Ridgewood for a spell due to a Bible-sized, though, given our history, more than passoverable, argument dating from Pesach, which was the most amount of time Rach and I had spent together in a while. After the seder at her mother's, we drove to mine's, and stopping at a backroad farmer's market had bought a tree and given it to my mother who'd wondered aloud, who spends money on a tree? and then criticized the pot and Rach had taken that as a snub and refused to stay over and yelled at me all the drive back and yet all had been forgotten until we received in the mail a thank you note Rach took as begrudging—though that's just what Rach would've done, sent a belated thank you with gritted teeth—enclosing a photo of a fresh pot thrown as criticism.

I could say it was a disagreement over how I'd acted at Dr. Meany's, refusing to talk about "trust as fatherhood/fatherhood as trust," instead ranting about Jung, Lacan, hypergamy/hypogamy, gigantonomy/leucippotomy, modern male childhood as berdachism, modern male parenthood as couvade, or over how I'd acted at her mother's house when the woman, who knew everything/thought she did, told me to wear looser underwear to promote sperm motility and I—exploded.

I could hand to Bible or at least Haggadah swear on all of that, but the truth was—we weren't having sex anymore. We weren't trying anymore. Not even trying to try again. Trying to sneak in a jerkoff sessh on the toilet. "Don't mixup the toothbrushes." But both of them were green, which, because the brushes sold in twopacks are always different colors, meant Rach had bought two packs—"I'm not provoking you."

Cig out the window. No bourbon after toothpaste.

Rach and I had been touch and go, no touch and yes go—since fall? check the archives—Rosh Hashanah/Yom Kipper 2010? Conjugally making each other's lives unlivable but getting off on the correspondence. We'd flirted briefly, on chat, over email, another Meany suggestion, and so it was innocent, or it felt that way. Opening different accounts under different names, getting back in touch with each other and so ourselves by communicating our fantasies, her writing me something salacious or what for her passed as salacious as sexrach1980 or cuntextual (an injoke), as rachilingus or bindme69me (a cybernym I picked for her), but then just a moment later writing something serious again about her thyroid hypochondria or the decision of which dehumidifier to purchase, from her main account, her work addy identity.

We'd even taken to posting personal ads on a personal ads site and then responding to what we guessed were the other's—not following through unless—I'm sure she never followed through.

It was early or still late when the ring woke me up—it was darkness and the only light was the phone, which displayed either number or time, never both. The ringing stayed in my head. I'd been drunk, I was still drunk, there was a cig burn at the cuticle of my middle finger. I never turned my phone off, when we were together and even apart, because Rach still called with crises and if I didn't pick up, there would be wetter blood and trauma. She called between home and office, between meetings, at lunch's beginning and end, from the lockers at the gym, between elliptical slots, before and after freeweights, in the showers at Equinox with her newer improveder phone wrapped in a showercap and kept on a ledge above the sprinkler on speaker, from the supplement aisle at Herbalife, while smoothieing in the kitchen, while abed dream-dialing. This flippity phone Rach purchased and programmed and forced me to keep charged and carry at all times, vibrating my crotch—for potency's sake I wasn't supposed to carry it in that pocket—or intoning L'chah Dodi, from the Shabbos eve service, her choice.

Abandonment issues, resolving in engulfment. In stalkiness, if a husband can be stalked by a wife. Rach's msgs as shrill as the matingcall of whatever locustal species mates as foreplay to the woman smiting, devouring, the man. prsnlty dsrdr is how I'd abbreviate for txt.

This tone, though, wasn't anything prayerful, just the default, and though I couldn't program, I could still recognize the digits.

But Aar didn't want to talk. He said, "Let's meet?" and I said, "Let's," and he said, "Just come across or, better, I'll come to you," and I said, because he didn't have to have all the grindy geary details of my situation, "Best is for me to do the traveling—noon?"

He said, "Now."

(212) faded to clock, 6AM.

Manhattan was accessible by train—I'd have to change only once—by bus—I'd have to change all of twice—just as I was about to blow up the bike, the phone resumed its default panic.

"Take a cab," Aar said, "I'll pay for it."

Cabs in Ridgewood weren't for the hailing. There was never anything yellow not lotted. But up the block was a gypsy service and I'd like to be able to say I'm fictionalizing—they took their time serving me because all their drivers were directing another driver reversing a hearse into the garage. If I were fictionalizing I'd say they put me in the hearse, but it was a moving van and I was seated up front—take me past Ambien withdrawal, or on a tour of the afterlife according to Allah.

We hurtled into the city before the rest of the rush with the sun a sidereal horn honking behind us. Manhattan was still in black & white, a sandbagged soundstage, a snorting steamworks, a boilerplate stamping the clouds. This can be felt only in the approach, from exile. How old the city is, the limits of its grid, its fallibility. Fear of a buckling bridge, a rupture deluging the Lincoln or Holland. Fear of a taxi I can't afford.

Off the FDR, I dialed Aar, who said, "Un momento, por favor—she's taking forever to get slutty," though I wasn't sure which she he meant until 78th and Park, and it was Achsa—I never remembered her like that. But it takes just a moment.

Aar paid the driver, "Gracias, jefe," and we chaperoned Achsa to school—her last patch of school at an institution so private as to be attendable only alone, which was her argument. "You don't have to drop me." But Aar was already holding her dashiki backpack, "Not many more chances to ogle your classmates." Achsa said, "That's nasty, Dad, and ageist." Then she laughed, so I laughed, and Aar was our unfinished homework.

The sky was clear. The breeze stalled, stulted. We talked about graduation. About Columbia, which was closer, but too close, and anyway Princeton was #6 overall and #1 in the Ivies for field hockey.

Achsa's school was steepled at a privileged latitude, a highschool as elited high on the island as money gets before it invests in Harlem. Girls, all girls, dewperfumed, to blossom, to bloom.

"This is where we ditch her," Aar said, halting at a roaned hitchingpost retained for atmosphere. "You studied?"

"Argó, argoúsa, árgisa," Achsa said, "tha argó, tha argíso."

"He/she/it has definitely studied." Aar swung the backpack and unzipped it and wriggled out a giftbox.

"What's that and who's it for?"

"I'm not the one taking the tests today—you are."

Achsa shrugged on her straps and said, "Hairy vederci"—to me.

Aar said, "No cutting."

But she'd already turned away—from a shelfy front to a shelf of rear, enough space there for all the books she had, jiggling.

"Blessed art Thou, Lord our God," I said, "Who Hath Prevented me from Reproducing."

"Amen."

"But also she resembles her mother."

"My sister," Aar said, "the African."

East, we went east again—away from fancy au pairland, the emporia that required reservations. Toward the numbered streets, to the street before the numbers, not a 0 but a York—Ave.

Pointless bungled York, a bulwark. Manipedi and hair salons. Drycleaning. Laundry.

Outside, the doublesided sandwichboard spread obscenely with the recurring daily specials still daily, still special, the boardbreaded sandwiches and soups scrawled out of scraps, the goulash and souvlaki and scampi, leftover omelets and spoiled rotten quiches, the menus inside unfolding identically—greasy. The vinyls were grimy and the walls were chewed wet. A Mediterranean grove mural was trellised by vines of flashing plastic grape. A boombox was blatting la mega se pega, radio Mexicano.

The methadone girl was working, and so the methadone was working on the girl. Our counter guy wiped the counter.

In this diner as in life, nothing came with anything, there were no substitutions—it was that reminder we craved. A salad wasn't just extra, but imponderable. A side of potatoes was fries. We always went for a #13 and a 15—which was cheaper than getting the #s 2, 3, 4, and 5—a booth in the back like we were waiting for the bathroom.

Aar ordered from the methadone girl, "The usual," and then explained again what that was, and then explained the job: "Just your average lives of the billionaires vanity project, the usual."

I didn't even have water in me—nothing to spit or sinuose through the nose. Just: "This is the guy who haunts me?"

"Who called me directly and Lisabeth put him through, saying it's you, and straight off he's proposing a memoir."

"He wants me to be his ghost?"

The caffeines came, and the juices—an OJ agua fresca.

Aar went for his giftbox trimmed in ribbons. An expertly tied bow resembling female genitalia.

He took his knife and deflowered it all to tinsel, tissue—"You're the only one he wants." Champagne.

"We're popping bottles?"

"What do you suppose they charge for corkage?" He held the magnum under the table, until the radio repeated its forecast, a chance of showers onomatopoeia—no fizz, no froth, just a waft at the knees—and he took both juice cups down and poured them brimming and then setting the magnum at his side offered to clink chevronated plastics:

"To the JCs! The one and the only!"

"But which am I?" though I was sipping.

"We're dealing either with a dearth of imagination," Aar swallowed. "Or an excess."

"I thought he hated me—I thought he'd forgotten me before we even met."

"May we all be hated for such money—Creator of the World and of all the Universe, Creator—may we too be forgotten under such munificent terms."

"What do you mean?"

"It's already sold."

"A stranger's autobiography I haven't agreed to write yet has already been sold how? To whom?"

"I wasn't sure you'd agree so I went ahead," and he reached for his pocket, for a napkin, a placemat.

A contract stained with waiver, disclaimer.

\

Sign and date here and here and here and here, initial. I have to fill them in—the what else to call them? the blanks?

By now I'm through saying that my book changed everything for everyone around it, around me—I'd recognize the smell of burning ego anywhere.

Not even the events—the explosions—changed everything for everyone. But still it's unavoidable. He is, Finnity. After my book, he never went back to editing lit—meaning, he never again worked on a book I respected.

Out of favor with the publisher—a press founded as if a civic trust by dutiful WASPs, operated as if a charity by sentimental Jews, whose intermarried heirs were bought out by technocrats from Germany—Finnity transferred, Aar said Finnity told him, or was transferred, Aar maintained, to another imprint, a glossier less responsible imprint where he acquired homeopathic cookbookery, class-actionable self-help, and a glossy, Strasbourg-born associate editor who also happened to be the only daughter of the chairman of the parent multinational, the top of not just the Verlagsgruppe but of the whole entire media conglomerate, getting intimate with the business from the bottom (missionary position).

Two children by now, a house in New Canaan.

He's become a revenue dude—a moneymaker.

Anyway, Aar—vigilantly sensitive to the vengeance of others—had gone to him first, and Finnity hadn't believed him.

"I'll be straight with you," Aar said to me. "First he tried to talk me out of you, then we both got on the phone to conference JC2, let's say, and Finnity went naming all my other clients."

"But you insisted?"

"He insisted—your double."

"He doesn't assume from that dead assignment I know anything about online?"

"What's to know? You go, you hunt and peck, what comes up?"

"Twin lesbians? My bank balance?"

"Words, just words. You know this."

"Did you know he read my book?"

"Joshua Cohen is always interested in books written by Joshua Cohen."

"Joshua Cohens or Joshuas Cohen?"

"Or maybe his hobby's the Holocaust—why not? Whose isn't?"

"Or maybe it's another gimmick, like to keep it out of the press that he's not writing it himself—or like for marketing."

"Actually the contract provides for that: strictly confidential. He worked it out himself, no agent on his behalf. You're nondisclosured like a spook. Like a spy. You can forget about any duple credit on the covers, or the two of you breaking names up the spine. No 'As told to,' no 'In collaboration with'—we're talking no acknowledgment, not even on copyright."

"Actually that makes the offer compelling."

Aar went for my bagel, caved it. Laid on the creamcheese, waxy mackerel, frozen sewerlids of tomato and onion. To eat one bagel he had to have two, because he only ate the tops. The tops had all the everything seasonings.

Poppy, sesame, garlic, gravel salt: his breath as he said, "What compels, my friend, is the money."

"It's a lot of fucking money."

"What we'd be getting paid is a lot, what the publisher would be paying is a fucking lot—for him it's just snot in a bucket."

"How much would he get?"

"How much I can't say," but Aar took up his knife again, pierced one of my yolks, and scribbled in the yellow.

A dozen times my fee.

The waitress came by not to clear us—we weren't through yet—rather to plunk down two styro cups, and so the magnum was brought up and poured, settled on the table.

She smiled to demonstrate her braces—all there was between the trackmarks at her jugulars and her bangs held back with bandaids—and took the full cups and gave one to our cash register guy and they ¡saluded! each other and us from the takeout window and drank and sparked a swisher cigarillo and passed it. Enjoy.

Aar was in the middle of saying, "Even them—¿comprende? ¿me entiendes? you can't tell anyone—anything."

"I get it."

"Not a word, he was adamant about that," and Aar was too. "He wanted to contact you directly, wanted to do this without me, represent you himself—he's even insisting that the publisher not announce the deal."

"Finnity's complying."

"Doesn't have a choice, and neither do you."

"Book of the century. Of the millennium. I get it—what's next? An age is a million years? An epoch 10 million years? Or what's beyond that—an era or eon?"

"Be serious—there are penalties if anyone blabs."

"Penalties?"

"Inwired: if word gets out, the contract's canceled."

"Abort, abort."

"Autodestructo."

"So not a word."

"Rach."

"No Rach."

"Shut your mouth."

I shut my mouth.

The diner just had pencils—I picked my teeth with a pencil, until a pen was found.

A caper was stuck in my teeth.

://

I left Aaron in a stupor—Aar taxiing to his office to process, me to wander stumbling tripping over myself and, I guess, cram everything there was to cram about the internet? or web? One was how computers communicated (the net?), the other was what they communicated (the web?)—I was better off catching butterflies.

I wandered west until, inevitably, I was in front of the Metropolitan.

I used to spend so much time there, so many weekend and even weekday hours, that I'd imagine I'd become an exhibit, that I'd been there so long that I, the subject, had turned object, and that the other museumgoers who'd paid, they'd paid to see me, to watch how and where I walked, where I paused, stood, and sat, how long I paused at whatever I was standing or sitting in front of, when I went to the bathroom (groundfloor, past the temporary galleries of porcelain and crystal, all the tapestries reeking of bathroom), or for cafeteria wine and then out to the steps to smoke, whether I seemed attentive or inattentive, whether I seemed disturbed or calmed—as if I were carrying around this placard, as if I myself were just this placard, selfcataloging by materials, date, place of finding, provenance: carbonbased hominid, 2011, Manhattan (via Jersey)—a plaque and relic both, of paunchy dad jeans, logoless tshirt untucked, sportsjacket missing a button, athletic socks, unathletic sneaks.

I visited the Met for the women, not for meeting them new, but for the reassurance of the old. For their forms that seduced by soothing—for their form, that vessel shape, joining them in sisterhood as bust is joined to bottom.

I visited to be mothered, essentially, and it was altogether more convenient for me to get that swaddling from the deceased strangers buried uptown than from my own mother down in Shoregirt.

The physique I'm feeling my way around here is that of the exemplary vase: a murky womb for water, tapering. I'm remembering a certain vase from home, from the house I was raised in: marl clay carved in a feather/scale motif, the gashes incised by brush or comb, then dipped transparently and fired, and set stout atop the cart in the hall. That was the pride of my mother's apprenticeship: a crudely contoured holder for any flowers I'd bring, which she'd let wilt and crumble dry, as if measures of my absence. Yes, coming to the museum like this, confining myself behind its reinforced doors and metal detectors, and within its most ancient deepwide hushed insensible receptacles, will always be my safest shortcut to Jersey, and the displays of the Master of Shoregirt—Moms the potter—who's put together like this, like all the women I've ever been with, except Rach.

\

Just to the left of the entrance of the Met, where civilization begins, where the Greek and Roman Wing begins—there it was: the dwelling-place of the jugs, the buxom jugs, just begging to surrender their shapes to a substance.

Curvant. Carinated. Bulging. The jar girls, containments themselves contained, immured squatting behind fake glass.

I used to stop, stoop at the vitrines, and pay my respects—breathing to fog their clarity, then wiping with a cuff.

I should say that my virgin encounter with these figures was in the company of Moms, who'd drive the family up 440 N across all of Staten Island for culture, for chemo (the former for me, the latter for Dad, whom we'd drop at Sloan Kettering).

But that Friday this past spring, I didn't see any maternal proxies. Coming close to these figures, all I could see was myself. At each thermoplastic bubble, each lucite breach, I hovered near and preened. I was shocked, shattered, doubly. My chin quadrupled in reflection. My mouth was a squeezed citron. Stubble bristled at every suggestion. What had been highbrow was now balding.

Returning from that first chemo visit, Moms went and bought some clay, a wheel, some tools. Impractical platters, flaccid flasks: she'd been inspired to pot, moved to mold, vessels for her depression, while I had been, inadvertently, sexualized.

Moms had intended to inculcate only a fetish for art, not for what art must start as: body, the body defined by waist.

Dad, weakened, shriveled—a mummy's mummy—had six months left to live.

\

That day, signing day, I took my tour, conducted my ordinary circuit by gallery: first the women, then the men. Rounding the rotundities, before proceeding to those other busts, those heads.

Staved heads—of the known and unknown, kings of anonymity with beards of shredded feta, or ziti with gray sauce—separated for display by the implements that might've decapitated them. If it's venerable enough, weaponry can look like art, just like commonplace inscriptions can sound like poetry—Ozymandias, anyone? "this seal is the seal of King Proteus"?

The armor of a certain case has always reminded me of cocoons, chrysalides, shed snakeskin—all the breastplates and armguards and sheaths for the leg just rougher shells from an earlier stage of human development. The armor featured in an adjacent case, with its precisely positioned nipples and navels, sculpted pecs and abs, would've been even stranger without them. The men without bodies were still better off than the men just lacking penises, or testes. Regardless, statuary completed only by its incompletion, or destruction, resounded with me, while the swords hewed through my noons, severing neuroses.

But then I returned, I always returned, to my women, closing the show, a slow, agonizingly slow circumflexion.

Fertility goddesses, that's what the archaeologists who'd dug them up had said, that's what Moms had said, and I'd believed her—these women were the idols of women and women were the idols of men and yet we kept smashing them (I understood only later), smashing with rose bouquets, samplers of marzipan and marrons glacés, getaway tickets, massage vouchers, necklaces, bracelets, and words.

It strikes me that Moms herself might've believed that these odd lithic figurines were for fecundity, because everything else had failed her—the inability to conceive (and the inconceivability of) were fates she'd share with Rach, or else the problem was mine.

And Moms might even have been so distraught by Dad's decline as to have placed genuine faith in the power of that petrified gallery—guiding me through rooms now changed, antiquity redecorated since 1984—because suddenly I wasn't enough, she wanted another: a boy, though what she needed was a girl in her image.

If so, then that studio she had erected at home—her installation of a kiln in Dad's neglected garage—must be regarded as a shrine, a temple to opportunity lost.

\

Now, when it comes to art, and I mean every discipline: lit, sculpture, painting, music, and theater (but only Rach liked dance, because she danced)—when it comes to any medium, I'm divided. Not between styles, between perfections. Mark my museum map with only the oldest and newest. Roll me in scrolls, volumina of vellum and parchment, papyri. But then also pile up all the new books appearing, seasonally stack the codex barrage—how else to live, without contemporaries to hate? Forget their books—I mean how to live without their bios, their autobios to peruse and hold against my own?

Beginnings to romanticize and endings to dread—I'll take anything but the middles, all that received or established practice crap. Because the middle was where I grew up—bounded by house and garage filled with clay—a cramped colorless room filled with clayey boyhood, which my mother was bent on modeling not for greatness, but for portability and durability and versatile use. Moms's hands that were her English, the puffy wrists behind the pads digging in, poking holes in me so I might perceive life only as she perceived it—threatening, but beautiful if I'd be careful. This was her way because from earliest age she'd been foreign to even herself, as the youngest and the only girl after six brothers, dumbsy, clumsy, inconcinnous, a dreamer, whose family fell in the snow around her, around Kraków, and who'd lived like "an extinct girl dinosaur"—meaning arousing of a hideous pity—until my father married her home.

She'd had difficulties having sex, and so difficulties getting pregnant. Her baby was late, was me. She'd told me about the drugs. Pergonal, Clomid. The barren superstitions. Don't sit on snow or ice or rock, do bathe in water infused with moss from the walls of the shul on Szeroka Street. Dad had mentioned, only once, as he was dying, that Moms's war had been "tough," "hard knocks," which was how he'd recount each tax quarter. A solo CPA after being laidoff as an auditor with Price Waterhouse, he'd never applied his actuarial MS but kept it in a depositbox at the bank. Moms is a public school speech-language pathologist/audiologist, retired. Anyway, Dad's instructions: "Help your mother out," "Kaddish if she insists."

Moms: what she lost in family, she gained in body.

She was dense with her dead—with Dad's passing becoming ever more solid, ever more embonboobed, rubicund. Zaftig, not obese.

Steatopygous—which doesn't have to be italicized, it's already my language—all italics do is make what must be native, not. Anyway, it's not from the Latin, but Greek. Steatopygous meaning possessed of fat buttocks, and implying fat all around, the thighs, hips, waist, a gluteal gut, even adipose knees, unfortunate but vital. That's what Moms's lady statuettes are technically called—steatopygi, or steatopygia. Thrombosed bulges, throbbing clots—my mother's hindquarter was always a veiny maze, a varicose labyrinth, though not just hers: weighty were the bases of all the women in my family, my mother's family. My grandmother, my greatgrandmother, every aunt and cousin—Holocaust fodder. Heavy Jewesses, thickly rooted Jewesses, each swinging a single pendulous braid. From Poland, the Russian Pale, that settled and mortaring mixture. Upper Paleolithic, Lower Neolithic, lower and swollen. Marbled in calcite, schist, steatite, striated with stretchmarks of red rivers, the Vistula, the Bug. They were made out of stone and many of them even had hearts of stone—not Moms, though, despite how tough Rach found her. Yes, yes, Rach—she was the hard one, the skinny, the taut, all rib and limb, a spindly wife more like a plinth, like a pediment.

://

Coming out of the Met with all those gods on the brain—all those haloed faces seared into my own—it's an adjustment to sense normally. That's why the museum abuts the park, so that its patrons can walk in solitude—"walking in the garden in the cool of the day"—to get their glaze back.

Or—in the collecting heat of that Friday, a freak faineant warmth that unnerved me. I wasn't myself because enriched, beyond the pecuniary. Distracted by the thought of a second self. Distracted by the thought of a second book.

I was so scattered, I'm still not sure what to write: About my back aching from where I'd slept? my head still gauzed, Pharaohnically wrapped, from when I'd been woken up? about the cut on my neck? the slit from chin's caruncle to neck like an against the grain shaving mishap, just healing? Rach had responded to Moms's thank you gratuitousness by throwing a bisque dish for our keys, which struck a sill and splintered all over me.

The window had broken. Rach was expecting me to replace it. I was expecting her to replace it. We both were aware of this, but only she might've been consciously waiting.

I was—instead—counting my bounty.

Writing mental checks, but not for windows, before I'd written a word.

I still haven't written a word—just musings about museums, snarks about parks, observations to obelize: two frisbeeists freed from their cubicles—a professorial but perverted uncle emeritus—a Caribbean nanny strollering her employer along the reservoir. I was imposing topiary on trees, and rhymes between their branches and trunks.

I'd rather be procrastinating—I'd rather be doing anything—rather jog, rather run—than record that moment.

When I approached the bench.
When I recognized him.

\

Now what I like about lit is that though you feel you know the characters involved, you don't—you get all the benefits of having a relationship, with none of the mess. The fictional, the factually nonexistent, don't leave msgs or txt. You'll never have your own story about meeting Raskolnikov shuffling the aisles of Zabar's, or about bumping into Werther or, more bizarrely, Bouvard and Pécuchet on line at Han's Fruit & Vegetable—anyway, if you did bump into them, having been exiled from home yourself, like a fairytale knight errant sent out to seek not your fortune but tampons, how would you know? From their "teeth gnashing"? their "furrowed brows"? all those antique gestures? or just those antiquated translations? Forget the fictional characters—how many authors are being stopped on the street?

Another feature, but of the Victorian serial novel: They always doubled up, they repeated, reviewed, just in case the reader skipped an installment. Or was diverted by a major business decision.

I'd just made a major business decision, having contracted for a book for which I had absolutely no qualifications.

Or my only qualification was my name, the JC halfloops I stopped strolling—I stopped.

I'd just quit the presence of immemorial Basileis and marmoreal Caesares—the likenesses of infamous men who'd raped and plundered Europe and Asia as if only for my entertainment. Yet this—he—was what jarred me. This guy who'd always played the shrewn but happy hubby, the patient catchphrasey Pop. A minor B-celeb, a situational tragicomedian.

He was sensitive, but gave the impression of impersonating himself. His handsomeness was stilled, like the lines of his face were just distortion in his reception. In terms of painting: chiaroscuro cheeks, a worried craquelure mouth. In terms of sculpture: the nosetip curiously chipped, puttied cosmetically.

This cameo was atop a bench off the reservoir path, crowded by pigeons pecking at the matzah slivers he tossed. A proper picnic was spread in the grass.

I gathered myself and approached him, setting the flock to flying, a claque clapping its wings and wallaing west—like in film when directors seeking indistinct background chatter have their extras, forbidden by union rules from pronouncing anything scripted, repeat the same word at the same time but at different speeds and in different tones, *walla* supposedly being the most effective or just traditional choice, which happens to be an Amerindian word for "water," as well as slang for "really?" in Hebrew and Arabic—really?

Because sitting next to him was Rach.

\

I started fabricating immediately—as if I were Rach—began peddling their presence to myself: this was just a routine appointment enlivened with nature. A meeting negotiated into a harmless park outing. Their commercial was about to be shot, had been shot and was about to air. This was crunchtime, kinks had to be smoothed, geriatric touches retouched.

I remember thinking that their conversation—this situation—was itself a commercial, an infomercial, a public service announcement warning: you're not as witty as you think.

The actor noticed me before she did, and he recognized too—two stars in rare midday conjunction. His face tanned a shade deeper, and went rumpled as if by a gust, like the dewed pollenstrewn picnic blanket—a bedsheet, one of ours.

Rach collapsed into her lap.

She'd been complaining about him since the fall. He'd been forced on her by a director, by an agency exec. She'd never been more harried on set, she'd never dealt with talent more demanding. So old, hard of hearing, glaucomic, goutish—just getting his travel arranged was an account in itself, a nightmare.

But the way Rach kept her head in her hands told me the truth: that he'd been her true campaign, or she his, all along, and that all her whining to me had just been a prompt or cue—to be something, to change something, perform my regret, make amends.

What's my line? Did I have any lines?

Otherwise, his presence would've been nothing but scenery to me—he'd existed strictly in bitparts, never as a whole. Until then, I'd thought of him only as a supporter, a walking dead rerun, I'd known him only as a man who—a generation after appearing as the first teacher cannibalized by student zombies in the last installment of a horror franchise, as the smilingly wisenheimer outtaboro accent of an animated knishcart in a popular afterschool cartoon series—didn't even work with my wife, but worked for her.

A face without a voice, a voice without a face, though even if both were retained, I couldn't remember his name. I hadn't expected him to feature in my marriage, and, moreover, even if I had, I could never have suspected that the character most natural for me to portray—Jewish Husband #1—would feel guilty about it.

"I'm sorry," I said, "I'm interrupting."

Rach raised her head, said, "You're not," but too formally, as if our next meeting would be with our lawyers.

"Decided to take the day off?"

"What about you—keeping tabs on me?"

"I had a meeting."

"We're having one too," and she bowed to the actor, who was friendly, or who was trying to be, I'll give him that—when he held my face with his and said, "You're the husband."

Rach, helplessly, laughed, "Take two."

He repeated, but did so reluctantly, "You're the husband."

Rach, out of control, shrieked her teethbleach, "Isn't that fantastic?"

"Isn't what fantastic?"

She shrilled, clogstomped, applauded, "You never watched our spot?"

"My apologies," I said to him, and to her, "I'm sure you never told me to watch it."

"I did," she said. "A couple's like asleep in bed—does that ring a bell?"

My sneaks sunk in the soppy turf, grass engrossing, growing over the heels—"Ringing nothing."

"Like a couple's asleep in bed," she said. "At least they're presented like a couple in bed, in the suburbs—when suddenly an alarm sounds loud from downstairs, it wakes them up and the woman whispers it must be a burglar, like get up, like go downstairs and be a man—you're positive I never showed you?"

"About the only thing I'm positive about."

I was honestly ignorant, yet I loathed her describing ads to me, her scolding me for having to describe them.

"So the guy steps out like with a baseball bat on tiptoe, only to meet like a stranger prowling around the den and shouting who are you and the guy's screaming who are you and like he's got the bat cocked and is about to take a swing but like hesitates just perfectly because the stranger, the alleged burglar who's all balled in the corner, he whimpers?"

"I'm the husband," the actor gave an imitation whimper.

"That's who you are?" I said. "You're the husband?"

"The other guy," Rach said. "It's our spot for Skilling Security."

\

I've since rectified, viewed it online:

After that line the camera pans disinterest across the cozy den, taking in a row of photos of the wife from upstairs alongside the second man, the supposed burglar, plowing the ski slopes, hippie fab at their wedding, babyboomed flabby on an anniversary cruise.

After a cut to the logo of Skilling Security like a coat of arms with a Yield sign, the ad cuts again to EMTs, fire, two burly cops cuffing the adulterer.

A final tense shot of husband and wife, confronted by infidelity, cozened by den and moon.

The commercial's wife, the actress, appears to be younger than Adam but older than Rach, who cast her, I'm sure, so as not to attract him or be threatened herself. Or just so the relationship would test appropriate agewise. As for the husband, he's not my type, but not Rach's either. She had the egalitarian audacity to cast a Vietnamese, who's ageless.

But it's Adam who has the last word, in custody overdub, police cruiser voiceover, though now I can't recall what it was, rather I can't differentiate it from the last words of his other commercials I clicked on (for razors, deodorants, cholesterol meds), nor can I recall him, for that matter, in any of the made for TV dramedies, or the direct to video aliens vs. robots action thrillers I torrented (always portraying the reliable neighbor in the former, and a rabbi in the latter), as having been wardrobed or madeup at all differently than he was just then, a gentle goof in suede, an endearing streak of sunblock down the nose stump.

"I'm Adam," he said, finally rolling the credits.

His sitting height was my standing height. His hand was damp, but the body behind it was muscle.

"No doubt," I said, "Rach's told me everything about you."

"You might as well join us."

"Already?" Rach said.

I said, "Since the weather's so nice."

"It is," Adam patted a slat.

Rach said, "Already?"

Adam said, "A pleasure."

"I'd love to," I said, "but I have writing to do."

Rach said, "No doubt"—like she was flinging a crust, as I hurried off for Ridgewood.

Cut.

One last repeat, one last syndication:

Another man's career is revived, only because of his relationship with my wife, and I'm supposed to take that as material. A suggestion for Adam's next vehicle: an adaptation of Rach's life, in which I play him and he plays me.

How am I, a writer, supposed to feel about having lost you to a reader? Not even—a memorizer?

What to say, Rach? Will you tell me what to say?

://

May through to June I spent my time deciding how to spend my time, which is the first, second, and third through nine thousand seven hundred and griftyfifth items on the agenda of every writer, or neurotic. I was getting ahead of myself, fretting whether the book would have to have notes or sources cited, fretting whether I'd be allowed to decide anything at all.

Meanwhile, the sweater layers came off and then the women put on shorts and then the men put on shorts and everyone became a child. The appliancerie threw up bunting declaring preseason priceslashes on BBQs and ACs, and all the children were out on Atlantic Avenue slurping challenging snowcones in flavors like tripe.

I, no surprise, was camped inside, grilling windowless. Heinekens, pinching the filters out of Camels.

The desk had to be cleared, but then what—go clear out any unmatched gloves I'd left uptown? pack out Ridgewood's Rach clutter and return it? Spring cleaning—my neighbors, my floor of nine thousand seven hundred and griftyfive units, were into that too.

The unit to one side, the trove of an Albanian who peddled arts recordings mailorder and in person, DVD, VHS, Regions 1 and 2, even rarees on reels, 10mm, 8mm, of concerts and operas, tours of the Hermitage, the Louvre, Gemäldegalerien, both samizdat shaky cameraworks he produced himself from the back rows of Lincoln Center, and classier documentaries duped from public broadcasting, all for homebound infirm or dying oldsters who couldn't be bothered with or couldn't afford a system upgrade. The unit to the other side, the vault of a dire Sri Lankan trying to become the exclusive stateside distributor of only the worst products of his island: floppy slabs of irregularly cut rubber reclaimed from sparetires, coir, peat, microwaveable pouches of a prespiced rice—Sprice.

I wasted a lot of that stretch with them, out in the hall in plastiwicker patio chairs from a patio furnisher, and a homeshopping supplier's rotating fans.

"You can have shot the actor for $10,000," according to the Albanian, "or for that you can have also two new womens and not the Tirana bitches but the healthy country girls from Kukës."

The plaintive Sri Lankan, "You will write for the CNN about my rice?"

I didn't know what I wanted, Rachwise, and I was as angry at her as I was, I'll admit, turned on—by the thought of her wanting that actor. After my hallmates left for their own domestic disturbances I got onto wifi and clicked past Adam's ads, trafficked into his filmography, his televisionography, his large and small screen oeuvre or at least his performances not expressly endorsing rugged yet sensitive colognes, refreshing, switching among the networks—Proven Nexports, WinsumGypsum, AY86MNO22, Readyornotherei1111 (in order of reliability), some from businesses whose proprietors had given me their wpas or wpa2s in order to facilitate my redaction of debt consolidation/collection correspondence, others I'd just guessed (either the names of the networks themselves, or abcdefgh, or that CAPPED, or 12345678, or a combo), but none of his films or shows I found had any sex scenes, rather he, or his characters—because a writer has to be careful about confusing a person with his characters—weren't involved in any of them: always it was his son fucking someone, or his daughter fucking someone, after which he, Adam, might have a benignly erotic talk with her about it, or a stern but supportive discussion with her partner. *Revenge of the Nasteroids* I liked. Also the complete Season 2 of *Fare Friends,* except for the episodes "The Bantling Commission" and "Dolly Dispatch."

In *Daaaabbb!* and its sequel *Daaaaaaaabbbbbb!* he was animated again—busy, active, but also a cartoon—some type of anguimorph in length trailing a long scorpion's tail without a stinger. He was, I realized, some variety of lizard, and then a franchise fansite's posting clarified, he was a mastigure, of the genus Uromastyx, and another posting debated which species. The head, because I'm not sure whether lizards have faces, had Adam's dry/wet features, his slitherine expressions and gestures, and, of course, his voice, conventionally rugged, with fugettaboutit dabs.

But that must've been relatively easy—for the rest, it was just a matter of having him strip and slapping nodes on his tits, letting a computer model his motions.

I clicked through the clips and, in the midst of loading part 3 of 21, I must've fallen asleep and the signal must've too, because waking up it was frozen, and I was in a sweat.

The phone. Aar was checking in, "How's it going already?"

I said, "Nothing going," and I told him no one had been in touch, and then I told him about Rach.

"What am I supposed to do?"

"Don't contact him, he'll contact you."

But I'd meant—about Rach?

Calls also came from Finnity, but I ignored them, and the msgs were: "Is this your phone, Josh? It's Finn," "So this is the number Aaron gave me, just wondering if you've gotten any sense of the project timeline or maybe you're already working?" "It's your daily obscene phonecall from your editor, just wondering what you're wearing and what the plans are if you've made them?" "Regrets OK if I'm wrongnumbering you but that's the price of an automated greeting, or else OK if you're there Josh I'm just going to have to conclude that your not picking up or ringing me back is like some fantasy tantrum about something from way in the past that neither of us had control over—it's Finnity?"

Rach didn't leave any msgs, just called.

\

Important that I explain.

Some, not all but some, of my avoidance of their calls was about as basic as psych ever gets: with Finnity, I was delaying a reconciliation with the editor who'd abandoned me and my book in our time of mutual distress and yet whose meddling I'd now have to stet again due to a perversity of Aar's—a perversity I'd have to appreciate—and then with Rach, I was procrastinating the final total squaring of even more convoluted, more vulnerable, accounts.

But the rest of my evasion was professional in nature.

I had, contrary to the terms of the no conflicts of interest clause in my contract, another client. I had a single active client. My last, and special. Especially demanding.

She was a curator, and a perennially tenuretracked assistant professor at CUNY, and I'd been ““““““working”””””” with her off and on for a desultory year or year and a half, and also working on a vague ms. vaguely concerned with archaeological controversies that if it doesn't make her scholarly career will at least make her scholastically notorious as it's intended for a general audience. In practical terms that meant helping her edit the indefatigable writing she did for various archaeology and Egyptology journals and exhibition monographs—which became, as I got involved, duographs, I guess—recasting the required academese for mass appeal while retaining the authoritative tone. She had a cubicle at the CUNY Graduate Center, in Midtown, but preferred to rendezvous at home, specifically in her bedroom, Tribeca (bought when the market was down, when the towers went down and only the ruthless were buying beyond Canal Street). Her name, not that it's important—Alana, or Lana, which is "anal" backwards, which is how anal's done (I initially noticed this reversal in our cheval glass reflection—her lucubratory loft was otherwise bare).

During the second week of May—after having been out of touch, and then away again on perfunctory fieldwork in South America—she called. It'd been a while. It'd been ugly how we parted. Then she called again, and left another msg, but now about having been invited to deliver a lecture at a summer institute—a seminar series held in a pristine mountain state that presented the work of diverse scholars and famous public policy types to the busy and wealthy who required an educational justification for their leisure.

All that was required, she said, was a breezy summary of her blown uncollated messy ms., though she also said she'd decided to focus her presentation on mummies—nothing pleased a crowd of the retired rich like mummies, apparently. So, she wanted to meet. Then, fourth week of May, she needed to meet. Unfortunately, she knew how to find me, and unlike Rach didn't have an aversion to multistop, multitransfer, masstransit.

We labored (I did) on something that would air aloud, something oral, but had to finish—prematurely—and told her I'd email her the rest.

She never paid me—not cash. It wasn't that type of relationship.

There was hardly any work left to do on it—but still I let it drag, the lecture (there were other conclusions I'd always put off).

Until after she'd dialed, and redialed, if-I-get-your-voicemail-I'm-going-to-act-like-my-phone's-in-my-purse dialed, I-just-happen-to-be-driving-a-Prius-on-the-way-to-a-coworker's-parent's-shiva-in-Nassau-County dialed, and I had to pick up to avoid another surprise. I was laying on the curses like I was protecting my tomb: I couldn't meet, not here, neither in her corkwalled cenacle between two cenacles each shared by a dozen prying prudish anthropology and sociology department adjuncts, I wasn't feeling well, I had other deadlines—I couldn't stop by her loft to primp her in the mirrored center of the bed amid all that white Egyptian cotton, reaching over only now and then to the bedstands to languidly spin her globes and point—stop.

It would've been disastrous—getting into that again.

Instead, gut spilling over my laptop's lip, I screened more of Adam, but more of his earlier vehicles, from when he was my age, when he was younger, a child, becoming dissatisfied with clips and even sequentials and so going to torrent the entireties, torrenting illegally, getting dropped, returning and resuming, .ph, .id, malware centrals, poisoning my computer, giving it fullblown whatever's worse than AIDS, now that AIDS is treatable.

Anything to divert me. Anything to distract.

\

All books have to be researched, but readable books have their research buried. The facts have to be wrapped like mummies, in the purest and softest verbiage, which both preserves them and makes them presentable. Instead of straight explanations, analogies must be pursued—like mummies. Examples, instances—next chapter.

I thought the other JC had forgotten me, or that the job itself had just been a thought—a whim of his, or mine—my "imagination," which is how a writer phrases a mania or pathology. I'd get to his book in the afterlife, if then.

June. I sat laptopped amid the doldrums, the slowdown, the season when traditional publishing takes fourday weekends at Montauk, when even the sites are updated only sporadically, remotely. I finally returned on Finnity, but in the plasmic midst of night, leaving 2:37, 4:19 msgs on voicemail, and when he'd call back in the morning I wouldn't pick up. The msgs I left were just, "No news, I'm assuming it's off," and he'd voicemail in response, "No news on this end either but still we have to talk," and my next call would be, "Let's try to get an extension—also ever catch *Daaaabbb!*? or *Daaaaaaaabbbbbb!*? They're about this lizard and lizards are reptiles, which live on land laying eggs as opposed to amphibians, their ancestors, which are born in the water with gills only to grow up into lungs and die on land, but I'm not sure with them about the egg thing," and his reply was, "The terms were no contact until contact's made, but once it is I'll try for an extension, which means we have to meet—me, you, Aar," and I'd just capacitate his box, "I can't, I'm deep into drafting this thing starring this NY Jewish kid who while on a class trip to the White House wanders off by accident and finds in a bathroom a telex using the Soviet GOST block cipher, and he deciphers it, just like that, just like nothing, and tells the president what the telex says, and whatever it says, I haven't gotten to that yet, it's enough to convince the president to end Cold War ICBM brinkmanship, and the West is saved and the kid's father who's from the USSR and is now in the numbers rackets down on Orchard Street is proud—I've been getting into this one specific actor, but also into 1980s and 90s representations of mathematicians and scientists onscreen" (I was cut off, I'm figuring, around the recap of the president).

I sat spotlit by the homepage, Tetration.com, boring my head into its underdesign, the whole shallowbacked templatitude of it, trying to find out what was going on, and even once tetrating, "where is joshua cohen?" and "when will he get in touch with me?"

I went to the Midtown library, and read—but bury the algorithms, the histories of tubes, transistors, circuits, of processor architecture and the invention of memory—maxed out my understanding and turned to Egyptology, borrowed the techbooks for later along with a Theatrepedia in which "Adam Shale" was mentioned.

I came out of the main branch and past the tarred trunks to Broadway, which anytime I'm on it I'm amused is also "Broadway"—at least to the prairie herds of fannypackers that roam between shows. This is the only sort of mental masturbation that gets me through Times Square.

Because someone was behind me, and someone was, millions. But in among them, the stands of balloontwisters and calligraphers who are paid to write "Peace" and "Love" in Hanzi but instead write "Scum" and "Twat," the chula churro carts and that truck that does nachos and roofies, the same person, again, on another block, an Asian—in an intemperate sweatsuit and cap, Red Sox and red crocs.

An Asian of indeterminate everything: intention, gender, age, even Asianness. Indeterminate even if he or she were the same entity each time. Rach, at this point, would've condemned me for racism, though not only don't I care and write this for myself, but as a reader I'd surely enjoy a book by an Asian in which he or she suspects they're being followed by a white person, but can't be sure of that white person's intent or gender or age, or whether that white person is the same person every time or even white. I'm perseverating, I know, but thoughts have to be followed to their ends, the end of next block, and then keep going, to avoid being overtaken.

By the highway, the Hudson—the library books straining at their delibags, corners poking. Straining my arms, throttling my hands, the numb rewards of literacy. The Paronomasian, let's say, turned to close the gap to the curb. A whiff of brine, a swank trestle adumbrant, Loading Only No Standing, 14th & 10th—this was Tetration's NY HQ.

I went through the doors and stood facing anything but the street, until a Tetbot treaded over to make inquiries. I stood behind a rubberplant. The Tetbot reversed and treaded after me. It was a clownwigged trashcan that barely reached my lowest hanging ball yet without compunction it was demanding my credentials: Tetrateer? or Tetguest?

Since last I was here all or nothing had changed: there was just a new type of new in evidence—all novelty has this feeling, this rush. A provisionality. Something to marvel at, not something to trust. The bot was trying to palaver with me in a crepitant creole, increasing its volume and titling itself and then treading away.

A monitorbank mounted on the crosstown wall showed activity at every subtetplex, where there was day, like here, and where there was night, like Amsterdam, Copenhagen, Moscow, Tel Aviv, which were nonetheless still busying. Everyone was being scrutinized, but denied ultimate access, the access to themselves. Everyone was being made reciprocally vulnerable. All lobbies were onscreen but this one, which existed strictly in my poses. It was my duty, then, to be conspicuous. I flung my limbs bagladen just so that someone in some other life might choose me. But I was chosen from just behind by a guard. (A human.)

"May I help you, sir?"

"I sure hope so," I said, realizing that to him I was a transient. "I have a reservation for the Circle Line Cruise?"

\

Maintaining that I hoofed it back to Ridgewood would account for the next week, give or take, though I paced that distance inside, ordering in until my cash ran out and running to the ATM at the Comida Fresca Cada Día—leery of any Asian not affiliated with the nearby Tianjin Trading Ltd., or Lucky Monkey Lumber & Millwork. I read a lot of news, which I liked to read because text, unlike newer media, didn't tell me how to pronounce it: "Jamahiriya," "Ansar al-Sharia"—the Arab Spring seemed an issue of *Vogue,* the *Times* was so into wiretaps and leaks it'd become an electrical or plumbing manual. I studied the techbooks, which had underlinings and highlightings and in one a frayed crocheted bookmark from what had to've been a little old lady striving to master her little old PC. I searched Rach's blog with the thought of identifying our pseudonymized friends, Rach's friends who might've known about her affair, who if they'd ever reach their mentions themselves would have to search for the scarf they wore or the wallet they lost on their last lunchdate with Rach, in the very terms Rach used in her posting (searching online becoming a writerly endeavor: the search for the perfect detail, or error).

6/6, I got an email from Cal, replying to my own email of drunks ago. He wrote me about how "optimal" it was that this Muslim unrest had coincided with his book hiatus, and how "unabatingly obligated" he was to his editors and the reporters who'd taken his beat. As for the unrest itself, it was still undecided "whether the oppositions will do the governing required." Anyway, it was "awesome and poignant that technology that was so manipulative is now so cheap it might level the playing field for civil disobedience." However this was merely his transition to fiction—rather to mansplaining wisdom about fiction. Cal wrote that while technology itself might be "naturally ambivalent," he was certain it was "anathema" to novels, "to the vicissitudes of the novel," in that for a novel to "function properly"—as if novels were like a tool, not a bluntness—its characters had to be kept apart from each other, "separated into missing each other and never communicating," and that now in this present of pdas and online, people were rarely ever "plausibly alone," everyone now knew what everyone else was doing, and what everyone else was thinking, and the result was a life of fewer crosspurposes and mixups, of less portent and mystery too—and I agreed with him, I'd already agreed, because I'd recognized the ideas as having been plagiarized verbatim from an interview with a decrepit South African literary pundit just published at the site of the *NYRB*.

Anyway, Cal signedoff by asking, as he always asked, whether I was working on anything, and I answered that I'd just completed an email, nonfiction.

The next email to slip from my hands (two fingers, hardbitten nails) was sincerer.

I told myself I had to finish the last lecture page for the professoress by midnight, be done with it, and at midnight I uploaded and clicked send, and she wrote back with such speed it was like she'd responded before I'd sent it, or at least like she'd had her response already prepared and saved under Drafts. Lana wrote to thank me with an invitation to the summer institute—apparently she was allotted one guest and it "has 2 b u."

I wrote another email declining—don't waste the keystrokes on how, why—and Lana wrote me back, "lets chat."

"I don't have chat."

"just download it here," a link to Tetchat.

"You can always just call me. But I'm not sure I'm ready for another trip. Need to sort things w/ Rach. Need time."

"download prick dont be such a

"a

"a

"a

My laptop was colorwheeling, so cursed to its cursor that force quit had to be skipped for the nuclear option, Off/On.

Then the phone rang and though it was a regular ring and the number wasn't listed, I went for it, "No patience."

But the voice though expectedly female was Asian, like reared in Asia, "Excuse? Hello, Mr. Cohen?"

"Speaking?"

"Please pack a single piece of luggage, including only materials important to your process—everything else will be provided. Waiting outside your studio residence is a Lincoln Continental, black. You will meet it within 10 minutes. Your flight departs JFK at 7:00."

"To? I'm guessing Palo Alto?"

"Palo Alto does not have a commercial airport. Delta 269 nonstop to SFO. San Francisco. 10:18 PDT, arrival."

"Oskar Kilo."

"Excuse?"

"That just means OK."

"Please, one precaution we ask: take your phone or pda and remove its battery, leave both the battery and chassis at home. You will not require it."

She didn't have to ask twice—she didn't.

Goodbye (646).

://

The shift to Palo Alto was—I'm already regretting this—tectonic.

Not because there was this apparently extremely minor earthquake or tremor just as my flight was being cleared for landing and we were delayed, an hour, hovering, two hours—the last time I fly commercial—nor because all my typical eastern negativity toward the West always threatens to break and chunk and pile up into violent incoherence.

Rather I'm talking a totally personal, emotional rupture. Coming to the other coast, single, oneway, felt like a permanent upheaval.

Also, I was all sorts of pilly.

I have what's called an addiction to Ativan, and Xanax. Which is preferable to admitting to an aversion to planes.

The livery smartcar had a partition between me and what must've been a driver, but the switches just lowered the windows and a platelet of GPS. Our destination was La Trovita Lando, which I took for a city, or for a neighborhood. It was a slough through brackish marshes, a ping at a gate, and we stopped. And I stepped out into the snaring web of a twentynothing woman, covered with spidery henna, her hands just slobbered with cobs—spinning me through the grounds to a lavish stucco cottage, unlocking the door, handing me the key, then sticking around spraddled in the doorway, one hairy armpit aired by the jamb.

I'm proud of myself for not mentioning until now that she was Asian. She was. Now hatless. Braless vest and culottes.

"It was you on the phone?"

Nothing.

"Or at the library—but isn't there a library closer to home? Like in your lap or whatever?"

Or in her vest. She took from its midzip pouch the house pda, a Tetheld.

"Your guestwork is paltoguest0014," she said. "For access you will have to create a uname/pword, each a min of eight alphanumerics, the pword to contain a symbol and CAP."

"I'll try," taking the Tetheld from her, klutzing the keying, creating both out of my former accounts.

Her Tetheld informed: that uname is not available, and I said, "That uname is not available," and she said, "What does it suggest? Can you follow the prompt?"

It suggested Jcohen19712, which was also to become my email.

I chose the dollarsign to close my pword—$ finishing what'd been my pword for all.

In other accommodations the bellhop points for his tip to the thermostat, or offers to lead you up the lilypad slates toward the saunas, but here the orientation was only: how to get online.

She took back her Tetheld, "We have been instructed to apologize. Today will be busy."

"It will? What's the schedule?"

"Party prep. Invasion and occupation. Caterers. Florists. Amusements. Petting zoo."

"I don't understand—party for what?"

The face she purged was disgusted.

"His birthday?"

"His?"

Principal's, she informed me as she flicked, finalized my account. His 40th, tomorrow.

Was I supposed to have mindread? or have been previously briefed?

She had an @ bud pierced above her lip. Her Tetheld shook, "You are affirmed."

"Confirmed?"

"Affirmative."

"Confirmative?"

She buttoned again, "May we have a moment with your computer?"

My computer—two years old? two generations and an operating system defunct? A present from Rach from my own birthday past, a generous provocation to earn. As I dug through my bag for my laptop, I considered the immediate gift politics—what to give a quadragenarian who has everything? besides donating to a favorite cause? Besides myself, I mean.

"We have been instructed to transfer everything—your .docs, your contacts—all will be the same."

"Why?"

"There is a requisition order."

"Requisitioning what?"

"A new laptop."

She left, I pottered, lasers raved across the windows and mariachis tuned. I'd only just unpacked and was resting on the cot when there was a knock at the door, and without me responding she entered, "We are sorry for keeping you waiting, Mr. Cohen."

I took the slab from her, "Thank you, Miss?"

"You are welcome, Mr. Cohen."

"Miss?"

"Myung."

She turned to go so I went grasping: "It's smaller."

".72"/1.8 cm × 12"/30.4 cm, × 8.2"/20.8 cm the depth."

"Lighter too."

"2.4 lbs/1.08 kg."

"Brand?" because none was evident.

"Tetbook prototype."

"You've moved into computers?"

"No."

"I don't understand."

"Prototype."

Drop it, rather—don't, "But everything's still on it?"

"Everything."

"You sure?"

"Even the apps you will never use are on it."

"Appreciated—but where's my old unit?"

"Excuse me?"

"Larger, heavier? My oldie?"

That flustered. "Most guests do not want theirs back."

"Most everyone hasn't a clue what they want."

"Please," resetting herself, "you are also completely backed up to servers. Clouded. Nubified. Nephed. Your files are now protected online. Accessible to your account only."

"Jcohen19712 then my password?"

"Precisely. If that is what it is, precisely."

"So this is mine to keep?"

"All yours."

"As for the oldster?"

"Yes?"

"You've trashed it already, haven't you?"

"Do not worry. We recycle."

It was only when my deliverer had departed, when I was alone with this foldable tablet where all my files, or copies, were nestled nicely again, or anew, into folders, that I realized just how much they had the goods on me, how much intel was available on my preferences, vice. I had no secret, I was no secret, to be Principal's guest was to have nowhere to hide—not just the laptop but, beyond the panes, the surveillance outside, the tall strong stalks of spyquip planted amid the birch and cedar, the sophisticated growths of recognizant CCTV, efflorescing through my bungalow's peephole, getting tangled in the eaves. I bawled myself out, got cotted, covered my face with the dresser's doily and scrolled schiztic for what to disclaim, for which self to accuse of what inclination: the offlabel oxycodone and hydrocodone ordered scriptless from British Columbia, the minoxidil reliance legal though mortifying, all that screengrab analingus. Meanwhile, vans and trucks were offloading dusk—a carousel clattered from a trailer, ferris wheel assembly clamor, a log flume hosed, trampolines inflated.

\

Waiting to be collected by dark. Waiting mopey for Myung. As the helicopters chopped my sleeping into naps. As the gusts balmed in chatter between the blinds.

Finally I got up, showered and shaved and toweled over to my wheeliebag to formally decide (wrinkled old City Hall ceremony suit? wrinkled older bookparty suit?), ineluctably jeansed it below a tshirt Rach'd gotten me from the Mark Twain House in Connecticut: black, "Mark *This* Twain" in graffiti white, an arrow pointing dickward.

My presence aside, I still hadn't come up with anything as tribute—again, what do you get the Founder of everything? besides flattery? Beautiful. It was just beautiful. The trail to Principal's back 40 acreage had been redcarpeted, a door policy was in effect.

At trail's terminus was a cupreous voluptuous Chicana. The thing in her hand must've been an unreleased Tetheld, judging by how it disturbed attendees into fussing with their own models, noting equivalencies, compatibilities, breathing screens and wiping them clean.

The Tethelds were scanned—touchless mating of machines—the attendees were admitted, returned their devices to their pockets, patting, reassuring: like it was the last time they'd make love to a spouse they'd have to abandon.

The invites were surveys, apparently—digi.

Waiting for approval, I recognized: the chairman/cofounder of America's most popular eTailer, a crowd theory academic from UC Berkeley, the COO of a premier iConometry site, a venture capitalist/immediate past California state controller, a Congressperson who'd been advocating for the establishment of a Department of Online (DO) within the next president's cabinet (the president of the United States), and then—far in the front, past cyberpunkadelic bodimodis, transdermally implanted proboscideans, vulcan jedis with diversified portfolios and freshly filed teeth—was the alternative to the alternatives, was Finnity.

I wanted to sign off, I wanted to sign out—whichever had the most hits, or provided the least traceable exit.

Which flight had he been on? the red eye or brown nose? The rest of him was a ruddy blond—and perfectly unfolded, with not an extraneous crease—tweeded like a lordly hunter.

I might've guessed: Finn never missed parties—he would've hitched if he'd had to.

He scanned, was admitted, indifferently seamless, but because I didn't have a pda or even a rotary dragging an oinker's cord all the way from NY, the Chicana guided me under the privacy of a willow, "I'll have to take this actinally."

"Take what?"

"Your dietary requirements," clicking her screen. "So: vegetarian, vegan, pescatarian, lactovo, or macrobiotic?"

"Are you serious?" but as her thumbs huddled I answered myself, "I'm an omnivore."

"Now do you mind eating out of the Greater Bay? Or do you insist on zipsourcing—94/95000s?"

"Anything goes."

"Any allergies?"

"Just to being interrogated."

She put me down for seconds of testiness, "This is only because you didn't respond online."

"You asked this on an invite?"

"It's just protocol."

I was Table ${}^{\pi i}e$—which was difficult to remember atechnically. But if the seating arrangements were what I suspected, that would be the one to avoid.

The festivities were centered on a capacious bullfighting ring patio flanked by Moorishish fountains reviving ponds. Hubs of eager earnest convo, politics too optimistic for opinion. Mass delusion. Mass hydration.

The patio: La Korto—every notable architectural element was labeled, was to be referred to, in a slurred Spanish that was just Esperanto. La Trovita Lando, the compound—the main house above us (La Domo), the guest huts beyond (La Domoj), enshrouded in fog.

The xeriscaped rear descended into the vast gape of a wildlife refuge: a semiofficial preserve and so another tax dodge to Principal, a religious life—mission farmland and clergy R&R—to the Spanish, but originally a religion itself—animism, totemism, dendrolatry—to the indigenous Indians, whom the Spanish called the *Costeños*, or "coastal people," but who called themselves *Ohlone: Ohlo* = "western," *ne* = "people."

All information offered by my employer, sin costo.

The info both explained, and became, my surroundings: The darkness was cypress, juniper, madrone. The trailside eruptions were of manzanita and sage. The interfaces scattered around the property obtruded with names, in English, in Spanish, their Native American names and *Genus, species*. I trackballed one: "Tell me more about *chaparral*."

The interfaces served dual functions: to educate, sure, but for the more curious—to mark the perimeter of the wild. No Trespassing. Be content with what vantage you have. Go beyond, get a foot stuck in a conquistador helmet, a tomahawk wedged in the head.

I had the sense, though, that those woods were where the real party was—the real debauchery, I mean. Those woods were made for culty fucking, if not for fucking then for fireside circlejerking, critter sacrifice—who had the coke? what's a Cali dally without pot (without unrefined hemp utensils, dishes, and stemware)?

I was about to make a break for them when the apéritif/hors d'oeuvres sampling was called by the perky MC, Conan O'Brien (*Late Night with Conan O'Brien*)—the only chair vacant was mine. I had to either leave or confront—a round table, Finnity counterclockwise from me, lagging always a moment behind.

"Yo," he said.

"Eloquent," I said. "Yo back."

He took it, he grimaced but took it. Perspiration down my crevice, already.

"So," he said, "a surprise?"

"I think our host knows it's his birthday."

"You know what I mean."

"Sure, my life's been nothing but surprises—for what's it been for us? A decade?"

"10 years Aar's filled us both in on."

"What's left to say then?"

"That ever stopped you before?"

"It wasn't you I was avoiding in line, it was definitely Gwyneth."

I didn't mean to be so rude, just I felt—cornered, even at a circular table. Babysat, boosted.

"You want to know why I'm here?"

"I want to know why you think you're here, Finn."

"I thought it would be nice to talk."

"I was going to say frequentfliers, I was going to say points."

"I trust you're keeping your receipts."

"You came to intimidate me into getting to work—but you're staying for the favors, the swag?"

Conan (*The Tonight Show with Conan O'Brien*), loosened tie, hair swept up like someone had jizzed it, told a joke about some Silicon Valley Social Media PR summit happening now "at the Best Western in Menlo Park," but empty, unattended—not because everyone was here, but because it hadn't been publicized.

"One dork, one geek, one nerd, all male, just hanging around polishing the icecubes."

He told a Gwyneth joke funnier than mine—when Finn leaned in: "You might've made time for me in NY."

We got sommeliered by a guy with a cowbelling tastevin. Finn went white, I went red, both of new autochthonous vintage.

His cheers: "To your book," mine: "To your book."

To ours, to theirs, earthy, hints of bile.

"Josh—this is us doing the mending, OK? Healing up? It's enough. No more grudges. No more blame."

"Sure, why not? How to argue that? Edit away—you're the editor."

"Keep lying to yourself—you're the writer."

"Finn, you can return to your prixfixe friends at Café Loup in peace. Your ambush was successful."

"Enough, Josh? What did you expect me to do back then—take out a fullpage color ad in *The New Yorker* saying ignore the tragedy and read this book?"

"I get it."

"Fuck it, I tried for you—OK? I had the *Times* chasing you for a feature, didn't I?"

"The angle was like author victimized."

"OK?"

"Wasn't exactly dignified."

"Nothing was dignified then except to shut the fuck up. Still I leaned on them to let you write it."

"Promote myself—not exactly tactful either."

"That was the choice—whore or be whored. But you went lofty."

"But there could've been a rerelease. There could've been a goddamned paperback."

"That was shit luck—it's not like I landed so smoothly either. The quarterlies came around and we all had to explain our no sales and why we hadn't been signing up Islam books all through the summer like we had warning. The publishers were acting like they'd all known about the attacks forever—why didn't we know? Why weren't we prepared with books on how to cope with jihad or the infrastructure of hawala or a comprehensive history of the House of Saud, or, fuck it, a Guantánamo tellall by the fucking 20th hijacker, OK?"

"Got it."

Finn iced himself down and sipped, whispered, "You haven't met our Principal, have you?"

"I was expecting you to introduce me."

"He doesn't know I'm here—I begged an invitation off an exgirlfriend from Gopal," and he nodded a radius through the table at four brunette romcoms.

"Get her to introduce us, all four of them."

"She doesn't think he's here."

"I don't think I'm here either."

Our server approached.

She was wearing a stetson and roper boots, denim overalls underall which I'm not sure.

"Your preferenced meals will be out momentarily," she said. "For now, does anyone need anything?"

Finn said, "Nada."

"Just as an update," she smiled, "for dessert you'll be having the birthday cake, which is glutenfree, the candles are sustainable beeswax."

"Muchas gracias." Finn reached out to tug straight her bandana.

"Also keep in mind," she was saying as she swatted his hand, "with continued climate change, drought will affect over half of the world in this century alone. That's half of the whole world, not just the developing. So, we're doing all we can to moderate our water waste. By not changing your plates, you're changing lives. Snap the QR on your napkin rings to get involved."

I excused myself behind her: pretense was the toilet, purpose was the bar.

I trailed, and turned past the wagonwheel tables of every industry's pioneers, destined for the dimming. Passing fame, passing actual fame. Not the observed in the park, but the celebrated globally. People—what's more than people? more like businesses, companies, corporations, states unto themselves?—whose reps, even, whose lowliest brand ambassadors, would never return my calls.

It was a reality show—an actuality show—a making of a behind the scenes collision. Two Nobel laureates (Physics, Peace), two models whose models, unlike the laureates', I understood (thanks, Rach), the actor who got top billing in something Adam was in (won't drop a name, but rhymes with "Mom Thanks"), another who won an Oscar for directing a host of somethings Adam was never in (rhymes with "Even Spielberg"), an andrologist with an infomercial system, a copyright attorney who commented on extremist cable, and Oprah? Fat Oprah and her skinnier double? Everyone lounging, chatty, bingey purgey—entouraging one another, giving interview, posing, thronging the serapedraped vitamix stations, mingling the dancezones, Tethelding selfies in pic and vid while decrying the paparazzi.

If they were invited, they were a celebrity. Even if this was just a job for them, they were a celeb. They had to be, the fame was contaminating. The wraithy freckled red bandanafied servergirl, all the servers, they were moonlighting microphenoms not only by moonlight but in their true industries too, with even the busboys, the prides of Sonora, maintaining their own stalky followings.

I joined, danced through—no one else had my moves—toward a holographic bonfire lighting up the forest. Finally, a pit of the party's only stiffer provision, a makeshift cantina camp pitched twinkly out in the night like the last settlement before everything went savage—calling a younger crowd, guzzling heirloom beers and heritage cocktails of one part freerange to two parts forage, muddled into mason jars out of the back bays of circled Conestogas.

A girl bordelloized to impress asked, "When's Lady Gaga showing?" A ranchhanded guy said, "It's Dylan & Jagger," and the girl asked, "Who's that?"

I waited for my hooch behind a pornstached chillionaire and his two brogrammer friends, by which I mean his coworkers at #Summerize, according to their shirts and shorts and hats.

One said, "You can't change the scale without scaling the change."

Another said, "Evoke transcendence."

The chillionaire said, "Will you stop reading that neurolinguistic reinforcement pickup artist shit? This party's got mad fucking latency to it."

His coworkers nodded up from their Tethelds and the transcendence guy said, "All paradigms can be realigned, modulo a pussy deficit. Because if we don't count the nontech women, who don't count us, we're dealing with 6s, the same as always, mid 6s."

"Get positivized," the scalar change guy said. "Or just get beyond the systems integration analysts—the ad rep girls are 8s for def."

The chillionaire said, "For me, this birthday's all about trying to get an audience with the boss. I mean, he bought us without even meeting us, who does that?"

His coworkers clenched smiles at me. The chillionaire noticed and answered himself, "A fucking genius is who. What are you guys feeling—the no carbs rum horchata punch? Or the Red Bull Añejo Paloma?"

But his coworkers' faces shone expressionlessly rapt again in the glows of their Tethelds until the chillionaire said, "Before your batteries are cashed, are you guys checking in with your Tetsets?"

They keyed, and the scalar change guy said, "This says there's a quidditch game for new acqhires happening over by the stables."

The transcendence guy said, "This says if anyone finds a yellow/black GoreTex GoreBike windstopper cycling shell, please reply, reward negotiable."

"There's a capture the flag tourney for vest & resters that's voting now on team captains."

"This says P Diddy's taking all the ad rep pussy to the sweat lodge."

"Hey, sorry, disruption incoming," and the chillionaire was talking to me now. "Can you just take a square of us?"

He handed me his Tetheld, the only one I've ever held, and it was anodized cool. I tried to get them all onscreen. But I wasn't sure what to press, or if there was anything to press. Or even whether the recording was still or in motion, with sound. An Asian, an Arab, and an Indian, all speaking together in questionmarks like white girls. Such were my unspoken thoughts, which only I can record, I think.

The Asian thanked me and posted the groupsquare crossplatform from his Tetset and the Arab and Indian reposted to their own Tetsets, and read the replies as they blipped in: "giddyup you cutie cowboys," "fuck u and fuck the startup u rode in on."

It was their turn to order from the Conestoga. They ordered waters with electrolytes.

I had the fringey coonskincapped hipster pour me an artisanal vodka with artisanal rocks.

As I went for a cig he said, "No smoking."

"Where?"

"Nowhere on property."

They didn't need a sign. They needed a sign for everything else.

"La Bano?" I pointed, "the toilets?" and while the frontierster was pointing them out, I swiped a bottle, biomash rye.

I headed away, swerved for the trees. Forgive me. Fine me for tossing my lighter. It was empty but I still had matches.

I staggered, rolled like a stone. It was all a ball of feints, disguises. Power masquerading as responsibility, stewardship. Excess but slim, trim. Spiritual emaciation in good citizen costume. Wastefulness spun as ethical consumption. A party in honor of health, which improved health. Nothing could fool me, or could fool me enough.

Still, I couldn't get no satisfaction—the leaves rasping hey hey hey. Cause I tried, and I tried, and I tried, and I tried—to distinguish between the rustic and the epic style art: a Calder stabile like a girdered ferruginous rhododendron, and what was either a Richard Serra or a Donald Judd or a boulder.

I couldn't shake a certain bumpkinish feeling, that sense of being a hick, a rube, an unacceptable regression. I spurred myself sloppy, smoked and drank with the roots.

Just ahead was a stand of trees, just tremendous trees, mossy antennas, redwood but pulsing black—their monitors were black, and their bark was livid brown, quakefissured. They too had to acclimate after being transplanted. Weldmesh fence prevented my touch. The path went around them and pebbled away and was panned into sand by the grass.

It was a spit of beach along a salina bayscape. A dimidiate moon, and stars falling darkly pacific.

From out of the nebula and down the beach, a desperado was approaching. I didn't have a weapon, I was freelance. I dug in, sparked the pack's penultimate cig, contemplated another message for the bottle besides breaking it. On his skull, on mine.

He swayed, wary, rolledup pants, rolled shirtsleeves, suitjacket looped around neck, a sockstuffed shoe in each hand, whiteness, Finn.

"Can I get a taste?"

"Taste the empty?" I tipped the bottle to grains.

"Then a smoke?"

I passed the butt, "Why not share?"

He dragged, "You've been making the rounds?"

"I've had people to meet—putting faces to names and names to faces. The next round I'm putting bodies to bodies."

Finn ashed, returned what was left, for me to snuff.

He said, "I'm not keeping tabs."

"I am?"

"But Aaron just happened to mention—something about the wife? She got you down?"

"Mine or yours?"

Finn clapped his heels, "You want some advice, Josh?"

"About what—always be a friend to your friends? Never go swimming on a full stomach?"

Finn grinned, "The book: it can't be a book—it has to be an option. Write it for the screen. The game version. Whatever."

"That's it?"

"I need a property," he mooned. "I need an adaptation."

\

I felt it the next morning. Noon, after. Nothing but hangover fog, a lukewarm front of quit throat. Giving way by evening to arrogance.

Nobody came.

I checked my new account: one email, my first. Jcohen19712@tetmail.com. An invitation to yesterday, a link to a dietary survey. Made another resolution: quit drinking and smoking, check email more or less often.

Drag. Dump Trash. An empty inbox, an empty outbox. A pure, an impeccable, soul.

I went out to get something to eat, and some head analgesia. Just when I had my hand on the handle, a voice said, "Hungry?"

I turned.

The voice said, "Aspirin or ibuprofen?"

"What?"

Voice circumambient, modulated with viperish reverb, then a panel withdrew, the monition of a monitor face. Just opposite my cot. Principal's face. But frozen, cryogenized.

I assumed a malfunction, a fritz.

"It is just a still," the voice said. "Official as like for a book."

"As like what?"

"Or perhaps this one is better?" and the monitor regressed: a Founder's shot, him next to a—I'm just going to call it a server. "Or this one?" a yearbook shot—highschool? college?—teeth agleam amid pleiades of acne. "Or maybe this?" a newborn frame, squashed and jaundiced, clawmarks at the cheeks. "Or?"

"Whichever the fuck," and again, the first familiar image was restored.

"Come back toward the cot—hang out."

"You can see me?"

"Confirmative."

"You can hear me?"

"Confirmative, though on the cot is better—hang loose."

"You're fucking snooping on me?"

"We are doing no such thing. We are offering naproxen? Acetaminophen? Depends how your stomach is—you should not need an anti-inflammatory."

"I'm just trying to avoid taking the hard shit."

"The hard shit?"

I gestured around at all my stuff stowed, "You should know—you think I moved in myself?"

"Pfizer is in the dumps, trading down below 20, indicating low consumer confidence in ibuprofen. Johnson & Johnson is holding steady in the 60s, aspirin is on the up."

"Were you even around for your own 4-0?"

"Around, yes, in attendance, no."

"Did I jerk off?"

"Unclear."

I wanted to wish him happy returns on his birthday, but also I wanted to keep that sentiment pounding in my head, to determine whether it registered.

"We cannot read thoughts."

"Try."

"Think of something."

"Any something?"

"Any."

"Am doing it—you got it?"

At the door was a knock and a black but white goth buff transgender person entered—an XX or an XY or a chromosomally spliced Ze bearing a metal tray. I had not been thinking about its contents. But I did not have that thought until I'd consumed its contents. The tray was divided into quadrants, and all were of composted mush.

I used one of the quadrants to ash in. I wouldn't have minded a beeeeeeeer.

"Go to your Tetbook, the desktop, open the folder Dossier."

The only new folder, "Dosser?"

"There is no *i*?"

"Guess not."

It contained: Tetration site txt, public domain .docs, junk. But then also internal reports. Personnel intel. Official Tetration capsule bios of its prez, its vps of VP (Various Projects), Finance, Futurity/Devo.

Quarterly assessments. Performance reviews with nothing smeared out. How many files? More than scrollable—inscrollable?

Everything has a beginning, or needs one, and if the beginning's identifiable but not dramatic enough, it needs to be deidentified—located elsewhere. Creation stuff, cosmology, a founding myth, lore of origin: light separated from darkness, the wind inseminating the aether—the earth is balanced on the back of an elephant, or held by angels standing on the shell of a turtle—but what was that turtle standing on? was it just tortoise on tortoise forever?

An apple plunging from a tree and inventing gravity, volume determined by water displaced from Antiquity's jacuzzi, a dream about the structure of the solar system being the structure of the atom, a dream about a snake consuming its own tail being the ring structure of the molecule benzene, relativity conceived in a tram as it passed a clock-tower in Bern, coordinate geometry measured by the relationship of a flitting fly and the floor, ceiling, walls of some sordid dorm in Utrecht? or Leiden? A suburban garage with Dad's camper parked out in the driveway—make room for the racks, clear the toolbench for the switches. A grant or degree. A mentor, a mother.

I took it as my job to discern something similar—to search in the way www.searching couldn't, to find in the way www.finding couldn't—which is to say, to conceive, make it up.

Like say I'm talking to myself—how to substantiate the claim? how can anyone but the author authenticate? I had no way of corroborating whether it was or wasn't Principal, talking. His feed could've been recorded in Myanmar, in Burma, prerecorded in Siam, postproduced in Thailand, he could've been coming to me live but two hours behind, eight hours ahead, on whichever side of excruciation's meridian, 36 TbPS streaming straight from the 36th century.

From then on we met constantly, continuously. I questioned, I didn't. Answers were dirigent, direct. This was our background, the setting of scene: the hut monitor displayed graphics resembling the Himalayas (spiky unscalable linecharts of number of urls indexed by year, number of tetrations by year, number of new/unique users by year, number of tetrations by average user by year), resembling the planets Venus and Mars (πcharts of ownership structure) and Bay Area bridges (bargraphs of ad revenue)—thermodynamical models of the tech protocol itself or just organigram tutorials in managerial flow, squiggly doodly retiaries that rendered concepts like vertical or horizontal omnidimensional, unhelpful.

I had access to stuff I shouldn't have had access to, but then Principal shouldn't have had such access to me—cameras, mics. Interfaces: beaming cracks in plaster.

But it was all about others. Nothing about him. None of the material was personal. An interface has no profile.

He spoke to me as a grownup to an infant. A brat pubescent to a rutting pet. Would I be allowed to interview the others? No. In person? No. In writing? No. Can I speak? Talk to the wall.

I had clearance like it was going out of business, but the cost to me was guilt. Families and financials. I knew how many dependents people had, how many savants and seniors, their salaries and dividends, bonuses and dumps. Their incentives for retirement, their splits. Class A, one vote per share. Class B, 10 votes per share. I knew everything but what all this meant to them. How they spoke. Stood and sat. How they groomed.

Were they people? Not to Principal. Not even employees? They were more like digits, widgets, sprockets, more cogs on the command chain.

He guarded his privacy but flung open the doors to the lives of others. His underlings. Their underthings. What's privacy to the employee is security to the boss.

All this factuality grated, was a grate, a veil, a screen—a firewall. There was a firewall between us.

Tetrate "firewall." Though how to decide which site to hold with? the most popular or most reputable? and if reputation shouldn't be popularly decided, then how? and couldn't this question be better asked of politics (management), or religion (ownership)?

Class A knowledge is not as powerful as Class B knowledge, and all the managers be fools and the owners, doctrinaire.

Tetrationary.com, a userdriven site, defines: "Firewalls can either be software-based, or hardware-based, and are used to help keep a network secure," then digresses into types: packets, filters, layers, proxies. Entry last updated by "Myndmatryxxx."

Correction—last updated by myself, as I rejoined the verbal phrase: "Firewalls can be either."

Whereas a more authoritative site, which I'll define as one that employs professionals, at minimumwage, but still—pride counts more than maternity leave or sickdays—states: "1. A fireproof wall used as a barrier to prevent the spread of fire. 2. Any of a number of security schemes that prevent unauthorized users from gaining access to a computer network or that monitor transfers of information to and from the network."

Correction—the site, lexility.com, just freeloaded the work of old print dictionaries and encyclopedias whose compilers are dead and whose compiled kin don't receive any residuals.

Another site says "firewall," in its architectural usage, dates to ca.

1840, in its computing sense, to ca. 1980. Yet another site gets strangely specific, 1848, 1982, on the dots.

Austro-Hungary, apparently, designed the firewall. The Austro-Hungarian theater. Where it was armor dropped from a proscenium to prevent a conflagration onstage from spreading to the audience. No mention on the site as to what might've started the fire onstage—the effects, like the fake cannon that ignited Shakespeare's Globe, likelier than anything textual.

In German, this barrier was called *der Eiserner Vorhang*. "The Iron Curtain." Which another site attributes to Churchill. Whose own source is cited by yet another site as having been the Muslim belief in "the Gates of Iron," "erected by Cyrus the Great to keep Gog and Magog out of Persia." Still others assert that Cyrus is actually Alexander the Great and Gog and Magog are really the Scythians. "Not even a wall of iron can separate Israel from its God," Rabbi Joshua ben Levi, 200 CE. "Iron and steel were called the same in ancient Hebrew and Arabic, and both cultures believed the element fell from the heavens."

Both Judaism and Islam speak of God protecting with, or as, "a wall of fire." "This relates to the desert practice of keeping oneself safe from predators by surrounding oneself with fire."

\

During breaks my hut's screen oscillated a koan. It was a clock, but with just a single hand, and the clockface had no divisions into minutes or hours. It had no divisions at all. Was it a timer? and if so what time did it tell?

Mornings, or whatever, I'd be woken by Principal's voice shrilling over a hearth of incombustible logs that might've been another screen-saver.

That morning, however, I woke up on my own to a screen that was off, so I fell back into a dream in which I was shopping for the antithrombosis travel compression braces that Moms had recommended, but the stores were gypping me and I went into a frenzy because each pair contained two and a pair for me, I can't explain it, meant three, and then Rach and I were going to Dr. Idleson the fertilitist who was also Meany the shrink, who told us that what we'd been having wasn't sex and was about to tell us what to do instead—but then I was jolted up and out of the cot by an error msg honk. Abort retry fail honking.

The screen flickered an external feed—a clubcart was at the door.

Two men were jammed inside—two big men, giants, juvie and cruel, special in the sense of special forces: Jesus and Feel (Jesús and Felipe).

I rode deck as they let the cart drive us, in swampy compound circles.

"So you the visitor genius?" Feel said.

"You think?" I said.

"Never met no genius."

I said, "Only a genius would know what you're talking about."

"What else a genius do?" Jesus said. "You get the mother and father—los árboles?"

"Meaning what?"

But Feel was saying, "Also in my family the primos, the cousins segundos. Not like when my cousin has kids, but like when my two brothers marry two sisters and they both have kids—they would be how related?"

I understood: "Genealogist, you mean."

Principal had told them, hadn't told me, my cover was as genealogist.

I said, "And what do you do—seguridad detail?"

"No importa," Feel said.

"Stunt driver," said Jesus.

"Are you from here or Mexico?"

"Afghanistan," said Jesus.

Feel said, "Two tours."

We went ramping down into the mound of La Domo—a subgarage of charging stations and inductive mats. A mechanics corps was sponging a Tesla X, a car that didn't exist. No other boytoys though. No racers. All electric. And no motorcycles. Scooters. Bike-bikes.

Adjacent to the garage was the mechanics' locker room. The next room was a box, like a boxroom, just heaps of packaging, addressed to me, myself, and I. Deliveries oneclicked—one guess—online. Principal's no different from the rest—he orders and so he is.

The boxroom, the bagroom, the room of guitars, the room of drums, of charcoal and chalk, of splintered easels. Room of wood. Room half carpet half grass just because. Room in which the scissors were left. Room of nothing but the loss of a button.

Rooms: there must be something to call the room in which everything in it is supposed to come off as causal, but, in fact, has been calculated down to the threadcount. The room into which, before someone visits, the householder hauls everything significant or representative, so that even if this is the only room he—I—will visit, everything will be communicated: essential personality, selfhood. Gist, pith. Taste.

There must come a point when a house has so many rooms that it becomes pointless to name them. There must come a room—where the homeowner just wavers at the threshold, and fails it.

Principal had made a shrine, and so enshrined himself. An altar awaiting a sacrifice. Rotund Asian deities in speedos. Incense censer. A sutured set of sutras. The Dharma lode, block and mallet, beads, wheel, ghanta, vajra, mandala.

Principal lotused on the floor. His face, the skin that showed, was haggard. Wrung. He'd aged double what I'd aged since our last.

His chinpatch was now the color of static and the shape of Long Island. A short wiggy bowlcut, as lustrous as laminated bamboo.

But, as he gradually rose, as he ritually twitchingly rose, what got me the most was his size—how fat he was or creepy with muscle. Massive pecs and quads. Pumped bumps for biceps. Bulgeous calves.

Rather what got me was more the disparity, between whatever it was that made him so swollen imposing and the head that hovered above, the floating face shrunken, wan, marasmic, insucked brittle cheeks, bone straining through nose—the presentation was freakish.

But also at least halfwise intentional. Because as he breathed and commenced with a ceremonial stripping, all that bulk turned out to be clothes, just clothes, bunches, rolls, layers, breathable filters. The heat was on and there was no call for the heat to be on. Principal stripped and shivered.

All of it was branded, [T]T Tetgear: he unshrugged the kasaya robe to expose a unipouched hoodie, tore the tearaway trainers to sweatpants—not in academic gray, but silicon gray. The plastic toggles that capped the drawstrings of both hoodie and sweats had been gnawed to shreds. He tugged them loose, tried not to gnaw. Underneath was a neoprene wetsuit. Thick wool socks overwhelming the sandals.

The wetsuit peeled away to a belly bloated white but of the same substance, that squishy squamous thickness, that reptilian or amphibian give—like if I would've poked him, the indent inflicted would've remained for life. His limbs were tentacularly downed powerlines, livewire distensions. He was a nonviolent resister, of himself. On a hunger strike, protesting himself. That's how ill he was, that's how Gandhi. An ascetic, or ascitic, revealing to me scars, stitched slits all ragged red inflamed like the marks of the great, the markings by which one suffers for greatness, also revealing his penis—testudinal, pinched, sacs sagging like they'd been punctured, hairless—and he was hairless too under the wig.

"What the fuck? What happened?"

"A second opening, all of life is but a second opening, or it can be," he said. "That, and only that, is the fuck."

He trembled back to the concrete floor, relotused himself stiffly.

I settled just across.

"Please," he said, "our sandals are still on us."

"Off?" I said. "You can't take them off by yourself?"

Or he wouldn't, so I undid the velcro and got him discalced, shed socks from feet, rigid toes horned coarse and crustated.

He seemed relieved: a man at rest after a powertrip.

"A man is born royal," he said. "His father is the king but he is no prince. Or he is on the outside. But it all is just outside, exterior."

"This is you? Or are you talking the Buddha?"

"We are not talking Buddha. Or we are but he is not Buddha yet. He goes. He seeks to go outside of the outside. From the palace to the walls, through the gates. Out until the gates and the walls and the palace are all behind him."

"So you're becoming the Buddha? Considering a career change?"

"We are no one. We are the horse and the chariot both."

"But in the different accounts I'm trying to recall, isn't there also like a charioteer—a guy who's steering or whipping? The Buddha, or whatever he is, whatever his name is, wasn't alone."

"We are all alone, always. No matter accounts. Whether a charioteer or no charioteer. Immaterial. Does not matter. There is no horse and the man is just walking."

"But he's walking in orienteering socks and nubuck archopedic sandals."

"As like he goes, he is followed: men seeking money, to be repaid only in hatred, women seeking money, to be repaid only in sex, and he ignores them and goes on. He meets an old man, very old, on the verge of death, and laments because age awaits us all and all the world does not lament every moment. He meets another man, afflicted not just with age but with disease, and laments because infirmity awaits us all and all the world does not lament every suffering. Yet another he meets. Or he does not. Because this man is not a man, not old or infirm anymore, not living, a corpse, and the man who is a man, who is still alive, healthy and young, laments nonetheless, because death awaits us all and all the world does not lament every death."

"I'm with you," I said, and I was.

"So the old, the infirm, the deceased," he said. "They get into his head. And the head is shaped as like the bowl for alms and all its faces are the same in vacuity. The man is incapable of love, incapable of emoting anything. He is depressed and seeks the trees. He sits under a tree and waits and attempts to cure himself of waiting as like it were a disease and attempts to destroy his waiting as like it were a life. Then through the trees, enter the fourth man, the beggar. And the beggar would have passed, this is the point, he would have passed the man at the tree, and would have respected that peace and asked for nothing. Because true beggars never ask. They are beggars because they are given. There is something in them that compels the alms, something saintly. They might even refuse. In reward or punishment. The man asked the beggar who he was and the answer was not a beggar but a wanderer—we wander, he says, we search."

"And then the man attains enlightenment and becomes the Buddha and the beggar goes to heaven," I said. "All beggars go to heaven—they never refuse."

"But maybe we can say it is better if the man never asked and the beggar never answered," Principal said. "The man becoming Buddha just knew. Basically. Maybe from the presence of the beggar. No. Or from the existence of the beggar. Yes. Because begging is giving too is the point that communicates all the knowledge that is ours."

"I don't follow." I didn't.

"We are becoming bhikshus," he said. "Itinerant, mendicant. Sadhu to the Hindu. Monastic."

"Do you have an itinerary in mind or is that against principle?"

"Europe, that is all for now. 25something° N, 55something° W."

"You can't get specific, or won't?"

"Immaterial. Not divulged."

"That's supposed to be reassuring?"

"We know."

"What do you know?" I asked.

"Without asking," and he reached for his kasaya, that white wound-bind slopping the floor. He took from a slit in it a blueblack scab.

He gave, I took. It was a passport.

"We have our charioteers after all. Payrolls of them. Part men, part chariot, part horse, all inclusive. Expediters."

"This is possible?" I turned the passport around in my hands.

"What is not possible is to go wandering the earth as like a Class D motorist licensed by the state of NY."

I opened it up. My date and place of birth were accurate. And unfortunate. The proceeding pages were as blank as an alms plate.

The pass I already had, I tried to remember when it expired, and where it was stashed—in Ridgewood's hoarder forests? with Rach?

The photo on this pass was even worse, though, from spyquip: me stumbling back to my hut from the party, out of my mind and unretouched.

I couldn't tell—I couldn't.

Which of us was not himself.

://

9/7–8, BURJ AL-JUMEIRAH HOTEL, DUBAI

total time of Principal recordings: 146:07:09

total number of Principal.Tetrec files: 58

their size: 2.9 GB

their content: *In consideration of the disclosure of confidential/proprietary information ["Information"] by the Disclosing Party ["Joshua Cohen 1"], the Receiving Party ["Joshua Cohen 2"] hereby agrees:*

> *i) to hold the Information in strict confidence and to take all precautions to protect such Information (including, without limitation, all precautionary practices/technologies employed by Joshua Cohen 1), (ii) not to disclose any such Information or any information derived therefrom to any third person/party, (iii) not to make any use whatsoever at any time of such Information or any information derived therefrom except to evaluate internally its relationship with Joshua Cohen 1 for purposes covered under Section 2 of the contract ["Contract"], and (iv) not to copy or*

Emails received:

UNIT #610 OVERDUE NOTICE, from VanderEnde officespace mgmt.

OVERDUE NOTICE, from the New York Public Library.

No Subject, from Moms.

why arent u returning my calls? from Lana.

Autoresponses sent: "traveling for work through september at the latest, replies might be slow."

How else to reply? I can't write about what I'm doing with Principal even here in this .doc, so what can I communicate in an email?

If you're ever unable to discuss the main events of your life, you have to rely on all the bits you've somehow always missed.

Managed some fruit. Shit an hour.

Insomnia, nausea, sinuses aching, still can't shake this plane cough (avian pertussis? or is that for the birds?).

Vocabulary: *orthogony, heuristics, traverse vertices, exocortex, autonomia, transclusion,* "the embedding of one document or part of a document within another by reference."

tetrationary.com/transclusion

But tech's not my only vocab problem in the Emirates. There's *ménage,* which isn't quite how it's said in French, then when I don't understand, there's *zimmermann,* which isn't quite how it's said in German, and then when I don't understand that (my sinuses having imparted to my replies an enigmatically European accent), they say *room keening.*

Language itself is a *burqa,* an *abaya*—so many new words! so much chancy chancery cursive! The garments that blacken even the tarmac, that blacken the lobby (irreligiously lavish). Words are garb. They're cloaks. They conceal the body beneath. Lift up the hems of verbiage, peek below its frillies—what's exposed? the hairy truth?

Alternately, click here: *dubai.ae*

Click until this page wears out, until you've wiped the ink away and accessed nothing.

\

A remote control should indicate the existence of another device to be controlled remotely—to be uncovered, certainly, within range.

The remote is typically the filthiest object in the room, according to Principal. 100 billion bacteria per button, on average. Each bacterium's DNA containing the equivalent of approx 1 million bytes of information. Meaning the average remote control button has the data capacity of approx 100,000 terabytes.

According to Principal: streptococcus, staphylococcus, meningococcus, coliform.

Aerobic, anaerobic. Microbes.

Roomservice—because I can't bring myself to go down to the restaurants alone. Jump. But window won't open. Shouldn't be smoking anyway.

I ordered the "Four Been Soup"—bean soup with regrets. Cramps 2.0.

Tetrating transgulfane: pancreatitis, the difference between communal and equitable distribution of assets earned by one party before divorce but after separation if separation was never legally sanctioned (New York Consolidated Statutes, Article XIII, Domestic Relations, §236B).

Other sites: *nytimes.com* (to check whether Cal had written, he hadn't), *nybooks.com* (to check whether Cal had written, he had), *haaretz.co.il* (ERROR), *haaretz.com* (ERROR), *guardian.co.uk, lemonde.fr, a-bintel-b .tlog.tetrant.com/2011/01/09/doc-n-law-1.html* (Rach), *escortzrevue.com /dubai, escortzrevue.com/abu_dhabi, whitedicksblackchicks.biz* (ERROR), *whitedicksblackchicks.biz/whitezilla-slaughters-her-ass* (ERROR), *the national.ae, gulfnews.com, a-bintel-b.tlog.tetrant.com/2011/02/09/doc-n -law-2.html* (Rach), *hoodratlatina.biz/ass-to-mouth-teacher-on-student* (ERROR), *hoodratlatina.biz/cumpilation-blonde* (ERROR), *poetry foundation.org, poetryfoundation.org/article/16129, jewsy.com* (ERROR), *jewsy.com* (ERROR), *a-bintel-b.tlog.tetrant.com/2011/03/09/doc-n-law-3 .html* (Rach), *a-bintel-b.tlog.tetrant.com/2011/04/09/doc-n-law-4.html* (Rach), *bangableblackteens.com* (ERROR), *bangableblackteens.com /mixrace/fave/orderby+mf&timeby=today* (ERROR), *tetration.com /search?q=Thor+Balk, tetpedia.com/tet/Thor_Balk, maid4jizz.biz* (ERROR), *maid4jizz.biz* (ERROR), *maid4jizz.biz* (ERROR), *maid4jizz .biz* (ERROR).

Each instance of HTTP 404ishness occasioned a buzz, a buzzing.

My gut knocking too (getting fatter off roomservice).

A deft young dark boy in a resort staffed exclusively by same, wheeling in more lentils. Occipital headache, sneezy.

I hadn't gotten around to getting any of the currency (either *dirh*am or *dihr*am—tetrate it?), so gave him €4 (too much?).

\

On every flight I've been on since the invention of wifi the attendants are always saying, don't go online until we tell you. Then they tell you, at what they call cruising altitude, which some sites have as 30,000 ft/9,100 m, and some sites have as 35,000 ft/10,600 m. Whichever, no online, and no phone either, during takeoff and landing especially. Passenger signals interfere with the cockpit's communications with the ground. I'd always accepted this, until aboard the Tetjet, which has no attendants, no announcements were made, and electronics were being used all the time. By Jesus and Feel. Not Principal. But still. This had me skeptical. I'd rather be brought down by glorious jihadi or a flock of sphinxes screeching into the engines than by some amped mercenaries playing some app game matching lozenges.

Principal's coding ("Principal" is itself a code, for me to avoid having to type "my name"). When Principal says, "The Sims are ready to fly," he means he's ready to fly (both of his pilots are Sims: Simon Prentice, Thomas Simons).

"The Gulfstream 650 is the largest elite jet in the Gulfstream fleet. Its maximum operating speed of .925 Mach makes it the fastest civil aircraft flying, and its maximum altitude of 50,000 ft allows it to avoid congestion and adverse weather," but then I gave up reading *All About the Tetjet,* and switched, dismissive flick of screen, to Media, streaming everything conceivable but also featuring a selection "curated this quarter by Kori Dienerowitz, President": 80s sitcoms, *Jeopardy!,* Scorsese, Westerns all'italiana, Korean Wave, Mecha anime, 20 episodes of a show called *Xun Qin Ji.*

When Principal says, "Gaston wants to cook," he knows that all meals are docketed, but isn't hungry.

In London, Welsh radix box with a side of sprouts (both raw), in Paris mixed kales below purée de betterave crapaudine (both semisteamed), muria puama, saw palmetto, reservatrol. For dessert, his nutritive of twos: vitamins A_2 (retinaldehyde), B_2 (riboflavin), C_2 (choline), D_2 (ergocalciferol), supplemented with hazelnut oil, cedar berry, turmeric, borage, selenium, γ-linolenic acid.

When Principal says, "Lavra wants to exercise," he knows that all workouts are docketed, but isn't motivated.

40 elliptical minutes listening to a podcast on diamond synthesis using hydrocarbons, another on Malthus (London), watching a clipathon on the extraction of precious metals from waste electronics using

plasma, another on the physiocrats and François Quesnay (Paris), Lavra alongside him on the twin machine, then leading him in 80 light squats, correcting technique. Midplantar/lower palmar reflexology, cranial electrotherapy (Lavra insists, no acupressure or brain stimulation without the cardio).

I've been with Principal through every meal and workout, but have never participated in any.

When Myung says to Principal, "Doc Huxtable has got you booked," she means—forget it.

This is exactly where a code's required, extra shorthand, an abbrev: like how red ink indicated lies in memoranda sent to and from the gulag, like "an inlaw" meant "an SS officer" in the partisan encryption of the Warsaw Ghetto, while the Nazis themselves used "solution" to mean "mass extermination."

\

Code.

There are two great innovations to recall: (1) all relationships between two or more quantities can be expressed as equations (the algorithm, which enciphers the name of al-Gorithmi, the Persian mathematician, astronomer, geographer, and Judeophile, eighth century CE), and (2) all numbers, no matter how large, can be expressed by the sequential combination of the smallest numbers: zeroes and ones (though the original binaries weren't numerals but short and long syllables, combinable into every conceivable meter of Sanskrit prosody—Pingala, fourth century BCE).

Binary code—an encryption that's simultaneously a translation, in how it renders two different systems compatible, equitable. "Bits"—the term itself is a contraction ("binary digits")—are the fundamentals of any expression: not just of integers but also of language, and so of instructions, commands.

In international unicode standard, by which every conceivable character in the universe can be represented by an octet, or a sequence of eight bits, Principal's net worth would be signified by 00110001 00111000 00110010 00110000 00110000 00110000 00110000 00110000 00110000

00110000 00110000 (or $18.2B, as of 2010 taxes), and the value of my advance for this book by 00110100 00110100 00110000 00110000 00110000 00110000 (or $440K)—though I'll get only half that up front, or Aar will and then he'll take his commission (00110011 00110011 00110000 00110000 00110000), and then the IRS will take its too (00110001 00110101 00110100 00110000 00110000 00110000).

Principal has directed our publisher to pay his own fee to an undisclosed organization, or so he says.

The only records of prior largesse are of $2 million to endow a computing exhibition devoutly aggrandizing Tetration at the Smithsonian Institution, and $252 to the Santa Clara Council of Dharmic and Abrahamic Religions, which has become a for profit yoga studio.

He never says our name if it refers to me, not even the nickname, the lame abridgement, "Josh." Bash it to bits, you'd get 01001010 01101111 01110011 01101000, though if the "j" were minuscule, were lowercase, you'd get 01101010 (01101111 01110011 01101000).

Thanks, biconversion.com.

Point is, we're all made differently of the same ones and zeroes—the ones our fortunes, the zeroes our voids, our blacker lacking places.

Ultimately, then, Principal and I do not compute, and all the imbalance between us can't be attributed to just the swollenness of his bankroll, or my fatter tits and ass—or to the facts that only one of us was given a middle name, and only one of us was given a future. How to express the extent of Principal's nullity? how else but code to write around his holes?

://

The time and/or distance required for luxuries to become staples, for wants to become needs, for consumption to consume us. London's just around the corner, a floor up or down, Paris can be ordered, ensuite, round the clock. Our access is bewildering, not just beyond imagination, but becoming imagination, and so bewildering twice over. We can only search the found, find the searched, and charge it to our room.

The only thing that grounds me is the beach—the ground before the oil, the oil money, the derricks bowing, rising, bowing, rising, the gusher skyscrapers, the rush on the roads.

I feel the sand, the salinity, the limit, the edge—they're in me, they're in everyone.

Mortality is a mesh for sifting water and quartz.

All of humanity washed up on the beach, but I stayed a span later to dry. I wasn't always bridges and tunnels, huddling under scaffolding in Midtown waiting for the storms to stop or for the stripclubs to be demolished—I wasn't always NY.

No, no, I'm Jersey, sprung from the Shore. And that basin is contiguous—all tides are my territory.

Fridays, try to leave the city before noon, turnpike to parkway past the loading and lading, our own crude tanks and refinery towers, toward the barrens, the pinescrub ceding to reeds, marshgrass and weedy tails. Take any exit south of 114, and take it to the end, to the dunecrash, the salt scarp, the lick of the sea. Low tide uncovers the loss—snapped surfboards, ripped rafts and tubes, jetties black as if soaked in creosote through winter—high tide covers that loss again only to hazard the driftwood piers, threatening to flood the rentals masted up on their struts as the vacationers flee with summer—this was how I grew up.

Shoregirt.

Let me reel in that life, like a fishing haul, winching back the lines for concessions, cranking the queues to catch battered flounder, hook pizzas and gyros, burgers and franks, fries like bait, and funnelcake like tangled tackle. Or else, like a gull drops a bivalve to smash its shell, then swoops down to beak up the meat—my memories:

Beachfront, we had resorts too. Hotels and motels. A boatel. Then four blocks in, off the touristed strip, lotto bodegas and pawns. A decent taco drivethru. A gas station.

Another four blocks inland and it's already the other side of the island, the bayside, where Shoregirt—a city in summer, a town in spring and fall, a village in winter—dwindles into wharves. At the top of the island, sandcastle timeshares, at the bottom, tenements teeming like conches on the verge of being outgrown, kept by chainlink fencing trawling fortybottles, sixpack rings, and butts. The ocean goes in, the ocean goes out, east to west. The boards, the promenade's planks, curl to crash north to south.

Home was in the axis. Between the two waters, the open ocean, the closed clammed bay. My house, two floors of wind between the shingles. Giving directions, my mother would say, "By the gas station."

Do I trust myself in this garden state? With the heart all rusted like an abandoned Mister Softee?

To Moms, I'd never be "a beach person." At best I'd be "a shoebee"—which was as far out as she'd swim into slang: a local term for all the poor Polish Jews who hadn't moved out of NY and married American, who'd come down the shore for the day with all their necessities—cold leftovers, balms—packed into a shoebox.

My necessities were books. I read a book at school, another to and from school, yet another at the beach, which was the closest escape from my father's dying. Though when I walked alone it was far. Though I wasn't allowed to walk alone when younger—so young that my concern wasn't the danger to myself but to the books I'd bring, because they weren't mine, they were everyone's, entrusted to me in return for exemplary behavior, and if I lost even a single book, or let even its corner get nicked by a jitney, the city would come, the city itself, and lock me up in that grim brick jail that, in every feature, resembled the library.

I'd be sneaking around, then, until my father quit his chemo, and Moms resolved to spend our final family time together by the wake down the street. I dressed in long sleeves long pants long face and brought along whatever I was reading bound in its municipal cellophane.

I'm recalling a stretch of grain as a single day—Dad yelling at me, "Stop that, enough with the words. I have one word for you—Atlantic, get in!"

Kaufman and Laufer were digging moats. The Tannenbaum sisters buried each other. The Gottlieb twins wore baseball mitts on their heads to guide their mother cutting their hair, then they had a catch with their father—not even, their stepfather—while Dad, sclerotic, was sputtering, "Get out there, bodysurf! Goddamn it, ride a wave!"

After that didn't work, it was, "Here's a dollar for the games"—the gambles a kid could take, the gambles not even a kid could take. Skee-Ball and Whac-A-Mole, or the forceps submerging in plush, always surfacing empty.

"I'm too old for that," I said.

"Leave us, amuse yourself, enjoy."

Moms said, "Just this once you'll do this."

I was 12.

Money meant that Dad had made mud in his diaper.

It must've been mortifying for him to have to use wide waddling Moms as a cane, hobbling him under the boardwalk, to change.

Though I was reading I didn't comprehend all this until after.

"Enough with the book!" and Dad, churning, gathering his strength into swells, threw himself out of his chair and atop me, ripped the book from my hands—a sentence, in the middle of a sentence—and, limping through the froth, threw it to the Atlantic, far out, not far enough out, its pages splayed like an injured pigeon.

The book splashed, and surged, and a wave brought it in and so Dad, wailing, stooped to his soil, picked the book up and tossed it again, but another wave brought it in and again, until he fell by the tidemark—only for Moms to claw for the book before dragging him in.

The book before the husband. I cried the whole way home.

Out amid the spindrift tears, by boardwalk's midpoint, between Eustasy and Orarian Terraces, there's a bench: a slatty construction anchored in tar, with a plaque engraved on the back dedicating it to my father, *1924–1984, Yevarechecha Adonay, v'yishmerecha*—the inscription translating as badly as a stranger's dream, or sappy reminisce.

Dubai. If I would've drowned off the coast of my childhood, and my body had sunk to the bottom of the ocean as dead as my father's, this is what that bottom would be like. Truly, the furthest shore. Where there were no poor, and certainly no shoebees. Just children, or the childish. Foreigners whose very foreignness was childish, demanding exorbitant juicy red orange yellow iced quenchers be traipsed to their wombish white caravan cabañas between sucks on their flaring cigars—they'd become adults again only when the bill came.

The Gulf sun does that, it reverts, regresses—unthinkable to be a thinking person amid all this light and heat.

The resort curved up, like a fin or wing, a dhow's sail giving shadow: Eurotrash littering, their guts and asses and tits heaped rudely, extremities flung out to grip the towel tips, the corners of the plush horizon. The men spilled from their trunks. Hairy but soft, bodies the consistency of flaccid cock, sticky testicles lolling. The women were counterpoised, compensatory, lean, bronzed upgrade wife and mistress trophy, bones propping up the skin tent, shaylas for the bust and crotch, burqinis.

This was a private beach, then, and not cheap. Barbicans segregated it from the public beaches, which segregated themselves by gender—you have to pay for equality.

I stomped to an unclaimed chaiselounge, and ratcheted it back to an obtuse degree, sat, lay—washed up.

I tugged down the visor, repositioned the shades. More Tetration freebies, more items lettered with corporate glyph.

No one around me was doing anything, even making conversation. They were all just perfectly inert, laid out prone or supine as if submitting to autopsy or dissection. Only the dead or the lowest of species can bask, I'm convinced. That basking was making me suspicious—and turning me into my father: Why don't you diddle a racquet? go fly a kite?

I rummaged through my Tetote—also company complimentary, brimming with brandwater, brandpretzels and chips, "fresh" dates and figs, that commonest variety of nut called "mixed," yogurt or no, that's sunscreen—for my Tetbook.

But nothing else was getting written.

Just like it's impossible to be around words without reading—try not to read the next words as they turn—it's impossible to be around the naked without gawking.

\

As I closed my Tetbook on a .doc unsaved—it was replaced by another mirage. A bland white guy whiteguying up to me, in flipflops.

He was familiar, but I wasn't sure how. He had this ambling and amiable coach demeanor, and the agglutinated fatness of the entire Eastern Division of pro football, American football. He was in slumpy trunks and a tanktop from a Beat Leukemia!! 5K race he definitely hadn't run, and then the tanktop was off, and was over his head like a kaffiyeh. As he settled into the lounger beside mine, his flab extruded between the slats.

He grinned buckteeth and said, "Hiyo," aggressively genial, content with his content. He produced an identical Tetbook from an identical Tetote, set it in what had to be his lap.

He showed me his, I showed him mine—or just went to remind myself whose was whose: I reopened and, angling my screen away from the glare, and from his glare, went toggling through files.

Kori Dienerowitz, in the copious flesh—Kor Memory—Tetration President, and presidentially sized. What'd prevented me from an immediate ID wasn't the context, but the dread of him. He was all clickety-clackety, "Crap connection," dug out the same tube of sunscreen. "Would I be interrupting you to ask a favor?"

"Yes?"

"I have a tough time reaching my back, my shoulders and neck—it's fine, you can laugh, but would you mind giving me a slather? Strictly hetero, one patriot to another?"

"I'd rather not."

"Don't burn me."

"You're not going to lie stomach up the whole time?"

"You're right—a true American would choose a side, but this is a matter of survival."

"How?"

"Allegiances have changed—tides and times. We live at the pale, the fade of the unmelanized. The white man's hegemony is over. The future belongs to those who tan, or those so dark they never tan."

"Doesn't that leave out the Asians?"

He closed and toted his unit, "If I have to try myself, I won't be able to work—you have any idea how annoying it is, typing with slick fingers?"

I closed and stowed too, toed my tote closer, as Kor stretched over a shoulder and squirted a lump—a thick chunky load leaking down his back's already medium rare hairless center and it wasn't that I wanted to help him, it's just that I couldn't bear to witness the trickle. The sheer smooth presence was the goad, that dollop dribbling fusiform, taunting, luridly viscid.

No, not any secretion: the lotion was like a perspiring prophylactic, a condom he wanted me to tug over his pudging—and I tugged, I applied my fingers and thumb, put my wrists behind it. I rolled, twisted, pinched, slapped at his spinelessness, went for the deepest tissue—rubbing whiteness into whiteness as the glabrous pores absorbed, until I couldn't tell what was zinc and what was just Caucasian.

"Obliged."

I wiped my hands on the sand, the sand on my shorts, and mentally waded. Pretended to study the lifeguard's bunker. No lifepreservers, no rowers, but gathered around the bunk the guards chattered into walkie-talkies, prodded jellyfish with Kalashnikovs.

"Tell me," Kor wasn't asking, "has he mentioned me yet?"

"Who?"

"You're the genealogist, you figure it out."

"I don't know what you're talking about."

"Are you sure?"

"I am."

"Good, very good—we can trust you."

"Who's we?"

"You know—I'm one of the guys with the creditcard. What's your beverage—seltzer?"

A beachboy abjected himself, and the order came, "Two big waters with bubbles—975, no, 976 bubbles in each."

As he scampered I decided, "What brings you to the Emirates?"

"You."

"Me?"

"We have similar interests," he said, going through his Tetgear, putting on the shades, the visor.

Just what I needed, another clone. "I guess we have a thing or two in common."

"Though you'd prefer vodka, and I'm sober. You smoke and I'd never. You're about to be divorced, or are you trying to reconcile by telecuddle? Making passes at your lady by wifi?"

"Fuck off."

"Fair enough."

The resort was a blade that cast darkness to the dial, that clocked. But now there was no time. Now there was no shadow. It was noon, and that great incandescent beachball was directly above. Behind us, far on the elevated concourse, a crowd went about its static, like spray spumed from an unattuned screen. Men in robes, white terry. Women blacked between them. In front of us, the abyss lapped at the corniche, as if gorging out of boredom.

The beachboy brought the seltzers, and Kor tapped the charge away.

"So what's the point?" to let him sip.

"I'm only trying to stress confidentiality, reminding you how important it is to keep whatever you're doing to yourself."

"Genealogy."

"And just generally making myself available."

"And you do this by intimidation?"

He burped, let him.

"I've been trying to convince the FTC that any protocol we develop that allows our devices to communicate with those of our competitors doesn't have to allow those of our competitors to also communicate with ours, and so must be regarded as free and clear not just proprietary, but benevolent. I'm hiring an operations guy in Johannesburg, firing an operations girl in Belgrade, mediating a discrimination suit in Ottawa, monitoring coups throughout the Maghreb. China's about to embargo my ass. Japan has two, count them, two, national intelligence agencies, and they don't get along, and yet what I'm telling you is, I'll make time for you."

"I got it."

"Tough for the both of us."

"Yes."

"Your wife, that actor—stupes."

Then—I'd like to report an air raid, but no: it was the muezzin. Cutting us off, an ululating breeze.

It was the call to prayer, Dhuhr, and one person, but only one, turned over on his towel to face Mecca. Not east but west.

\

It's disgusting, how I've been managed: the surveillance hut and passport, then this moment's notice trip—and now to be lubbered up against an intertidal watercooler for office chitchat with Kori Dienerowitz.

That was the straw that broke this camel's back, to get all local about it.

Roomed again, I opened my Tetbook for the nth time to ensure he hadn't switcherooed his for mine, and it was automatic—it's in my hands, or like how my hands breathe—I typed in the address.

Tetra—I didn't even have to type it fully. The addy autocompleted: tetration.com.

I have, I admit, visited before. It knows me like a good conciergerie, knows me better than my wife.

I checked in on camels (no spitting for them, they "gleet," and it's the bactrians that have two backs to break—two humps—while dromedaries have only one), checked up on Rach, who she linked to, who linked to her and left comments and what their comments were and the comments on the comments—We're always trying to improve our service, Tell us how we're doing.

The latest post's latest reaction wasn't to Rach's choice of curry joint (a takeout I'd found, which she was claiming she'd found), nor was it an opinion as to whether the best thing about breaking up was that now she was getting a pet (but which? vote below: guinea pig or fuzzy lop bunny, a chinchilla or mink?). Rather, it was just a fuzzy irrelevancy, a spam-curry bot sequitur or whatever, courtesy of username "KORDIE":

"*if yre not 2 busy genealogizing & if yre down 2 continue our convo im hosting recept 4 prince @ 20:00 bani yas suite*"

Fuck you in your Bani Yas, Kor Dienerowitz.

But then without intending to I was tetrating that. The Bani Yas were "among the founding tribes of the trucial United Arab Emirates"—another window—I clicked, and kept clicking through the autoloading Burj site if only to keep from tetrating for sites that have never existed: what-do-you-know-about-my-sexual-history.com, which would tell me how intimate Kor had gotten with Rach's raving, do-you-think-theres-a-pattern.biz, which would tell me whether Kor had been tracking me all along or was just taking a chance on this invitation—if-he-had-been-tracking-me.org might explain why, then-why-invite-me-to-realize-this-so-blatantly.org might explain itself (but there's always the chance that I was totally misaligned and that somehow msging someone through their estranged spouse's blog had become a newly permissible mode of communication).

It was the heat on me, it had me clicking through the Burj surveillance feeds: out_beachport, and toggling to where Kor and I had sat, where the sand had no traces of our sitting. Saw the waves. Heard the waves. Streamed the data. The number of miles (km) of beach outside, the number of miles (km) of beach inside. I clicked the in_beachport, to remember an experience I never—membered: the sand set firm under the tanning lights, a gunite wadingpool of water piped in and then waved into froth by machine.

Another toggle, to the four chlorinated lap pools beyond its negative edge, each the size of four Olympics, veritably.

Next, soothing myself, I connected to a tour of the golfcourses both outdoor and indoor, linked around the links. I splitscreened between them and the volley with a robot tennis pavilion. Cricketcam. Wicketcam. The sports snowglobe. Keyed in my room number to find out if I was eligible for discounts on any XXXtreme bungee/skydiving/kitesurfing/jetski/abseiling/assorted parasports "adventures" (I was).

I, who'd actually been in the lobby, could understand the lobby only now, immersing, submerging, and so discovering its décor with a diligence that in fleshlife would've required a dubious protracted loiter by the guest services station consulting reference texts on textile history and rubbing lasciviously against the drapery. I could explore the provenance of the provincial antiquities displayed in the perimeter encasements (one I thought was real was a repro, and another I thought was a repro was—guess).

The restaurants I'd never dine at, serving which cuisines at what hours, locations, with directions—with directions from within the resort.

Stats on all the rooms not mine, inclusive of their rates I'd never pay, stats also on their interior design with links to the sites of their interior designers, the furnishings' brands listed with multicurrency pricing and even the option to "add to my cart" (delivery options, next page).

My experience was beyond the vicarious—I myself was autocompleted (I don't recall getting dressed and out of the room).

The elevators were each the size of an Emirate, each with its own culture, weather, official tree (ebony paneling), official animal (ebony operator). I took a car from the same bank I'd been taking to Principal's suite—but passed Principal's, into the open.

The doors withdrew, as if in the presence of majesty, with every guest a royal, and I found myself in what can only be described as a purple passage: literally a passage of purple mirror etched into damask, tossing petals at my steps across a roofdeck—behind me shafty minarets cupolating with moon for the delectation of the sheikh on the jumbotrons—ahead of me the Gulf and its isles, dredged drifting replicas of all the earth's landmasses, the Antarctic a sandbar of bulldozers and dumptrucks, Greenland a flurry of speedboat launches.

I took a stairwell of chrome and glass up to a helipad, beyond the roundel of which a tent was pitched and inside the tent was a room. A suite double the size of Principal's, the standard layout zoomed to enlarge, deep into the fabric of night. Hircine, rough, and nothing to knock. The furnishment was all divans draped in antimacassary, pillow pyres obscuring the brocades beneath. A mixed bag showcase, then, as cluttered as Orientalism, as patchwork pastiched as the choice of whether to relish or critique it. Shelves held alcohol distilled by types, within types, by vsop, xo, cigs American and British.

The mess was hubbed by a vast mannered table, marquetried in fractals of pearl but inlaid with an unmohammadian felt swath for games with cards and dice. It was staffed, but also patronized, by cleancut young achievers.

They were natives, though, and so only nepotistically ambitious, twit sycophants attitudinized by privilege: twentyeightsomething, twenty-eightandahalfsomething at the far end where the tentflaps were staked to expose the starlessness.

Kor motioned me to a propinquous tassled tuft. A Slav built like a pole flying a blackstriped bandeau swimsuit like a flag laid out the snifters and cohibas.

The natives were Arabizing and I didn't understand—anything beyond, they were freaked by the Slav.

"This is Josh," Kor said. "He's a biographer, a writer—can any of you name any writers?"

Each member of the fraternity auditioned his own laugh.

"He didn't mean just American," I said. "Any Emiratis or Emiris or whatever? Anyone in Arabic?"

Nothing, so I named a few—a few poets, ghazal guys. That gal Scheherazade.

"And these," Kor intervening, "these are the programmers we were hoping for."

"Programmers?"

"Apparently we're negotiating a server facility, and this is the local talent."

"Is that why we're here?"

"You tell me."

"That's why we're here."

"Just us and the fauxgrammers—their English gets a D, and I'd bet even that's better than their C++."

"And now I'm apparently a biographer?"

Kor patted their cheeks like valets pet the sleek sides of cars, soothing assurance for a smooth ride: "You tell me."

"Do they at least know how to update a résumé?"

Menus, rivetbound, were passed around, listing not the fare but the etiquette: everything would be sampled. Shareware soup, cybersalad of packetsniffed florettes dusted with a terabyte of truffles. Herbes de POP Palmiers. Tarte à l'Terminal et aux apps.

The fauxgrammers studied, breaking off their fastidiousness only with Kor's foray: "Any of you familiar with orthogony? Orthonormality?"

They weren't—they were brainless. They grinned.

"What about mengineering?" Kor pressed on. "Are any of you mengineers? Smellecom experience? B.O.-tech?"

I raised a glass and toasted Kor and the fauxgrammers gladhanded at their glasses to toast him too, or else to keep him from pouring them Krug Brut—only the best for them to abstain from. With his blubbering jollity and tonsure Kor now seemed like a wily friar brewer, like the mascot off a label for cider or ale.

"Did you know our programmers back in the States do all their consumption from a vendingmachine?" he said.

I said, "Did you know they're also forcibly neutered?"

"Guess who else is staying at the Burj?"

The fauxgrammers kept murmuring, "Burj?"

Kor said that current guests included a girlgroup called Broadband, a catalogue raisonné of Biennial curators. The fauxgrammers were blanking.

"Jerry?" I said. "George? Elaine? Kramer? Omar Sharif? Batman?"

Half the fauxgrammers chinned excitably, "Spidey?"

Kor said, "Stupes."

A whole roasted lamb—stuffed with lamb sausages, organ and glandbreads, dried fruits and currants, tomato/garlic/onion mush, the entirety cardamomated, corianderized, cumined, cloved—was brought out on a spit, danced around. The carcassbearers were women, further gorgeous bursting Slavs, just as anorexstretched tall as Rach but otherwise her bulimically inverted opposite—modified, with satellite dish breasts of an antennary perkiness. Globoid, global. When a woman's loveliness was through and the Burj would cast her out to sea to drown into bait or chum anew, only her tits would survive her, nonbiodegradable pouches of saline floating loose to bob in saline, silicone buoys choking dolphins and sharks.

Some Ukes, some Poles, Czechs and Slovaks, Yugos, but the lingua prostituta was Russian. There were only a handful, at first—one for each of the fauxgrammers? leaving two for me given that Kor would go for the drove of slaveboy fauxgrammers themselves?—eventually over a dozen, as women I'd never been around offscreen and without masturbating unfolded their limbs in scopic sections like the stands that steadied amateur A/V equipment.

Their English was better than the fauxgrammers', was better than any of our Russian—if anyone can ever speak universally, it's whores: Sveta, Svetka, Svetichka, names getting diminutively girlish by the toast, the dregs upended. Throughout, their protuberances were immovable, their faces paused impassive. A despondent lover might jump from their cheekbones, noosing ropes of waistlength straight hair peroxidized or crude black dyed or both. Sharp stilettos under the vexillological twosies, in the national colors: Abbasid black, Umayyad white, Fatimid green, red spilled of al-Andalus—each piece of each twopiece no bigger than a napkin, stained and tenting in my lap.

Eastern females: there's something to be said of them definitively and I'll try for it, allowing the fauxgrammers to get done with dessert, allowing Kor and myself our postprandial brandies—Cognac, Armagnac, liqueurs of French cantons extant only in the cartographies of marketing—to refuse coffee for tea, in homage to our waitstaff.

Chai, chaichick—what among the Arabs has to be cultivated, among the female Slavs grows wild: when young they steep the testicular bag in their tight sugared mouths, when old they turn bitter, sour, take on the silhouettes of rusty samovars, and wrinkle from smoking—as if they stubbed out their cigs on their foreheads—as if, whenever they weren't drinking their tea, they set their glasses atop their chins to leave behind tepid impressions.

I knew some women like this, knew how to resist them especially, women who with the fall of communism, went west—they were Aaron's obsession. He had a girl from Brighton, a girl from Forest Hills—give him one each from Staten Island and the Bronx, if just to preserve a sense of socialist equity among the boroughs. Long drives to Long Island, detours into metro NJ, compulsive, he was always ferrying them to Whitehall, ferrying them back to their parents' apartments slummed so far out in the city that their transit stops were the train muster yards and the bus maintenance lots, returning them nervous, flustered because just fucked, in the Saab convertible fucked, to do mealtime with the folks.

Immigrant families, emigrant families, codependent, claustral—Jewish girls unable to make it through dates without their mothers calling, or without expecting Aar to father their children.

They'd invite him up: for bruisey melon and disemboweling kvass, to sit on the sectional en familie and peruse the photoalbums scattered (this is Odessa, this is Kiev, the future mother inlaw, the future father inlaw, as kids), to give a word in Yiddish to the grandparents farting the stripes off their tracksuits in the corner, farschimmelt—Aar always halfway between the parents and grandparents in age—he'd oblige but never return.

The Slav slaves strutting around this aerie harem, this high houri lounge, were different. At the least the one on my lap was. Olya. It's not just that she wasn't Semitic, it's that she wasn't even Slav, or not fully. She had that Asiatic horde hybridity, that Tatar sauce Mongolic mix. Kazakh, Uzbek. Or from one of the randomer stans where feminine training included not just cooking and cleaning but how to put on a condom with the mouth. Olya, though that was just a conjecture: taut, tensile, cold in her bones, tempered ice, her back blades so severe they sliced against my face, shaving off what stubble I'd grown since—last I'd shaved? today or yesterday?—her ass like a heel crushing my crotch, as two men entered the tent, like they owned the place, or were about to burn it down.

\

Spend enough time with the überrich and spotting the bodyguard species becomes a cinch—they're almost physically inhuman: the legs of a police thoroughbred, the torso of a firetruck, the arms of a steroidal ape, steeringwheel heads set on no appreciable necks—noctivagant, and foul of mood.

There are two ways these specimens dress for the wild: one is to differentiate themselves from the party they're supposed to protect, while the other's to blend with him or her, choosing camouflage similar or same. Designer pelts. Couture pelage. Pistols by Glock.

The latter's the classier adaptation—Jesus and Feel, a floor below, dressed down because Principal dressed down, presenting a uniform exterior of exclusive brandwear.

But these two had opted for the former. They were gangstafied as turf enemies, one cripped in blue doorag, blue puffy over blue beater and blue jeans slung to show the blue briefs between, the other blooded in red flatbrim, red puffy over red soccer jersey and matching shorts as long as pants, all for a counterfeit team—the San Francisco 94ers.

Nothing made less sense than the duffelsized puffies—nothing made more, when the crip punched a console and the blood kicked a vent, activating the AC.

The tent whirred, Olya's areolas poked.

The gangbangers had bags from the dutyfree, tokens to distribute. They hulked around the table, handing each fauxgrammer a filigreed manacle of a watch in the souk dreck style, oudh in a glass spritzer blown into the borders of the UAE, both labeled "un souvenir pour votre femme/ein Souvenir für Ihre Frau." Also a trackpad. In the style of a Bedouin rug replete with nonslip rubber backing.

As they went dexter, another man made the rounds sinister—the bodyguards' body, their charge.

I hadn't noticed his entrance, and not because I was so taken with my—what was it? an electrophoretic shatterproof Sinai tablet?

The olive beret, plumped as if to give him height, just made him even slighter, twee. A bad narco's crinkled white linen suit became, in the climatized bluster, inappropriately lightweight. Sockless. In little tiny loafers.

He had a temperature problem, obviously. There was a seethe in his greetings he didn't intend. He sweated, dousing each obeisance. One kiss to one cheek in America, one to each cheek in Europe, whereas in the Emirates, or just to him, it was a threepeat, with a return to the cheek of origin.

Or four, with a kiss to Olya's scalp—he was leaning so close to me it would count as a hug in any culture.

Everyone was standing but me—Olya was standing, preventing me—everyone had bowed.

Kor, minister of whores—man with tricks up his portfolio—sunk so low his gut scraped crumbs off the table.

"Salam alaykum."

"Wa alaykum salam."

A director's sling was produced, hinged out for the sitting—it was the highest chair around, and the fauxgrammers lumped around as he spastically scaled it.

"What do you say, Prince?" Kor asked. "How's my Arabic?"

"It's like we grew up together, quite," the prince said. "Oxbridge? Le Rosey?"

Kor laughed.

"And my IT Emiris," the prince went on, "how progresses their English pronouncement?"

I chewed a cohiba. "Quite."

The prince frowned and Kor to the rescue, "If you're just as generous at hosting servers as you are at hosting us, we might have ourselves a deal."

"I am chuffed to be considered. To conduct this facility—this cluster." Then he Arabized and the Emiris blushed into full cups. Zam-Zam colas, Mountain Dews.

What I knew at the time: there was a king, and the king had sons, and so there was a line, but not like of foaming techies camped outside select retailers just to overpay for an undertested Tetheld 4. Rather a line that stretched for eternities, for grudges—throneward.

I took this prince and his presence at this function to communicate the succession: the son at the head of the pipeline would handle the oil, the next son would handle the gas, the son after that the shipping, and only the next after that would get online—and if that's who he was, he could afford, perhaps, to act princely—depraved.

His protection placed before him a heavy cutcrystal decanter, poured him a tumbler he gulped clear down—either a louchey anisette or a malarial water. I prayed for water.

Emirati royalty, what could I know: his father was the sheikh, or one of the sheikh's brothers, whether the crown prince or another. He himself might've been the son crowned with a PhD, administering the free trade zones in Fujairah and Sharjah, or the son with a MEcon, or MEng, developing a transhub in Ajman. Or he'd been the prodigal abroad, who'd tried to stick it to every busted ugly daughter of the 20th Earl of Diddlesex, before being recalled and betrothed to a Qatari sheikha who'd never had a wax. Or the son accused of a homicide that became a suicide only when the bank transfer went through. Or the cerebrally defective son still favored over his sisters, who were mere baubles like their mothers. Like all their mothers, who, if not sisters to one another, were otherwise related.

He might've been any of them, or none. He had some of that sheikhy jumbotron to him—some of that lizard snout, but then lizards are all snout—darting, sensing.

He said, "I trust my Burj you find sufficient in terms of modcons, nothing dodgy."

I almost expected a tongueflick, a forked tongue flick, when his protection served his dinner.

Goblet refilled and drained again.

I said, "To be honest, Prince, I've been having trouble accessing certain sites."

"Which?"

"American sites, mostly. Politics, mostly."

"Only such?"

"Only."

"Cheeky," the prince said and then Arabized and the fauxgrammers chuckled.

Kor tried to join them but just showed teeth.

The prince asked, "So what politics have you been craving? I will do everything I can to accommodate requests."

"Nothing in particular—just the sense that I'm not blocked, is all."

"You are saying you are blocked—at the Burj? Or in all the Emirates?"

"Forget it."

"I will not. This is unacceptable. What is it you lack? Certainly not cunt?"

"What?"

"Cunt—or do you prefer to pleasure yourself alone?"

"I don't follow, Prince."

"Bollocks. You have the real right here—right now—but all you crave is fake?"

"I don't, Prince."

"You Americans always think you have such progress—you think that you are libertized and the Emirates are not? That the Emirates censor and you do not? Wankers. What you have to search for online in your country, in my country is already found."

Kor said, "He's sorry," and then he said to me, "Apologize."

"For what?"

The prince Arabized to Olya, who genuflected and leched away from me, to lift his dinner's cloche.

What was exposed: two rawly moist strips of bacon as skimpy as the two elastic strips that gripped her, and as she reached French tips out to grab one, the prince smacked her hand, and Olya shivered, flushed baconcolored, and the fauxgrammers gasped.

Kor said, "What?"

The prince said, "This is not for her—she must keep her figure."

Kor said, "Forgive us, Prince."

Then the prince pointed at me, "Here, you have the honor of tasting. Tell me it is good, tell me it is salty."

"If you please, Prince, I'd rather not."

"Do not worry, you cannot botch this. Tell me how scrummy it is—I can smell it."

"Taste it yourself," just a suggestion.

"But this honor is yours—it might be poisoned."

"So feed it to your thugs."

"They eat what I tell them to. Animals must not eat other animals."

"Go ahead, enjoy."

"You."

"Why me?"

"Because you are a Jewish—you must be."

"And you're Muslim—pork isn't for you."

"So I am accurate—you are a Jewish—but not religious? Is it for religion that you refuse?"

"No, not that, I just don't like being coerced. I don't like having my face rubbed in another man's dinner."

"But this is soy, this is curd, imitation."

"So we shouldn't have a problem."

"We should not," and he unsheathed a dagger—hilt all bedizened with precious twinklings—cut the fake meats in half, stabbed each slice into his mouth, then set the glistering blade pseudogristled on the table.

"A bad habit from abroad," he said. "All my education it was bacon, hams, and sausages, but here it is back to the soy. Do you not think, Jewish, that religions are quite like soy, like tofu? You let the good natural essence curdle, until what is left is without taste, a substitute?"

"Prince, how can I argue?"

"You are a Jewish, yes, but also of Israel?"

Kor said, "He's not, Prince."

I interrupted, "Fuck—you're Kori fucking Dienerowitz. And his boss just below us is also a Jew."

The prince thumbed at his neck.

Kor said, "But only my father's a Jew—so technically I'm not."

The prince turned and groped Olya, who'd been leaning on his chairback.

"Israel," he said. "Jewish, indulge me."

"I won't," I crossed my arms, my personal cutlery.

"Indulge me and say this woman is Israel—can we agree? Foot to head, this woman, Israel, yes?"

"Isn't that demeaning?"

"According to who demeaning? Later you will fuck her and that will be demeaning but now she serves a purpose."

"Demeaning to fucking Israel too, I meant."

"Negev to Golan—how would you distribute?"

"I wouldn't."

"You want me to cut?" again he brandished the dagger.

"Enough."

"Do you want me to cut her? Be serious."

"I don't know—I'd probably give her away, all of her, you can always find a new one."

"No, you cannot, this is the rub. This is the only one we both want, we both want her whole. What do we do? What say the Israelis?"

"We share?"

Olya, who understood I'd say about half—cut, divided in her comprehensions—trembled.

"I am the host and you are the guest, it is my hospitality so it is you tonight and me tomorrow? Or we try to coexist, bugger her at the same time the two of us?"

"We could. But I think we should let her off. A woman isn't land. Affections aren't an issue of territory."

"They are the only territory. The Israelis think this. They say here, the Jewishes take the knocker tits and holes, the cunt and bum, the oases. And here, the elbow, the shoulder, the knee—my arse—the Arabs take the desert, quite."

"You said Jews—and it's not Arabs, it's Palestinians."

"The same—or not even the knees, but the more rubbish parts, the pinkie or thumb, the mingy hair, the cropless arid cellulite portion—that is what you do."

"Not what I do."

"But what say the Arabs?"

"The Palestinians."

"We accept, we compromise—we say have the holes, the reproductives, have it all foot to head, even the face, just leave us with the navel."

"The face you hide under veils because you're too weak to resist?"

"The face we conceal out of respect."

"And you fuck instead the Russians?"

"And we fuck instead the Russians—and we take our electronics from Asia, our online from America. We agree, assent, assure bloody right we will be your ally against terror, bloody right we will cooperate with your trade agreements, your military drones—bloody right all your energy needs will be met, even though bloody right all your foreign debt obligations will never be met—bloody right a stable industry because bloody right a stable government."

"Stable because oppressive, Prince—stable because allowed to be."

"Jewish, we are not Africa. Arabs are European—we believe in bargaining—we haggle."

"Prince, yours is a theocracy criticizing a republic, a monarchy critiquing a democracy. Anyway, arguing the Emirates is different from arguing Jerusalem."

"But it is not—regardless of our government you would treat us the same, it is politically expedient. If six million Emiris suddenly settled your America, policy would change in a snap."

"I'm not convinced."

"You are already convinced—you came from a failing empire to this desert, only to take advantage of us, quite—then it is back home to a second mortgage and the one woman marriage."

"Not for me."

"But just like you wank online and never touch, you preach a freedom you never practice. Your libertization is a fiction, which must be maintained so that particular pressures can be exerted upon particular regimes, in order to deprive them of their resources. What Israel does, what Jewishes have always done, is just perpetuate this lie. In the media especially. This falsehood is not just your god but also your idol. You are enslaved to it, and so you enslave us too."

The prince, still holding Olya, stood, shoved her to the floor, where she huddled, heaved.

The weapon's sharpness outglinting its jewels.

He wasn't going to cut her empty head off, he didn't have that in him, though he might've been capable of severing a toe. Instead, abruptly, he sheathed the dagger, and staggered out, his thuggery trudging behind him.[†]

://

† This dagger would be the very last thing I'd tetrate—later, in Berlin, on an overcast noon at the Staatsbibliothek (library). Everything following this note was written entirely from my head, entirely out of what I know and think and saw and heard, without any technological verification, or direction. Any slips are solely my own. Correx and/or corrigenda may be sent but not received. The prince's dagger was a *khanjar,* a scythey, severely curved—verging-on-90°-curved—weapon, reminiscent of a penis at rest. *Khanjarha* (the plural) are carried "in a[n] ivory or leather scabbard and decorated with jewel, gold, silver, etc., etc., worn on a belt similar[ly] decorated." While the hilts of the most precious specimens are of rhinoceros horn, more common hilts are of sandalwood or marble. Design variations—hilt type, # of rings attaching scabbard to belt—denote different privileges enjoyed by the wearer. Though the steel used to fashion the blade was traditionally Yemeni, its ornamental silver was obtained, at the turn of last century, by melting down *thalers,* a popular bullion issue of Austro-Hungary. The prince's model was gold or heavily gilded, its hilt definitely horny.

Insomnia, nausea.

Shit.

—I've been having some name grief—I don't mean with my homonym, or Tetwin, but with the aliases we've been registered under. All standard operating procedure, of course, and it was fun though somewhat defamiliarizing initially to be calling down to the reception desks and have them say, "Fine day, Mr. Immermann," or, "Bonsoir, M. Yaarsky." Though it's not obvious that any of this duplicity would be effective for celebrities of the first results page rank, who if they're staying anywhere, even at the Burj, would certainly be noticed by employees, and then it's just a matter of when the tip's called in, to the press crews, or the protestors. It seems, then, that the only guests for whom this handling would make sense wouldn't be recognizable by face, but only by name: the primeval way of being famous.

—An indication of the failure of our aliases is that neither Jesus nor Feel can keep them straight, checking Principal in under what mine was last, and checking me in under what'd been Principal's (the ultimate indication is that none of this fooled Kor). Myung's the one who picks them, the aliases, and so she's the one to ping as to whether I'd become "Moises Binder," meaning that Principal was "Chaim Apt."

Think back to the time my name was still mine, all those aughts ago: 1999. Think of my feelings, as online associated me with people with whom I shared that name, and yet nothing else. Idempotent nomials, mutual onomasticators, whose lives would otherwise never have disappointed or cheered (me), or even been counted (against mine). I've spent my whole entire virtual experience subordinate to Principal, reloading my name as it became his, reloading it into becoming his—but it's only now that I can regret my collaboration: that the more I clicked on him, the more he became me and I became nobody.

It's no neat psych trick to explain why I'm reliving this now—the anticipations, the anxieties, all the dreamshit especially—with the traveling I'm doing, the traveling for a book, interviewing again, gathering materials.

This was in Poland, fall/winter 1999, and I was driving, for research, not lost, asking in Krasnystaw how to get to Piaski, asking in Piaski how to get to Krasnystaw, asking this goitrous streetsweeper for directions to whichever town I'd just left only to calm her hostile claim that the destination I was originally asking for never existed: the Trawniki concentration camp, which I was sure was midway between them, Krasnystaw, Piaski. But the only thing between them was a sign for the highway to Chełm, and on my last pass through, as the road narrowed to a toppled chimney of darkness, I turned, and found myself trapped by the snuffed timber and thatch of what might've been a granary, and I stopped and got out to piss.

I dropped trou in the weeds, above a septic depression rimmed by moon and the headlights of my rental Daewoo. Just as I unleashed my stream I noticed the stones, I was pissing on the stones, a cemetery of nubby slabs askew and overgrown, desecrated by the weather or Poles, and just ahead was my own, it was my gravestone, rather it was a sandstone marker belonging to Yehoshuah ben David Ha-Cohen, whose dates had been abrased yearless though the rest was still legible, Adar 14–Tevet 4. This wasn't just my Hebrew name, but also the deathday was the same as my birthday by the Hebrew calendar. By the time I'd made the calculations I was trickling. Zipping, buttoning up. Yiddish might have a word for "both strange and expected," or German, "expectedly strange": the banality of names, the banality of numbers (I went to make a rubbing but it didn't take) (and my camera's flash was broken).

\

Archaeology—that's what I'm doing in the Emirates—what else is there to do in the desert? except excavate through bone and bed, toward a terminal stratum, an inaccessible anticline depth? I won't fully love a woman unless I've done this, unless I've dug between her legs. A site. I have to wave my spade around seeking the who and where and when of her. Who was here, or there. First, last, longest, shortest. The Chaldeans? The Sumerians or Akkadians, Assyrians or Babylonians? One of the Canaanite tribes, like the Moabites? Or just a bluechip Jewish Philistine from Central Park West?

This was my field—I'd fuck someone new, some casual bar score from Barnard, or The Factchecker for Bloomberg News, who held that title for an unprecedented 1994–98, and the moment I was finished, with her lying next to me unsatisfied or in the bathroom already flushing and clitting off, I'd be asking about her partners, asking what she liked, what she didn't, and if she'd answer at all it'd be abashedly—but still I'd press, barter, bribe, shovel atop my own carnalities, overplaying myself until my mid-20s, downplaying intensively by 30, not because I was so experienced, just wiser. But then by that age my women were too, and they understood and manipulated my appetite. Giving me the grittiest on exactly precisely how many men they'd fucked before me, how many times and in what locations for what durations, simultaneously, or separately, ages, races, physiques, with what appendage sizes in which positions in which orifices—was it good? who was better? grand total of orgasms? their intensities? and whatever their pasts, I'd suffer through them, until I'd find the strength to live up to them.

Which was the thing with Rach—with her I dug harder than ever, and turned up all of what? Comedy club stubs from dates she'd had with retirement age tax lawyers and radiologists, a taxi receipt in return from a tryst with her graymaned counterpart at a competing agency, the baggy condom of a dentist and family friend.

They treated her like an equal, that's what she swore—that's the truth of it. Just like everything she writes for her campaigns is true—it has to be. The best electronics won't obsolesce with their production. The top refrigerator/freezers won't expire before the eggs inside them. The acclaimed bouncy bath toy will never suffocate a child. Rach, of the monochrome suits, the locavore dairies and cauline greens, the classes in bhangra, hatha yoga, and the Audi whose space rented for twice my office—her talent was for enthusiasm, with a specialty in revisionism, in her men as in her ads, and if she didn't find the explanations she was after, up at a client's HQ, or down in its labs, in the market testings, or at the brandjob rounds of her fellow creatives, she didn't hesitate to invent.

\

History has always privileged the civilization—shunning nomadism, tribalism, all the existential bachelorhoods.

A people's legitimacy is derived from its artifacts. Even a relationship isn't a relationship unless it's left behind its trash.

Knives, forks of diverse tines, spoons, a ladle. Shards, sherds—from the same or different pots? did this dish catch the spray of human sacrifice or was it used to prepare a corny gruel (I had similar quandaries at the fancier spots in London and Paris)?

Impossible to grasp the development of the handle: that improvement that made handheld blades of basalt, which before had cut only the closest things, now cut violently at a distance, as axes, spears, and arrows—the handle, the innovation that made vessels move. Impossible to come to grips with how its perfectability endures: the wheel becoming the halfwheel of the handle? metaphorized into the handle that posts and chats, gropes virtually?

In that sense, women, vessile women, posed a threat.

The wife I was supposed to fuck, but had no desire to fuck, had no handles (ancient, modern), whereas the nonwife I wasn't supposed to fuck, but had this uncontrollable desire to fuck immediately in one of the Met's least frequented galleries—#547 for the bergère, the #400s of Mesopotamia, rattling the ewers in American Wing parlor interiors—had an abundance of handles: she had a waist and clefts, posterior juts, a jug's taper beneath the jugs, and it was death to decide which to hold, and how (very ancient, very modern).

Once Lana wrote an essay for an exhibition catalog, which means I helped, inhibited. The show concerned an archaeological controversy, and presented a pair of prehistoric remains from Chile's Atacama found intact, but evincing no sign, or no "evident sign," as we phrased it, "of having been purposefully mummified or otherwise preserved."

The remains were of a man and wife, a couple, presumably, and, if so, their serene condition was doubly inexplicable. Some scholars pointed to the geochemical composition of the quebrada cavern they'd been found in/buried in, something to do with salts. Others pointed to the holes bored into their skulls, as being too alike to have been the cause of their deaths, and to the fragments of hair found in the brain cavity of the male, which defied all tests until one finally identified them as a llama's. Our walltext, at least, had no agenda—it just stated the case, the state of the research, the arguments for and against intentionality, cagey.

\

My own Pharaonic entombment, a Caliph Suite at the Burj:

—clothing, the basics concierged in Paris from American Apparel, from London an outrageous suit in barcode gingham, an albion basket-weave shirt, and a tie frauding me in the regimental colors of the First Royal Dragoons, Savile Row.

—a cache of Europorn, bilingual and lesbically bisexual, purchased in London and Paris (Great Windmill & Brewer, Soho, Rue des Archives, Fourth Arrond.), after Aar had emailed a reminder that the Emirates curtailed access to certain niche haunts online, which didn't stop me from tempting that access: trying workarounds, proxy IPs, any way to evade (any way not to consult Principal).

—purchased from the dutyfree, four cartons of cigs (Camel Lights), and a bottle each of scotch, whiskey, and vodka (I'll identify the vodka, which was Gorbachev, which was horrid), after Cal had emailed that the Arabs who'd invented it—al-Cohol—now sell it only to foreigners, not in bottles but by the bankrupting glass.

—one pill left in the bottle of Ativan, a half going to gauze in the bottle of Xanax (the tradenames for lorazepam and alprazolam, which remind me of genie or djinni incantations, abracadabra, alakazam).

—a candybar, put on a creditcard, a receipt for a $6 candybar (Toblerone the size of an alpenhorn).

—two pairs of shoes, dressy and less, an unmatched aquasock crept in, Dad's watch.

—a wallet I haven't much used, keys to an apartment I'll never use: W. 92nd 2 br/ba, prewar/newly renovated, move-in condition, spare room prefurnished with a crib and daubed in a pink that insists on not just a baby but a girl, even as Broadway dawn and Hudson dusk ensanguines.

—travelbag with matching toiletrykit, which were wedding presents? from whom?

—Tetbook, have to mention the Tetbook.

—two books besides the Koran.

I'd noticed when heading beachward—copies are given away in the lobby for gratis. I want to hoard heaps of these, cairns and dolmens of these—I want to die in this facility wrapped in a rabbinic beard as quilly soft as this duvet so that when Security (dial 0) slams down the door I'll be buried under this monument: 1,001 Korans.

://

9/9, HOTEL PALACE KHALEEJ, ABU DHABI

total time of Principal recordings: 168:53:51 (the amount of time a Jewish male is alive before he's circumcised)
total number of Principal.Tetrec files: 72 (the number of names of the Jewish God)
their size: 3.5 GB (the Jews fled Dubai for Abu Dhabi in the year 3.5 GB)
their content: *This Agreement imposes the same obligations upon Joshua Cohen 2 with respect to Information or any information derived therefrom that (a) was available to Joshua Cohen 2 prior to the time of its receipt from Joshua Cohen 1, (b) is or becomes publicly available through no express fault of Joshua Cohen 2, (c) is received by Joshua Cohen 2 from a third person/party with/out a duty of confidentiality, (d) is disclosed by Joshua Cohen 1 to a third person/party with/out a duty of confidentiality, (e) is disclosed by Joshua Cohen 2 to any agents and publishers and their employees with Joshua Cohen 1's approval as covered under the agent and publisher NDA ["NDA 2"] and Section 2 of the Contract.*

Failure to comply with the above will result

The time and/or distance required for luxuries to become staples, for wants to become needs, for consumption to consume us. London's just around the corner, a floor up or down, Paris can be ordered, ensuite, round the clock. Our access is bewildering, not just beyond imagination, but becoming imagination, and so bewildering twice over. We can only search the found, find the searched, and charge it to our room.

The time and/or distance required for luxuries to become staples, for wants to become needs, consumption to consume. London's just around the corner, Paris can be ordered, ensuite, round the clock. Our access is bewildering, not just beyond imagination, but becoming imagination, bewildering twice over. We can only search the found, find the searched, and charge it to our room.

The time/distance required for luxuries to become staples, wants to become needs. London's just around the corner, Paris can be ordered, ensuite. Our access is bewildering, not just beyond imagination, but becoming imagination. We can only search the found, find the searched, and charge it to our room.

The time/distance required for luxuries to become staples, wants to become needs. London's just around the corner, Paris can be ordered. Our access is bewildering. We can only search the found, find the searched, and charge it to our room.

Principal thrives on consistency.

Every accommodation, each site of a sessh, has quartered his Buddhas, and patchouli wafters, the tantra appurtenances: vajra and ghanta, mandala.

Vajra: a small bolt capped with pins like an antique mainframe's vacuum tube. Ghanta: a small bell that dinged histrionically. Both objects of contemplation. Brass.

Mandala: a large papyruslike scroll psychedelically emblazoned with a square pierced by four gateways shaped like Ts that grant access to a circle of four subsidiary squares whose plenitude of applications and meanings—including directing meditation and symbolizing the universe—I can only slight by explanation.

Anyway, responsibility for this domestic Dharma fell to Myung.

She was our prepper, and her mysterious tesseractical talent was for already being at every destination before us, despite leaving after us—having all of Principal's surroundings broken down in one country, only after he'd departed, and set up in another country, before he'd even arrived—as if she'd transcended aircraft for teleportation.

She was in Dubai before us, she was in Paris and London before they were founded—it was like she had multiple Buddhas, it was like she was multiple Myungs. Each with her own white bodystocking, ballet flats, the lobes dangling unattached, which is rare for an Asian, the epicanthic folds enclosed in aviators with barely a nose to hang them on, @ stud in a nare, arachnidan henna across the hands, hair granted extensions hanging coaxial to the waist, clipped at the sides with barrettes of memorysticks.

An advancewoman, front female, avant of the entourage, a vanguard of one, furnishing Principal's life just a leg ahead of its living, ensuring that anything he would have to adjust to, instead adjusted to him.

Never once since I've been with Principal has he commented on his immediate surroundings—nothing about transit facilities, or life beyond windows, climates and biota of disparate timezones. But then it was Myung's job to ensure he wouldn't have to. She enabled his detachments. Whether they were from religious principle, or developmental disability, or just the preference of his richness. She was the caretaker of his temples, his travel agent along the autism spectrums, specifying to the relevant guestologists his linen requirements (Mitetite® sheets, 1200 sateen, 2.6 micron pore size, no pillows, no comforters), conforming lighting fixtures to house style (Ecoxenon® bulbs, which would outlast the combined lifespans of all subsequent occupants). Consult attached specs on installing alkalizing purifiers on the taps, bath/shower inclusive, Alqua®, on installing the airfilter of choice, Hepass®. Arrange Gaston's salt block, spiralizer, dehydrator, soak/sprout set. Arrange Lavra's resistance bands, plyo harness, quigong bolster, tabata stool. Even unpacking, herself, Doc Huxtable's protein machine, the vial valise of cytokine boosters. Move all media outroom (no draping). Remove telephones/computers (remove jacks, no draping). Just so that with Principal's appearance he'd be able to function as if he had no preferences, no demands, whatsoever.

A bustling recreatrix—who'd left in each one of my rooms a fresh pack of appropriate adapters/converters.

The UK plugs are bulky, rigid, threepronged with two up top, that absurdly big grounding knob at bottom—indicative of a bulky, rigidly grounded country? or a country ridiculously overcompensating, seeking to overpenetrate, for lost power? The French plugs are expectedly more attractive, softer, rounder, twopronged but with a hole at bottom because the grounder, in France, is not incorporated into the plug itself but into the socket—indicative of a more attractive, softer, rounder country? or a country that surrenders its hole and enjoys it?

The Emirates are equipped for both.

The time was a beseechment between Isha, the prayer to be said after the sun's red recording light has faded from the sky, and Fajr, the prayer to be said at the pulsing return of its luminance.

I kept getting roused out of sleep by a dream or a line memory, which had me backtracking all the way to Palo Alto—through tracks I never imagined having to Play, I can't imagine transcribing, rewriting, being read. Rewinding and Playing again: "[. . .] the time/distance required for luxuries to become staples, wants to become needs. London is just around the corner, Paris can be ordered," "[. . .] wants to become needs. London is just around the corner, Paris can be ordered. Bewildering. We can only search the found, find the searched, and charge it to our room."

A knock at the door interrupted, and Jesus let himself in like in an extraordinary rendition, which it was. Except there wasn't any chloroform towel, the pillowcases stayed on the pillow, under my head and smothering it "in quotes."

He wouldn't let me pack myself, but it wasn't a security measure, it was a haste thing. He rolled my bag for me.

Feel was in the lobby with a single suitcase.

Principal had either ditched, or forgotten, his toupee. In his hand was a begging bowl from the buffets.

\

I'm not sure I understood what, but something got screwed up with our transport: something about how we were supposed to leave from an auxiliary garage, but how as an extra precaution Jesus and Feel had waited until now to inform the Burj concierge, who was apologizing that our transfer had already been routed out front and the auxiliaries all reserved for the impending visit of the ruler of whichever nation had a white flag with a crown and a serrated edge, waving.

So while Feel and Jesus tried to hash out a compromise in a way that kept the concierge from alerting his supervisor, and I turned my head for just a moment to rustle for my drugs—Principal got impatient and wandered unattended.

The dudes in turbans and S&M leather and chains slouching across the lobby must've been affiliated with that visiting ruler as like valet dungeonmasters, or executioners. Because they weren't doormen: the doors were automatic, sliding glass.

Principal was heaving himself over the gul rug and Burj medallion until, just as he was about to crash into the glass, he stopped—the panes wouldn't part for him, his presence wasn't sensed, and he was shocked. He barely even had a reflection, just the ghost of a ghost, of an insatiable paling, and an amniotic and alien baldness.

Then the sadomaso dudes mobbed him, and bowed to him, and their bows were detected, and the doors stood aside. Jesus and Feel, just sprinting up, dropped their hands from their holsters.

Outside, and into the heatblast. Convoys of Range Rovers and Escalades were idling, and whether Feel or Jesus or the dispatch itself was to blame, ours was the black tacky stretch prom limo.

The chauffeur—Afric, vitiliginous—tried to wheel my wheelie but Jesus refused him. He tried to take the suitcase from Feel and Feel handed it over with a palmful of dollars that if they didn't buy the limo itself bought the right to drive it.

Jesus rode shotgun reading directions off his Tetheld.

We had no sirened escort or motorbike gang—just speed, lanechanges without a signal, tires bucking us unpaved.

Principal, throughout, was just this loosely seatbelted breathing, which intensified with and then surpassed the AC, by a mindful circulation, simultaneous in and exhalation like he was resuscitating himself nose to mouth. I sat alongside him and bumped knees with the chauffeur sitting abstracted and sad on the opposite banquette.

A sign put Dubai airport one way, 20 km, Abu Dhabi airport the other, 100 km—as one airport ended, another began, with nothing between.

Construction sites, stalled. Construction completed in the style of stalled. The cranes indistinguishable from the towers they built. For sale or lease or rent, both the towers and the cranes. The sky was blue. The lights were green. Until, at Port Saeed, traffic honked stopped. A yacht had floated off a flatbed. A sideloader's shipping containers barged by the guardrails. Gulf Navigation, Hanjin, Maersk, P&O Nedlloyd.

Helicopters hopped and buzzed like locusts over Al Quds Street. Baggagetrains wormed through the snail drips of refueling tankers. The tarmac was uneven, as if asphalt had been poured directly over the dunes, the airplane hangar an oasis, roof planted with radar fronds. We slowed, and stopped, and just left the limo running, the doors ajar and the chauffeur sitting amid all that calfskin and burnished trim, and as I walked under the hangar's ribs, I turned—he was still in the limo, just sitting, hands brooding gloved by his flanks.

This wasn't our plane, but was—it was the same but Kor's, Tetjet Two. Another shrewdly nibbed Gulfstream 650.

An Arab in a spotless salafi jumpsuit that marked him as foreman sprung at us with a folder of paperwork, and went up between Jesus with our bags and Feel escorting Principal shaky on the airstairs.

I lit a cig, procrastinating. Bibbed mechanics flipped wrenches. The rest of the groundcrew sat around on a conveyor. That the scars of their faces were different might've meant their tribes were different, or their troubles.

The foreman returned and I assumed he was going to have me put out my cig, but he bummed one, and as I was lighting him he said, "Next time you give advance notice? Avoid rush charges?"

As I boarded I popped the last of my pharmacopoeia. My beverage choice wasn't a choice, kombucha or lukewarm Corona.

I sat across from Principal—I wondered which seat was Kor's. Between Feel and Jesus we had at least one pilot, apparently.

Principal lotused his legs, and wedged them under the armrests, the arms at rest, he was breathing into becoming breath, he was ridding himself of ballast.

The Burj bowl was overturned in his lap.

Samadhi—I don't know if that's how to spell it—iddhi—I don't even know what that means, what it can mean to the spiritual.

I've never subscribed to the miraculous: a Samaritan turns water to wine with artificial colorants, tugs extra fishes and loaves out of bottomless hats, a leper dances across water in shoes with stilts attached. Still, of all the miracles of all the religions, Buddhism's are the only ones that make sense to me, because they're the only ones I've at least technologically experienced—seeing over long distances, hearing over long distances, passing unimpeded through walls, doubling, tripling, and quadrupling the self—and especially, levitation: going up, and staying up for a bit, coming down.

Principal did this every time we flew but this meditation must've been especially focused. Or it's just that I had nothing else to notice. The portals were shaded. Principal rumbled in a fluent enginese—either Sanskrit or Pali.

The self must be escaped, or ejected. The fuselage must be cleared for takeoff, and the wings must become mere excrescences. Heavy metal on the ground becomes airborne, hollowboned birdflight, featherlight. A vessel for impurity becomes a vessel for purity, without claim to creed or even the corporeal.

Principal chanted, but this time did a version translated for me: "Dwell so that the above is below—shed skin, go, pass organs, go, shit, piss, bile, phlegm, blood, sweat, and fat, go, go."

We went—Principal disburdening for lift, and lifting us weightless.

Until—I felt this genitally—the landing gear deployed. We were back on the ground in about 18 to 20 minutes.

"Dwell so that the below is above," Principal still aloft even as the wheels skidded, skipped, and the semaphores yielded.

He left his bowl, bottom up, in his seat.

\

I'm not sure how to write about this, not sure whether to still be writing at all—I've been trying to screen and block so much out, so many confidences throughout, classified stuff, government stuff, might even get me imprisoned stuff, that it's become systemic with me, to the point that I find myself trying to withhold on this confession even. Principal's mouth wired to my ears, his eyes becoming mine, a monitor, a common prompt between us blinking, unblinking, at this sense of having become so irrecordably joined that the only way not to write about him is not to write about myself. I'll have to spread and type around. Furl and reach between Del and Esc.

I'd been hoping that this diarizing here would be for me what our sesshs have been for Principal—a reckoning—and that the role he'd play in this would resemble my own in his: a standard, a measure, irrelevant where ignorant, relevant when desired, and if intrusive then only as a punctuating mantra, Am, Em, Im, Om. I guess, um, the difference, um, is that I'm the one who's getting paid, and already in breach of contract by this acknowledgment.

We were alone, but if I can't get into why, I'll have to turn that omission into a virtue, like the way handicaps are treated, or like scriptural restraints. At least what I'm omitting is professional, nothing personal.

Am, Em, Im, Om.

We were in Abu Dhabi, having been checked into the Hotel Palace Khaleej under our names assumed, and ensconced for a sessh in Principal's preposterous enfilade, which even with its crazy brecciations and carats and enough room in each closet to sepulture the shame of it, was empty. Rather it was disarranged, like the qtips weren't in their dedicated holder, and the glasses on Principal's face weren't the unhinged rimless squares that he preferred and anyway were grubby, and there were no protein potion or granulocyte macrophage booster shot reminders, and there were no potions or shots without reminders. He'd left Myung behind in Dubai, along with the rest of the away staff, our normalcy. I'm fantasizing they're all helping dismantle that topfloor temple at the Burj, and demolishing its idols.

Now it was just Feel's toothaches, Jesus and his restlessness about not being able to contact his wife, who was pregnant.

At the courtesy call for Asr (that prayer recitable in this season at this latitude between ca. 15:45 and 18:15), Principal told me I was sleepy, which meant he was. I asked the time of our next meeting, I asked what time he had to meet the sheikh, but he was asleep in his chair—I didn't take off his sandals.

I retoted and let myself out, relieved Feel from sentry. Jesus was out making a phonecall, or as Feel said with kulfi popsicle lips and a mordant stick between them, "encrypted phonecall," which, as a status update, I interpreted as twitchy.

I went out to the elevators, pressed the only button, the down, until it turned into a fiery bindi—if only salvation were as summonable as an elevator, if only redemption were just a mechanical designation, an assignment. The doors closed behind me, and I swiped my keycard, which was coded for floor access, for room access—rubbed, and blew on the black stripe, rubbed, swiped again—demagnetized, which is what happens to everyone who works with laptops, I guess, they lose their hair and muscle tone and magnetism.

None of the other guest floors or reclevels would admit me. Not even the lobby. The underground parkinglot. The ground under which admits everyone. I pressed open, but the doors wouldn't open, then went for the help button that in all languages is red and in braille is a rash. Sweating, dizzy, stifled.

I struck out at the walls, the antiscratch padding and weather touchsplays. I jumped but was short of the ceiling, took out my Tetbook—no wifi—had this urge to cringe inside my tote, as the elevator's lighting dimmed and the thrum of its mechanism quieted.

I was karmically stuck, a floater. It was my breath. I had to ease my breath, and then empty it. Void this car containment.

I tried to fold myself up like a map, to compress myself like in eastward travel. To become the time lost to flights, the time lost across longitudes. The differences between Palo Alto and London and Paris, and between them and the Emirates—I'd go where they went, when they went. Into nonexistence—into neverexistence.

The doors would glide away then and it wouldn't just be the Khaleej again, it would also be the Burj, de Crillon, Claridge's, all their ambiance mingling, their couture scents and muzaks merged, the corridors turning one way into London wainscoting below Victorian wallpaper flocked with paisleys, turning the other into Paris parlor boiseries wreathing Empire urns with moldings of laurel, a cracked soaking tub bashed through a rainforest steamshower, hometheater systems dunked in the toilets, gardens growing into beaches to kelp the Gulf, the desert strewn with broken crockery from The Foyer and Les Ambassadeurs—bent knives from every restaurant I've stayed above, with Doc Huxtable, the piloting Sims, Gaston, Lavra—and all Myung's Buddhas staved and dashed, the prayerbeads off their threads, the wheels unspoked, the sutras dismembered and blowing scattered. It was as if by evacuating my mind, I found this was my mind, a room of all my rooms, assailed by all my planes, or just a car in flames, and a voice, which was its capacity, shrieking.

\

With Maghrib (ca. 18:30 to 20:00) I was moving again. Descending. I had to be called, being unable to call myself. But then the car stopped, around the Khaleej's midlevel, the doors fell away, and there's no other way I can explain this sensation—of identicality but wrongness, of unicity within displacement—this was, but wasn't, my floor.

Only the numerals distinguished.

A man crouched by the elevatorbanks, his back to me.

He was an Arab, clad in a kandura like a bedsheet filched from housekeeping, straight off the cart. Bright brilliant just from the shrinkwrap white, still creased shoulders to elbows, rustling at toes.

He was close enough to obstruct my exit, and was stooping over as if to pick up something he'd dropped. Some hankie or submissive tissue—a woman.

But not white—she was black. She was a wadded tossed abaya, a smutty black abayayaya—trill it through the nose, like a jihad ululant.

She'd fallen—mucous sniveling through her nostril slit—she'd been hit.

As the doors went to shut, the Arab pivoted and kicked a foot out, a foot clad expensively crocodilian, and wedged them open.

"Stop!" I yelled, "Lay off, asshole!" or its panicked equivalent—it's not enough to look ridiculous in action? I have to sound strangled on the page?

The Arab just tried to drag her into the elevator with me.

But she struggled, and so the Arab let go, only to hit her again—smacking the sniffling girl backhanded. She thrashed away howling.

Or that was me, urging her on with stupey nonconfrontationalisms: "Get away!" (I'm sure there's a security recording), "Run!" (I'm willing to negotiate terms for the erasure of any security recording). My sneaker might've grazed his wingtip still holding the doors, and the Arab whirled around dervishly.

We faced each other, and I can only imagine what he took me for: a burnt paleface, a paunch in its decline, into financial services, *Homo americanus consultantus*.

Then again, my impressions of him were just as imaginary. He was some fictional character from transit lit, some thriller villain spun from a revolving rack in an international terminal. I only wished it were a better translation. He was introducing himself as the girl's husband, or father, or brother, explaining that whatever the nature of their relationship, it entitled him to beat her, explaining that it required him to beat her—and just as the elevator doors were sliding shut again between us, he lashed out with pointy chinbeard and charged.

He choked me by the totestrap and I went for his thumbs, until everything in the tote was falling and we went after it, into the hallway. We fell like dictators. Slowly, messily slowly, crashing into curios and rolling into benches. I punched his jaw and his head hit the wall, bent my knee between his balls on my way to getting upright, lurching amid the wreckage of lamps, braziers, kashkul of sawdusty potpourri.

He was out. Not just unaware, but unconscious, and not in the psychoanalytic definition, but with blood in his goatee.

"You OK?" I said to the girl. But the cowering napkin just wailed.

I stumbled to the elevatorbanks, pressed the up and down buttons. I rocked him loose from deadweight and turned him over and inside the car, pressed every floor.

The elevator closed, opened: a flap of his bedsheet was stuck between doors. I tucked him in and took out my wallet and swiped him down to the pillow of lobby, and thank the gods of maintenance or inspectorship, or of magnetic coercivity, he plummeted.

My sessh effects were sprawled along the hall, Tetbook concussed from tote. "If you're seriously OK, help me pick all this up?"

The girl stayed just a heap, of grieved cheek and lusty gutturals, so I bent to collect my adapters, converters, pink highlighter, and then went to haul her up too—but her hands wouldn't have mine—she refused to reach out and meet me. Though this wasn't because of trauma, rather it was because the touch of an auslander male was prohibited: her daddy or hubby or whatever could touch, he could strike her, but her savior was—haram.

"What room number are you?"

No reply or no number?

"Speak English? The zimmernummer, your numéro de chambre?"

But why would she slink back to the suite of a beater?—beyond that, would a controlfreak batterer let her have her own key?

"Let's call Security? Do you have any family you can stay with?"

Nothing, and I even tried in Hebrew—gevalt.

She stayed down on all fours just wiping her face with a black cloth, which then again became her veil—and her face was gone, and then she was gone, spurning me crawling around a corner.

Her mouth, at least, was beautiful. All of me that was not my mind was virtuous, blameless.

Rewrite this all. Bottom to top.

://

The Khaleej's stairs were strictly service, in case of emergency, power outage. Their utility proved a moral instruction. An ethics of exertion. The soul antipode of the resort leisured around them.

There was no carpeting so profanely plush that rougher rugs had to be placed upon it for prayer, no marbles so carnally veined as to recall the flesh—they were purging, spiritually purifying. Unventilated, sweltering.

10 flights of 10 steps each, count their discipline down.

The fluorescence hummed penance, absolved the walls of their materials: scuffed, costcut, asbestic. Breathe in, breathe out, relax. But my wind wasn't up to even an intellectual exercise. My lungs were tight, legs, feet, it's my hand that I'm sure was broken. Typing with my nose. The last two flights were huffed.

Back in NY straggling home from the office, I'd do the burp fart shuffle four blocks south from my stop, trying to forget which building was mine, trying to forget which apartment. I could live anywhere, I thought, I could put my key to any door, not a card to swipe but a dagger to stab and turn—wounding any door, wounding any lock, and the insides that would weep for me, the roomy rumen and innards viscera, all that bark and sap and heartwood ringing, would be similar or same. They'd heal, but even when they wouldn't, I could always exchange them, I could always upgrade—with no regard for brand if new. The new—once the time of the unprecedented, now the time of the compatible.

It's mortifying, but this also went for women—the thought that any woman could accommodate, could give me what I expected from a life. The fault, then, would be with the expectations—downsized, reduced—the fault, then, would be mine.

My landing was temporary, hard on the heels. Junior Caliph Floor #2, North.

I leaned against the jamb. Against the bar. Open Sesame. If no one's around, no alarm will sound.

\

I hadn't realized I'd left the sink on. I washed my hands with my hands, cracked my knucks from numbness to stinging—if only minibars carried Vicodin or Percocet.

Admit it, I was smitten. Me, the stricken party.

I'd been aroused by a woman wearing a sweaty tent, a woman I don't know, can't ever touch to know Biblically let alone get proximal to for a chat in a neutral language—it's absurd. With a husband too. To whose swart cheek I'd delivered democracy. Four fingers of unrequited democracy, not even the thumb opposable.

Her husband? who else? Next corridor please let it be a widow I encounter. A cripple. May the next corridor be so empty I can only save myself.

I was desked again, chaired again—the primal scene.

It's difficult to concentrate—difficult to pay attention, though it accepts any currency current.

I downed trou, tried to get a honker. Tried to beat my cock like it was leukemia. Twisted my scrotum like the wallsafe knob. Then I switched to stroke my shaft with the hand that bled and throbbed. I managed a half honk, a sputter. A corpse's lean on the wheel.

If only I could shrink like my hair into a single follicle. If only I could zip into my wheelie and mail myself flatrate, at email rates, on home.

I rooted around the nethercompartment of my wheelie, surfaced with my smut—these pages too glossy to gloss. I surrounded myself with the porn, flicked, flipped, unstuck the pages to loosen me up.

I knew as much about these women as I did about that girl. I knew more about "Agnès," pp. 20–22 her spread, in French. At least I know "her name." Better to know her name than her herpes.

Masturbation feels different with different hands and without a ring, which I'd left behind in Ridgewood, jarred in clay with the clamps and clips, Moms's cloying amber glaze. To compensate, then, I rolled the pages around me, positioning their binding staple just at the seam the ring once touched, and stroked, as if I were scraping away a model's hipbone mole or removing jiggle from her thighs.

With this I managed a bit of length, of longness. A width that wouldn't flatter girth. Trying for an elevator shaft, straight up and down, getting the incline of a stairwell. Trying for Rach's shape, narrow and hard, but getting that girl's—a swerving curviness.

The lamp stood straight in the corner, its metal stanchion staunch, incorruptible. The table with the ice bucket rose immovably, stiff. Two glasses erectly stemmed, unbreakable bottles of booze. Cigarettes, matches, undisturbed smooth. Her bawdy chaudey lips léchouille, bouchey coochie coo. Her khaki hands cupping my sac.

But then the imam interrupted and the call for Isha was all that arose: Allah hu akhbar, chafing, Allah hu akhbar, chapping, Allah hu—my cock bowed over my thumb.

\

I went for my Tetbook, dented and loosed of a Return key, which went chattering around the tote like a tooth. Everything was running slower. Walking, crawling, load. Its cord, its powercable, raveling, unraveling. I weaved it between my fingers to make four insulated rings for the friction, for the frictive pleasure, and wrapped the rest snug around my base—what to call the connection of cock to scrotum along that seam like a perforation on old printer paper with the holes? Don't tetrate, resist the urge to tetrate ("what to call the connection of cock to scrotum along that seam like a perforation on old printer paper with the holes")—and, while I'm at it, what's the difference between *raveling* and *unraveling*?

No, memory will not be, cannot be, refreshed—is it the Chinese or the Japanese socket that has the slitty slanted eyes and slashes for ears? or is the proper term not *socket* but *outlet*?

The computer's coolant fan was squealing at pitch with the room fan, with an equal frequency of rotation.

I thought I had to have some porn in storage, some neglected impulse stuff I hadn't called upon in forever, and, according to tech, according to psychoanalysis, everything transferred. Metaphor, its literal meaning is transference, but tech doesn't think in metaphors. In similes, maybe, which are like or as math. Regardless, the originals, if ever originated, would've remained from my former setup. Time to rouse the past. Raise the clotheless ghosts.

I opened a window—not a real actual window, rather an otherness or alterity—a sill for my filth. I browsed internally by all the cumskein verbiage that occurred to me—blowjob pov, reverse cowgirl, reverse cowgirl Arabian Indian Pakistani teen, curry pussy, spicy biryani pussy, French maid proctolgia purring barky British boardingschool accent—no results. Then browsed by types of files—.avi, .flv, .mpeg, .mpe, .mpg, .mov, even went for the .jpegs, .jpgs, .tiffs and .gifs, .pngs and .raws—zero (0) results. I'd modernized too precipitously, adopted too early, never saved my vulgarity to memory, relied too much on streaming—how much I had to stream.

I emailed Aaron: email me some porn. I emailed Caleb: email me some porn. I emailed Finnity: email me some porn. I emailed them all again, not cc: but bcc:, my preferences. Tried some social profiles, the Tetsets: Lana's square, which featured just professional headshot pics and shaky footage of her lecturing, was socialized with the square of a Patagonian preservationist at the Met, who though she was too old to get me up was coupled virtually with the square of her darkfeatured daughter, who though she was too young to keep me up was coupled virtually with the squares of maybe cousins or friends of intermediate ages whose unprotected images extended from last springbreak to last weekend's MDMA excursion culminating in a mass makeout in the middle of the Pulaski Bridge.

I tugged my wire, charged myself.

But then another window opened, to shut my own—the prayer of Fajr. There is no God but Allah and Mohammed is His slayer of boners.

I clicked away, to Rach's blog.

What was new wasn't the vid of a client picnic—Governors Island, all leis and tikis, account execs wattlenecked sweating the BBQ, multistrawed canisters of daiquiri and piña colada sweating pixels—I sat through all of it but Rach never made an appearance. Neither was it the pic of the rental condo we'd had in the Hamptons, "Steatite counters!"

"Miele appliances!" shelves of salty cookbook, the landlord's romance and detective novels, the only thing human a suede docksider shoe disembodied on the maple—Adam's, it had to be.

Rather what was new was a comment. If I can call a thing a comment that has nothing to do with an original. Rach's blog is offered for free, which must be taken to mean: only at the price of reaction. But I wouldn't react—not yet.

I scrolled down below the dross:

uy387456: "*perfect post!! 2 increase yr traffic* click here."

therightfootfwd: "*i subscribed to this feed and will check new posts. for bargain footwear and related content* click here."

StrongL80s: "*happiness happens. be yourself today tenaciously.*"

I'd always presumed StrongL80s—and Nokiddushing, and Challahatyourgirl, and others—were all just Rach, cheerleading herself tenaciously.

The next and last was it: the only comment I hadn't already read, the only comment I hadn't already reread, was another from "KORDIE":

"*wtf? taking my plane leaving me behind in ras alkhaimah ummmm alquwain wtf? im just concerned 4 the both of u. the truth must not be evaded. trust me yre in waaaay over yr head.* download this *2 contact me now.*"

\

I got up out of the chair, tried to find the remote—where was it? if I were a remote where would I be? Wriggling myself across pins and needles to the entertainment system, to switch it on manually, then reembedding myself, constantly switching my alignment to face the east that was west, the west that was—comfort.

Insomniac, I defaced every direction—every qibla, or mihrab. All prayers point to the Saudis.

Each time the muezzin came through the curtains—sounding throughout the city, resounding and vibrating—each time he pronounced, I heard Rach. Her old ringtone.

That voice. It wasn't recorded, but live. Both bodiless and hoarse. Arabesque. The voice that turns lattices to speakers. That speaks the very fretwork. While rising and falling like an arch. The sound of calligraphy, of cacography.

I listened, I lay and listened while watching the default channel, as the face of the sheikh wiped onscreen—a screensaver, a sheikhsaver.

Then a dissolve, to a stock image of Medina. Minarets around a vert dome. The sheikh returned, superimposed. A dissolve again, to a stock image of Mecca: caravanserai encircling the Kaaba, that brute granite tabernacle that holds paradise inside it and grants wisdom to all—in its big black squareness it even looked like a datacenter.

Again with "the sheikh"—or "king"—the lexicon kept changing, or else the man himself refused to be defined. Ruler of the petrols we're passing for flight. Ruler of the electrified high celestials. Guardian of freon, and of the urinals that flush in the sky.

I wondered how he'd receive Principal: desert hospitality mandates feetwashing, the watering of camels, a meal (the guests served first and best), the best bed and first choice of concubine (supplies limited). A prudent host would also provide the translation.

The sheikh would speak, would describe an immense palace of utterance, and only when finished, only when utterly finished, would he let the interpreter render. A dictatorial practice, Koranic in a sense. Unless the totality has been communicated, nothing has been communicated. A single misunderstanding flaws it all.

Or else maybe the sheikh would break his speech into units, bits and bytes and girih tiles, pausing between each to demonstrate his authority, in the guise of generosity—pausing between each to allow his interpreter, scrounging on hands and knees, tongue thrust in concentration, to clean it up. To lick the words up from the limen, and spit out again a perfect reproduction mosaic.

But then perhaps the sheikh would say nothing at all, and just sit enthroned, while his interpreter stood and spoke for him: either words the sheikh supplied the interpreter with prior to this audience, or words the sheikh never supplied—the interpreter recast as a prophet and the sheikh becoming an oracle or dream.

Then again, the ultimate would be if there were no sheikh whatsoever: the sheikh could pose as his own interpreter, or the interpreter could pose as the sheikh, who was absent from this audience because too important, or too senile, or even deceased, and so the interpreter who claimed to represent him was just representing himself.

I wrapped my hand in a washcloth, prepped for my next sessh with Principal. Stretched for the ascent.

There were a lot of steps ahead of me. And each vital to mastering the next.

://

9/10

To fall for this Arabess is forbidden, but nowadays to fall for any woman you can't search up online is forbidden. How else to snoop her? how else to send her around?

Her life had been set to Private.

Her mouth, a pool of jewel set in bodied blackness. The modesty mullahs sure know what they're doing, insisting that the less I know of a woman, the more I want to know, I need to know.

She'd reserved a full floor in my memory, without giving a number, without giving a name. I had no wasta, and only this chance. Though even if I'd manage to baksheesh the compjockeys at resort IT, it'd be too suspicious to ask after her, I'd have to ask after him, the rolypoly ayatollah, the offensive effendi. Claim him a prospective investment partner. Invest him in my claim. Either that or I'd appeal to Principal to hack the Khaleej dbase and ransack the records. No other sources to cultivate. Just desert.

Instead of excavating around the site, exposing its ramparts, I decided to go down, foundationally. I dug myself into the lobby, and sifted through the drifters, the dunes motioned around me—humpy dumps in full hijab.

The women who passed compelled attention by tighter fits, which were pregnancies, and heelless shoes, so as not to slight their escorts. Kitchen slippers, or wrung through the laundry slippers and then, open toes.

Hints of tint from the fingers. Ten drips of an esoteric ultramarine.

The purdah population must've boomed overnight (or else I've just grown the appropriate antenna).

I was muftied again in my predistressed jeans, flannel over I heart NY tee, sitting on a tulipary divan between the elevatorbanks and pretending to compute. I clicked for a speech I'd consulted on for the mayor's office: New Urbanism & the Future of Energy. But energy has an unlimited future, and it's humanity that doesn't have even a horizon on the horizon: "The city seeks Albany's pledge to develop solar, wind, and hydroelectric capabilities in both the Hudson and East Rivers within the next decade"—this was laughable, rather, depressing, reading this in a Gulfside palace powered not by sun, wind, or water but by fossils, whose government ownership would go sustainable only if that meant going nuclear. Scrolled through a few old journo squibs: reviews of books about homosexuality and Cubism, about German dodecaphonists in America, and then a profile of an Israeli novelist dedicated to answering "The Palestinian Question," a kaddish eulogy overpraising an overpriced deli upon its shuttering.

Went through my résumé, exaggerating credentials for the main search—the job search—to come. I rattled the filechains, unfettered the inbox. Wrote: draft emails to two lawyers Lana had recommended, ridiculous (one Levin, the other Levine), to decline a Rosh Hashanah dinner and/or Yom Kipper break fast invite from the managing ed of jewe.com, to thank Cal and Finn for the porn. Loaded the porn. Cal—gratitude retracted—had sent a pic of a grossly obese man having his foreskin licked by a dog having its foreskin licked by a cat. Finn—apologies in order—had sent a vid. Long. Loading. Taking so long to load the old me could've buffered twice already (the new me couldn't fathom ever buffering again).

Black. She emerged from the car. I knew it was her, because she knew it was me. She startled—facelessly—turned away, turned back but clung to her guide.

She was being minded not by her husband but by a more voluminous rotundity—a floating dome, like of a mosque, but undergoing reconstruction. An old woman scaffolded with a cervical collar, and an ungainly plastic and titanium orthotic—a bootcast.

I shirked my Tetbook into the tote, approached. Sidled up alongside.

"Hello."

Closer than would be considered normal even if she weren't a she, or Arab.

They made a show of ignoring me, her most of all.

"Speak German? Speak French?"

She said nothing and her escort was just a gentle dumb hemisphere orbiting gravely.

I said, "Pretend no one else is in this lobby—you with me?" I tried to hold her pace, her general area of face. "It's just the two of us, remember?" I gestured at my chest, sashed by the totestrap in the getup of a eunuch.

She whispered what I took to be "English."

I said, "What are you up to today?"

The equatorial plumpness next to her shushed, Arabized a spate comprehensible internationally as disapproval.

I said, "Today?"

"No English," she said, mine.

"Mari?"

"No."

"Frau oder Mädchen?"

"Jaloux jaloux mon mari."

This was like a Russian novel already, this French, this German—excessive, dumm, imbécile.

The chaperoning mother—or mother inlaw? or an eldest prima wife who'd been hurt in an unpreventable domestic accident of her own?—scolded in gutturals, tsks, and sped them ahead, her boot's clunkery punctuating my failure.

\

No matter how much they've traveled, most whites have had this experience abroad—especially in the darker countries. These people—these dimnesses, darknesses—are interchangeable, the white tourist thinks, they're cognate, coincident, synonymical. The inner life as impenetrable as its outer pigmentation. Black is bad, the color of evil, a stain or taint. A cancer. Red is bestial. Brown is shit. Yellow is piss timid.

But then inevitably our traveler comes to know someone—maybe only his waiter, maybe only his maid. He might even, let's hope, come to have sex with someone, for love or money, for both, and—when the fascination ends, when the package tour ends—is either confirmed or disabused, ashamed of his initial bias or not.

I followed—what should I dub her? should I set up an online presence for her, have Aar and Cal vote on a name?

Like her, dislike her, track her as favorite—through the Khaleej's lobby, through a garish consecution of kufic script scannables and projected ads that connected practically and thematically the resort complex with the mall.

Gaudy antiseptic fountains, cacti to deter loitering, boulders whose size trafficked toward sales. Palms marked the passageways fronding radially from the central bourse. The mall had planted only species native to the Americas, as if to boast, to brag, to demonstrate what was feasible—not just the acquisition but the thriving. The trees grew, amid the frigidity, they prospered and grew, and the abayas were their fruit, ripely contused—the proper plural of abaya? abayat?

Their color scheme was basic black. The fall collection, also the winter, spring, and summer collections in this desert without season. They were bolts of black cloth unrolling. Items strayed off the rack. Some silk, some chenille. All blended.

The women made a hajj to a windowdressed concourse, whose mannequins matched them in chador before lightening up and becoming hysterical, gruesomely festooned in chiffon plastron and crape carapace, billowing with metalline polyester, lycra strapped to masks—garments that called attention to the fact that their wearers weren't supposed to be calling attention to themselves. Fashion was taking chances so these ladies wouldn't have to—these ladies swathed in pockets to be worthy by comparison, still devaluing themselves by comparison.

If a girl was just in an abaya and shayla, she judged the girls who were in veils too, who judged others of their retinue for having veils with more or less stylish coverage.

My girl's covering was just some bag. Some upsidedown insideout unadorned bag. She was wearing its reflection in every display. She was wearing the windows that reflected her and the vain commerce behind them and then instead of a face, my own.

Her old woman companion finished unbunching her beardy niqab from her collar, and swiveled her head around its scant range—but I stepped behind a kiosk.

\

Decency protocols flashed me—from the HD panels battenmounted above, whose programming looped Islam's conduct and sumptuary guidelines and a fanatic advisory about creditcard addiction and the abominations of debt. A You Are Here dot danced on an interjacent panel, damning me to the haram department—an annex beyond ahkam, a demilitarized or greenzone accepting dollars, its boutiques stocked with wares that on the homefront would be considered tame if transgressing only of taste, but that here transgressed nature itself and were risky even when folded, when hangered. Dresses cut to skirts, lingerie barely exceeding the size of the average customer's vagina, what it'd take to muffle a mean set of nipples. Negligees, bustiers, girdles, diaphanous whisperweight giggling. The ladies stopped to admire, never to touch. At least I'm assuming it was admiration, though I wasn't sure of what—the merch itself? or the confidence to be its consumer?

The outfits outfreaked only by the foreigners who purchased them: a eurobimbo bureau of diplobrat jetettes, drafty castle heiresses, and serial divorcée alimony phonies. Still, it takes volition to decide which products to buy. As my ladies passed, the parties exchanged glances, nods, sophisticated gynics. My ladies had no volition, and by contrast seemed like products themselves.

My abaya's consort embraced her, then left—clumping that boot toward the domestic appliances arcade, accompanied by two other mosquerading matrons.

We were alone now, though still among a dozen. I had to focus. On her hefty swell, the way she shuffled at turns. Otherwise her abaya was so flowing that it trailed along the tile and obscured her stride, giving her the appearance of hovering.

She boarded a conveyor. I scurried alongside, tarrying at every passage break as she disembarked toward free sample demos of jewelry detarnishing solutions, displays of boudoir organizers, pyramid placements of woks and pans, rotating installations of cognoscente cutlery, magic flying bakingtrays and bathmats.

The ultimate stretch of pathway rose, became a ramp—I boarded—an ascending escalator of an escalating steepness leading to the mall's upper tier, the uppermost skylit.

If stairs are the model life—prepared for any fate, whether up or down—the escalator is a step in the wrong direction. In one direction only. Like each day, like every day, its steps begin by staggering, only to end by flattening. They stagger, fall flat, then repeat.

I sought the highest sharpness.

As we rose, her shoes were exposed. Aqua heels. They were low heels, the lowest, which she stood in as if splashing around. They got a rise out of me nonetheless.

I clambered up the climbing—staying always four abayat, three abayat, two, behind.

\

Language is acquired only for the purposes of further acquisition—my abaya, my burqa, my burq. How much does this item cost? how much larger can it get than xxtra-large?

The ancient mystery faiths all held by this, that whosoever knows the name of a thing, owns that thing, and I'm convinced that's true only by the truth of its reversal: that if you don't know something's name, that something owns you.

Because I was hers, and my tongue was the receipt. I kept pace to better appreciate belonging.

Her featurelessness was of a supernumerary tit atop tits, though in her strain to speed ahead a waist was shaped atop that ass. Swishy hips, thighs that rubbed. Becoming again all ass. Even her feet were ass. She was an ass in heels. One cheek to each, wobbling for balance.

In the foodcourt there was a pub called Hybernopub, theme of Dublin. Its façade was fêted with shamrocks, bows rising crassly from cauldrons. Outside the premises an animatronic leprechaun jigged on a plaster keg and listed, in robotic Arabic and this language, robotically but with an Arabic growl, not beers but nearbeers, missed beers, close but no dice beers, pints of simulhops, the demalted and wortless unfoaming, and runed on the keg itself were their bankrupting prices in chalk. Dollars, euros, AED/dhs—that currency whose slick prismatic bills, denominated in every pigment of the oleaginous spectrum, depict skycrapers, sports stadia, falcons? sturgeons? antelopes? rams?—malls, definitely malls.

The chalk.

It was a short thin length like a finger bone, a pointer. I emancipated it from its string, approached her—the other ladies noticed, or didn't, but parted, humped on.

I quickened, she quickened, tensed from my tension. My shadow crossed hers and was lost.

I was hurrying alongside her—swinging arm and leg caressing her cloth, as if stroking her hair, as if her garment had grown from her scalp—reaching out to her, once more.

It wasn't a pinch I gave—I'm no pervert—but a mark, a chit, between the shoulders, chalking her for the ease of my stalk.

Just as I did, the ladies—the handful or so remnant, after most had peeled off for meals with their men—exited the foodcourt, and entered the tech sector. They went left, toward the A/V side, featuring televisions (how antique), and stereos (how antiquated)—to the right, the side for computers.

I dropped the chalk stub into a trashcan atop a waxpapered basket of chickpeas.

We passed through a pair of weighted black curtains—like I was passing through the ladies themselves. Suddenly it was night again.

There hadn't been enough prayers—there would never be. All was frozen dark.

A vacuumsealed interior—it took time to adjust, it took the ladies dispersing. I stood behind woofers, tweeters, subpurrers, gluglugers, supraribbiters, hissers.

My abaya was caught, contained. Glassed plasmatic. She stood in front of a camera, which captured her image, and then sent it to the screen she stood in front of, scrutinizing herself. She moved left, her image moved right. She turned her back, turned her back on herself. It took her—it took all of her sisters doing the same at their own sistered stations—a moment to realize that the cameras were built into the screens.

As they groomed their monitor selves, I monitored them—as they realigned, adjusted. Fascinating how their abayat resembled screens—black screens struck from the walls and curtained around their curvatures.

Still the chalk on my girl's back shone through, from deep amid the mediaroom mockups. She'd strip before bed to wash that body beneath, the skin the permanent abaya, and find this sign singed into her skin, and take it as intended and find me? though if a symbol was all I could afford, how could I be sure it'd be interpreted correctly?

I considered returning, retrieving the chalk, to outline my body in a very public atrium.

The girls trembled before their trembling, while I wavered undecided between signal and noise, feigning interest in a gadget.

It was a Tetheld 4, a successionary replacement device as new in relation to preceding Tethelds as Allah is to Yahweh: with every capability of spoken life (it had a phone and SUI, or semantic user interface), and of textual life (via Tetsuite), and was equipped for music/pics/vids (multiformat/polyshareable, via mOEs, or mobile operating ecesis), and for any other experience purchasable online (4G). It had a health monitor that took blood pressure, pulse and body temp, body mass index, tested reflexes—I'm sure it even legally notarized.

An Emiri tween—torqued by gym and sleazily pimpsuited—approached sniffing commission, "Any assistance?" And while I was declining his attentions, she vanished—my abaya, disappeared.

I glanced from the flash in my hand, and she was gone, they all were.

Only their images remained for a breath, then faded.

Strike this.

Strike this like an Arab bride.

://

I was back in my room switching channels, too wasted to pack. BBCs 1–4, CNN Int'l, Eurosport (volleyball), Al Jazeera (unrest). I sat through a documentary about the Khaleej but clicked away during a segment on its dining facilities. The weather was a rerun too.

Black and white manna crackled across the entertainment system glass.

It's like with the Korans I've been reading, it's like with any other paradisiacally dictated book. There's enough of everything for everyone, there's never any call to hoard or grub. When you're wandering the desert, you get to decide what your manna will taste like. Then you eat it, and whatever it tastes like it is. Pick any verse, interpret it into any texture, any flavor, sweet or savory. Corny honey. Matzah brei. Milk schmilk. Bdellium and coriander dew fondue. Any verse can be historicized, analogized—made palatable.

I paged through my Korans to the sura that one edition calls The Banquet and the other calls The Feast, which concerns—dilating on the dilemma of how to sojourn among strangers while preserving a sense of unblemishedness—Islam's dietary laws. Abu Dhabi's free copies were preferential to Dubai's, more archaic, more Thous and Arts—neither copy credited its translators.

Following the prohibitions against consuming prey, raw blood of any type, any porcine product, and the meat of any oblation dedicated to any god not Allah, The Banquet/Feast serves up a delight—by decreeing that Israel had been deeded to the Israelites, the Jews: "the Followers of Scripture" (Dubai version), "the People of the Book" (Dhabi version).

"Enter the advantageous land [Dubai]/the blessed land [Dhabi] that Allah has assigned [Dubai]/hath ordained [Dhabi] for you." It's incredible: the text says just what I want it to say, just what the Muslims, I'm sure, don't need it meaning.

Revisiting the gastronomical proscriptions had whetted my appetite. But I had no patience for the restaurants. The linen flap. The fork and spoon routine. Oppressive. By the second course even the disdain, the derisive scorn, has spoiled to stale formality.

I was having inexplicable tastes, slavering for a porkwing, like a wing from a pig that flies, the blood of beef roadkill consecrated to Baal, the paschal ewe for two, a chicken flipper—the special?

What on the side? Survival's just a matter of taking every side.

Pastures of greens, eggplant swords beaten into ploughshares. Starches.

I hung up the phone, went for another dram of brown, then stood on the bed and disabled the nimbus of smoke detector, lit a cig—where's my drink? atop the minbar or bottledwater minibar? There it is. Water down the brown. The same sura bans this booze.

Towel under the draft to block the smoke.

\

The chime at the door had me cowering. What happens if you choose your manna falsely? does the divine chef intuit the heart's hunger and modify the menu?

I bundled all my *Hustler UK*s and *Club Derriere*s into a drawer, doubletapped the doorcom monitor, nudged away the towel, unlocked, unbolted, unchained. On the other side was the boy. The bringer and bearer. He was polite and neat in a stealth tuxedo, his moustache pubescent fascist. Ratib, in English at least, his nametag printed in two alphabets, Ratib. He fluttered a napkin, set a chafing dish atop the table, formerly the desk.

He was older than I'd remembered, or younger—point is, how can I be expected to distinguish between the Ratibs? given that they, the Ratibs, aren't incentivized enough to distinguish themselves? All the Khaleej's servants, and the Burj's too: their faces contort in my mind, like wet sand trampled to dry and harden into brick, and I mean that as praise, if management will pass it along.

"Shookrun," I said, which extended the full courtesy of my fluency, transliterating "thank you." I tipped him one euro and one quid, the last linty currency I had, and he sneered, withdrew shook running.

The offering, uncovered, was all garnish, preservatived herb celebrating a premature gestation. Not yet brought to term and so borne with dill and parsley.

Rate the Catering? One star charred. Cleanliness? 10 out of 10, but only because turndown's been forbidden me, by Principal.

Please remit any suggestions in the space below provided:/S'il vous plaît donnez des suggestions dans le champ ci-dessous:/Bitte geben Anregungen in das dafür vorgesehene Feld unten:

Merci, danke, thanks—sheikh's rume? chic room? Standardized transliteration of pleasantries might empower guests, and encourage their engagement with local culture. Elevator 2 of the north bank should be fixed. All mall escalators should be steep enough to get a wisp of female crotch in purdah. Countries that practice online censorship evince a higher incidence of sexual assault, and a lower level of political literacy, or else it's vice versa. Ratib was quite simply the best Ratib I've ever encountered.

That survey card was my bookmark. I covered the inedible creature as if extinguishing an altar, returned to the Korans.

But the Don't Disturb had fallen from the knob, was sticking its laminate edge through the draft.

\

Just as I was about to replace it, another knock. Once, timorous.

It was Ratib returned, I guessed, working up the nerve to blackmail a better gratuity out of me. Good for you, Ratib! go get him (go get me)!

The doorcom monitor showed only a fuscously cloaked dessert cart.

I opened, and made way for her. The chalk was still at her back.

She was a darkling abaya bag, with a cheap overbuckled overzippered velcronated aluminum missile of a case she dropped by the closet.

I leaned into the hall and the rooms numbering upways and the rooms numbering downways were peaceful, and outside their doors platters of blistered doughy pistachio sweets slumbered through their rots alongside the drycleaning and laundry and men's shoes awaiting polish.

Inside again, lock chain slotted deadbolt, I said, “Your husband?”

She was standing between the chairs, speaking Arabic to them—to me. There are some people who pick up languages fast, there are some people who pick up love fast. But I can be only one of them. Too late.

I said, “Mari?”

She held out her hands, held her fingers apart like her nails were still wet from their dip in the sea—and she went for the stitching, and revealed her face.

Or what of it there was around the sunglasses she was wearing: giant outlandish mosquito moonspecs, their pricetag hanging by a thread. Her injuries seeped a shade matching their lensing.

I’m going to try transcribing what she said, I’m going to try doing every other thing to her, decently: “je veux divorcer,” and then she said something “rien à foutre”—and then something in Arabic again? “khanith”?

I said, “Did you decide to get divorced before he hit you or is this just today’s development? Peut-être he’s been hitting you forever?”

She cried, and my arms led my steps to her, but she recoiled and took off her glasses, and her eyes—haven’t I read that certain Semitic languages never distinguish blue from green? Hebrew does—but what about Arabic? Her ears had no earrings, no holes.

“You sure you weren’t—vous a-t-il followed here by anyone?”

“Je serai toujours seule.”

She stood by the east of the bed and I stood by the west and what was between us was all that sharia blanket she was tangled in.

But even switching directions, changing the poles—stand me by the east, stand her by the west—what was between us was blacker: our ages. Also the sense that my interest in her was erotic because she was also, or merely, exotic—though Rach would knock that down and call racism, if she’d burst into this room just now to find this woman, this girl, Muslim, pretty young and gorgeously wed, facing me across the bed and quivering.

She’d been gathering up her hem, and I circled around and helped her lift it over her head. All she had on underneath was her underwear, which was torture: iron maiden panties, spiked bra.

She took my hands, and laughed, the laughter swollen, "Lentement."

Don't worry—"Je ne vais pas hurt you! je ne pourrai jamais hurt you! No pain, no pain."

Her cheekwound blushed, and yet that blushing was also its bandage. Below the unmentionables she was still in her heels.

She was warm to my touch but how to say shy? just traduce to timide?

Still, let the opposite room eavesdrop, let anyone peep into our window from a wraparound suite. I didn't care—I didn't drop blinds or slip drapes.

Her mouth was intensely ovoid, an almond mouth, of citrus crescents. And under that sling, her breasts were like young fawns, sheep frolicking in hyssop—Psalms were about to pour out of me.

"Vous?"

"Josh," I said.

"Vous habillé."

"Je vais me undressed, clothes off, unhabillé, déshab."

She fussed with her hair, braided it into a fuse. "Lentement."

Slow, but slowly, I declothed. Though I was shit unfit, though I was every bit as fucking fit as her husband.

She had to her an overbite of hesitation.

\

Meekness, humility—terror. She sat on the bed terrified in puffed diaper and padded bra. And seizing the elastic, and faltering. Squeezing at the clasps. Like she'd never worn undies before. Like someone else had put them on her, some enemy. Packed her nylon cups to an underwire straining, rigged posterior casings with C-4 plastique. And I wanted her to do it now, I wanted her to just detonate herself and get it over with—launch all the lethal payload that was fertilizing her: shrapnel nail and screw and poisoned syringe.

Blasting me away, blowing us both through the floor, and ticking through the igniferous floors below it, bombing the lobby at mortal checkout—bringing the hypostyle to crash, the arches to collapse, atop a cuneiform of limbs and kilim tatters and fragments of the monogrammed blazon of Allah that'd pendulated over the interactive pillars.

Imagine, amid the settling dust, a providentially inviolate vase from which a single peacock feather—drifted.

"Vous étrange," she said.

"Non."

She shuddered. "Oui, vous."

"Non je ne suis pas regardez you strange."

My last wish before I submitted: let her explosion scramble this diary so that everything will read like my French.

She shimmied out of the bra, let it fall—without a flash, without immolation. No martyr.

Then she tugged the panties down, stopping at the calves to shed the heels before continuing.

She wasn't shaved. Not in any of her pits.

I was holding in my hands this wild mother of a bone.

Rach would be familiar with the feeling, Principal would be too. This feeling of unveiling. To unveil the next product. To lift the curtain on the new.

I went slowly with her below me and then I was behind her and not slow.

Her name was Izdihar, so Izi, so Iz.

://

0

No one is spared the betrayal of a biographer: not his ostensible subject, and certainly not his truer subject: himself. "All books are autobiographies," can be found in books in nearly every language, in nearly every age. How else can a man survive having dedicated his one life to the lives of others, to reading them and especially to writing them—isn't betrayal the only noble choice? [. . .] Which is why I can't decide about a child—what material will I have to bequeath? [. . .]

Diaspora Jews have inherited not a tradition but a rupture. If we were enslaved, it was to fashion; if we were liberated, it was by wandering the deserts between channels; if we fought wars, they were against our own parents; if we had any true enemies, they were our selves. All generations are condemned to end in death. Only ours was lucky enough to have never lived to begin with.

—*POLYN: A LIFE OF MY MOTHER*, JOSHUA COHEN

Yehoshuah Kohen was born in the shtetl of Bershad, on the Southern Bug, halfway between Kiev and Odessa, Russian Empire, presently Ukraine. The old century was dying, and the new century ~~lurking just beyond the fields, lying in wait in the snowy woods~~ would be no consolation. By the ~~goyim~~ Christians, it was 1870/71. In an heirloom Bible, the family Kohen recorded only FUCK ME BEGIN LATER

://

from the Palo Alto sessions: We were born in the year of the microprocessor, LGBT Pride Month, the Day of the Death of Mohammed [June 8, 1971]. M-Unit a retired gender studies professor at UC Berkeley, D-Unit an engineer, Xerox-PARC. Basically he was one of the inventors of personal computing. Which meant, he used to say, he took computing personally. We grew up in a white splancher in Crescent Park [Palo Alto]. A good neighborhood too überaware of its goodness. Lots of cool subdued kids. Lots of cool hippie parents. Kindergarten was at Berkeley. A totally egalitarian viro. M-Unit and D-Unit alternated breakfasts, spelt pancakes, stevia quinoa. We had chore charts, surprise room cleanliness inspections. We collected dinosaur eggs, coprolite, ambered insects, pyrite. We memorized the chart of Mendeleev, which hung on our ceiling. We were picked on at school for our [INCOMPREHENSIBLE—wardrobe?], which was sewn by parental friend [INCOMPREHENSIBLE—Nancy Apt?], the back fabrics of the chinos and buttondowns different from the fabrics in front. We were raised to mistrust brands, to be a proactive consumer, a prosumer. All adults were academics. Primiparousness was the norm.

://

~~Communication is a useful [tool [way] to understand Cohen's family.~~ Cohen's was a family [consumed subsumed] by communication [communications/communications systems]: His father, Abraham, ~~was one of the prime innovators of~~ ~~laid many of the most important foundations for~~ worked on a team that helped establish a few vital technical specifications for the internet—before the web, before the technology had any commercial, industrial, or even military? applications. Not many companies can afford a pure research arm, but Xerox, the photocopy giant, could, and endowed PARC (Palo Alto Research Center) in 1970 ? thousands of miles away from Xerox corporate headquarters (in Rochester, New York). The PARCys, as employees were called, were free to pursue their projects with minimal supervision, but with minimal support. The innovations that came out of their labs, particularly from the Computer Science Division, set the standards for modern computing. ~~Though Xerox invested in developing none of them, though development costs would've been prohibitive.~~

In 1972, the Computer Science Division built the Alto, the world's first personal computer [IS THIS TRUE?], which featured a wordprocessing program called Wupiwug, which its programmer Hal Lahasky always claimed was a monster from a scifi book by a writer he'd never name, though it was only an acronym for "What U Press Is What U Get," an indication that the keystrokes a user made were reflected directly onscreen, and not on a teletype printout. [INSERT HERE A LINE ABOUT LANGUAGES: BASIC, LISP.]

Nascent computing displayed its output on a tick of tape. The monitor followed, a face to face the user's, light hurled at a pane of glass. The last frontier, or what was regarded as the last frontier, was also the first, paper again. The laserprinter both continued and undermined the Xerox tradition: in that it reproduced, but from a nonexistent original, putting to paper the page of the screen~~ (parenthetically, the laserprinter was the only PARC innovation Xerox ever brought to market, in 1977 debuting the 9700, which averaged TK?? pages per minute, and retailed for $??K)~~. (The output of nascent computing was just text, and not its formatting—to Abraham, the two were inseparable.) The problems he had set out to solve involved what today is called "desktop publishing," or "design"—namely, how to perfectly reproduce a print artifact onscreen, and then, outrageously, how to render it manipulatable, perfectly printable again.

[However, building on phototelegraphy, which had been around since the 19th century, and the shift from wire to wireless facsimile, which occurred just after the turn of the 20th, Xerox's main interest in documents remained in their reproduction, and in their reproduction through transmission, not in their manipulation. All distances had to be bridgeable, as far as Xerox was concerned—the distance between PARC and ~~Rochester~~ Stamford, CT, to which Xerox moved its HQ in 19??, was not.] While Abraham's colleagues were focused on [creating the] transmission protocols between computers[, and computers and printers], and constructing the Ethernet—a local area network [explain] that allowed machines, and the people who made them, to communicate with one another virtually—Abraham was alone in his fixation. He spent 14 years at PARC huddled with scanners that still functioned with tubes, surrounded by hunched engineers who'd already been graduated to transistors and circuits.

While the character recognition program was relatively simple to code [WHAT WAS IT CALLED?], as were the modifications to Wupiwug that allowed user modification of the recognized characters, it was the image that proved frustrating. The images scanned well [do scanners work the same way as photocopiers or fax?], but Abraham was never able to code an interface that pleased him. Every graphics program he invented was either too rudimentary, or [the opposite of rudimentary?] intricate. He experimented with raster and vector, with dividing the graphics into 2D "spatches," into 3D "layers," but his lack of progress led to a lack of resource availability, and in 1984, with PARC reorganized under new management, Abraham's unit was mothballed, and he was transferred to another [BUT WHICH?].

He would joke to his son that this was the fate of the Jews—to be stymied by the image.

[[**OPENING VERSION 1 BIOGRAPHY:** ~~One hundred years before PARC's inception,~~ Yehoshuah Kohen was born in 1870, in the shtetl of Bershad, on the Southern Bug, halfway between Kiev and Odessa, Russian Empire, presently Ukraine.

Bershad was a textile town, and antisemitism was a familiar thread. Upon returning from a spell at the yeshiva of Koretz, Yehoshuah married Chava Friedgant, the youngest daughter of a family of weavers, and it was weaving that supported Yehoshuah's life of study and prayer, and the life of their son, Yosef, born 1895. In 18??, however, a pogrom was sparked [a pogrom sparked how?], and burned the Jewish textile warehouse [but only one warehouse?]. Theirs was a tragedy so common to the milieu that it can only become banal by repetition.

Regardless—wagon to Uman, trains to Lvov, Warsaw, Berlin, Hamburg—the family took a steamship to America, bundling with them a single trunk, and Yosef. Ellis Island records attest to an arrival of April 4, 1901. The year of the Edison battery and the transatlantic radio, the death of Queen Victoria and the assassination of McKinley, *annus Rooseveltus*. The first day of Passover 5661.

They settled on Orchard Street, on the East Side of New York City, where Yehoshuah—now "Cohen"—found a job as an iceman, initially cutting that substance from the East River, before being promoted to assistant deliverer (an innate sense for horses and geography), to chief deliverer (developing English and manners), cut manager, assistant payroll. But when his payroll chief married the daughter of the ice concern's owner, he left. The man was a fellow immigrant, but from Uzhgorod [, Ungvar in Yiddish], who considered Yehoshuah a peasant[, which he was]. But he was also a natural businessman.

In 1909, with money he'd saved and income from Chava's lacemaking, Yehoshuah purchased a building in Coney Island, Brooklyn—freezing cellar down below, living quarters up top—from which he'd deliver his ice to every borough, and even unto the wilds of New Jersey, where he buried Chava in 1918 (influenza).

A year later, their only son, the Americanized "Joseph"—who'd spent his late teens working nights for his father while attending Stuyvesant High School during the day, and his early 20s working days while attending City College at night—was married to Eve Leopold, a German American Jewess and fellow student at [City College? whose family, all of whom were involved with industrial refrigerator/freezer manufacturing, disapproved of the match, and attempted to snub Joseph by not taking him into the business, instead granting him a nonexclusive license to retail their products, which he did, to outstanding success, by exploiting the newly emerging home market, introducing puffs of the Russian Pale into American households by van and truck as far afield as Connecticut].

[Yehoshuah died in 1967, Joseph in 1977. Colon cancer—both?]

In 1930, Joseph and Eve had a daughter, Lily (accountant, d. 1998? how?), and, in 1933, a son, Abraham (named for Eve Leopold's grandfather? great-uncle?, Abraham Leopold, a pioneer of gas absorption technology? or aqua ammonia?).

"Abs" was a loving, and beloved, son—in true immigrant fashion, Joseph and Eve would have done anything for him, but in true first-generation American fashion, "Abs" had required nothing, and had accomplished all he had on scholarship: Harvard (bachelor's in electrical engineering), MIT (SM, electrical engineering), Stanford (PhD, electrical engineering). 12 years of education had cost his parents nothing.

~~If Abs ever disappointed his parents it wasn't with any computer coupling, rather with a coupling more personal [more what?].~~ Joseph and Eve still held out hope that their son would return home after he finished his PhD, and Abs seemed to placate them throughout 1969 by interviewing for positions at IBM, Honeywell, Multics, and Bolt, Beranek, and Newman [was he offered any?]. But he had no intention of taking a job with any East Coast firm. Either because of the women out west, or the war in Vietnam.

Joseph's pedes plani (flatfeet) had earned his deferral from WWI, and Abs had been too young for conscription into WWII, too II-S (enrolled in essential studies) for Korea~~, and old enough that by Vietnam he wasn't~~

~~fit for anything besides servicing mainframes[, which were the size of jungle temples, and brought napalm from the sky]~~.

~~On Christmas Day 1969, Abs had accepted the only offer he'd been waiting for[, from the celebrated Computer Science Laboratory of Xerox-PARC]~~

On New Year's Eve, 1970, two men wandered San Francisco's Haight-Ashbury in a celebratory mood. Abs and Hal Lahasky had been rivals at Stanford, but now that both were newly minted PARCys, the time had come to be friends. Firecrackers were going off in the streets [WERE THEY?]. Love-beaded flower-children danced in the gutters with sparklers [DID THEY?]. The house [DESCRIPTION OF WOOD BOHEMIAN GINGERBREAD TRIM SF HOUSE] belonged to a cousin/friend of Lahasky's, but the party going on inside it, spilling out onto the porch and the street, was so packed that Abs never met her/him, and lost Lahasky within a moment of arriving [REWRITE/CUT: NO LAHASKY].

Marijuana was being passed around, which Abs was used to, but then, judging by the [crazy bucknakedish people], there was also LSD. He avoided the punch and went for beer. People stood [at a distance from the hifi?] "drinking draft." That's what they told him the game was called. You drank the number of drinks of your draft number. Until you hit it, or died. Luckily, also unluckily, the numbers were low. Still, a guy [in a Mao suit?] had to be held standing by, or was trying for a piggyback ride from, a [pretty young] woman.

"Let me help," Abs said.

"I got it," she said, and slumped the guy up against a banister. "Chivalry is misogyny."

Then she turned away just as he said, "And chauvinist on a double word score is 36 points in Scrabble."

She paused, "Heavy."

"And a pair of Yahtzee dice can be rolled in 36 combinations."

"So you're a [spaz/square]?"

"I'm 36."

"That's your draft number?"

"I mean I'm 36 years old."

"Bummer." ["far out"?]

A month before, on the first day of December, the Selective Service

System—an agency of the US government responsible for staffing the armed forces—[had reached its omnipotent eagle's talons into a dimestore fishbowl] and chosen 366 blue plastic capsules, each of which had been [impregnated] with a paper slip marked with a number corresponding to a day of 1944, which was a leap year. The first number drawn was 258, and the 258th day of that year was September 14. The last was 160, and the 160th day was June 8. Anyone born on June 8 got the highest draft number, 366, and would be among the last to be inducted, while anyone born on September 14 got the lowest, 1, and would be among the first~~—the other 364 days of 1944 all drew draft numbers between them~~.

A subsequent drawing was held with the 26 letters of the alphabet, to determine the order in which the men born on the same day would be called. The guy [in bellbottoms/pirate shirt] groveling at the woman's [quilt skirt] had a birthday of October 26, which was the seventh number picked. His last name was Negrón, and N was the fifth letter picked, and his first was Witold, and W was the ninth. Witold Negrón had done seven shots [of rum?], then five, then nine. ~~Then pounded a beer[?].~~ He was going to smuggle himself to Vancouver, and the woman told Abs she was considering tagging along.

Her name was Sari Le Vay, and she was a PhD student of comparative linguistics at the University of California, Berkeley[, at which she'd later teach linguistics and gender studies]. She was just finishing up her classwork but was finding it difficult to begin her dissertation [WHAT WAS ABS'S DISSERTATION? DID HE HAVE TO DO ONE?], she said. Her academic field was not respected, women the world over weren't respected, the current party Central Committee in Hanoi had the lowest number of women of any socialist or communist governing body worldwide, zero, and beyond all that, it was like America had already slaughtered her boyfriend, whose body was laid out on the stairs. She rolled her own Bali Shag, drank Mohawk ginger brandy, popped bennies. She had opinions on how Bundists treated their wives and Trotsky treated the blacks. Self-determination was not a transitional demand. She'd registered Chicanos to vote in Oakland and dated them. Men and women both.

Out on the porch they pondered space. She had theories beyond

MLK and the Kennedys. NASA landed on the moon, but it also controlled monsoon season. Kissinger sabotaged the peacetalks to tilt the election from Humphrey.

"Like this lottery shitcrock," she said. "Like we're all equal and even and fair in America and who gets picked to go die is just one big serendipity—I don't think so. It can't be an accident that everyone I know numbered low is either a minority or an immigrant. You're a numbers guy—you check the numbers."

That's what Abs did the very next morning [BUT WHAT DID HE DO THE REST OF THE NIGHT?]—he found the numbers in *The Stanford Daily* [IN HIS APARTMENT OR?]. But they had nothing to do with minorities or immigrants. Though there was something about them still perturbing. Or something about Sari had left him smitten. He got her number out of the phonebook and wrote it down at the top of [a page]. Under it he listed all the draft numbers, in 29 rows for the shortest month, 31 rows for the longest, across 12 monthly columns, making a crippled square of days with 18 extras dangling at bottom [like orphans trying to hang onto a Huey whomping out of Saigon].

He got up and into his [car type?] to find a computer, because the sooner this got done, the sooner he could call her. But Stanford's lab was closed for New Year's and PARC wasn't finished yet and didn't have any computers. The IBM 360s and SDS Sigmas were still trucking on the interstate. He shouldn't have shown up at work until [?].

He went back to Perry Lane [his neighborhood?], and took the integers by hand, put together scatters, chi matrices, demarchic distributions. He called up Lahasky to hash it out at the Nut House [WHICH WAS?], even bothered their mutual dissertation advisor [UNINTELLIGIBLE NAME]. The math was just elementary statistics, the advisor's encouragement was exciting, the rest was galling. [As a computer person] It was galling that the US government had entrusted such an undertaking to anything but computers.

"Lottocracy, or, Casting Democracy in with the Lots" was carried by all the major news outlets, in reduced layreader form, over the second week of January [(the days of draft numbers 101, 224, 306, 199, and 194)], though the complete article was published only in July, in a special War

Math issue of *Science*. Abs's scrawled charts had been typeset, and the epigraph was from the Book of Proverbs: "The lot causeth contentions to cease, and parteth between the mighty." The paper opened by [IN THAT PEDANTIC AUTODIDACTIC SNIDE WAY TECHNOCRATS HAVE OF KNOWING, NEVER THINKING] surveying Biblical and Classical literature pertaining to divination by lots (or cleromancy), before recounting the supplanting of deistic caprice by the laws of nature and rules of logic [erudition supplied by Rabbi Maurice Fienberg of Congregation Beyt Am, Palo Alto]. It went on to define differences between the "arbitrary" and the "random" (the former a determination of will/discretion, the latter hypothetically indeterminate, or chance), and the basic principles of sortition (the differences between chance samplings of volunteers and of the general population): ["QUOTE"]

The second section explained the Selective Service regulations for the draft lottery[, the third was tragic, the fourth, a farce]

The third section opened by asserting that in a year with 366 days the average lottery number for each month should be situated in the middle—at 183. But in this lottery the average draft number for the first six months of the year was higher (for people born in January, the average draft number was 201.2), while the ADN for the last six months was lower (for people born in December, the ADN was 121.5). The correlation between one's date of birth and draft number indicated a regression curve of –.226. An unflawed lottery would've maintained a level correlation at zero, a straight flatline throughout the year.

~~[In sum, the closer you were born to the start of things, the better.]~~

The paper then pointed out that people are not born with uniform distribution throughout the year[and especially not with uniform distribution in the leap years]. It proved this by parsing datasets from the US Public Health Service to determine that the birthrates in the first quarters of each year between 1900 and 1940 [EARLIEST RECORDS? TO THE WWII DRAFT?] were a mean 12.2% above average[, confirming that summers between the equinoctes have normally been the busiest periods of conception]. Further[—through a sinister twist that might only be explained through a syncrasy of biochemistry, sex trends, and God—]an average of 64.2% of all babies born during the first quarters of 1900–1940 were male. This meant that early year male babies were doubly insured against conscription—firstly by their birthdates, and then secondly by their disproportionate sample size.

All [samples of] men who shared the same birthday were inducted by order of their names, last, middle, and first weighted accordingly, and ranked in the lotteried sequence: an alphabet that began with J and ended with V[for Victory]. This policy spelled discrimination for men who lacked middle names, and made no provision for the grading of men with identical birthdates and names.

It was this nameranking that comprised the lottery's purest bias, apparently. Equations weren't required to understand that the scores of Johnsons and McNamaras and Nixons and Mitchells and Hoovers and Helmses in America tended to have middle names while the singularly ethnic Witold Negróns tended not to.

The paper's fourth section, its conclusion: In preparation for the lottery drawing, Abs wrote, the days and so the months had been encapsulated consecutively. Meaning that the capsules containing the papers with the January dates were assembled first, the February capsules were assembled second, and so on through the calendar, with each month's encapsulations poured into a handcranked drum, a mechanical bingo spinner [like a wheel for a gerbil or hamster], upon completion. This meant that the January capsules were mixed with the others 11x, the February capsules mixed 10x, and so on, through the November capsules, which were mixed with the others 2x, and the December capsules, mixed only 1x. A final condemnation cited the Selective Service's own report that the capsules had been poured into the fishbowl from the side of the drum that'd held the earlier days of the year, so that the latter less thoroughly spun days remained atop[floating like a scum].

~~On the day "Lottocracy, or, Casting Democracy in with the Lots" was published in a special War Math issue of *Science* in July 1970, six months after Sari inspired it~~ Abs proposed to Sari. Theirs being an engagement very preoccupied with numbers—figures, equations—it bears notice that though they were married at Congregation Beyt Am, in Palo Alto, on January 1, 1971, their son and only child was born on June 8.

~~Witold Negrón, 8th Battalion, 4th Artillery, was mortally wounded in Operation Lam Son 719 between Khe Sanh forward supply base and Tchepone, Laos, March 1971.~~

[[[[**OPENING VERSION 2 BIOGRAPHY:** Sari's parents, Imre and Ilona Le Vay, were Hungarians to the Americans, but Jews to the Hungarians. Above all, though, they were Budapesters, geographically and culturally marooned between Joseph's [Abs's father's] ghetto origins and Eve's [Abs's mother's] haughty ancestry in Cologne.

To them, Joseph was just a [coarse] peddler of frozen water who'd tried to socially elevate himself through his union with a [wealthy snobbish] yecca wife, Eve, who invariably played the same EZ piano arrangement of Mozart's Variations KV.265 ("Twinkle Twinkle Little Star"/"Baa Baa Black Sheep"/the ABCs), dabbled in depopulated watercolors (kitchen still-lives, insipid landscapes of the wildlife preserves around JFK), and in lieu of financially solving whatever problems their daughter was having with her monkeywrench son, preferred to waste her fortune on transcontinental flights, to offer her opinions in person.

The Le Vays would have sudden fevers and lymphatic surgeries whose recuperation periods would last the durations of Eve's visits. They called her "the princess gourmand [Princesse de Guermantes] of the synagogue women's league." Or else "the doyenne of the mooing bourgeois [la doyenne de la moyenne bourgeoisie]." They mocked her Shalimar perfumes, her Scherrer suits worn always with the gloves, her inaccurate recitations of Heine that never aspired to more than the first two couplets of *Die Lorelei,* and were just the malapropic asyntactic expressions of the trait that most provoked them: Eve's Deutschtum, or the conceit of her Germanness. Though it wasn't just that she persisted in a vain attachment to that identity, it was that she hadn't suffered for it—she hadn't suffered like they had. The Le Vays had cultivated the full European education and with such unflagging intensity~~ the continent had no choice but to plan their genocide so that~~ they embodied its quintessence.

The Le Vays were the conjugation of generations of linguists, etymologists, philologists, and lexicostatisticians who'd been querulously cross-referencing one another ever since their forebears—who on both sides included Lévais and Lévajs—Magyarized their surnames in solidarity with the Kingdom of Hungary following its fraught unification with the Austrian Empire in 1867. [Their grandparents?] had learned how to speak, read, and write all the Germanic, Slavic, and Romance languages, and how to speak, read, and at least write about all the Baltic languages too. [Their parents?] were capable of griping about the dissolution of the dual monarchy in its every single tongue, and in the Ural-Altaic, the Finno-Ugric-and-Permic, Samoyedic, and Oghuric—in everything but the Semitic. ~~The stiff leatherskinned and authoritative edition that was their family would go to its death incomplete—the Le Vays the missing volumes~~.

Imre and Ilona had been doctoral candidates at the University of Budapest, where they'd maligned each other's talents so publicly that when their professor paid a university janitor [how much?] to shelter them both in the janitor's dacha [Hungarian equivalent?] outside Sárospatak, the beneficiaries, even with the Nazis at the door, interpreted the gesture as only partly altruistic. If the other part was a joke, though, the professor never laughed. Dr. Péter Simonyi died fighting with the Resistance. He never got to meet the couple's daughter, born in spring—or witness its nuptials, civil in fall—both 1945.

But then neither did their parents and siblings [how many?]: Imre's family had perished in Auschwitz/Auschwitz-Birkenau, while Ilona's had been executed and left to the Danube [by the Arrow Cross?].

Following the war, the couple was unable to find employment—despite Imre's formidable achievement as an Esperantist (his dissertation sought to officialize the artificial language's first natural phonological evolution, the replacement of the phonemic *ĥ* with the *k*), and despite Ilona being one of the great hopes of Hungarian bibliography (her dissertation had proposed conversion mechanisms between the author/title taxonomies then prevalent in Hungary? and the various faceted? international standards). They labored, instead, in the dissident underground, as translators, interpreters: in Russian, *vragi naroda*—"enemies of the people."

In 1956, with a popular revolt roiling the boulevards of Budapest, and columns of Soviet tanks about to roll in[, stretching like the lists for arrest they were on], Imre and Ilona took Sari on a train to Szombathely, and telling her they were just visiting her new Gymnasium, slipped across the border[—parted the Iron Curtain—]for Vienna.

In Vienna they renewed contacts with prewar colleagues, now adjunct émigrés abroad~~ suffering from visa problems and pleionosis~~. Jobs were arranged~~, nonetheless~~ [how?], and in 1958 they moved to Saint ?,

Minnesota, initially to teach a discipline called Sovietistics at the Lutheran Bible Institute?, and then to Berkeley, to teach Magyar language under the auspices of the Center for Slavic Studies at the University of California [but Hungarian's not a Slavonic language?].

Sari attended Berkeley for what she then called her bachelorette's, mistress's, and PhD degrees, initially studying applied linguistics, though under the guidance of Professor Debora Laklov she chose to do doctoral work in the specialized field of sociolinguistics, focusing particularly on the confluence of language and gender [on the genderlects of disclosure? second-language intimate differencing/contextual integrities?]. "Iceman," to her, was more than an occupation, but not in the sense that it might've been to her future father inlaw, while "Icewoman," which term Eve might've used to describe her daughter inlaw, would become similarly reprehensible. "Iceperson" was less deterministic, preferred. Sari's dissertation, "Male without Prefix, Male without Suffix: Volapük, Esperanto, Ido, Interlingua, and the epicene misnomer in international(ist) language(s)," became a chapter in her seminal [no, no] book, *Toward a New "Neuter": what is ideal about the sexist, and what is sexist about the ideal,* Berkeley, CA: University of California Press, 1979.

In September 1973, Sari traveled to a Reassessing Animacy summit at the University of Texas, Austin, leaving Abs with their two year old son, and prompting a visit from Eve. Abs insisted he was managing on his own, but Eve refused to accept this, and wouldn't pass up an opportunity to spend time with her grandson~~ who at the time was two years old~~.

Eve had strict ideas about the proper way to raise a child, but none approached the method by which Abs and Sari split their parenting duties: divvying up the caregiving by tallying, individually, at the end of each day, and together, at the end of each week, and then again monthly, their changings and feedings, playtimes, and sessions of counting and reading, to ensure an utterly equal distribution of responsibilities. ~~Eve was not aware of this~~ Had Eve been aware that her coming to take charge of her grandson would not redound toward Abs's total time spent with the child, and that, quite to the contrary, he'd have to make up whatever time he'd been relieved of upon Sari's return, she might never have made the trip.

Eve would usually spend her visits sitting in the den of the splancher on Fulton Street[, bobbining mundillo, or reading only the best new American fiction][—Leon Uris, Herman Wouk—]while Cohen slept in his playpen, or toddled on the floor. But on this visit she decided that her grandson's rompers were no better than rags, and that there was no one better than her, there was no one else but her, to dress him appropriately.

As the Le Vay-Cohens had only one car—a Ford Pinto, which Abs had taken to work—and as Eve wasn't able to ride a bicycle, especially not with a grandson atop, she called for a cab, raided the pantry for supplies, and the note on its door for the address of Sari's parents~~, whose atopic dermatitis that'd prevented them from stopping by was surely noncontagious~~. Eve wasn't familiar with the greater Bay Area, so might not have expected the hour drive, the traffic, the toll bridge, or the $48 that got her to Hillcrest Road, in Claremont. After the Le Vays assured her she hadn't been swindled~~ but didn't offer to contribute to the fare~~, Eve gave them stringent instructions regarding Cohen's regimen[—the Le Vays had never been left alone with their grandson before?—], had them repeat to her his feeding times, on what foods in what portions, which she'd provided in a diaper bag along with diapers, wipes, powders, creams, told them she'd be back in two hours, apologized to the driver for keeping him waiting, and asked to be taken "downtown." [Why didn't she ask the Le Vays to recommend a children's clothingstore?]

She was let off in San Francisco[, paid the driver another extortionate fee], went shopping. It was while exiting a Family Wearables on Page Street and turning onto Market, having purchased a pair of overalls and onesie pajamas, that she walked directly into a VW Combi, described only as "tiedyed," its drivers never described and so never identified—a hit and run [she was left to bleed to death on the sidewalk].

The body lay at the UCSF Medical Center and, since Eve's driver's license listed her residence as New York, and the Le Vays' address was the only local contact contained in her purse, it was Ilona who got the call, and it was Imre who called Abs[—imagine the amount of energy being used in enthusiasm control]. At UCSF Medical, Abs could identify the body only by pantsuit and purse. After, he went to pick up his son from his inlaws', and call his wife, who convinced him that an earlier flight could change nothing. Finally, Abs called his father, who broke. Joseph was unable to decide whether to have the body sent back to New York or buried out in California, and Abs was unable to tell his father that there wasn't much of a body left to bury, and so Eve was cremated, on Sari's recommendation. [COMPRESS.]

Joseph never recovered from this trauma. Cancer, the family's remontant curse, developed. Colorectal. Adenocarcinoma of the bowel.

Joseph arranged to sell Cohen Cooling Solutions, Inc., to his employees, liquidate and sell the locations of his two Chilliastic outlets—one in New Jersey, one in Staten Island—to Lowe's? Walgreens? and to the Staten Island Mall (Sears was built on its ashes), retiring to oncologists' offices and New York Presbyterian for a colectomy and two rounds of chemotherapy that left him uncured, without options, and so weakened that he stayed most of the time not at his too oppressively large splitlevel in Valley Stream, Long Island, but in that small bungalow he also owned on the beach in Far Rockaway, Queens.

The decline of the iceman was tragic [REWRITE]. Joseph Cohen, with his cold [business sense?] and warm [heart?], had exerted an indelible influence over his son, and over his grandson too, who regarded him as a wizard, with the power to change the elements[, to turn the states]: liquids to solids, to liquids again, to gas.

Joseph Cohen [might've been a greenhorn but he had a green thumb, a man] who grew apples from asphalt, berries from tar. An inveterate tinkerer who [FILL ALL THIS IN].

~~Cohen, who founded his career on memory, on the notion that memory is the future's greatest commodity,~~

~~The time Cohen spent with his grandfather in the last summer of his grandfather's life comprises Cohen's only memory of~~

Summer 1977, Joseph was ailing, and Abs took a leave of absence from PARC, and took his only son, then six years old, to New York. Cohen's memories of that trip are myriad. The trains submerging and surfacing, the pneumatics of the bus. How whenever he entered and exited a deli it rained [the dripping air conditioning?]. How wherever he was, even at night, it was daytime—neon, the commonest of the noblest gases. His grandfather's plot: the raspberry and blueberry bushes. The feel of the house—a cottage, remote, damp, decaying, in no way accessible to masstransit [the A train back then too?]. Two bedrooms, a livingroom—a tiny garage in which Joseph kept a white Plymouth

Duster and a workbench. Tools were kept in pristine condition, orderly. Mason jars had been saved from neighboring trash, meticulously labeled: “screws,” “nails,” “nuts ’n’ bolts,” “good nuts.”

One morning Cohen only remembers as having been about a week before his birthday a last issue arose? regarding the pending sale of Cohen Cooling Solutions, and Abs insisted on going into Manhattan to handle it himself. Joseph, surprisingly, agreed. ~~He’d never felt healthier. He’d spare his son the job of minding a child so that Abs would have the tougher task of minding the lawyer, ? Dubin, a Park Avenue Litvak.~~

Abs went, and then called from the law office to check in, and since his father’s positive report was convincing he took the opportunity to have dinner with ? Ramirez—formerly the cooling business’s supervisor, now the president of its ownership cooperative—and a few friends from Stanford who’d just been hired at Columbia?

That evening Joseph took his grandson for a walk on the beach. The setting both was, and was not, unusual [THIS SENTENCE BOTH IS, LAZY AND RIDICULOUS]. Abs and Joseph had taken Cohen out for a walk along the beach each day of their stay. Cohen liked the air. He liked being under the sky. What impressed Cohen the most was how his grandfather knew the names of all the trees on the way to the beach, and even knew the names of the rocks and stones, and the game was that Cohen would point at one or pick one up and his grandfather would tell him what it was and in doing so would bring it into being, into a better or clearer being [UNLIKE THIS WORSENING AND UNCLARIFYING SENTENCE]. Joseph was also familiar with the shells and related to Cohen how they were the homes of animals, huts of protein and mineral, keratin and calcium carbonate, though they weren’t homes in the human sense in that the ocean creatures didn’t hire architects and contractors but made them themselves, they made them with sweat, he explained, or by sweating, and when they outgrew them, they left to sweat out a larger one, and when they died, they left their shells behind but no other ocean creatures would touch them because, he said, “It is indecent to dwell in a shell you haven’t sweated for.” Cohen remembers his grandfather always trying to take his hand whenever he went to touch something, to take it. ~~“This is the story of the Jews,” Joseph had said. “The story of the Jews in America.”~~ He remembers his grandfather always removing from his hand that something he'd taken and placing it back on the beach, placing it, not letting it fall, exactly where it'd been taken from. ~~"Seagulls are goyim—they pick up and drop, pick up and drop~~."

Joseph shocked his grandson by telling him that sand was made out of rocks and stones—"ground down into dust," he told him, "grinding is their working"—and Cohen was skeptical. Joseph also shocked Cohen by telling him that the clouds were made out of the same stuff the ocean was, water, the same stuff that he and his grandson were made out of, and that water was two parts hydrogen to one part oxygen brought together by covalent bonds, and then he told Cohen to take off his flipflops and wade, and that the water was as old as the earth, billions of years old, and that the water they drank was billions of years old too, all water was, even the water inside him and his grandson. When they purchased a knish from a boardwalk vendor and Joseph requested water and the vendor charged him a nickel, he said to Cohen, "Remember when you drink it this water is billions of years old, that you have stuff billions of years old in you, and that the chances are that the molecules, the atoms you're drinking, have been in you before and so are now just coming home." And then Joseph said, "You should never pay for water—you should maybe have to pay for the cup but never for the water."

Then it was fully night and the stars were in full relief and Joseph pointed out how they too had shapes like clouds, or were as shapeable as clouds. Joseph pointed out Ursas Minor and Major, the bears, and Orion, who could never lose or gain weight because his belt had only a limited number of notches, and the clawing crab, which he said had given its name to the disease he had, Cancer, because the marks it left on the body were like pincer pricks, and then he said, "And that's the lobster thermidor, and that's the shrimp scampi."

He said, "They're incredible, the constellations, how random they are, how arbitrary—the Chinese think Orion is actually a white cat playing with a purple bird, or else it's really the Japanese who think that but about the Canis constellations, the dogs."

Then, though Cohen was only dimly aware, his grandfather continued to invent them: "That constellation," but Cohen wasn't able to follow Joseph's finger, "is the davening rabbi," and Joseph waved his entire hand and pointed out, "the negligent mechanic—there, there, there, there," and "the criminal nurse with the catheter needle—just here," and "the east-west yarmulke, also called the angry beard," and he encouraged Cohen to find his own and Cohen tried.

Joseph went on to mention Europe, which was "there, then," and Cohen was aware that his grandfather was talking about a landmass now and not stars.

Joseph had never mentioned Europe before, but Abs had, a bit, and Sari, to be cryptic, would speak in its languages to her parents~~, "Ma and Pa Le Vay. Ilona and Imre, the elders I."~~

"Think of our ancestors," Joseph said. "They knew the very same stars. As old as water. Older maybe. Then again maybe not. Same stars."

He said, "Pick one," and Cohen, when faced with all those fantastical animals and archers, those electricians and plumbers, settled on the shiniest, and Joseph said, "Polaris, the North."

"Common," he said. "Never be ashamed of the common. The common is useful. Common understands."

Joseph said that just as Cohen had a father, he, Joseph, had a father too, he still had one. "Other people are unlucky and have never had a father, but anyone who has ever had a father will have him forever."

Joseph's father had been named Yehoshuah, Joseph said, which was just Joshua in Hebrew~~, though his family had spoken Yiddish and called him Heschel, and his wife, Chava, called him Shy~~. In America he cut ice, this was before refrigerators, before freezers, he would have to wait for the freeze—"it froze more often back then, it froze more thick"—and then when the ice was sturdy enough he'd venture out onto it, the ice over the river, ice over the bay, and cut it out in blocks, cutting the ground out from under himself, like how the Israelite slaves built the pyramids.

[REPETITION: In Egypt, Joseph said, the Egypt of Europe, his father, Yehoshuah, had been a rabbi—in Bershad. Cohen asked what Bershad meant and his grandfather answered it meant Bershad. It was a city the size of a city block. All of it might fit inside Grand Central, or Port Authority. Yehoshuah didn't have a congregation, but instead navigated the territory around Bershad delivering rulings on kashrut and fair labor practices, performing weddings and funerals. He'd be gone for days, even a week, at a time~~, like a traveling salesman, offering women brushes, combs, fertility incantations, fiduciary spells~~.]

"He had many brothers and sisters," Joseph said. "In America, people don't have that many brothers and sisters, even though they have the money to have them. I could never understand. My mother, and Evele, never could."

Joseph told Cohen that Yehoshuah was the eldest of eight or nine children and Cohen asked how it was that his grandfather didn't know whether the number was eight or nine and Joseph answered, "Old people have trouble remembering, young people have trouble knowing."

Cohen was confused and Joseph said, "We left so young I barely knew how many hands I had, let alone how many fingers. Such a rush we didn't count."

~~But Yehoshuah knew the numbers, Joseph said, he was the type who always knew. "If you don't keep the numbers in your head, they keep them for you on your forearm."~~

Joseph said his parents, Yehoshuah and Chava, took him out of Bershad but left their family behind. "Uncles, aunts, brothers and sisters on both sides, cousins—the family was now what is called nuclear."

[FUCKING REPETITITITIOUS.]

But it was difficult to stay in touch with the rest of the family, Joseph said, especially given all the turmoil. It wasn't like he could just pick up a telephone, or send a telegram so easily. Rather he could, Joseph said, but it wasn't like the family was always available to pick up the other end, or reply. The post was unreliable too, especially for packages. Instead, Joseph said, we could only think certain thoughts, and they could only think certain thoughts and, but this was important, "Each half of the family had to know that's what the other half of the family was doing." Joseph said, "At least, that's how my father explained it."

"He told me he'd picked his own star," Joseph said, "like Polaris—lots of people pick Polaris, especially if they're young, especially if they live in the north, in the cold. And he told me that if he was in the mood to communicate with his family he faced this star, not at a certain time or from a certain place, but whenever, wherever, and he talked to that star, or he didn't even talk, he told me, he just poured himself into it, all his life and frustrations, all his feelings, his dreams, he just poured all of himself into that fire.

"Then he told me," Joseph said, "that I could do the same thing, that I could just find a star, any star—I could find my own or I could use his star, because any star has the capacity of all of them—and I could invest this star with my emotions, I could make this star the outside pocket for everything inside me, and that the family still over in Europe would have their own stars and would do this same thing too, all of them, all of us, sending and receiving."

[REMOVE FROM DIRECT QUOTATION]

Joseph told Cohen that these communications would become stored in these stars, ~~turning them into mutual archives, common caches, omnipresent and yet evanescent~~. From which they could be accessed, not at a certain time or from a certain place~~—"people have to work, after all"—~~ but at any time, and from any place, and ultimately not just by the relations and friends they were intended for but also by anyone sensitive enough to go seeking. Anything ever communicated to a star, Joseph told Cohen, could be accessed even after the death of its transmitter, and, unlike with the spinning satellites and their transmissions, could be accessed and even altered by the dead themselves, and then he mentioned Oma Eve and encouraged Cohen to speak with her in this way, freely, and then he mentioned himself and encouraged Cohen to speak with him in this way too, freely, once he himself passed, to that light on the other side of the darkness.

"Your father does this kind of thing now with machines, which I don't have to understand. Because what they do isn't new to me."

But returning back to the bungalow, Cohen turned to his grandfather and asked about daylight, pointing out that this system worked only at night, or in darkness, and furthermore he'd studied at school how the sky was always changing around in circles and if in some seasons the stars decided upon were present, in other seasons they were absent, and so access was not as universal as his grandfather had said it was.

Joseph turned to Cohen and said, "Tell it to Polaris."

://

from the Palo Alto sessions: We went to Montessori, both D-Unit and M-Unit were active in the PTA. Basically we won everything at maths and sciences. But math really. Math was really our thing. Age eight was algebra, geometry. Age nine was trig and calc. M-Unit and D-Unit packed us brownbag lunches. Lots of veggies and fruits, pita crisps, bean dips, major beanloads. 1x/weekly an egg, 2x/weekly a yogurt, only if we insisted. Though there were vendingmachines at PARC and the Berkeley Linguistics Department and we would p/matronize them depending on whether D-Unit or M-Unit would pick us up from school. Basically just Fritos at Berkeley. But Twix and Mars bars at PARC. We did not consume them but bought them to sell to fellow students. Our best customers were Ricardo Boyer-Moore, now of Aquarius Initiatives, Bjorn Knuthmorrpratt, founder/CEO thebestof.us. A line taped to the carpet in the den marked how far we had to sit from the TV in order not to be irradiated. We were raised on a halfhour of TV per day we were allowed to choose ourselves though we had to justify our choices daily either in oral argument or writing [ANY OF THOSE WRITINGS STILL AROUND?]. The same policy obtained for the body, if we wanted to be exempt from the vegan dinner diet of our parents [THOSE WRITINGS?]. Rule #1 was do not waste water, only turn the faucet on to rinse, do not keep it on while teethbrushing or facewashing. Rule #2 was the same applied to energy, turn off the lights upon leaving a room, always keep the fridge and freezer doors shut, and memorize not just their insides but the insides of every room so as like to minimize ajarage and not waste electricity. M-Unit and D-Unit told us we could not have a pet until our 10th birthday when they brought home a lemming we named Chomsky. M-Unit lovehated Chomsky [EXPAND?]. But the lemming died and was replaced by a vole because it had an even shorter life expectancy and was largely monogamous, though we could only have one at a time, and the first we named Zuse [EXPAND?] but then it also died and was replaced by a second vole whose name we cannot recall and when that died too D-Unit brought home two computers. M-Unit chose the Tandy 2 so that left for us the IBM 5150. We also had an Alto in parts in the basement. Or we had so many parts of so many Altos D-Unit called the heap of them "Tenor and Bass." FORTRAN, 1983. PASCAL, 1983. M-Unit was disappointed we were never too proficient at language-languages. Except. Give us a piece of paper, a writing thing.

://

1984 was a dystopia. Life had become confusing, especially in the suburbs. There were simultaneously too many options, and too few. Everything was the same and different, at once. The supermarkets had every food and drink conceivable, but Cohen's home had only certain foods and certain drinks, and his parents shopped at only specialty health stores. The candy Cohen was not permitted to consume came in more varieties than the fresh produce from his parents' garden, but then the fresh produce had more vitamins than the candy did, which despite its branded array all contained the same ingredients, refined. To further confuse things, if the ingredients of an apple were just apple, it didn't make any sense that his parents differentiated between organic and nonorganic varieties, or that apples were retailed with labels stuck on them alerting to pesticides and waxy preservatives. Water, the substance within, became particularly perplexing, because it came from the tap until it was delivered in jugs, which were initially plastic, then metal. Television and movies proved bewildering too, in that the same things didn't just happen in different movies and shows but also in different episodes of the same shows, the same plots were always recycled, and during every commercial break the same sports drinks madness recurred. All the shows and movies began wildly enough—teenagers played with matches, snorted drugs, and appeared to enjoy doing both—but then they'd all end tamely, caged, contained in the frame, and even if the teens died tragically they'd return for a lesson, out of character and after the credits, telling their peers don't pay attention to pressure, stay away from firearms, pederasts, drunk drivers, just say no, and notify an adult.

Sari wanted her son to attend private school, Abs wanted his son to attend public school. But not just that, Abs wanted his son to become a bar mitzvah, Sari wanted her son to avoid that[, calling the practice "a spiritual circumcision"][CAN'T RECALL: DID PRINCIPAL EVER HAVE AN INITIAL—PHYSICAL—CIRCUMCISION?]. Deliberations ensued. The costs were high, in drama and financials. Palo Alto High School[, staffed by PhD washouts from Berkeley,] would be forsaken for the coeducational, awardwinning [WHAT AWARDS?], $10K/year Harker School, whose infirmary was run by a Yale/Harvard MD DrPh, and whose track & field squad was coached by a medallist in the men's 400m dash at the Munich Olympics. Which meant that instead of a weekend in middle June hosting the usual round of gaming—the forbidden Karate Champ, Kung-Fu Master, Montezuma's Revenge, Drugwars, Dunjonquest, Wizardry, but also 1K Chess, and Tetris—it hosted instead the ungameable Sabbath.

The Torah, like a computer's memory, is divided into compartments, parts, one to be read for each weekend of the year. Cohen read from the portion called Shelach Lecha, though he didn't read from the scroll itself, but from a book. Rather, he didn't read at all, but had memorized the verses phonetically from a cassette recording prepared by Lay Cantor Tawny Fienberg of Congregation Beyt Am. ~~Though the Torah is divided into portions, one to be read for each weekend of the year, the divisions aren't marked in the scroll itself, and neither do the verses feature any punctuation. It was the rabbis who compiled the Talmud who established, yet refused to physically separate, the sections, and so consubstantially commanded the reader, who reads aloud, with mentally tracking all classes and clivities of that separation, from section breaks and sentence breaks to, within the sentence, the pauses of phrases. The units the rabbis defined became referred to by their incipit, or opening clauses, and even today Cohen can remember the opening clause of his and chant it with the traditional cantillation: *veyidaber adonay el Moshe leymor, shelach lecha anashim, veyaturu et eretz Canaan.*~~

Cohen didn't study for his admission exam to the Harker School[—on which he attained a score more perfect than anything achievable in Tetris—], but he couldn't help but study for the bar mitzvah: Hebrew was the first subject that gave him trouble, and he could never decide whether it was that trouble or the language itself that fascinated[, and kept him from coding modifications to Tetris that allowed two elements to fall at once, that allowed two elements to fall at different speeds, that previewed the next two or more to fall and allowed the player to exchange them, and that expanded and contracted the playing surface both vertically and horizontally, and flipped it 360°, both by player whim and parametrically]. To be sure, Cohen wasn't frustrated by the Hebrew language, but by its alphabet. Cohen never learned to read, speak, or write Hebrew fluently, and certainly never learned any grammar. His interest and experience were cut from semantic context, purely characterological. ~~While bar mitzvah preparation required an emphasis on the letter as phoneme, to be reproduced orally, subsequent to that event the graphic or glyphic aspects prevailed, an approach that denied the letters their aggregation into syllables, the syllables into words, and favored instead their pictogrammatical or ideogrammatical identities, as if Hebrew were an Asian language in which each sign was a pantomime of arms and legs, ascenders and descenders, bars and stems and ties, in kabbalistic permutation. This pursuit of a symbolic or representative Hebrew was what inspired Cohen to develop his own written language, an unpronounceable language that would never be named, but that would serve as his sole mode of expression for an entire year after his bar mitzvah, until the summer of 1985.~~

[GET PRINCIPAL TO ELABORATE ON HIS MOTHER'S BOYCOTTING OF HIS BAR MITZVAH.]

[GET PRINCIPAL'S FATHER'S REACTION.]

Cohen's initial impulse in creating his own language was to avoid what he considered the central paradox of all languages, both human and computational.

This paradox could be expressed in two ways:

1.) In human language an increase in the number of characters (or letters) means a decrease in the size of their utile aggregates (or words), until an alphabet gets so large that to be utile its letters must have their functions foreshortened, and returned to the primacies of the glyph, whose basic constituent is the stroke. English has an alphabet of 26 letters, and the average wordlength is an unwieldy 4.5 letters, while the Asian languages each have hundreds of characters that function as standalone pictograms (images of the things they mean), standalone ideograms (images of the ideas they mean), and thousands if not hundreds of thousands of pictoideo combinations and phonetically radicalized aggregates.

2.) In computer language the opposite of all this is true, in that a decrease in the number of characters (the On or 1 and Off or 0 of binary code) means an increase in the size of their aggregates (strings or lines), so that though any given computer program must be made of millions or billions of positive integers separated by negativities in one unrearrangeable sequence, what is rendered is perfect, and perfectly understandable.

Human language sought precision, BUT became *less widely translatable*. Computer language found precision, AND became *more widely translatable*.

Cohen's father's coding meant nothing to Cohen's mother, while his father couldn't understand his mother's specialist linguistic jargon—this resulted in "strife." Things only got worse if they had to give directions, on masstransit, in Spanish.

Cohen was appalled by the fact that human processing unlike computer processing was not and would never be universally standardized. He resented that human languages could merely describe a program, they couldn't execute one, and had to resort to metonymy, analogy, simile, metaphor.

Contraction from expansion, expansion from contraction: It was Cohen's ultimate conclusion that human language had to be computerized—for each user individually. It occurred to him that his language's proportionality should not be between the sum of its characters and the relative length/shortness of its aggregates, but rather between his parents' interest in him and his own interest in privacy.

This led him to develop the following resolutions: 1.) His language had to be written, not spoken, because the intimate intricacy of his expressions would be lost to time (the time required by human processing), and 2.) It had to engage that processing in a way that convinced his parents he wasn't frustrating their ability to comprehend, or respond—instead he was encouraging their interpretation (what his mother called "active communication").

What Cohen decided he needed was an alphabet of a single letter—

something familiar, something recognizable[—a grapheme for the wall of his puerile silicon cave]. The letter he needed had to have a shape that allowed for representational or symbolic variance—many points, many limbs.

After auditioning and discarding the Hebrew letters *Shin, Mem,* and *Ayin* (שמע), Cohen settled on the W. [The fourstroked digraphed double U, which evolved from the V—the dubya, the last ligature remaining in this language.]

A normal W, as it would be read in this language, would indicate Cohen himself, in the nosistic or firstperson plural [a note: Cohen always speaks plurally—at what point to mention that?], but rotated 90° to ⋞, it would indicate Cohen's relationship with his father, rotated another 90° to M, it would indicate Cohen's relationship with his mother, and rotated yet another 90° to ⋟, it would indicate Cohen's relationship to the both of them[, and to everyone and everything else?]. All pages of this writing had, at their fundament, a variationally turned W, ⋞, M, or ⋟—all expressions founded on the kinship of possession. But, notably, each glyph also served as a chronometer, a timeline of a pastless futureless single day, with each of the four prongs divided into six hours, for a total of 24:

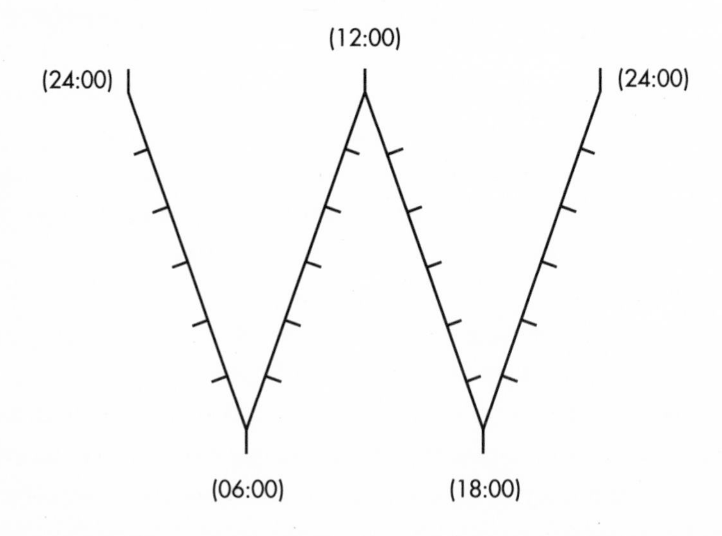

Primary rotations of the W had secondary modifications: W^2 indicating the happy/sad continuum, $⋞^2$ the sleepiness/wakefulness continuum, M^2 hunger/thirst, and ≷^{2} health/infirmity, with the intensity of whichever condition being expressed by the location of the primary's junction with the secondary: ¯W indicating very happy, _W moderately happy, W signifying apathy or a median mood, W_ indicating moderately sad, W¯ very sad, and the same scaling applying to the rest: _M very sated with food/drink, ¯M moderately sated with food/drink, M again the baseline, M¯ moderately hungry/thirsty, M_ very hungry/thirsty.

At the refined culmen of his language's development Cohen was operating at 28 fully rotationary levels of physical, mental, and even psychological elaboration [NO NEED TO ELABORATE], supplemented with a variety of auxiliary markers providing spatial context to the foundationally temporal and intensive: a solid circle indicating school, an open circle, home [NO NEED BUT REPRODUCE AND ANNOTATE AN EXAMPLE].

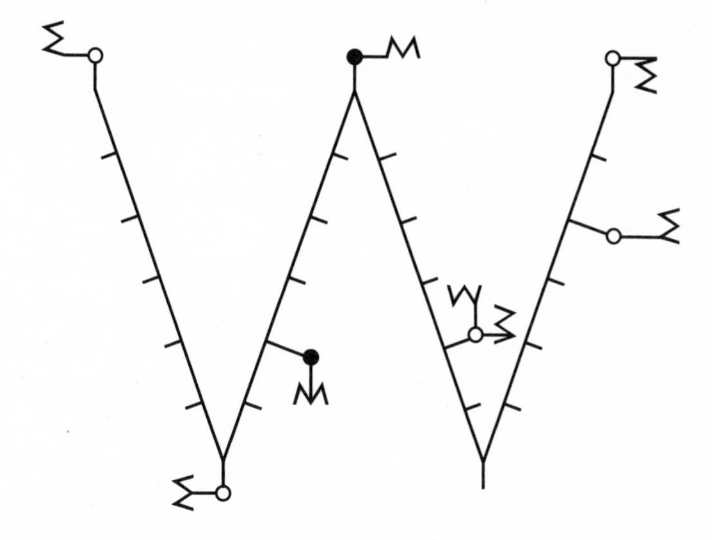

Above would be a typical day, translating to: Cohen [W] at 24:00 [timemark] at home [open circle] was hyperawake [junction marking the ⋜^{2}, or secondary sleepiness/wakefulness continuum, at its alert extremity], at 06:00 was tossing between waking and sleeping [⋜^{2} marked at midpoint], at 08:00 found himself at school [solid circle] and indifferent to alimentation [M^2 at midpoint], though at noon had forced himself or been forced to eat/drink until he was full [M^2 at its satiated extremity implying an intervening lunch], by 16:00 was back home again and feeling moderately unwell [⋝^{2}, junction at third apex] and moderately depressed about it [W^2, also at third apex], by 22:00 was 25%/1 prong more awake than the median or 25%/1 prong less awake than he'd been last midnight, but by this midnight, he was undisturbably asleep [implying, perhaps, that a homeopathic soporific had been administered to him in the interval—Cohen's was a language of elision and duction by absence].

A single expression, then, might easily fill a page. But if a page of Cohen's language was laborious for his parents to decode, it was doubly laborious for them to reply to, especially by hand, and as the word-processing programs of the period weren't yet capable of typesetting such convoluted hierarchies, Cohen had to code his own, and he did, producing versions for the IBM PC, Tandy, and the Commodores 64 and Amiga. Upon distributing this unnamed or unnameable free langware to his parents in summer 1985, he gave up the language entirely, and never wrote in it again. [Cohen's mother never installed her Mwriter.] [While Cohen's father installed his ⋜writer, he found his son had failed to equip it with the marks expressing approval ('-), and disapproval (-').]

Cohen's most significant initial coding, however, appeared under the auspices of another letter—C. [SHITTY TRANSITION] That language—~~developed in the late 1960s and early 70s at AT&T Bell Labs~~—reprogrammed his life, involving him more deeply with the concept of the algorithm. [EXPLAIN ALGORITHMS] At the time C was best learned from a book, and books were best available in libraries. But the Harker School's library also contained the only two computers it made available to students. It was there that Cohen could be found on most mornings, before school began, and on most evenings, after school ended, and, increasingly, skipping class, at all times between—waiting for a no show, or for a scheduled user to quit a session prematurely. According to school policy, each student could use a single computer for only an hour each per day. The slotting sheet was clipboarded at the edge of the circulation desk, and the librarianship behind the desk was responsible for enforcement. Cohen convinced the librarianship to let him automate the slotting, and they agreed, allowing him exclusive use of Computer 2 until the program was completed.

But Cohen stalled, complained, stalled and endured the complaints of his fellow students waiting, until the librarianship approached him offering condolences for his failure and gently requesting that he move aside and let other students take their turns, at which point Cohen unveiled ~~a palindromer and an anagrammatizer—which rearranged the letters of any input, not semantically yet, but sequentially, a program he called "Insane Anglo Warlord," an anagram of its dedicatee, "Ronald Wilson Reagan"—and finally,~~ two different schedulers, one that would run on the librarianship's computer, and was merely a database of times and student names, and the other a gameified version, which would run on the two student computers and allow users about to complete their sessions to compete for more time by answering a battery of SAT questions, with the user answering the most correctly in a two minute span declared the winner and awarded a session extension related to their score.

~~Cohen's life beyond a computer terminal was minimal. He joined no athletics teams and only one extracurricular—The Tech-Mex Club [WHAT, IF ANYTHING, WAS MEXICAN ABOUT IT?]—which he dropped out of after one meeting. He chewed tinfoil once—"it tingled the tongue"—he did whippets once—"it was on TV"—both alone. He never smoked and throughout highschool was convinced that caffeine was alcoholic. He [WHEN?] shoplifted [WHERE?] topical benzoylperoxide acne treatments his mother had told him were cancerous. His father noticed the creams in his room and gave him empty toothpaste tubes to squeeze them into for storage. He read through the Achs (Asimov, Clarke, Heinlein), (Avram) Davidson, and avoided romantic attachments [EXPAND?].~~

~~Any other justification for leaving the house, besides school, had to be computer-related. He'd ride his bicycle two hours to rummage the dumpsters behind the Santa Clara Intel plant, riding back with a backpack of faulty chips he'd use to assemble computers that wouldn't work [WHY NOT?], and then he'd upclock his own machine and participate in overheated rating wars in area diners [TO UPCLOCK IS TO RESET~~

~~THE CYCLE, AND/OR TO MODIFY THE PIEZOELECTRIC CRYSTAL, OF A CPU'S CLOCK, SO THAT THE COMPUTER, NOW PROCESSING AT A SPEED NOT ENDORSED BY ITS MANUFACTURER, CAN FIGHT BATTLES ROYALE WITH OTHER COMPUTERS SIMULTANEOUSLY EXECUTING THE SAME MATH PROBLEM SET: THE VIRGIN WARRRIOR WHOSE OVERDRIVEN HOTROD SOLVED FASTEST OR JUST DIDN'T MELT DOWN GOT GLORY AND TAPIOCA PUDDING?].~~

In winter 1986, with Cohen a sophomore, Harker invested in a networked computer system of IBM ATs, and a program called N-rollment, which integrated student information and grades. Cohen, irate at having been banned from library computers for session abuse [EXPLAIN?], waited for the viceprincipal [NAME?] to leave her office, went in and inserted into her computer a diskette containing a program he'd coded, which instructed the computer to log the viceprincipal's keystrokes. The next opportunity he had, he entered her office again, saved the strokelog to diskette. At home he managed to identify two strings, one of twelve characters, the other of eight, that, being "vpdernfurstl" and "hearken1," didn't seem to have any function in an administrative memo.

A week after the end of the quarter, the day after grades were due, Cohen skulked into school by explaining to a janitor he was a member of the jv beach kabaddi or innertube waterpolo team who hadn't cleaned out his locker. He picked the lock on the library, whose main computer was patched into the network, hacked into N-rollment as vpdernfurstl, pword hearken1, registered his Social Studies and Language Arts teachers as students in their own classes, failed them and had reportcards sent to their home addresses.

Further, as Cohen had determined that viceprincipal ? Dern-Furstl? used the same logname and pword for all of her access, he was also able to hack Paymate and have all the staff's paychecks mailed to an erotic wares outlet in Redwood City.

Viceprincipal ? Dern-Furstl? was contacted, and she contacted the PTA for recommendations on whom to consult on a sensitive computer issue in midsummer, was referred to Abs Cohen, who, just from the phonecall, had his suspicions [WOULDN'T SHE HAVE HAD THEM TOO, IF SHE'D BEEN APPRISED OF THE LIBRARY SCHEDULING STUNTS?]. Abs came into school, went through the viceprincipal's computer, and found the strokelogger [WHICH HAD BEEN KEPT INSTALLED FOR FUTURE NEFARIOUSNESS?], recognized a few things in the rogue code that seemed familiar from mealtime conversations, and, without hesitation, fingered his son as the culprit.

Cohen was suspended, and threatened with expulsion, unless he developed a network security system. The school, essentially, gave him a job—"Harker prided itself on fostering creativity, they made us their IT guy for nothing." Cohen set about synthesizing a number of security protocols already on the market, "but too sophisticated for any school, too expensive for even a WASPy private school to license." His only truly original contribution he called Doublestroke, a 1987–88 keylogger logger, a program that could detect programs that kept track of keystrokes and, rather than purging them, shuttled them false clists, or character lists, that, if used to gain access to the network, gave access instead to a decoy in which the intruder could be studied.

Abs was so proud of Doublestroke that he tried to license it to Symantec, but Symantec became ambivalent after the patent provisional admitted that he wasn't its author, rather his son was, a minor. Finally they outright refused after they received a letter from a lawyer claiming the trapware they'd been considering was the legitimate property of the Harker School. Cohen had boasted too much. Ultimately Doublestroke was sold, not licensed but sold, to Prev in 1988. The price was $8000. Split two ways, and less the lawyer's commission.

://

from the Palo Alto sessions: We had so much anger back then, so much rage, which psychoanalysis might claim comes from our parents or from the parent of society, the crass materialism of the 80s assaulting through media that was matched in its destructive violence only by the counteroffensive of our domestic life. The strict discipline, the rules and regs. The bylaws. But our rebellion against them was not a slacking. We were much too young for the hippie thing and much too old for the punk thing. School had every demographic. Cliques were Bimbos, Himbos, Nerdlings, Geekers, Dorklords, Fagwads, and Whegroes but we complied with none of them. We were not even dweebazoids though we could have been if we had not been resistant, basically, to all category and class.

We felt more as like hardware, mauve, taupe, beige, boxcolored, putting in an intense amount of interior hot effort only so that our exterior, our skin, would appear jointless, seamless, cold. We felt more as like software, writeable, rewriteable, if not compatible, we would adapt. Point is, we had secrets, we hid. Our rebellion thing was that we were aware of it, our compatibility or adaptability thing was that we worked through that awareness, though both impulses might be genetic and if so in regard to work ethic it could be cur to examine dopamine levels in the striatum of the brain, ventromedial prefrontal cortex, anterior insula.

But our ultimate repression or suppression was just so überwestern. It was that we were doing all this work in the service of not doing any work and, if we accomplished that goal, that would be our revolt. It is überwestern to be conscious that this was what we were doing and to feel bad about it, to try not to feel bad about it, to feel bad about feeling bad, to try not to feel bad about trying not to feel bad. It was as like we were getting revenge, but on ourselves. This attempt toward automation. Or better toward autognosis.

Hardware, software. Both used to come packaged, not readily unpacked. Now everything installs itself, feeds and grooms itself, selfexplains. But we were not that 1D propellerhead tech d00d you want us to be who needs to hack the drives of Gorbachev before he can POP3 his cherry. Before this all was math. After just math. When we applied we were pure. When we were pure we applied.

We refrained from accessing records of past GPAs and class ranks and comptrasting them w/r/t college admissions. Our personal statements, which M-Unit helped write, mentioned only our facility with numbers. The recommendations D-Unit got for us did too. We were going to restart and core dump ourselves of computers.

Let Trey Kerner [?] who still played the arcades bust open the Pac machs to change our high scores manually, let Mat Plokta [?] brag at school about reprogramming the barcoder at the GalaMart to read the Marlboro Reds and Olde English 40s as like $1 discounted each, only $1 to keep it plausible, we had higher scores and sums in mind.

Acceptance envelopes came daily from Cal Tech and the Ivies and even phonecalls as like the one that asked for Mr. Cohen and we answered that we were speaking and the voice told us that we had won the Reverse Turing Award. Cowon. [FOR WHAT? W/ WHOM?] This was spring 1989 and we accepted the prize on behalf of D-Unit and even made the travelplans for him to attend the banquet ceremony in Washington DC. We wanted a direct flight from SFO, we wanted a corner room at the K Street Sheraton.

That day we were admitted on full tuition to MIT, and D-Unit went to get the prize on his own and while on a visit to the Mall, the National Mall, had a mild myocardial infarction. A heartattack. 04/20. M-Unit visited him in the hospital in DC. "The unshittiest," Aunt Nance said. "Of the shit hospitals." GW. She had come over to take care of us. Dr. Nancy Apt. Berkeley, Econopsychology. We had always known her as like our aunt, though we also knew her only sisters were the MFs of the Bay Marxist Feminist Coalition. She moved in and never left. She was on the foldout in the den between D-Unit on the memoryfoam in the kitchen and M-Unit in the parental bedroom. Then she was in the bed too and sharing it with M-Unit and D-Unit might have joined them, he had always been invited to join them before. But now he was too weak.

He was weak as like the memoryfoam he dragged all grumptious into the hall.

Aunt Nance was basically applying all her knowledgebase in conflict/resolution, to mediate. Between D-Unit and his physical health. M-Unit and her mentals. Aunt Nance was invigilating bloodpressure, the betablockers and nitrates, the inhibitors and statins. Transitioning herself from babysitter supportive friend and lover, to babysitter lifepartner wife. Nurse practitioner UN peacekeeper dean. She negotiated both halves of the parental chores, and our third half. Cooked noncholesterol taro callaloo and tzimmes, and took us to the Army/Navy surplus in Campbell to get outfitted for Stanford.

For graduation she gave us a Nintendo with Zelda and Zelda II and Metroid, and though we had outgrown all that we were gracious. But then one night it along with the 16" Zenith had been relocated to their bedroom and M-Unit who had cried about Nintendo being a brain pollutant was now giggling playing a Donkey Kong, with Aunt Nance Player 2ing her. Parent child role reversal. Precipitated by Kreem Kush, a midgrade cannabis hybrid. The next morning when they went with D-Unit to a cardiologist checkup we retaliated by wiring their clockradio into the console flap where the cartridges go until the Zenith picked up KQED and the LED 12:00, and though the system was unusable they were back before we had figgered how to set the alarm. After that M-Unit acted busy with her scholarship, ignoring us except for that once she remarked on how our leaving would mean D-Unit would have his own room.

Do not interrupt. Let us tell how it was. Two plus one does not always equal a threesome. Recall the isosceles fallacy, how the midpoint P is outside the triangle. Some nights D-Unit who was not enjoyed by the Is, the parents of M-Unit, would drop us at their house, and in the mornings collect us, and M-Unit would be doing yoga out on the lawn and Aunt Nance would be recycling winebottles and composting joints. Just to get away we went to second *Ghostbusters,* second *Back to the Future,* third *Karate Kid,* and went on fieldtrips to the Artificial Intelligence Center in Menlo Park because no one else ever did and Calonis, the robot that led us around, seemed lonely.

Computer scientists make good husbands for polyamorous increasingly lesbian feminists because of how functional they are, how booley, steady and quiet as like fans.

No, do not say that. Rewind, record over. Take two. Compscientists make good first husbands. It is true how silent they are. Cooling fans.

08/22, what we considered that early in our life to be early in the morning. We had finished packing ourselves doublebagged into trashbags we cinched altogether and rolled down the hall. D-Unit was already waiting outside in the Ford. But we had octalfortied our dorm assignment and had to get the address from the letter magneted to the fridge. Off the kitchen the door was open to the bathroom and in the tub a man was sleeping and on the tile were wrappers and in the toilet a condom. We neglected to mention that M-Unit and Aunt Nance had thrown us a goingaway party the night before.

On the way we asked D-Unit who that man had been and D-Unit answered, "Him—he is the Laureate."

Solow. [?] Stigler. [?] Anyway. Jewish.

All we can tell you.

D-Unit had slept in the Ford. Or garage.

://

[A NOTE RE: STANFORD. HOW IT WAS FOUNDED IN 18?? BY THE RAILROAD MAGNATE? LELAND STANFORD, WHO HAD TAXPAYERS PAY FOR THE RAILROADS HE PROFITED FROM, AND HOW THE WAY TRAINS CONNECTED THE EAST AND WEST COASTS OF THE COUNTRY WAS VERY PROTO ONLINE.]

[CF. *TETRATION NATION,* JAMIE GLEICHE (MACMILLAN, 2010), *SEEK AND YE SHALL FIND: THE GOSPEL ACCORDING TO TETRATION,* MATTHEW KJARR (HACHETTE, 2008).]

The only thing Cohen liked about Stanford was the architecture. [Though he never appreciated the main campus itself—the Mission revivals of darkening porticoes and lightening arches, the dull pious sandstone cloistered below bright terracotta—]He was in all likelihood the only freshman ever grateful for having been assigned to Stern, a student residence facility constructed just after WWII in a style that, when Cohen moved in, was all over the TV news—sternly, brutally, Soviet. ~~It was as if an Eastern Bloc tower had been cut up and scattered, a floor at a time, across a landscape of encina, bristlecone, gum tree, and asphalt. The Wall in Berlin was being chipped at, and smashed, but Cohen's dorm had been built already broken, and whereas the prefab slabs of concrete halfway across the world were smeared with peacenik graffiti, the local décor tended toward posters offering $10/hour to participate in sensory deprivation studies and ads for cheap student sublets.~~

Cohen's dormroom was small and blank and the smallness appealed to him, because it meant less to clean, but the blankness, the scuffed emptiness, provoked. He couldn't understand why the school provided each student with a bed and chair and desk, but didn't continue that determinism into wall decoration. Beyond that, he couldn't understand why his was the building's only single, and suspected it was because he had just enough personality to be left alone, but either too many or too few personalities to have a roommate. Or else, he suspected, the registrar or bursar's office regarded his unit as vacant—because he wasn't even enrolled—he hadn't accepted, hadn't been accepted, to begin with.

Cohen's neighbors were roommates, ~~a double~~—Cullen de Groeve and Owmar O'Quinn [INTRODUCE LATER]. On one of their walls was a map of the Bay Area, on another was a batik likeness of Einstein, and so after a visit to the Salvation Army on Veterans Boulevard that's how Cohen furnished his own, with an MTA map of New York City, and an 8x10 glossy photo of "Dick Feynman," whom he wouldn't have recognized without the autograph, "To promising physicist [sic], best wishes, Dick Feynman."

Cohen's major was math. Class was Mondays, Tuesdays, Thursdays, and Fridays, while Wednesdays were seminars rotating around a diffuse array? range? of topics—logic, number theory, algebraic and symplectic geometries—followed by research group: he worked in probability before the possibilities of game theory lured him [WITH WHAT/HOW?]. ~~["We worked on statistics. Decidability, duction. Pattern recognition, precision and recall. Allocations, nomials. If you want to get granular, ergodicity, Gaussian distributions and masked Markovistics, processes and models. If you want to get übergranular, asymptotic properties of the entropy of stationary data sources with applications to data compression."]~~

Cohen applied that education to his own private scheduling but found his interests and commitments difficult to reconcile with classtime and his major's requirements. He'd be awake for days, "jagging" lists of things to do, then doing the things on the lists, "jagging" lists of the solids he ate and the liquids he drank, lists of his urinations and bowel movements, of his Carson and *Family Ties* catchup consumption on the TV nextdoor, and his inability to sleep, as publicized by his nextdoor neighbors, who, wall and door aside, effectually became his roommates, caused the other students in Stern to presume he had an addiction to amphetamines, and caused two upperclassmen who presumed he was dealing amphetamines to try and get him to pledge AEPi [until what?]—which resulted, in turn, in the alternate personas Cohen assumed/adopted: speed addict, speed dealer, and eventually, a third persona, speed pharmacologist, which itself became, soon enough, the fourth, the inventor of a new speedy drug whose name he kept changing [to/from what?], and whose substance he refused to sell to anyone.

~~Cohen, who hadn't yet resigned himself to not having an identity, would assimilate the identities of others:~~ He was also a horticulturist Buddhist (he kept bonsai junipers), a retired skateboarder forced out of the competition circuit by knee injury (he affected a limp), a manically verbigerant mediaphile—in which he spoke only in the dialogue of female characters from John Carpenter and Wes Craven movies—and a brand ambassador, in which he would monthly choose a new product, an edible or drinkable, a wearable or widget, and would buy it and use it publicly and remark on how great it was to everyone around him in inordinate terms such as, "Powerade is deliciously refreshing, dude," or, "Powerade is refreshingly delicious, dude," enough so that people began assuming~~—he never disabused them—~~that he was a paid spokesperson, an influential marketing covertly to students.

["]The roommates["] were in on this, and would help with the ruse: Cullen de Groeve's parents were [astoundingly?] wealthy executives for Timex, living in Hong Kong, and so always had new gadgets they'd give Cullen, who'd give them to Cohen to show around [de Groeve's father had been an engineer with Casio and Seiko who'd sequelized the calculator watch before being hired as senior vicepresident, manufacturing/supply chain, with a mandate to bring Timex into the digital future, while his second stepmother, who'd been *Playboy*'s Miss December 1976, handled the company's Asian press relations]. Owmar O'Quinn was a scholarship case from [which?] Philadelphia projects[—his father worked Sanitation, his mother for Corrections—]who out in California had to support himself working for a market research business, Concentives, as a mystery shopper, browsing through regional shoppingcenters, falsely p/matronizing their stores as a fake consumer in order to collect information and make report on the behavior of retail staff: whether they offered assistance, or attempted to upsell him, whether they offered free wrapping or shipping or respected feigned allergies and lactose intolerances. ~~To maintain his cover,~~ In each store O'Quinn was supposed to buy a small product, an item under $5, and though the $5 and under items he bought were usually just sneaker shoelaces or sweatbands, energy bars or weightlifting shakepowders, he also managed to shoplift, advantaging the eccentric costumes he'd designed for himself to conceal goods more expensive and so more likely to garner bids on the secondary market~~, though the fragrances he stockpiled, in the unlikely event of a girlfriend~~. He'd dress as a woman, or affect a traditionally ~~black~~ African American manner of speaking—O'Quinn being half ~~black~~ African American, and half Irish—in a bid to remain unrecognizable to the staff on repeat visits.

The merchandise O'Quinn lifted, like de Groeve's gizmos, served as props in Cohen's campaigns.

~~[A SENTENCE OR TWO RE: THE EVOLUTION OF "STARTUP CULTURE"? BECAUSE WITHOUT IT THIS'LL SEEM WEIRD?] "Startup" culture hadn't even begun yet—it was online that enabled that, and launched a billion geosocial sex apps and digital currencies [developed in rented frathouses fetid with ass and backyarded with lenticular pools]. Before then, students and even faculty were content to collaborate on products the university would own and market: CAD modelers for the automotive industry, analysis and trading platforms, system emulators, military simulators. With the university's computers prioritized for class projects, personal projects had to be pursued on personal computers—inadequate, DOS incompatible, RAM/ROM inexpansible, intramural. In 1989 [or 90?], the year online debuted, Cohen, O'Quinn, and de Groeve had only one unit among them—de Groeve's: a Gopal Ovum 1000, which retailed for $4800[, which today would be over $9300?].~~

~~["It was this 16 bit at 2.8 MHz 1.125 MB 256 KB round white cow egg. Fugly. We do not mean to fellate our competition by confessing that our future partners executed their juvenilia on its equipment. As like Gopal does everything else by itself, from its chips to the antitampering sixpointed screws that entail an antitampering sixpointed screwer, let it administer its own fellatio. All the rich kids at Stanford had a Gopal, all the kids at Stanford were rich, RAMateurs, ROMateurs, who craved the shelter of an impermeable shell OS and whose only other computing~~

~~requirements were to sound and look cool with 32 oscillators, 640 x 200 resolution. Anyway, we were not in competition with them then or now, and never will be. Gopal already had over $2 billion in annual revenue but our dominance was math, we knew bigger numbers, we knew the biggest. We tasted our dominance even while economizing on a daily diet of one pineapple nectar and one pita sliced midsagittally into devaginated halves and spooned with marshmallow fluff."]~~

Both de Groeve and O'Quinn were compsci majors and by the end of first semester had cowritten a program for Concentives that enabled the mystery shopping company to automatically tabulate upsell results and implement a general rating system, both by mall and by franchises of chains among malls. However, they were still having a problem with standardizing, not to mention automating, the evaluations of the written portion of each assessment and, having related the particulars to Cohen as they packed for the holidays, left—de Groeve to Hong Kong, O'Quinn to Philadelphia. Cohen remained in his dorm throughout winter break, and by the time his roommates returned for second semester he'd engineered a solution. The roommates were stunned. Cohen had broken through their wall, and not just figuratively, but literally. Requiring their stash of written assessments and unable to find his copy of their key amid his mess, he'd borrowed a sledgehammer from maintenance and bashed a crude passage into the plaster shared between their rooms.

In Cohen's estimation, deriving and automating [automatizing?] ratings from written assessments was merely an extension of listing, a matter of sourcing an urlist of keywords, which could be accomplished either by management designating approved verbiage for reportorial use ("topdown"), homogenizing and so narrowing the expression of the reports, or by culling the reports themselves for the verbiage ("bottomup"), relying on the reporters to provide a heterogeneous and so wider expression. [Obviously?] this latter option was preferable, but it could be implemented only if the assessments were made searchable.

Cohen had written a [descriptor algorithm?], pen on quadrille paper, which totalized the frequency of term use both across the entire spectrum of reportage—by all reports, by all reports within mall, by all reports within type ("apparel," "appliances"), by all reports within chain ("McDonald's," "Burger King")—and within the oeuvre of each individual reporter. This approach generated ratings both of the stores and the shoppers or pseudoshoppers themselves, whose written assessments were rife with [ambiguous proportions?]: "very"/"extremely" being positive values when applied to "helpful," but negative values when applied to "unhelpful," not to mention the double negatives ("not unhelpful"), which were only halfway positive, and the double positives ("too helpful"), which were only halfway negative.

De Groeve and O'Quinn coded the algorithm in C++ [INSERT JOKE? "THE ONLY GRADE ANY OF US RECEIVED THAT SEMESTER"?]. Cohen would have nothing to do with the programming besides suggesting that the better language to use might be Perl, in which each line is prefaced with a dollar sign—a "$" [CLARIFY USAGE/DIFFERENCES, BETWEEN CODING AND PROGRAMMING, AS NOUN AND VERB].

Cohen completed his freshman year without visiting home, which was only [#] miles away, and without even taking his finals, which were only [#] yards away. That summer he turned down an offer from de Groeve and O'Quinn to live in an apartment with them in San Francisco's Mission District and hone the program, now officially called Repearter, for Concentives, and instead opted to stay in his single, and accept recruitment [WHY?] into a panoply of university projects [WHY RECRUITED?]: memory and cognitive studies (on efferent discharge, synaesthesia, subitization), and a psych manifestation team that trained participating students to embody certain characteristics of certain psychiatric syndromes and comorbidities to test the ability of trainee shrinks to identify factitious disorders (as team members included both "authentics"—those with genuine syndromes/comorbidities—and "healthies"—those without—and as admission to the team required screenings by mental health professionals, whose findings were not revealed to anyone, no team member was aware of which they were, or were supposed to have been, until the collation of the professional and trainee diagnoses that marked the study's conclusion).

Cohen's sophomore year was, if possible, even more disastrous. He was generally regarded as the most promising [undergraduate?] mathematician at Stanford, and yet he was failing all of his classes except for a course in information theory. He wandered the campus perpetually, somnambulistically, and his attempts to count the numbers of windows and doors in each of the buildings, and his unwillingness to move from Stern into another dorm [WHICH?] he was assigned, were all taken as indicative of drug dependence.

The hole hammered into his wall[—over which he hung an ersatz family shrine featuring a Chinese New Year's card wishing a lucky Year of the Horse 4688, which depicted the de Groeve parents dressaged from jodhpurs to helmets on horseback atop Victoria Peak above Pok Fu Lam and bay, and an unframed group portrait of Philadelphia's own Local 3, which union did not identify but unequivocally represented O'Quinn's brothers—]was rumored to have been the result of a methamphetamine lab explosion. With de Groeve and O'Quinn informing him that even the faculty had been gossiping about his hallucinogen abuse, Cohen went into Math 234/Stat 374, Major Deviations, obstructing and so invalidating a toss of either fair or loaded dice ["TO DETERMINE WHETHER STOCHASTIC PROCESSES WITH DIFFERENT TRANSITION MATRICES PRODUCE THE SAME STATE DISTRIBUTION"], and introduced himself to the professor as Inigo Zweifel, which was the professor's own name.

Cohen's second sophomore semester was spent ~~further investigating indeterminacy [EXPAND],~~ in an office repurposed from the dormroom in Toyon Hall assigned to de Groeve and O'Quinn, who at the time were finalizing Repearter for Concentives in their Mission District apartment, commuting to campus only for classes. Cohen had refused his share of the $20000 the roommates were paid to deliver the program, but counterproposed nothing except this office. It was filled with decks of creased playingcards, Thoth tarots, lotto tickets and scratchers labeled by purchase date and location, snapped pasternbones and yarrowstalks, all of which kept him from his cryptography problemsets for aleatory variables. Library books on Confucianism, Taoism, Shintoism, and Muism [KOREAN SHAMANISM AND NOT A TYPO], overdue and never due because stolen. [Breaking into 208 Sequoia? to protest the student incident report Professor Zweifel lodged with the ombuds?,] He acquired a black magicmarker and a white dryerase board, which he [back in his quarters] installed incorrectly—with the board's scrubbable surface facing the wall, so the corkwood backing facing out—meaning that anything he'd write on it would be permanent, so he waited, and was patient.

There was a knock at the door and Cohen ignored it but the knocks kept coming. He went to the door and asked who it was and the voice on the other side answered, "Acting Dean of Student Affairs Kyle."

Cohen was sure he was being expelled but then Acting Dean of Student Affairs Kyle asked, "Are we speaking with Mr. de Groeve or Mr. O'Quinn?"

Cohen answered, yelling, that he was speaking with both of them.

"Will you open up, please?"

Cohen yelled they were both undressed.

"We have been trying to get in touch with Mr. Joshua Cohen. We understand he is a friend of yours."

Cohen confirmed.

"Mr. Cohen is not in his dorm and famously not in class—will you at least pass along a msg?"

Cohen pressed his mouth up against the door, said nothing.

"Please tell him to be in touch with his mother. An emergency family situation."

[DIALOGUE VERBATIM FROM PRINCIPAL—REWRITE ALL W/ SINGULAR PRONOUN AND W/ CONTRACTIONS.]

[ID TIME AND LOCATION AT TOP? OR BOTTOM?]

Cohen unlocked and turned the knob. His father had had another heartattack, in the sauna at the Belmont Hills JCC, 04/01/91.

Two ceremonies were held—a funeral, which Sari planned at Alta Mesa cemetery without a rabbi and without having notified any extended family or friends and, a month later, a memorial service at Abs's favorite restaurant, Prime Asian Tacos II, held by his former colleagues, who were furious with Sari.

Cohen was barely sentient throughout the funeral, having taken [only now] the first drugs of his life—two Valium, the prescription courtesy of Nancy [Apt].

For the memorial, Cohen took four Valium and, approaching the restaurant's sombreroed dragon that served as a makeshift lectern to read a selection from the Tibetan Book of the Dead [WHAT SELECTION?], passed out, and hallucinated his father being mauled to death by a dragon in a sombrero. He came to in a cramped untidy condo [WHERE HIS FATHER HAD BEEN LIVING?], in the midst of Abs's shiva, and when the mourners had finished their prayers[, they left]—they left Cohen alone[, and there he stayed].

://

from the Palo Alto sessions: Toward the end D-Unit had been working on the touchscreen. Do not interrupt, we do not digress. Tactiles. Haptics. It must have been that he was forced into this, or the PARC touchscreen group had been short an engineer and asked him and he could not refuse, D-Unit could never refuse. But his true cur, toward the end, was printing, still printing, but not in 2D anymore, in 3D, and he would have printed in 4D if he could, but no one could, least of all a Xerox employee. His condo was filled with attempts, cracked half shapes and crumbling forms, in plastic, metal, glass, ceramic, foam, powders, pellets, waxes. It was a lot to go sorting through, a lot to determine which was a model and which a modeler, which was a machined part and which a part of a machine that machined the part, from a photofabricator, laser sinterer, deposit fuser, and we spent our time totally consumed with this sorting and did not return to Stanford.

We did not drop out, we just stopped going in, never answered the letters that came from the profs and deans who knew where we were living [HOW?] and then the letters stopped coming or just the box got too congested because we stopped going outside, never answered the phonecalls that came in either from the profs and deans who knew where we were living [HOW?] and then the calls stopped coming or we stopped getting them because the line was too busy and even now, we read once online, Stanford still lists us as like being on leave.

We just hung around the condo and avoided the computers, mutant x86ish PCs D-Unit had clunked himself, monitors surrounded by boxes of Kleenex and spritzers of Windex, keyboards surrounded by pressurized air containers, for blowing out the dust from between the keys, and the other periphs he clunked himself too as like joysticks and steeringwheels and the double mice he called rats surmounted with babywipes and kleengel antiseptics.

D-Unit must have abhorred the touchscreen. All that work to splenda an image only to let the user foul it up with sweaty fingers. Printing their grimy genes. Sacrificing clarity for convenience.

Basically this is the problem.

No matter how much we wipe our hands, no matter how much we disinfect—any way we can remember D-Unit just ruins the resolution.

We had not known that D-Unit had been condoliving at The Clingers ever since we left the house. D-Unit had never told us and we are not even sure whether M-Unit or Aunt Nance had known. Of the mail we took in, what surprised us the most were the catalogs for exotic gamemeats and kits for homebrewing. Of the msgs on the voicemail we checked, what surprised us the most were the appointment confirmations from gun ranges and attendance requests from Hasidics seeking a minyan.

Either this was the true D-Unit, free from having to split everything with M-Unit and so free to psychically compensate by evincing a split within himself, or this was a newly single engineer in the midst of über-crisis. We will never have confirmation. Unit 26 at The Clingers. Apostrophe, possessive.

We were alone with the computers and we tried to avoid them. We tried to convince ourselves we were above them, beyond them, we were pure and they were applied, we could work with just our head and they could work only with processors and electricity though still they required our head to give them tasks. But the truth, we realized, was that we were afraid of them, we were scared of getting into trouble again and to be honest being left alone with that many computers in one condo was as like being abandoned as like a pedophile in a sandbox during recess. Bad analogy, but appropriate.

But again this is the problem without resolution. We could say we were not able to help ourselves and were bored and so broke. Or we could say we were just cur about D-Unit. This career vegan who after his wife left him for a woman stuffed his freezer with enough cuts of venison to make $1.\overline{33}$ deer, this atheistic azionistic Jew who after his separation scrawled on the wall by the Xerox photocopier/fax the tollfree number for transmitting a prayer to be printed in Jerusalem and stuffed into a crevice of the Kotel. The Western Wall. Überwestern.

We turned on a computer and went through its files. We turned them all on and investigated. They were networked, so we stayed on one and went through them all. There was a genealogy he was investigating. There were recipes in a .doc called *EZ_Meals_for_the_Single_Cook*, there were inspirational anecdotes collected in another .doc called *therabbinicapproachtodivorce*. Another we remember was a scientific study on midlife, or secondlife, lesbianism.

On the floor by the CPU chassis was a flaking mass that, we had always thought, was just another faulty tridimensional printjob, and in a sense it was, because it was a cardboard box and we were always kicking it. But then we kicked it once and it spilled over and we, leaving off reading about the process of gittin, or Jewish divorce documents, but you know that, or the pseudoscientific relationship between lesbianism and premature menopause and the resultant excess of stress hormone and dearth of estrogen that affects the amygdala, got up out of the swiveler to examine the damage and what it was, it was the future.

It is inconceivable now. Not just that we had not experimented before, but that this was the way access was packaged. That access was packaged at all. Now everything just loads, streams, flows, automatically, but back then software was indistinguishable from hardware. A program came on a disc. A round rainbowized flatness that came in a box. Remember. There was a handbook, there was a manual. Containing instructions to heed, for installation. The program had to be registered, there was a warranty, there was a terms of service that had to be agreed to and signed, and both had to be sent through the mail. The old mail. Remember. But D-Unit had taken care of this. We cannot conceive of having missed this but have no rationale. The icons were there all along, there in plain day on the desktop. Press us, press us.

The net, the web. One a way of talking, the other what was said. We would have hacked if D-Unit had not stored all his IDs and pwords in memory. We dialed and the hiss came through and we came through the ascending levels of hiss as like progressively being swallowed by a cobra. We were connected, had msgs, mail, the new mail.

D-Unit had CompuServe, Prodigy, GEnie, America Online, and though we forget which one we used, it was a service. Mortifying. Commercial. D-Unit was an early adopter for a rec, having opened his accounts in 89, though also a late adopter for a tech given that we are describing 91 and serious presdigitals had been dinking around with modems and phone exchanges not even in their offices but at their homes from the 80s, the 70s.

The D-Unit we knew had always been a hardware guy, meaning that he regarded software as like unserious, or pretentious, as like the gynolinguistic pedagogy of his wife. He had spent his life around machines and if he at least tolerated the code that programmed them it was because it came on discs that came packaged in envelopes, in boxes. The D-Unit we knew never had any patience for the service economy, but was fundamentally a maker, a producer, consumed by stuff and things. To him, legit computing could only be accomplished in a workplace with other professionals, in the flesh and on a schedule, time and space were physically shared. The engineers replaced the tubes, replaced the transistors and circuits, by hand, the boss had a desk with only a paperweight on it and could not even type. The home was the home, the office was the office, and to bring a hugenormous mainframe back into the house, even in a better color than mental ward offwhite, was as like committable an offense as like bringing back into the house another lover to introduce to your child and spouse.

We are not implying that D-Unit was a company suit, we are just trying to convey that for him the home office dichotomy was a quasireligion, just as like his parents had kept glatt kosher and his grandparents had kept the Sabbath. He would never have read the Rationalists in the lab, he would never have soldered on the toilet.

He would have been appalled by all this realization of the virtual, communication becoming transactional, customers exchanging money for air. He would have considered it a scam, as like having to pay an admission fee at libraries, or having to pay a multinational corporation for admission to his brain. A multinational corporation that made its money licensing his knowledge to others, and, in turn, by commodifying, commodizating, their thoughts. He would never have listened to the movements of the fourth Bartók quartet out of the order of their intention, he would never have looked at the Rubens Calvary except in person.

We should also say that he always insisted on matinees at the Aquarius Theater.

But that D-Unit who was totally capable of achieving his own access instead chose to subscribe to a cruft of rectarded netservices whose chief goal was to keep their users within the walled garden by providing a sense of community, along with local news and weather, only so as like not to lose them to the wilds of the web—that this was his choice meant he was depressed. We read his emails first, the first emails we ever read, and confirmed, depression. Online was not a hobby for him, but an attempt to spend himself unsad. Companionship at 14400 bits/second, 2400 baud, $6/hour on evenings and weekends, $3/hour on weekday days.

Venturing into the online activities of abco, abco33, batchelor, and cuddlemaven did not bring him or them to life, but brought us to become them or him, which prevented any mischief. Initially. While the rest of userdom was liberated by alias to chatrape girls or cybercheat on husbands, to meddle in any way as like D-Unit or his selves was to transgress a commandment. Respect the name. Respect thy parents even unto their proxy reputations. Initially.

D-Unit had posted to boards about the Dodgers, about seismology. To a room called Bay Singles, a place for people to flirt while discussing the dangers of meeting people online. To a room called Bay Singles: Jewish, a place for Jews to flirt while discussing the dangers of meeting goyim online. He also gave advice at Querytek, and at 1-900-Trouble. The desperation was overwhelming. He had helped a woman fix her modem by telling her to restart it. He had also accessed pornography. We would prefer not to discuss it.

It was ultimately the census that broke us, a room in which amateurs made recommendations for a digitization of the census and in a thread titled "1990 Last Paper Census??" D-Unit had posted a warning about the ease of data manipulation and uploaded a paper about accusations of electronic voting fraud in the 1972 presidential elections. The thread then split into two, one a discussion of Nixon, the other a discussion of the history of data manipulation, beginning with the punchcard and its tabulator and ending, as like all discussions end, with the Holocaust.

D-Unit had been attacked for defending the deathcamp totals. The thread had been dormant for eight or nine months. We posted nonetheless. We posted as like abco33, then created our own avatar and agreed with ourselves. Posted as like abco33 again, with thanks for our support. Then we argued about the Dodgers, a team we knew nothing about, a sport we knew nothing about, and were informed that, in baseball, there was always next season.

In Bay Singles, batchelor had explained his situation to troglodyke_Y, a selfidentified lesbian who had collapsed midway through and written, "what else 2," number 2, "expect from women?" then admitted he was a man. In Bay Singles: Jewish, cuddlemaven had explained the same or a very similar situation, which had garnered a single response, "abs?" and so still as like cuddlemaven we took the thread offboard and emailed the responder directly, wondering why s/he had thought it was "us," and the party who turned out to be a retired PARCy responded, "abraham cohen is deceased. whoever you are you are being reported for violation of your ToS," and so that account, the CompuServe, died too.

We flamed the PARCy with emails, as like other avatars, as like the same avatars but registered with other services. batchelor but now @Prodigy, cuddlemaven but now @GEnie. We even went trolling for him among the dossy BBSes and subscribed to leetish listservs and wrote posts or comments or whatever they were called then to autogenerate and hex all the sysops down. It was an addiction, because the self is an addiction. We placed orders just through chatting, with paraphiliac feeders who lived in the Bay and were willing to drop takeout Asian fusion at the foot of our stairs with no strings attached, or else we explained and this we regret that we had cancer and so normcores took pity on us too and delivered pallets of cane sodas for nothing, never taking the bill or coins we left wedged under the mat. Our deliverers did not even want to meet us, certainly not after we insisted that we did not want to be met in our condition, and this let us assert was ultimately more important than the start of ecommerce, this was more as like the start of freecommerce, though not even that claim can justify our behavior.

We joined all the religious fora because back then the only pages that existed, smut aside, were about two things, basically: one being the absolute miracle of the very existence of the pages, as like some business celebrating the launch of some placeholder spacewaster site containing only contact information, their address in the real, their phone and fax in the real, and two being the sites of people, predominantly, at this stage, computer scientists or the compscientifically inclined openly indulging their most intimate curs, their most spiritual disclosures, as like experimental diabetes treatment logs and conversion diaries patiently explaining ontological discrepancies between Theravada and Mahayana Buddhisms, interspersed with kitten and puppy photos, a Christmas tree growing at syrupspeed from starred tip to rootless trunk until filling the window.

We tracked what we could, as like much as like we could. We trafficked, unable to stop. We had to know everything, to not just know everything but to have it, to keep it all under wraps, under banner. We correlated pages with profiles, crossreferenced profiles based on similarity of subject, of style or time of expression, but each time a connection was made, another connection appeared, and the number of sites grew too large, and so the number of their links grew too big, and so the database we were producing went onerous.

This is how history begins: with a log of every address online in 1992. 130 was the sum we had by 1993, by which time the countingrooms we were monitoring had projected the sum as like quarterly doubling. 623, approx 4.6% of which were dotcom. 2738, approx 13.5%. There were too many urls to keep track of, so we kept track of sites. There were too many sites to keep track of, so we kept track of host domains that only monitored or made public their numbers of registered sites, not their numbers of sites actually setup and actually functional, and certainly not their names or the urls, the universal resource locators of their individual pages, but what frustrated more than the fact that we could not dbase all the web by ourselves was the fact that none of the models we engineered could ever predict its expansion.

Computers had grown smaller by the release, shrinking to lapsize, and were shrinkable further until the limit, the entropy point, at which it became feasible to make a computer handsize, fingersize, too small to be humanly usable. The web had reached something of the same limit-point but from the opposite direction, it had become too big for any one user to feasibly navigate. We identified only two ways to bring about re-alignment. Either to limit its size, which was censorship, or to map it and make that map searchable. The future was and will always be ahead of us, but also behind us, and to the sides. The future is the client, the past is just something to find.

The wallpaper of the condo was testpattern CMYK, cyan magenta yellow key black stripes curving shoddy toward their tangency at a mon-oxide detector whining the sinewave of its battery drained. We covered it all with lists printed on printers and legal pads, lists of sites and sitemaps described, but it was only with the phoneline conked and the electricity just after that we were finally able to get to work. Before we were too close to the screen. Too near to the potentials to equate them.

It was harrowing just going outside. The other condo units shone dusk to dawn and phones rang in the sky. We had octalfortied that sound and the look of gravel and hedges. At the foot of the stairs our mailbox had lacked the bandwidth for all the bills from PG&E and PacBell, four figures of bankruptcy. The condo was accessed by a staircase as like a fire escape, and the storage enclosure under the stairs contained a cage, and the cage contained a putrefied pet skeleton. It might have been a hedge-hog. We went back inside. Just swiveled. It had taken a year and a half, 1993, for us to realize that the chair we sat in was adjustable. Which was helpful because either the desk was too low or we were taller than D-Unit.

Or else it was AOL that finally cut us off. Because that too was billed separately. We cannot recall precisely. And we had no clue that D-Unit owned a hedgehog.

Point is, we were returned from practice to theory and paper. It is unfortunate that you will have to transcribe this.

[SARI CONTACT?]

[CONDO MGMT?]

://

~~Tetration's genesis~~ The Clinger's, Abs's condo complex at 100 Muralla Way, Pacifica, CA, consisted of 26 identical units, all of them two bedroom condos below second floor one bedroom condos, with the exception of Cohen's, which was a second floor one bedroom condo above the maintenance shed.

Visitors had to navigate ruptured mulchbags, rusting rakes, shovels, and a wheelbarrow to access the outdoors staircase, which [suspiciously] resembled a fire escape. But if visitors were infrequent with Abs alive, with his son in residence they

Only once a month, from July 1993 through July 1995~~, just after Cohen had completed each month's second update of his site, diatessaron .stanford.edu, and clicked Send on the month's second email—addressed to 92 recipients (01/94), addressed to 736 recipients (12/94)~~—would a rental minivan show up, and two men—still boyish—would hazard the stairs, and knock at the door.

Summer 1993 was a decisive time for both de Groeve and O'Quinn. They had [been] graduated from Stanford, offers were on the table from Microsoft, graduate school beckoned, and

Diatessaron, hosted at[?]/by[?] the Stanford domain due to the entreaties of recent graduates de Groeve and O'Quinn, was a site comprised of two pages [EXPLAIN THE DIATESSARON NAME]. One listed [≥400 ≤600] sites ordered by main url alphabetically within category. The other listed [≥400 ≤600] the same sites ordered by domain or host alphabetically within category. All listings were suburled, meaning that each site's pages were listed individually, until that policy had to be abandoned for practical considerations [REMINDER OF EXPLOSIVE GROWTH OF ONLINE], summer 1994.

Its categories remained fairly consistent throughout: Tech, Math, Science, and the omnivorous Arts & Culture & Oriental Culture & Recreation/Miscellaneous/Food & Drink/Gaming, each of which contained White Pages (personal sites), Yellow Pages (business sites), Blue (governmental), Red (academic), the colors being the highlighting around the links and so the governmental and even the academic were unreadable.

Access to [the] Diatessaron was free—it was not equipped to process payments online—neither was there a fee for the [daily? weekly?] email, which was a hyperlinkdump of all the sites that'd appeared since the previous email, both alphabetized and crossclassified by url within host/domain. Admission to this elist, however, required each prospective recipient to file at least eight unique site identifications and descriptions, while to remain on the elist required filing a further two IDs and Descris if not uniquely then [biweekly? bimonthly?]. The updating, and the compiling of the email, were funded by subscriptions to a print directory, published [irregularly], which didn't just reproduce the site in intransitive hardcopy, but synthesized it too. This was "The Rainbow Pages" (O'Quinn). Or "The Online Phonebook" (de Groeve). It contained both halves of an updated Diatessaron, but unlike the site it interpolated the emails **by bolding,** *or italicizing,* <u>or underlining</u>, depending on who was doing the wordprocessing/design—de Groeve favoring bold, O'Quinn favoring italics, Cohen the underliner—all the urls that'd appeared since the previous edition.

All this for just $12, postage not included, or a 12 volume subscription, postage included (domestic only), for $100.

But then why pay for something available for nothing online?

Because of the incentives—"Why pay for something available for nothing online?" was a note Cohen wrote for the original edition, and his question was answered by the features that followed: coprographic site correspondence reprinted under the rubric "Dear Admin," the swift merciless judgments of "Editorz Pickz 'N' Prickz," which de Groeve and O'Quinn issued under the collaborative cybernym "Dr. Oobleck Tourette OB/GYN," a centerfold with interview column called "Femailer Daemon," and the regular but vague and so never fulfilled promise fonted above each page in Helvetica: "all members get h&jobs."

The backcover, initially, was an ad for The Clinger's—whose management had not requested it and had no site to publicize and rejected a proposed trade for rent reduction—and folded behind it was a subscription envelope preaddressed but not prestamped to a PO box in Pacifica. Checks were accepted, but not creditcards: "If sending ***ca$h*** please fold ***discretely***" [sic or not?]. ~~[“Being in business meant reordering our lives: the file could be sent to the printer, but not via email [[then how?]]. The proofs had to be approved, and even that could only be accomplished in person. On distro days whoever rented the minivan, drove it, or so ‘Cull’ and ‘Qui’ insisted after they had an accident when whoever was not registered was driving[[?]]. We had to be at the printer in Oakland by 08:00, in order to load up the books—in our prime we were selling just over 2000 copies per volume—to get to Bay Stationery by 10:30, in order to pick up the packaging, to get to our unit by 11:00 or so to print out the labels and pack the books, to get to the Pacifica PO by 13:00, when it was relatively empty just after lunch. At the PO we would check the box, collect the checks and cash, stop at the Wells Fargo to deposit it all, and if we still had time stop for agave shakes and mock duck pockets at Bigestion. We had to be dropped off at our unit by 16:00 at the latest if our partners were to regas the van and have it back in its lot by 16:30 to avoid the night fee. ‘Qui’ and ‘Cull’ would then bicycle home. They were still living across from the The Irish Phoenix on Valencia.”]~~

[First quarter?] revenue was about $16—after the sunk costs sunk in, after Cohen paid his partners back for helping bail him out of utilities debt—before the threeway split. But by summer 1994, they were making enough to pay for the hiring of two employees, the daughters of Raffaella and Salvatore "Super Sal" [Trappezi/Trapezzi?], the bookkeeper and superintendent, respectively, of The Clinger's. ~~[“Salvatrice would have been about 20 then, and Heather about 16.] [[They would become employees #1 and #25 of Tetration, after Heather insisted on skipping the intermediary numerals in favor of 25, the number of Barry Bonds, the leftfield lefthanded slugger of the Giants, apparently, and so even today Tetration has 24 fewer employees than the personnel ops spreadsheets would indicate.”]]~~

Salvatrice, then 20, and Heather, 16, were paid $8/hour for data entry. Salvatrice would check the synop@diatessaron.stanford.edu email, verify "first level uniquity," as a new site was called inhouse, or "second level uniquity," as a new url was called inhouse, and copypaste to the DDbase appropriately. Heather, who was still a junior at Oceana High School, would report after school and relieve her sister. It was her job to update the dual subDDbases, crediting subscribers and prospectives with finds. The Trapezzi girls were diligent workers, and if they ever exasperated Cohen it was only because they failed to understand that the work they were doing could be done anywhere and at any time. Though the business's first major purchases were two computers Cohen set up in the Trapezzis' unit, Salvatrice persisted in arriving at Unit 26 at 09:00 promptly, and Heather in arriving at 17:00, on Mondays through Fridays [I AM TYPING OUT A SCHEDULE]. They couldn't be persuaded to use anything other than the same mongrel workstation of Abs's design [SUCK MY FUCKING BALLZZZ].

But neither Cohen nor de Groeve nor O'Quinn was content with being a publisher. Semesters came and went and gradschool was deferred. The Microsoft offers were off the table. With the Trapezzi girls now taking care of the business—entering data, updating the site and the emails, regularly checking for deadlinks, even taking over the print edition's layout and negotiations with the printers, and then hiring employees #26–30, Heather's classmates, to canvass the Bay soliciting subscribers—Cohen, de Groeve, and O'Quinn spent 1995 developing the algorithm.

This equation would become the foundation of Tetration. It was mapped out on paper by Cohen, and [coded] by his partners in two [programming] languages, Python and Java.

Its first iteration found application as an internal searchengine, which allowed the Trapezzis to find any link by name, category, domain, date listed, and user contributor.

Its second iteration was embedded in the site itself, though its appearance there was ~~unfindable~~—it was not for external use. At this stage—mid-1995—the algorithm was set to track any link *to Diatessaron,* to follow it back to its origin page and determine whether it was listed or not. If not, the page would now be listed, and would be linked *from Diatessaron,* though none of this would happen automatically but rather required approval and manual inclusion, due to "a Biblical swarm of quashless bugs" that caused the algorithm to confuse incoming and outgoing urls of the same name but at [different domains], resulting in a failure to relate individual urls with their [hosting sites]~~, "and that does not even take into account the equifails as like disk crash."~~

This type of autosearch—in which an algorithm, conceived of as a "bot," or "drone," would "crawl," or "creep," "crustaceate," or "spider"—required an increase in computing power, which, at the time, was expensive. July 1995, they took the site offline and sold their contributor elist [FOR HOW MUCH AND TO WHOM? I AM WRITING ABOUT A MAN WHO SOLD A LIST!!!!] to a new emarketing firm called Schlogistics~~, whose CEO, Randy Schloger, would marry Heather Trapezzi~~. With that income and the proceeds [HOW MUCH MONEY AGAIN? BECAUSE I MOTHERFUCKING CARE!!!!@#$%] from the last four editions of the Diatessaron, Cohen, de Groeve, and O'Quinn bought three Ultra Enterprises and three Intel Pentiums, both loaded [right word?] with Linux, which they racked [right word?] in the maintenance shed below Cohen's unit. The Trapezzis refused to accept any rent for the shed [but weren't they just the management, not ownership?], so Cohen drafted an agreement on the back of a Shell gas station receipt [though at which point did he or anyone else get a car?], giving the accommodating couple a 1% stake in whatever resulted, subsequently turning them into multimillionaires~~, which is why today "'Super' Sal Trapezzi" is still listed on Tetration's About page, and even in SEC filings, as "Head Janitor 4 Life."~~

Raffaella Trapezzi set about cleaning out the shed, and Super Sal, assisted by Salvatrice's husband, insurance adjuster Ronnie Giudice ~~(later the impresario behind Ronnie G's Best Braciole, which had ?number locations by ?date)~~, constructed makeshift desks, bolting extra warped unit doors atop sawhorses. Following Cohen's specifications they lightproofed the one window with flypaper, soundproofed the entirety by covering the walls with layers of bubblewrap atop vivisected eggcartons, and partitioned it in particleboard, with Cohen requesting that his own cubicle in the very center be boarded from floor to ceiling to create an enclosed shaft [how would he have gotten in and out?], though he was never to be found there [because there was no way to get in or out?], and preferred to work upstairs, in Unit 26, which he called “The Brumbellum,” “The Brain,” and later “The Fourth and a Half Estate,” and then “Getit D-Unit.”

~~By early 1996, they were set—they had everything but a name.~~

THIS IS JUST POINTLESS FUCK FUCK FUCK FUCK

FUCKQW

FU

Q=013847IE;A bv,.ghhgty qp83ur j ;j ‘’ 1aa0;2s9l38ddytvnm,.// bhgddk4f7j\|^%5g6h{}

://

from the Palo Alto sessions: It was as like a dream. Or hallucination. As like when the comp digirecorder shuts off when its condenser mic does not detect our speaking voice for 1, 2, 3, 4 seconds and so the recording will become nothing but an artificially compressed memory omitting the time in which life is lived, the times of blankness between the redlit sesshs just lost and irretrievable. That is how we perceive that existence today, as like a vast unrecorded emptiness. We were not sleeping and not awake. We were convinced that we were writing everything wrong and had gotten everything uncombobulated, that we were writing the algy as like it were the businessplan, and writing the businessplan as like it were the algy. The algy a sequence of specific commands executing specific operations, the bplan a sequence of nonspecific goals and objectives or just subjective projections that would execute only if we failed to convince the VCs, or worse, if we succeeded at failing them totally. The algy used sequences of numbers to represent functions, the bplan used sequences of letters to represent the dysfunctionality of its intended readership, manipulating prospective investors according to sociocultural filters and career trajectories, levels of greed and their enabling inadequacies, significant degrees of gullibility too, or just plain unadulterated stupeyness.

We had set a full functionality deadline of September 1996 but we were behind schedule by April so we revised for December, but then it was May and we were behind the revised schedule. If stage 2 completion was unfeasible we would redefine and make that completion stage 1 so that everything was feasible. The aim was not to be workable. Not to be presentable. But to achieve seamless genius, no raphe. Only the rec investors say done is better than perfect. The techs say perfect is better than done. We were blessed, in that we had no rec investors and were the tech itself. We were always prodding, nudging one another subtle with our fists. Cull would say, "Cunts do not drip on deadline." Qui would say, "It is too difficult to coordinate the squirts." We talked as like this even with the girls around, and the girls were always around, The Friends of the Trapezzi Sisters nerfing it up and tossing the frisbee indoors and the only way to get rid of them was to send them out on errands, or if they had a date. "No that is not the correct surge protector, and no we do not have exact change." Qui and Cull asked all of them out and the answer was, "But you never change your pants."

Never. We shared even the undies, just took what was folded atop the unit washer/dryer. We were all the same size back then. Fruit of the Loom was the best for extended sedation. No socks. Raffaella cooked but if she ever went aggro against our herbivorism and tried to convert us to sausage we sent The Friends of the Trapezzi Sisters to forage. Cull and Qui both ordered Greek salads but Egyptian Fuel was a mile closer, though OrganoMex had faster response times despite being 2.2 miles farther away. Smoothies were the optimum delivery system but we were never quite satisfied with our formulas for determining whether the time it took for us to make them was more or less precious than the money it cost to order them and anyway Raffaella did not have a blender. Qui and Cull stopped driving back approx twice a week to San Francisco but still had to drive approx once a week to Stanford whenever our test-site would crash its servers and no one else could fix them or could apologize both so well and disingenuously. To make up the time Cull would ignore stopsigns and stoplights and Qui would ignore even the roads and once drove straight out of the parkinglot and through the condo quad and ruined the sprinkler system and so had to waste a weekend helping Super Sal and Ronnie G dig up the heads and replace them. We were so fritzed that once when we had to go to Stanford ourselves to tender our regrets for once again crashing their servers and to try and retrieve the latest corrupted version of their financial aid site, we forget because we were passed out whether it was Qui or Cull driving the car, but one of them was passed out with us and the other got lost in Monta Loma or Castro City and sleepdrove instead to the old apartment they shared in the Mission and even sleepwent to the door but the key he had did not work and the new tenants woke us up by giving us directions with a crowbar. For models of how best to present this period consult any national intelligence whitepaper on the behaviors of terrorist cells or besieged messianic cults.

Still, the hours were no longer than at any other startup. The hours were no longer than life. Cull and Qui would code and crash and then we would recode until crashing. We would work on it as like online would work on us, which meant perpetually. In the beginning it was a site, and then it was a program to be embedded in other sites, and then it was a program to be tabbed in a browser. But would we license it. Or sell it outright. Or just diversify it all as like our own company. Which would require which systems. Requiring funding of what amount and engineering by whom. Was search even patentable. How to recognize a question. The appropriate time to incorporate. How to recognize an answer. We had a title but no name. We were the founding architect of nothing.

We kept failing, our own computers kept crashing and kept crashing the servers at Stanford and then Stanford threatened to banish us from the servers but Qui and Cull appealed to Professor [?] Winhrad who interceded and then we failed again and lost some of their admin and even some faculty email and then they threatened us again and Cull and Qui appealed again and Professor [?] Winhrad interceded again and then they put us on probation, gave us a second chance squared, after which, hasta la vista, baby.

We had a problem but it was not us and yet neither were we the solution. Our problem was time and not because we did not have enough but because we had too much of space.

We had so much of this space and all of it kept growing but by the time we could crawl even a portion of it everything had grown again so that we could not have kept up even by walking or running. But that is not how to understand it.

If the internet is the hardware and the web is the software

If the net is the mind and the web is the body or the software the body and the hardware the mind

Think about it as like knots. Shoelaces. If you tie them but the knot is no good you can either tie another knot atop it or just undo it all and start over. But if you have never experienced a good knot in your life all you can do is do the both of them. Tie another knot and start over. Or think about it as like shaving your face. If you use a razor you might miss a hair or not cut it completely but if you use a tweezers and tweeze each hair you can bald your face to even the follicles. But then the rash. You cannot do both. Forget it. Or as like losing a wallet. You can retrace your steps or you can, forget it. Or as like losing a button. You can either retrace your steps and try and find it or you can just sew on a fresh one. But to do both you have to have two broken shirts or two broken pants and the needle, the thread. You have to realize the order. People wrapped themselves in skins that fell off them before they invented a needle and thread to sew them better before they invented a button device to clinch them better, and all the fits just worked. But imagine if everything was the reverse and you had to invent a clincher before inventing the equipment to sew an animal skin before even inventing the animal. That was search invented by how to search. Invented by how to tailor the results to the user. Not to mention that "button," in another context, could refer not to a clothes clasp but to a key pressed to launch a weapon. Not to mention that in still other contexts "needle" could mean "annoy," or "bother," and "thread" might not be a literal string or twine but figurative as like a "drift" or "stream" whose speed is measured in "knots," "a train of thought" just "flowing," until it was "brought to heel." The choice was to both needle the thread and thread the needle. Through its eye. In one ear, out the other. To know the polysemy of tongues. We had to code a searchengine to check our own code for a searchengine. That should tell you everything.

Or better, understand this by what we are, by what we have postulated as like our axiomatic expression. Separate, divide. Categories, classifications, types. Genus, species. Clades. It is history, it is historical. The world was discovered, the world was explored, and it was all so round and immense that it confused us. We reacted by formalizing ourselves into becoming botanists, zoologists, and so the plants and animals became formalized too, the botanists and zoologists arranged them. But they arranged them by how they looked, how they sounded, where they lived, when they lived, by character. How our humanity, taxonomized at the top of the pyramid or tree, perceived them. But then the universe that could not be seen and could not be heard was discovered and explored. Cells were observed. Mitochondria. Genes. DNA. It appeared that not all the animals and plants were as like they appeared. A whale was biologically closer to a panda than to a herring. Turtles were biologically different than tortoises but they both were closer to being ostriches than snakes.

Point is, what was important was not the organism itself but the connections among the organisms. The algy had to make the connections. We figgered if we could index all the tech links, and apply to each a rec link, whatever terminology we mortally employ, we could engineer the ultimate. The connection of connections.

How a single user regarded a thing would be comptrasted by what things existed. Not only that but the comptrasting of the two would be automated. Each time each user typed out a word and searched and clicked for what to find, the algy would be educated. We let the algy let its users educate themselves. So it would learn, so its users would be taught. All human language could be determined through this medium, which could not be expressed in any human language, and that was its perfection. The more a thing was clicked, the more perfect that thing would be. We would equate ourselves with that.

Now let us propose that everyone out of some psychosis suddenly tetrated for "mouse," but chose results pertaining only to "device for menu traversal and interface," or if everyone tetrated for "rat," but chose results pertaining only to "snitching to the authorities." Auxiliary metonymic or synecdochic meanings would become primary, while the displaced primaries might have their meanings reinvested in alternative terms.

It took approx millions of speakers and thousands of writers over hundreds of years in tens of countries to semantically switch "invest" from its original sense, which was "to confer power on a person through clothing." Now online it would take something as like one hundred thousand nonacademic and even nonpartisan people in pajamas approx four centiseconds each between checking their stocks to switch it back.

The connection is basically the point. Or the motion between two points is the connection. Basically nothing exists except in motion. Nothing exists unless transitive, transactional. Unless it joins. Unless its function is its bridging.

This is what we meant by mentioning the blankspots on the recordings, the empties. The gaps, the missing gaps. What is omitted from our recordings is all that links. Relations.

The algy itself was base 4, though not in the normative sense but in the way it expanded, the way it optimized by expansion, extending, stretching, from describing the world to prescribing the world, from connotative to denotative, mapping to manifest becoming. We had four criteria. Or better four questions. Four basic foundational questions the answers to which were transfinite to infinite.

Is what is being searched for *a prescription,* as like a name or title? "Vishnu," say, or "Carbon Capital"? Or is what is being searched for *a description*? As like "an engineer," or "someone who can build our systems," a "venture capital firm," or "some entity that can finance us"? Could this description and/or prescription instead be *linguistically proximal,* to a most perfect result? Which is to say is the name transliterated scifi style, as like "vYshnOO," or are we dealing with a typo, as like "caBRon capitOl," "n gineer," or "fin anceus"? Finally, and this is arduous, could the searchterms be in any way *conceptually proximal,* to a most perfect result? "Not Krishna but other god but Indian human," "person whose job it is to build things," "entity whose job it is to roll bank/bankroll," and so on into subquestions pertaining to whose concept of "god" or "job" are we using? What is the sample size by which, and what is the scale by which, proximity is being defined? Our ideas of "job/god," and/or your ideas of "god/job"—how to make them, how to make anything, mergeable?

We searched among the numbers for a name. Not among the numerals but the integers, which name the distances between.

A quadratic is a square or pertaining to squares, to both the object to be squared and the subject of squaring. Quadratic algys output in a duration proportional to the square of the size of their input. Applicable to algys simple, not complex. Used for kinding and sorting. The relationship of any 2D curve to any curved 3D form, whether spheroid, ellipsoid, cylinder, or cone, is quadric. The same as like the relationship between the value fluctuations of our respective portfolios. The Babylonians squared all shapes with quadratic equations, the Hindus and Buddhists with cubic equations, because they understood the worth of negatives. Angling with quartics had to wait for Europe, polynomials.

The deadline we had set for a name decision was our birthday, 1996. The day approached and we still had no storms in the brain, only in the algy, and Qui and Cull would not even respond to their own names let alone to suggestions.

The names Cubic, Cubics, Cubix, Cubiks, Cubicks, and even Q-bics were all already taken, both as like company names and dotcoms. All registered to a military contractor who bounced our emails.

The name Quartical did not test well with father and stepstepmother de Groeve who kept dangling a watchmaking future in front of Cull as like a hypnotizing pendulum and neither did Quadration impress the parents O'Quinn who kept reminding Qui he could always get back in touch with Microsoft while his brothers insisted that brogrammers genius as like he was should be getting paid by the codeline or even by the character.

Salvatrice Trapezzi would read the news, each new incorporation filing, for Affine, for Infdex, but if they had $10 million in capital we had 120 million documents identified. The narrative plot of online is that as like the number of sites that made the web increased, the number of hosts or domains that made the net did not, and it was just at this point in time that their stasis or even decrease was being felt, with capitalism and so democracy too in thrall to just a handful of corporations. We had to be one of that handful. The forefinger, which starts words, the pinky, which ends them. The ringfinger, which is bound to shift and second functions, as like in programming to code parentheses and brackets. The middle finger, we would be the middles if lucky. Not the first, not the last, but the strongest.

Raffaella proposed Etude, and Perspective.

We were partial to E-tude, with a hyphen, or Perspektiv, with a k. Also, Indagator.

Salvatrice: 2gether, GathR.

Heather: FrisB, Boomerang, Poprank, Rankpop, Demogz, Dmogz, Yoyo, JoCo, Juggle, Buggle.

Cull was suggesting CoCull (which is Latin or Greek for a cowl), or CullCo (bastard Latin or Greek, "to inculcate"). Qui went for CoQui (which is a frog or toad native to Puerto Rico), and QuiCo (bastard Spanish, "to glut").

Nobody could spell Diatessaron. But even if they could and we used that there was still the fear, but an unsubstantiated fear, of Stanford suing us.

But by trying to think words all we were thinking were numbers. As like language was a problem and we were solving for name. We were always returning to math. Operations. All the ways two numbers can be manipulated are essentially the same. They are just depths, or nests, recursions. Addition, a quantity that has been followed, or succeeded, by another, is contained within multiplication, a quantity that has been added to itself x number of times, while multiplication is contained in exponentiation, a quantity that has been multiplied by itself x number of times. Practically, all computers can do is just add and comptrast, though theoretically, the number of potential operations is illimitable, and the sums generated grow too large for a human to compute, even too long for a human to write.

The operation after exponentiation is called tetration, the fourth order of magnitude, a quantity exponentiated by itself. Also called iterated exponentiation, hyper-4. By the time we got to Stanford this question of what to call the operation had been answered, not so the question of how to calculate and notate its results. The mathpeople were all cur about Cs, or complex numbers, which are numbers represented by x + iy, where x and y are real numbers and i the imaginary unit equal to the square root of negative one. Essentially this number does not exist. But its speciousness enables the modeling of chaos. The systematizing of chaos and the differencing of that from the random and arbitrary, which given even an infinite or eternal timescale or space might never evince determination or design. Applies to morphogenesis, phyllotaxis, biochirality, and fractalization, how leaves and shells are proportioned, how the human face is proportioned, econometrics, oscillating chemical reactions, dynamics of liquids and gas. This is a ridiculous explanation but. Encryption techniques. Quantum mechanics. Ridiculous but.

Because it is only in the tetration of complex numbers that results become so large and long as like to allow for the identification of repetition, of pattern. Of deepest nested recursion. Once every C would be tetrated all the disciplines would be united in singularity and day would be night and night would be day and no inbox would ever again give evidence of anything but an integrated self. We have read through your email, sorry.

Anyway, at Stanford every mathperson we hated because they were also a compsciperson was cur about how exactly to calculate that—the repetition, the pattern—so they kept writing code

```
}
void setBit(u_char byte, u_char bit, bool v)
{x[byte] = setBitOnByte(x[byte], bit, v);}
void setBit(u_char b, bool v)
{setBit(b/8, b%8, v);}
bool getBit(u_char byte, u_char bit) const
{return getBitOnByte(x[byte], bit);}
bool getBit(int b) const
{return getBit(b/8, b%8);}
ALInteger operator ~() const
{
```

writing programs whose tetrating kept overloading the computers, segmentation faults as like fatal, choking on kernels.

The lawyer did not appreciate this either.

The lawyer was Mendel Gutshteyn, who had handled the estate of D-Unit. He was an émigré who had met D-Unit at shul, the Hasidics shul. He had read a kaddish at the shiva. He had a grody plateglass office on Geary Boulevard in the Richmond.

Tetration Inc., the name, was to represent our automaticity, to symbolize our selfgeneration. The way we would equalize ourselves with data and data with ourselves, by sprawling out in our search through the prolific irrational until we found recurrence, redundance. Cull signed and Qui signed and then we did too, but just before we slashed the date Gutshteyn stopped and reminded us. It was 06/10, not 06/06. We had lived in advance, we had been living ahead. We had miscalculated and missed our birthday.

It is unfortunate that you will have to transcribe this.

://

LONDON

Ohlone.

[How is that spelled?]

O H L O N E. Forget pixels, write it in blood.

[Ohlone.]

He was a madman, a full stack fucking madman, apologies. Make sure our voice is in the red. Boost, decompress. Ohlone, fuck, Ohlone. This is evidence, this is proof. We are not sure in what order to tell it.

[From beginning to end. Leave it to me to disentangle.]

But what we knew before or what we knew after?

[Doesn't matter to me. You're the one who thinks thought has an order.]

Indian. His name was Ohlone. His name was but was not Muwekma Ohlone. Mohlone. Moe. Any index of knowledge is also an index of ignorance, except that knowledge is finite and ignorance is not. The myths could fill a book, though no one would want to read it. They could be algyed. An algy for the most popular myths. For the myths mostly true. The myths mostly false. Legend and lore ranked by our or his need for their indemnity.

Goa was clear as like Portuguese to us. Goa State, Konkan Region, Western India. But we did not know the degree of poverty involved, the no electricity conditions, or that the water for shitting and pissing was downstream from the nonpotable drinkingwater for livestock, which was downstream from the bathingwater for humans, which was downstream from the also nonpotable drinkingwater for humans, which, all that, was just downstream from the water for shitting and pissing of the neighboring slum. We did not know how or even if to credit that then. The water that caused hep A and E. The insect vectors that bred fevers that blinded and deafened. It was either 1 OR 0, or 1 AND 0. True and also false.

But what we can verify is the motivation, the drive. We will never have that, not as like he did. We will never understand what exactly it took to beat that system, a system not even imaginable by an upper middleclass or upperupper middleclass Jewishish kid from middle Palo Alto. We were physics homework, papiermâché models of meiosis, mitosis, we set magnesium on fire. We were Math Masters of the Month. We blueribboned at the fairs. If we hacked it was for the thrill of it, the attention. We were overparented, underautonomized, überwestern.

Our major challenges in life were college acceptance, peer group acceptance, leveraging our abilities into a slot on the Forbes.com listicle, and incubating or at least simulating emotional intimacy. Though our life has had its positives and negatives, even a negative number has more magnitude than zero, and no one was more a zero than Ohlone.

He won India. Ohlone. He won the game of India and he did it by surviving, siblings stillborn and dead in childhood, parents survived only by him and their tapeworms. An orphan. He never mentioned his siblings or parents beyond confirming their deaths and their tapeworms. The orphanage put him to work. They had a type of half school, half factory, all slavery. This was not beachy Goa, not Arabian Sea Goa, but far inland slammed against the Ghats. He would escape to the resorts to scavenge. Holidays living off the wastes of hippie tourists.

A billion people in that country, millions more than any continent deserves, and annually sitting for the admission exam to the IIT, the Indian Institute of Technology, which was this Nehru scheme, there are something as like two, three hundred thousand students all the same age, of whom something as like only two, three thousand are finally accepted and that, even a humanities grad can figger a .01% acceptance rate. Harvard go fuck yourself, Yale go fuck yourself. Stanford, sit and spin. Factor into that equation the number of graduates that merit fully sponsored #H1B work visas for the States, no more than a few, the best few, 10% of the .01%, and even a humanitarian can stack up the odds.

.001% of the total.

Two people, three people, in each class.

Ohlone placed second overall the year of his exam. Or so Ohlone claimed. Do not request the year. He also claimed that his disappointment was due to his not having eaten anything that day and that the first place high score boy, Vikram somethingrajan or swami, who always had something to eat, whose cousin serviced the grading machines, had cheated.

He called all cheaters that, "fucking Vikrams, Joshua Cohen," "fuck that Vikram in his tokenhole, Joshua Cohen," he would always use our full name.

://

But again, we did not know any of this—we knew diddly. We were still trying to master the unicycle or sneaking into matinees of *The Terminator* or *Dune* and Ohlone who was only a decade or so older was wasting no time in achieving Valhalla.

But to understand Ohlone you have to understand—what is your fluency with remotes?

[I know how to use them. What you said about the germs.]

You know how they work?

[You zap like a beam. Not a laser but like a laser, a beam.]

So, Paz, this crap company out in Santa Cruz, does not exist anymore. Paz does not. Santa Cruz still exists, unfortunately. Ohlone, this was his first job in America. First serious adult engineering job, that is. It did not make him into who he became, it broke him into who he became. It was a disaster. White slavery but for an Indian.

Paz was set on creating the universal remote control, the universal remote, the unimote, the unmote. We can relate to this concept, admittedly, but some things that work in theory do not work in practice, as like some things that work in practice, do not work, for <i> in <seq>. Consummate control had been a dream ever since the exchange of wire for wirelessness. Ever since Torres-Quevedo lacking any military support retired his project of electromagnetically guiding missiles and bombs and applied himself instead to creating a robot to play chess with, and Tesla died alone in a cheap New York roominghouse after having lost the AC/DC battle to Edison and given up the war to deliver even current through the air.

Throughout the history of this technology, though, each device had to have its own controller. This was the Nazi standard for remote zeppelins. This was the American policy too, for remote submarines. Each device would follow its leader, bound to its controller by proprietary signals and waves. Call it the Führer principle, or just call it monotheism, or monogamy, under Eisenhower and the rise of the home electronics industry, this was law. Though even the most wealthy or most attuned 1940s and 50s consumer still had to make do with a cabled control that would tangle the pets and trip the children, all just to work the radio, predominantly.

And this was the situation through the 60s, until the market penetration of ultrasonics, or the control of TVs by audio frequencies too high for anthroperception. Then came our decade, the 70s, by the middle of which major advances had been made in infrareds, or the control of TVs by visual frequencies too low for anthroperception. This was the break, the redshift. Standards, as like the universe, only expanded.

Now you cannot think about online. In the midst of the 70s nobody thought the future was going to be this nothingness, this immateriality that stores everything and the software that links everyone to it and one another. At the time that was fiction, pulp sciencefiction to everyone but the tech insane and US army researchers. The rec pop was out shopping for fridges and freezers, dishwashers, TVs, and so it was booley that the hope for the next new advance would be for a device that connected them all, for that one single item of hardware that connected each average user to all of his or her domestic possessions.

Back then the future, the only future, was the remote. The remote, its hope, was the original online.

Around 1980, each home electronics brand went about developing its own remote, one remote that would control its every product, which was easy or relatively easy and even costeffective because all it meant was that all the controls for all its products would all be contained on a single slab. A remote would be divided into trays keyed by function: the TV controlled in row 1 with volume and channel, the videocassette recorder controlled in row 2 with Play, Stop, Rewind, Fast-Forward, in row 3 the button for the stereo cueing the synth muzak, in row 4 the switch lighting the sex candle—together comprising a multifunction remote no larger than unifunction remotes because everything was getting smaller and reduced except the options, the expectations.

But then the next innovation would be about, we are not sure, 82, 84, when the idea gradually became to make a remote that would work across brands, to make it not just compatible panbrand with regard to TV formats—NTSC (America, Mexico, Canada, Japan), and PAL (South America, Europe, China, half of Africa), even SECAM (Soviet Union, half of Africa)—and videocassette recorder formats—VHS, Betamax—but also to clunk it scalable to any and every product/standard conceivable. This was the goal of the independent remote designers, the mavs who inspired by the phenomenon of the corded telephone becoming cordless were trying to do the same for other devices, trying to get all the entertainment wires, all that wirelessness, to fit onto the tiniest number of the tiniest chips that could sit comfortably or not on the tiniest slab that could be manufactured at the tiniest cost so that it would not matter when it was lost, and it would be, between the cushions of the sofa.

We might stress that since their very inception cordless phones, by which we mean phones just without cord, not portable or mobile much beyond their base station chargers, had been compatible with most if not all telecom providers. The chips were the enablers, limited pellets of silicon that served an apparently unlimited range of functions, as like a single snackfood delivering the tastes of chocolate, vanilla, pork rind, popcorn, pretzel, and chip in every bitesized bite.

Ironic that this gadget, so simple to imagine, turned out to be so difficult to develop. It takes a whole lot of labor to keep the customer lazy, but the price of this was higher. Adjusting for inflation it was a height between the costs of launching satellites into orbit and laying the transatlantic cables. Both of which had worked. This, however, was all false starts. Snafus. Unfixes. Incompletes. Approx a dozen design firms going raped ape over plurassigns, simclicking. Approx 100 engineers, couched in advanced degrees, all dedicated to improving the couch experience—what a way to trash a life.

The most soulwasting project in the history of tech. The stupiest and most wasteful expenditure of money, time, intelligence, and energy project in tech history.

E. Ver.

://

Now initially the way the unimote business went was custom, bespoke, and so never very profitable. High end always begins high pricetag, given the R&D and STailing, the specs tailoring altering by device, with features always being taken in and out, given the manufacturing costs, and the vendor percentage, which can cut into margins considerably.

An A/V vendor with more overhead than sky has would sell a home entertainment system of mixed brands, the best of each brand because one does TVs better, and another does speakers better, to a decent earner with the spouse equivalent and the two point fives and the four floors mortgaged out in the parklands, ready to blow an unexpected bonus on better picture than from an ocean vista and better sound than from a splash in the waves. The vendor would then contract with one of the many indie design outfits staffed by disgruntled engineers hired away from home entertainment equipment manufacturers for their familiarity with the proprietary wireless frequencies used by different brands, who would cobble together a remote that conjoined the features of all the devices of all the brands, devoted.

But even if this could take weeks, for the designer and manufacturer, or a month, for the consumer, and even if again the costs were crazy all around and for the consumer could be equal to, for a full domestic theater remotegration, or remote integration, the expense of finally having that missing point five of a child, what was beyond all that, what left that dissuasion far and distant behind and rendered the devoted remote business not remotely remunerative or even feasible, was that its products always broke, even if just dropped on the carpet, or sat on by a sitter, or else from having been handled roughly by the post. But because this was Western suburban consumption in which everything including life itself was held to its warranty, the customer would call the A/V vendor and the A/V vendor would have to provide service, would have to jeep out and try fixing the remote on location, not because the post was untrustworthy but because it was both cheaper and kept the customer satisfied if the vendor did not have to package the remote off to the designers again, for them to repair it, or to the manufacturers again, for them to furnish a replacement.

Half the complaint calls that came in were from customers with units so broken the vendors were at a loss, but the other half were from customers just wondering about proper usage, and so alternate tollfree numbers were set up and operators were underpaid in India, every Indian who had never been accepted to engineering school following the troubleshooting/FAQ script—Does the unit have batteries? Does your unit have separate or joint On/Off buttons? If separate, are you pressing the correct one? Or both simultaneously? If joint, are you sure the device is not already Off? Or On? Are you operating the remote within 28 feet or 8.5 meters of the equipment you wish to control? Are you pointing the remote correctly, in the direction of the equipment you wish to control? The lines busy, the holds long, clients calling from their carphones in traffic, put on hold for longer than traffic, only to be disconnected, getting picked up on only to yell about how previous calls had been dropped.

But it is not our intention to survey the history of subcontinental customer service.

Not that the topic is ungermane or uncur.

Now, 1988. Out of Santa Cruz nowhere, Paz—this business that before this could not get arrested, that could not even get picked up on radar—announced they had a unimote ready to launch.

But whether they did or not, and they did not, this was marketing genius. The competition was saying, "Works with *any device*." Paz said, "Works with *every device*." The competition was saying, "Generic." Paz said, "Universal." Though as like any tech can tell you, there is nothing more frustrating, nothing more generic, than the universal.

Paz, having been late to the party, reinvented the party by spinning early and wizard. Advertising in the trades before they even had a prototype. Issuing a statement about production commencing on an unfinished product. Imposing internal discipline by external publicity. Setting deadlines by the press release. Nothing so motivates the engineers, who if they fail will not only be fired but will also have to explain to their families and friends how a device so intensely anticipated, as like it had always existed, never did.

A good artist ships. A great artist lies about shipping and no one notices. Paz even made a TV commercial, what better way to target their audience, which aired in select markets in central California. The remote used in the spot was a dummy, just a plastic prop, and so each TV in it had to be controlled by its own remote operated out of frame.

It was with this commercial that Paz shifted their businessmodel from hype to fraud: they announced they were accepting preorders.

Basically, the original recipe Paz product, we forget what it was called, was billed as like not just programmable but easily programmable, capable of storing up to 10 favorite channels, including cable, the commercials always mentioned, as like insinuating that it was more difficult to go changing to and from the channels of cable. But only a few tubers ever dialed in their orders and after nothing was delivered they called again demanding refunds the engineers paid out of their own salaries, that was how guilty they were and how stressed and tense with management and ownership becoming more involved with infomercializing baldness tonics, denture whiteners, and shammies.

At the time a cruft of Paz engineers used to hang out at Kompfs in Sunnyvale, exit 394 off the 101, a ragbone junkshop of spare parts and spare time the dimensions of a dumpster. They had hung there as like kids or had worked there as like kids, which was the same thing, hanging, working, acquiring their trade by mend and patch and now they were broken and had to be unwound again. They had lost all confidence in their project. In their methods even. Which were all reversals and backmods. In both their profession and selves.

To compensate for having failed to do a thing as like negligible and yet unnegligible as like making a remote that was universally programmable, to compensate for having wasted their talents on infrared transducers and ridiculous niggling 4 and 8 bit microprocessors, issues of command segregation, firmware retention—whether the uremote should be programmable manually, whether it could be made to autoscan specs just from aiming its interface whether at the target device or its branded remote, whether the uremote should include a coupling to a computer, and how that coupling could best be accomplished—and to buck one another up for having missed out on making a fortune with Microsoft, even IBM, or Hewlett-Packard, they chatted up Kompf, traded homophobic Kirk and Yoda jokes, "To boldly go where gone before no man has," and rummaged for versions of themselves among all the rusted desuete electronics in stock, only in order to modify them, to control them remotely.

Now this was entertainment. Taking an antique coil toaster and electric kettle and slapping sensors on them only so that toast and hot water might be made with a click from across the room. Just for the fun of it, or the consolation. But then, as like always happens, the hobby hypertrophied, with the engineers proceeding to attempt the same hack with nonelectric devices. Forget digital vs. analog. Mechanical. Machinal. To remotely control a pedal sewingmachine from Podolsk or a Kashmiri abacus required motorization.

There was a clock there, at Kompfs, something European, we would not know which make exactly. An archaic dusty clock that had stood throughout its grandparenthood until fashions changed and its coffin-size casement was axed for firewood and the mechanism with all its gears was taken out and pinned to the wall, and the current challenge was to somehow remotecontrol its winding, and the decision was made to use say the Zenith TV remote, we would not know exactly, with say the Power button the winder, the button that would control the motor, which would be powered, as like all remotes, by battery.

Whatever interval separated their meetings is a mystery to us, but when the Paz engineers returned, whenever they returned, they were shocked.

Not only had the clock been outfitted with a motor triggered by sensor that was controlled by the Power of the Zenith TV remote, but the Channel up and down buttons had been assigned to respectively speed and slow that motor to affect the winding rate, and the Volume up and down buttons had been assigned to trigger the strikers wrapped in scaled amounts of gauze, effectually raising and lowering the volume of the chimes. Finally, ingeniously, the Mute button did not mute the chimes, but engaged the wound power of the clock to recharge the 9 volt or lithium cells, and so energy was conserved. Though not in the engineering.

The Paz engineers, who had assumed this clock mod would take days or even weeks, asked Kompf who was responsible and were answered the guy who had been browsing in the back while they had been discussing the challenge.

None of them had registered his presence and Kompf though this is not surprising could not even remember his name, could only describe him against type. An Indopak, but unshaven, untucked, and maloccluded as like he was grinning about it, who would drop by not infrequently to source parts and talk failures and deternatives.

Kompf, whose nationality was a German accent though we have never been able to decide if he was also a Jew, was universally recognized at least on the newsgroup he moderated, genysym.grimoire, as like the expert authority on defunct tech, and discredited alternative energies. He blogged treatises on the wunderwaffen and the remotecontrolled but not unmanned kamikaze vehicles. On orgone, the power generated by the orgasm. Odic force, the power generated by the will of Norse gods. Shakti, Prana. This guy the engineers were cur about was, apparently, the best informed about such and other hermetic matters that Kompf had ever met, offline. Do not think we would know anything about Tesla on our own, do not think we would know whether Torres-Quevedo was one person or two people. One.

The Paz engineers asked how to get in touch with the guy and Kompf said the guy had told him that either he had just turned down a job or been turned down for a job at Raytheon. The engineers asked around but nobody at Raytheon would admit to not being able to differentiate among their myriad subcontinentals, and in that viro, the engineer hab, for someone capable of such leisure robotics to be essentially anonymous was so preposterous that the Pazzers suspected that the guy they were after did not exist and that Kompf was just pranking them, or involving them in some elaborate scavenger hunt whose rules they did not understand.

But then one night or we are just imagining night one of the engineers, a Gregory Rundle L E or Rundel E L, who before Paz had worked at Samsung and after Paz would work at Samsung but demotedly, got a call from Kompf, at the office or home the same, "Your guy just came and went all flustered, requesting a recommendation letter."

Apparently Kompf had asked what it was for but the guy said nothing beyond, "Just a letter of reference in re: evident engineering prowess and loyalty to America." Kompf asked for his name and the guy answered he would fill that in himself and gave an address out in the 95030s that was certainly not residential. Other fusses. The letter had to come in two copies: To Whom It May Concern, and To the Honorable James A. Baker III, US Secretary of State.

Kompf typed up the letters chockfull they had to have been of praise but also conjecture.

Greg Rund EL or LE picked them up in their unsealed envelopes and took them to the address, but having brought no other offering was made to surrender the bag of macaroons he was snacking on along with a lock of his receding hair to whatever gods they had then at that Hindu mandir in Milpitas.

The Indian, who prayed there daily, was propitiated.

He was unemployed and his visa was expiring, he explained to Greg. He was amassing testimonials for his deportation proceedings in the event he was unable to find a job.

Greg then offered him a job. The interview was strictly a formality, except for the negotiation of terms, including but this might be baseless the stipulation that half his salary be transferred, concurrent with paycheck issuance, directly to the orphanage that had raised him. We do not think that orphanage ever existed. But as like with tax law, it is for others to know.

Health benefits were exercised immediately, prescriptions were obtained and cortisone shots for carpal tunnel.

He was made Associate VP of Engineering for a business that had eight other Associate VPs of Engineering.

Paz, 1989.

://

But this was beyond even him: a remote that could be programmed by purchaser alone, a remote intended to be friendly enough so that even a mentally rectarded pet child could instruct it in less than 12, 10, 8—in less than 6 steps per gadget in the widest variety of TV and VCR functionality, in the configurations of stereos and surround sounds.

It was the very breadth of that variety that inspired what we later called the Law of Moe, which states that if universality were ever possible in space and so in time, life would become utterly impossible for everyone but the patentholder.

Though Moe had other, related, formulations: "Not even the globe is global, not even the galaxy is universal, Joshua Cohen."

Also: "The longer the search, the wider the find, Joshua Cohen."

In each interim between his team of Pazzers designing a mod feature and testing it out, as like a Power button that turned On and Off every product made by four brands, 8 or 16 or 256 new products would be brought to market, and another consortium of bargain brands from Japan would establish another competing remote lab to coadunate proprietary specs. The Pazzers had to match each progressive advance, but even if the success rates were equal, the operations were not, and if the Pazzers were adding, the Japbrands were multiplying, and if the Pazzers were multiplying, the Japbrands were exponentiating, and this situation of a small team of good scrappy engineers vs. a big evil capitalist universe was not a fictional media property as like a ninja telenovela available on the equipment the engineers were attempting to control, but was instead real and actual and hopeless, and no intenser degree of application or polytheistic divine intervention would have helped them, or anyone, keep up.

Innovation does not wait for standards, it sets them. To innovate is to be incompatible. But business was bad. Then business was übervikram.

By 1990 Moe had clunked a multiverse of universal demos, a semiversal for audio, a hemiversal for video, a demiversal for TV, meaning that each worked on approx 50% of each product, crossmodel and panbrand, half that percentage programmed by scanning, the other half by manual programming so serious as like to require a code glossary of function assigns grouped by model and brand that was illegal for Paz to have even compiled let alone to publish and monetize.

There was a Sharp remote with a timer mode, which allowed users to set the VCR recording of future TV shows, a JVC remote with an edit mode, which allowed users to edit recordings, both of which just a gen later would be claimed by and would enrich everyone but their inventor, and also a crossbreed Panasonic/Magnavox remote with the commsense function, which sensed commercials by their distinctive mixrates, turned channels to another show, and returned to the original show only once its commercials were over. Ultimately, Moe invented, he would always claim, or he only modified, he would never claim, 108 remotes, 108 versions of what was supposed to have been a single remote. An Amote. We just remembered what it was called, the Paz A M O T E, and some said "ah mote" and others said "ay mote," and 108 is just a Hindu euphemism for "many," or "much," 108 the sum of the Upanishads, the amount of gopi or cowherds of unconditional love, the number of the beads of the mala, so the breaths of the japa, the names of each ceaseless god.

Moe needed that practice, which is Buddhist too, that counting, that numerical mantra. He needed a break. Even another job would have been a break. He was leveled. Everyone else was on permanent vacation. Always off, working remotely, taking meetings in Porsches in the middle of carwashes. Out in back of the office, his parkingspot had been taken, the entire lot was taken by a trailer that quarantined a furtive clan of Indonesian pribumi assigned to different projects. No windows. His paychecks came from Spazz, and then from Spazz Telecommunications, and with each the signature changed. We are not sure if the orphanage got its share. We are not sure in general about the orphanage. New managers were brought in and they were always on the phone. With new ownership. With parole officers.

Rund, Greg, who had returned to Samsung, got Moe a Samsung offer, generous. Other coworkers who had quit tried luring him to Canon,

Nikon, Sony, and offered him equity in GPS tritels that would be so clovered by the millennium that even the receptionists would be able to platinize their lawnmowers. But Moe had not come to America just to work for Korea. Or to give suburban paleface parents driving directions between stripmalls.

Fall 1990, Moe was the sole engineer still assigned to the Amote. His manager was the son or nephew of new owner/CEO Nicodemo Merlino, who was never in the office, but then neither was the nephew or son.

Except the night before Christmas Eve, they both burst in, sweating, rushing through and clutching at cabinets and leaving a papertrail out to the lot, too panicked to notice their last legitimate employee, or so Moe would later hope.

The FBI, we are fairly sure it was the FBI that arrested the Merlinos burning files in a trashcan atop the one remaining handicapped space with enough accelerants as like diesel fuel and insecticides in the trunks of their Mercedii to torch the rest of their workplace too. All the Indonesians were taken into custody. All the descrambling illegal cableboxes they had been assembling in the trailer were seized. The Merlinos were accused of trafficking, were already out on bail posted by the virtually unindictable Emmanuel Figlia, San Jose mafia, by the time Moe finally emerged from hiding.

He with a handful of his remotype Amoti had squatted secret above his cubicle in a corner of the dropceiling, its panel browned from leaky HVAC.

://

PARIS

Now we are about, 1997. Skip ahead. Tetration was through with academia, or else academia was through with Tetration, our domain needed hosting and everything, as like our posture, needed support. Based on reviews, our own reviews, we chose Grupo Escudo, Santa Clara. This was how it went before we groundbroke on our own DCents. Datacenters.

We took their least expensive barbedwire enclosure and stuffed it with our production serverack, the Ultra and Pentium IIs, a cruft of external driveage. Basically it was a maximum security humane society in heat. Locks were not provided. Next on one side was the cage for eBay, next on the other the cage for Hotmail, all of us were still just unprofitable toddlers in hefty mental diapers, but only we were not growing to scale.

That was why, in fugly winter, Cull and Qui were in Las Vegas for the consumer electronics show. The CESS. The notion was to go and license our algy, or corner someone to buy it flatout. Preferably one of the portal boys, some pitboss of the winners circle. We would have granted sublicensable transferable interminably renewable rights in every territory, we would have swallowed any nuggety lump sum. Our combined assets were then approx $8K: $4K from Professor Winhrad as like to say a faretheewell from Stanford, the rest what was left of the Diatessaron profits, along with the Christmas windfalls, the $800 courtesy of the de Groeve parents, still less, always less, than the $60 the O'Quinn parents had scraped.

We had decided not to go along out of thrift, or so we had told Cull and Qui, but the truth was that perfecting our algy had to take precedence over any bachelor industry spree spent parsing the activities of Datum Millennium from the activities of Millennium Data, Datamex, Datamax, Datatec, Datatek, Datatron, Datatronic, Datary, Dataria, whichever it was that had paid women to stalk the tradeshow floor wrapped head to foot as like mummy zombies in wires urging attendees, on average 92.4% men, to Go Wireless, and then stripping down to nipples, no pubes.

It was in Vegas, baby, that Cull and Qui met with Microsoft, Netscape, OmniWeb, Mozilla, Captoraptor, Peruser, and Moe, a guy whose name had not always been Muwekma Ohlone.

He had a crappy berth beyond reception, where even the newest Motorola demophones had no service. Where typically the coordinators stuck lunatics and hobos. Not businessmen. We have been there since at least once and this was what we encountered.

Sad fat bald Kompfy dinkaround tinkerers peddling their chemtrail detectors, subaqueous treasure wands. Redates, a company specializing in putting the innards of newer and better products into the skins of older and worser products, and in making the innards and skins compatible. They rotarized touchtones, and remediated a VHS cassette with a lid that lifted not to tape but to a DVD player, the customer inserted the disc, depressed the lid, inserted the cassette into the VCR, everything converted. Marketed to senior centers, retirement communities. E-fterlife, a company marketing a gravemarker embedded with a screen, which looped clips with optional audio from the life of the departed. A keyboard below the screen let visitors type msgs, for public display or privately protected by PIN.

A somber zone. Basically a cemetery.

Moe had not been told to bring his own décor, or else the coordinators were fresh out of foldingtables. No chair. Just a poncho laid on the floor as like in a silk road Levantine antique and spice bazaar. Moe sat on the poncho and presented. A bulky creditcard he was hoping Visa/Mastercard would pick up with a graphic window that showed the balance owed on the account. It was the same size as like the beeper he was flogging, which featured a bloaty red button for 911.

Another of his offerings had some elegance, some grace. It was an attempt to redress the greatest undiscussed blight of globalization, namely that not all computers around the world can recognize or even detect all attached devices. An auxiliary keyboard made in Russia or Ukraine and so completely in Cyrillics might not be compatible with a Taiwanese PC clone whose OS was a pirated Farsi edition of Windows 95. To remedy this, Moe had designed a box, a small white apparatus cubed as like a craps die at bottom, rounded as like a roulette pill at top, to dongle between whatever periphs and plugnplays, Chilean lasergun, Brazilian joypaddle, and the computer itself, and that would render the devices usable on it.

Software configs and coalescing manufacturing parameters would make all this hardware obsolete by 1999, but still it was admirable. Few devices get even a year between usable and admirable.

But the one ware Moe had brought to the show that alone entitled him to Valhalla was just a proposal, and is fundamentally too involved to explain to a rec, given that even for a tech, even now, it is still too unicorn dreamy. Especially given the physics. Engineers tend to change their arch levels and switch their packets if ever confronted by timewarps and wormholes. The only way they can face the quantum is with the munchies.

Basically our lives are not reversible and yet physics is, the laws of physics holding true whether time moves forward, as like we perceive it to move, or backward, as like can only be observed through equation. The only exception to this reversibility is courtesy of mechanics, thermodynamics. Ice can be turned to water, which can be turned to gas, but every change of state requires a transfer of energy. The energy that does not or cannot effect each change is dispersed. But where and when is the problem. Or else it is lost. But energy cannot be lost is the problem. The solution to both is entropy.

Yawn.

FYI: Yawning, as like laughing and crying, is only socially contagious.

Now physical entropy is the measurement of that available but unutilized energy. If with more time comes more change, and if with more change comes more entropy, it follows that entropy is perpetually increasing. Booley. This makes entropy a statistical property. Measuring change and waste, change and scatter. Information accrues with each transaction, because each transaction itself becomes information. Order increases but only as like disorder. The universe tends toward chaos.

Computationally, statistical entropy can be reduced with an increase in parity, the more input equals output, the more output equals input. In principle every operation can be done and undone, executed and unexecuted, with the same booley, the same algys, circuits and gates, nothing different regardless of direction.

Physically, though, is the difference. Computers work on electricity, on battery. Each bit processed dissipates energy, kT In 2. Even just trashing a .doc creates corresponding entropy or drag somewhere or somewhen on the system.

That was what Moe was up against. His pig flying to the end of the rainbow goal was reversibility, specifically to perfect a type of inverter gate that allowed any operation passing forward through it to pass backward again, as like a one lane but two way freeway, along with the charge recovery circuits that would serve as like a tollbooth but a freeway tollbooth that instead of charging the input to go through, converted it to output, to charge, turned it around as like input again. To put it more directly, he was trying for a computer capable of turning all the work that was ever done on it, as like typing, or just clicking around online, into energy, with 1:1 transmission, without any entropy, no loss. To put it most directly, he was trying for a totally reversible computing, to be powered not merely with human effort, but with the absolute minimum of human effort, solely by its processing.

Reversibility, an Eastern conceit.

Imagine two bows that share a single string that can shoot a single arrow headed and fletched at both ends in two opposite directions at equal speed simultaneously. Imagine an archer who thrives entirely off his aim, and who can sustain himself physically by aiming forever, but who with the gradual release of his grip will gradually die.

To be clear, all this is possible only on paper or modeled on a computer charged or socked into an outlet. But in life, this might only be possible in Vegas. Moe was proposing a new paradigm of DCent, a facility not as like the one we were renting but open, as like to balance with access the way all other systems were, are still, autarkically closed. It would be a place full of fully reversible processors, routers, a local server, drives, operating all by themselves. A business of, by, and for computing, and the most anyone would have to do would be to make a contribution. This was conservation, this was ecology, more. This was a second nature requiring a god and not a man. The hope itself was selfsufficient.

He would call this facility the Tabernacle of Isentropic Synergy, or the Dedicated Hub Tabernacle of Collaborative Coopteration. Which, no doubt, is guano, batshit crazy, but also as like Stockholm or Oslo material, the ambition level that gets a man inducted into Boulder, Colorado, the ultimate frisbee hall of fame.

The presentation that Moe had taped to the floor around his poncho explained that some California Indian archive, but Indian as like Native American and not Indian Indian, some repository of historical manuscripts concerning indigenous life in California, did not have the funds to digitize itself, and the state would not help, the state was going broke too. His plan was to raise enough capital to pay the elderly or handicapped along with any cur volunteers to digitize its documents, its reams of scholarly paleography, notes on diet, trapping practices, fornication customs, birth and death folkways, and tralatitions of oral religious lore, for input into the computers of his Tabernacle, which would proceed to sort and kind them, to analyze them and other tribal and municipal records to enable any future research, though the research was not the point, the point was that all of this processing would generate not just enough electricity to power the Tabernacle but also to output heat and light, which would be distributed at no cost to the descendants of the archived on local reservations, and then to illegal Mexicans and the Afromerican poors, ultimately to everyone, globally.

Moe already had a location scouted out in San Mateo, as like an offisite scanning office, while for the inaugural Tabernacle itself he was set on one of the populous ancestral counties, either Sonoma or Mendocino, so as like to maintain maximum proximity and so transmission fidelity between the natives, who would upload their cultures themselves, and the downloadable power their cultures would generate. We will conclude only by noting that with classic Moe counterintuity the cardboard model of the Tabernacle that held down the hem of his poncho was not in any indigenous reed and grass wikiup style but was apparently an adobe or pueblo, and beyond that the little tiny people on the cardboard sidewalk whose purpose it was to humanistically scale the rendering were just green plastic soldiers as like toys.

It was Qui who told us none of this then, in his call to Unit 26 not from the room he had with Cull at the Desert Inn but from the Bellagio. We had been waiting for a report on their summit with AOL, waiting to be told we were being procured, and so it was serling that the first figure out of his mouth was not the $12 million we expected.

Serling. Rod. *Twilight Zone*. Strange.

Instead, Qui explained, first they had met a guy, his name was Ohlone, then they had grilled cheese sandwiches for lunch, then AOL was not offering because it was deving its own search, Microsoft was doing this, Netscape was doing that, and Yahoo. Then they had dinner, which was grilled cheese again and soupflavored soup.

After which this Ohlone guy just happened to bump into Cull again in the sportsbook at the Bellagio. Cull had just gotten on line, not online, but in a cloggy human queue. He was waiting to put his name down for a nonsmoking table, but this Ohlone kept a seat by the VIP screens, Qui said, Cull said, and was just headed over to lay down a bet. A major race was slated next. Moe had handicapped all the relative weight calculations by jockey, means of speed at distance weighted by recency on turf and dirt. There was some tendonitis afflicting the favorite being covered up, and then he mentioned something about an unfamiliar strain of alfalfa in the paddocks. He had reduced the semiofficial odds from 37.9:1 to 16.2:1. Cull basically figgered he had to trust an Indian about a horse, and so inquired what stakes the guy was in for and then doubled them, handed over all his cash to be wagered for him, parimutuel.

All that after just a chance meeting and one lunch Guinness and two bottles of Zinfandel with dinner.

Qui explained that while Cull had been gambling he had been in the toilet. Not doing number one. Number two. He had not been fast, but he was at least faster than Filly Up, who finished sixth. Of 10. Qui found Cull tangling with the rope dividers between the smoking and non sections. The Indian had never come back. Cull would not tell Qui how much he lost. But then Qui insisted, and Cull obliged him, though he would not tell us how much. But then we insisted. It was more than gas money. More as like horse or used Humvee money.

"But only $2468 of it was from the common account," Qui said.

"We told you not to gamble with money from common," we said. "And the rest was from what?"

"Cull and I took in $220 in stud."

"Which you also lost?"

"This Ohlone dude is doing fascinating shit with circuit adiabatics."

"And with adiabatic prostitutes he is paying with our money, certainly."

"The phone just told me to insert another quarter," a pause for him to pat himself down. "No more quarters."

"No more drinking," we said.

Just before the call was severed he said, "All beverages are complimentary."

://

The Vegas news had interrupted us while crunching solitary in Unit 26 in front of a terminal in front of an algyshell, which is a programming interface, just window and cursor. Lines of language lined, a Cullion lines of code, a Quinnion lines of code, which we had been purging of breakless switches, ampersandless arguments, (is) instead of (==), (_dict_) instead of (_slots_). But now all our code that had been right was suddenly wrong. Which left only our code that had been wrong as like right, though what there was of it was just dropped colons and closed bracketing omissions, unfindable. The conditionals that operated, and the conditionals we had implemented to obscure the operations, seemed interchangeable to us, and then even the spaces that gaped between the characters and the characters themselves seemed interchangeable, because no space is ever blank, so everything is flawed.

We had to sit down though we were already sitting and so we just got up and moved to the next terminal. Its comp was hibernating, suspended. The glass of it was motey. Then the glass had our face, as like we were touchlessly communing with it, and then calming to its mode. Outwardly neutral. But inwardly still volatile and cycling.

find (Indian)

find ($$$$)

if (amount of $$$$ Indian has left < amount of $$$$ that was ours)

then# beat him down

else (he can bring us our $$$$ within start=datetime end=datetime with interest compounded daily for range at rate_float)

else (we would derive > satisfaction from having him beaten to death). Let The Friends of the Trapezzi Sisters bury his corpse under some soddy landscaping job outside some McMansion in Montara.

We decided, this Indian would be the victim of the first nonsimulated living breathing execution of our algy.

But all we had to go on was the name. Not even its spelling, just phonetically.

We took the comp out of hibernation and tetrated variations: "A Loan," "Aloan," "A Lone," "Alone."

Just imagine what results were returned to us. But then add "Indian."

Qui and Cull returned from Vegas. But we had no use for their apologies or tears or promises of payback or all the swag souvenirs they brought us of Engadge tshirts and Isruptious hats and Acer tshirts and hats and drinkcozies and Compaq tshirts and hats and drinkcozies and flyswatters and the Continental Airlines plastic wings pin designating us as like Captain.

All we had use for were the data.

We wanted to know whether anyone had found any email or phone for this Elone or Ilone before we had. We wanted to know whether the Vegas cops had outstripped our algy.

But Qui and Cull had never even called the cops, and so our algy was spared.

Then we called CESS, the electronics show organizers. But they would not relay exhibitor info over the phone and suggested we consult the official commemorative catalog. But we already had. We had an unlisted Indian situation.

We clenched, we had been waiting to clench. Everything Cull and Qui were telling us was a repetition. Either the Indian was this master who absently mixed up his horses, or grifted, or both. He made interactive creditcards. He made crappy dongles. But he was also working on a vanguard type of total computing in which what went in and what went out were sustainably equilibrated. Reversibility in computing was as like letting a bet ride through every race without ever winning or losing but also without paying a vig. As like a sex act between two bodies that never aged and whose minds were equipped with the Undo/Redo functions.

Cull and Qui hit the showers. We went back to getting aggro about the inprogress site of the Bureau of Indian Affairs whose only unbroken link on its linkpage was to a url broker trying to sell virtual reservations to every tribe, apache to zuni.com. We decamped for the unmoderated engineer hunting grounds, WbStrZ.org, Netikit.org, @omic@araxy, 73h

.wh157l3bl0w3r. We read about nodes and electrodes, capacitive coupling, bistability.

We posted msgs with handles as like ISOLone and VegaSageV with offers to hire an engineer for a reversible experiment that made a weeny affirmative action claim about especially welcoming applications from Native Americans. Just by reading and msging we were feeling proximal already, if not linguistically or conceptually proximal, then mystically, religiously, as like in searching for him we were feeling that tingle of being searched for ourselves.

Super Sal woke us up at the terminal by saying, "The Chief is on Line 2."

We took the call, assuming we had been preemptively found, but then Line 2 introduced itself as like, "This is only the acting chief of the council of business elders." He was just returning the voicemail we had left after tetrating "Indian+O'Lune" had brought us to the tribal site of the Ohlone, or to be politically PC the Muwekma Ohlone, descendants of the original inhabitants of the Bay, since dispossessed, halfassedly genocided.

But none of the members of the Ohlone tribe were called Ohlone, the chief said. Or they all were called Ohlone. They were the Costeños, "coastal people," to the Spanish. The Ohlone, "people of the west," to the Miwok. The Muwekma, "people of the Miwok," to themselves. People of the Miwok, people of the west. Western Miwok. Überwesterners.

The chief told us we were eligible for a lowprice genetic test that might establish our membership in up to 18 federally recognized tribes. Or our money back. And our money back. Reparations might be attainable.

Finally, a TendR VC cur about our having applied for and received US Patent 5835905B, "Method for relevance prediction," rang back with two asks:

Firstly, would we explain the parallelism formulas governing Fig. 4D? And secondly, would we explain why we were getting so publicly inquisitive about this character Ohlone?

We answered that our partners had met him in Vegas and got cur about him but never got his contact, and the VC said, "Next time write an algy that can, with all respect, call bullshit. Anyway, Muwekma Ohlone. That is an alias. Legally his name is Vishnu Vaidya."

Our terms, then, became clarified.

"He tried to get us involved in a scheme for invertible computing," the VC said and we said, "Reversible."

The VC then reminisced about a snazzy anorak he used to own, lined on one side in cotton, for the theater, the other in water repellent Tyvek, for hiking home.

"He is Indian?" we said.

"With a dot," the VC said. "Not a feather."

"Vaidya?" we said.

"But he came to us with that bullshit inversible scheme calling himself Vishnu Fernandes."

"With a z?"

"Fernandes with an s," the VC said. "But then how the fuck would a dot Indian get that name?"

"From Portugal."

"You can say that again."

"From Portugal."

Then the VC told us all that montage about the remotes and the mafia, backtracking, and how the Vishnu identity had been disclosed during diligence on his reversible papers, backtracking. "The suspicion," the VC said, "was that he stopped being Vishnu because of all that cablebox fraud and being foreign especially was trying to not get arrested."

We thanked him and he said, "No prob, just keep our name out of it."

But we told him we did not understand why and he said, "If you hire him, you can forget about our support."

We hung up.

The VC. His name was Bretton Cleaver.

We tetrated again using "Vishnu Vaidya," and appended "the Bay," because back then to trim by coordinate consilience or zipcode was a Vedic fantasy.

The results stack came back paltry.

One result was a gambling site, one comment below many and most of them gibber, "nice turnout last time. chuck u left yr asthma inhaler will bring," left by the uname Vishuponafern at the bottom of a thread called "Poker In The Rear."

The READ THIS FIRST post advised that getting in on a game was contingent on responding correctly to a riddle: "Four men sit around playing blackjack. The first man gets up, leaves, and lives. The second man gets up, leaves, and lives. The third man gets up, leaves, and lives. The fourth man gets up, leaves, and expires. Explain without accusing anyone of homicide."

The last line of the riddle was hyperlinked to a moderator/admin email, and we clicked it and replied: "They were playing on an airplane to determine who got the last three parachutes, or on a boat to determine who got the last three lifejackets, or else the guy with the lowest or busted hand had a brain aneurysm," and the moderator responded immediately with an invitation.

At the Wells Fargo we withdrew the sub $6K still in the account without telling Cull or Qui, went out searching the way our ancestors searched, with the only other cards we ever had, with our name on them and the title embossed, Founder, Tetration.

The game was held outside Portola, on a foreclosed duderanch this Amazon lady from Amazon.com had bought just to flip, an egregious driveway to a villa, cardtable and saddlechairs the only furnishings. Already we were down in the hole thanks the taxi.

We went with the Fresca, left the other players to their single malt doubles. Let them read us or try to.

Vishnu Vaidya, Vishnu Fernandes, Muwekma Ohlone—Moe—he came in late, a groundless current bursting from this just heinous flasher trenchcoat. His teeth were all caried crowded funk mesiodental, his tongue as like a pinkslip splotched white.

He stunk, reeked to tell the truth foul.

The game was Texas hold em, 2/4 no limit, which dealt from the top suggests the obfuscation at stake because to win most of time is to fold em. We were better than most but worse than him, tight.

Moe had half the table buying in seconds by the second full deal rotation, and immediately post antemeridian the other half just left.

By last Fresca it was just us and a scruffy cruft of simoleoned emotionals, who played not too strong not too weak, but unpredictably predictably reckless. The type to wait out, let them cope, come senses or tantrum.

But Moe did not wait, shuffling a pocket pair as like a toolbar. He did not even take off the trench.

His play had been tame wild until it suddenly became wild tame, without bluff, which was the bluff, but not. Basically any bid to define strategy yielded tactics, any attempt to refine his decisions into levels or stages, degrees of the mind, was the biggest mistake an opponent could make. Rather the biggest mistake after not cashing out or not being Moe himself. Or boozing between pots. Moe might have been Hindu but for poker he had Buddha face. He bet low on big hands either because they were not big enough or just to keep us or him still cur. He went all in 44 times. He was little blind holding A-J just anteing up until the J-6-4 flop had him going in as like gangbusters, which left only this dotcomster comedian still in the game miraculously seeing not raising, the turn was 10, which meant a straight or flush could still be in the cards because both the J and 10 were of some manly finance suit, some clubs or spades flushed straight away in an ace cascade and fuck you, Yahoo from Yahoo.com, $8K for an ace high on the river two pair.

Moe quit approx $10K up at the end of the night that was morning, while we had managed, just, to make exactly $3.379K, though that was nothing because he still had not acknowledged—you will not laugh? Promise?

He still had not acknowledged us.

Our self.

Not until we were both outside amid spring 97.

Moe popped his collar. "So we are square?"

We said, "The name is Tetration."

"We are money square, that is my meaning. Tell your Tetration bros—I have lent back to you what I have borrowed from them."

We stopped our slog through the driveway clay and dung hung in the air. "You think you let us win in there?"

"I think I let you win a profit."

"What about the DAS Capital associate or that Gaymer GM who folded on queens over eights?"

"It was queens over nines."

"Eights or nines."

He poked his ignition key between our ribs and said, "What about we settle this in Los Angeles, Joshua Cohen?"

://

The best thing about search is you always find what you want. The worst thing about search is you never find what you do not want. As like Los Angeles, as like a drive to Los Angeles. But we were helpless. We were in a dustbrown dump of a soccer parent van with a fluorescent red bindi decal on the hood and a back bay lending library of leaflets and pamphlets as like "Cellphone Brain Tumors Exposed!" and "Beware the Monoculture: the PC virus and the viruses that can bring down the system!" A lot stub from Vegas was wedged between spring coils in a gash in the upholstery. The talkradio was tuned to Republican. Moe drove not toward I5 but stayed on the 101. He chainsmoked a figment cigarette, just bringing fingers to lips and pinching the lips and breathing in, breathing out, windows fogging. It was dewy and cold and he could not figger the defroster. We will repeat that. He was a trained genius engineer who could not figger the defroster, so he rolled down his window to the breezes, route scenics.

He knew everything about us, knew everything about Tetration. He referred to Cull and Qui as like our "bros," and to us as like his "rakhi bro." Everyone at the game had called him Moe, and that was the only name he ever mentioned having. Moe picked among his toothcrowd with our businesscard.

His driving was not erratic if we followed his thoughts, because his driving followed his thoughts and veered and passed. Cut off. He was telling us about India, which had invented online. The Vedas, the Upanishads. He rehashed the Ramayana, stalled, the Mahabharata, stalled. Rather, he said, Hinduism had invented the cosmology that had been plagiarized online. The net, the web, just a void and in the void a wilderness, a jungle of hardware sustaining a diversity of software, of sites, of all out of order pages, a pantheon to be selectively engaged, an experience special to each user. Each click was a dedicated worship, an act of mad propitiation that hazarded destruction.

Altogether, never altogether, online comprised a religion of bespoke blue plural gods that could also be goddesses that could also be customized in any alternative to gender and blueness, not a religion but a flux of cults, temporary sects, routing allegiances, provider alliances. The user as like the Hindu can ping whatever divinity is best convenient for whatever purpose, can ping the deity of the specific moment or location, or the one pertinized to a particular task, without any core theology, without any central control, anything goes.

What guaranteed this access was search. No one understood search as like an Indian.

We stopped at a tarpit outside Paso Robles and Moe got out and pumped gas and went into the conmart and returned with a carton of menthol cigarettes, buckled up, then unbuckled and conmarted again and returned with a tank of gin in plastic. He put his incisors to the carton, a pack, bit a menthol and struck a strike anywhere match anywhere, breathed in and out and swore he had quit. He uncapped the gin to wash down two whitepink pills whose pharmcalls we noted, M575, do the detectivework, go sleuth it. When he swallowed it was with the Gayatri, that mantra that clears the astral nerve tubes. We have no clue how to drive. We have never had a license.

We got into LA around 18:00 and went to get some dinner. After our steaks he gave us a pill. We took another after our sundae. The steaks were gushing in that rare to raw style that homophobe kitchens hash out to men on dates who request medium. The icecream was brownbutter lardon nut brittle berry. We had never eaten as like that in our lives, but had no guilt.

Though we had two, but only one each, martinis. Because Moe was taking us along to his regular game, and we had to stay upright to knock it over.

"You go in and just ask the reception for Rosebud," Moe said, "who will tell you the room. Come in calm and be yourself. Sit how you are told to sit and get your cash out. Pretend you might have met them all before but you cannot remember. Pretend with me just the same."

The waiter offered cappuccino, espresso, and Moe said, "You are awake enough?"

We said, "Are you asking us or just the waiter?"

Moe said, "You are awake enough. Check, please."

Modafinil retails as like Provigil in the States, but the whitepinks we had taken were some Canadian version, Alertec. A eugeroic, a nootropic, which IT twerks and the Green Berets prefer to amphetamine and methylphenidate because it is nonaddictive.

Moe insisted on paying for dinner, as like he had paid for the gas, and we got back into the van and drove and stopped and he lit up a menthol for us from the dash.

"That mansion," he said, and through the smirched windshield was a mansion. "You will get out here at the Liquor Locker and walk slow down Sunset, so I will have time to park and go in before you. We do not know each other. Remember."

"But that is not a lie," we said and got out on the street.

Then Moe leaned over and unrolled the window. "Trust me," he said. "I always know a rakhi bro. I can sense our wheels turning back through the samsara, Joshua Cohen."

He waved all the honking cars around him and said to us, "But if they ask, only if they ask, tell them you are the guy who runs the game out in Venice Beach."

Moe crept into the lane and we went on slow for blocks, doing the base vs. adjusted probabilities for holding an 8/8. Preflop against one player was 2%, 2.9%, and by increasing by one player per block we had mentally calculated for up to six, a situation in which there was a 16%, 16.3% chance that one of them had a larger pair.

Then we spit our autograph onto the sidewalk and crossed the street and up the drive. We had been prepared for everything except the Chateau Marmont.

We dropped Rosebud and were shown down speedbump carpet halls and opened a door to the celebrity 1990s. We are not sure we should be more specific.

But suffice to say someone as like Keanu was in the room, someone as like Johnny Depp, a Damon and an Affleck, the wrong Wahlberg, who could have been wasted from a protracted wager sessh or just from more of better drugs than we had.

The one who was Affleck or Damon was yelling at the one he was not for leaving the door unlocked, while the other was yelling that the last to leave the room had been the butler. The Wahlberg was approaching as like to bounce us out, but we were recognized.

Moe recognized—"You are that guy," he said. "We met him out in Brentwood, Johnny?"

Then Depp claimed we were familiar.

"Not Brentwood," we said. "You came to our Venice game."

With that Damon and Affleck relaxed and put their arms around us but also they were frisking us and the Wahlberg said, "This guy is famous?"

Keanu said, "For losing."

Seats were rearranged to give us next hand first position, or not rearranged because the only seat available was the bed and so the table was nudged in our direction. Action heroes nudged it, and put us in the chips. We were dealt and folded and lost to establish credibility at first. But then we were betting middlingly, after tipping our hands to Moe using chipstacks to signal our facecards. Ten of $10 whites a jack, ten of $20 reds a queen, ten of $100 blacks a king, nine of the white or black an ace just to miff it, cutting a red stack for a warning sign if his raising verged on patterny. A crude system but comptrasted with manual collusion as like finger taps, effective.

Pathogenic duvet, walls venereal with mold, polluted cash, but we never washed, we never even had the urge to wash. No bend or crease or soil would spoil our royalty. The bartender was knocking and Keanu was trying to undo the chain with his mind alone until he folded and the Wahlberg helped carry in the bar trolley. Moe kept ordering gin and tonics but we held with martinis despite the bowtied guy repeatedly belaboring our options up or down and dry or wet, dirty with a twist, and smirking because we ordered them with vodka.

We had to get drunk enough so that our loss was convincing, but not too drunk so that we betrayed our cheat, just running out the clock until a watch was on the line. Moe won but did not have the wrist to wear a Bulgari Ellipsocurvex Tourbillon. Two pairs of courtside tickets to the

Lakers next season. If Jerry Buss had been there Moe might have won the Lakers.

Keanu was busted. The Wahlberg was broke. There was no air, only smoke. There were no glasses that had not been used as like ashtrays. Everyone was yawning that they were due at a party. We were not invited to the party.

Moe had left his van in Marmont Parking but was in no shape to drive it and would not let the bellhop call us a cab. He did not trust anyone that any venue would call to pick up two men who had just won their karma at duplicitous cards.

He led us down the strip to hang outside a bar until two guys, all gel-spiked hair and cacti muscles and torus piercings through Celtic tatts, got dropped off by a cab.

Moe yanked us in and across the backseats and directed the driver in a mellifluous Hindi, "He will take us to women," he translated for us. But we stopped at this sportslounge with a grungy chalet debased out back as like it had slid down from the hills and the driver said something and Moe shook his head and responded something else and said to us, "He misunderstood that we wanted prostitutes," but we said nothing again and he said, "If we maintain this luck we will have no need for prostitutes," and then he spoke to the driver who banged a sharp U, let us off in the lot of a stripclub.

Moe said something to the driver and translated for us, "I told him to come in with us, we will treat him." But as like the driver declined, Moe pressed, saying something about it not being a hassle or condescension. Or about how we would pay not just for the cover charge but also for the dances and lost time. Moe got out of the cab and removed from his jeans his naugahyde wallet spilling a wad of bills across the asphalt and as like we stooped to reclaim them from the wind more $100s fell loose from the pouch of his lumberjack plaid, and Moe gathered them up himself and offered them to the driver.

The driver then declined again by delivering a canonical poem in Hindi until Moe got soberer and solemn and held his hands to his heart and then hugged the guy and kissed his lips. Moe must have told the driver he had to take the money because the driver finally agreed and accepted the bills smoothing them as like to soothe them into a roll to fold into his pocket and the total was definitely more than $2K.

With the cab turning around we stood separate from Moe in another slotted emptiness of lot and asked him what the driver had said. "He said his wife is to have her surgery tomorrow."

The cab slipped back onto the boulevard and sped through a yellow. We asked, "What type of surgery?"

But Moe was already grinning past the bouncer. We caught up with him and inside the club he flipped his trench over his head and spread it into the frill of a spooked dinosaur and hopped around yelling, "Cardiac cardiac cardiac cardiac."

The club was loud and crowded gagging from the smell of bowling-alley antifungal footspray and was called 98.6°, if we did not already mention it. It was 360° all around us that hot, in Fahrenheit.

The coatcheck girl offered to check the trench by asking, "Am I taking it? Or not?" Moe said, "I was hoping you would just give me the hanger," and she said, "Lick my cock," and Moe said, "Why?" and she asked, "What about you?" But we kept our jacket and msgrbag too and the girl shrugged, "Whatever, I dance next."

A bar and stools up front, banquettes toward the back, all the walls except the curtained one behind the middle stage mounted with TVs as like old and bulky bodied as like the audience, riveted to a replay of the NBA quarter or semifinals, the Dow, the NASDAQ ticker, NASCAR, Seattle or Portland up, the Dow down, the NASDAQ down, NASCAR at the finish. At the completion of each circuit a fresh young flatscreen showed the Hollywood clipnews.

Six girls took their turns twirling germs around two stainless steel poles. We cannot recall anything about them except how blatantly diverse they all were as like in an ad for democracy. One white, one black, two in the middle, two Asians. The martinis were watery and on the cutting, the bleeding edge of expensive, but we drank them and were crashing, we were core failure crashing.

Moe stubbed a menthol out on the table and covered the burn with the acrylic placard, No Smoking. Then he shrugged out of his trench and went for a lapdance. Then he came back for a second pack he had stashed behind the placard, left again for a double Asian lapdance. The trench hung on the chair in a manner suggesting it was skin that had been flayed from its owner. We were teetotaler nonsmoking veganfuckatarians, feminists, proponents of female bodyhair, enemies of glass ceilings, of the mirrored ceiling above us, supporters of equal pay for equal work that extended to a fair wage for domestic chores for the stay at home parent. That was the milk we were raised on. We hated strobes and fucking hated being recalled to the genre distinctions between hiphop and rap. But this must not be construed as like racism. We had never been to a stripclub before. The flesh was live, not just live on the monitors.

Our share, all our poker money from the Moe split, was in our msgrbag, which would not leave our neck. We had not been able to count it all exactly.

://

Moe returned to the table with the coatcheck girl and picked up his trench and huddled into it and sat again to take out some bills. He paid her this fistful of cash she was fanning us with as like it was our turn and though we only shook our head it was as like she was angry with us not for denying her but for being ourselves, and so she left, and we were left to correlate an increase in stiletto height with an increase in length of stride.

Moe was kicking at the denominations that had spilled to the tile, he was kicking the $50s and $20s into a mound and then leaning as like to fall and stuffing them back into his pockets.

Then he took out something black, contoured round and smooth as like a lingam, and he pointed it at us and we put up our hands. "Either I rob you or we rob this joint together," he said.

Then he laughed and set the remote down on the table and tugged the trenchflaps around to his lap and dug through unloading the other pockets.

The exterior pockets held cash but the interiors held remotes, a different failed successful remototype in each pocket, rather no type because all universal. Also packs of batteries. AAs. AAAs.

Moe lined some remotes on the table and some on his lap but a bigger one was in his hand and he pressed at a button and nothing. Or anything that happened was just not discernible to us, because we had been transported to another time so faraway that the future must miss us and the present was only the waveparticle excitement of the past.

Moe repocketed the biggie then and picked up a smaller one instead and pressed a button but nothing or just the undetectable happened again, and so he repocketed it and went for a third, which had come from a breast slit, a fourth, which had come from a hip slit, a model even smaller than the models preceding it, and with a strand of DYMO plastic label tape peeling: the Amote 2niversal.

Moe pressed, and up on the TVs stockcar crashes changed to the sitcom *Friends,* pressed again and changed foulshot recaps to the sitcom *Seinfeld.* Pressed yet again and the stereo system hiphop got louder to rap. Pressed the TVs that were muted unmuted. A movie about a woman who fell in love with her vacuum or how much plasma a papertowel absorbed or how baby gentle this roll of toiletpaper was or else it was a commercial.

We took another remote, took another that worked and we worked it more too, in a History Channel war documentary, and the girls onstage below the switching were caught in the crossfire, the changing flame colors and shrieks of the laughtracks, and they slowed their dancing toward the screens, they stopped their dancing and then the hugenormous penitentiary brawny bouncer who was the only untelevised personality not fixed on the girls or the screens was waving a truncheon as like to smack the plastic from our hands.

We turned to leave just as like he was clearing the other remotes from our table and cracking a few between boot and floor.

Outside he was saying, "Gimme those fucking things!" because this was something a bouncer would say and because we were drunk and menthol was burning our lips it was Moe who said, "These are the property of the federal government," and the bouncer said something as like, "Fuck you, gimme," and Moe said, "We are fieldtesters and this is the field." But it was a full parkinglot of the cheaper SUVs and the type of sportscars that are just sedans with spoilers attached and the bouncer yelled in essence, "Do not make me call the police," and Moe yelled, "Do not make me call Al Gore."

A fight but with blood would have erupted had we not dragged Moe away, and walked off down the strip.

We were the only pedestrians in the universe, pointing randomly, pressing buttons randomly. Most of the bars and restaurants we passed had projectors flinging shows onto walls, and they were not affected, and most of the karaoke monitors were not affected either, and because the streetlight never changed and click as like we might we were unable to change it we waited long to cross at the crosswalk, so long that a homeless pixel had the time to get near with its shoppingcart of recyclables and Moe pointed his remote and pressed and said, "You are dead," and the homeless said, "Tell me about it," and Moe pressed again and said, "You are alive," and the homeless said, "Give me a cig," fundamentally.

Then the light changed and we crossed and once we got residential it was just splenda. Moe fell and in helping him up we fell too and Moe helped us up and led us down Cienaga. We are not going to pretend we know LA. We had four years at Montessori but we are not going to pretend we know Spanish. But La Cienaga was as like a swamp or drowning. We have not had a drink since. We are yoga practitioners and reformed adherents of the revered Master Classman. We are Stage IV terminal bardo. We are clean. We maintain a monastery in Noto.

We took Holloway or Hollow Way the street might have been down to Hacienda, we recall Hacienda. Bungalows and cottages in the mission style or as like the Moors had wandered off from the studios and conquered the rest of Hollywood. The residents of all the terracotta around us were not the poors who are never asleep, yet neither were they the rich who are never awake, instead they were the middles who were always getting stuck in the middle and paused between. We put ears to their sills, eyes to their drafts, cupped at their panes, peeked through their bubbles, passed unscathed through their walls and with our remotes went flicking their switches ghostly.

Moe messed with one guy in a groundfloor unit by flipping his Indiana Jones to either softcore porn or a nature show about the beach and how undressed a girl had to be to enjoy it. We were arguing which but the guy blocked our vista and gave us another show by getting up from his beanbag and searching the shag on all fours for his own remote, and not being able to find it, crawled over and rechanged the channel and sat back down but Moe pressed again, and it was either softcore again or just a show about the harmful effects of pederasty on coral, we did not stick around to find out. Instead Moe flipped a neighboring woman onto some frequency, no way of telling whether it was some special mod or just a glitch, but we got her from an MTV or VH1 grind into fuzz, pure flakey rain she could not get out of, we could not get her out.

On the next house his channel up/down did not work, or did not work with the consistency of our volume and picture, so this matching monogrammed robe couple had their domestic soundtrack shrieks blared as like we hued and tinted the picture, turning all the whites and blacks to yellow.

We cut across a yard and Moe got snagged in a mesh for volleyball and dropped his remote and then we got snagged too by our msgrbag and dropped our remote and we both scrambled around just searching. But we decided to screw it and keep moving only as like a siren drove past, though the loss enraged Moe who said, "It is just a false alarm, people panicking that they have lost their entertainment."

But maybe he or we had dropped our remotes earlier or maybe later in a pool, point is we had the big remotes in our hands, basically the biggest ones and the only buttons they had that worked anything approaching universally were the Powers and because one click that would turn off an on TV would also turn on an off TV, we canceled each other, we canceled the couples, in darkness or colorbar light. We plugged and unplugged from a distance removed. Then either a scream from a resident or a scream from a speaker but whichever it was it would fade, their echo would fade, or just blend into the next as like we bolted. Garagedoors opened but nothing would be inside except kittylitter and a hose. Nothing would be inside except bulk granola bars and a Chevrolet Blazer. We buttoned them closed and bolted. Our msgrbag was gashed and leaking cash and Moe was dropping cash too and the gusts blew the bills across the patios and lawns and we chased them. We ran past a mailbox shouting about how much we hated mailboxes, with their weeny flags, obnoxious. We ran past a villa whose mat was mounded with advertising circulars shouting about how much we hated advertising circulars and the sprinklers turned on and soaked us or maybe we fell into a Jacuzzi or maybe only Moe did. Then an autolight switched on and we crouched in a hedge until it switched off and we emerged but it detected our motion again and pitbulls barked for our throats.

Toward the back of the property was a sleepy casita and Moe went to wake its screens but his remote did not work so we tried ours and ours did not work and Moe fumbled for batteries and replaced his and nothing and replaced ours too and again nothing either, and so we leaned against the trunk of a palm and kept smacking the remotes against the palm, and sliding open their back casings and taking out their batteries and shaking the water out of the casings and replacing the batteries again. New ones or two old in the other direction, plus to minus and minus to plus, sliding the covers back until clicking.

But the moon could not be raised and the sun could not be lowered and the night could not be rewound and the day could not be fastforwarded. The sky was still dark to the west but getting light to the east and the casita was just the alleyed trash vestibule for a dump of apartments decorated with archways and turrets and CO_2 emissions, the Alhambra, it was called, or the Alcazar. We crept into the courtyard and people were stirring and so their TVs were stirring too. We clicked and off they went.

But then this was cur, unexpected. The TVs that were on would turn off but the TVs that were off would not turn on, at least not the ones we discerned through the screened windows that were both off and on at once because toward the west they reflected and shone and toward the east they absorbed and were shadows.

We had become crashers, blackeners, goodnight monitors. We pounded for that last surviving function of our last surviving button, pounding harder and faster to keep up with the wakers, putting them back to their sleeps as like dreaming.

We were in a fit, rolling along a lattice fence and slamming that only button in its only function, shutting the apartments down, shutting the city down, snapping and zipping everything up, putting everything off off off off, forever.

We came to a caretaker cabaña whose window had no shade and through the window was all junk hefty wood rung around with cola sweat and not retro or vintage but just sad floral print upholstery stained with seepage from the foam noodle containers, but over and above it all as like lording was this new expensive polymeliac idol screen showing news, which nobody was paying any attention to but a wheelchair.

Or whatever was in the wheelchair was still asleep or just dead as like the body on the news we could see, we could hear it—a body as like of a child, crisp and bleeding and wailing in stereo, and yet before we could be told who this was, or how this was, before we could be told when and where this was—we clicked it, we cut it.

"Shiva," Moe said, he said we were Shiva, but only the two of us together were, the ear that hears the ear, the allseeing infrared third eye of the consort of death.

://

DUBAI

[recfile 58 hello hello.]

Testes testes 1 2 3. Do re mi. Pop goes the sibilance. Red leather yellow leather. Aluminum linoleum. L M N O P.

Do not leave your Tetbook unattended. We repeat, do not leave your Tetbook unattended.

[So we were dealing with how you got involved with Carbon Capital.]

It was fairly straightahead, at least it was at the sniffing of asses. Basically no one wanted to fund us. No one even wanted to discuss our funding, which we to be honest took personally as like a presentation issue. We were unwashed, which was borderline normal. Malnourished, insomniac, rude, all borderline normal too. But also we could not explain what we did, or could not explain how there was money in it.

Keep in mind this was a time of major seeding, major sowage. Sums were being strewn to the breezes, and reaped. But every firm had responded firmly the same. Profitability implausible. Not just for us but for any of our partners. Everything was still vertical then. Not horizontal but vertical. We would drive traffic away just when the wisdom was insisting on users being kept inportal or at least onsite. Domains had to be protected, hosts prioritized, content would never be mutual. The VCs still considered sites as like stores or casinos. Do not let them out, the users. Do not let them leave to consume or even peruse the products and/or services of competitors. But in our model coming would be going as like going would be coming. No difference ever countenanced, because we were just the conduit. Expose the users to all competitors because the exposure itself will be the shop of life, where users become their own products and/or services. That would be our gamble.

Basically it was Moe who made us profitable, but accidentally. This we have to stress, it was never his intention.

He was an artist, an engineer, no rapacious dick tasseler graduated from B School to a Series A. He could count cards, up to four decks, but he could never even balance his checkbook. It was just something he said. Something for us both to regret.

[I don't understand—regret what? And how do you make money accidentally?]

Backtracking. We were just heading back to the Bay from LA whingeing to Moe about our lack of offers. No bids on purchase. No bids on license. All rejections were accompanied by referrals to consultants. But then we had no money for consultants. Every VC hinted that things would be different if we had advertising. Paid banners up top, paid sidebars. But we were against any advertising. Unclean, violative.

Moe, who had no appetite for businesstalk, stayed hungover autopilot silent. He got off at the right exit but in the wrong direction, permuting the 680 into the 280 as like we were going to his place. We were going to our place, though, to drop us off. Backtracking was, though all of San Jose was, ponderous. But then we passed a billboard.

[What billboard?]

That is the point, it changed. We cannot recall what exactly it was at the time. Some local place. Some fuel place with a family zoo and swings and slides and a ballpit. Moe said, "Did you ever notice that on billboards on the highway they never advertise for crazy shit as like a pit a hundred miles away?" and we said yes, "but that every ad is made for parents passing fast and having to make quick decisions pertaining to where to stop for bathrooms or gas or balls for kids to swim in?" and we said yes, again. "The point is just what is expeditious and convenient, what you need, and where you need it," and we were with him all the way.

It was as like there was a redwood tree always just in front of our fender and though we were speeding we would not have hit it otherwise. Inexplicable. No one would have even grazed the thing but leave it to Moe when we told him this, weeks later, when we told him we were algying a version, months later, and went with him to Gutshteyn to patent the thing just the two of us and partner him to Tetration, to downplay his involvement. Summer 97.

[Adverks?]

Confirmative. Everyone was still thinking about onvertising, online advertising, as like a phonebook. As like the Diatessaron. Whitepages in the middle, yellowpages all around based on whatever, on whoever, would pay. But then to take the terms a user searched for and respond to them with ads, to respond to them individually and with only the ads that pertinated alongside our free results, which would inadvertently demonstrate the supremacy of our free results, that was total Moe. Wasted nothing. Perpetual motion. Reversible.

Leave it to Moe, captain machine, general mechanics, to deliver such sagacity from just a billboard.

[Adverks—this was what lured Carbon Capital?]

Dusty. For serious, Dusty.

He was hayseed localish, with a family just a generation or two off the thistle farm, tightwad inspectors for the USDA, Dustbowl grim.

But Dusty did well.

His address, but his treemail address, growing up, had been the splitlevel of a nulliparous uncle and aunt in Fresno, the last on the culdesac that still zoned him into the charter school district, which then scholarshipped him to Berkeley, which then shipped him out east to intern the P/E desk at Credit Suisse, but basically his significant other at the time left an email out on his computer and Dusty read it and uncovered an auxiliary relationship the SO tried to rationalize as like research for an NYU cosplay or furry fetish social science study, immaterial.

Dustin now that we are remembering. Something stupey as like Smith. Point is, he moved back to the Bay, started grappling at a dojo, started a grainsifting shift at a coop, landed a desk at Carbon. The lowest desk all the exes would land on, with all the prospectuses that Carbon was about to pass up but still was cur about only because a rival might be stupey enough to go for them, and so the public might be too, if the businesses went public. He was not allowed to make decisions, but had to take responsibility for misdecisions and chances missed. The worst job a VC can have, to be the CV, meaning that if someone else ever makes bank on a prospect snubbed, get ready to update the résumé.

So Tetration settles on his pile, meaning the partners had already passed and after this last review Tetration was reduce reuse recycled.

But Dustin was a gamer. Dustin understood. It is not just math and science that are relational. We are sure the same must hold in its way for the humanities in which something in one context means something else in another. In gaming, in the fantasy realms especially, each avatar has a quest and improves his or her chances of success in that quest by alliances. Trolls are short but smorgs are tall, so a troll can squeeze undetected into a tubehive but cannot reach the tubehive and so must be boosted by a smorg. Once inside the central lair it takes a human male to slay the ouroboros. The human male wants to save the human female, the smorg wants the scepter, the troll wants only an ouroboros tooth whose magic powers can save the shire. Elves can also help, with archery. Also wizards.

Each quest is different. And though each quester might not want to participate in the relative subquest of the other, participation is necessary for the ultimate quest of each to attain completion. Each roam from the goal must also be an incentive. Do not aid the smorg just to be aided by the smorg. Rather, trust destiny, trust fate. Help the human male rescue the human female because it is she the prophecy refers to, Princess Wyvern, whose power is her ring, which before her capture she had entrusted to the Norns, who had entrusted it to a Teut, who is currently imprisoned by a Hun who, immaterial.

That is how Dustin talked about it with us, with his superiors. Each search would find its own result, but along the way the terms of the search would be generating other results and each would have its price. The main search would never be lost, and the subsidiary searches would always be strictly demarcated. They would be intersections, byways.

Diligence was due, and so we were called in to demo the algy.

Way back then Carbon was still used to prospectives hauling in their own gear to show and tell, that is the deep history we are talking, the buggy whip era.

But we just had a memorystick.

Carbon founding CEO was John Bates, JBates, most famous for having basically invented silicon, which comprises as like a quarter of the earth and so he basically invented the earth. There was a massive hunk of that element in the middle of his desk and clear crucibles lined along the mantel in which crystals were being grown out of hubris, unwaferable ingots and boules. He was as like a semiconductor himself and though a digital oracle to the media not many know of his analog activities administering the shipping enterprises that allowed the political and business elites of Greece to float approx 80 times the GDP of their country through Cypriot accounts. He wore gray slacks and a white dress shirt with a gray number 14 ironed on the back, the atomic number of his tetravalent metalloid.

We loaded Tetration.com onto his Gopal N-Ovum, a machine that without his investment would not exist. We searched for the Carbonites and found their site, in the version just updated. Then we let the Carbonites try it themselves, and all the searches they called for were for "marathon training" and "knife collecting," "arbitrage" and "the euro," and other topics they knew preoccupied their boss. Sites were found and we were raptured, because this was the first time, the first presentation, in which nothing had crashed.

Then JBates searched himself and found a distinguished benefactors page for the Claremonts mentioning his donation of auditoria, and a page for the Hellenic League of America mentioning him as like the recipient of the Ribbon of Daedalus. There were profiles in *Wired* and *The Wall Street Journal,* and a flash animation of him as like the devil with horns pitchforking Gopals and gulping them whole, which he played for us twice.

Apparently, he was also the volunteer tech for the Sacramento County Historical Society, and had even designed his own GeoCities page—"The contents of this page do not reflect, refract, diffract, or diffuse the opinions of the Sacramento County Historical Society"—which documented his genealogy with particular emphasis on the life and career of one Ioannis Baetylus, who came to America in the early to mid 18somethings, came west in the mid to late 18somethings, and pioneered cyanide leaching at the gold rush around Coloma and the silver boom of the Comstock Lode, which left him rich, then paralytic, then dead.

And it was the corresponding ad that sealed the deal for us, as like tetrating "Baetylus" solicited a banner for a deal on Mediterranean cruises from the newly launched triparian.com, just contracted with by The Friends of the Trapezzi Sisters, which in turn derived thirdparty sidebars for Kodak.

JBates signed the check that day.

This was still the age of signing checks so we had to take it to the Wells Fargo and wait in line as like everyone else to fill out a slip and deposit it.

But then also he handed us two caveats.

://

[Let me guess—no Moe?]

Not quite.

[Compulsory bathing?]

AMOR, AROM, MARO, MORA, OMAR, ORAM. Administration. Management. Organization. Responsibility. The Reign Of Multiple Acronyms, ROMA. The Regency Of Authoritarian Maturity, ROAM. Carbon demanded a Culpable Adult Reliable Bureaucrat Overlord Normalizer and had us sign an agreement to the effect that we would hire a suitable executive by a suitable date that was as like now, as like yesterday. An exec subject to our nomination but their approval. This was a lesson, indubitably. Let the others canvass but always retain veto power yourself. Saves the upperhand party the time and energy of vetting, saves the lowerhand party from trashing the basement and themselves.

According to the agreement we signed not only did we have to conduct this search for a Tetration chief with the help of headhunters, the choice of which was up to Carbon, but also the fee for this cannibalism was our responsibility. Organization. Administration. Management.

Never let a firm with only 4% equity suggest anything, especially not a lawyer. Gutshteyn learned on the job, was taught even the finer sartorials by Mintz, Mintz, Parce, & Hashing LLP. The education was relentless. For Gutshteyn, for us.

Deepcast, that was the name of the headhunting group. Carbon had to hire and pay them whether they got a scalp or not and would bill us once our earnings had reached a certain threshold.

Which threshold pertained to caveat two, which disagreement we still

Or our order has gotten all mixy because we must have disagreed before any check or chief casting

Maybe it is unimportant?
Maybe skippable?

[What? Deepcast?]

Adverks. Its algys were copatented between us and Moe. But Carbon wished to have the patents transferred to Tetration. We and Moe were against it but had no leverage. Cull and Qui ensured we had no leverage, after Carbon had informed them that if Adverks was our only profitability, then it had to be ours, in the inclusionary plural. We yielded.

[Carbon was afraid of Adverks going out on its own as a separate business? They didn't trust you or Moe?]

Both, 100%. But stop. Bear this. Everything will be related.

We fantasized about being able to type all the qualities we desired in a corporate boss into a searchengine that would just spit out the result, his/her title and brief, spew a figurehead to that Aeron throne that tilted precarious atop the nominal cap of the company pyramid. CAO, Chief Amnesia Officer, CBO, Chief Borderline Intellectual Functioning Officer, CCO, Chief Catatonia Officer, Chief DSM IV. Qualities as like Facey, Gladhandy, A Suit, No One. Quantity, 1. We settled on President. Start Immediately.

But if there was no extant tech to auto this, there was another model. A game, a lark, a larp. Basically. A live action roleplay.

The Deepcast Group kept mailing us prospect dossiers through treemail and we would read them and group accordingly. All the candidates were presented as like Hogwarts alumni, veterans of Gondor and Gandalf the Whites, but that was just sheer cloakery. They were more as like B and C class asuras and rakshasas. More level six stridlers, vikrams disguised. Some had intense lanthanide reserves of experience, others just the faintest lilypulse of texpertise. And their armor and weapons training varied wildly.

In choosing our President we had to cloak ourselves, which meant doing laundry. We were set up on dates in the depths of fusion pits, grills in the round, cushioned across from liminal lusers trying to impress us by having saki or soju made special, a rare hybrid breed of tuna or salmon flown in. Or by bringing their own lapsang souchong, ordering the kitchen to resmoke the duck, ordering in Cantonese to show that they knew, that we knew, that the waitstaff was not from Kyoto. There was the woman who explained to us how menus were assembled, with a very expensive item listed just above a cheaper item but the cheaper item would have a higher profit margin as like $50 for Wagyu beef followed by $24 for General Tso chicken, the cost of which was nothing. Then there was that other woman who brought her capuchin monkey along for the meal and ordered another placemat to place on the floor by our booth so the monkey could practice its pilates. Once we got the same fortunecookie as like our prospective, "Confucius say, market penetration should begin with dessert."

We realized then that our decision was becoming more complicated. All the toolbars we were interviewing were more obnoxious than anyone tech. They were not smart, just articulate, mouth vectored, conventionally staffable. Wharton quants accredited by Brooks Brothers, displaying their lobbying aptitude to such a degree that we had to remind them we were not Congress. Copula function approaches to default correlation were not math, because debt was not a science. We realized then that if we were being forced to take this for serious, we would hold out for what we lacked, not a connoisseur of cryptoasian gastronomies but a bonafide compliterate vizier on the ultima thule tier.

But then Deepcast sent

Rather it was Carbon that had Deepcast send us Kor

Though who sent Kor to Carbon we do not wish to guess

Or perhaps you will or perhaps through Balk, though Balk is not

We had become frustrated, not by our regular gluten and alcohol abstention, but by the mimicry of the rectards interviewed. Some of them skimped on their entrees while others skipped appetizers and dessert altogether, and as like we declined wine and beer, they did too and in doing so betrayed their weakness, politeness. That was why it was refreshing that Kor suggested a bikeride but would not divulge anything regarding distance, duration, or route. Kori Dienerowitz.

All he told us was to meet him by the Searsville marker, which we were not familiar with, and was not online, and already enough of a ride to get to. We took 84 up and around Bear Gulch, back around Skyline to

84 in a loop. Kor rode a special titanium bike made for titans, fitted with large allterrain tires and an xxtralarge seat of the same circumference made by a guy from Texas and intended for obese motorcyclists. A business Kor was invested in.

Our gut reaction had been he would never keep up, but then he did, and we were impressed until he was at our side going up a slope and then passing us going down and keeping the lead. We were still impressed, but ailing. It was Mountain Home or Sand Hill and then across the freeway into Woodside, Atherton. We were pedaling ourselves to dehydrated death unhelmeted in cutoff denims and a polo on a lesbian basketed greenmarket bike borrowed from M-Unit and Aunt Nance, just following or trying not to lose that fat ass cracked between the two pieces of maximally stretched pink spandex below a helmet reminiscent of the heads of the aliens in *Alien*. All the way to this café, Au Natchl. Which was his choice but only because it would have been ours. We, heaving, were the ridiculous party. The only thing he said to our gasping, "Never make excuses for your equipment."

We got the counterfeit chorizo scramble, soy replacement fries, etrog juice, chia chai.

He went for his bellyworn fannypack, unzipped a plasticbagged cheeseburger.

Warm. Hot. Jack in the Box. Soggy bun stuck melted to patty.

Basically, as like he usually told it, the paramount tragedy in the life of an army brat was that the family never stayed put in any one locale for enough time for him to develop at football. Individual skills were developed, team skills were not. Kor had attended four different highschools before joining the army. Rather he had been forced to apply to, and been accepted by, West Point. He was unable to make the football team. But then he exercised, gained weight, gained glutes, adductors, abductors, and tautened the hamstring. Then he made the football team. This was an unprecedented feat as like Vietnam. 1968, Tet Offensive. His position was linebacker. But then he played a game and broke his coccyx. Then he was rehabilitating, on leave, dropped out. He moved in with his mother in Eugene. His mother moved to Seattle but left him the RV. All he did was follow football. Not teams or players. He followed the coaches. He felt at last as like he was living for himself and his goal was to become either a coach or referee. Which required psychology, kinesiology, early childhood education. He swapped sports for the liberal arts, infiltrated the humanities. Though discrimination was another explanation for the trade. West Point did not exactly embrace his sexuality. Granted that he explained it this way belatedly, only after being named gay business leader of the year. 2004.

He enrolled at Reed College and then transferred to Evergreen. He was a reformed cadet jock undercover amid the counterculture, studying gay athletic history, carpentry, blacksmithing. He bounced around communes that raised their babies as like they raised their eggplants or rabbits in hutches, collectively. Then at some point whether being pursued by or pursuing some lover or job he rode his motorcycle to Bogotá, Colombia.

He related all this to us vaguely, in a way that implied not squander but wonder, the sense that were he to be honest about what he had done at our age, no one would ever credit it, we would be ashamed of ourselves. Still we were relieved that it was not just us, that other customers were reduced by him too, by his size. The customers and staff at Au Natchl. He patronized the waiter, matronized the busboy, corrected their Spanish, and as like to the question of what he had been doing in Bogotá, Kor answered, "Trying to stay young."

But then you will have to suss all this out for yourself. Doubt, struggle, coast. Trust, coast, struggle. Pedal to turn the wheels until the wheels are turning the pedals. Miss the landscape regardless. At a certain point, motion alone becomes truth.

"How did you get into tech?"

"My father retired from the army in 76," Kor said. "Founded his own outfit. He was fed up with my being a bum. He paid my way back to the States and hired me at son rates."

"To do what?"

"Time travel. Meaning I arranged meetings for him in the future, and paid the bills from the traveling, the past."

"For serious though?"

"The airplane recorders, the blackboxes that record flight data and cockpit activity, keeping the info on anything that goes wrong, just in case everything goes wrong. Dad had adapted them for car use and was trying to get Detroit onboard. Then it was the Japanese, the Korean chaebol. 200x the number of people die in car crashes than in plane crashes annually. Dad was sure this was it, his ticket."

"But?"

"No one went for it. Not the consumer advocacy groups, not the manufacturers. It was invasive, they all said. This was before everything was invasive, 1980 or so, a recession, gas rationing, mandatory sentencing for marijuana. We moved to Chicago. Dad went to work on stenographones, which would transcribe conversations. In the interim he set up an operator interpreting service. It was a number to call for doing business in another country, another language. Both parties would call in and the operator would translate the negotiations live and record them, produce dual language transcripts. Chicago had lots of Polacks, Krauts, Québécois, lots of foreign women seeking work, Dad married every one."

"But what did he do in the army?"

"Radar, sonar. Use your imagination."

"Explain?"

"He used your imagination," and then Kor laughed, and his laugh was a dialup, a modem communicating with another modem as like another life, the two setting the synack, hissing into parity.

We have searched and there are records of him at Evergreen and Reed and West Point, but then we are talking about one of the guys who controls the records. A Merlin manipulator, who bluffed us into thinking he could code, and then bluffed us into thinking he could not, even after we had proof.

Every time we would visit a city together it would turn out he had lived there. He knows Iowa City, Milwaukee, Madison, Americans Central and South, he knows how to fly helicopters. Once, but this was later and we were not there, this was the Tetbook launch in New York, he was with Qui and Cull who told us this, that a man crossed Fifth Avenue and called him Terry. Kor just ignored him and got into the Prius. Once, but this was later in the midst of our depression, he told us that his dead mother had been bipolar until Prozac. But Prozac had not been available until the early 80s and earlier he had said his mother had died of a stroke in the 70s and with his father still in Saigon he was sent to live with a cousin in Utah.

Stop us if we are getting too warm or hot. Or if our buns are sticking melted to the patty.

But if nothing else is factual, Scrutor was, and Matosz. Scrutor was based in Santa Clara, and in or outside Salt Lake. It was an attempt to regulate online but without the appearance of regulation. Whatever the government does is spying, but if businesses do it for them it is research. Basically Scrutor was a paleo archive, as like a steam or internal combustion searchengine. It was tasked with storing a copy of every url, but because of the state of the tech Scrutor had to do everything manually, as like we had to do the Diatessaron, with the difference being that Scrutor was financed by TendR and an outfit called Keiner Sequirities. It was VC money and not book profits that afforded all that manual labor, American manual labor. Mormon kids just off their missions knocking at virtual doors and ringing virtual doorbells, visiting urls on a regular schedule, on a regular rotation, only to store images of them, not active or interactive live versions, just records, screengrabs, captures.

In 96, just after Kor resigned as like VP, his immediately previous position, the project was abandoned. Scrutor had documented approx two million copies of approx one million urls, a fraction but an appreciable fraction. About six gigabytes of content downloaded. Their printed matter, not the index but the documentation itself, would have stretched for about 60 miles, Palo Alto to San Franciso and back.

Scrutor we had been apprised of but Matosz was new to us. According to Kor, Matosz had been a division of Scrutor and the only reason he was a VP of Scrutor was that Matosz did not officially exist. Scrutor was guano wasteful, pointless. It had no crawlers, no bots, just Mormon boys with creepy fingers.

Matosz, though, did the same work as like Scrutor did, just automatically. Without Mormons, no brakes, no hands. This meant, booley, that Matosz was formulating an algy. This meant they were, had been, our competitor.

Throughout this explanation Kor was very clear about having received clearance from the Scrutor family to tell us about Matosz, that it was defunct. He was very clear about everything in Utah and outside Utah being not just finished for him but for everyone, tanked. Though he would not say how they tanked, so we asked him why and he answered that he was big on honesty, and big on loyalty. Then he admitted he did not understand the algys. His role was managerial. He wore the interoffice communications hat, the intraoffice communications hat, the cheer up the mahatma engineer who is getting divorced because he is never home hat, laceless Keds. None of the Scrutor family had truly understood search, he said. He was loyal and honest and that meant telling the truth no matter what, he said. By last quarter 95 they were paying hosts $10 a whopping pop to image and report all their new domains upon registration. With approx 14000 new sites appearing each week, approx 56000 a month, the only businesses that can lose that type of money are governments.

The check came, and Kor reached for it.

"What else to do with ourselves but search?" he said, examining it, "I mean, being human?" and that was what attracted us, not a shift or sudden gearchange but a simultaneity, a symbiosis, of practical and theoretical, finance in the mists.

It struck us as like very mature at the time.

"Freud thought our cultural pasts lived in our present minds, while Jung thought it was not just our individual cultural pasts that lived there but every past and present too. Now, though, our innerlives have become exteriorized online, creating the first truly universal unconscious or subconscious. Think of the burdens we have been relieved of, think of the traumas transferred out. Bestial instincts, barbarous urges. The appetites of criminals. That is why search is important. It is the last direct connection to our primal darkness. It is the last link of light between evil and our awareness of a better self. It must be respected, protected," he said, or to that effect. It is a pity we cannot do his voice.

"Search is a conduit," he later said, "all notions are related through it, somehow, but some notions are only related through it."

"That is also one definition of intelligence," he said. Kor would later give us other definitions of intelligence.

We took the check from him and from out of our pocket, we have never had a wallet, the Diners Club card Carbon had given us, for interviewing purposes only.

"Please," he said. "My treat."

"Carbon pays."

The waiter came, took the card.

"But you know who is responsible for paying Deepcast?" Kor asked.

"We do," we said. "We are."

Kor went into his fannypack for a napkin and asked, "But you know who owns Deepcast?"

"We do not."

"James Bates, second cousin of John."

We nodded but not at this. That a VC firm required one of its investments to retain the services of another of its investments did not shock us as like what weighted the middle of the napkin or rather paper Kor held, apparently a tax filing for Deepcast. It was a rod, and Kor was confirmative, it was platinum. He told us it was exactly 14.8 ounces and that with platinum now trading at $1515 per ounce, the price of this rod was precisely equal to the fee owed to Deepcast.

"Hire me, let me take care of it," he said. "Consider it this way, you get a President who pays for himself."

We shook on it, and our signature on the receipt felt as like gratuity.

://

After the backgammon board has been set up, before anyone has moved or even rolled the die yet. After everything has been problematized toward the left of an equal sign, before anything has been solved on the right. Moments of tantric potency. Potentiality held in reserve. This was our situation. We were funded and had a new den mother. Who was about to move us into a new office den with enough capacity to hibernate everything online 100x over. Beyond, Moe was already poised to scale toward 100^2, toward ^{2100}.

[What year are we in again?]

Worst. Year. Ev. Er.

[Which?]

97 through 98. But also not. Rather it was Beta. It was perpetual Beta.

[You're at the Tetplex, the office?]

The core of it. A bay tract by the sloughs. Sedge, rush. Muck. City land. Palo Alto. The building we were in then, former garaging for the Department of Public Works, has since been cleared for parking. We bought the rest of the acreage from NASA Ames, adjacent marsh. Expansion in 2001 through 02, fitness center, kindercare center, yurt. Major renovations in 08 and 10.

[All the servers at the time were onsite?]

They were. Kor would not put Moe in his own barn or silo unsupervised. That was the issue. At first.

[What?]

But we are not sure what was first. It was hiring Kor, then the Tetplex core, The Lesstel. But they all overlapped, they lapped. Even a few things we had not been apprised of.

[Namely?]

Sometimes secrecy is secrecy but other times it is just that we have octalfortied the fact that other people as like you do not have access to everything we know and think. Many people have this problem, most of them not trying to hide anything. They just assume everyone can read their minds as like a book. We presume you understand this.

Point is, we found ourselves up to the waist in wetwork. Blackops, glomars, skunks. We moved to the marsh and suddenly stunk. This was what it meant to be managed. To compromise, and to be compromised, to dwell amid decay. Amid the pervasive waft of methane as like everyone in the office were locked in a continuous fit of farting.

As like we expanded Kor would take us to inspect the perimeter, out to the point that our clogs would just sink. "Freedom is water," he used to say. He meant that it has the behavior of water. How it takes any shape, because it cannot make its own.

We have to be the shapers of freedom, Kor would tell us, as like our concrete shored up the basin. On the rain days. The fog days. "Tetration is the air."

We planted public land with capital and harvested it private. We bought from the city, bought from the county, took credits and abatements both state and Fed for setting aside a nook for a rookery. We sheltered the least tern and brown pelican. Eggs of smelt and tidewater goby.

We took a disused building and renovated it, built a building nextdoor, each to its use, different floors in the different buildings, different sectors on the different floors, each to its use, quintessential Kor. Multitasking, polypronged productivity initiatives throughquarter. The lefthand ignorant of the right, as like in typing tutorials to develop finger independence. Compartments, compartmentalization. Cubicles. Tetricles.

Businesses predicated on unicity had to function by secernment. Employees now had to swipe in and out. They had security clearances. Even we had to swipe, but we always lost our card, and anyway later the Tetplex switched to facial/vocal recogs, connating cepstra and isometries.

Even we had a clearance level and though it was the highest we were not assuaged. It was still a level, it was measurable.

Previously we had all been not just on the same page but the same page itself. We were inured to our proximities. The engineer who started a project, finished it. Delegation was for rectards, and the techs were treated as like they treated themselves, if only they were the boss, everything would be splenda. But now we had been severed, dissevered, cleaved apart. Disarticulated, boxed. This and not any speculation was the worst bubble of the Valley. Specialization, which made a speciality of nothing but boredom, the integrative duty descriptions, which institutionalized that boredom, the windy command catenations, the recirculated air of assessment, filling the corridors of every office and the cavities of every engineer until the only way to remain sane was to pop.

Previously we had all been down in the niggly bits. Qui and Cull and the original Tetrateers #s 26 through 33. We will go through them alphabetically, rather in hiring order. Gushkov, Lebdev, émigrés who never appreciated us mixing up which one was from Kiev and which from Akademgorodok. Posek the Jaw, Japanese Jew. Syskin the Chew, Chinese Jew. Roland who was Roland. Toole, the youngest living person with an Erdős number of 2. Tiiliskivi, who had epilepsy and was allergic to wood. Yazyjy, who at 18 was our youngest hire and was still wearing his varsity badminton sweatband from the U of Jordan, Amman.

Now what we had to do was relevate. Move up the foodchain, evolve. Qui was responsible for supervising the writing of external code, userside, what you get when you use us. Cull was responsible for supervising the writing of external code, tetside, what we get when you use us, and how we use you and ourselves, backend. We were above and between them. And Mondays and Fridays we were at lunch with our Chief Engineer.

We met Moe at The Jaggery, Kokum If U Got Um, Daal Central, and the Seed Factory. We talked Tetration. Mnemosystems, mnemotechnics, sperance. How to not just bring users to sites or sites to users but how to store all of online ourselves.

How to store online, not how to shop it.

We would begin with the concept of existing space vs. new space, proceed into talking through the entailments of each w/r/t data and electricity, racked mountables per cabinet, and cabinets per corridor, seismal dampering, algidities, praxeological redundancies. W/r/t electricity and data.

Then Moe would end at least the work component of our powwow by reviewing.

About how it would be more energy efficient and so less expensive to install latitant 12 volts in each server so that if only a few of them conked he would not have to crank all the backup ancillary power, but how Kor who knew fuckall had kyboshed that as like unstable. About how seamless it would be for him to father the conversion of AC to DC inside the motherboard itself and not outside and so attenuating the supply, but how Kor knew he was fucking Moe by kyboshing that too.

Moe lamenting the oversight, the underlistening. Moe lamenting his Tabernacle ideal.

We will be sincere, we will be veracious. We never entirely credenced anything Moe said about his Tabernacle of Reversibility. Rather we would have credenced his ability to build it, had it been buildable by anyone other than the intelligent designer of the universe. Though if anyone could compete with that supreme engineer it was Moe, which was why our time together was never merely collegial. This was the one scintilla of transcendence we had to have in our life in order to tolerate the rest of it. This was, or used to be, the purpose of lunch.

Moe talked about Guadapada, Govinda Bhagavatpada, Adi Shankara, dharana and dhyana. He talked about his own mental sorbency and respiratory practices, "But only in America the more you practice respiring the more shitty you get at it."

We as like rookie Buddhists had been encumbered by counting our breaths when we should not have been counting them and not counting our breaths when we should have been counting them, and Moe took up his glass and poured water in our mouth and told us to breathe it out of our nostrils and then poured water in our nostrils and told us to breathe it out of our mouth and after lavaging as like that a number of times we had no chance of being encumbered.

"Is that a Hindu breathing technique?" we asked as like we wiped ourselves up.

Moe answered, "That is a Hindu technique for getting thrown out of a restaurant. But now you are breathing and the numbers have stopped."

Moe always said that the cycle of in and exhalation was a reduplication of the cycle of birth and death or samsara, which could be improved only by an improvement of karma, which depended on our guarantee of an autonomous engineering division for Tetration, and our marriage to either another human or tree, as like humans without love can marry in India. On our returns to the Tetplex Moe would try to set us up with a tree. But being unable to find any eligible baobab or even tulsi shrub he would say that this was just the Indian tradition, and that the contemporary American equivalent might be betrothal to a discarded curbside microwave. And though a Westinghouse was not our type we appreciated the sentiment.

Wednesdays were for management. We met outside by the estuary, way before we had a commissary. Kor would have us sit in a T, but there were not enough of us to form one. He would present a chart or graph of a T for us to emulate. We had to be broad in our disciplines, as like the horizontal bar of the letter. But also we had to be deep in our passions, as like the vertical bar of the letter. Then we all brought out the blenders and made disciplined passionate smoothies. Our favorite we called Fierce Enemy of Yeast. Ice crushed, not cubed. Size medium, with two straws for maximum suction.

It was seleccess then. Select access, invitation only. The site. Our focusgroupies were an even distribution of recs, as like The Friends of the Trapezzi Sisters, and techs out on disability leave whom Dustin conscripted from the Market Street coop. Then we admitted the Stanford students, the cardinals of the ordinal trees, the full roster of Ubicomp 101, Professor Winhrad. We assigned them all proprietary unames and pwords tied to dedicated IPs. But they were careful what they tetrated for. They were too careful, which is a solecism now.

Ours was a testmarket tetrating wholly for wholesome things, educational things, nothing real, nothing real and sebaceous. They tetrated for Stanford, the SF Centre Nordstrom closing times, meteorology 94301, 94303.

They knew we were tracking them, we knew they knew we were

tracking them, and they knew we did they did too. Knowledge sheds prejudice with increase in sample size. It was expectancy effect, assumed bias, and they tetrated for "expectancy effect," "assumed bias," as like they were trying to impress us or applying for jobs. The most telling thing, though, was that at the most improbable but also probable times as like between 02:12 and 04:16 at night they tetrated for themselves, repeatedly, despite knowing that nothing was there.

Beta. To the West Beta justifies mess, excess, otiosity, sloth, and only the East understands it for what it is, the basic prime condition. To be unable to finish or be done with a thing is not to be blocked. It is to recognize no safety but in process, no security but in flux.

That is why ours was not true Beta, but false. Ours was the Beta of appearances, but we understood this only later.

In a true Beta there are no distinctions between recs and techs, user and provider. In a true Beta everyone must be both. Our false Beta, our Beta 2.0, was just another instance of a business putting its customers to work, a Beta by approval, a Beta that surveilled. This was Kor 100%. His justification. The public can never be fully employed under capitalism, but they can be fully capitalized in the sense of being employed without salary or benefits, just cred.

True Beta, 1.0, is life. Is human. Opening all the windows, opening all the doors, knocking down the firewalls to let the bugs out. Some butterflies, some moths.

All existence is Beta, basically. A ceaseless codependent improvement unto death, but then death is not even the end. Nothing will be finalized. There is no end, no closure. The search will outlive us forever. We as like a species will just shrink and wear.

We were tired in our minds, the software. Exhausted in our bodies, the hardware. A wreck even before a crash. Fit only to be sunk for a reef.

We were wasted far from April, and too near August. The softlaunch would go hard. Cull was complaining about "link flaccidity," "conflab." Qui kept muttering about "chaingangs," "intimacc:ing." We had selfdiagnosed shingles. We had selfdiagnosed everyone. Prodrome, aura, ache, postdrome, migraines have four phases. 1998 did too.

We could not remember where our office was, we could not remember when we had been in it last and so we just chaired a terminal in whatever room in whatever sector on whatever floor of whatever building until its assignee would return and we would move on. We were lucky in that not many would lay claim and displace their Founder. On every terminal surface were Diet Snapple bottles, churro wrappers, and the glomerations of wet tissues that in drying resembled little tiny furrowed desiccated mouse brains. Everything smelled of semen, and the Trapezzis aside, our one female employee who was also our second Afromerican had quit.

We glitched, we grated, broken links would not be purged, debroken links would not be reprised, header text was weighted too heavily, or comptrastingly had light relevance to body and/or anchortext. That being the basic text that was linked, 80% of which accurately described the nature of the link, as like Visit Tetration, which linked to tetration .com, meaning that 20% inaccurately described the nature of the link, as like Visit Tetration, which on a blog maintained by an Adverks rep fired for time theft linked to fagsuck.com.

We were disturbed, not at the vengeance but at having to recalibrate our favor/disfavor ratios.

Spamsites abounded. Phisheries, grouseries.

The address given for Au Natchl was that of a competing organobistro on the Alameda de las Pulgas. The phonenumber of the kasha joint was that of a salon also on Castro, called Kashas, possessive, not possessive.

Hatespeech, we slaved on that. Racists were rectarded but had figgered how to post. The issue of how to keep a search for "negro" not pejorative but historical. The issue of how to keep a search for "jew" a noun and not a verb.

How to keep a tetration for "penis" or "vagina" clinical, not porny. How to keep the user from being misinterpreted or worse, misadvertised to.

Also we were hacked. Malevolent techs were cur. We went chasing down their viruses, their worming. Crackbabies, the first people who had ever seemed immature to us, broke into our systems and we caught them. We set traps and caught them and spanked them hired. Tetrateer #36 Mark Garnisht seemed fetal, zygotic, immaterial.

We debugged but they were as like exterminators. They smoked out cocoons. Squashed roaches and ants one line at a time. But because they were hackers we had to ensure that in fumigating they were selective with their poisons.

That was our life. Work was. Fail reports, patch recommends, distro to uside or tetside accordingly. This might explain our response or nonresponse to The Lesstel. An external off the record subsection of Tetration. We were crunching, we had deadlines to die for, we were busy, the truth was busy. 04/01/98, which we missed. 06/08/98, which we missed. And so if in the midst of this frantic T minus countdown just to make launch by 07/01, by 08/01, Kor approached us to mention that he was going to czar a special discretionary security unit, what were we supposed to reply. We are not asking a question.

Kor took us into his confidence. He said the cyberattacks were slowing us down. We were not equipped to keep up both with them and our algys simultaneously. Sitting by ourselves had sapped our force posture. Construction crews were ubiquitous, employees were being hired without adequate background checks and assigned duties without adequate monitoring, external threats would become internal, inevitably. The best action course would be to diversify our vigilance, at least until the Tetplex was finished with enough capacity and safeguards in place to reinstall this unit. The VCs had already granted approvals, operating under the principle that all intel we uncovered on new viruses and worms along with all patches we developed would belong to Carbon, which would split any revenue generated, 60/40 in their favor. No worries, Kor said, this would not require any Tet or Adverks teams to be reassigned, he would be staffing this himself. Then, and this was sneaky pirate of him but we did not register it then, he asked if we had any names in our Rolodex for him to vet. We did not answer. We did not even break screen. It shames us still that we just shook our head and smirked, "Rolodex."

The Byx B&B Inn was summarily converted into the Lesstel, a motel, a notel, no telling. Its addy and moribund phone have since been seared into our memory, synaptic burns between axon and neuron. 816 West Ahwanee Ave, Sunnyvale, (408) 734-4607. Just off the 101. It was a bleak strip of grimy pink stucco over cinderblock all vacancy rooms that had gone out of business with telegraphy, but now it would house a copy of our systems, along with a terminal or two. We admit that we gave it no thought, we had already given all our thought away.

It was owned by a bank, we cannot recall which, and Kor ensured it was purchased not by Tetration or even Carbon but by a shell, Accommodations Made, Inc. The bank had repossessed it from its owner, Ian Byxby, who, immaterial.

We are not sure who did the setup for Kor, because, again, we were not present. They were not staff, that is certain. They were tenants at full occupancy. We do not know how they were paid, or what, by whom. We do not know whether room and board were included. We imagine a vestibular ice machine on the fritz, a drained pool the color of chlorine to fall into.

We had octalfortied it clean from our drives by the time it was recalled to us. But we will return to this, we promise.

://

[After that invitation phase, what were your expectations
for admitting all users? What was your
experience after the site had gone live?]

Understand that Tetration as like every other searchengine, basically, was predicated on the assumption that establishing a presence online was analogous to the first word or first step of a baby. Infants, toddlers, do not want to just lie around unvisited in their earliest sites, they want to grow and move and communicate, they want to connect with and be connected to others. Apparently, however, this was not always the case, and people who had put up sites would routinely request that we delist them. It was not our meniality to answer such requests, but they were answered, by others, and for each instance of Kor mentioning a user registering an inappropriate content or intellectual property infringement objection, we are certain there were hundreds or thousands or hundreds of thousands of petitions for us to remove from results pics or vids of users with their exes, not even compromising pics or vids, just distressing, or distressing exspouse blogposts. The legit objections went to Legal. The rest just got form mail. You will excuse us. Please. We presumed that everyone wanted to be public. But not just that, we presumed everyone also wanted to be popular.

This principle was fundamental, due to the algy. Which we had made to order, and only to order, not to resolve any dramatizing ambivalence about the public self.

[You're sure it was the math that convinced you? It
wasn't that you had your own taste for fame?]

Psychoanalysis again, überfaulty. Fame is just measurement, proportion, a weight, a number. But then everything is a number. There is no way to separate sums from our experience, and if there is a way then even that separation itself can be summed. You. We are sure you have difficulty doing double digit multiplication or converting the quotient of simple division into a fraction or percentage. Regardless, you still exist in this system. You contribute to many fractions and many percentages. Unwillingly perhaps, but then you become counted among the unwilling. Your appetites, attractions, desires.

Anyway, you write, and what you write cannot be judged by any individual. The criteria become quantifiable only in the mass. Genre or medium criteria. Social, ethnic standards. All in perpetual flux. Which, with time, delineate metric. But now take out of the equation all the history of books, take out of the equation all of history. Without precedent there is no metric, no expectation. Now all you can rely on is what is marketed to you, retailed to your senses, and, also, on the instincts inside. The animal. Tell us, then, what will be unleashed? Imbue the users with the anonymity of animals, what will become popular?

[The same lowbrow lowest common denominator junk
of offline TV and film, but on a screen that folds?
Unreadable ebooks instead of unreadable books?]

404. Abort. Retry. Fail.

[Brands? Whatever's advertised?]

AOL, Yahoo, Disney. CNN too. No doubt they were popular sites. Still are. Among the most visited. But still never among the most uniquely visited. Users just type the urls into a browser, or click a bookmark. No searching, no finding, no cur.

We mean something else, something novel, neolatrous. The popularity that cannot be purchased, only earned, or bestowed. The fantasies in aggregate, the figments in common. Not heuristic or empirical for all users always, but rational. Statistics. The number of links, not outgoing, but incoming. The maximal repetition rate of a minimal set of terms. That is how rank is determined. If two parents love each other, and get others to love what they make, then nine seconds, nine minutes or hours later, another meme is born.

Name us someone famous.

A celebrity, someone A-list.

[You think I'm in touch? Why not just list your friends?]

Do not snob us. Natalie Portman.

Surely Natalie Portman still trends.

[But why her? Don't you think you're every bit the celebrity she is?]

We met her once.

Or she met us.

Point being, she was popular, the terms of her were. "Natalie" alone, not much. "Portman" alone, very much. In her fullest iteration, though, "Natalie Portman" was unstoppable.

But not in any of the ways you might predict.

She was not Natalie Portman+actress, she was not Natalie Portman+celebrity, she was not even Natalie Portman the symbol, rather "she," the "she" in quotes, more than anyone else, more totally than any other famous person or brand, so simultaneously served as like signifying and signified, in M-Unit language, that there was no use in defining designata.

Or, to put it directly, we were at a loss for what to do about, quotes again, "her" results, given that approx 82% of all tetrations of, quotes one last time, "her" name, were accompanied by smut, and approx 24% not accompanied by smut resulted in clickthrough to dubious sites rising rapidly through the rankings.

Everything was, you will forgive us, her vagina, her anus. Rather they were just the ideas, the conceptions, always better represented in the vernacular. Pussy, asshole. The pussy and asshole of Natalie Portman.

Tetrations for Natalie Portman topless, bottomless. Natalie Portman sex scene. Natalie Portman blowjob scene. The mouth of Natalie Portman. Semen, whatever the prevailing slang for semen, on her lips, on her teeth. "Natalie Portman 34B" OR "Natalie Portman 32B" OR "Natalie Portman 32B..34B" OR "Natalie Portman ~breasts ~boobs ~tits | jugs | knockers | honkers –pitchers –doors –cars filetype:jpg, mpg."

This was the most craved escape in, or from, our universe. This was the most craven. Users tetrating for things they admitted were frauds, "natalie portman fake horse rape," "natalie portman fake gangbang snuff." Users tetrating, "how do i fuck natalie portman?" "natalie portman will u fuck me?"

The bias crap intruding, reinforcing. Hate kinks becoming our new normal. Questions we would never consider answering, even online. "why does natalie portman date fags?" "how big a nigger cock can natalie portman fit in her little jew hole?"

This was the basic lesson of the launch. On 09/01/1998, 06:00 UTC, we welcomed the public to itself, and this was how it returned the greeting.

The tetraffic altered pronto. It skewed. Hashtag understatement. The datasets we crunched concluded that our info w/r/t relations as like they were conducted offscreen had become comptrastingly tenuous.

Admitting users without registration was getting us abusers, and that was wounding. They moved into the neighborhood to find the doors open, not closed, and their temptation became our agony. They burned their crosses out on our lawn, then broke into the premises and got into bed with our family. It was Moe who offered the domestic analogy.

We had to move against the very users who with their every greedy purchase sustained us, who with every tetration for a pacifier or mobile or stroller to add to their cart, had multiple, exponential, spic MILF cumpilation tetrations. Same user. Same IP. This must have been, for anyone who shared that computer or head, dissociative, fragmenting.

Just a moment ago we ourselves had been concerned for the site, but now were concerned, or pretended to be, for people. We sat alongside Cull and Qui at our terminals and it was as like we each became our own business or employee, NSFWing constantly. We sifted and sieved, labeled and rated clickbait, as like online engendered through vulgarity, and diversified by hate, until the only consensus left was obscenity. For which we each had our own definition. Our own indefinability of its primacy. Our first mutual culture was becoming our last, a default devolution to simian sex and violence, which our algys were staging amid the personalized commercial identities of food, clothing, and shelter.

A person would consult linear algebra about how to terminate a pregnancy in a way that appeared accidental. Their spouse would seek advice on infidelity from differential calc. How to hide a body. How to acidwash all DNA traces off a body and hide it. This had not occurred to us as like risky before, the advice received no better than the deeds. We reasoned that our users were researching for a novel or screenplay. We rationalized that everyone in America along with half of the rest of globe was writing a novel or screenplay. Rather than passing prurient IPs onto the authorities, we filtered their sites, blocked them if illegal. Though a censored online could not represent existence. But an uncensored online should not. We told ourselves we were saving users from themselves. But we were also saving ourselves. We were soothed by recalling that even our online was not genuine, authentic. If the average user had limited access to childporn, we had no access whatsoever to the NSA, CIA, FBI, the IIA of NATO, though we guess we might have hacked them. We were soothed until we recalled that the life we were living was also not total, not full. The life we were living was empty.

[Wait—what you're saying is that Tetration is or was engaged in active censorship of nonillegal sites?]

In what country—America? Or in China?

Bottomline, the point now is our feelings. Again, as like for the rest, we will get to it.

[So, your feelings?]

Do not condescend, we will return to this. For now, though, we were manic.

[How?]

We had selaccess from our office, but office is whatever. We had selaccess to an encrypted algy that tetrated without filter. We toggled between modes, between online as like it was, and online as like we were changing it. Flagged pages flew incessant. We never delegated, every decision was our own. This site was evil, that site was borderline evil, this was satire, that was parody. Making distinctions to make the rubric, delivering verdicts to write the lex. We tried to establish gradients and hierarchies, to formalize a protocol to reprieve this automatic. But nothing would equate, because nothing was equatable. Art was porn and porn was art and every joke was defamation, libel. We were stuck in a recursion, going loopy, doomed. Obsessive compulsives always have to match obsessive with compulsive.

[The pressure you were under was because of the politics, or guilt? Or just the workload?]

The pressure was us on us. If we experienced guilt it was not from violating any ethics or morals but the magnitude of the second eigenvalue. Tetrate it. Do not. Deploying emotions without matrices distressed us. Human intervention was the crime. Lack of system was the crime. This is all about our eternal failure to have deved a viable semantic algy that translates, interprets, and reads between the lines to appreciate intent.

[What about the launch itself?]

No party we recall. No circus bread or smoky mirrors. Just a press release by Kor. There was no call to fly in New York journalists only to demo a product already numinous at no cost.

[Your role was limited?]

The servers, we mean the Tetplex servers, were crashing. We were not handling the site queries let alone the media requests. Every time Kor opened his mouth our volume doubled. Every time we crashed Moe would hectically sweat as like the white crept up his sideburns and the wrinkles from the stress and tension rung wild around his mouth in the yelling of four languages to the 10 engineers he had hired for diversity, but diversity of expertise, because all of them were Jains. Cull and Qui would have to intervene while we rollerbladed the parkinglot. Doing grinds, fahrvergnügening. The AP took a photo that was faceplanted all over the press and the gist of the accompanying article was Tetration .com will keep your online inline, which was neither very funny nor accurate despite. Point being, that line in the piece was taken verbatim from our About page.

[Remember the publication?]

Does not matter. Just gossip, rumor, coupons.

[If I'm remembering correctly, the press had a particular animosity toward Adverks?]

The press. Depressing. No single server institution not a college or university pinged us more, might even still ping us more, than *The New York Times,* which alternately praised and damned us, and used us for its research. The technophobes will always be a loyal demographic. We recall someone at *The Atlantic* tetrating copious reference shelves about Yugoslavia, clicking for the Kosovo casualty stats at this émigré site that turned out to be a project of the State Security Service of the Federal Republic of Yugoslavia collaborating with the Kremlin. We read the feature, but we never read the corrections.

Adverks got journalism revved. Reporters accused us of faveranking links to advertisers. No. They accused us of faveranking sites linked to advertisers. No. They covered our every diddly lawsuit, neglected every judgment but their own. They demanded our schematics, without knowing which or for what, they only knew schematics. Environmental impact assessments of the Tetplex. All our IRS 1120s. They demanded full transparency for everyone but their readers who, just by using us, became their competition too. Journalists took our hardware to store the news, our software to lay it out for publication, then they used our email to spit on the rest, and lost their pages, jobs, and pensions. They went cheaper than we ever did, cheaper than free. We just strained, they catered. We will never feature any celebrity pregnancy exposés, for those who do not want them. We will never publicize a guide to the worst foreign vacation spots, for those who do not need one. Libel, defamation, and slander are merely available through us, not originated by us. Protecting copyright must be the responsibility of the host domain and not the engine. We were honored to consult on the redesign of the US Patent and Trademark Office Database, for gratis.

Truth is, media were worse than we are. Publisher money determines editorial determines content. You have told us this yourself. Certain expectations obtain. In newspapers and magazines especially, conformity is institutionally imposed. Contentproviders are censored until they selfcensor, for which achievement they are elevated to management. There are two warzones just north of us, involving approx 68 million civilians, and approx 140000 US troops. American broadcast and cable news organizations cover all this with a total of six fulltime correspondents. Blood is rarely shown. Footage of mourning parents is preferred to that of their amputated children.

Tetration is accessed approx 1 billion times per day by approx 600 million users from approx 180 countries in approx 140 languages. The exchange is immediate, and priceless. Rather each user sets the price, by deciding what to tetrate, and what results to click, setting in motion a process by which the vids or pics taken by the surviving member of a family that might or might not have been accidentally bombed can grow to rival and even dominate press accounts of the incident. No doubt you can choose to click strictly conservatively, or liberally, but click independently and you will find blood, limblessness, the carrion of drones, without commercial break or advertorial confusion, just sidebars, banners, sponsored links in gray. We show how foreign children die from our taxes, we are not sure why it matters if we purged from our index a site that staged lynchrims. Which are, true or false, situations in which one human hangs lynched without clothes from a tree while another human stands just below and rims their anus.

://

[How did we get off on that tangent?]

Remember 2000?

[If you mean the year.]

We mean the century. The millennium. 2000. Remember?

[If I have to.]

You do. Please. The end of time, the beginning of time. Panic. World historical Orson Welles World War III. The apocalypse. ATMs out of money. Cans of Spam and bottledwater in the basement. Gun sales up 62%. Explain it to us.

[It's my fault?]

Explain, please.

[It was. Everything was just exaggerated. Hype. A boost to circulation.]

The computers. Recall what was happening with computers.

[All the computers were going to crash for being set to the wrong date, I guess.]

Elaborate.

[What I read was that computers tell time by two digits for the month, two digits for the day, two digits for the year, but the years were all 20th century, 1901, 1902, 1903, 1904, second millennium of Christ. At midnight on December 31 or I guess January 1, it

would be 01/01/00, and all technology would be
blasted back to 1900.]

Before the filament bulb, gaslight. Horses on the cobbles. Women and Afromericans disenfranchised. All the vaccines would be voided. Polio returns. Confirmative.

[Alarmism.]

Media again.

Stations were losing the air and so were scrambling to fill it, reclaim it. The more they claimed with their filler the less they would lose. Chat shows. Nonstop cable news. Every channel demonizing the computer as like it was not a tech who invented TV too, it was an emcee, it was an anchor. Online was about to take the ozone from TV and TV was out to avenge itself. That was the scoop. To survive, TV had to go after revenge in advance. A common fantasy in the West, a religious tenet in the East. Preemption. But to destroy a thing can also mean to destroy yourself in the process. All you have to do is respect the inevitable.

This was not mysticism, however. This was what happened.

Basically, media were just reiterating the partyline of nonstarter nonentity startups, rewriting marketing eblasts from the inbox. The news they broke came from the publicists, who were employed by the businesses, which had been founded to remediate, y2K.

The remediation outfits had hired only the worst programmers in the Valley, inferiors, ulteriors. But they had also hired the best PR staff in this language, and so in every language, virtuosos of suasion. They scared global conglomerates into retaining their y2Kludging services, they frightened the big clogged artery hearts of the big three producers. ABC, CBS, NBC. The PR wunderkinds billed by the assignment, but the coder poseurs were paid by the parameter. They made an Altoid, a Tic Tac, a mint. There has never been or will be again such a splenda syzygy of business and calendar. Opportunity costs opportunity.

Point being, all that clock resetting zeroing quandary, if it affected any hardware it was only the mainframes, bulky IBM corrugated boxwork due for replacement regardless. For any software the update was only a flourish. A line. A line they took their time with. It would have been cheaper to begin from square one than to have hired nonentity hacks to nonsolve a nonproblem in a nonexistent timecrunch. If the nuclear warheads launched anyway, at least existence would have ended in the black.

[You weren't taken in for even a moment?]

We tried to be, gave it our best. But, basically, zero.

[So why weren't you speaking out to debunk it all?]

Spring 99.

Second round funding had been obtained, $20, $22 million, the bulk courtesy of Carbon and Keiner Sequirities. This was money to pay off the Tetplex, continue expanding the Tetplex, develop adforce, identify potentials for a DCent outcampus. A DCenter. A datacenter. A project tacitly promised to our Goan bro. Topology by Moe, infrastructure by Moe, his pick of hinges, and any red he had ever dreamed in for the sprinkler system.

But the VCs had their own project in mind. One was a Sapp. A StorApp, a StoragApp. Properly a Storage Appliance.

We are not sure how to tell it.

Basically, there was this company, Moremory, y2K profiteers. They were deving memory, drives. Nonvolatile drives. Imagine a downscaled shrunk portable DCent, your very own warehouse of servers, to keep with the mops in the broomcloset.

The idea was that when everything crashed, all your files would still exist for any future civilization, if, that is, they would have the wherewithal to reboot compatible computing.

Functionally, there is no difference between the device we have described and any other midrange moderately tricked out external hard disk. Except that this was an early one and would be marketed directly to rectards and rectarded businesses with a guarantee in graffiti font along its side: "y2Keeper."

Its design resembled an Incan timekeeping disc or, honestly, a thermostat.

But then everything about the Moremory Sapp was basically stupey, überstupey. As like it was conceived without a modem, and so would never go online. No doubt this was why Moremory was finding the device so appealing. The very thing that made it cheap to produce, the very thing it lacked, was its major safety feature. No online access meant security, reducing if not eliminating chances of infection. Which was sure to be important to any Sapp owners trying to survive the millennial calamity, who would have no computers, and no telecom, only a scorched plastic orb containing all their spreadsheets.

But the more proximal disaster, the true compocalypse for us, was how many of them were selling. Units moved, retail, wholesale. The severity appealed. The expensive severity.

Morememory was owned 14% by Carbon and 6.8% by Keiner, making them partners to each other before partners to us. Operands were operating venal. Keiner proposed a product, Carbon brought it to us and we balked, but then Carbon balked, and the termsheet Keiner submitted turned it into a precondition for funding. Dustin ran interference but his superiors had run the numbers, leaving us no support or alternative but to walk.

They proposed a drive to be equipped with our algys, which would render all files searchable, findable, for posterity or holocaust. Take the price and tetrate twice. STrapp was the workingname. A Storage Tetrating Appliance, a "y2Kreeper."

Kor was going pro on this but we were neutral, but neutral for us means con.

We still had a cruft of algy tweaks on Adverks.

We were trying to arch a system that enabled bloggers to embed ads on their blogs so that if a user clicked through to vendor and made a purchase the directing blog domain/host and/or the bloggers themselves would garner a share of the proceeds.

Further, we were trying to figger how to divide that share, whether by a set percentage or a percentage escalating in proportion to clickthrough from among the total of all purchases per quarter.

[Slow it down, one thing at a time—are you explaining Adverks or this storage device?]

The risks of assetizing and/or equitizing preferences. The costs/benefits of rendering recommendations transactional. Exploitation. Anthropreneurism. We are just trying to explain our mind. Summer 99.

We had been falling asleep in whichever was our office, whose AC had been set to autoadjust and would wake us up to Monday, 08:00. We had just signed into a terminal and clicked up an Adverks algyshell and there was a crash, there was an offline crash and then our phone rang. We did not pick up and then it stopped but then there was ringing by the next terminal, to our left or right, and then to our left and right, but then they stopped and our phone went again and though we were sure it was not for us we picked up. Tiiliskivi was on the line reporting a meltdown, apparently Kor was melting, down.

"Why?" was what we had to offer, basically.

But Tiiliskivi just stuttered, "This is not Yazyjy?"

No, but now we had to assume it was his phone, his terminal, his office.

We quit the algyshell and refreshed our email.

Yes, we had email back then, we had emails, from Gushkov, from Lebdev, all subject: BLDNG 2 FLR 1 STAT, CAPSLOCK CAPSLOCK EMOEGENCY.

That was a floor below a building over. We took the stairs, and counted the stairs, one step demote Tiiliskivi, the next demote Yazyjy. For violation of the Tetplex ToS, 82:6: discussing anything w/ colleagues before discussing w/ us.

The meetingroom, still unfinished, was plastered over with contractor tarp. Extra swivelers had been hauled in but there was no table yet to center, just carpetlessness. Down the corridor was a banging. Dustin and the Carbonites were pacing as like they had to use the toilet. Keiner the VC exec was consoling two females presumably affiliated with Keiner the firm. They were crying and he comforted them without touching or being touched.

The Soviets, Gushkov and Lebdev were the Soviets, were by the bathroom door and trying to slip the lock with their new black Amex Centurion cards, contorting paperclips and attempting to pick and then switching, as like whoever of them was not engaged debriefed us.

Apparently, Moe had shut himself inside the bathroom unresponsive. The gender neutral bathroom, because it had the only flushable toilet on this floor.

Then the water in the watercooler was rippling, the plants were rustling, as like Tetrateers and guests backed away into cubes. We were hooked by a beltloop and brought along too.

Kor was charging down the corridor toppling processors, wielding a hammer and screwdriver as like to chisel the law into the door.

Super Sal was rushing just behind him flailing either in a protest of access methodology or merely trying to retake his tools.

[What happened? Moe picked a fight with the VCs or with Kor?]

Basically, Kor had called a VC meeting, had not invited us but had invited Moe. This was the first we had been informed about any of this. Apparently, Moe had been under the impression that the purpose of the meeting was to examine his plans for the DCent, which, for him, was culminant. Anyone else would have resented the lack of notice, but he was primed. He had been primed since birth. His first birth. This was why he had endured the quibbly servers and Tetplex delays, this was what he had been mounting and sealing and soldering and suffering for through every karmic deferral, countless reincarnations counted as like retroincarnations until the bodies released their egos. All existence had been just a mobilization for this, the mindful manifestation of his sadhana, his purpose, this slideshow presentation.

After Moe finished presenting Kor applauded and said they were tabling on the absence of table the DCent for later. For now Moe had to focus on this thing called a Sapp.

Rather, he had to turn it into a STrapp. To make it searchcapable. That was the agenda in its entirety. In this, Kor was the decider.

Moe was speechless initially.

The rationale was revenue, Keiner said. An outcampus server could wait, but a tetrating storage device could not. It was y2K sensitive. And y2K was sensitive.

Waiting, Dustin said, is what servers do.

The decision, not as like the commissioned product, made itself.

Moe yelled in Hindi, and if you recall your Mahabharata or Ramayana, how the bowstring is said to snap and the arrow is said to wail through the air as like the god Rama slays the king of the monkeys, that was the yell with which Moe fled the meeting.

Or basically.

Out in the hall, the Keinerites kept crying about an "asshole Sikh," which at least the Carbonites refuted. Moe was an asshole, but never a Sikh.

We squatted by the bathroom door attempting to mediate. We suggested to Kor and the VCs that Moe would only have to supervise the STrapp, not dev it himself. We suggested that if the future solvency of Tetration required Moe to temporarily transform his role, it was only fair to define a time commitment and profitshare fraction. But there was no response from the other side of the door and from this side there was just Keiner who clicked his dentures, "Every now and then, boy, you have to STrapp one on."

It took until noon, and the exchange of hammer and screwdriver for fire extinguisher, for Kor to bust the door.

But Moe was gone. The bathroom was voided. There was no window to slip through, there were no tiles or insulation panels pried, staff had been present around the clock and yet. He must have gone for the ducts again and shimmied.

It was so hot that summer that even the flies were in heat. Anyone in building 2 who had to piss just went outside in or around a contractor bucket but for shitting they had to go to building 1 until Super Sal had reinstated the door.

://

[The way Moe reacted, wasn't he just
protecting his pride?]

Moe was only four below us on the corporate totempole. He barely tolerated working with others on his own designs, and now he was being bullied to work on theirs. The DCent was his maya project and not the STrapp. But more to the point, more salient.

He must also have been disappointed, as like his reaction to this treatment had set him back transmigrationally, rather set in front of his atman soul further benchmarks of deaths and undeaths he had to meet before ever again being admitted to a meeting with VCs. We are saying this for serious, positing that if the situation had been less spiritual he would have contacted us or returned our contact, he would not have gone off the rez.

[But didn't you intercede with Kor—I mean,
aren't you the boss?]

But Moe was also our friend.

And he reminded us of D-Unit. In that they both were engineers who put metal to metal welding the devices on which we just used and were used and typed, and if that idolization had always insecured us, what insecured us now was how that idolization was causing our lenience. We were accused of being lenient. By our two other cofounding partners, whom we pinged preliminary to Kor, though Kor must have pinged them both already.

This was a test, Cull and Qui argued, a popquiz even a rectard would have anticipated. Moe was being sent to discipline school, a postgrad class in detention. The subjects were teamwork, reciprocal priorities. How respect for authority can confer authority itself.

Qui had never wanted to deal with phrasal identification and relation through bit vectors, Cull had never wanted to waste himself on interteam/intrateam Tetmail. They pointed out that our own ambitions had not always pertained to Adverks algys.

Moe was a genius, we said, but they said that in business a genius was replaceable. Moe would have to prove himself as like a prerequisite to being turned loose on his own server Taj Mahal.

Today Tetration has 12 resident beekeepers, four affineurs, two ongoing emoji valency experiments, and a lab dedicated solely to honing a 3D printer that itself can be 3D printed. Today we are able to afford a Moe, but at the time we had no budget for integrity.

We returned to our office, the office of Posek and Syskin, or Roland and Toole, to mull alone for a jag until we were found, within that standard deviation between Thursday and Friday.

We were the only ones around, but then a nose poked as like a talkingpoint just above our felt divider. Kor entered, squeezing, and while he pondered what of nothing but us and our terminal to sit down on, we told him we agreed, but told ourselves we regretted it.

[Why?]

Because he was not coming to persuade us, he said. Which is überindicative Kor, the confidence that his own conviction is enough to convince anyone of virtually anything.

We have that in common, us and Kor, and perhaps you too.

[So what was he trying to wrangle out of you?]

After the weekend. Hindu month of Shravana, late August. It was a mandir sessh but we forget which. A holiday. A major. A biggie. Putrada Ekadashi, when you pray to Vishnu if you are single for a wife, if you are a couple for a son. Or Janmashtami, when you celebrate the natality of Krishna as like the eighth avatar of Vishnu. Fasting. Insomnia.

Kor wanted to make an offering, to Moe, and of all things, he wanted the billboard.

The billboard Moe had passed every day or even twice a day for two years now to avoid traffic and tolls between home and the Tetplex.

The billboard that had inspired Adverks.

On our previous and only visit, on our way back from remotely controlling LA, the billboard that had inspired Adverks had advertised some local petting zoo or playland, then we recall Moe mentioning fashion, an ad featuring the model Lena Söderberg or someone resembling the model Lena Söderberg, and though we would just be inventing its next iteration it was comptrastingly bland as like for a mayoral campaign, or just for itself, Imagine Your Ad Here. This iteration had been especially enraging, to Moe, who must have taken the detour past this billboard only to feed that rage, or else to provide fodder for his interstitial work banter, because he would always be delivering us updates about it, verging into diatribes about the lazy wasteful Americanness he had taken it to represent.

But then just earlier that spring, toward the end of the fiscal year and the start of all our trouble, a new ad had finally gone up.

As like it was a sign.

It was a billboard, which now promoted a languageschool.

Kor had sent us out with the Schloger nephew who was interning for us that summer and was president of the mountain climbing club at Cornell, and Ronnie G who had a catering business, but a landscaping truck, and we drove all the lanes of tar that become Calaveras Boulevard as like they cross the 880 in Milpitas.

To recap: Ronnie Giudice, husband of Salvatrice Trapezzi. Randy Schloger, husband of Heather Trapezzi, uncle of the intern.

We drove along the chains of Verizons and AT&Ts and the Wells Fargos and the odd weird indie Thai restaurants that buffered the parkinglots that buffered the stacks of big box stores that would never be properly malled. We passed Best Buy and Walmart and an intersection of Mexican laborers, as like the access road wandered toward the freeway again, in that stunned and desperate way a dying coyote approaches a dumpster.

And then we stopped. At the last stoplight before the coiled ramps and cars. We were pinched between Ronnie G at the wheel and the Schloger intern nephew, and we were feeling their pressure, and feeling their doubt. Just after the light was the rear of a landfill. A planting of wan sapling evergreens and a fence at the rear of a commercial landfill. Then, attached to the fence and between the evergreens was a blue that was not the sky.

Rather, it was the Bay, billboarded up in the air in dramatic panorama, and though the Golden Gate Bridge was arching across it, the calibration or transfer was off and the result was less golden and more a silver gray as like ash, while the Bay itself was the color of all the weeds outside the frame. Bottomline, though, what was truly distinctive about the image was that in the oozing middle of the Bay, and half on one side of the bridge, half on the other, but also just erected through it, the Statue of Liberty was photoimposed in malfunctioning printer and monitor-scalding electric blue screen of death.

The face of Liberty was not her face or even the face of a woman but the face of a genderless and racewise indistinct person neither old nor young and not even just one person but a composite. The blended American in flubbed retouch.

In the raised hand was still the torch but the other cradled what appeared to be a Dynabook. The earliest but unproduced tablet computer from Xerox-PARC.

The English text was "Study English With Us And Live Your Dreams (Both Conversational And Technical)," above text in every other language and a 1-800 number but no online presence just yet.

The Schloger intern nephew whistled as like Ronnie G gunned his truck. "Not going to be a problem," he said.

The Schloger intern nephew set the ladder in the grass and said, "That German is whack, that Chinese is whack. The thing is falling down anyway."

As like they had been stealing billboards all their lives.

We suggested it would be easier to razor and roll the thing but Ronnie G and the Schloger intern nephew insisted on detaching the billboard from the aluminum bracket full and complete in its plywood frame.

We trucked off with it propped between flatbed and cab.

It just occurred to us that it would have been easier to buy it.

Moe had a slanted rhombus shanty house at the edge of the Asian diaspora, Centerville, Fremont. Which explains why he spent time at the mandir. Nothing explains how he spent his money. We reversed into the driveway and honked and Kor came out to the stoop and across the tanned brown lawn. Ask us how he got inside. Ask us how he was sweating.

The doorway dimensions would not accommodate the billboard, and the garage was sealed at every threshold by a keypad whose combos were, Kor had found them to be, uncrackable. We were considering giving it a go just to show him up, but the Schloger intern nephew was already up on the stoop holding the billboard aslant and Ronnie G was revving his chainsaw. He sawed clean through the frame and bridge and even through Liberty, the paper chunking into papers and the paste that bound them brittling away to exfoliate ragged sooty rainbows. Every one of the ads was still there, apparently, providing backing, providing weight, as like each next ad had just been stuck atop the prior, as like for the benefit of the prior, to stick, bubble, lump, and make whole by the concealment, because now in their surfacing all that remained of whoever had or had not been elected, of Lena Söderberg or her double, and of that foundational inspiration of happy healthy parentless California children playing around a sandbox and monkeybars, was just a mass of acidburnt skin peeling twisted.

Kor directed the halves inside and had the Schloger intern nephew lean them between the walls as like to obstruct the window. They took up so utter much of the room that we and Ronnie G had to keep to the hall, and then he went outside to wipe down his truck.

We felt around for a lightswitch. A burro blanket was tacked to the wall and the plaster around it scummed with swatches of the deserty hues, evidence of a previous occupant deciding on, then abandoning, an upgrade. The linoleum was stripped. In the kitchen was a spork/knife, soysauce. The fridge was not plugged in. The efficiency tag was still on the range. The bathroom had just gone paperless. The bedroom was so unfurnished it did not even have a computer.

Circling back, Kor and the Schloger intern nephew had angled the billboard halves to fit in a diptych as like an altar. They had lined the baseboards along the hall with banded stacks of sacrificial cash, a $10K advance on the STrapp.

Not much, and not even generous as like an insult.

Anyway, Moe concluded his holiday fast as like he always did, with a japa prayer to Vishnu, Krishna, Devki, Devkikrishna, and froyo. Frozey yozey. Frozen yogurt. Moe was a freak for froyo. Every cup was a different system error blend. Kiddie cereals, gummis, dodol. He never used a scooper but his hand, two fingers. Not just for toppings, for gorging.

Before he even finished, though, he called the Tetplex. However by the time the Trapezzi Sisters had determined which office extension we were currently using, which was the office extension of the Soviets, Gushkov and Lebdev, Qui and Cull had patched in too. We listened to the licking. All that was hearable was inveigling and slurps, ambient clank of van.

We were trying not to announce ourselves just yet but must have been respiring because Moe without a swallow said, "Do you know what is rectarded?"

We said we did not know what was rectarded specifically.

He said, "STrapps."

We agreed.

He wanted to know why not task, insert engineer here. He wanted to know why not task, here insert another.

But all we had to give him was what the VCs had given us, a flatterjob. No one else had his artistry, we said, no one else had his tenacity, that was what we told him, and it was while blowing that down the phone that we might have had the sense, we might have but did not, that this insistence on Moe was if not stupey then stupey suspicious.

Finally, Moe said he would do this suckalicious STrapp. But under four conditions.

One. He would never again be forced into a project. Two. He would not be listed in the patent filings for or be associated in any way with any STrapp product. Three. He did not want to report to Kor directly and if he had to report at all it would be to Carbon or Keiner and strictly via email. Four. He wanted Kor to personally restore the billboard to its original location, and replace the locks on his house and the bedroom alarmclock that was broken.

Kor unmuted his speaker just then and joined the call, assented to the first, assented to the second, and got Moe to compromise on the third by agreeing to his emailing the VCs but insisting he work out of the Morememory facility, though with total independence. Four Kor had to reject or rather accept as like a provocation.

We did not recall an alarmclock. Kor did not recall breaking one.

://

[Kor's always been manipulative?]

Psychology is for trophy spouses and corpses. Even now you are wasting our time.

[But he always gets his way?]

Kor had gotten Moe, the one human responsible for making us profitable, relegated to the Moremory incubator just to hatch this hunk of STrapp, while without telling anyone he had Cull and Qui out on a nationwide fieldtrip searching for a location for a tentative DCent. We ourselves would not be tapped into this until the next genexec in September. The general executive meeting. September.

They were visiting visnes with an appetence for data. Our founding partners were in LA, meaning outside LA. New York, meaning New Jersey. They were in Illinois. Maryland/Virginia. Assessing the expediencies of the Texas/Iowa border. Data occupy no space but place matters in proximal terms. The closer the users to servers the closer the users to being served. Come for the speed, stay for the algy. If we supplied speed, preference would be won.

They were back for the October genexec. On the agenda was a discussion of two new cartopositioning sites and which one we would either have to dev against and compete with or compete with others to acquire. Penultimate item was the formation of planteams to improve our foreign semantics, which devolved into a wonky procon debate of Cyrillic rootzones, .рф. Then Qui and Cull stood bashfully offering their surveys of the renewable energy compatibility, but just gray drab dull inclemency, of Celilo, Washington/Oregon.

Moe did not attend this meeting either, but should have. The drive should have been going into production already.

[You were in touch with him? I mean—what were you doing all this time?]

That was just about the time of the letter, which had been addressed to us and brought by post. A globally synched humanbased delivery system.

Point is, a letter had been delivered but not to The Clingers, where we still had the condo, neither to Sierra Vista, where we had rented this vinylsided cyanobacterially roofed crashpad to be maximally proximal to the Tetplex, nor c/o the Tetplex whose treemail has always been envelopes of anthrax flour and lipsticked postcards from deathrow, but c/o M-Unit and Aunt Nance. M-Unit, who had called Super Sal who had called us to his phone, was apologizing for the snailish delay. The letter had been posted to their previous Palo Alto addy and so had to be fwd:d to their current Berkeley addy. Also, they had been away. M-Unit had never told us she was going, but insisted she had. They had mediated Eritrea, sabbaticalized Ghent.

We told M-Unit, drag to trash, it was just another beardy luddite demanding a ransom on our sanity. Though if she were feeling in her citizen mood, she might dial the FBI or the CDC.

Either way, we said, she would have to get used to our new profile, inure herself to philatelic harassment and Safeway bags of ricin left on the porch.

M-Unit countered with accusations of Chomskyism, or megalomania, and said that any fellow creature who had gone through the trouble of postage was due an audience, respect.

"Open it yourself."

"We do not open mail that is not for us," M-Unit said.

Aunt Nance, on the study extension, "But you steamed that Dutch envelope of mine, just for an offer to lecture on Baathist Clientelism at The Hague."

"We do not get involved in conversations that do not involve us," M-Unit said.

What Aunt Nance humped downstairs and unsealed was a normcore AAA roadmap to Delaware, DC, Maryland, Virginia. A handwritten line joined Fort Meade to McLean, from the middle of which another line went south to drown in the Potomac and make a T.

M-Unit offered that the postmark was San Jose, CA, 95126.

But the return addy was Pruristac, which does not exist except as like a midden of shellfish shells, a lost original Ohlone settlement on the margin of Pacifica.

[So Moe or someone impersonating Moe sent you some roadmap of the nation's capital? Why through the post, though—he'd never heard of email?]

He had.

This was toward November. That cold warm clouding toward November. Fog in advection, wet light deresolutioning into darkness by noon. The Bay getting to resemble itself on the billboard.

Everyone was feeling this weather as like confirmative of STrapp fail and so a Keiner renege on the balance of our funding. That at least was the chatter in the corridor and at the end of the corridor the office of Kor was empty. Kor was never around. The claim was the common coryza. Or a stomach flu. Everyone chattered and wheezed.

The office of Kor, we had always avoided going inside.

[Wait, hold up—I'm not seeing the connection. What does all this have to do with a map?]

The office of Kor, we had always avoided going inside. A showercurtain hung over the threshold, indicating a total availability to staff. We approached that clearish nylon sheet, and handled it carefully because the rod was not bolted but wedged between jambs and so would fall if tugged. The shelving units were empty then, as like they were waiting for their contents. Groundbreaking shovels from the African techschools we would finance, Taiwanese Olympic pingpong team jerseys, putters that decided the Masters, the key to the city of Sderot. Nothing Kor had any relationship to, just fealty from admirers, dignitary tribute, rubberplant, spiderplant, fern, ficus.

We picked up his phone and called Moremory in Cupertino, asked for Moe, who was not available.

We asked for Kor, and the lobby bot without any sardonics replied that Kor was available only at the number we were calling from.

November the policy changed.

[Fucking stop—you're going to have to slow the fuck down and explain this to me. You suspected Kor of hanging around Moremory to crack whip on Moe and make sure the product shipped?]

November the policy changed. The new deal was no meetings. Kor had sent the email, which Cullqui fwd:d approvingly, and Quicull fwd:d disapprovingly, but we had also received the missive directly from Kor. We responded to such redundancies with an email reminding them of their founder status, which, if it had no other perk, at least signed a blank check re: scheduling. Cullqui replied all complaining about our tone, cc:ing Kor, bcc:ing Moe. Quicull replied all complaining back, cc:ing Moe, bcc:ing the Soviets.

We neglected to mention that we had taken to regarding them not as like friends anymore but a conformant unit, which we called Cullqui if they sided with Kor, and Quicull if they sided with us. We called them that mentally, then increasingly aloud.

We found ourselves unable to control our impatience and so went into the shared Tetcal and filled a convenient blankness, which turned out to be Thanksgiving.

The meeting would be a Culloquium, a Quiocullum, calendared for Founders Only, and for everyone else not a founder to worry about. Its only agenda would be to assert that it was still our prerogative to have one. A meeting or agenda. Cull and Qui canceled tofurkey carving with Roland, Toole, Posek, Syskin, and their consociate SOs. We had not been invited to that potluck. M-Unit and Aunt Nance spent their holidays of Puritan hegemony at the Korean spa.

The building 1 meetingroom had just been finished. It was paneled in slabs of gleaming serpentine that approx 140 million years ago had erupted from the mantle of the earth to become the crust of the Pacific that deformed it into greenness and receded, as like California rose. The mineralizations matched across the slabs, their quartz as like polished static. Everything, carpeting to knobs to handles, gave shocks. The table was sequoia, a crosssectioned stump obtained sustainably from a tree timbered dead outside Yosemite, the rings showing evidence of approx 620 years of fires and storms, after which we always lost count. Its glossy varnish was set with saddlethemed leather chairs.

Qui showed, and he stood, until Cull showed, and they sat, opposite each other, and so we sat too, but because the table was round all us CoFos were at opposites. CoFounders.

We opened by announcing Tetrateer of the Quarter, Salvatrice, who had just had a baby. Super Sal had Tetblasted about it, which was next item, a zero tolerance policy for all vanity Tetblasts.

Qui and Cull said nothing, so we declared a moment of silence to reflect on the genocide of the precolumbian peoples.

Kor, who would ordinarily facilitate our meetings, had introduced a practice of docking the pay of any Tetrateer who interrupted him, prorating the sum by time lost to interruption weighted by employee number. So, as like he lumbered through the door leveling our concentration, we figgered he owed us, despite his position. He had on jorts so short they were as like nonexistent below a long pouchy baja emblazoned with the Tetgram. We hated that insignia, ^{T}T, and hated its font, Fellahin Serif, designed by, immaterial. We hated "Your Site Never Dies, It Just Loses Rank," "Never Hesitate 2 Tetrate," "We Work 4 Free," and "Tetriffic," and hated the office contests too, Best Varint Reduction, Best Alt Use of Staplers, both of which we would have won except, immaterial. All were Kor initiatives.

Our President sat straining against the pommel of his saddle. We tried to decide whether his ruminant gumchewing meant that he was, or was not, expecting a meal.

We ceded the floor, and the single dryerase wall, to our CoFos, who had reconsidered their recommendation of DCentering Celilo, apparently, and were now unanimously in support of DC. Rather Maryland/Virginia. Celilo would never be feasible, they explained. Even if the Columbia River would scale, hydroelectrically, if the Columbia Gorge would be scaled, anemoelectrically, and regardless of all subsidies and tax credits.

They were revising their projection of average DCent power consumption to exceed 20–22 megawatts/quarter, an amount unsustainable on renewables alone. An amount unsustainable even if American forces would annex and refine all the fossils in Iraq.

The goal for now, they said, had to be to serve our Beltway customers, whether from a base among the Amish farms of Mechanicsville, MD, equidistant to two Mirant coal plants, or Newport News, VA, by a Dominion Resources coal plant that supplied NASA Langley, which had granted them a tour.

Throughout this report of our CoFos, something was nagging at us, something was off. It was Heather who had just had the baby, not Salvatrice. Anyway they both had off. They were stuffed together with the rest of the Trapezzis making gravy.

All our other employees, even our employees who had only just pilgrimed to our coast on probationary visas, were away and giving their thanks.

Kor chewed as like he was mouthing grace. Outside our meetingroom the Tetplex was all barren open plan bullpen and deserted pods, halogen for no one, and the hum of things unused but still plugged in.

Which explains why he was not spotted, this courier, why he was not stopped, this rider from across the Bay.

Someone, Moe or someone, must have let him into the lobby.

He must have wheeled straight through. Taken the stairs. Stepped them with his bike. The elevators, biometric now, at the time would have required a swipecard.

Our door was ajar and he was dizzy skidding through. Hispanic, Latino. Indo. Chaingrease on his denim and the wrong cuff was rolled. The smell of his sweat was of frying. He tried to slot his bike between the hinges, then leaned against the handlebars and huffed.

Rather, he was struggling with his backpack. A cinch string backpack. He shrugged to get loose of it and twisted in his windbreaker, writhing the pack around to his front until its toggle was in his teeth and he was biting to slacken the strings, to extricate a clipboard. He shoved it at us with both hands but without a pen.

As like we had a pen, or would steady him.

But Kor snatched the clipboard away, read our name from its sheet and asked, "You order food delivery?" and asked the courier, "What do we owe?"

The courier though was bent over sucking air, delivering us a seizure, or tugging out what appeared to be the lining of his cincher, but was a trashbag. He tried to unziptie its ziptie and then just slashed through the black shiny plastic with his nails.

Kor waved the clipboard and yelled, "Oye ese, what are you doing? Quién te ha enviado?"

But the courier was oblivious, he was on his knees, wriggling partially out of the bag and dripping this slimy rank squircle, a device shaped as like a square circle. This panicked Kor, who wound up with the clipboard and smacked him on the back and everything just spewed. The device flew across the room amid an acidulous piñata confetti of huevos rancheros and arros con upchuck, semidigested plaintain rounds and frijole flak and cola. For serious unmelted chunks of cola ice soaking the carpet a darker fawn than we had paid for.

Kor tossed the clipboard at the courier, lifted him by the pits as like he yelled, "Lo siento, lo siento, no se lo digas a mi jefe, no hacer que me despidan," but we do not speak Spanish. Kor crashed him into his bike, which he crashed into the door, frontwheel bucking, rearing through, pedals scraping processors already slated for service toward the stairs.

Barf treadmarks down two flights to the lobby.

Qui had tipped his chair into a fort and huddled behind it. Cull was atop the table on his mobilephone with 911, which kept asking the Tetplex addy, and he kept shrieking the answer, Tetration.com. The only addys he ever retained were online. In frustration he threw the unit, clunky and weighty and totally state of the art then with its extra sharp retractable antenna fully out, not at anyone specifically, but at the ceiling, which scattered it down the hall as like components.

Even now that nick is there. Up on the ceiling between mediate track fixtures since replaced, and though all the furnishings are different too. We told Super Sal to tell his migrants not to touch it, and Kor just let it pass. We can praise him for that at least.

Now, the delivery. The bloodcolored package in the corner.

This was the STrapp, the y2Kreeper, the only model that existed or that we had ever encountered and yet we recognized it, which in other circumstances would have been the certification of smart design. But this was just a sloppy handpacked brick, contouring at its extremities into hooded vents influenced by snakes. Its middle was split, though the split was ragged as like it had been done manually and not manufacturally standard. This midunit gash exposed a motor, rotor, stator windings, readwrite headstack and magnet, spinless disk. Two stray sopping coils were centered. A slick conjoined pair of wiry wrinkly spheroids.

Then Kor was just next to us flicking the dense retch from his hands, wiping his face with his baja. He leaned over and bared a patch of his ass, white, round, reddening. But the sodden orbs were redder, rounder, and hairy. He picked them up and let them dangle.

By December the Tetplex had contracts with every able vet of Gulf War I as like security guards, and we had gone on leave. Discussing this meeting was never discussed. Except, through the US Postal Service again, c/o M-Unit and Aunt Nance again, Kor sent us the results of the analysis. Courtesy of the UC Berkeley Museum of Vertebrate Zoology. It was bull scrotum, they concluded. Gouged into the circuitry were two balls in a sack.

://

[You get yourself all crazed about office politics, Moe's been hijacked to put this drive together and then what he turns in has a penis inside? Am I with you? Because if I am, then I don't understand.]

Not penis, the testes.

Please, we did not understand it either. Rather we did, but wrongly, on the novitiate plane. In the way we can understand that all humanity is inviolably one but still not realize who our friends are. Or that the guy carting his recyclables down La Cienaga is God.

The suddenness with which life can scale expectation. How the most essential secret is how to live among lesser secrets never disclosed. How what we hide best from ourselves is not our own ignorance but how that ignorance sustains us. How trust can become another method of control, how even the future of openness is closed.

We were swiveling around in a postlaunch tizzy pretending we had transcended Beta and attained nirvana. But then Moe went and changed the OS on us, he changed the platform. As like to say, you think you have passed through all the realms already, Buddha boy, think again. You think you have broken the cycle of rebirth and redeath and are now exempt from its traumas, think again.

Moe was showing us that no one was pure, because he was showing us the sign of Kali. Of Kali Yuga. Meaning the final phase. The very last. Extinction, the postscript. Which makes all that karma and feedback loop of the soul stuff fairly moot.

For Hindus, the world goes through four stages. In the first stage, the world was ruled by gods, and in the second, the gods fought, in the third, the world was ruled by humans, and in the fourth, ours, the humans are fighting, terminally. In the beginning, purity is signified by a fourlegged bull. With each subsequent stage, the bull loses a leg. The time of demon Kali is the time of the onelegged bull, which will never again chase its own tail. At the end, the bull with only one leg to stand on will be slaughtered, and along with it, the world.

[You got all that from Moe shoving bull testicles into a searchequipped storage device?]

Confirmative. We wish we had kept it. The STrapp, not the scrotum. But by the time that had occurred to us it was gone.

[Kor?]

But we certainly kept the post. Though Kor must have a copy of it too.

Here. This memcard. Here. Just a STrapp on a chain.

[What post? What's the deal with this memcard? I'm just trying to make sure you don't lose me.]

To take content down from online is almost impossible now and anyway even if taken down in terms of accessibility the content itself almost always remains, it just stays clouded. Nubified. Nephed. But back then it was possible to destroy it.

By comptrast, to take a person down has always been easy. People take down themselves.

For example, the itching. For instance, the scratching. We basically spent all our time disambiguating whether we were scratching at itches or itching at scratches, our migraines extended to seize even our abdominals, our skin tasted as like salt. We had come down with a bad case of psychosomia. Though after tetrating for our symptoms of rashes, fevers, chills, and fatigue, we found that we had ringworm, shingles, scabies, and mule lymphangitis. Comorbid cutaneous infections fungal, bacterial, viral, mule. Chronic circadian rhythm disorder. Tendonitis. Carpal tunnel. Our fingers would go numb and then our hands would go numb and then our entire arms would flail as like rashy dying parasites.

The prime salience was, we were home again, though not at Muralla Way or even Sierra Vista. Rather this had been the home of Ma and Pa Le Vay, the elders I, whose generation had been able to afford two floors with a baud of yard, Claremont Hills, Berkeley. M-Unit and Aunt Nance had moved in after moving them to that assisted living facility close by and even resembling the university. To be clear, neither Ilona nor Imre Le Vay were dead yet, but now one is, though we have never determined which.

It did not help that the relationship between M-Unit and Aunt Nance was healthy. We were unhealthy while they thrived. They cuddled in the lounger covered with shawls reading conlang morphologies and the Asian syllabaries used only by women as like hiragana and nüshu. They had friends, academic friends, gardening group friends, LGBTQ youth counseling center friends. We just had them, and their shared study the Jamaican eldercare aides had used for changing into and out of their scrubs, second floor. Propped along the bookcases were photos of two Hungarians we barely felt any relation to being amicably restrained by middleaged husky Jamaicans. Aunt Nance had hung her diplomas on the wall along with a gonfalon that explained all the different types of dispute resolution. One type was legally binding settlement, another type was also settlement but not legally binding, the third was about getting each party to understand the other emotionally, while the fourth was just about getting each party to recognize the existence of the other.

We lay on the foldout sofa and refused all fuel and hydration and so lost weight and were convinced also our mind. Aunt Nance asked us whether our actions or inactions were a protest for or against any particular cause, and we yelled that she had asked us that already, but she had not, she said, and M-Unit said that it had not been her either, and we believed them.

We stayed offline completely. Qui and Cull visited and talked about investments they were considering and offered us tips because we had no investments. They had purchased for us a Muppet at auction. A rare authenticated Elmo.

They took turns operating it as like to cheer us but we just turned the talk to Moe and so ultimately it was a puppet telling us he had gone missing but that Kor was pulling every string to have him found. Kor would pull everything unraveled.

El Moe. We believed in losing our mind.

M-Unit left small plastic UFOs of salad and small tetrapak milks outside the door. Aunt Nance slid under it a book, *The Little Adventurer*

Atlas of Sexual Orientation. They kept calling us to deck the tree with dreidels. They had never gotten a tree before. We never got up from the foldout. Merry Chanukah and Christmas.

New Year. Remember the New Year. Cull had apparently met his father and stepstepmother playmate at a reception Timex was holding for the Hong Kong Secretariat. Qui had apparently at the suggestion of his brothers chartered the USS Chesapeake to take all the delinquents who had beaten him up in the Philadelphia schools and strand them in Rehoboth. JBates had purchased a former US military bunker sunk under the Mojave Desert and refurbished it to withstand polarity shifts, comet impacts, 50 megaton nuclear blasts. All Carbonites and friends of Carbon had been invited to hunker down.

M-Unit and Aunt Nance were having a party. A scholastic coven bash. They were busy unfolding rental tables and chairs on the fully enclosed, fully heated glass porch out back, which was a renovation we had paid for to mark no occasion, and also they had put in a request. $28735 had seemed a fortune then. M-Unit and Aunt Nance were rearranging the market greens so intricately it was as like they had not only marketed and mixed them but had grown them too. They were clattering platters and chasing chestnuts across the talavera. At 20:00 or so half the Berkeley feminist department showed. The half that M-Unit was still friendly with. We cracked our window to snoop, let the cold in. Cracked into the conversation.

Some shrink from Stanford, who might only have been the spouse of someone, wanted to talk to us. Everyone else wanted to talk disaster. They were drinking as like everything was going to y2Krash and so were convinced that everything was going to y2Krash even though the aughts were already being lived in Lahore. In Karachi. Delhi, Mumbai. On the darkside of the dateline, light not from fission or fusion rising over a new event horizon. They drank port and Aunt Nance passed a joint and M-Unit abstained not because we were around but because it was hash. Which, she said, always confused her libido and destrudo.

Though M-Unit and Aunt Nance had liberalized in this house to the point of finally owning a TV, they kept it off in favor of the hearth clock. They did not want to witness the carnage, but they still might have wanted others to experience it. Newt Gingrich, Exxon and Mobil, which had just become ExxonMobil, the WTO, HMOs, supporters of Prop 187, President Clinton even though he was against Prop 187. Time measured nothing but a failure to change. Someone told Aunt Nance her son was destroying the culture and someone else said he was destroying the human and Aunt Nance replied it was M-Unit who deserved the compliment. The shrink said he would talk to us about it. His was the only male presence, and someone said only males would confront in that way, and someone else said that historically psychoanalysis itself was nothing but the sublimation of masculine confrontation. But neither this nor the waist squeezes of his spouse were stopping him from hauling in from the porch. It was the clock that was stopping him. A crowd of tenured feminists counting, 4, 3, 2, 1. Icons of the triumph of the male orgasm, signifying the cessation of coitus and the onset of death. Popped corks, the froth, the smoke, the fireworks in the sky toward the Bay.

But as like everyone was still alive at a Pacific Standard hour into the first day of the year 2000 they had no way to avoid clearing dishes. They cleared and we lost them from our window. Then M-Unit was at our door. We did not want scraps. But she was offering the phone instead. We had a call from Russia, Soviet Russia. We did not want to take any calls, but Gushkov and Lebdev were insistent. M-Unit thrust the phone at us and paced hiccupping in the hall as like we were getting doomsday news from the Kremlin, and Aunt Nance waddlingly joined her and steadied her wobble against her and burped.

The Soviets had volunteered to work prowl for the Eve, to maintain site vigilance, expecting nothing, but poised. y2K itself was not the threat, it was whether or how it would rally the hackers. Denial of service attacks so broadly distributed they had to be Martian, Venusian, ping surfeit of a stratospheric bandwidth, untraceable, or fribbly to trace. But the Soviets had none of that to report, all they were wondering was the last time we ourselves had visited.

"Do you mean visited the u or checked in tetside?"

"Either," they said. "Both."

"A month, six weeks, way back in 99—why?"

"Get online," they said.

We got up and grogged past M-Unit and Aunt Nance and down the hall to the Mistress Bedroom, eased down onto the physioball and powered the IBM clone. A crappy bullshitty unit, constipated processor, swollen registry, bloated drives, just fragged. Loaded every program ever at booting, a tertillion .docs on the desktop, and half of them named Test. Our patience tested as like the Soviets jittered. M-Unit drifted up and shrugged a robe around us. We had, we neglected to mention, never dressed.

The computer finally booted but could not find its modem, the modem could not find a signal and the helpscreen automatically loaded. Diagnostic scan in progress. Rotating hourglass, grains in the queue. Quit everything, restart. Quit everything, shut down, unplug, burn the house, build another house, replug, restart. Aunt Nance said she was glad we were feeling better, and wondered whether we would give her a brief tutorial, did not have to be now, it was just that she had never been able to get online.

The Soviets, though, the Soviets said that if we had no access we had to come oncampus.

"Tell Kor," we basically told them.

"With respect," we will not try the accent but maybe the vocab and syntax, "with for your situation, respect, we come only because is crucial."

The cruciality was this. Apparently we, meaning an entity or entities with our ID, had logged into Tetsys at quarter to midnight PST, using an IP from a Delaware eCafé called My Cup Runneth Dover the Soviets had gotten through to enough to determine that it was a proxy for an IP from a Canadian eCafé called Mountiebank Delectables, which we had to suspect was a proxy too by the first, last, yet never just only general law of conspiranoia, which everyone will always refer to, but no one will ever quote.

They, our assailants, had all our tetokens, wardwords, passhibbols, and skelkeys, which meant they had all access, which they used to mod.

"How mod?"

The only change detected, the only change detected so far, was so minor and negligible and immediately remediable as like to render its quiddity alone of major concern.

It was a redirect. All tetraffic was diverted.

"To what?"

All they would tell us was to redirect ourselves to the Tetplex.

Which did not compute, nothing computed. How recy of a hack it basically was, yet how techy the hacker had to have been to execute it.

Then they said it was Moe, which diverted.

They requested permission to take the site offline. "Be smart, this must to do."

Permission granted.

://

[Moe's revenge part 2—where were all
the searches going?]

He who insists on having the end before the beginning will still only have the beginning. Who said that? Vagary might be requisite to life. What about that? Enough. Let us speak.

M-Unit sat lapped atop Aunt Nance, a mesosociologist sat lapped atop a social anthropologist, the shrink was at the wheel and because his spouse had staged a tantrum yelling that we would all be arrested for driving under the influence she had called for a cab and waited moping on the lawn while the car swerved out of the garage. We rode in the seat alongside.

Validate hate if deprived of love.

Breathe greedy.

[When you're through quoting bumperstickers
you'll tell me?]

We terminaled, and because Gushkov was already logged into Tetsys but because two confirms were required for keyswap we had Lebdev log and so were able to regain our access, the only way to begin ending a compromise. We were us again, if just in that.

We set about checking the site, currently extant only tetside. The hpage loaded uncorrupted, but everything searched for detoured to this post.

Before even reading it, though, we screenshot and duped it external. Manipulables must be preserved.

Then, as like Aunt Nance cut us a slice of napoleon leftover from the Eve feast of the Soviets, we read.

[A post Moe wrote?]

Though in a sense we wrote it too.

[How?]

Give us your Tetbook.

[It's yours.]

You will read it.

[No problem.]

Krishna.tet. Save it, read it into record. This memcard is ours, but after this it will not be ours, or yours, because truth belongs equally to all and none. Go.

[Now?]

Better. We will hold it for you, the Tetbook. That is better for us both. We will scroll along and try not to shake.

[Why don't you read and we'll do the scrolling?]

Go on. We do not have the breath.

[Om! Krishna Gonzalez, son of a bitch and a workers hero engineer, was an engineer born himself and so in this caste that is the greatest in the world he was rised! That it was the greatest caste in the world he was rised to believe! Equal to a Brahmin he believed! At the time of his life the four castes were everything and at the top was hard engineer, below that soft engineer, below that the users, and beyond that at the very bottom the untouchable. The hard engineers the bodies made, which allowed the soft engineers to put their minds into them and the users to operate them and the untouchables had no electricity and were pariah. "Harijan." "Dalit." This was the world at the time of the life of Krishna until the age his parents died. He was so deprised he wandered. He was all alone in the age of the world and so to a new country he wandered, Cali. But Krishna Gonzalez found that though the jobmarket was good, the market for making friends with his fellow jobbers was bad especially with the Pakistanis who all had friends from schooling and athletic associations and even this one Pakistani who asked hello how are you doing at the bank and Krishna answered we are doing fantastic when after the transaction Krishna got a sourdough prune danish and beer and they met in the parkinglot where the Pakistani was on smokebreak Krishna greeted him this time but the Pakistani did not recognize him. Also the fellow Indians who had Cali flagged were demissive and cared only about property mortgages and voted the Democrat until they owned and then voted the Republican but just to prevent other Krishnas from downgrading neighborhood economies. They were in favor of quotas. No one to have the opportunities they had. He went on a date with one who was not born in Delhi but in Cali for which he had to beg, the date, and she who worked the cashier at a carwash spent the full time at the dinner theater whingeing about a psychiatric disorder that caused her to go into a druggist and buy a product no matter what and come out again and just in the closest trash toss it immediately, and that was her syndrome that shamed her but also made her feel chosen and proud, she bought things and then not out of shame or chosen proudness but just automatically threw them out, profligia or prodigia was the official psychological diagnosis. Her family who was from Delhi did not comprend either. They wanted her to marry not just any Indian but a certain salary fitness type and she said this was wrong and everyone said this but in personal practice was racist and she would not visit him at his home because at the time it was black Oakland. Krishna should have trashed her on the corner! Krishna should have bought her from her family and tossed! It was not that she or anyone else in Cali had no caste and were premissive but what they had was backward. Role inversal. Krishna went to the movies but not with her and what Calis worshipped were the actors and actresses and not the innovators of celluloid or even of charged couple devices and complementary symmetry metal oxide semiconductors. Famous for praise were the demons who sang and played or the devils who just pretended but not the craftspeople who made the sarod and shehnai, who without microphonics or camera crews went out to the trees to split the wood and the special keywood and mined the metal for the strings and pedals to make a piano, not to mention the inventors of ragas and talas. Famous for praise the painters and sculptors and the architects of museums in the images of banks but not the crushers of berries for the paint or the weavers of leaves for the paper or the collectors of the rodent manes for the brush, not to mention the technicians of quarrying equipment or surveyors. They in Cali celebrated the users of sites above the programmers of code for the sites and them celebrated even above the engineers who designed and erected the machines that do everything and on which everything is done. Krishna dispaired of this but not enough and so was himself tempted to tend his checking account at the very expense of the puranas. It was while in this dispair that a cloud visited Krishna and this cloud was blacker than Oakland and out of it emerged with the tongue out not the female but male gaysexual Kali. The Lord God Kali.]

That was a link to a universal gods directory. Continue.

[Kali the destroyer had a commission for Krishna and it was by this commission that Krishna would fall in caste and be turned upsidedown to become worse than a Lockwood Gardens project shelter leper. Kali the destroyer ordered Krishna to propound a memory device so that with it everything would be rememberable. But though Krishna did not want to agree because for him memory was not a static device of plastic but of volatile flesh and with magics of transmission, he also did not want to earn the disfavor of an armed and dangerous transgender Kali. Also the business that employed Krishna in this life, this business operating the site that roots to this post, encouraged. All his friends who were not friends but just jobbers gave him their kudos and bravery. Krishna accepted. In the spirit of the team. He was locked behind a great gate in the unwashed corner of a startup called Remomori. In Coppertino. A Pakistani handed him specs and instructed him to put them in a betelnut. To erect a betelnut to contain both the specs and also everything, this was what the Pakistani instructed. The specs revealed to Krishna were incredible. They were not what had been stipulated by Kali. Though the memvice was supposed to be equipped with the search functionality of his employer Krishna doubted that anyone familiar with that functionality was familiar with the storage specs because if they had been the storage was so incredible they would have told him. They did not tell him lamentably. Also his employers or their adventurous capitalists had mentioned that the memvice was not to have a modem, but this was to have a modem though not one equipped for the internet but for an intranet, internals. Normally this would make no sense or be a software issue but for Krishna the exposure to this was hard. He was tasked with propounding this feature himself, but then the task kept changing and so the feature kept changing until it had to be both a modem to access and also a server for a proprietary web. Also according to the Pakistani its weight had to be less than 2.2 lbs and its dimensions less than 16" x axis by 5" y axis by 7.25" z axis, meaning mobile. Physically portable. But still durable because it had to be made of this polypropylene copolymer material, waterproof, crushproof, falloffcliffproof, able to withstand temperatures up to 210° F/98.88repeating° C, which is an impertinence, Fahrenheit. In case of its use in situations of not just no signal or current but combat. It had to have an average of 48 hours of rechargeable batterylife. It had to maintain full search functionality while offline and full online functionality while on battery. But what made this combo difficult was memory. The size the Pakistani was stipulating. RAID, redundant array, independent disks. Four drives, removable. 2TB capacity. Blocklevel striping, distributed parity. Each drive fortified by a server blade too. Removable too. Krishna was up to his "pupik" in dualcore processors and working toward double distribution. To ensure that failure of one would not be failure of all, which is drivers and serves aside an important lesson for the citizens of Cali.]

Moe always referred to white Americans as like Pakistanis and conversely referred to Pakistanis as like white Americans. Continue.

[Krishna would complete an ectype and leave the Remomori lab at night and return by morning to find it had been taken for testing with the search capability, and so he would complete another and never again leave the lab. At midnight the time of this posting but last month or six weeks and two days ago a car came. Last century! Last millennium of users! Not just a car but a Caterham Rover K Series MG X 1.4 liter engine 16 valve double camshaft six speed gearbox operated by an adventurous capitalist for a firm called Kinere took Krishna to a motorist inn. This inn did not have an identifiable name but everyone called it the Lesstel. 816 West Ahwanee Ave, Sunnyvale. (408) 734-4607. Outside except for the no name was typal for motorists. Parklot without lines or curb barriers. Rebar on shuffleboard court. Gluetraps and for opossums. Structure itself built out of Lego. Inside was all computers! This cannot be stressed enough people, computers are not furniture! Everyone inside the room was Paki. They had buzz haircuts or dreads and eczematicous and pimple conditions for which the best treatment is the distillation of trees ashoka and peepal. The Pakis who worked with Krishna did not introduce him but were polite and divergent from how they were typal because they had broken the ectype. They had brought the memvice to this room for testing and had not told Krishna about it until they had broken his work. Until they were unable to fix it and they had tried but they had just made it worse. All the doors of the room were open, except the exterior door to the patio vendingmachine, and through them were other open rooms with other computers not furniture in them but staffed by Mormons from Karachi and Lahore. They were writing on their computers code and Krishna had to presume it was programming for this memdevice that was not being accomplished by his employer. Also sensitive papers were taped to the walls. Transfer protocols that even to a lowly but high engineer were comprendable. The Pakis Krishna worked with were called by him the OPs standing for "Orson" and "Parley" but were called "Willcox" and "Bobblehead" by their coresidents in the motorist inn who ordered them to close the doors. They did. Orson and Parley closed the doors. Papers blown to the floor appeared to deal with normalization, entity extraction, morphgraph

analytics, and how to search unstructured txt in
Arabic, Persian, and the terrorist language of Urdu.
The OPs instructed Krishna to fix the unit and he tried
because of vanity but the tools were inappropriate and
he told the OPs and so the OPs offered to get him the
tools and Krishna told the OPs that anything they
expected him to repair had to be brought back to
the lab. But they would not let Krishna go with the
memdevice and advised him instead to go back to
the lab and assemble his tools and return with them.
Krishna was driven back to the lab by the adventurous
capitalist from Kinere and assembled what he
required. The same Caterham was taken the yellow of
rancid ghee. Which despite his pleas he was prohibited
from driving. Krishna was returned to the motorist
inn of Legos and installed with his tools in another
room and Pakis who were foreign to him brought the
broken device and required him to not only fix it but
also to modify it so that within the searchable storage
there would be a further detachable subdrive that
would not only be protected from the rest but also if
detached would destroy the rest in the manner of Kali.
The hero of this epic worked and was not given leave
to depart homeward. But home was not an option in
other terms because his employers whoever they were
had installed in it a surveillance billboard. All the
windows were shut around Krishna and no
conversation was had. The food they brought was
poisoned to nosh. The only noshable food was from
the vendingmachine, around which was the only
conversation. Though the Pakis never spoke with him
but strictly with each other. Krishna intuitioned how
unimportant he was. How unappreciated a menial.
Hard was not crucial. Soft was crucial and was failing.
The Pakis were being utilized to write the code for the
device. That itself was obvs. But the program was not

working. That also was obvs. The only explanation for such an apparatus being custom made by an organization not his employer was that it was for the government of Cali America a memdevice. Further and beyond that its propositioned ability to store information to be shared and searched within a system of closure pointed to the involvement of a number of different agencies. Krishna attempted to demagnetize from his mind who set the founding protocols. ARPA, Advanced Research Projects Agency. DARPA, Defense Advanced etc. etc. Agency. Search clients and find entities that do not endorse collaboration. CIA. NSA. That would explain the tribulation involved. The faces Krishna encountered arguing over popcorn on the patio. THIS WAS A HORRID SECRET KRISHNA HAD FOUND! HE KNEW HE WOULD NOT BE ABLE TO HIDE IT! HE KNEW HE WOULD POST IT AND NOW THIS IS HIS POST! THIS WAS OMINOUS IN THE SUPREME! The algorithm promulgated by the employer of Krishna in this life was being modified to search across the archives of all different agencies so that the intel would be comparable and contrastable. Each agency to a dedicated drive?? Each of them copying to a clastic subdrive and autodestroying its original in case of capture or a seizure emergency for an agent in the field???? But because success and not coopteration has been the priority in Cali America the agencies must have been unwilling to adopt the protocol or methods of processing the archives of others out of vanity. The Pakis all of whom must have been TS/SI COMINT must have had to create one. A single. A standard. The agencies are noncompatible. They are jealous and envious and prise success and abdere their specs. IC. Intelink. "They are at throats," that was all that was explained to Krishna after inquiring how are you doing to this Paki compforensics specialist name of "Hinckley."]

Never skip the parentheticals. "(To the OPs we were Krishna but Vik Ram was how we introduced ourselves to 'Hinckley.')"

[Krishna constructed this interpretation while building the Kalidevice because he was not able to make deficiencies. And this oppressed him, how pride is as instrinsical to a creator of things as amorality and aethicality are instrinsical to the thing created. That is how you become irrelativistic and monotheistic. Make the thing until the thing makes you, which is not a cycle but a spiral. And so he took what he had become and on a holiday celebrating the death of the natives of Cali America departed. He went to a farm to imagine the farms he was not working on and attempted to purchase a castration in rupees. He said the gonads were a folk remedy, he said they were glands to rub on the body of an unmarriageable sister in order to obtain for her a mate, and that if he would have had an unlucky brother he would have paid to clitorectomize a cow. The farmers even with his rupees in their rags treated him strangely. All he had inquired was whether a cow would be able to milk on one leg. He fled the farm. He was pursued and so trusted no one because everyone was a verifiable .gov. He had reached out to friends before through the quasigovernmental mails but no one reached back and so he had no friends. He too became a map refused, no key. And that is what it means to be an emigre of color. You are a cipher no one cares to crack or can crack. No one even recognizes you as a cipher. The Contra Costa sheriff speedgunned my 1988 Dodge Caravan doing 73 in a 55 and so as not to get properly shot I stopped, but was let go with just a $214 fine and that was the worst because that meant Kali had not yet contacted the authorities. I tried to contact the New York Times, CNN, Time. But my calls were not returned to the only payphone left in Alameda County. Charlie Rose was not at home. The metal of the billboard played Hot Talk 560AM KSFO to my teeth fillings and adjusted warmer the climate temperatures. I stayed off email. Traveled by moon and avoided the clouds and the mandir. The agents of darkness even in the showers of the El Camino Y lurked. By the sex novelties dispenser at Capital Launderland were staked. The lottery telemetry was openly rigged. Pumps did not give my Caravan the gallons they asserted. The suffering of my stomach due to nacho poison grew. I fell in the cheese and so fell lowly in the varnas. It was not again my ulcer. It was my body being left by "my jiva." I became a programmer to code the access to what is in this post that had been in my head and also my mind. Then I denigrated even lower and became a user by opening this account and posting this very content to survive. Beta is not samsara. Incarnation. Transmigration. Beta is not even one single punarjanma transcarnation of samsara because everything ends but the cycle does not. The cycle only goes so fast until it is the same as slow and the same as still and withholding. Moksha. Find our exchange attached and below, downloadable as .tet files but also plaintxt because this is the inside of me, guts. Peace out. tetrak -tetrail= IMPORT-PATH –cpp_out=DST_DIR –jv_out=DST_DIR –pyth_out=and just forever gibberish.]

That is not gibberish. That is the sourcecode. Programming compiled. In executable file format. But then also in a document of language, tuples forever. At midnight PST Moe had posted all of this online, and to seal it exfiltrated the fulgence of our algys.

[Give away the algys, give away the business?]

Confirmative. This was everything, the whole company.

[But is there even a bit of fact in what
Moe was getting at?]

To have faith, to require faith, is an admission of lost power.

Credence fills the vacuum of control.

The post was hosted by a Konkani news portal, *Vavraddeancho Ixtt,* or *Friend of the Workers*. It was 02:30 on the West Coast with everyone still partying so 05:30 on the East Coast with everyone just slithering in from partying. All of Europe was still sleeping it off. The portal was able to handle our traffic, oblivious at Indian midday.

Until we were going after its domain as like remorseless, with a hack hash salt concat at md6 spread across four computers. But getting all impatient with the processing we instead set up a dummysite and account for a travel industry tipsheet we invented called the *Wwwayfare Gazette,* typed up a reprint request for a current *Vavraddeancho Ixtt* article about millennial festivities for Westerners in Goa and emailed it to every @v-ixxt.com addy on the masthead, routing it through the same proxies Moe had used, which the Soviets had already tracked through Delaware and Canada and into the UK and certainly, given Moe, gone further. The email linked to our dummysite, which was just a download of a virus we had been studying, petulant malware from Pyongyang. We had been getting homologous viruses also from Seoul, though such masking practice was the traditional dragon dance of the Chinese.

Among the Eastern cultures the only way to truly earn a contagion is to purposefully pass it along.

The editor in chief clicked at 16:50 IST, Goa, and that got us his access, and we wrecked it. We wrecked that mother joint down.

Then we restored all Tetration sourcecode from autobackup and inserted the url and even copypasted snippets of the post txt to index, searching for page mirrors or any other reflective body with same or similar txt, found nothing. If there was a translation into Konkani or any other language that scripts Devanagari or Kannada either there were no repercussions or the agencies got it. TetHindi had not yet been deved. Neither Tetranslate. This was just 01/01. This was still 2000.

Then we decached and rode mod on the algy to block anything with the algy itself from being transclused in future results. Not buried, blocked. If this were just a year later regardless of whether the intel agencies had or had not found a way to play nice together and share, this would have been diametrically impossible. This was the last time possible.

Aunt Nance was a backgammon game up over Super Sal who had dropped by to recaffeinate the Soviets. The shrink was over in the estuary phonecall niche talking on the phone to his spouse.

The sociologists had left.

Our brain was making no sense as like sociology, which is just egalitarian anthropology plus math. We had median nerve palsy in the wrists and yet every keystroke was excruciating because though we had been typing without break our nails had been gnawed to festering paronychia. It was the time all tech shows twice a day and after a reset, 12:00, but the noon one, and we were just about to go live again. Super Sal lost another game and got up to flip the calendar page and we were all just, how quaint, a page.

Outside it was storming. Not winterwise but as like the academics had been correct, the world was ending after all, the universe was over, despite all our work or because of it.

The black cumulus of a helicopter descended, but just before wrecking in the marsh, it hovered. It floated above the reeds bent low. Kor jumped out to make a splash all formally disheveled in a forktailed tux, bowtie snapped, burst cummerbund. He marched straight in to fold us around his belly and squeeze. His shirt was stiff from having been sweated through and then drying and then being sweated through again. He wiped his forehead with a towelette embossed with the grizzly Great Seal of the State of California. He greeted the Soviets humanely too. Even embraced Aunt Nance.

We were about to tell him what happened. But then he grabbed our robe, dragged us toward his office and through the curtain to sit on the futon he on one side and we on the other of M-Unit asleep. Then he told us what happened, and touched our neck, our robe fallen open. He said Moe had been found. Just now. Dead. Committed suicide in Canada. Hanged by a belt from Montreal.

No one would be contacting us but if they did, no comment. No one contacted us. Ever. Never.

Then Kor woke M-Unit, had his copter take her and Aunt Nance on a rainy turn around the Marin Headlands, snow up on Tamalpais. The shrink drove himself. But before, the pilot came inside menacing in how strong he was, and in asking a question called us Sir, in the military style. He asked to use the bathroom.

://

[You never cornered Kor to substantiate Moe's claims?]

Balk not. Virtue is a patience.

[What?]

That was a joke, laugh. Balk, Thor Ang. You might be familiar. Tetrate him if not.

[I'm familiar with him, with b-Leaks, which relates to all this how?]

You will know. We will scroll away into just a squircle parcel for the dirt, but you will know. You must, you will, understand that. That is your privilege. Do not concess the process. All time in its time.

Moe had liquidated through the mesh. He had vaped himself. The balance of his direct deposit Chase Bank checking account had been transferred and all future payments to it had been set to autotransfer to a savings account registered to the Goa Orphanage of Achievement Trust, Oriental Bank of Commerce, funds that had remained untapped until their seizure by the India Reserve, whose inquiry determined that no such orphanage existed. No images were provided to us and since the Americans refused to take the body from Canada because it was not clear that Vishnu Fernandes was a citizen and India refused to take it from Canada because it was not clear that Vishnu Fernandes ever existed, or was Vishnu Vaidya, or was a citizen, he, Mohlone, whoever, was cremated in Montreal. All this according to Kor who brought us the cremation report along with the files of the Vishnus obtained from various Bay Area hospitals pertaining to treatment for dissociative identity, formerly multiple personality disorder, and depression. Brought them to us in Berkeley, audience denied.

[That's all the investigation you did?]

The Soviets scootered out together to the addy. The Lesstel.

They reported just a pukka blacksite all condemned boarded up. Not even a vendingmachine.

On Kor edict Tetration bought the house of Moe from Chase Bank, which gave access to the garage, from which we were sent just tranches of scrawled papers and matchbooks and coasters, random arbitrary disintegrated μCs, disassembled shields, linear regulators, crystals, interferometers, junctions and loops we had such limited bandwidth for that we did nothing to stop M-Unit from trashing them out. Kor had picked them all over beforehand infallible.

And then just a year ago, approaching a decade after the demise of Moe, Kor organized our quantum computing syndicate with Stanford, with its tech all pilfered from the garage, with its elementary particle inspired by Moe having tried, for our sake, to give practical form to his reversible computing theories.

Moe had been inventing the tetbit, as like Kor calls it now, a bit capable of two expressions, superposited, subatomic.

In the way computing works today, a bit can represent EITHER 1 OR 0. But in future computing based on the work of Moe, each tetbit would represent BOTH 1 AND 0. This would speed everything up by a factor of confounding while redimensionalizing all storage. But still this system would always be entropic, which is to say it would use electricity, which is to say it would use electricity without ever regenerating it.

It takes a lot of electricity to keep an elementary particle stable. The kind of electricity whose unsustainable generation might even destroy the planet.

All because of a collapse of significance. As like everything collapsed.

And so it was a compromise. Moe had been compromised, by having normalized his natural madness. He put aside his Tabernacle for quantum pragmatics. And he did it for us.

Moe was a computing genius who is not even remembered for his only realized genius contribution. To advertising.

Tetration donated his house for asylum, some quasigovernmental initiative providing transitional accommodation for political refugees as like hijra fleeing the Pakistani Taliban and last we checked in it was apportioned to some Lhotshampa activist from Bhutan.

We have no clue what became of the billboard.

[So you just closed the books on him? Put Moe behind you?]

If we ourselves did not press to your specs it was grief, bandhu. We were physically pressed worse than ever before now.

Our friend, our partner. Our Injuneer bloodbrother. Had deleted himself. Was erased from our life. We craved contact to such a degree that with every hack aggressed against us subsequently our initial instinct was to hope it was Moe. Schizoid Moe. That his jiva has returned to defeat the Pakis. Jiva is the soul.

[You're feeling what now? Guilty?]

What we feel now was what we felt then but now it has become even worse. We were turned into a child. Unappreciated, depreciated, not fledged. Dwelling still with M-Unit.

We pretended we had never seen or even heard of a computer.

Cull and Qui inquired about what they might do to assist us and M-Unit decreed we would enjoy studying papermaking and so they dispatched who they claimed was a papermaking artisan to Berkeley who entered the study and took her breasts out.

We did not bury our face into them.

To be more open, we would not have preferred a man.

To be as like most open, at this juncture we are basically sexless.

Point being, the letter with the map keyed so uninterpretable, the bull balls chiming as like temple bells, everything Moe ever did was instruction.

Moe was instructing us in how to open, how to be open, as like a lotus getting pollinated, or the cloaca of the gharials that once dined on corpses in the Ganges, the one hole they have for pissing, shitting, fucking, laying eggs, and that might also help with respiration and mobility. A single twoway orifice. Lubed. Ironically never a totally accessible lesson.

Comptrasted with Moe we were closed.
Shut down, broke down, pent.

Users give themselves away
by giving away their only asset, he said

the self in exchange
for selves, he said, but then

[What users?]

There are no users, he said, just, or
No winners or losers
There are no somethings
No victims

He had some line about the first world beginning with educating everyone into accountability, but ending and becoming the last world if that were ever accomplished.

No victims, just users.

[You're still quoting Moe?]

Strain to record everything. In America, even the smallest portions were too big for him, except with "frozey yozey." His favorite places were always selfserve and charged flatrates for small and large cupsizes, regardless of the amount of yogurt and toppings. Moe would stagger in vast crockery to fill, and the staff was unequipped to charge in excess of the maximum. It was not as like anything was returnable, melting probiotics crammed back into dispenser, the carob chunks replaced. It was because of this that all the places switched to retailing by weight. Spring 1998. This was always our prime directive at Tetration. Our actions were the higher law, the lower law either adapted or was abolished.

Summer 98, walking in SF from what had become so suggestively called SoMa onto Ellis Street to pay a visit to his ghee guy, he was stopped by an officer for resembling an AfroMexican suspected of a burglary. In answer to questioning Moe said he lived everywhere, worked nowhere, when asked his name he asked the officer when. Hauled in, he told the entirety of Southern District Station how he owned them, their holsters, their weapons and ammo, and that though they certainly owned them too, as like fellow taxpayers, the injustice was that while he, Moe, had no authority even proportional to his burden over how such things were used, they did, police authority was total. Moe had been picked up on a public street, in public air, under public weather, at public twilight. Non-proprietary, unlicensable, the commons. He did not require the courts, he claimed, the gods had already ruled in his favor. Still he called us and we called Gutshteyn, who met us. No charges were ever filed. As like we left, the arresting cop said, "Still not satisfied with the system, fucko, even you can run for mayor." Moe said, "I wish just to run for mayor of your brain."

If you meet the Buddha along the way
destroy him
by obtaining his confidences
and then making them available publicly.

Fuck Kali
the headseverer

[Are you feeling OK?]

Whatevs. Or whatever your wife would say.

[Why don't we break?]

No, no. Here, take your Tetbook back, here. No. Keep the memcard, the stick. No. Eject it and return it.

://

[Feel or Jesus tell you yet? Or Myung? Fucking Kori
Dienerowitz's flown into Dubai. He just
ambushed me down on the beach.]

Rovery. Ranting. Rambling gamblers gambol in the brambles. With ferry fare fairly free travelers trip with fashionable frequency twixt two temples on the Terekhol.

[OK—but what's Kor doing, besides fucking this up?
What have you not told me?]

About what? Can you name us another multinational corporation tech or rec assetized at north of $90 billion that has not done a favor or two for the governments of every country in which it operates, just hoping not to provoke conflict with the foreign policy of the country in which it is based and the majority of its investors hold citizenship?

[It's time that you came clean.]

What did we say? We are never without a system. We are telling according to plan. What did we leave off with?

[Moe, the hanging, you still have to finish that, hold on,
". . . destroy him by obtaining . . . the self
in exchange . . ."]

We hate our voice. We hate the babiedness in it, the infantile spanked whine, pedolalia. A lacking something sound. An always disagreeing with something sound. To rewind, to replay, the loathing just procreates. As like to be reborn, which is also to redie.

The alternative is to avatar, replicate the self, which

Moe used to say, whatever happens in life always remember that the worst tragedy is already behind us, the end of immortality with the beginning of sex. Once there had been singlecelled organisms capable of eternally replicating by dividing, by splitting, and the replications gradually sought protective symbiosis in colonies that civilized into multicellular organisms. But then an evolutionary drive to succeed emerged among them, and ultimately compelled them to mate with others of their kind in order to eliminate mutation and competition in the propagation of the very best of their kind. Though with each reproduction the essence of the progenitors was becoming less and less evident in their progeny, who grew into separate lifeforms entirely, conscious of their mortality and aware that their only consolation for that and for having their own offspring who would be so different and ungrateful was the fact that reproduction was sex for them, and sex for them was pleasurable.

But then to be able to enjoy the sex without receiving that propagation benefit, that might be the next phase in evolution, homosexuality, which Moe never pursued, or bisexuality, which we

Moe thought future humans would become as like the ardhanari or Hindu intergender gods, but with larger and thicker skulls that would shield their brains from being microwaved by wifi.

Another thought Moe had was that because humans were now able as like a species to digest lactose past childhood, in the future they would be able to breastfeed themselves too and survive through adulthood on that alone.

Telephone poles always made him pensive. With everything going mobile, he worried about what would happen to them.

Maybe they would become effigies. Maybe they would be worshipped.

The cardinal difference between Buddhist and Hindu incarnation doctrines is that Buddhism does not believe in a soul, but in a mind that transfuses our successors, and in a body that decomposes as like biosphere. Hinduism, however, believes in the soul, which determines

Moe related the situation of the individual Buddhist to the situation of a computer that lacked a memory. Which would not be a computer at all, but

Dire, our condition was dire. M-Unit brought in the Stanford shrink, who was cur about investing in a Tetration IPO, the Stanford shrink brought in homeopaths, naturopaths, acupuncturists, aromachologists, who were cur about our investing in their research. Pulse electromagnetic field therapy. Enerpathic and liquid mineral stimulation of adrenals. Entheogen solutions for aboulia and immunocompromise. Bhang, ayahuasca, venoms.

We fake slept through Aunt Nance, weak without her sarcasm, consulting a chelationist for advice on how to treat her joint inflammation. Then we were asleep.

We had dreams. We will not discuss them.

Mat Plokta and Trey Kerner chased us through an arcade while calling us "cholesterol." They threatened to beat us until we turned into "testosterone." Then we were in this stadium cafeteria that was not at Stanford, but it was, there were tons of students and every time anyone recognized and was recognized by anyone else, both of them grew taller, wider, everyone scrambled for their friends, which was awkward, as like everyone grew, they bumped one another, bumped heads. We had to dodge their shoes, we were friendless, we reached up to their shoelaces. Next we dreamt that Moe would not let us play a game that involved arranging very small cards, facedown, on the squares of a chessboard, we asked him why, he said, "Because it is unfair, you are a computer." We asked him to at least explain the rules, he said, "You either obey me, or you obey me while pretending to understand me." Next we had a dream about a taco, D-Unit was the vendor, it was a bull taco with guac and salsa and yellow shredded cheddar wires, and just before we bit into it D-Unit snatched off a papertowel and placed it atop our head as like a yarmulke. He said a blessing, but he said it in BASIC, or LISP.

Then there was this low rumble, and a whiny grating. The sofabed shook, the entire room shook. It was the garagedoor, below us, grinding along its track, opening, closing, remotely. M-Unit and Aunt Nance drove off.

They had their volunteering to do, counseling the families of queer minors, coaching tolerance, coaching love.

We got up, folded the sofabed, folded the robe. This was all robotic, this was the fanaticism of the robotic. We went downstairs and dredged the drawers for the phonebook. Flipped through to Places of Worship. We skimmed the entries, recognized the addy, the number associated. We must have put on clothes, because we had our rollerblades on and were blading to the rabbis.

We rolled out of the BART station at Powell Street and through the Tenderloin, from Market, to Turk, to Laguna, and Bush Street. We did not know what we were doing, but then we did not know what D-Unit had been doing either, praying with the Hasidics, or praying to the Hasidics, driving the 20 minutes, 40 minutes in traffic, each way, just to make a minyan. He did not believe in anything. But he believed in showing up.

It was a grand old slammed to shit synagogue, littered, tagged, bird shit and bird nests around the decalogue windows. We knocked until a Fujian janitor was at the door telling us to come back at no time we comprehended, and so we coasted around until dusk or so, the momentary jolt of passing under lamps and having them flash on.

The far curb was all comppeople peers of peer age with incomplete facial hair, chip earrings, 3D glasses type glasses. They hung apart from the hippie men bald but with gray ponytails, hippie women gray to the knees. We crowded between them into a foyer smogged with incense. The signage was Sinitic. Half the people might have been half Jewish. This had definitely stopped being a synagogue.

There were bins by the inner door, and the hippies took pillows and bowed to sit, and then with all the pillows taken sat on mats, and then with the mats gone, the floor. The way they bowed, we would never be that flexible, the way they realigned their spines, we would never have that posture, how they stretched and rolled around. The comppeople stayed by the walls. Deployed the meld effect.

We rolled to brake against a pillar posted with reiki ads and bulk offers on rhizomes and herbs. We have tried to impart this, how receptive we were, how divestable.

This was not the state in which to meet the Master Classman.

Tetsugen Kenneth Classman, the Master, Zen roshi to the Valley. Something had brought us to him, and whatever that something was we would venerate it. He was born in the Bronx, 1946. His parents were unionists, tailors, Jews, in that order. They were Left, very Left, though we have never been sure of the Trotskyist distinctions. He went to U of Chicago. Philosophy. But the war or the antiwar movement was already escalating, and he got involved with SDS. That he dropped out is clear, not so what forced him underground with the Yippies in San Francisco, with trips above to study at the SF Zenter with Shunryu Suzuki, from whom he received Dharma transmission in 1970, just before or after they called his draft number. He stowed away on a ship to Japan, to resume his studies at Sōji-ji, and Eihei-ji, a Sōtō summit brought him to China, from which he hiked across the border to Laos, Cambodia, smuggled US military defectors across the border from Vietnam and resettled them in Bangkok. We have been told he was caught and turned informant, or that he had worked for the MI Corps in another unspecified capacity and was pardoned. We have been told he was never even caught. Bottomline. He repatriated and established a vet soup kitchen, 74, vagrant bakery, 76, the inevitable gentrification of the Haight. Possession of LSD for personal use, 1980. Multiple counts of unlawful assembly and obstruction, for organizing nonpermit marches protesting CDC apathy toward HIV/AIDS, 1984.

Founded Zend0, 2002, now the #2 Buddhist nonprofit according to do-n-donor.com. Transcendental Unlocking, a potential cultivation method extremely popular in Hollywood, ongoing. Dynastatic Shikantaza, or ScreenSits, the focal training intensives that became serious industry schmoozles, ongoing. Four books of koan, *Selfhelp for the Helplessly Selfless* I–IV. Two cookbooks. Cowritten. All. A bikram fitness regime, Chakra Till You Dropa. Udderly Yummy, his organic dairy collective. 2010 revenue $18.2 million. Not quite Zen activites. We are shaky only on the arrest dates and Nam, the rest is kosher.

Physically, we never remembered if he had a beard. Or if he did, which one. He worked all the angles onstage, but it was as like he dwelt in stillness and the stage instead moved for him. Nothing disturbed his wraps, which were not black monastic capes, rather papal dictator satin and Thinsulate polar fleece.

He kept saying the group would do a guided meditation but then kept talking through it.

"Unplug yourself, and boot belief. Let faith fail, and blankness."

"Concess nothing, process all. You become the deadline."

His devotees, true to the school, laughed, as like they were practicing laughing. This alone was going to have to suffice as like both meditation and guidance.

The Master Classman beamed, and his beams were for us, rather we realized that everyone else was claiming them too, for serious reaching out their hands and clapping down around the experience, everyone was clapping onehanded.

"Zen is mystic Buddhism," he said, basically. "Zen is the elite, it influences the current, and sets trends in the wind."

"Now you have become the teachers. But it is not just one student who is telling you this, today everyone is a student and is telling. Our wisdom has always been dependent on the wisdom of our teachers, but now, everything depends. We are not in the Valley, and yet you are the Valley. We are just Buddhists. You are the Zen of Zen."

"The world of email is the world of attachment, the world of sites is the world of design, the speaker is speaking, the monitor is monitoring, screens impede and cannot be lifted."

"A peasant, out plowing the field with his ox, died, and was born again, but online. That was his world. He did not know anything else, or have any memories of any existences prior. But this is the world in which all the peasants around you live currently. They are living online, but they think it is offline. They will wander unsettled until they are taken offline again. But even this will be just another design, or attachment."

Then, just to our side, we noticed Rolf Schadborg. He was working for Treap then, who were no competition, but was about to breakaway and found Quineisha.com, which would resolve the crosscultural timelag by bringing urban street fashions out to white suburban sprawl while still at the peak of their freshness.

He was surrounded by other Treapsters, terminal jockeys from Go, from Flooz, who would not have jobs in another month or so, or week, or day, or their mobilephones were about to ring with the news, the market flux, the dotcom snap and crackle. Or maybe they did not have jobs already and that was how they were able to be here, the 200 million vicepresidents of Pets.com, which was about to lose $200 million.

Techs, dejected, susceptible, who, whatever they were up to then, went later into bitcoins, their investment and exchange, anticounterfeit bots combating minting. Startups as like Urrgency, Eastern Union.

Any one of them might have introduced us to the Master Classman. Reintroduced us. Because he must have been prepped for us. Because neither of us would have recalled the last time we met, in our prior incarnations as like ginkgo trees or leaves or beetles.

The Master Classman finished. Rather he had been dramatizing the precept of mandative inertia and the techs had interpreted that lull for his finishing, and they mobbed him, pressed around him as like magnetized. He had this stickiness to him, this retention.

We bladed circles around their glomerate.

The Master Classman bowed to them and blessed them, bent again to Schadborg, light whispers, heavy guruing.

It was out grinding curbside that he appeared to us. Appeared. From nothingness into flesh. Not kitschy as like flickering from a cheap desaturated color Obi Wan transported to the Starship Enterprise effect, but manifestation. We had been crying. He had that ability to out of nothing cry along. He said that we were sick and our sickness was of knowing. Also of not knowing. Ignorance was making us ill. Our willful disregard. He told us to sit and we sat. This was at a fundraiser in Menlo Park. He told us to stand and we stood. This was at another fundraiser in Los Gatos. He introduced us to his acolytes, including the rabbi of the Bush Street congregation, which after the retirement of its Jews rented its facility to the Master Classman. The rabbi offered a parable about a forest getting lost in itself, and then an anecdote about D-Unit.

We were with the Master Classman all the way, even to Noto. We went to Noto, no away msg.

[You just packed up and left?]

First trip. First trip out of the country.

[But where to exactly?]

Noto Peninsula. Ishikawa Prefecture. Honshū. Japan.

[When?]

Spring 2000. April, do not quote us, or do, but we stayed through the summer, September.

[A monastery or what?]

Zen. Sōtō. Order of the rice sorters. Sect of the jeweled mirror in which all substances and images merge.

[That's why you went, to count the grains?]

We are going to barf. Pass the bowl.

[Wait, which?]

Pass.

://

[So you can't tell me what made you drop it all and go monastic? And you won't tell me what's up with your health, the vomiting, the Doc Huxtable injectables?]

Balk not.

[Thor Balk again—what does he have to do with you finding religion? Or with the Master Classman?]

What the windbroken pineneedle has to do with the earthworm halved by a hoe. What the dragon howling in the wasted cedar has to do with the grains that fill a kalpa. Nothing. Gibber. The Master Classman was full of that on our arrival. He was very proud of the nature too, but that was fair, we had not expected the nature. We will try for local scenics. It was a monastery. A kakuchi. Pagodas with tiers all stacked, pagoda atop pagoda atop pagoda. Mountains we were told not to wonder which. Waters we were told not to wonder whether the bay or sea or ocean. The nearest neighbors were just jungle and beach. Closer to the beach was a decommissioned nuclearplant. For two months or so we went unrecognized. For 10 weeks we donned a diaper robe to toddle around behind the diaper robes and bibs of vivider colors. Sandals, timekeepers. Click-clack as like keys. The Master Classman was in and out, being driven to and from the airport in Komatsu. Approx two hours away, though not in sandals.

We were allotted our own eight mat hut. It was weatherized and had electric. We took a vow of silence, which was pointless, we took a vow of celibacy, pointless. We were never very capable at being a novice. It required a backengineer, a reversal. This might have bothered the Master Classman, but he was off pursuing abandonment.

Neglect the monk who seeks approval, true approval is neglect. Just a basic Western psych thing, not a koan.

All the monks who supervised our zazen and cooked and served and cleaned up from our meals lived two to each four mat cell, two cells in each hut. They had no electricity, no doubleglazed windows or vents, certainly no private tile bathrooms. They worked, not prepping for rice season or raising livestock, or making indigenous handicrafts, lacquerwork, halite pottery, but readying the guest facilities surrounding ours, doing repairs, vacuuming. We would sit for zazen in the zendo, and then the jikijitsu, who supervised our training, would bash the gong with the butt of his drill and go away to fix sinks and toilets and outlets.

The snows melted, the river thawed and flooded. The grounds were muddy, and even the monster trucks stuck.

Execs showed, from Vitol, Glencore, Trafigura, Saudi Aramco, Gazprom, just in time for the sakura. They were unavoidable, they were chatty, quadlingually chatty. The Master Classman took over zazen, two sesshin a day. He taught "greedy breathing." He taught a technique called "median digit lust mudra." But we would skip one or both or the sesshin, to kinhin along the river to the top of a hill and just sit there lotused and yet even there one of the newbies panting and thornpricked and searching for phone reception would inevitably solicit up to us as like we were the shike, asking us if we were going to Burning Man, or Davos, asking us how this experience comptrasted with Burning Man, or Davos, wondering if we would recommend a regression ashram or matha or yeshiva, seeking advice on a pesky archival digitalization issue, seeking advice on synching emails across multiple devices. They would request our presence on philanthropy boards dedicated to eradicating autism. They would make confessions about having autistic children, estranged wives, about how they had come out here to forge closer relationships to family they had left back home, or to recover from mysterious diseases, affluenza. They were men, and under the direction of the Master Classman they did manly bonding things to also get closer to one another, carrying bronze keman and umpan and even gravemarkers extreme distances, samurai fights with rubber katana, sumo fights in rubber fatsuits, waterfall trustfalls. At night girls tramped in full geisha regalia from kimonos to whiteface would be jeeped in from Suzu and Wajima, and we would be awake and out early enough in the morning on kinhin to catch them leaving, and half of them were boys. We refused the ones that came to us, and then an oshō, a priest, showed up at our screen with one or two and an emoticon frown insisting we were getting him in trouble by refusing. We let them stay, the boy and girl, and so as like not to get them fired we performed sexually, but incompletely. So much for our celibacy. So much for our silence.

The oshō kept visiting, having taken notice of our conflict. Anything we say now is flattery, but he recognized us for pure, for attending-intending-to-pure. He took us under his instruction, explaining the writings, the Shōbōgenzō of Dōgen, and even the sutras by which Damo had explained India to Asia, the Prajnaparamita, the Avatamsaka, the Lankavatara. He explicated the Sanskrit, which he could only partially read, but in this language, which he could only partially speak. A child of his had suffered worse than we had and the writings had spared him, had spared the oshō. He got that we were not here for recharging, or hermitage pampering. He confided in us, his ricecloth-wiping-mirror-retaining-reflection. Our essence was communicated, he said, not just by our sexual tact, but by the fact that though we experienced shame we never stopped anyone from their duties, from laundering our koromo, from beating our mats of dust. We understood. Tipping would only insult.

The oshō, who had served at this or another kakuchi before the loss of his child had him joining the Master Classman, snuck to our cell for tutorials. We sat, no zafu, no zabuton, sat smack in our center and zoned. It was as like programming, but deprogramming. Our heads were monitors, our arms extended to hands extended to fingers, our legs and feet and toes were power. If any code inputted on our upper display, the middle converted it to output, which the lower expelled. The ultimate result was not clarity, kensho, or revelation, satori, but just the flinchless acceptance of a thwack, open palm, back of palm, rod of cypress.

The Master Classman disapproved, or so we thought because he sent an unsui to collect us, and though we were not supposed to think or refrain from thinking, this was what we thought, let it pass. He mentioned nothing about our informal sesshin, however.

He just reminded us of the schedule for the impending tech retreat. The Valley visiting the valley.

Then he handed us a parcel. Our luck has not been strong with parcels.

It was an SFO dutyfree plasticbag containing a Canada Post box stuck with customs stickers and addressed to Kor at the Tetplex, which contained a permit to transfer human cremains from the ministère de la Santé et des Services sociaux du Québec, taped around a canister containing Moe, or what was left of him.

[Fuck—but this was legit?]

Every field for name in the documentation had been filled that way, just Moe.

[Are ashes even matchable for DNA?]

The lid was sealed. Glued.

[Kor was using Classman to make his peace with you or what?]

We shook it. There were contents.

[Or did Classman get this together on his own just to fuck with you?]

He who insists on having the end before the beginning. Vagary might be requisite to life.

://

[You're hanging around a monk monastery in rural
Japan with your burnt friend in a thermos?]

Sitting lotused for the welcome meal with staff from Gopal, Dell, Qualcomm, Texas Instruments, Cisco Systems, Comcast, Verizon, Sprint. Threading rice on hairs. Not boring. Unbearable.

[Or just with what might be your burnt friend
in a thermos?]

This was living Buddhism, with the bone confetti of a Hindu saint just at our side in a container that resembled a water tumbler. Everyone was cur about why we got our own special water tumbler.

Moe had hated Buddhism, incidentally. He would always remark, if any Tetrateer mentioned meditating or practicing yoga, that they had the wrong tradition. It was Hinduism, not Buddhism, which was relevant. The contemporary was about multiplicity, not the unicity of void. The void was the easiest thing, or nonthing, to commodify. Or commoditize. Tetrate which term is currently popular. Do not.

All around us the talk was of popping, of bursting, who was going out of business, who had already gone. The atmosphere was that everyone present would survive, had been karmically intended to survive. What might once have been the will of the JudeoChristian God had become sexier, wiser, as like a destiny or fate. But our face must have disagreed with them, because we were asked, by the Gopal people, whether we felt our being here was preordained, and we answered no, and then the Gopal people asked how else to explain how we got here, and we answered we flew United.

Point is, that meal made it clear to us that 1.0, the first online generation, was over. The stocks had dissolved, if the businesses themselves were frauds shares of them were doubly fraudulent, hallucinations of hallucinations. Now that enlightenment had arrived in the form of the NASDAQ Composite in spiral, gratitude was called for, they were calling for a reevaluation of priorities. Young companies, they said, young execs as like us, had to respect their elders, learn what the market was teaching. We had to put off going public, stay lean, buckle down, attain profitability through ubiquity. If we did that, they said, we might just be the ones inheriting the lineage, becoming the online manifestation of IBM, the second bodhisattva emanation of Xerox.

Haiku, only haiku, got us through dessert, because now the kakuchi was serving dessert, mochi and red bean tarts.

The risen bubble
subsides in seven ripples.
Sun and moon in none.

The talk turned to antitrust law and the Microsoft precedent. Citigroup being fined for misleading investors.

Crane and carp make peace.
No violence can equal
bubbles drowning air.

The execs were talking Gautama Buddha and the differences between renunciation and moderation but as like they related to diet and exercise, the middle of the Middle Way. The affinities between Buddhism and capitalism. How compatible they were, how adaptable. If mindbody was a product, meditation was an unparalleled interface. Access was intuitive, direct. Divestment of material possessions would become simpler than ever online, even temporary, reversible, everything we owned would live on "the cloud." "Aesthetic ecology," "cultural conservation." But put them and "the cloud" in quotes.

In the future we would have total storage, all of us would, our media libraries would dematerialize and just float above us, books would no longer sit on the shelves reminding us that we had not read them, music and TV and film formats would no longer clutter the den reminding us of all we had not yet listened to or watched. Also reducing domestic mess, the many devices on which we might ever decide to read or listen or watch would become integrated, merged, fewer.

We would not be bound to our possessions, nor would we ever be forced to produce them ourselves. Between the time we are recounting and now, everyone at that meal, drinking gunpowder tea but also café au lait, would go on to outsource and offshore their Buddhisms. Even us, betraying. Our Tetheld and Tetbook processors are made in Dalian, Guangzhou, the batteries and casings in Thailand, Malaysia. Our design sensibility was to buy design sensibility off Nokia, which we did by buying Nokia. But that was later.

Some tech obsolesces, some has been engineered to obsolesce, all is basically nonrecyclable. Moe was manic about that recursion, the tech afterlife, the device eschatology. When products die, they are exported back to where they were made, to the nativity of the East, to India. This being the true cosmic cycle, the pdas and comps and printers illegal to dump in the West instead leaching their mercury, lead, cadmium, beryllium, barium, into the foreign groundwaters, and rewarding the same populations that manufactured them with silicosis and neurotoxicity, just enough to numb against irony. Meantime corporate atrocities are offset by quarterly donations. 10% of gross to related causes.

[Atrocities aside, disingenuousness too,
aren't we way offtopic?]

Moe. His hatreds, his dichotomies. To him, hardware was Hindu, each machine an integrated system, software was Buddhist, repetitive series of flawed instructions. The net was Hindu, the underlying protocol, the web was Buddhist, undesigned empty sites, framed nothingness with noodly chanting.

[You agreed with him?]

We had to agree. Except about JudeoChristianity, which Moe loved, but in that same exoticism way. The way you love cancer patients, not relations or friends. He felt for the irony, the cynicism, the turning the other cheek while turning a buck, the imperative to monetize, capitalize, whether a material or intangible asset, the mania for advantaging, for leveraging one into the other. The regard for worth, exchange value. Valuta, the catallactics.

Transactions, he had a sweet tooth for transactions.

We are trying to remember the last time we met.

Not at the Seed Factory. He would always order the candied cashews, which though they are definitively seeds

Not in the lot. Harassing the Trapezzi Sisters into giving his van a spongebath.

Maybe we just passed in a hall, or maybe only he was passing but

[Just hold up. You mentioned cancer?]

There were tumors among the monks, there had been tumors. Environmental radiation from the neighboring plant. We did not mention. You did.

[I didn't mean the monks. Can we talk about it?]

We would prefer to talk about every other omission, as like your own. The porn and the pill consumption rivaling ours, by prescription at least. Your career before this and after. We would prefer to talk about your wife.

://

[Prompt?]

Please.

["... The atmosphere was that everyone present would survive, had been karmically intended to survive. What might once have been the will ... they said, we might just be the ones inheriting the lineage, becoming the online manifestation. . . ."]

The meal. After the meal the monks clattered the trays, and the jikijitsu gonged for a calligraphy workshop, but we grabbed the putative ashes of Moe, set out on our regular kinhin along the river.

The canister, even the canister had a taint at bottom, Made in China. We stuck it down in the pouch of our rakusu.

The route of our kinhin was always pine-tree-slicing-serpent-belly-river, the bridge to the cemetery to the hill between the mountains to the south, the hyperboloid coolingtowers of the nuclearplant and the evacuation drill beach to the north, out to the flies-aggravating-mouth-tidalpool, and then around again, returning. But this time we were interrupted. The Master Classman. He was the gate itself.

He asked to accompany us, which was to accompany the current. He asked if the people from, he mentioned an acronym, DBA, had mentioned his proposal. Wind shattered everything into acronyms. The current switched. He talked about DCents, talked siting, the top six concerns, top four concerns, energy costs, cooling. He was familiar with our specs. We sped up and put trees between us. Transmissions lost efficacy with spatial gain. Information over distance weakened as like a voice, an echo. All that buffered us was green.

He caught up on the hilltop, laid out his proposal as like the vista.

There were realestate opportunities, he said, also religious preservation opportunities. There was a chance to ensure a bold future for the kakuchi, by investing in the surrounding grounds. Someone was going to do it, and a monk was a someone, if he had to be. If Tetration purchased certain lots from the Ishikawa Bureau of Land Development, and DCentered them, contracting with TBA, or TBD, or breeze, the Ministry of Economy, Trade, and Industry would surely accelerate efforts to convert the nuclearplant to geothermals. Electricity would be green, cheap, and just below us, a mangly contamination of oxidized pumps and pipes, a single siren spinning mute light. The whole peninsula would benefit, Kanazawa especially. The Master Classman too, who would receive a fee for the brokerage.

He told us to meditate on it. For serious he told us. We were still atop the hill but facing the mountains. Then he was gone, smacks of rain and righteous sandals.

The massive trees were dripping, had us missing Palo Alto. A scurry through the branches had us recalling that primates were the only mammals whose behavior did not predict tsunamis. Only mammals besides humans. Fact, no fact ever contradicted a tree.

We made our way down to the beach. The descent steepened us into feeling as like we could leap and begin again, we could just jump and land, splash stars or sand. Startover. The tideline was vast with trash, wet reactor core trash, washing in and out and in. But just beneath us on the slope and tangled in shrub was a runningshoe, a neon and 10 other types of fading yellow runningshoe, gel midsole/heel, meshed vamps crisscrossed with kelp and logo bolts, all phylon pronating lacelessness. This is immaterial. It was just us out in the rain above a single runningshoe. A moment. Not kensho, not satori, this was just being conscious, aware. This was our maturity. Our disabuse. A discarded runningshoe out in the midst of nature was our nature. We held a culm of bamboo, reached for the shoe, struggled to unshrub it and slid, but it was as like a misty vine binding all the culms hauled us up and steady again. We reached into our rakusu for the cylinder, fitted it down into the shoe and under the tongue and then, aiming for the rainy waves, we chucked it, and whether it even made the waves is immaterial.

We had the oshō drive us to the station, took a train for Kanazawa.

The Ishikawa Bureau of Land Development informed us that all Shinto shrines were owned by the prefectural government. Buddhist, Confucian, and Taoist temples and monasteries were the property of their respective sects, all except the kakuchi we were cur about. In 1992, Sōtōshu Shumucho, the official body of the sect, had deaccessioned the kakuchi, and put it up for auction, citing reservations about its proximity to the new nuclear powerplant in Shika. It was purchased by a company of gaijin, Americant Unholding, S.H., which traded on its history and shukyo hojin, religious nonprofit, status but staffed it with unaccredited monks and even laypeople and operated it as like a tourist enterprise, eliciting complaints from Sōtō roshi in Fukui and Hyōgo. But the Sōtōshu Shumucho practiced detachment, the prefecture refused to get involved. Americant Unholding, S.H., was registered in Tokyo. We took a train to Tokyo.

The current owner was the half Japanese, half Sacramento exwife of the Master Classman, a cosmetic surgery nurse with her own taxes in arrears. She had won the kakuchi in the divorce in 96, kept the Master Classman as like director out of mawkishness and torpor, but given how paltry and sporadic the transfers had become was now convinced he was skimming. We called Gutshteyn collect from her pebble garden, got Carbon or Keiner to recommend a local lawyer to negotiate purchase and structure the deal. We installed the oshō and shike in cocharge with the sole stipulation that they let the Master Classman stay on as like an unsui. Basically, the Master would become the student, but he refused and so had to be escorted off the premises. Immaterial. After our death kakuchi ownership will revert to its board in perpetuity, immaterial. We emailed Kor who rented a plane for us and already in midair we decided we would purchase one too, a better one, and an airport. You are still wondering about the source of the ashes. Whether Classman or Kor. But we are too. Fall 2000.

://

ABU DHABI

Buddhist calendars are lunisolar and delay their approach to our secular time, adding extra months only every approx 20 years. Hindu calendars are lunisolar too but keep up with ours in realtime, adding days to weeks as like necessary, adding weeks to months as like necessary, each with their own unbooley appellative. The fundamental unit of the Hindu clock is the breath. In Buddhism it is the thought, or nonthought, because time is actualized only in its absence.

The turn of the century procrastinated, lagged, as like we did. 2001 was the millennium returned. The cable channels had transmitted the fall of Wall, and of the Soviet sputnik satellites, by satellite. The towers went down pure online.

[Speak for yourself.]

We do.

[OK, fuck it, where were you when?]

We were with you, that is the salience. We were the pressed suit and tie plunging curbward and the rubbled pit janitor crying refresh. We were every impatient pick at the groin while the footage was still loading. Every on the clock officewide click.

[But what about you physically?]

It was 06:00 on a Tuesday morning, physically. We had been awake all night. We had a foreboding. That something would prevent the delivery, that something would prevent the enjoyment, of a never plugged in 1984

Bally Midway Spy Hunter arcade console. Not the standup but the sit-down fully immersive cockpit version. Which was finally delivered to us, but not fully enjoyed, at noon.

[Fuck you, but I was always a fan of the pinball version.]

But the tower events were not just online, they were all communications. More sites, more gadgets, more wars. More of the government seeking to resolve domestic policy abroad and in the process merely finding new markets for us and not even requesting a kickback, at least not directly. All this was just collateral damage.

Kor called it, called each new product launch, "Bringing democracy to the Arabs."

But the for serious offline impact of 09/11 was the continual contact, continuous contact, it encouraged. On 09/12 everyone went out and bought phones. The mobiles, the cells. Suddenly, to lose touch was to die, and the only prayer left for anyone who felt buried whether under information or debris was for a signal strong enough to let their last words outlive them on voicemail.

Nothing had indicated this. There were no predictions. Take a small elite cadre trained to dev a plan, keep it quiet, then go big on release. The results had to be instructive.

Buying out blogging platforms, to neutralize or plagiarize into the one your wife uses. Turning the toil of others our own or just profit. We were good at it and glad we were good at it. We found we had this penchant for business and happiness.

In our absence we had accumulated approx 24000 emails in our inbox unchecked or we are assuming unchecked and we went about responding to each one. Unfortunately we will not be able to make the bart mitzvot of the son and daughter twins of the chief compliance or compilance officer of tendR that anyway was held weeks ago, months ago. Unfortunately we must also decline your invitation to audition Menumancer or MassTransicle. Because apparently in our absence we already bought it.

We replied to all, and shut the account. We never had another.

Though for a while if there was an email we had to send we would just open a new account and send it and the footer would disclaim no one responded to this account. Then opening new accounts got to be a hassle so we created an app, but this was later, that just let us send msgs, clancular, from any idle pda. But then we stopped. Entirely.

Backtracking. While we were gone Qui and Cull had become our Acting CoCEOs, but though Qui offered to relinquish the position and Cull offered to share it, we let them have it, we put a stop to their acting. They were our CoCEOs fullstop, and we were The Shuffler of Titles, trying Chairman, Deskman, Founder Person, but rejecting them all, realizing none was required. Everyone had equal vote but so did Kor.

Backtracking. He, Kor, went pressuring us to do press, and rehab our rep, which at this point had become as like Howard Hughes with a Unabomber haircut. But instead of replying to any interview requests we interviewed for hire. Assistants.

We asked them to imagine the mythological web or net of Indra, woven of precisely 600 monkeypubes warped horizontally and 600 monkeypubes wefted vertically. Now calculate the number of nodes, meaning how many times the pubes intersect, along with the number of voids, meaning how many openings dehisce between intersections. Next we asked what is in the middle of China. The answers were 360K, 359.4K, and in the middle of China is "i."

The only candidate who got that was Korean, Myung. So we gave her the vitamin test. No math was involved. We just had her grade our vitamins. Then we had her script the commencement addresses we gave for our honorary degrees at Stanford Business and Caltech Engineering. Myung responded with material about how our religious search was enriching our online search. How finding ourselves was finding our users. We surveyed Asia, waggled at American overregulation and undereducation, but closed with, "We are ecstatic to be home."

[No—you were ecstatic for your IPO.]

08/01/04, we were public. Do you know what we initially traded at per share?

[I've had enough of trick questions.]

We ask because we do not know what we initially traded at per share.

[2004, my friend, Cal, invested in you and was after me to put money in too.]

Did you?

[No, unfortunately—my conflicts of interest have never been that lucrative.]

But they were for everyone else. M-Unit, Aunt Nance. Deans, profs. The no perchloroethylene drycleaner. The cleftpalate waitress at Au Natchl. Recs never met or octalfortied. All invested. Tetration split, divided, dividended, it was as like a cell before sex and better than sex, or a god whose potency only increased with each embodiment. Parents of Cull who were already flush got a fourth pied à terre in Copley Square, parents of Qui got a Rittenhouse manse with a dumbwaiter. They had never been so excited.

Our CoFos, their homes were our offices, and our offices were their homes. They were our family, and we, for <i> in <seq>. If we had a juicer emergency and Myung was off they would dispatch a young woman replacement to take us for produce in an ethanol Corvette C5 metallic pearl with baseballglove seats tan as like her, and later after she had returned us to Sierra Vista or Pacifica they would call to yell at us for having sat in the back and not recognized Natalie Portman. Cull or Qui was fucking her and the other was fucking Rogue from *X-Men,* Anna Paquin, and they both were doing the same recurring characters on *Stargate SG-1,* but not at the same time.

There were a lot of opportunities around then. All of them small with ombré hair atop heads shaped as like Reuleaux or Meissner tetrahedra, spheres squeezed to the smallest volume while still retaining a constant width.

The percentage of their bodies that was fat was the percentage of corporate income we paid in taxes, approx 10%, until we got that down to approx 2.6% by transferpricing through Tetration Ireland Limited, a subsidiary of Tetration Ireland Holdings, Bermuda.

We purchased a lot, hired and fired starchitects, designed La Trovita Lando ourselves, exterior, interior, domotics. Started, finished. Got involved in litigation over unfair use of plans, settled, decided it was unfinished, started again. We lived on the property in a trailer throughout.

10 figures we had, and a portapotty without a permit. La Domo, what existed, became warehouse, storage.

Guitars and drumsets once owned by the Keiths, Richards, Moon. A prototype Moog, KRS-One turntable. Some plaster cast suitcase, sculpture. Some goat embalmed and varnished clear with glitter, sculpture or installation unclear. Who the artists were we had not been apprised prior to bidding. We resisted independent appraisals. A Rothko, another Rothko basically identical, anything modern but as like the old modern. We managed and still manage our money ourselves, liaisoning with M-Unit and Aunt Nance who retired. They run our interference, run blitzes, scrimmaging against the memorabilists, antiquarians. 50% of a T206 Honus Wagner baseball card but under the terms of our custody split Kor has his turn to hold onto it.

We have a first folio Shakespeare, the Schlechter Schneider Stradivarius, a Bruegel. Did we show you?

[Nope, disconfirmative.]

2005, the last we transacted with the Arabian Peninsula. We had keynoted a cyberterror exchange at UCLA, and a visiting Dhofari Omani general approached to sell us straight from the tomb in Salalah a toe of the prophet Job. Though there are at least four other tombs asserting sole possession of the prophet, who anyway never existed. But it was definitely a toe, a middle, which we later had carbondated to approx four centuries after the Book of Job was composed.

Why did you not get us to show you?

[Because you never offered.]

Malibu surfshack, Aspen cabin, duplex coop in Manhattan, 740 Park, close by the museums but still far from getting zoning approval for a rooftop livestock enclosure.

We purchased a defunct volcanic island at the edge of the Revillagigedos, approx 170 nautical miles S/SW off Isla Clarión, as like a tax shelter. Though we refused to decide on a name until the Mexican government retracted its claim.

[This was the scandal?]

We would have been better off owning a planet instead, even with the extraterrestrial banking laws so undefined.

[I hope you're not expecting me to interrupt?]

You have to realize how stealth we were, especially in comptrast with our CoFos. Cull and Qui were more out, more liable, giving the commentariat interactive tours of their spreads, for serious prime acreage. Kor appeared less but made his appearances count. Plying Congress with the next quarter tech haruspexus, and writing opeds on our stewardship of the Fourth Amendment.

2006, he flew us to New York. Our new offices were opening up, in his mind it was time we opened up too. Intimately. To reporters.

You remember our sitdown. Debacular, catalaminous. We wore clothing appropriate but approved. We prepped, Myung had prepped us, but then we withheld, which is as like writing up a profile but never publishing it.

Click "About." Click "Tetstory." We had committed that official history to memory, revisionism Kor had commissioned this PR firm with the secondlongest client roster ever to keep short for us. Moe is mentioned but popup window note minorly, as like a mascot engineer who died discreetly after a prolonged illness while on Canadian vacation.

Not journalists, they were pingers. All, what sports do you do to relax. What causes, what candidates. Relationships, marriage, for <i> in <seq>. No Moe. The most intense, most deep dig anyone undertook was you interrupting our mediacoached byte about our tech enabling you to take control of your life to say "nobody has any control" and so we understood, you were not doing what you preferred to do either, but also, though we realized this only later because your quote stalked us after we wrapped, Moe himself had always said that.

The outlets that cited sources had to factcheck, but all the gotchablogs had to do was go through our trash. wwjcdo.com and jocohenspiracy .com did that literally, and the biohazard receptacles we were renting were no deterrent. He uses quilted papertowels. Flagrant. He tossed out a jar of lysine with two capsules left inside. Even this must have its meaning.

tetricity.com and tetspionage.com at least tried to cover the industry, by letting disgruntled unable to hack it exTetrateers announce forthcoming projects that either did not exist or we never intended to dev. Accuracy subordinated to rate of update, style.

But b-Leaks was different. Approx 100000 hits from approx 88000 unique IPs per day and that was just through us. Their credibility was documented, unredacted documents. b-Leaks was a dump.

Basically, the second Count of Revillagigedo, scourge of pirates and viceroy of New Spain, namesake of the inarguably Mexican archipelago, bequeathed a neighboring anonymous uninhabited island to the dukedom of Medina Sidonia, in appreciation of its having insured the voyages of Bodega y Quadra, which searched Alaska for the Northwest Passage and attempted to capture Captain Cook, though no Passage was found and Cook, who had been unable to find it himself, was already dead in Hawaii. 18th century, late.

Immediately after our purchase of the isle in 2008, Mexico contacted the State Department.

They sought to nullify the deal, by asserting that the grandees of Medina Sidonia had never held title to the property but were merely its "gobernadores," "guardianes." Ceremonial positions. Ruling rights and privileges neither intended nor implied. We had Myung email the deed to State, a fancy scroll expressly granting sovereignty. The specific inheriting marchioness we had transacted with had scanned it for us but insisted on holding onto the original out of curatorial sentiment. State relayed to us that Mexico had requested the original but that the marchioness had left Ibiza for equestrian season and was currently unreachable. Based on an expert evaluation of the scan, however, the deed appeared to be forged. No paper analysis required, period Spanish would never have spelled it "cuando," but "quando."

According to satellite, the Mexican Armada, or what can pass for it, sent two Huracáns to blockade the only usable inlet on the isle. We introduced ourselves to the head of Tetration Mexico, fired him, hired another, and then went out to a reception to help reelect Representative Eshoo for the 14th District, and to solicit the intervention of the emcee, Senator Feinstein, who had not been previously apprised of the situation and would make no guarantees.

We had Myung write a report and email it with the scan attached to the senator. The senator was never in contact. But her aide fwd:d the email to a friend who was a Congressional page, as like in the spirit of incredulity or humor, compensatory reactions to insecurity, basically. That Congressional page then fwd:d to her boyfriend, in the same inane vindictive spirit, and that boyfriend to another friend, a fellow PhD candidate in media studies at Brown, who clicked it to the b-Leaks general account, and b-Leaks posted everything.

Charges of undue influence were rampant. In exchange for assistance we would publicly endorse a cyber coordination act, which would include a stipulation that authorized an executive sequestration of online in declared states of national emergency. We would support an online infringement and counterfeit act, which would empower attorneys general to blacklist sites perceived as like fraudulent. The aide and page resigned and Senator Feinstein disclaimed ever having extended preferential treatment. Mexico took control of the island, and set up an observatory, no staff. The marchioness has yet to refund our money.

Myung wrote our statement, Kor edited. "We have never sought or expected preferential treatment."

This was how we became familiar with Balk.

://

Thor Ang Balk. The product of the inadvisable coupling of a Norwegian and a Swede. But childhood is over, and whatever he did before pressing the button on b-Leaks we missed. Virtuous hacking and masturbation, epitomizing the righteousness of the social welfare state. We heard of him at the same time you did, and saw the photos. The US beating hooded Arabs photos. We clicked, zoomed in to resolve them unblurry. Then the intel memos he leaked from Afghanistan. Renditions. Detentions. Waterboardings. Torture.

His residence was Copenhagen, but Denmark had no grounds to prosecute him, and extradition was not an option. He had not broken any laws. He was a naturalized EU citizen, he had never even visited the contiguous 48. Still, enough other countries with militaries in the region or just with violations of the Geneva Conventions to conceal were angry or feeling the pressure, so he went fugitive. Rather there was a warrant out for his arrest for something sexual, nasty sexual. The consensus was confusing. He had raped someone, or he had not and the charges were trumped up. He was a free speech hero or international threat or both and either being persecuted for that or a pervert. Point is, he shopped around and got asylum. At present his residence is a compquipped closet in the Russian embassy in Iceland.

This is nothing new to you.

Balk not.

[What's your take on him personally?]

Transpaque, oparent. So transparent as like to be opaque, we cannot tell what he is made of, if anything at all. Gray noise. So loud and quiet at once, ideology becomes a substitute for mood. Point is, if it had not been him, it would have to be another. It still will be, even with mirror servers and AES256 bit key encryptions. b-Leaks is not a person but an organization, and not even that, but a brutalist .org, a discipline of releasement. Upload shame, download liberty. A coordinate to confide in. A platform for all spills. Imagine a shrink practicing group therapy on the UN. Imagine if your wife and mother collaborated on a blog. In comp-language, Balk himself is merely a statement, a conditional. If then else and else if then. Representative of the modern choice. Whether to disclose yourself to no one or to everyone, exclusively.

We have avoided being so principled all our life. Balk lives shut into what would have been a luxury cell at the Lubyanka, eating consulary blini and drinking vodka without ice, waiting for soldiers and diplomats and intel and military contractor types to get bored or depressed and blow their whistles. They are his friends, as like penpals. They are his only friends. Along with his intermediary and hausfrau, Anders Maleksen, his laptop, a treadmill. Sometimes Balk works on the laptop while working out on the treadmill. Sometimes he even uses our site. We have no such information about Anders Maleksen.

[That's your take or the official Tetration line?]

The official Tetration line we are through with. Our terms of service we are through with. We Work 4 Free. But we do not. Balk does. For him there is no platinum parachute retirement.

Balk is basically open and we are basically closed. As like Kor says, "Open is not what open does. Closure is for closers."

Throughout 2010, Cull and Qui were deving Autotet. This would be their last contribution to the business. We worked on it as like an advisor only. Comptrasted with them we felt as like the old dude.

Both our CoFos had married and reproduced, yet we were the ones getting draggy. Juncle Josh, their kids would climb all over our stacks, we were Juncle Josh. A graybeard wandered out of the Bible. Out of their *Bible for Children* ebook.

Basically, Autotet is an app that searches without having been instructed to find, collecting terms from Tetmail and Tetset, from all our products and services, and then generating a unique online experience for each user, by directing them to pertinent sites they have never before and might never otherwise have visited. It has what you want/need before you need/want it, delivering you in advance.

Such a thing can only be used transactionally, to sell and buy, we were all clear about that, Qui and Cull were.

In Tetmail or Tetset you used to ask your mother how her pottery had been going, and an ad immediately appeared to the side asking you to buy some vases, or two for one, but always something massproduced, commercial. Tetrating "spouse/user with online addiction disorder" would get results alongside counseling offers covered by Kaiser Permanente. But that was in the past. Before gays could marry widely and Afromericans could be President.

With Autotet, each tetration has a secondary function, or dreamlife. The terms you pick become the accidental expressions of an automated dream. Say that you once typed in a chat or mentioned even on a call having enjoyed "chain bookstores in Paris and London." On any subsequent visit you pay to Charing Cross Road your pda will ask, "Remember Foyles?" or the next you are shopping for clichés on the Rue de Rennes it will ask, "Remember FNAC, only .6 miles ahead?" but in French, if you prefer, or Basque, in which the distance would be .96 kilometers. The display would announce a sale on select stock of the langue anglaise section, "Act in the next 20 minutes and get an additional 10% off," and it would even do this in celebrity voices, or yours, which you have instructed the semantic sampling feature to reproduce just by calling normally. You will be able to remind your greatgreatgreatgreatgrandchildren to get a parka, if ever again the temperature falls below a preset 42° F/5.5° C.

Autotet predicts what you will do based on what you have done. Not predicts, but determines. Destines, fates. Entraps your future in your past.

This doubling, this doubling was also his nightmare. Moe, we mean, it would have been. His hope for recursion. For reversibility. Input to output to input again. The only entropy the intel we have accrued on you. Per lustration. Posterous.

[You're gloomier than Balk, then—you're saying we don't
even have to be surveilled, because with proper
incentive we all bare ourselves voluntarily?]

Biochemically, neurologically, confirmative. We want to see and be watched, to listen and be heard, and even a cave needs to be famous, if only among caves, or to the fighters it hides, to the fighters who storm it, if only to itself. Our appetite for secrets is our appetite for fame. How many we keep is how much we lack. Then we divulge around the fire. Then we only have others to live for.

The exposure of bombing targets and dronestrike locations merely reveals, by the inaction inspired, how alienated we have become from our governance. Balk is just facilitating the inevitable breakdown of yet another system we were forced to respect, however fraudulent it is, or was. He is ultimately just proving arithmetic, the arithmocracy. That what happens to us happens to you, our institutions, all things civil.

The desert, octalfortied.

Imagine all the grains, the tribimillion grains that make up the ergs, the barchans, the dunes. Imagine the dune on which Arabic numerals were first traced. Not ////, killed, but 4, murdered. We have always had the suspicion that this abbreviating method was invented because of the wind, because of our brief time before everything is blown away from us.

[So Kor—I assume we're avoiding Kor because of this.
He wouldn't be pleased that you're putting this
on record, would he?]

Confirmative.

[But if Kor himself were telling his side, that would be
OK with you, even though you'd disagree with it?]

Let him provide his own account. Better that he does before the law compels it out of him.

[What do you mean?]

That we will not be around to testify. With all respect to the shareholders of this and any other court, by then we will have been assigned to another judge.

[Does that mean what I take it to?]

Difficulties. Extenuations.

Except Myung. We were never involved.

Let her determine her own involvement. No. Let her decide her own pseudonymity. No.

Leave everything, trust nothing, and as like D-Unit would say, may you always be able to convince everyone but yourself.

[Of what?]

All.

://

Tibet was next. Recall Tenzin Gyadatsang, the dissident.

[Gyadatsang? Wasn't he a poet, though, also?]

Is. Poet, playwright, activist.
Persecution does not always come with a job description.

The past is the well
the future is the bucket
the present is the rope
we have taken to hang ourselves.

[Next you're supposed to say it rhymes in the original.]

or

the present is the rope
reappropriated to the gallows

[All dissident verse is the same.]

All oppression is too.

[And all roses are red? All violets are blue?]

A FedEx arrived at La Trovita Lando, mailed from generic LA. All it contained was a book, xuan paper, corrugated covers, staplebound, limited edition, #168/200, Editions Nirvanasa, Varanasi, India, 2010. That frontmatter was all we understood of it. The language of the rest appeared to script in Devanagari but turned out to be Tibetan. We were typing everything into Tetrans, whose Tibetan is now fluent. "Rope

Poems" had to be the title because "Tenzin Gyadatsang" was a bad title. Though "Rope Poems" was such a good name for a poet that we were considering taking the name "Tenzin Gyadatsang" to mean "Upholder-of-Buddhist-Doctrine Enemy-of-the-Chinese," aliases both. "Nirvanasa" did not mean what we assumed it did, but "exile."

We even typed the poems out into Tetrans. We got their meaning, but their significance eluded.

we are srivatsa srivatsa
we are our border
we eye and ear and knot and knot!
we pray for an equality of not independence!

knot mouth
mouth knot

[So what's the explanation?]

Nothing. We got treemail all the time. Fan portraits of us in acrylics and oils. Fan R&B operas of our life. We researched Tenzin and he was poetry famous. There had not been a note. He had not requested us to write a foreword, or afterword, or note. We put it aside.

But were haunted by it every time we went past it to the toilet. So we went to another toilet.

[What does this have to do with Balk?]

A week or even month later, which are just %ds, or placeholders for the true integer/interval, poetry was making news. After the jump and keep scrolling, there was a link under the Global rubric, UPI, or Reuters.

Tenzin Gyadatsang, the alias of poet Lhundup Jamyang Tenzin Gyatso, had been in Hungary. He was attending a Writers of Conscience summit to accept a citation, a consolation type Nobel.

On his way back to Tibet, the Chinese detained him. He had been flying, of course, through Beijing. The trial was over before lunch. He was in prison just after lunch. He missed lunch. No lunch since for Lhundup Jamyang Tenzin Gyatso.

He was being accused of having abused the privilege of travel abroad by plotting, alongside EU resident Nepali citizen subversives who had visited him in Budapest, to undermine the Party if not to overthrow The Great Firewall of China itself, through the staging of illegal performance art and lhamo flashmobs in Ngawa. To mark the second anniversary of the 2008 Tibetan Unrest, which resulted in %d jailings, and %d definite deaths. There was no mention of the evidence against him, no mention of how that evidence had been obtained.

[What about who sent the book?]

We preferred to regard it as like a coincidence, as like someone organizing some Free Tibet gala had misjudged our tolerance for unintelligible sherpa verse.

[Why?]

That was the question, booley. Because if in fact it was not a coincidence, then only why would answer who.

[A hint?]

We had been sent the book as like a notice. That whatever happened to Tenzin Gyadatsang, we would be responsible. Us. That, at least, was our translation of the translation.

[But what cause would anyone have to blame you?]

In the beginning it was casual. Clandestine, no chalance. North Korea, Russia, and China especially were always gambiting with us. The Liberation Army had agents stationed at the factories we had then in Shenzhen snarfing viruses into our circuits directly. Unit 61398, the advanced persistent threats, the APTs, Chinese cyberwar special forces. They targeted us and Symantec and decontractors as like L3 and SciApp and CompPsyience, basically everyone who has ever loaded Minesweeper or done over $20 billion of business with the last Department of Defense, with that hardcore softconfig management attack that just seclused itself as like an SSL, minesweeping the sourcecode, reprogramming the sourcecode, immense infectious worms from Shanghai wriggling their havoc from the Valley to the Beltway.

Or pick a country. Any country. Iran. They will not let Tetration in, they will let Tetration in but the president wants only certain features. The Majlis, which is parliament but also for all practical purposes the directorship of Telecom Iran, wants certain other features. Nobody is being more specific or can be more specific until the ayatollah farts, meantime fucking South Korea is demanding users register for all our services under their legal names, fucking Russia is demanding we remove all content that purportedly glorifies homosexuality, suicide, and drugs or face the prospect of getting interdicted, and here in the Emirates they are insisting we not just block the amateur dickpics or vids but also immolate their posters, and we will not even try to account for the presumed offenses to Mohammed that lately result in up to a dozen other nations rioting in our lobbies and flipping us on and off all switchy.

But no matter what it was, the government, by which we mean the American, would help. That was why we paid all that tax we did not dodge. The Department of Homeland Security CERT, the Computer Emergency Readiness or Reaction, we cannot recall which, Team, would fund groups of independent techs who otherwise would never have swiveled on the same transport layer together, to crack a rollback or reneg, to crush the red hackers, the black hats, the pointy sabots, the Baltic and Balkan hacktivists, the Trojan horses and the elephants of Carthage. Even State, which did not have to do us any personal favors after our tantrums over what was not Mexico, what never was Mexico, would regularly intervene for Tetration abroad.

In return we complied with requests. A government or agency, by which we mean the courts, would petition a tetrequest panel to crook a set of Tetmail or Tetset msging activity or tetraffic from a particular IP within a range of geolocations and/or dates. Whatever they served us, a subpoena, order, or warrant, would determine what they would get. Might determine. Requestwise, say we received approx 4000/month, approx 48000/year, involving between 30000 and 32000 accounts, approx 80% of the requests domestic, we would comply with approx 60% and contest the rest. Anything too broad we would challenge and narrow, and any users affected would be informed unless we were explicity gagged. Internationals had similar recourse. Dependent on reciprocity agreements. Treaties of mutual aid. Say that Monday an identity went astray in Jerusalem and wound up associated with another #tet, on Tuesday the investigating detective filed a request with the Israel Ministry of Justice, which went Wednesday to the US Department of Justice, on Thursday a US attorney went to a judge, and Friday they got in touch, we disabled the account and surrendered its deets, the wicked were punished, the lost identity restored, and then it was the Sabbath and we rested. This was our patriotism. This was the cost/benefit of success. Legal required its own tower at the Tetplex, and a single nerve fiber between our prefontal cortex and temporal lobe. We had doctors for everything else.

[Which was what exactly? Not cancer
but neurological?]

Judicial, strictly judicial. Stay focused.

Because even allies hack, and if China can take a shit in our systems, cadging an individual account is just a wipe.

If the Tibetan winner of the 2010 Poetry Wreath of the City of Szombathely amasses approx 8660KB of data while on his winning trip, even the mistresses of the Politburo will be able to access it, be sure of it. Images of ruined impregnable castles and the beautiful blue Danube. Threads of seditious txt. All of which had only been sent to other Tetmails.

The account we had tetrated and were snooping through had been opened with us just recently, as like the week before in Hungary recently, tengy@tetmail.com. It had not been accessed by anyone outside Hungary up until four days before the arrest. Then there was a guest ostensibly from the Philippines. A blatant Chinese hab.

Though even if we had been broken into that still did not explain how we had become a dedicated reader of stanzas about wells and buckets without pulleys, prior to the arrest.

Sitting at La Trovita Lando, turning pages, it was as like all that white space surrounding the incomprehensible strained to fill us in.

This had to have been a bilateral hack, we realized. The Chinese had to have broken into the account of the poet, but then another party, either already ensconced in our systems or ensconcing itself through its pursuit of the Chinese break, must have confirmed this and decided to alert us by posting us this poetry.

Which was not the least explicable aspect of it all. Because the least explicable aspect of it all was that despite having access to our systems, this party did nothing to try to crash or even change them, according to the Soviets.

Meaning that whoever did this was pure, was Moe pure. Meaning political, religious, truther.

Balk.

[Then what? Suddenly the migraines came back and
you were vomiting blood?]

182 days in prison, to date, one hour outside every two nights in an exercise yard 12 × 12 m^2, 1100 calories/day, 1 liter of water/day, no phone, no email, no writing materials, no books or even Chinese media of any type, two one hour conjugal visits every six months, 44268 signatures on eight petitions, 3468 days left in his sentence. **不人道**.cn, the Not-People-Way however you pinyin it, disproportionate, unfair, Bu Ren Tao, not any way to treat a homicider let alone a weibos junkie, a lurker at an obfsproxy tor to the Forbidden City. A poet. Tenzin.

"We have always evaluated access requests on a case by case basis, forever endeavoring to be of service to our nation, while remaining convinced that our best service consists of protecting the privacy of our users worldwide." Ladies, gentlemen, Kori Dienerowitz.

://

[Can you recall a time the government filed a request with Tetration and you didn't cooperate? You refused?]

Next. Felix Ranklin. @clitmechanic, #clitmechanic1992. None other.

[You wouldn't hand over his what? Did they threaten to contempt you?]

You misunderstand. We had no inkling of this Ranklin even as like a user. We had never come into contact with any clitmechanic, 92 or not. He did not exist to us, least of all as like human.

Anyway final decision regarding contesting requests falls to Kor. The government just settled the case.

[Did they? Am I that out of touch?]

The countersuit. No one can discuss.

[You can?]

Also 2010, last year. Just at the break of spring US citizen Felix Ranklin was apprehended at the condo he shared with his paraplegic widowed mother in Dover, Delaware, the FBI barging in and custodying the pimplepopper and impounding his as like decrepit Gopal Pro. They summarily charged him, an 18 year old fryer at a reststop Burger King, with a count each of conspiracy to support/inflict terror, and asserted that his computer had been surfeited with plans for the DIY recreation of Kinepouch and Kinestik, basically binary explosives of ammonium nitrate/nitromethane, blank applications for materiel, unsubmitted queries for shocktubes, blastingcaps, and the jetfuel hydrazine, for commercial/industrial purposes. But instead of reporting that among all that there were no logistics even circumstantially interpretable as like indicating achieved capability nevermind an impending attack, the agents chose to grossly emphasize other sites he had visited regarding Asperger syndrome, subthreshold pervasive development disorder, dyslexia, and "macroclitorides," which are female sex organs whose protruding tips have been so naturally or artificially engorged as like to resemble "micropenises."

Fall, we flew to DC. The Smithsonian. We were being fêted. Again we were working for free. Doing a favor for the homeland. At Smithsonian request we had donated our earliest server unit to them, the rig from The Clingers and later from Grupo Escudo, but scoured of its stuck gum and nosepicked patina. They had requested our attendance too. Kor required our attendance. You give them a server, they give you a banquet. The ante is upped and you have to reciprocate with a $2 million contribution, deductible.

We had not appeared in public in six months or even spoken to Kor in two, approx. We had been having trouble eating. Our weight was down to levels totally pre IPO. The blogs, ratetion.com, jculate.com, speculated a theological relapse. They wrote we had gone Brahman again or were changing our gender. We were studying the Zohar with a talking donkey at the gates of Dagestan.

Other intuitions were closer.

We had to be photographed, Kor said. In public, he said.

Also there was a new Congress to meet. There is always a new Congress to meet.

We stayed at the, we feel the urge to say the Watergate, at the Mandarin Oriental. Überproximal. Our skin was dry, our mouth was dry, we had nausea and the swells. We were only trying to get away with not wearing a tie and so were experimenting with other neck adornments as like a deluxesize button or bolo but the swells, the neck, and then we cut ourselves shaving but never healed.

Kor was arriving from fill in the blank. Again. We had not been in touch. From Orlando, why not, native city of the Ranklin mother.

We supposed it was him at the door, Kor. We flushed, rinsed, and opened, towel to our chin. But it was Myung, and Jesus and Feel, and with them was another man the proportions of all of them. He was built as like IKEA. Faelid, dalofaelid furniture. White laminate. With blonde and blue. Anders Maleksen, the msging face and adjutant hausfrau of Balk.

Maleksen had just approached our detach, which had directed him to Myung who had directed him to us. He would only speak to us. They would only let him speak to us if escorted. As like it would take all of them to keep us from being accosted by a 220 lbs 6'4" home gym colder than the Arctic Circle.

If Maleksen had said anything, he would have had an impenetrable accent. He left a bulging manila envelope on the bed, and left. No answering our questions, no regards. No purpose but ensuring our possession of the envelope.

Inside was a Russian model of external solidstate hybrid drive, essentially a nextgen Sapp. It reminded us of a detonator or gaming buzzer.

We dismissed our detach. We never travel with a computer but we always travel with Myung. After she set us up with her computer we dismissed her too. She was about to shut the communicating door, but then we must have been a mess, because she warned us as like we were a n00b about viruses and timeline, slammed. We were due to leave for the event, imminently. With Kor or without.

We plugged, loaded. The drive was split into tranches. One just contained a .pdf of the Ranklin indictment. The other was a double, a carboncopy of the Gopal Pro the FBI had seized. Felix Ranklin, the defendant at that very moment on trial, had duped a clone, a backup not just of files or whatever but of histories too. Either that or b-Leaks had done it for him, filching his browsing, his cache, off the Hoover racks.

A Korean American, Myung, had loaned us a Taiwanese Tetbook, unfolded a Japanese chair, a cherrywood tatami zaisu, and left us alone with the Ranklin desktop.

Everything except the suite and the city outside was Oriental, Mandarin.

Bottomline, nothing stored on the Ranklin computer pointed to his manufacture of dynamite, or plotting of massdeath. Not anything in Tetmail, which he used to email his instructors at Dover High, re: assignments. He was stupey diligent. Not anything in his Tetset squares, which registered only his participation in the Robotics Team, Variety Show, Escoffier Club, Anti-Bullying Initiative. He was stupey active. Not in his .docs, which were all school reports labeled as like How_Controlled_Burning_Aids_Forests.doc.

But with all the visits to all the sites of the demolition and blasting services firms, firecrackers and fireworks suppliers, tunneling and quarrying listservs, thousands unique, and tens if not hundreds of thousands multiple, Ranklin had never downloaded anything. Maybe he sensed it was wrong. At least maybe wronger than the glansular XXX. Which he did download. Lots of macrohard clitorides, microsoft penises. But in terms of smoking guns we found nothing. We found nothing besides an application for dynamite purchase, and the Armed Services Vocational Aptitude Battery. Both only half completed.

[Meaning Ranklin was careful not to save anything incendiary?]

Meaning all of it was tetraffic, metadata winnowed to minilife, and the only way the FBI would have been aware of any of it was if they had filed a request and we had decided to oblige them.

[You're implying that in violation of policy someone on the inside was volunteering suspicious tetraffic to law enforcement?]

Not someone. Rather Ranklin had been using Autotet. His Gopal Pro had synched multiple mobile devices he must have spent his entire Burger King fortune on. He had gone nosing into explosives, basically, and our algys lit the fuse by suggesting the rest.

[You're implying that Autotet has a monitoring and reporting function?]

All who read us are read.

[But by humans or just machines?]

Myung was at the door again, with Kor and Nicky, the casual encounter partner of Kor. A textbook innocent bystander. Panamanian, drove towtrucks and helped motorists who locked their keys in their cars, you get the type. He got their keys out of their cars.

Kor never brought him with on travel and yet the Smithsonian was an exception. Nicky was a Lincoln buff and keen to tour.

Point being, the banquet.

Kor ordained a stroll. We tripped at curbs, barely kept it together. Kor went praising the monuments as like they were monuments to him. He granted approval to the duraturf, validated the marble horses.

It was lost on no one but Nicky that the server we were donating had last been modified by Moe.

He should have been with us in the greenroom, Moe, should have been onstage. He was. Hardware, the body left behind. And software is God, wandering, doubted, bloodless, able only to describe itself. Everything else from that vantage was niggly rectarded. Hi-res to the point of lo-res, distorted, overundercalculated. The vicepresident of America smiled, but it was not at us, it was at how guano crazy he had to be to assent to existence. Congress was just a gray repository that got its OS replaced with each election.

We were too small for a too big suit and our braided leather belt was extraneous. We had pronged an extra hole but it was too wide and the buckle kept slipping. We hate all belts. They stop us from being seamless.

Kor was the one who spoke. He had our PR rewrite Myung. Just for the record, Tetration employs struggling writers. We, for serious, give back. We would never have worked with any of them otherwise. Lax procrastors, writing their thrillers on the clock.

We got all woozy, after. Sweated over our salad, steadied ourselves by holding the breadplate. Held the airplane filet but we were grounded. Getting too close to the ground. We managed to arrange our napkin nicely before basically asking as like a baby asks to go to the bathroom. We had already made number one but then made number two balled in a corner halfway. The only reason we mentioned Nicky is because he found us on his way out for a cigarette. He had quit but it was difficult to stay quit while drinking. This was between us. Our head was also between us.

We sent him to get Jesus, Feel. Myung would tender Kor an excuse. E coli, salmonella. No hospital. Rest. We had passed out, this was the Smithsonian, in an alcove below a case displaying what we had taken for a basket but was we swear the headdress of Soto, grand chief of the Pomo tribe.

://

[Let's take a break. We can order up a bite, and I can tell you how I got my hand all mauled.]

Ibrahim Albadi.

[Who?]

Your friend from the elevator. From the hall. Franchisee, British Petroleum. Owns every BP station in Marseille. Or many of them. An Omani, flew through Roissy CDG on Etihad Airways Flight 340 with his Yemeni first wife.

[First wife?]

He loves her.

[He was beating the hell out of her.]

Do not let your fantasy jeopardize our book. He loves her very much.

[My fault for bringing it up . . .]

[. . . But it's been a fucking ordeal, OK? This whole thing. This whole fucking desert of a summer. And now I'm supposed to what, assure you I wasn't the one picking the fight with a polygamist polyabusing Arab? I have on the one hand, which might be broken, Rach, whose emails I haven't responded to because of how busy we've been to where I'm sure she's convinced I'm avoiding her because I don't want to get divorced. But I want to get divorced, that's the truth, I honestly do.

And not just to please Lana with the tongue and
museum patience who if I'm going to be single again
might be the only thing left. The only person left.
Which is my fault. All of it's been my fault, OK. So it's
not like I don't understand what you're doing, that
you're treating me like I treated them, controlling the
contexts, omitting, withholding—until what? Until I'm
finally ready? Or I find out on my own and resent you?
You're seriously going to act like I hadn't already
guessed the cancer you've been keeping in reserve like
a fucking birthday surprise? Don't talk to me like I'm a
child, but like another suffering fucking adult too
flawed to have a child, the same as you. I was 10 years
old when the diagnosis angel visited my house—my
mother—]

Noto, not the kakuchi but the reactor, might have been a contributing factor, because though we were screened for radiation and certified normal immediately after, the effects

Diet and lifestyle pressures might also have been responsible, the rolling deadline stress and tension weakening immunity, and though we tried antioxidizing ourselves through veggie and especially fruit juicing, all that did was elevate our fructose too, and promote cell senescence if not

[My father—]

D-Unit was always clunking around the basement with toxicish components. Though he died before the current state of genetics research and we have not involved M-Unit, we ourselves do not possess any of the BRCA2/PALB2 germline mutations on the q arm of chromosome 13, or any of the ATMs or ataxia telangiectasia mutations either, of any genes on the q arm of chromosome 11.

We hate that science is not fully conclusive. That this might be gibber within a year or even six months. That this might be gibber and we will be dead. It is not fair that we will die before science has concluded.

[My mother said it was unfair of my father to leave her still alive, before he got around to replacing the stormwindows. For him it was his lungs, then liver.]

Or else, and we admit that of all the idiopathies this is the stupiest, but the summer just before DC, Cull and Qui invited us along with their children WynWyn and Varian and a cruft of friends to fly a dronekite in Shoreline Park, and after we managed to smash it our CoFos called a toiletbreak and took half the kids with them and left the other half with us. Immaterial. Or one took the kids to the toilets and the other went to collect all the smithereens of the dronekite. Immaterial. Anyway they were gone and stayed gone and we fell asleep on a bench. We had been falling asleep a lot at the time, and were lucky no one strayed into the lake, but instead WynWyn or Varian picked up a bug and let it crawl around our face. A caterpillar. As like a caterpillar. They must have prodded it or just flicked it into our mouth, a black hairy wriggler struggling to get all its legs aligned down our throat as like we woke choking and spitting and yelling until everyone cried. Our CoFos came back with the others and assumed the crying was our fault.

Point is, we still cannot shake that sensation, of a larva tracking its goo through our system, squeezing toward our darker warmer recesses to spin its cocoon, pupating, bugging up our relays and switches and sticking together our tickertape guts, only to emerge as like a monster moth, fluttering around inside us, wings beating our heart, pincering our stomach and sucking dry our gallbladder. No butterfly. A moth. There are no butterflies at the end of this.

%d after returning alone with Myung from DC we consulted with Dr. Majer Gupta, Stanford Oncology, who examined. A scan of 10/01/10 noted a tumorous growth, basically pancreatic ductal adenocarcinoma, localization ectopic/head, 2cm. That was resected 11/02, in a Whipple or pancreatoduodenectomy performed by Gupta. A scan of 12/04 demoed metastasis, pancreas removed in its entirety by Dr. Nikhil Mehta, Stanford Oncology, 12/10. A scan of 01/28/11 demoed multiple metastases to the peritoneum, carcinomatosis. If this was the future, chemo might have worked. If this was the future, radiation might not both cause and cure cancer. Pancrealipase for enzyme replacement, AKA Zenpep®, a drug derived from pig pancreas, just the type of trivia our readers will enjoy, and metoclopramide for gastroparesis, AKA Reglan®, which is responsible for the tremors, why we cannot type, why our handwriting is even worse than the crushed arachnid egg shit it was, why we were unable to write this ourselves, why you are writing this instead.

We intend to discontinue both medications, both ineffective, effective immediately. Also the alternative treatments, cow colostrum, sheep placenta, enemas/bowel cleanses. Doc Huxtable provided them. His specialty was to keep us just energetic enough to mention him, while fasting. Call him Dr. Zaius, evil orangutan, *Planet of the Apes*. Call him the ineffable name of *Dr. Who*. All we know is we do not know his name, only that José Canseco called after our Whipple to get us to participate in a charity teeball event but we declined and said we were injured. Canseco recounted his own chronic pain, we responded by pretending to similar ailments, and then this guy with a syringe briefcase just showed up at our house.

Recommendations for next stage care include the retrial of an experimental macrophage protein vaccine that has failed us once already and is still a year or two away from being adapted to fail better. Prayer, estate planning. Remission rate w/ treatment, .26%. Remission rate w/out treatment, 0%. Median survival, 8.2 months from diagnosis. Time elapsed since diagnosis, going on 12 months.

Neither Aunt Nance nor M-Unit are or can be privy.

://

It was while we recovered at La Trovita Lando after the utter removal of our pancreas that b-Leaks was back in touch. An encrypted torchat from Anders Maleksen to Myung. The salutation was just SORRY FOR YOUR CANCER, which we had not spoken to Myung about, and now we had a chat to answer, other things to answer for too. Of course she knew, but now she knew and left in tears. The chat proceeded to outline 12 new domestic and international arrests based on Tetmail and Tetset monitoring that, because the intel was obtained illegally, were made to appear as like accidental arrests, fortuitous. Drug and weapons busts. Two new cases of Autotet entrapment. The feature actually recruiting, actually aiding and abetting, by autosuggesting the user from browsing into action, with the sense that only then was a human involved, an agent cracking knuckles to type probable cause. The affidavits were sealed. But our site was already a search warrant. All this was January. February.

Balk threatened to post, and he would have, except nothing was conclusive. He had all of the onus, none of the gun. No evidence, no proof. He threatened to disclose our disease unless we provided that. But never once were we forced into this. Or we were but under terms we set ourselves. Balk never anticipated anything not online, and that is why this is a book. Everyone will get their chance to post and post about our documents.

Refusing to dwell we collapsed again, but now in the room at La Domo reserved for the possessions of D-Unit, reserved for his books, which had been intermixed with ours, and from the floor we noticed our name, and concentrated on it until Myung found us, and that is why this is a book, will be, because it was as like D-Unit who had read everything about Jews had read your first book too and neither of us were privy.

Myung contacted our agent and publisher.

We could keep going on forever, until. We could relate the joint hurt and weakness, the swelling, the lounger and dustbunnied powerstrip tangling with the IV drip, *Family Feud* on mute. But time. The time on the TV topleft and the Tetbook topright, diverging by a minute, two minutes, drifting. We would not drift. We would not be left behind. But we had not programmed solo in a rec decade, tech century. Programming now had become too reliant on tools, plugnplay in a blackbox. The work now was just puzzlefitting, snapping into place sharpnesses of mirror, curation. Making your own app required only a rectardedness of will that was virtually the will to enrich us, because we had already coded all the templates. All you had to do was pop in the snippets, insert the peon widgets. We owned the platforms, we owned the portals. We ruled. We were the inventors of language and would not be criticized by, or in, subsequent fluencies.

We had not played with the sourcecode since diapers, which we were wearing once again. But we sat down in it. Into the shit and piss and swivel sweat. We are trying to avoid a scatological snark about backdoors. We were a child again. A romper kid among the algyshells, Python, C++, Java, and Simping, that language we came up with in 2004–05, to improve metadata granularity and named, given that Java was the largest of the not yet sunken islands of Indonesia, after the smallest of them, Simping. Beachy granularity. If we would have been able to keep that exalted boulder just off Baja, not Mexico, that was what we would have named it, once the original submerged.

It was there that we searched and found the inexistent. b-Leaks had already defined the terms. It was an easy autoreporting function, clumsily glocal, obvious. At least obvious to the person who had written all the rest of the code and had his days free, weeks free, and months to live, to go through by the line. What it did was autoreport all tetraffic to what had to be a DCent, not ours. To two of them, neither ours. The same or similar functions obtained for Tetmail and Tetset. The reporting was realtime, but really. With the mass of data being shuttled proxying was pointless. The IPs were bareassed with just a mask instead, but that mask elasticated away from Utah and Texas and Alaska and Hawaii locations to uncover straight intranet, the Intelinks, the systems that prop up the intrawebs of the CIA, through the Operations Center Analysis Group, the NSA, through the National Computer Security Center, and US-CYBERCOM of US Strategic Command. And so we figgered, stop there, cease, desist, better not to trace any further, better not to hack or even, what else, report it. We had been surrendering our users directly to the government, but the way we were doing it was consistent with our principles, at least. Automatically.

Kor did not code this snippet. Or not by himself.

Even the simplest program must accomplish two things. It has to make something happen, and then it has to store the making of that something happen to memory. The event, and then its memorial. Its marks, signs, indicia. But this function ensured that the reporting was not stored. That it was forgotten, by us, as like it had never transpired. All of our amnesia had been ordered by a single conciliable command/statement, which though it could negate everything, could not negate itself. That command was <LESSTEL>.

The motor inn lived on but totally DCentered, its buzzy neon dimmed and its rooms cleared out to separate coasts, underground, in caves, and becoming listening stations, watching stations, wiretap archives, no vacancy spy quarters greenlit in mass SIGINT.

We are just going to spell it out for you, because this is not paranoia, this is not the Nixon Administration.

This foreign function amid all our familiar grammar and syntax had to have been the work of the white Pakistanis Moe had posted about. The same white Pakistanis for whom Moe created a STrapp, which if we still had the prototype and searched through its firmware we would surely find similar functions. Meaning that all our millennial consumers convinced they were entrusting their information to an overpriced blinking beeping storage device were also entrusting it to American intelligence. And American intelligence was so dedicated to protecting that data, or consumers, or itself, that it might even have invented y2K.

We bled for Moe and from our bowels, pivoting on the porcelain cryptchatting Balk. We did not tell him what we found, just that we had been searching. Bull droppings, he said. Balk gave us until September to go to the press, but given the recondity of the material we proposed this prose and so extended the deadline. We made no changes to source, but only signed off, signed out, signed our deal, signed with you. Pivoting London, Paris, Dubai.

We did not need to meet British staff to discuss removing the UK Only option from the hpage. We did not need to meet with French staff to discuss the .fr launch of Autotet. Perhaps a small part of us, the small part whose metastized cancer will be our death, perhaps, wanted a last reminder of our successes. Mostly though, the mostly functional portion, we wanted to escape Palo Alto. We could not have spoken in Palo Alto. We could not have been so

Sincerely yours,

Very Truly Yours,

as like our lawyers are always writing.

Dictated but not read.

://

We had hoped to have this time alone with you. No Kor. Two days in Berlin, two days in Moscow-Skolkovo, two days in Seoul-Teheran-ro. With Dubai and Paris and London, enough. If you ever find yourself at a loss for recalling how we left it, remember. This is how we left it. We had not even told the local offices about our trip until the night we departed for London, meaning that Kor would have been told by the morning we arrived in Paris. We had not expected him to free himself immediately. He had meetings arranged, with lobbyists, consultancy chiefs. Myung had made sure to schedule by his schedule.

No wonder no antitrust motions have ever tractioned, parenthetically. We used to drive ourselves conspiranoiac over Tetration being cut up by the Feds, never suspecting we would be the one cut up instead, in a substitute sacrifice. Death is the only monopoly. Nothing can compete, parenthetically.

The purpose of our visit to Dubai was to scout a location for yet another DCent, but this was never the purpose. We did not have to be present to scout, but that we were present made Kor cur. But what is more fucked than the fact that no court will ever find him guilty of having violated the Fourth Amendment, and/or the Foreign Intelligence Surveillance Act, what is more fucked than even his violation of plentitudinous international conventions, is how blatantly his new mode of pursuit transgresses a basic commandment. He bought the same jet we bought. No asking permission, no asking forgiveness. He did not even use his own money. Thou shalt not covet the jet of thy boss. Commandment 10.5.

Our intention in visiting Berlin was to inaugurate a freshly completed DCent, but again, not. Regardless of whether we would snip a projected ribbon with a pair of digiscissors, the DCent would function, the champagne and flecky charcuterie atop square pumpernickel hors d'oeuvres would still be served. Moscow, we had not figgered that yet. We would have gotten Cossack furs and danced outside the Kremlin with Tetbooks on our heads. Seoul. We would have found a garden with lotus ponds and a comfortable pavilion.

Out in the desert everyone suddenly has more to conceal or has to work harder to conceal it. Nothing, no one, has more clearance than the desert. Kor had just landed and we were both crisis panicking. He called the suite at the Burj and we ignored his calls, and then he knocked himself but Jesus or Feel told him we were snorkeling, or scubaing. Myung told him we were in DCent sessh with the Dubai clan, and that was true, partially. Lavra and Gaston were honestly paddleboarding. You were out on the beach. Disgusting to imagine Kor all slouched out roasted pink and stinking of sunscreen carcinogens.

The sheikh himself came back with an estimate. He would sell us 2 km^2 or 200 desert hectares assessed cheaply at $10 million USD, and provide construction according to our specs at $200/$m^2$ for up to 180000 m^2, an entire DCent for $46 million, a bargain.

Exclusive electricity and water contracts would go to the official Emirati provider, the Dubai Electricity and Water Authority, administered by the prince whose friendship you enjoyed.

That was two nights ago now.

While you defended Israel we were calling the other Emirates, which had never even been on the map.

We called the princes of Sharjah and Fujairah, both Mohammeds, both cousins of your Dubai friend. We sought to deal, individually, offered to pay the Dubai assessment to each, explained that Sharjah and Fujairah synergized better with our goals. Dubai was so 2000. In the 2020s the minor Emirates would flower.

They would become as like Switzerlands, we said, but for the future money, which is information. They would become datahavens with new laws, or no laws, they would overcharge the Saudis for fiber.

If our DCent experience was satisfactory, we might even consider opening a local Tetplex. Employee shuttlebuses shimmering by a wadi.

Yesterday. We pilled, went down to visit Kor in his suite and dismissed a nude twink fauxgrammer who had apparently taken up residence. Sand was pooled on the carpet. Kor was in flipflops and towel. In towels. He had burned himself.

But it was us who was acting wild. We launched into our new fascination with servers, talked geography, talked topography, dune and diaspore preservation, lizard dwindling, photovoltaics comptrasted with thermals, grid parity, Filipino labor working 6/12 and if or how to negotiate fair shifts and a living wage.

To be convincing we had buried ourselves in the deets and become as like a god who knows it all. But then a god would know how to create a replacement pancreas, how to make the islets and acini and insulin and glucagon and all that raging hormone and chymey digestive enzyme. The pancreas, being endocrine and exocrine, is the server of the body. Just now, just now that came to mind.

At this point Kor got dressed.

We told him about the Mohammeds. Sons of their Emirs, promotable sheikhlings on the Economic and Industrial Development committees of the Council, deputy generals of the armed forces, of the UAE. They were willing to match the Dubai price. Pay attention and they might even go lower.

Sharjah and Fujairah were the Emirates to bet on, we said. In every crash Dubai had evinced a withering. It was all prefab infrastructure afloat on silica, grainy towers slipping through the fingers, whole entire reinvestment zones and innovation districts just salty Gulf bubbles rolled up on the shore, the roads between them paved with oil borrowed from the Emirates that pumped. Sharjah and Fujairah pumped. Dubai had no oil, just reserves. Sharjah and Fujairah would survive no matter what.

All the billionaires we have ever met stand clasping their hands behind their back. Only Kor holds his hands that way while sitting.

He was basically disgusted.

"Stop micromanaging," he said. "Stop all this cockmonkey nano pico femto attomanaging." He asked us what reduction came after atto. Then he asked us to have a seat.

"So you flew all the way the fuck out here just to save dough with a petty Emirate? What the fuck is going on with you?"

We answered with the further reductions, "Zepto, yocto, nothing."

"You sound the way you look," he said. "Shit."

Then he broke out a bag of sourdough white, tipped a jar of mild salsa, pooling the gunk atop each slice, mozzarella, parmesan, prosciutt. Mexican pizzas, mezzas, two, and two minibar colas.

We should have abstained, should not have abstained, unsure as like which would have maintained the normal. We delivered the mezza to our mouth and chewed.

Kor asked, "This is Negam territory, no?" Referring to Monica Negam, who directs our DCents in Africa.

We swallowed and said, "You," not basically, verbatim.

Kor asked, "You ping Susan Rim?" Referring to Seo Woo-Rim, who directs our DCents in Asia.

We said, "This is us delegating. You."

"What?"

"You are going to go to Sharjah and Fujairah on our behalf."

"Why?"

"Because the Emiratis expect the works with extra cheese."

"You are telling me? With how you screwed us already, just by making this trip alone? It was enough of an effort to massage the fauxgrammers. To keep your autobiographer or whoever minding his manners."

We had a sip of cola and laid our trump. We said we were only trying to do something nice for him, "Korele, stop making this something we regret."

We told him that one of the Council negotiators had turned out to be a comrade vintage military freak who quartermastered the army depot in Ajman, collected vehicles and crafts, historical armaments. At our suggestion he was sending a helicopter. A mint condition Mil-24, a Soviet combat rattletrap, a cramping buggy Hind. Kor would be traveling to Sharjah and Fujairah in style.

But not just that, Kor would be permitted to fly the thing, and beyond that he would even be allowed, but this was not our suggestion, to fire a rocket or two along the way. Into the desert. At a dune. Oryx, ibex, gazelle, whatever leaps.

You will go suss both deals and return same day, we said to Kor, basically.

We would stay behind, not to spook Dubai. This Sharjah and Fujairah trip would be pleasure, justifiable.

Just after Kor went coptering off we put all nonessential personnel on our jet and flew them Stateside.

Then we took his for Abu Dhabi.

://

Josh, Balk not. We will give you our passport. Tomorrow you will go to Abu Dhabi International and buy a ticket on one airline with our passport for anywhere, Aeroflot has significant discounts to Moscow, then buy another ticket on another airline with your passport for anywhere, Korean Air to Seoul always gets tetpraisals of four stars. But remember, two different tickets to two different destinations on two different airlines leaving from two different terminals under two different passports. Pay everything in cash. You will have to backtrack and take out cash. Next. Check into one with one passport, go through security, go through immigration, go for the veggie kabob, no booze, then go back out and take the shuttle to the other terminal, check into the other with the other passport, security, immigration, another veggie kabob, no booze, then back out and take a taxi to Al Bateen Executive Airport, executive terminal 2, arranging to arrive by 10:00. We have hired a plane. Not a Gulfstream as like none were available but be assured it will be serviceable and staffed with a competent twoperson crew. They will fly you to Berlin. Upon landing, customs or whatever might assume you are us but in the event they request a passport, they will certainly not scan it. Jets make an impression, even if they are not Gulfstreams. Backtracking. Destroy our passport between the airports. Correction. Shred inflight and flush. Keep your own for a souvenir or an escape plan. Immaterial. In Berlin you will be met. And though you will not know this someone, they will know you. Someone with a car we presume. They will reimburse your tickets and expenses and drive you to a house apportioned to your use by an anonymous donor to Balk whose identity even we do not have. Neither do we have the addy. Not city or state. Do not interrupt us. Or country. You will stay until you finish our book.

Backtracking. You will have to transcribe our recordings yourself. Use no online or offline computational transcription service or product, and never employ assistants, secretaries, humans. Backtracking. Avoid your Tetmail account, never check it again from this or any other computer. Backtracking. Same goes for all other accounts, including Tetset. Backtracking. Do not transfer the recording or manuscript files to any other computer or take any other computer online. Backtracking. Give us your Tetbook. Help us off with our belt. It has the prong. To strap the strap. Shaking, there. Steady, there. We have just disabled your modem. You cannot take this Tetbook online. Upon completion, destroy it. Backtracking. Upon completion, print one copy and only one copy of the manuscript on a new and/or old printer that has never been and/or cannot be taken online. Load the printer driver by hard software and couple to the printer by wire. Transfer one copy of the recordings to either our agent or publisher not by stick but with a crossover wire with two male ends. Deliver a paper manuscript.

You will note that if you have not delivered a manuscript by 24:00 EDT, 04/01/2012, our contract autonullifies and you are forbidden from publishing in any media or way any work you might have completed. In that event Balk himself will contact you to take receipt of the recordings, an unedited transcript of which b-Leaks will post online. Regardless, the recordings must be retained, either by our agent and/or publisher or b-Leaks, and made available to press or court as like testimony, in a manner that mitigates their dissemination/reproduction. Once authenticity has been established we request they be destroyed. We are ashamed of our voice and would not wish its immortality on anyone. Upon what we are confident will be the print publication of a finished book, $14 million assetized to our shell Firstborn Equity, B.M., held in escrow by Bank Hapoalim, Tel Aviv, will be disbursed to b-Leaks accounts. This understanding will prevent b-Leaks from pursuing the matter independently, and will further incentivize its support of your work. Upon publication, the remainder of our estate will be entrusted jointly to M-Unit and Aunt Nance, all instructions pertaining to which along with suggestions for almsgiving have been arranged with Mendel Gutshteyn, Esq., 5290 Geary Boulevard, the Richmond.

We are going to find Ohlone. We will be taking Tetjet Two with Jesus and Feel, who will return to the States without us. We will be alone. We will be lost. Kor will have not even uncovered our routes by the time you are settled and we, all crossed. The crossing we seek does not countenance the passport. Moe never hanged himself with a belt from Montreal. But if he did it was only to return as like another.

We make this declaration while in full possession of our mental faculties for <i> in <seq>. We have had visions, bells.

Online has expanded since first we spanned it. There is a Vishnu Fernandes who sets up pennyante eTailer sites for as like tool and die and silk wholesalers in Goa, just some bad oneclick carting better subcontracted to robots. There is another just an entry on the rolls maintained by the Department of Social Welfare, Goa. A Vishnu Fernandes who appears to be a teacher at one institution, Indian Institute of Technology, Delhi, and a student at another, Kohinoor College of Tourism Management. Yet another in some orphanage in Uttar Pradesh, Varanasi, adoptable. We go. Moe claimed life open and we claimed life closed but neither is feasible because there are cows in the road. You can go and then smack. There is a cow. In the river of the road. You have to wait. You wait to cross.

Basically at that point it ends.

://

1

Rabbi Krikruker,

Today I was writing an email to my cousin and his wife in Israel (Kfar Chabad), to wish them a mazel tov on their first child, a boy. But then I was stopped by a sinful thought!! Obviously when I type anything that invokes the Hebrew for "G-d," I use the traditional euphemism familiar from the way everyone knows to pronounce the Name whenever they're not distinctly praying: "HaShem," which means, of course, "the Name." Like for a good luck on a new business venture email I might type: "May HaShem bless you and keep you," or for a get well soon email: "Blessed is HaShem, the source of healing," or for a condolence email: "HaShem, save us—may the King answer on the day we call."

But now that all of our communications are online, I can't help but wonder about rabbis like yourself who have to type out the Name of G-d, the true and perfect four letter mystical unpronounceable Name He calls Himself, for religious purposes such as instruction.

According to Jewish law—Torah: Deuteronomy 12:3–4, Talmud: Megillah 26b, Shabbat 115a, Eruvin 98a—the Name of G-d must never be destroyed. Any paper or other writing surface that contains the Name must be buried like a person is buried, not discarded. But what about on the computer? Can we erase or trash? Or do we have to bury our machines too? And what about servers or online like in the cloud?

Please advise, as my cousin and his wife are also interested. May your site go from strength to strength, b'ezrat HaShem.

I. Blitzer
New York, NY

Don't bury your old PC in the cemetery, Mr. Blitzer! Instead, dispose of it properly! Or better, recycle it! Donate it to charity! It is kosher to do so now that the Israeli chief rabbinate has ruled that it is permissible to delete the Tetragrammaton—the four letter Name of God—from both computer screen and file, AND from a server (meaning from anywhere online).

As the responsum explains, a computer cannot inscribe or be inscribed by anything, and the proscription against destroying the Name pertains exclusively to physical scripture, to writing by hand (though as dot matrix printer ink impregnates the paper, printed copies must still be interred). In a computer file, the Name of God, like any other word, exists only as a binary series of numbers, as 1s and 0s signifying the sequence of the letters—they are NOT the letters themselves! It follows that what is saved to memory, whether on your computer or to a server online—"the cloud"—is merely a representation! Onscreen, the Name of God is not even represented, but just perpetually refreshed. Light is beamed at the screen approximately 60x/second. In its every manifestation, then, the digitized Name is purely symbolic, and so, by the standards of Jewish law, lacks permanence. HaShem's light, by contrast, is everlasting.

—askandtherabbianswers.com

10/1, BERLIN

I haven't written in a while, I've been writing.

~~Factcheck: transcribing, what I've been doing is transcribing. Two .docs are open. This and the book, the book's. I have 80 recfiles open too, .recs. PLAY, PAUSE, type. REWIND, PLAY, type. This might be the only time in my life I haven't cheated. Every word out of Principal's mouth I've put down on the page (down onscreen). All I've been told to do I've done. I've earned this break, this vacation (though only a writer would ever consider writing a vacation). I'm speaking strictly for myself again, in my own words, talking back to Principal. To you—as of today I've copied all of you I have.~~

This might be the only time in my life I haven't cheated, except accidentally. By which I mean that every few hours:minutes:seconds, my employer's snakecharming vocoder voice has arisen from out of its 32 bit 44.1 kHz decompression with a statement of material fact so outlandish, that I had this gut or just opposable thumbs compulsion to corroborate, and before I knew it my fingers left the keys and were clicking on my browser, which loaded to remind—I was not online. I have even, without thinking, gone searching for signals, for nothing. I've been stranded, utterly abandoned, left wireless—rather, wirelessless.

~~Rosh Hashanah, Yom Kipper: a happy healthy year to you, Moms.~~

\

Izdihar al-Maribi—the only woman I've fucked whom I've had to remember, because she's untetratable.

~~Go ahead—slap me with a fatwa, make me famous, Insha'Allah.~~

~~That day~~ ~~Over two weeks ago~~

Fuck it—9/11—9/11 dawned with alarm, the robocall to a prayer of a day. There was so much to do, there was nothing else to do, so much of nothing else at 6:00.

Izdi, Iz—she was up already and out of bed, wearing her sunglasses and zipped ripely into my Tetration sweatsuit. As the roomphone rang on she was bawling in French, "Ne decrotch pa!"

I reached for the phone but she swatted my hand, "C'est mon mari!"

But I kept reaching. For how to say "courtesy call" en Français. Reveill? reveille? Coup de courtoisie? appel do wakeywakey?

I lifted the transceiver from its cradle but Iz knocked it away and cowered down to the floor—because, I realized, my sore livid hersmelling hand was empty in midair as if about to beat her, and so I just pressed the speakerphone option. The robovoice was repeating the date, as the Gulf sounds sloshed in the background, tides in and out and in. Iz recognized if not the meaning of the recording then its purpose, and calmed.

I offed the speakerphone as she went grabbing at her sweatpants and twisting the excess calf fabric around into knots—she wasn't used to wearing sleeves on her legs, I guess. The transceiver just lay there bleating.

And she was talking to me. And I couldn't understand—I couldn't understand because then she was on her knees and crawling under the bed and tugging out her abaya and spitting on the chalking still whitening the back of that blackness and rubbing it into a slime, and frowning, and spitting, rubbing, talking all the while.

Apropos of whatever she was saying, I tucked my abating prick under the sheets and recalled that cliché found in antedated Anglo-American translations of European novels, in which cravated Mediterranean lechers are said not to speak but to "have languages." "I had" no Arabic and only a bit of French, "Iz had" no English and only a bit of French. "We had" no language in common. It's an insinuative phrase—it's as if the very act of speech had once been possession, and innocence and naïveté and sincérité and intégrité each had its price.

Iz had turned her abaya insideout and now was patting it unrumpled. She was searching for a pocket, a pouch sewn into its insides, pudendal.

She took out a book of her own. And she opened it—and that slayed me with poignancy—how she opened the book as if to reassure herself of her identity before offering it to me.

It was an Omani passport whose red pebbled leatherette was consanguine with the stain spread on her face—that ruddier tenderness pulsing under her skin, seeping out from her glasses, still dangling their pricetag down her nose.

The pass's thumbnail photo had her face unbattered, in full. Muslim women must get special dispensation to unveil themselves to be photographed for travel.

I held the likeness up to the original and then set it facedown on the pillow and went to touch that cheekstain but Iz fumbled away and slit the blinds to put the sun on me. If I'd meant that touch sexually, I didn't anymore, I didn't bother.

I rolled over wallward and read—I read her passport. Which I mean in the idiomatic sense of "getting a read on that person," "taking a read on the situation," but also in the sense of "reading" being something even the inanimate can do, "the pass's ID flap 'read' *Sultanate of Oman,*" "it 'read' *Izdihar al-Maribi*"—examples that should give some notion of how automatic and pointless "reading" has become.

So pointless that even paper can do it. Paper can do it for us.

Here's how to read: take all the things that are on the page and apply them to all the things that are not on the page, and if that ever stops working, reverse it.

Place of birth/Lieu de naissance: Yemen. Date of birth/Date de naissance: whatever it was she was 20 years old. Sex, yes, please. I'm not sure height was listed, I'm sure, however, that weight was not. Eye color, brown? Hair color, brown? Married name: Albadi, which is how Omanis with Continental business pretensions spell al-Badi. Domicile: She had a Schengen Eurozone visa and French residency permit, titre de sejour temporaire but with an accent, de séjour, 76 Rue des Forges, 13010 Marseille.

Below it all the blank for her signature was blank.

I flipped it through—she'd flown only twice before this, or they'd only stamped her twice. Muscat–Paris. Paris–Abu Dhabi. Her marriage had been a layover. After wedding a wife you sweeten your nights by taking her on what's called a honeymoon. I wonder what it's called in Arabic, that trip you take your first wife on just before you marry your second. Because that's what this was. Because that's what her husband was doing.

I couldn't let her go back to him. But then I couldn't take her with me or even explain why. We weren't happening as a couple. One of us was going to fail us.

The ultimate page of the passport was unreadable with handwriting. Childish fistwriting, the Arabic script of a tongue thrust in concentration through the knuckles. It must've been the transliteration of an address, which only partially explained the slow deliberate heavy strokes. I got the numbers at least, the numerals, though they were Arabic too.

Iz dropped the walleted jeans and my vilest madras shirt atop me, pointed a nail at the page and said, "Unfrerch a Viend. Monfrerch a Viend."

That, combined with the only words in this alphabet, ÖSTERREICH/AUSTRIA, confirmed it: she was telling me she had a brother (un frère) who lived in Vienna (à Vienne). This was how to contact him.

Stupey of me not to jot anything down.

I got dressed so as not to be fat in her presence, got up out of bed and noticed that my wheeliebag had already been packed—everything folded, suit at the creases, shoes stinking up the nethercompartment. I mussed around for my undies and socks, displacing the twin Korans and even the porn she must've riffled from the endtable.

I went into the bathroom to cool shower myself and piss and not take my plane trepidation shit, not with her present.

I came back redressed just as she was raveling my Tetbook in its wire—I jumped at her—"No, non."

She huddled again until I was whispering, "OK, it's OK," and as I packed my tote myself I said, "You go à Vienne? Not me. You. Pas moi. Vous. I pay—comprendre?"

She said, "Oui."

I said, "L'aéroport we go together—ensemble?"

She said, "Oui. Mon passeport?"

I pinched into my jeans and returned it and then she went for the waistband of her sweatsuit for two other passports—Americans—mine and Principal's, warmed by her belly. We traded.

She said, "Avanty l'aéroport, lemall?"

"Le what?" I said.

"Boutiques."

But this wasn't romantic, or nostalgia for the site of our meeting—this backtracking of ours to the Khaleej mall, Iz in Tetgear and heels and me wheeling both my bag and her aluminum rocket case just as the boutiques were raising their grates.

We were in such a hurry and it was all so unplanned that I'm not going to describe it fairly. If I say (write) that it was Iz who led us into every outlet and down every aisle choosing the wardrobe I'd be buying for her, I'd be making her out to be greedy, acquisitive. If I say (write) that because I was doing the buying I did the leading and choosing too, I'd be deprivileging her, depriving her of agency. Either way, I'd be a monster.

Anyway, in terms of appearances it didn't matter what I thought—it mattered what everyone else thought, though this early the only other people on the concourse were maintenance Filipinos riding EV tile-scrubbers. I told myself Iz was Egyptian, or Jordanian, one of the liberals, and I wasn't her west but her center. We would convey our Christianity by paying retail. I posed between fittingrooms and tried to look like I wasn't looking. And tried not to hear as the poised blithe clerks—Caucasians but like from the Caucusus, the Khanates, who'd been addressing Iz in an uppity Arabic—cackled amongst themselves in Q train Russian about my "zhena," my "wife," my "doch," my "daughter," whom I'd struck raw and now owed for the damages.

A budget is a soiled outfit that has to be squeezed into. I was suggesting drawstrung leisurewear of her own, for her plane comfort, from Aéropostale (Fit & Flare Bottoms, €38, Sequined Fullzip Hoodie Top, €38).

But Iz wasn't interested, and she wasn't even trying to communicate why—whether her legs were feeling smothered, or she intuited that a transition as drastic as hers required glamour. Iz pointed to a dress in the window. Regardless of any outfits she found in the interior Iz seemed to prefer what was in the window. The clerks must've said there weren't any left or in her size, though—Chechens still lag in the customer service department—so Iz just teetered up to the display and nudged the dress down herself.

I splurged (Hugo Boss Metallic Two Tone Sheath, €790).

Skirts were next and priced equally though half the length to her dimpled kneelessness. And tighter than her own skin. Her walk runnethed over down the runway of aisle. She was showing off for me, but also not only for me, and I was doing the same just by letting her try the stuff on. And by buying it. We were showing off for the fellow shoppers so mortified they were pretending to be clerks and the clerks so mortified they were pretending to be fellow shoppers. Iz, it appeared, had that tacky rhiney sequiney taste that I'd always assumed, from Aaron's experience with the girls of NY's postcommunist boroughs, was Slavic, but was evidently common to new arrivals of every ambition. Blouses in endangered antelope prints that Iz must've considered sexy, but that I thought could only be worn ironically and Rach would've thought could only be worn cynically. Immigrant fashion. Social mores as brands. It's about finally having some money to flaunt. Money, which buys them the body they already own, or at least something of the body they've sold. Iz held the lovehandles of herself between mirrors. Don't go dressing for the passport you have, but for the passport you deserve.

Chanel Lambskin Leather Hamptons Bag (purse), €2,188. La Senza Microfiber Low Rise Lace Trim Thong, Medium, three for €20, La Senza Pushup Plunge Bra With All Over Geo Lace, 80D EU/36D USA, three for €28.

To the next man who'll be with her—you're welcome.

And though I tried telling her how cold it'd be in Vienna, she wouldn't even try the jacket, would only let them wrap it. A €340 Belted Puffer Jacket from Armani Exchange, but nonreturnable.

Makeup was by Dermalogica and Missha (€82.66 total), purchased at one emporium and slathered on in the fittingroom of another—and every time I attempted to sneak inside with her, other women, Rachlike, Lanalike, clashing embodiments of the Western femininities, materialized behind me, and they judged, as Iz emerged with turquoise lipstick on her teeth. To accentuate bone drama, or because it's never been the fashion for even an Arab woman to flaunt her abuse, she'd been zealous with the blush—laying the rouge across her buccal bruising, powder crumbing the corners of her pout.

A cab was taken to the grand mosque sheikh something or other, which perhaps wasn't necessary as an evasive maneuver—I just wanted to get a sense of the thing before leaving. No trip to Abu Dhabi is complete without a visit to the grand mosque sheikh something or other.

Then the airport, Abu Dhabi International—forgot what I paid the cabbie, forgot to tip the cabbie.

Went straight to the EgyptAir counter, and purchased a single one-way ticket to Vienna via Cairo (2,260 di*rh*ams?). For her.

I kept explaining she'd have to change flights in Cairo, as if nobody in Egypt spoke any Arabic or would help her. Or would out of chaste motives help her.

Bread sandwich at Starbucks, Terminal 1 (22 di*hr*ams?).

I didn't have enough clock to bring her to her gate and wait for her plane, so I just put her in line with her carryons and her carryon self and let her roll away until she was checked in. She turned around for the last, though not to me, I realized, after my limp wave wasn't repaid, but to what must've been a cantilevered screen scrolling Departures. I was so nervous about my own flight that we never did what even secular friendly uninvolved adults did and kissed or hugged or said adieux. I had to say that to myself, then—I do.

://

From: madamimadam@tetmail.com
To: jcomphen@aol.com
Wed, Sept 14, 2011, 10:08 AM
RigdeWood

I'm writing this email at Rach's request. She does not wish to make this yet a matter for the lawyers.
Rach and I have been intermediately receiving notices that expenses have not been paid on your Metropolitan Ave office for a period now of two months now (July, August). September's bill is two weeks overdue. October's bill just arrived. Rach informed you of this in emails of 8/16, 8/22, 9/1, 9/6 (below), to which she received no response. After receiving the second of two late notices (July August) we dully turned them over to Martin & Simon Eisen & Associates PC who according to them had no choice but to turn them over to your agent Aaron Szlai on 8/24 (copied below). We can only guess that Mr. Szlai's been in contact. What we can't guess is why you haven't been or paid? Rach is extremely insensed!!!! September's bill came 8/16 and was due 9/1 and October's came today 9/14 and is due 10/1 again. Against Eisen's recommendation Rach has as of today paid for July and August in full ($680 rent and maintenance x 2 plus $40 x 2 in late fees for a total of $1,440, below), only because the property's still in her name, plus an outstanding utilities bill of $216.64 cumulative (below). Rach does not wish to deprive you of a workspace that means your support. However she wishes to have the lease taken over and switched to your name ASAP and has informed Vanderende Mngmnt. accordingly (below). Please get in touch or have Aaron or representation of your choice get in touch with Vander-

ende ASAP, who told us you have not been on the premises. (Onders has been trying to contact with you also and we gave him Mr. Szlai"s phone.) If you do not assume the lease by 9/26, assuming you wish to and we do not wish to threaten, Rach will notify Vanderende of intention to terminate effective 10/31 (Bob Onders the manager stipulates two months' notice req. but is willing "to forgive September for October conversion"), and forward all damages/fees + moving expenses to you, or whoever. We're willing to write off our losses but no further.

Sincerely,
Adam Shale

P.S. I'd scrapbooked my entire career especially the stage to which I will be returning this fall and winter, PLaybills, critcial notices (the raves!!), cast photos and scripts, then the film and TV material to 1986, all of which I lost in a fire (Grove St., 1986), and yet I still miss this material touchingly. It was my whole life and the history of many others who miss it. I predict the temptation might be to forget the past but trust me if I say this is a sense you repent. Rach tells me you have many books at the office and papers,   p.p.s. also I don't know if you know but I grew up a bit in that neighbor   hood

\

From: madamimadam@tetmail.com
To: jcomphen@aol.com
Fri, Sept 23, 2011, 9:52 AM
Re: RigdeWood

I still haven't received a response from you to my email of a week ago but received a response from Eisen, to which I ccopied or bccopied my email of a week ago. Eisen wrote that he'd not received a response from Aaron Szlay and then did or a secretary called Eliza said no one has been able to reach you since August. I'm not prepared to repeat type what he said. What Eisen said

about the stalling that it was disingenius. But I'm sure you have a firmer opinion.
We're taking the opportunity to communicate to you that Rach and I have decided to revise our position on the office for termination instead effective 9/30. Vanderende has been very acomodating and is willing to cut a deal to forgive the dvanced notice if the office is vacated by the end of the month, and so that is what we'll shift to. You'll have to arange vacation yourself and if you don't we'll arange it for you at significant cost and not to mention loss to you.
Since I've been in rehearsals for "The Pryers"(Lincoln Center, previews Nov, opening Dec) I have not had the time to make an appropriate survey of the contents and for Rach it is understandably difficult. Also I have a lot of voice work on the schedule this fall/winter and another deodorant commercial too and Onders who HAS entered the unit (legally, within his rights as Vanderende management) also reports it is a mess and very daunting. It wi;; be understandably difficult if it's up to us do the clearance alone and though it might appear that I am in the best of shape even for me it would be expensive. After what you did to Rach! After how you treated her!
(to still leave her shoveling up your slop, even after)
Other issues: we would like to know your best delivery address for mail mail (Rach opened some of the envelopes thinking they might be joint concerns, not me). Some books Rach says are review copies and two cordial invitations she said you always got but at least they entertained me, for Dr. Joshua Cohen to address the astrophysics symposia in South Africa, and Dr. Joshua Cohen to participate in a "plenary" on "deliberative democracy" (I had to search that up), at the University of North Texas–Denton (when you search your name you get so many people no you but when for my name all you get is me for the first dozen more two dozen ro so resultant pages). But if you prefer I can just send them to your mother. If preferred.
Which brings me to a phonecall we received from a friend of Rach's at R ø t how do you change the font 9(used to be I&B),

head of global marketing who told Rach she remembered you from a xmas party two years ago but now recognized you in June at the San Francisco airport in June. Possible? You don't strike me as "a west coast guy." I am definitely not, though w'ere going out to LA for a weekend in October to record the voiceover of "The Fireplace" for a Pixar project I can't tell anyone anything about. But anything is possible. Judith Geller (Judy, her name is in San Francisco, black hair, dyed black, short, hair short and she is too, dresses funky)? Also Aaron Szlaw never returned my call about this either.

So you can mpathize that this fall what with the play and the dubbing and the spot for Refresh (deodorant but not na antiper-sprint) I UNDER NO CIRCUMSTANCES can let your affairs encompass our life beyond what they've already encompassed. Rachava was so kind and generous to you who were not kind and not generous and selfish. You begrudged her and kept your be-grudges all locked up for us to dispose of.

Case close.d

Also today going through a winter clothes container—second closet by bathroom—I noticed you left some nice condition sweaters. Assuming you're still around the city, it's only getting colder. Some nice bottom drawer sweaters and a few extra shirts including a very good insulated plaid. So, EMail me your best mail delivery address and I'll throw in a few pants that don't fitme anymore (too large), including a beautiful pair of corduroy I've never even wear.

Sincerely,
Adam Shale

://

10/2

—describe apartment/“flat” I’m in? describe Berlin?

—who’s it owned by? Balk?

—after I left “Iz” I hit two different euro ATMs in two different terminals of AD Int’l for €4,000 on my Bank of America Visa credit/debit, with which I purchased two different tickets to two different destinations on two different airlines leaving from two different terminals under two different passports, wheeliebagged in and out, initially as Principal, again as myself, passport controls, security checks

—took a shuttle to Al Bateen Executive Airport

—was flown to a midforest fascist boulevard airstrip that I still maintain was on the wrong side of the Oder, meaning it was Poland

—was met by Balk’s presumptive agent, Anders Maleksen, a mesomorphic Scando Nordo guy with a buzzcut and barcodey scars at his neck who drove me into Berlin in a beatup grayscale Mercedes, AND WHO STILL HASN’T COME BACK, OR BEEN IN TOUCH, AND HASN’T REIMBURSED ME

—so either Bank of America froze my account for suspicious activity

—or Interpol had them do it

—because of my double absence from the flights

—whose tickets I purchased in cash

— have €166 left

—and just coins in my stomach rattling around, THOUGH IN THIS COUNTRY COINS COUNT

—but then whenever I slot my card in a machine to check my balance and try to withdraw, do they know where I am?

—who are they?

\

Various things I'd like to tetrate: Whenever I slot my card in a machine to check my balance and try to withdraw, do they know where I am? Who are they? BoA? Kor? CIA/DIA/NSA? Obama? Cheapest closest grocery location? Hours? German phrases to explain I need to borrow a phone? German phrases to explain why I need to borrow it? The correct plural and caloric and fat contents of doners? How to insert umlauts in Tetsuite—Ö döners? The outcome of that football/soccer game the Copt pilots put on in the cockpit from AD and invited me to join them for and I did and there it was opening up in front of me, the sky? Russia vs. either Brazil or Portugal? Anders Maleksen, whether what he said was true about having never been told anything about reimbursing me or if that was all just subterfuge like his refusal to confirm even his relationship with Balk? Whether that treed airstrip he'd picked me up at was across the Oder in Poland like I'd guessed? Who that battered grayscale Merc with D plates BEI2628 was registered to if not to him or Balk? Whether Maleksen was from Australia or New Zealand, or just his accent in English? Why he wouldn't even stop for a bathroom break but just pissed into a 2L of Fanta Grape while driving? What or who was he afraid of or was it that he was scared I might run off on him? What was indicated by the recordingesque nictitating diode on the keyring he handed me? What if any repercussions will I have to negotiate for succumbing to my impulse to detach the ring from the keys and toss it to the trashcan on my corner?

\

QWERTY, n, adj: pertaining to the standard English-language keyboard layout, named after the first six consecutive keys of the weakhanded northern row. The computer keyboard is merely a copy of the typewriter's, whose keys triggered the arms that struck the letters to the page. But if the keys of the earliest models were depressed too fast, the arms would jam. Later models would integrate a lag, a drag. Letters commonly coupled together, like *t* and *h,* and *q* and *u,* were relegated to different rows or spaced apart, so that no matter how fast *the question,* the arms wouldn't tanglge, the letters wouldn't jumblbe, the page wouldn't blot. Users became so inured to the resulting keyboard that even as typewriters gave way to computers, it remained: a fossil, and any attempt to backengineer and develop a new layout, placing *Who, What, When, Where,* and *Why* in a greater proximity would be wildly inconvenient.

Point is, so it goes with our own human couplings: After a while, everything starts seeming logical. A failed writer gets used to being blocked. A Yemeni childbride gets used to being beaten. Both qwerty, if in disparate degrees.

\

Using Tetsuite, its wordprocessor—one feature I hate is how it senses you're typing an interrogatory and just automatically inserts the punctuation. Also, the Notes tab is lost in the clutter of the Typefaces menu, the notes themselves get lost if margins change, it reformats every numeral into heading a list, respells "algy" as "algae," and though I turned Tetration.com into a macro it keeps reproducing as a link, and I keep accidentally tapping it, and raising that unmullioned sill—that disconnected window.

Or I'm writing *cliché,* and it just autoinserts that accent? That acute or grave? As if cliché were French. As if it weren't universal. Publishers started out by setting their books one letter at a time. The type was movable (it was movable type), which was necessary given that all the letters had to be rearranged into every conceivable order, to spell out every conceivable word—necessary but also wasteful. And so the printers, always working toward efficiency, soon cast metal slugs of words and then, eventually, whole entire repeated phrases. "Love" was not composited of four separate sorts anymore—"l" "o" "v" "e"—but merely of one, "love." Phrases such as "as it were" or "for that matter"—their equivalents in the European languages—were confined to one continuous line. The sizzle made when a phrase was cast—when the hot hackneyed metal was dumped from its matrix into water to quench—was said to be, in French, *cliché*. The hiss of *clich, clich, clich, cliché*. In time, this onomatopoeia was shed, or rather acquired significance. Like: divorcing balding overweight broke male writer. Like: divorcing balding overweight broke male writer has sex with a younger female. Like: benevolent Jew, bewildered Arab. Like: if I remember it, it's true.

\

Other things I'd like to tetrate: Is the chair I'm in Biedermeier? Who's Biedermeier? Or is it Empire? Whose? Louis XIV was the furniture king? Louis XVI was the king whose only memorable furniture was the guillotine? This desk, what type of wood is it? Deskwood? How to pick a drawer's lock? How to determine whether a drawer is stuck or merely a glued cosmetic forgery? "Casement" windows? Or "casedment"? Is this ceiling "coffered"? Can floors or walls be "coffered"? Are the parquet plat inlays swastikas or is it me who's bent? Swastika is "hakenkreuz" and the plural is "hakenkreuze" but am I pronouncing either correctly? Who's the saint in that painting holding his own severed head as ink spouts out from the mouth? What are the pedals of this warped discordant piano called? How to determine whether a pendulum clock is broken or just unwound? How to wind it? No fireplace? No electronics so the remote I rummaged under the divan cushion is for what? That chest? Camphor chest? "Shoji" screens? Or "joshi"? Lacquer, how? Is there anything creepier than the Reich's kitsch penchant for the Orient? Are the three idols made out of crystal all Buddhas, or is only one of them the Buddha and the others Laozi and Confucius? Which one is wearing the hat?

\

—I have groceries now NO MORE FASTFOOD! NO MORE MC'D'S! STICK WITH RICE! PLATES @ 12:00/8:00!

—the Visa's been rejected by Deutsche Bank/Commerzbank/Volksbank/Berliner Sparkasse (multiple locations)

—who are Balk's contacts in Berlin (besides Maleksen)?

—contact Balk or Maleksen via Myung but how?

—better to go online at café or library or try by disposaphone?

—destroy Principal's passport or just dispose of it?

—hold onto Principal's passport

—clean up this shitpit

—pawn the flat's antiques at pawnshop, or "flohmarkt"

—wait until dark to take out the trash ("restmüll," the rest of the bins in the courtyard are recycling)

—rejected at ReiseBank/Western Union (multiple locations)

—€118.62 left

://

From: a@szlayliteristic.com
To: jcomphen@aol.com
Wed, Sept 28, 2011, 11:37 PM
checking

Dear J, stop reading this and get back to work. Two things are bothering me: should I be opening emails with "Dear," like a letter, and 2.) should I be worried about teensy mental slips like signs of aging? (like not flipping that formula around—it should read: should I be worried about signs of aging like teensy mental slips . . .) I hope your concerns are slightly more—slightly more—I hope you're writing. Give me news if you can but if you can't Just whatever you do don't come back to NY, where I haven't been able to sleep so Just up on the roof heeling the tar, clinking two rocks against the glass. The brownstones from here are green Achsa's settled into Princeton. But of course with her there's the car issue and she bitches that I'm trying to revert the insurance. She asks me if I know what the payments are. I don't know how to answer, besides obviously I do, you spoiled bratty bitch of my own raising. Her major will be Econ, which is now called operations research and financial engineering?! or is it !? Mir's loss was my gain. Now my loss is some asshole fratboy's gain, but she's not dating or wouldn't tell me. For the Econ major most students take a psychology minor. But she didn't say that. She said something like more than 60% take a psychology minor. Over the phone. Even with the car she don't come home no mo no mo no mo no mo.
Now, Rach. I can't have this. Fucking Martinize and Simonize (tetrate it) the Eisen lawyers call. Not to mention the actor guy calls twice a week and last time according to Seth this boy who's

been on phones giving Lisabeth a break—a break from what?—he even tried to pitch a children's book, a fucking series of children's books, because, the actor guy said, Seth said, he understands "such things are pitched in series."! Josh, I can't have it. I'm your agent, not your personal assistant. And I'm certainly not this kid power forward anymore running pick and rolls like Carmelo Anthony last season (they're going to regret the lockout, the players arguing over salary caps and revenue sharing while their youths tick away). Don't get me wrong, I understand what we're doing and why I have to tie myself and all the office up in phone lies, saying we've got no idea where you are, no idea when you're coming back, but now I'm realizing, with you not responding, it's true, I don't, I'm worrying.

You need to get a lawyer (because I'm not a lawyer and my dead parents are on line 2 saying "we told you so."). You're going to need Irv Feyer, or maybe like a Spence Rich. I'll think on which, you'll think on which, GET BACK TO ME and I'll handle it. Rach is trying to serve you with papers, and because she can't or for whatever other fucked delusional reason she's trying to shame you with this illiterate blog of hers and anything you can do to address it on your own will just exacerbate the situation. Do Not Fucking Comment. Keep doing what you're doing and DON'T CONFRONT. We'll get a lawyer to handle everything and make the removal of the blog a stipulation. But only a lawyer can tell you if that's viable.

The other reason I'm getting personal and legalistic is this: the check, first half, just came. I knew it was coming and I knew we had to decide what to do with it and trust me I considered every option. We need, the two of us, to talk, and if you end up retaining either Feyer or Rich as counsel as I strongly advise, we need to talk with him. Because it's my sense, again, not as a lawyer, that as the contract was executed and the half advance was sent before a divorce or even papers were served (it's not like I'm in the position to tell Finn how to time his checks, it's not like Finn after your fiasco with him in California would put himself out with

"the bookkeepers"), it's my amateur sense that this counts as earned income that Rach can claim, because this is NY, babele, up to 50% of, especially given indiscretions I'll spare the both of us, and the fact that she'd supported you financially for years, or like a decade. A judge would bankrupt you and a lady judge wouldn't leave you enough for funeral expenses. I was hoping you'd patch all this up or had been straighter with me.
So, two options to consider (I haven't taken my commission yet, I haven't even deposited the check): we can be what Miri used to call "home kosher" on this—meaning we ate whatever on our own but in our parents' house it was milk separate from meat and never a crustacean—and you get a divorce and only after the divorce the agency cuts you a check and you keep low like the mafia after a heist and don't flash foxes and Caddys, or we go full on treyf and impatient and you go now and open a new account with a new bank abroad and I'll have the money routed there and we pray (I have European junketing this autumn)—again, we can discuss this, even with Feyer and maybe Rich.
What else I wouldn't bother touching on unless I felt you might have a sense of it and would be willing to break the "radio silence" and please enlighten me. I'm also a bit trepidatious like I'm some Hollywood Adam Shale about to be popped by TMZ saying something racist and then I'll have to go on the Today Show to count up how many nonwhite friends I have. I have 12 nonwhite friends is how many (though Skip Gates has to count for like 10 on his own—my numbers were higher before Octavio Paz died). But over the last two weeks, or when I went to the Fulton banya I first noticed it, mid-September, wherever I went I was noticing this Asian person. It's more with Asian women and I'll never understand this and I bet I'm not unique in this regard but I can always tell from behind if a woman's Asian. Even with the hair bunned up. It's not like I've spent so much time parsing why, but it's consistently true, from behind, and I'm only secondarily an ass man, I can always get them. It might be just how they hold themselves. But I won't get into it. I hate this pc shit. I hate that I've

been cowered into this tapdance—I swear I'm so concerned for Asian welfare, I dropped Jolly Roger acid and 4F'd the VC, which at the time still meant VietCong.

So I noticed her from behind. At the Fulton banya. Then at Gourmet Garage, and I'm never at Gourmet Garage (I'd given Lisabeth a week off for a family reunion in Maine—because every weekend is a family reunion in Maine if you own Penobscot Bay—and she usually manages the menus). Remember Svetlana? Does this link work, tetset.com/svetlana.muzhikhoyeva or you're the expert do I have to put a www.? After you left I went online, and regot in touch with "Sveltelana," put her back on the rotation, but just the moment we'd gotten copacetic again, now that she'd turned 30 and turned her back on all the horrid shit women have to deal with in their 20s, not least of which their appraisals of themselves, their attempts to square their mothers' and then their own assessments of ability or beauty with their ambitions, and then further with their prospects, anyway, all of that crashed, we burned, and though the time before it was about marriage, or my refusal to ring her, this time it was about a wedding and wasn't my fault in the least, just bad luck though not nearly as bad as yours, no offense, my luck's the only thing I'm guilty of because otherwise, I didn't do shit. I just happened to have a lunch with an editor at Viking, junior editor, very young, very cute, Bard or Amherst grad handjob in the bathroom at a Paris Review party cute, but it was strictly a welcome to the business let's get acquainted lunch and as we left The Breslin who was it I met? "Svetlelana" was just out from getting fitted at David's Bridal with a lace gang of bridesmaids for one of their regular Russian nuptial orgies, and yelling at me, smacking me, stalking away with her fellow bridesmaids and the blushing bride, the junior editor fleeing crosstown weeping, and as I was about to head back into The Breslin to wash up and decompress another sazerac who was it in a Red Sox hat loitering on the sidewalk like she was checking the health inspection grade but checking me instead like a homeless harpy, and then she ran for it?

The Asian—stalking me to just about every other lunch and spending more time hanging around Achsa and me during her visits than Sveta my Svetichka ever did, and I'm sure you can put this into better Hebrew for me, but I was davening, God YHVH, Father of my fathers, don't let her shoot me down with Achsa around or before our tix to Merce Cunningham's farewell at the Armory. But then she's like God herself, this Asian, in all places at all times, though managing always to be far enough away from me and inconspicuous to cabbies that I thought she might be two Asians, or four, or more, and even jumping into Bill's on 54th and blarneying a bartender who'd once temped for me into letting me exit through the broken filing cabinets of the Prohibition sewer tunnel that let me out on 55th to come around Madison to get her face, head on, she'd turned, was gone. But then she's outside my office. Outside my fucking building. At the fucking cardiologist's, like she knows what she's doing to me. Always in that Red Sox hat, and that's what drives me crazy—also, can you imagine my bloodpressure coming through Koreatown?

I went through all the Asians I've ever repped, all the Asian women I've ever repped (so counting up my nonwhite friends nontheless), no likelies, so she's either a sub I rejected, or related to us, our us, which would be worse. Because I can say this with total confidence. I'm sure I never fucked her. It's difficult in life, to go against the conventional wisdom, to oppose all the entrenched norms and institutions and dogma, like Copernicus and Galileo, Spinoza, Marx, Pancho Villa, Rosa Parks, like Duchamp going readymade and Dylan going electric, and this is mine, my stand, my own two feet on the garbage day street with that scrawny flat just unfuckable ass always in front of me and then behind, face brimmed, averted. Unlike every other male American Jew, I have never had a thing for Asians. I've loved women of every race, and if I haven't loved them equally it wasn't from any bias, just my diet or circulation, poor sleep habits. But an Asian fetish? No. Have I ever thought of them as unobtrusive and subservient replacements for my mother? No. Have I ever thought of anyone as a replacement for my mother? Maybe my sister, maybe me for my sister's kid, maybe Elaine Kaufman, until we got into a fight over Norman Mailer, maybe Norman Mailer.

Have to go now. Calls to return to what was once called "the coast." Back in the days when 12 channels broadcast for only 12 hours a day, the pitcher's mound was 15 inches and the designated hitter didn't exist, the bestseller lists were 30% Jewish. When the pinnacle of technology was mutually assured atomic destruction, and women, who were basically typewriters—wait . . .

Really really can't wait for that away msg,

aar

://

10/4

~~To begin is how to begin, for the writer and reader both. The first sentence sets the rules, the laws, the measures, sentencing the second to its fate.~~

~~To begin with how to begin, I couldn't. I couldn't decide on whether to try some generalist baseline crap, something about how computers have changed our lives (the history of the mainframe or personal comp?), or how online has (explain the difference between the net and web?), or how search has (explain tetration/Tetration?), or to go instead for a more intimate approach, like with an anecdote, with people in it, a person, Principal, but I was unable to decide between presenting him as a child or as an adult, at a successful moment like the company's founding or IPO, or at a moment not more failed but sad like the cancer or Balk, though anything like that would mean that the book wouldn't proceed chronologically, which always requires an earlier germ, the earliest—Principal's birth and the lives of his parents and grandparents (the partition of Poland by Imperial Russia, the Roman exile, the Greek conquest of Palestine, the Babylonian exile, the sixth day of Creation, the void?).~~

\

~~The dream of search is the~~

~~History derives from *historia*, meaning "I search" [is this true?], which Antiquity [which Antiquity?]~~

~~I was [firstperson singular?] born in Palo Alto, CA, 40 years ago last summer. The neighborhood, Crescent Park, lay cradled in the crescent of San Francisquito Creek.~~

~~I am [present tense?] the 14th richest man in America and the 18th richest man in the world and my sole possession is a begging bowl.~~

\

All distractions, diversions—fidgeting, smoking, drinking, jerking to memories eidetic, echoic, Arabic/Semitic but fading like drunkenness, fading like smoke, until as empty as my Glenlivet and Jameson bottles and my last carton of Camel Lights.

I went reading through my old .docs for old inspiration and techniques (which voice to use for this, whether active or passive?), and I moved around (which tense, if not the present?), moving myself, the furniture, alternating nights between rooms, dragging the Tetbook's charger wire between my legs limp until finally settling—the past, the past was unavoidable, not as deep as the void, but proximal, basically, as like.

I forced myself to stay seated, at screen—no wifi bars to stick my nose through, with any other barrier just selfimposed—and then, after a day or two sleepless, I got into it, I grew into the writing and so found myself growing up too, alongside Principal, taking his life and making it mine or half his and half mine and so going through all that childhood pap and school crap again, maturing, or aging, but also, simultaneously, getting younger. Whatever, don't pay any attention, just get the words down on the page. Point is, that feeling was returning. That etherealizing feeling I'd assumed I'd lost forever of just losing yourself, myself, in another. Letting everything else just go slack. Hitting wordcounts, hitting Return.

The sky outside was a cloud, a metaphor or simile, a repository of all worldly files but mine. All the windows were on the same channel. Oscillating rain. Let lightning describe itself, and let thunder be its dialogue.

I had this superstition—never sit directly under the chandelier. No walls would ever be white again, next to or behind the whiteness of blank .docs. No silence would ever be as silent as the sibilance between .recs. It's bizarre that this flat doesn't have a fireplace, but I might've noted that already—pressing Ctrl+F would find that out, I keep pressing my sinuses instead.

If you think this is procrastinating, think again—because I also had the sensation of spyquip, and went about searching its concealments. In the tall thin coiled basketry that reminded me of Rach and the stumpy canopic jarlets that recalled me to Lana. In the sepia clock, the cameras and mics eloigned behind its escapement. In the small little Mongoloid trees, which if they weren't themselves recording devices were either dead or dying.

Going for a refill of ice, or a light from the burners, trying to block it all out—the kitchen. All that tile and stainless steel was just a rash of prepackaged foodstuffs in and out of prepackaging. The floating task station and chopblock, the handles of the freezer/fridge, the knobs of the range, were flavored with ketchup, mustard, mayo from teethslit packets. The double trough sinks cradled an afterbirth of takeout goulash, backsplashed even to the pot/pan rack. A sponge had been rended, which bothers, because I don't recall ever doing the dishes. A bite of the sponge was stuck to the wall.

Going to the bathroom was to navigate the McDonald's takeout sacks I'd intended to take out, börek and wurst wraps, polystyrene bivalves of dumplings, cardboard pails clotted with chiliflecked stirfry. €2 coins have a silver coating, a creamy gold center, €1 coins have a gold coating, a creamy silver center. Both feature maps of borderless Europe. Just desserts. Toiletpaper was wadded with all the laundry I wasn't doing. Tiny green hemorrhoids of toothpaste were affixed to the mirror and sink. Toothbrush gagging the drain. Thank Christ I'd boosted towels from the Khaleej, the Burj. No extra set of sheets has been provided. I haven't accounted for the bedroom just yet, that Charlemagne deathbed perfect for rugmunching and with a canopy so high no cumshot would ever reach it.

\

I've been realizing only lately what I've lost. I used to just sit in a chair at a desk and search myself up and suddenly I'd be sitting in a certain type of chair at a certain type of desk, on a certain date, at a certain time, and at certain coordinates, with a certain weather forecast outside. Those days are over, though, those days and their access I've been withdrawing from gradually, groggily, like from an addiction, a relationship. I've been realizing only lately the exact precise upholstery of my ignorance. Everything creaks. Especially in the dark, the dark trafficless silence—everything creaks, internally.

How perverse is it that thinking of Rach, with her fly's memory, consoles me?—how perverse that the only thing that calms me down is thinking of her in the same situation, unable to handle it, going insane? Her pda had this app that by the time I'll be finished with this job, finished with this thought, will already be outdated, outmoded—by the very thought that it might be, it is. She'd hold her pda out in front of her like a cleaver, and click to camera a pic or vid or to record an audio snippet, and by that alone the app would tell her what it is, or was, which intel she'd then use to preempt me, test me, correct me when she suspected I was guessing, when she suspected I was lying in the hopes of appearing better or smarter or sexier: wondering by the reservoir, "What kind of dog is that, sniffing around?" Click, "A Pomeranian." Wandering on Riverside Drive, "What kind of cat is that, grooming in the window?" Click, "A Siamese." That woman ironing is *La repasseuse* by Picasso, and that's a Morandi, I told her at the Guggenheim, at MoMA, and I was correct, but then later I called a Dix a Grosz or a Grosz a Dix and she checked and was irate—I told her the cab radio was playing *September Song*, composed by Kurt Weill, lyrics by (but everyone forgets lyricists), and she checked and yelled that it was James Brown, but then I yelled how it was a cover version, and though the app agreed she never apologized: "I wouldn't have to do this," she said, "if your confidence wasn't such bullshit."

\

A memory, unsubstantiated, inherently "unsubstantiatable" (is that a word? what site can prove it's not?). The first time Rach dragged me to psych, to Dr. Meany's office, I spent the entire sessh inspecting the office, telling myself that its decoration would tell me everything I needed to know about him or perhaps would tell me nothing I needed to know because he too must have had this thought and decorated accordingly, which, were that the case, would tell me everything. I'd get the same intelligence from his wearables. His wordchoices.

Another memory. Once I arrived early, or late, on a Monday but the appointment was for Friday—rather it wasn't an appointment with Meany but with one of the fertility doctors, though he was out, his receptionist was out, and I was all alone amid the indirect tracklighting and minimal tulips, and snooped. Or I tried to. The cabinets wouldn't budge—they were all childproofed, or adultproofed, they were proofed against adults who wanted children, proofed against adults who were acting like the children they didn't want to have (the greatest breakthrough I've ever had).

\

I'd forgotten just how much of myself I'd outsourced, offshored, externalized. To Rach and Lana, to Moms. Externalized online. I've become so reliant.

It's as if I'd presumed there would always be some woman or mother around, if not then some dusty storeroom in Ridgewood or even just a Jersey of unlimited storage that would hold everything for me, that would safekeep and recall me, so that no matter how far I'd go or how long I'd be gone, and no matter how many people I'd ghost, my own being or inborn self, who I was supposed to be, not who I was, would always be secure, if only in another's sense of how they've been frustrated, disappointed, or betrayed by me.

://

From: madamimadam@tetmail.com
To: jcomphen@aol.com
Fri, Sept 30, 2011, 10:24 AM
RidgeWood

We've been indated with rehearsals and gym and to have to deal with this I'm insensed but also pity you. Still we have had no response besides your agency's assistant, Daniel Maleksen, finally reaching out to me to state (in writing) (email) that because he hasn't been able to contact you if we were serious on the office front he'd have to hold onto your computer, though it's Rach's computer, but being over four years old it might as well be dead to her.
We are working to meet up.
You're lucky that tomorrow 10/1 is a Saturday—Shabbos Shuvah, or Atonement—and that today I had no time to deal with this or Bob Onders granted us the last—the last—extension.
So if you have any interest whatsoever in salvaging your office on terms that are your own you must get in touch now immediately.
We have also had to take issue with the Amex. This is either between us or between our laywers and you and the fraud department unless you can admit it and be absolutely honest. Rach's Amex has had a number of interesting charges recently that have only recently come to our attention, which none of the charges we have made. Rach does not remember ever having given you this card (copy of your own) and her own card she has in her wallet. But the fraud department has stupulated that a card for that account HERS WAS ISSUED IN YOUR NAME on 4/29/11 and

mailed to you not at the billing address I'm writing from but to you c/o your office. I was activated on 5/4/11 for a charge so negible we must have missed the statement at the time, which would be June, for Amazon.com, who would not conform or deny or eithr turn over an account or shipping destination unless the charge was contested in which case they would but directly to Amex. We are guessing books. And you. And this is unconsciousable that you would commit fraud like this but we are "hoping for the best" even after a period of no activity besides Rach's own legitimate purchases how it was lately brought to our attention (the account has since been canceled).
Namely (you might have had it stolen, or in loo of robbery had lost it, or the worst of the scenarios: you had it all this time and only now are using it impunitly): because now we received an irregular activity fraud alert for charges in excess of $4,482.62 from Baby Phat, Chanel, Dior, and "ASAQ" outlets, Abu Dhabi, United Arab Emirates. I tetrated ASAQ and got that it was "Abdul Samad Al Qurashi." Then again about a week or so after that attack of 9/12, the card was used at "Kaufhaus des Westens," Berlin, and throughout the month at Karstadt, Edeka, all Berlin, all tetrating as groceries, and then again repeated attempts at cash withdrawal including one just 9/ Monday that was rejected, according to the shah of the fraud alert team, "Teri" Lakshmi, for multiple wrong PINs, which you must have if it was you forgot. The Monday location was a Deutsche Bank AG, Kurf_rstendamm 182, and then a Sparkasse, Friedrichstra_e 148. We found this out only by luck because the primary number Amex calls to alert to fraud is our landline, which we just reinstalled after a full kitchen renovation (chelseakitchenry.com, maison-de-fantaisie-nyc.com), and the secondary number they are supposed to call with no response to the first is the cell, Rach's old work cell, which she had paid for you on her plan, and attempted to obtain back verbally by leaving a msg on it that was never returned and neither was the cell relinquenched. This msg would have been left, Rach's guesstimation, way back around 6/10. The cancellation of that phone from her

plan was 6/24, but she is very angry with herself that she didn't switch in her own cell as backup emergency with Amex, and you are cognizent I would hope of how it traumatizes Rach and gets her ticked to neglect something to neglect something.
Are you in Berlin? And in the Dhabi? If so, why? If not, why was Rach's Amex? And beyond that how can you justify doing that to her again, that extra insult of taking out another card for the account at the time you did,
in case you went broke alone and decided she'd underwrite you forever My character costarring in "The Pryers" (Lincoln Center) is about an "experienced," which is how I describe any character described as "old," "gentleman" who worked all his life in the pits of Virginia or West Virginia so he would be able to give his son the best, education, opportunities, and the son who's my costar is a major respected congressional leader, a friend of the poor and downtrodden like his father, which everyone is after to run for president, the son, but he won't run, the son, or won't decide not to until the accusations emerge of sexual improperties with a missing intern, and the media surrounds, and then fiscal improperties relating to the sexual and the media becomes unbearable. His wife has left him and taken the children just as he resigns at the press conference. Then with everyone trespassing his home in the capitol he has only once place to go, back home to the coal pits and father, and all throughout he has been unflappable but now he is flappable because he has to confront his father, which he intends will refuse to forgive him. He doesn't care about the constitutionts or about his fellow congress, just his father because his mother is dead. I am working like him on the forgiveness. You have to work on getting in touch about your office tomorrow (Sat) or at the very latest after tomorrow (Sun), because I have already getting varying quotes from different trash removers and DON'T DO NOT INTEND to make two trips. The voice of Pixar's "The Fireplace" I've created is an impersonation of Rach's impersonation of you. "Coming next spring to a theater near you." Rach does you like a vary enthic "nutty" "professor" liar who talks to everyone like talking to himself and the fireplace doesn't need

logs, it doesn't need kindling, it burns on its own. I'm going to do that with the stutter you had, which time we met in the park.

Yours during this holiday season that absolves us from sins,

shanah tovah,

Adam

\

From: madamimadam@tetmail.com
To: jcomphen@aol.com
Mon, Oct 3
Re: RidgeWood, 9:36 PM

Besides you know what (you KNOW), the main contention Rach ever counted against you was your lack of a job and now that you're through living off her sponsorship and have to get one let me recommend to you the trash business. It's a wracket whose worse aspect is that if the customer has any decency I can't help but help out, I'm too sensitive having had such jobs before, even though I'm paying through the nose not to. I couldn't restrain myself and lifted. I wish either of us could feel my spine.
You fouled up and today was the consequence. Fouled! Up! With Rach too emotionally busy to deal with this, because I would do anything to allevate her suffering. Today they and I (Bob Onders from Vanderende, management, and the assistant from your agency, Daniel Maleksen) were scheduled to meet at 10 to let me in, the Refuseniks—which I found online on the recommendaton of theater props and set design friends and for which I should now instead of this should be writing a testimonial to get a rebate—would come at 12, giving me ample time to go through your possessions before the Reuseniks would come, in case there was anything of Rach's property strictly. YOU CANNOT BE SVADE FROM YOURSELF!1!1 Having never been there before so how could I have known that the time was not ample, in fact, I could not have. Rach printed me a list of what she knew would be

hers and have made an exhausting list of your own items also that struck me and will retain them as collaterals (both attached, items to be disposed of pending what the courts will now determine). (final reciept attached too)
I'm trying to write this in your style . . .
Or I'll be honest, truthful's not your style: besides the airports and an event at the botanical gardens and I think another event on the QM2 at the cruise terminal I don't think I'dhave been to an outerborough since 1968, the very year I left my parent's house, which was only according to the tetmap about 2 miles from where you office. Still I'm Brooklyn and you're Queens I suppose, as if all that out of the way and distitute zoning laws or mileage still matter. I'll admit to the tepidaton I felt about the neighborhood. My parents moved down to Ocala (Florida) soon after I left and died soon after I hadn't been back but you recall the 60s through the Koch administration, or you don't because you're too young or to quote myself "inexperienced" from Jersey. ("Not from the "neighborhood.") Anyway it was a good place to live when my parents moved in but became bad when the—I was going to—but I guess it's a matter of educatin and opportunitie.s
The subway was off for the weekend. "they" always called it the BMT. The 10, the 16, Canarsie Line, Jamaica Line, I remember our phone number began with EV, Evergreen, then ST, which, don't get me started, and everyone was Jewish not like in books. Most not just small businesspeople like my parents but big strong men like barrels who used to labor in breweries, the women stuffed sausages. Germans toward you but Polish and Yiddish toward us, all Jews. But nowadays I had to get off seven stops out of Manhattan but the subway stopped at five and so I had to take a bus, because of a disruption in service. Everyone on the train was either "inexperienced" and white or "experienced" and not white and you didn't even have to look at them to tell which you just had to hear who do you supposed was grumbling at the service disruption announcement? the whites!! If it is a matter of education and oppoptunities that make priviledged "the gentrifiers," then no thank you. Originally "hipster" just meant anyone who

was exempt from fighting the Nazis, the psychological and gay. We got out of the station and they handed us free transfers to the bus. Free? But we paid for it already! (when you expect service and when you don't get the service you expected and so are offer an alternative they can't call it "free" but whats stopping them). News to me subway service is always off on weekends. But the bus was a bus bus not a shuttle bus so the stops it made were in between the stations. Though without a display the driver didn't announce any stops so I went to check but he pretended ignore me. This is the status of public servants nowadays except I'm convinced the MtA is private, like once on a bus from a director's house in Monticello, NY, which will remain nameless broke down and the driver wouldn't let us off as we waited for a new bus because of liability issues, and also on the subway every time no one gets up for the PREGNANT! A Mex lady with a full cart between her legs got off at the next stop and the driver drove away before she'd gotten off fully. But this would all have been entertaining if it was research for a role. I'm not sure who to contact about the driver, whether the city or his union.

I had because it was not a shuttle to keep track of the subway and I tried to find and count the stops out the window but lost them and we turned and got found them again and I knew it was my stop. I pressed the strip. I was sure I wouldn't recognize it but then I did and it was like the experience you know of finding a woman with another man, which I don't mean to be cheap about it but both of us can be direct that you are happier now. That happened even to me once, Barrow Street, a girlfriend "making out" with Ian Johnson who to me will always be Isaac Jacoby, his parents were on the last Yiddish radio, WARD, WBBC, which despite the broadcasts being over by our age got him "connections," for showing his paintings and strumming mandolin and doing antiwar pantomime blackbox down in the Village. He went on to host TV gameshows but only after he got his heartattack did they get married, Sonya Tubalsky, the girlfriend, which they inherited her paren'ts SROs and moved out to the Hamptons. I have never been married but would like to change, Josh. You are a bad person but if you too would like "to make a change," unless the more bad you are makes you the more happier and if that's the case, go ahead. No one got off with me and walked to my building. We were middle of the block. I walked into a dream sequence. The groundfloor used to be a grocer's then a stationary store then if you know what this is a notions shop, used broken clocks that customers paid for the repair and got the watch free, or paid for the watch and got the repair free, but now it's a locksmith but closed, I don't know whether closed permanently or if it also did a business in Our Lady of Guadalupe or else it had just a lot of plaster virgins and glass votives in its window behind the shutter and the window was shuttered. "Back when I was growing up" the owner of a business all they ever hoped to do was own the building so that downstairs was where they worked and upstairs was where they lived above it but our unit didn't appear to beinhabited. My father, not Shale but Shulinsky, was a failed grocer then a failed stationary store and notions shop owner then he rented the floor below to my mother's brother, who was my uncle to run "his junkyard," from money he had from an injury settlement from constructing the Goethals Bridge. Uncle Sruly who always played the sportsbook went to Aqueduct one Rosh Hashana and didn't come back not even for Yom Kipper. For my mother this was tough. He won too much or lost too much but they didn't find the body until I forget until. After. Washed up and leaking through his wounds the Gowanus.

I was standing outside recollecting my flashback from the sidewalk before realizing that someone was behind me on the sidewalk. I don't want to accuse and say this someone was Hispanic or Latino if there's a distinction because I couldn't tell and didn't want to turn around to tell, because he, I'm just guessing he was he, I could just feel his weight, he was very close to me. I decided to walk. A block. I walk fast and faster and if I was cold before now I was warm and though it was only 20 blocks but it was forever. The blocks are long are very long because industrial. The Mex was just behind me. It was always just an industrial stretch to avoid between the cemeteries of my parents who emmigrated from Warsaw as babies in the 1920s (emmigrated separately, the Shulinskys and Ratschelds—they were cousins and so Uncle Sruly was also my father's cousin).

I had the directions from my house in my pocket to your office but couldn't slow down to reach them but could find my way without them anyway. Linden across the intersection and under the L not running still to busier Gates, straight up, Forest, which I had never been on, Metropolitan, neither I had been on this stretch og it. I have to admit this to me is just a mystery what you do. Not what you do in this neighborhood so cruddy and all the clapboard out of vinyl. The halal laundromats and Polish not Jewish but Polish hair salons and Hindu destints, every dentist named Raj. But what you do with writing or used to do. All the time I was going up Gates north this Mex was following me. He was on my heels but that's difficult to communicate. It's very difficult how swift he was run. At leats on the screen there is music and sound effects and editing tricks especially to cover the time of the visuals and motion.

(I could already make out a white guy we would have entitled The Aussie in our youth down the block and waved to him and he waved back to me. I was coming closer. I didn't think this was Bob Onders from Vanderende because I didn't know how his appearance. Then I was crossing from Forest and on the corner. He was very white, which I will own up to it encouraged. Metropolitan was slow of traffic. Just the diesel tractortrailers and vans. I waved again to make sure he was "with me," and he waved again and the Mex must have realized I was "with him," because he just crossed Metropolitan toward the Carvel and either went inside or didn't. Your rep Daniel Makelsen couldn't even notice him.

I hope you are nice to this nice Dan Makelsen. Though isn't he too slightly old to be an assistant? He is so white but in wonderful shape, very worldly, with that politeness you find only in veterans. But isn't that a fascinating biography he has coming from Russia and not Sydney at all? He was giving me tips on postwalk postrun limbering out on the curb waited to be let in. He has the charm to be an actor so it's a pity how his neck's deformed. I told him that about the charm only and about my concept for a book series for children about the adventures of Dabb the lizard from that Dabb franchise I was did and he urged me to put together a proposal and then delinated how to put together a proposal. And we will work together hopfully.

And then in a flawless Chrysler Imperial Bob Onders arrived. Bob Onders who shook hands with me and Dan Makelsen is bald with limited sharp blonde stubble and his head is red, and the rest is eminently freckled. It is either a tan from working outdoors or hypertension, his head. He dons thick black plastic glasses and a gray jacket that says Vanderende Management, under which he dons an Islanders tshirt and careworn light blue jeans by Levi. His boots are Timberland. He chews tobacco and spits into the bottom sliced out of a plasticbottle I'm not sure was for water or soda but also smelled of vodka. He does not come off as the kind of guy who'd spend his cash on water. When he let me in with Dan Makelsen he held the bottle bottom in his mouth to hold the door, took the bottle bottom back in his hand and ushered me up the stairs, it's a lot of flights but we're in better shape and at the door to your unit he put the bottom back in his huffing mouth and took a keyring from his pocket and found the key marked with black electrical tape and put it in the lock and turned and turned the knob, held the door and stood around and spit (stage direction).

I can't believe it, Josh. I can't believe you put up with a place so unheated and where the light won't turn off, the light's always on and makes such a rattling and above all 40 watt. And you have so many books, so many that you by default don't want, by default. Such a goddamn mess. But then we were also shocked. Dan Makelsen packed up the computer. I have no doubt you won't be shocked. Because as we poked around I caught myself realizing how absurd this was but I was apologizing to Dan Makelsen, for you. The cartons, the fucking cardboard cartons, of pornography. Disgusting! I don't want to tell Rach but I'm not sure I have a choice for full disclosure. So much porn you have. The sluttiest! Reels, photos, dittos stripclubs hand out for the whore ads. Fist-fucking, chestshitting, cornholing, pissdrink. True vintage collectibles. Shit only an officionado would own. The labels were W (black) w/ Stallion (black), W (white) w/ Pony (skewbald), M on M cow (costume), M on M on F Dwarf "speakeasy 1929," which were disgusting for what they were but also for how antique and unlike your other piles organzied by theme, Bestiality, Gangbang, Minstrel, Red Army Sexual Hygiene Instructional Materials. I confess I was emphafically not going to sift this. I enraged at you. I we'd given you a chance. Rach had given you so many chances that I wanted to toss it out. Then I wanted to just take it all and send it to you COD. Send it to you COD destroyed. Take it and fence it immediately, one lot (though Rach's correct in that we'd get better prices on the other belongings from auction houses that will have to appraise and by putting the other belongings online).

But no, I became calmed down.

I have followed every law and then be courteous like a cherry on top.

Yes also I would know where to send it now. Or at least Rach has a knowledge as to your whereabouts approximately. Because her therapy blog has a stat counter that's counted traffic from throughout the United Arabic Emirates but also from Palo Alto, California, which neighbors San Francisco. Dhubai. Abu Dhaubi. Daily for a while. Consistent with Amex conditions.

Makes sense you are retreating us. All will be transmitted to Eisen our laywers.

Besides the porn the autographed editions of Wiesel, Bellow, Roth, Bernard Malamud. I.B. Singer, personalized inscription. Encyclopedia Judaicas, which can't be carried. Once a reference set is on the shelves the room can never be left, my parents called that "Jewish wallpaper." Basquiat napkin, laminated. The guitar pick of Slash from the rock band Guns & Roses, that's what's signed in sharpie on the ziploc. All will be authenticated. Brown-paper in plastic of magazines hoarded but the explanation as I went through them wasn't how into celebrity profiles you were but that your writing was in them, always in the back, always re-

views of books, and Makelsen who read through them also said you were "a very thorough reviewer." But he wouldn't take them with. Makelsen said he had copies of everything at the office his agency office already except for the files that were his intellcetual property in the computer so that's why he was taking the computer and everything else was your ordeal. I'm don't know what you did to anger a guy like that. Such a together guy except for the scalded throat thing that would barely be noticeable if he wore a tie, which for what we did together was inappropriate. Framed frontpage that says First Color Page of the New York Times, 10/16/9? So many copies of your own book I haven't read (but will). So many books on computers and the computing business new in their Amazon cellophane (I'll match up the invoices with our billing), just shelves of them called The Exciting Account of How Something Changed Something Forever? The drawers stuffed with crumpled tissue. Semen all on the underside of the desk. Your mugs, shrunken twisted penholders from clay I tried not to break, fountainpen, Mount Blank.
Which if any are valuable and what are they worth because they were in a separate special pile? The Education of Henry Adams by Adams, Henry, Brief Lives by Aubrey, John, The Life of Samuel Johnson by Boswell, James, Sartor Resartus by Carlyle, Thomas, Tischreden by Luther, Martin, Parallel Lives of Plutarch by Plutarch, The Playboy Interviews: Comedians, and then a book I was unable to read but Makelsen who held it said it was in Russian Programirovany economysomethingych y upravlensomethingych zaduck with total pro diction and said that meant Programming Economic and Management Tasks by? He's a very educated asset to the agency, Makelsen. My chair is much more comfortable than yours.
All this I took and put in designated trashbags with the assitance of Makelsen. I forgot to say I brought a box of trashbags. Then my cell rang. The Refuseniks were downstairs. This was the end of my salvaging time. I just could'n't do it anymore and Makelsen either who didn't have to assist me but did out of his own heart. We had ten bags full by that time. My knees and back were spasms, espe-

cially because I couldn't buzz them in so had to go all the way down the stairs again to open the door. But Makelsen who had publisher appointments you were keeping him from offered to go and let the Refuseniks in as he went. He handed me $200 in two $100s and said he wished the agency was able to do more but the agency wasn't able to do more and so I have to think this was from his own pocket, which would be gnerous. He said gday mate so I said gday mate too. I just love that. Then Makelsen picked up the computer that I never mentioned was Rach's so that I wasn't able with him holding it to even shake his hand. (I have profound respect for him and guess he had a car.)

Then the Refuseniks came on up.

The rest of your office is theirs now, which we can get a tax deduction and whatever they can't donate to charity will be offered to the dump. They will send a list of documentation for what has been donated and though it's too polite to you I will fwd: that too. All of this was explained to me again by their coordinator who mentioned he was getting a PhD in Urban, I'd rather not get it wrong, maybe just in Urban and so I asked if his two colleagues were also students and he answered they were graduate students in nonprofit while the two stayed silent strapping on their lifting belts. I thought maybe they wouldn't be phased by the porn but I thought wrong, because showing them around the unit but unable to move because all crowded in by your dreck your chazerai I said to be levity, "feel free to help yourself to this guy's porn," but they did not find it funny and acted insulted because their nonprofit thesis was on gender policy.

They were older than I remembered students being, certainly older than I must've been at City College, which I was barely shaving and they all had large mutton beards with moustaches, were big, burly, confusign. They certainly looked like movers or sanitation or other people in debt. Then talking it out with me they tried to sound like they were from the city with that accent I never hear anymore except in the crime procedurals I used to do, that Irish cop fireman or PS 475 assistant principal or Social Security office supervisor with the wife sore at him so he never goes home voice. All this but still they were quite transparentyl not from the city, they didn't have that city antenna, that you can't impress me sensabilty. I was once in a commercial for loans. But they didn;t recognize.

They began crating everything up indiscrimly, two packing and hauling with their dollys down the hall and one, the urban coordinator one, down the hall trying the elevator. I hadn't realized the presence of an elevator and the coordinator shouted if I had the key but I didn't and called Bob Onders but he wasn't picking up.

I took the two bags I was able to handle and took the stairs to leave them downstairs and search for Bob Onders or get better reception for the cell in the event he wasn't picking up because of the reception was better downstairs.

Or he was in the basement.

But just as I was about to leave a man comes jumping up the steps breathing and screaming, "stop! stop!" in Russian, "styop! styop!" and all I can say is where's Maleksen when you need him (Maleksen wouldn't need have to talk he'd just petrify him)?? But as he slams into me and we both have to hold each other to keep from flopping and he's breathing on me I realize the man's Tartar or mixed, which is all the worst of being Russian mixed with all the worst of being Muslim. You've been fortunate or are being covered for. A friend of yours, this Albanian, he said he was.

He said that all the documents were his and that you'd given him a spare key and that he was using it to store this extra inventory in your unit with permission. What documents? "The pornographies." For your sake is this so?

ALBANIAN (to me): I will remove immediately my documentaries.

I bestowed him the "benefit of the doubt," which appplies to you. This is why I have not told Rach about it despite how consistent it is with your behavior.

I told the chief Refusekin to let him keep whatever if it was porn.

CHIEF (fake hard): I'm not here to babysit anyone.

I went for my wallet to bribe him if that's what he would have come to but

CHIEF: Forget it, you'll just be overtime your estimate.
They bill by the hour but I didn't have it in me to negiotate the Albanian to pay. He was patheticly thanking
ALBANIAN: Thank you.
So the Refusekins would taken a break and we went down to let your friend or this con artist scrounge.
They helped me with my bags. All the bags and I was aching all over.
The bus and train would not be suffice. I'd have to get a cab or in that neighborhood a gypsy service because am I savvy in assuming no cabs ever come to that neighboorhod? Which serviced is yours? Gladly I had saved from online a number.
The coordinator with his assistants took the opportunity of my dialing to leave me. They scattered. They wanted a deli if there was a deli there or just not to be bothered. I was left alone and remembered but nixed going upstairs again to your porn con to wonder if he had a copy of the elevator key, because they wanted the key to the elevator.
The car service picked up, put me on hold, and I repeated them the address twice and finally they explained Spanish they'd be veinte minutos, which might have been 20 or 10 I froget. I waited out in front of the door alone except therefusenik truck, doubleparked at the corner. The Chrysler Imperial had taken leave of Metropolitan. The wind was It was cold. Check the weather today, it was freezing suddenly and I was waiting all freaked by the no pedestrians, which is not NY. All the cars with rims too ritzy for this neighborhood were passing me with my bags and scuffling, freaking me out to lug two at a time all my bags to the corner to wait by the truck, I amdit, to wait behind it. In the driver's seat of the truck the only Refuseniknikwh o wasn't a student. He was in distinction to them who were "inexperienced" white a black guy and very "experienced," dozing through the windshield it was all just a heap of laundry.
Half hour later the car service came and I dumped the bags in the trunk and told the Mex driver the city. But because he drove so hesitent on the LIE I took the wheel and told him to take the Queensborough and had to give him directions uptown and

across and was so irked that even though I was doing the heavy lifting the fare was still $44 and I wasn't feeling genrous. Still when I said keep the $60 he acted like he'd never been tipped before so that when he popped the trunk he got out of the car and got the bags out for me and some ripped with some sharp Tanach corner tearing through and all on the street was clay bits and loose pages from the broke Tanach. He stooped with me to the pavement scooping it all back into the holes and knotting the slack to be juryrigged enough to get them inside, which he also helped with too.

So tack that expense onto what's attached (below). Besides my time that I won't charge for.

Because I did this for Rach, which is priceless. But she'll be coming home in a moment and dinner's my responsibility, wash all this dust off me. We'll order. Prawnless vegan prawn rolls, two #2s, Bia Hois.

Yours in the book of life, gmar tov,
Adam (Shulinsky)

P.S. I took a mutliple copy of your book. Your mother's from Cracow?My people are Warsaw olev hashalom. Specifically Vishkava, the shtetl. If you have any experience with that I would be under other cirumstances fascinated. She was a reader and read until she died.

PPS: No bcc: but cc: to Eisen. If you are familiar with ironies what happens incidently in missing spouse cases after digilent search is undertaken "is divorce by publication." I refer you to New York Civil Law *§315-316 www.divorcelawxplained.com/ny/3, which states*

> *Contents of order; form of publication; filing. An order for service of a summons by publication shall direct that the summons be published together with the notice to the defendant, a brief statement of the nature of the action and the relief sought, and, except in an action for medical malpractice, the sum of money for which judgment may be taken in case of default and, if the action is brought to recover a judgment affecting the title to, or the possession, use or enjoyment of, real property, a brief description of the property, in two newspapers, at least one in the English language,*

designated in the order as most likely to give notice to the person to be served, for a specified time, at least once in each of four successive weeks, except that in the matrimonial action publication in one newspaper in the English language, designated in the order as most likely to give notice to the person to be served, at least once in each of three successive weeks shall be sufficient. The summons, complaint, or summons and notice in an action for divorce or separation, order and papers on which the order was based shall be filed on or before the first day of publication.

://

10/8

~~Fiction writers mistrust the truth, nonfiction writers swear by it, while ghostwriters—who are typically laidoff journalists with novels in the drawer—are divided down the middle. And even that division is split. By which I mean, the relationships I've had with my ghostees have always replicated. What happens is I end up rewriting everybody, and so I become rewritten myself. Haunt the lives of controlfreaks, egomaniacs, career narcissists and solipsists, your lovers, your wife, your mother, and you become them too, inevitably.~~

\

~~Banks again, then either a library or café. All my errands would be cut if this were fiction, but this is truth, so suffer.~~

\

~~It's like I'm writing for Rach. As if my accuracy in this ensures the accuracy of her blog. In Palo Alto I'd tried to get Principal to revoke her blog. He refused.~~

\

~~I've had this fear with everything I've written, rather on every computer I've owned—last laptop, the Compaqs and Gateways Rach took home from her agency, the Gopal desktopped out in Ridgewood. I go to open~~

~~up whatever .doc of whatever project I've been working on, one day, just any normal rainday, and find everything changed. Someone, though fear never fleshed this someone, had gotten into my computer and overwritten me and I wasn't able to tell the difference between what was mine and what was his. But it's only with this book, with Principal's—though also with this—that I'm finally realizing that's plausible.~~

~~So: if anything's bad, it isn't mine.~~

\

Out through the courtyard, jangling my Medieval keys, my last four €20s folded and frayed in my walletpocket. They were large bills, large in every sense to me, not just because they wouldn't fit into an American wallet.

Euros (a term, I might point out, that covers both the fake banknotes and the fake people using them). Euros (but I mean just the currency) don't advertise prime ministers or presidents or composers or painters but rather architectural treasures like bridges and windows, which might initially strike you as a liberalization of the elitist iconographies of the bygone mark and franc, until you realize they're completely false, completely conjured, that none of them are to be found on this continent whose every river is traversed by an actual bridge and whose every castle and cathedral and church contains an actual window to hurl monarchy and clergy through. And so a privilege once claimed by politicians and artists, who never appeared corrupt or syphilitic on their own money, has merely been extended to walls and gates, which now must be shown in their quintessence. The paragon of a Baroque or Rococo arch, the consummate Gothic steeple or spire. Not a style, but the ideal of a style, which can't exist, because style has to live too, style has to eat and sleep and make angsty concessions. Apparently, the EU Parliament reached this decision to feature archetypes as opposed to real edifices so as to avoid offending any nations lacking in culture, rather to avoid privileging any nations abounding in culture and beyond that, the monuments to it—and so preventing Italy and Greece, among the poorest of EU members, from seizing the cash both verso and recto with all their Colosseums and Parthenons.

The same effect might've been achieved, I'm proposing, by putting Berlin on the bills—Berlin's already perfect at being nothing. Ugly plattenbau, flattenbau, immane housingblocks the shape of bills, with the same sense of being backed by relentless brutality, yet just as fragile, frangible, crumbling.

As for the older houses still referred to as Jugendstil, the houses that'd survived the fires—to become cherished only because of that survival, because in their primes they might've been among the plainest façades around—next to their squat concrete heirs they seem memorial, like inhabited memorials to themselves.

\

Insert a line about the weather. Insert a line about how describing Berlin is like describing Berlin's weather—the moment it's set, everything changes, the wind changes direction, the rain stops, but only for a block of Mitte, the sun rises over a wan villa in Wannsee (west), and sets over the graves in Weißensee (east), and the only consistency is the mercury falling.

The lindens were being left by their leaves, and I blew through in a swirl of emergency colors. A drunk gastarbeiter in demidenim overalls stopped me to bum a smoke, but pretending to be a tourist, I turned him down—me, who never turns anyone down.

I missed the tramstop, turned corners strange and prefab, a prefabricated strangeness, encountering only signs standing for things I didn't need, only signs I didn't know what things they stood for and so didn't know whether I needed them or not. An ATM, or whatever that was in German—that's what I was after, though I would've settled for locating even just the full meaning of ATM at its source, automatic teller machine, automated teller machine, automatic automated I've never felt so removed or dissevered.

It wasn't that I had trouble finding a bank—I had trouble finding an untried bank. Until the FinanzCenter Moabit, a scruffy cashpoint behind decals and defaced perspex. I slotted my card to access the vestibule, which savored of wet German shepherds, unless in Germany they just call them shepherds. I swiped the card strip out. Geldautomat. Selected English. You can't go wrong with English. My PIN, why not write it? 179121? My birthday. Backward.

"Transaction denied," greened across the screen. "Contact your financial institution."

But I just did, sorta kinda.

I centered my face within the CCTV bauble and looked deep into my reflection like I was looking deep into an underground lair under the grounds of the White House, imagining my sleeplessness blown up to its pores on the defcon board for the edification of two presidents, Kori D and that other one, intel personnel and Congresspeople all taking a break from their mahjong to tune in, and though I was fairly sure that this Geldautomat didn't have the audio capability for them to also hear me, I said, "Library, Staatsbibliothek."

Read my lips why don't you.

Coming out and mind the bikelane, resist the urge to shove the passing cyclists into the passing smartcars, though the scrimpy smartcars might get the worst of it. I didn't know whether to ask directions in this language or try and ask in German, didn't know whether to trust someone who responded or someone who refused, and follow them like the street was following me, over the Spree and into the Tiergarten.

I avoided the paths to trail along the bisector road toward the roundabout's column, which bore a statue of a lady holding a wreath and staff all so goldsilver precious that it had me appreciating NY's Liberty for her copper, the metal that conducts our lives. Scattered crumbs, pigeons walking like Egyptians pecking crumbs, bench, condom in a bush. Keep walking, trying not to recall why I hate parks. Thank Rach and Christ I was out of the trees and back in the traffic again.

I went among embassies and consulates, and considered leaving myself on a doorstep and staying awhile like Balk, but I wasn't able to sort through all the tricolore.

Potsdamer Platz splashed ahead, and the crossing's white slashes on black asphalt reminded me that prisoners don't wear the striped uniform anymore, which must've been retired after everyone got lost behind the bars and electrified wires.

\

The Staatsbibliothek—a sleek airporty shell. Braze podlighting, hypoallergenic concourses. Switchback mezzanines jutted above the stacks. The ceilinged PA speakers were about to announce that boarding would commence to Belletristik, or last call for Flight 296.1.

That's the only decimal system thing I know—296.1, "Religion, Other & Comparative Religions, Judaism, Sources of." That's how to find Jews in the library.

I thought the hush of the place would take the edge off—it didn't. The modularity rankled me, the ranks of tables and chairs and the students too, interchangeable recessives, receding into their typing, without a backspace typing. All had laptops of their own, lonely and attentionless I can't be by myselftops. Whatever they were doing, it was too effortless for work. Every table, though, had its mechanical Turk, at the head or the foot, at odds. A guy or girl furrowing a textbook in either risk analysis or hospitality studies.

Beyond them were the public terminals. Radical queer crustpunk skinheads who weren't skinheads and just unaffiliated opiated homelesspeople, geriatrics switching between pairs of bakelite glasses and clamping down their headphones—they sat in neat interdigitated rows at new unibody Gopal Go 2.0s, searching.

All that Aryan lucence, the sham race purity of Gopal's product design—I kept spotting him, I kept hallucinating him. Maleksen.

Not among the users, but among the machines.

It took me a moment to understand why: Maleksen—there's no other way to say this—was like a Gopal device. He had that whiteness, that untouchably smug whiteness, that gloating, that crisp compact perfection. Everything so concentrated it was like his insides were his outsides and were muscle, and that muscle was always flexed. A processor torso curved into a nonadjustable head, a quadrat Gopal monitor. And that jagged scraping between them, across his laryngeal mass, like a hot knife had scarred him with thick and thin bars, was the barcode of his specs. Scan him and be intimidated by his dysfunction.

If he'd brought me what Balk owed me I wouldn't have come. Not that I had a clue what I was going to do besides maybe write Aar, maybe Cal. I looped around to the infodesk and signed for the next computer slot available. Cinching my tote closed throughout so that the librarian wouldn't notice I already owned a computer, and I'd have to explain how its modem had died, how the dying Founder of the world's most profitable because most complicit tech company had taken off his belt and used the buckle's prong on it.

The librarian wheeled around with my terminal number and time—I'm presuming it's acceptable to mention that he was in a wheelchair.

There was an hour's line to get online alongside unwashed Gypsies and jobless Slavs.

So I went browsing, or I guess it's not browsing if you know what you want. I wanted *Keine Familie ist ganz.* That's what the translator or publisher had titled my book. Retitled it for appeal, I think. They never even sent me a copy or review clippings, or royalties. I don't remember it surprising me that Germany was the only foreign market to buy the rights, though in the immediate aftermath of American publication I don't remember anything surprising me. Anyway, Germans buy everything Jewish, it's compulsory since reunification, it's in their constitution. It doesn't even matter whether the topic's Jewish, provided the author is, if only just half or mischling like Caleb, or if the book has at least one character who visits a rabbi in Brooklyn or a cemetery in Queens, to say oy gevalt chutzpah bupkes, amen.

Anyone of my generation with even the slightest Judaic taint can air their grievances in Germany—not for a fortune, or even a readership, but for a psychic reparation between hideous brown buckram covers—and as I thumbed at the spines of my consonant for the sole copy the Staatsbibliothek had in its catalog, I was imagining the cycle continuing: not just children like me chronicling how their parents survived the deportations, but grandchildren producing multimedia ebooks about how their grandparents were used as slave labor, greatgrandchildren generating interactive immersive lit experiences about how their greatgrandparents had been experimented on with phenol and cyanide—all to be sold at fabulous prices to futuristic Prussians, who'll still refuse to download anything for free, God bless.

And there it was, where it was supposed to be, where it'd been shelved since they'd ordered it. The original had been thinner than this edition, but then the original of me in the flap photo had been thinner too, my crown still sparsed with gritty city grass.

I checked in again with the infodesk clock and dedicated the 40 minutes or so left before my slot to reading myself in German, and didn't understand a word—which was good. That meant it was a good translation. Rather, the only words I understood had always been in German. Words like Aktion, Zyklon, and Judenfrei.

Keine Familie ist ganz—not a faithful title. But still it's accurate. No Family Is Whole? Entire? Intact? Together?

This trip—though it's absurd to call this a trip—is the first I've been back to Europe since researching that book. Not to discount my jag with Principal just prior to the Emirates, or that vacation Rach took me on to Athens, Crete, and Rome—after every meal sauced and cheesy reiterating to me, to the waiters, that she'd be paying, with her account management promotion raise—what I mean is, this is my first substantial solo return.

Because that pilgrimage I made 12 years ago, fall 1999, was weeks, was months, alone. Taking the grand deathtour, budget timetravel through ghettos and camps. I'd flown from having interviewed my Tante Idit and Onkel Menashe in Tel Aviv, to the setting of every interview's memory, Poland. Racking up expensive kilometerage on the Daewoo from Sixt Rent a Car in Warsaw, visiting the gravelessness of my family between Warsaw and Kraków. Swerving the Daewoo from red tollways to green freeways to yellow locals to the grayest byroads, as the map that was still wrought out of paper back then blew from the dash and around my face, and I skidded onto a dirtlane that muddied into a pagan grove of birch just wide enough for a uturn. Tailgating an ox and cart, unable to pass them, too timid to honk. Utilitypoles leaning heraldically like halberts on the shield of sky. And panicking that I'd already crossed the border into Belarus, even though I'd know when I had, they'd let me know when I had—there'd be a bridge, and a river churning like a wobbly tire.

This was (why am I even writing this? but then can anything about the past still be assumed?) before the zoomable livestream mapping, the captures and grabs and pinches and swipes, the make it bigger make it smaller fingers, tugging the corners of dewy pastures to a saturation verd. The only icons were in chapels, and if I hoped to obtain one's aid I had to make a donation for the restoration of a window.

I'd paged through my book all the way to the last chapter—the Vienna chapter, by chance. If chance can be invoked.

My mother and father met in Vienna. Dad was with the Army. The US Army. Moms had come down from the mountains of Czechoslovakia, from hiding in haylofts, and a convent in Małopolska that'd hid her from herself. The fields around Bełżec were fertilized with her parents. Her brothers were also ash.

Iz, it hasn't escaped me that you're there now, in Vienna—picnicking in the Prater, or promenading the Ring.

If we ever meet there remind me not to tell you this.

\

I sat, Tetbook in the Tetote on my lap, at a Gopal Go 2.0. Clicked the Union Jack/Stars & Stripes, which loaded up the Staatsbibliothek homepage in English. Agreed to abide by the Terms of Service. Only if I didn't have to read them, Yes.

My IP was what it was. Proxy this, Dienerowitz, bounce it off your ass.

The only precaution I took was, I didn't use Tetration.

Except, I did—I typed out tetration.com, was redirected to tetration .de, deredirected to .com again and tetrated, or the German verb is tetraten, I guess, "what are other searchengines?" And then I cruised the competition on another competitior's machine, and found both lacking, and I haven't been paid to say that, or paid for anything.

I broke my promise to Principal on opensourcers, semantics. With Clickb8, Sengine, Fravia, Phind0, Jerque, and Treap (in the order of increasing fatuity).

Whatever, their names were immaterial to me—I tetrated with all of them. Not every trademarked term can be chosen for genericide. None of us will treap. Or jerque it. What the fuck's a Gopal? Gopal fuck yourself?

I tetrated "Izdihar Almaribi": no results.

I tetrated "Izdihar Albadi": check spelling, increase number of terms, broaden terms, no results.

"Ibrahim Albadi": ("did you mean *Al-Badi*?"): site operations engineer at Sohar Industrial Port Services, no, executive VP for Takaful, Doha Insurance, SAQ, no.

So I added +"Marseilles"—which autocorrected to "Marseille"—and was returned two hits, beyond the usual snippety tetspam.

Iz's husband was listed as a member of L'Association des Stations-Service Franchisées de France, Provence-Alpes-Côte d'Azur Bouches-du-Rhône division.

He was mentioned again, amid plain Anglais, on the site of the Biannual Eurosummit of BP Franchisees, which would be held, had already been held, 9/9–11 in Abu Dhabi. He would be attending as a representative of L'Association des Stations-Service Franchisées de France, Provence-Alpes-Côte d'Azur Bouches-du-Rhône division—his honeymoon or whatever it'd been with Iz was a business expense.

"al-Maribi" ("did you mean *Al Ma'ribi*?"): but all were just Al Qaeda—inciter clerics and deranged bandoliered teens, the victims of other American results in Ma'rib, and of Shia militias in Dhamar—until what I recalled of the address—+"1210 Wien"—got me Iz's brother.

Yasir was a "Prozesstechniker"—"process technician"—employed by Birefringen AG, located in 1210 Vienna, and online at Birefringen.at.

Click, they were "the world's leader in glass science," click, "devoted to the best in architectural, automotive, aeronautic, marine, biomedical, and touchglass."

The "In Profil" page was dotted with enlargeable but not enlargeable enough official photos of the different "Geschäftsbereiche"—divisions? groups? There were about two dozen black and brown faces in the photo labeled "Prozesstechniker," and "Maribi, Yasir," was captioned in the third row five in. I counted and landed, because God is good, because God is great, on a forehead wound. Yasir had a scarlet birthmark at his hairline, but then the expression below it was quizzical, like that hematic crescent wasn't his, but was a corruption in the wifi transmission, or a blotch of phlegm on the screen.

"Maleksen": A Maleksen gøta in central Tórshavn, Streymoy, Faroe Islands. Maleksen Island, a glaciated constituent of the Arctic Russian Franz Josef archipelago. Norwegian sites tended to spell the name "Malekson," Swedish sites, "Maleksson." Pages in this language usually followed the Danes. Maleksen Spezialtransporte GmbH "specialized in transport" throughout Schleswig-Holstein and Mecklenburg-Vorpommern. Hilde Maleksen offered "online P2P healing" from ~48.13°N 11.56°E elev ~518m (Munich).

Anders Maleksen was a dual Swiss Australian citizen, who, incensed by the carnage inflicted on the Palestinians during the Gaza War of 2008–09, hacked into the computer systems of the Aman, Mossad, Shabak, and Malmab, exfiltrated palimpsests pertaining to Israel's second strike nuclear arsenal and submitted them to b-Leaks, which earned him the position of "amercement officer," which he parlayed into a spot as "adjutant"—the organization's #2.

"Balk," a verb meaning "to stop abruptly," "to refuse obstinately," a noun meaning "a hindrance or check," "a defeat," in sports both a verb, "to make an incomplete or misleading motion," and a noun, "an incomplete or misleading motion."

Thor Ang Balk, Danish national and the founder of b-Leaks who after allegedly drugging and raping a 16 year old Spanish "alt" or "alternative" model—with whom he'd been in sexually explicit correspondence, and who b-Leaks would later insist, without documentation, was an asset of US intelligence—fled his base in Copenhagen, was detained at Reykjavík-Keflavík airport, and spent a week dodging press while awaiting the verdict of the Icelandic authorities as to whether to return him to Denmark, until Andrey Vasilyevich Tsyganov, Ambassador Extraordinary and Plenipotentiary of the Russian Federation, dispatched a detachment that managed to surrept him back to the embassy's chancery at Garðastræti 33, his residence for the past six—the profile was dated—14 months.

Yet another—now that I'd switched to tetration.de, .com, to utilize its tetrans—I tetrated, proprietarily tetrated, myselves: Principal hadn't been reported dead or even missing yet, and no newsfeed mention meant me instead. Just Autotet fluff, and fluffy charticles about Autotet, earnings reports and predictions, stock flux. All the tabloid sites were sedent, their comments sections too. cohencidence.us was, reload, was down.

Then I finally did what I'd been waiting to do, I tetrated what'd been stabbing at my insides since Dubai, cutting away at my synaptic fray since Dhabi, I tetrated "what is that dagger called traditionally used in the united arab emirates"—no questionmark, no question, sharp demand—and was returned weaponsoftheworld.com, *khanjar:* "The khanjar was the traditional dagger of the Oman and the United Arab Emirates (but in Yemen called 'the jambiya'). It carried in a ivory or leather scabbard and decorated with jewel, gold, silver, etc., etc., worn on a belt similar decorated. Though today it worn as formal dress or as symbolical 'fashion statement,' in the history it was the regular weapon for revenge or assassining."

I loaded bankofamerica.com but had been brainvacuumed of my portpass. It was different from my PIN, and wasn't any other Rachy anniversary. I exceeded all my allotted attempts. BoA was sending an email that would let me change my portpass.

I put off checking Rach's blog, and went loading all my six million emails.

://

From: a@szlayliteristic.com
To: jcomphen@aol.com
Mon, Oct 3, 2011, 11:13 AM
call yourmother, myung

Knock knock? Who's there? Aaron. Aaron who? Why Aaron you replying to email? Though the other punchline is Aaron the side of caution. Dear, dear—this is your personal assistant again. Your Lisabeth. Telling you that your mother's been ringing nonstop. She's worried. You haven't been answering her emails, and she's been telling Lisabeth that the only reason she got involved with paying Verizon $54/month, and she can't understand why her first month's bill should be $88, incidentally, was to be in touch with her son! and then Lisabeth went through explaining her plan, the Quantum, 15/5 Mbps, 10 MB of hosting! I told her you were off on an investigative project, something about unfair wage labor practices in telecom manufacturing because that's what was in the NY Review under my latte (rhetorical latte), which was how I found out you'd told her you were doing something about scandals between donors and museums relating to deaccession policies and I apologized and agreed, you were overcommitted and overdue on both without an alibi, and she wondered how I held my soap, which was faintly erotic, and already today the answer's on my desk (your mother made me a soapdish).
Besides your mother traffic's been standard: Ad Shulinsky's now claiming you're charging lingerie and Arab whores to your wife's Amex (please use a rubber and also, DON'T CHARGE ARAB WHORES TO YOUR WIFE'S AMEX), and that you haven't renewed the lease on your office (which was relayed to me only on

Friday and I'm trying to intercede without involving Lisabeth or Seth but the voicemail Ad left says Rach's holding your possessions with intent to recoup your rent she paid—there better be nothing in there, in terms of P—"possessions" better just mean "the scattered grains of your neighbor's nukeable basmati"! and I haven't even mentioned the Eisenizers yet, or Alana, telling me she's been leaving msgs but your phone's off the hook or whatever the new hooks are, I told her get in line!

But Rach—just think—if her blog's a retaliation for what you've already done, think about how she'll reply to a felony. You're both behaving like fucking children. Ashamnu, bagadnu, gazalnu, fuck you. Dibarnu dofi. Forgive me. Or just trust me.

Bullet points, brass tacks, takhles:

—Feyer has been retained, informally. I had him pick me up on East End Ave so we wouldn't be followed and we weren't (the Asian) despite that he'd decided it was smart to take his Austin Healey. We drove to Jersey, in homage, or because if anyone followed us to the Brisket King of Linden, they could have us. They could have us with a side of kishka. I explained, not all of it, of course, just the divorce and money angles. Feyer tendered his advice. If you're indeed out of country, which I suspect you are, which you'd better be to be so incommunicado, and out of country for a protracted time (there are no definites on time), it's only logical that you'd require a foreign bank. Anyway, it's imperative we talk, either by phone or my preference is in person.

—My schedule: I leave for the Book Fair, in Frankfurt, Germany, 10/14–16, and I'm bringing along the final version of Cal's novel, which he just delivered fresh from Iowa after two years of revisions, dicking around with commas like they haven't already been paid for in the States, and spoken for by publishers in four foreign languages (German, French, Hebrew, and Dutch). I'll do my Fair business to shore up the rest of the rights and then if you're in Europe I'll rebook my flight or extend and meet you in Zurich and we'll go banking. Feyer advises that we found a company and not a personal account (under your own name). So pack for an incorporation vacation, all names pair well with the Swiss AG, we'll drink silver tequila tête à tête de cuvee, eat popcorn like gold teeth and write it off. In Europe there's Luxembourg, Liechtenstein, Andorra, before we're talking Cyprus, Channel Islands. What does P do? Query? Another option if the logistics go south is that I go ahead wherever and open an account myself and deposit the sum and then when you surface we'll make you a cosigner or even if you'd prefer remove me totally and cash me out. Now Feyer who suggested this mentioned that I wouldn't require your permission for this, or the bank wouldn't—because the bank wouldn't know that you exist, obviously—and if that suggestion doesn't shake you out of Arabia, even if just for a phonecall, I don't know what will. The IRS doesn't have quite the incentive of an embittered wife with forensic accountants. THIS MUST BE ATTENDED TO IMMEDIATELY. 10/28 I have to be back in NY for a routine coronary catheterization indignity but if you can't get together the week after Frankfurt or until later in the month I'm after any excuse to tramp around France with the NBA expats as they waste their lost season dunking on ASVEL Lyon-Villeurbanne. Beyond October, let's not get into. Beyond October, forget it.

—now: the urgency. You remember Tad Geary? Cal's friend once upon a time at the Times, and now with Wired? Anyway, he called Friday day and talked, because he always does, like an NPR segment, all about the death of print, and whistleblowing, and drones, before getting down to the salacious, genital warts at The New Yorker, herpes at The Journal, and from the venereal it's always been a natural transition to the topic of literary agency—because just as I was sure he was going to propose an ebook he slipped me a rumor that I'd been working with P. I denied, but must not've been as convincing as this rumor from sources unspecified, because Geary was already reassuring me that if certain access was given or blanks were filled in my identity and the "granulars" of my "partnering" would stay privileged. I didn't counter with what access he was after, but then the questions he asked explained everything (the blanks). Like, where's P? When's P back in Palo Alto? Is the health as awful as the gossip? What if anything are the plans for succession? I told him they'd just hire a computer. Then he took me to school on the health gossip. It was stomach cancer, he said. Or colon. That's not me being unsure. That was him. Then I had to call Cal, to coordinate blurbs with the comma czar and, I'm predicting, permanent writer in residence of Iowa, and while I had him on the phone said that Geary would be calling asking questions of him and that he'd be doing me a favor. If he'd pump Geary for his sources especially. I told Cal I wasn't involved in any tech projects, that not only didn't I know Bing from Skype, I thought lit agencies were cheapened by having sites, that's why we never got one. Geary called, because I'm a prophet, on Saturday, and told Cal everything he'd already told me and Cal feigned curiosity, but didn't have to feign ignorance, and probed, and promised to investigate for Geary out of interests of his own, because he'd just turned in a new novel, which would require my, Aaron Szlay's, full attention. The takeaway was that Geary had no indication of P's medical status, no verification, and the only news he had of P's potential book property was of my ostensible repping and Finn's ostensible publishing of it, both of which tips had been passed to him, independently passed, by some Buddhist guru, Master Tetsugen Ken Classman, and a VC named Dustin Something, who's tight, apparently, like they're sharing the same bunk on a yacht tight, with Kori Dienerowitz and, Geary told Cal who told me, he was finding it strange that not only had the same tips reached him, Geary, through two different channels, but also that Dienerowitz—whose stakes were higher than everyone's by degrees of magnitude, or higher than everyone's but P's—would have said anything about P to anyone, even intimately. Geary suspects a powerplay. A ploy or coup, but to what conclusion, Geary has no conclusion. I haven't jawed any of this with Finn (he'll be in Frankfurt).

—because, now, the Asian: I went out to Staten Island yesterday to explain myself to Svetlana (because she wasn't taking my calls). I took the ferry. You can't top for climax the Staten Island Ferry. Sveta wouldn't let me in and the mother whom I'd met all of once outside Macy's (Sveta once tricked me into going to Macy's to get a swimsuit only to meet in the ladies' swimsuit section a Soviet lady with Chernobyl growths on her chin and the cheeks of a circus cosmetologist who gave her daughter a crate of homemade beef cutlets and shook my hand and said, "You be glad forever")—anyway, Svetlana's mother, handling a difficult situation, came out to the stoop with a bottle of Evian for me, or not even that but the fucking bottle with trees on it, Poland Spring, and forced a smile and went back in and locked the door. Whatever. That isn't the point. Returning to the ferry, the Asian was onboard (she's Korean). She made sure I noticed her, the sweats, collegiate, crimson, Harvard. So loose on her, windblown at the railings. I decided, fuck it, enough cowardice and slapstick, and as the ferry launched I chased her casually up, down, and across the decks. But then I realized I wasn't chasing her. She was just trying to get away from the crowds. Away, windy. Starboard's the side that isn't port. I violated my policy of never engaging Red Sox fans, especially not from Harvard. But she had this together professional don't trifle with me thing that just cracked. That was her affect, cracked. A once organized type a ivy executive human now broken. She told me her name was Myung Unsui (she spelled it out), but I'll admit that ever since a certain site has appeared in my life, I've been having trouble with my manure detector. I'm just going to relate what she said, and let you be the judge of whether it's true or just, as the distinguished typo has it, "voracious," because I'm too frazzled—I can't sleep but if I do sleep all I dream about is apnea. She said she worked for P. Confirm this. She said she was an assistant and very close personally, and either it's all imagined in her head or they were fucking. By fucking I mean in love, confirm this. They were traveling together. She said they were traveling with a friend of mine, but she didn't say your name, or your names fungible. She mentioned the UAE. But how it checks is that she also described you, physically, accurately, but in that ruthless quibbling analytic metricsexual way. Don't shoot the messenger, just diet and shave. You and P were working all the time, she said. She was obviously jealous. She had that envy pout that so transcends all cultures and races and even our species that if the aliens ever contact me but I snub them because I'm writing an email to a client that's the expression the aliens will have, all their suctorial prehensile mouths petulant. Her job was that every place you went to she went to that place before you and set every-

thing up. But in the Emirates P told her to go back to the States and leave you two alone, just you and P. He told her to take the rest of his entourage back to the office "to await further instruction," which she said with airquotes and henna on her hands, like Achsa once had. She did, she took. But no instruction followed. P was misaligned, she said. I didn't understand. She hesitated and then said, cancer. The Battery grew. The statue and the bridges and everything and even with all of that she was crying.
She stood around the office doing absolutely nothing. She didn't sit because she'd never had an office in the office. She'd just shared whatever office P was in and now he wasn't in any and no one knew where he was or when he was returning and if she had a job anymore she decided it was to comport herself like she knew but would never divulge and above all wasn't anxious about anything. But then she didn't have a job anymore. She was fired. She was called in by Kori Dienerowitz himself and pretended to miss the voicemail but couldn't pretend again, she couldn't do anything but go in and get fired. She'd never been fired before. She said she still wasn't sure that he had the authority to fire her, but regardless her email was denied, her logs were closed, whatever the lingo is, they confiscated her computer and parkingpass, which I gather in California is rather severe. She wouldn't answer any of my questions about P's relationship with Dienerowitz. She just kept talking about "termination," about how being "terminated" was like being called "a witch," which her grandmother who'd been a shaman or shamaness I guess had been "branded," she said, in Korea. She was embarrassed, and talked fast, and then was embarrassed because her accent intensified. She had no friends in California, she had no friends except family in NY, and so she flew to NY and disguised the disgrace she felt by using her savings to pay off their apartment in the Bronx, Grand Concourse, so uptown in the city's math that the numbers collapse, with a 208th Street jumping to a 210th Street intersecting with a 208th Ave and a 210th Blvd. Having been sapped unconfident, and sapped by TV, and she had to share the TV with her grandmother, she now found herself the last two or so weeks commuting alongside her parents to the tip

of Hunts Point to help out with their deli. Balance the books. Make change to slide around atop the carousel behind the bulletproof partition. Acrylite. Like in a taxi. Like she'd done throughout Bronx Science, like she was a teenager again, humiliated. "The bills are filthy." "No one ever takes the one moment to unwrinkle." We docked. We went up toward Whitehall and approached my office and paused in front of it as if acknowledging that yes, this was a building, yes, this was a building acknowledged by both of us as my office, then resumed, went further, Bowling Green, the Bull getting its balls fondled by tourists. She talked about a job interview she had coming up. "Shit IT." But she couldn't even get her references together. If people knew her, she said, they knew her as P's, and worried about her loyalties. She couldn't stop chewing gum or cutting her hair, and she took off the Sox hat and showed me. Sometimes, putting the scissors down, she'd just suck on the hair, sometimes she'd swallow it. "There is nothing to do at a deli." It was a bad business model. No systems, so inventory's all by sense or by hand. Her father insisted on giving credit, microfinance for the parish, her mother on keeping a bunny despite the health department. The licensing, the taxes. Operating costs and insurance. Unreliable labor. Callingcards returns. The powerball machine always breaking. The hassle of cashing checks and regularly explaining to regular customers that prepared foods can't be paid for with stamps. The franchises and chain pharmacies that undercut pricing by stocking in bulk or their own productlines. 24 hours, two shifts of 12, seven days a week, and she insisted on the nightshifts so as to better follow me and then, letting her parents take off for some church and peace and a touch of the flu, she was by herself and went out to rearrange the produce and some bath salts maniac jerks around the corner and grabs the scissors out of her apron and holds them to her face. "He does not want money." "But he does not want to be alive either." I'm just typing what she said. I wondered if she'd ever considered a career in publishing. But we were on Wall Street. Bankers were out in the mild. She was about to go down for a 4 train. To Woodlawn, I said. Yes. Get out at Yankee Stadium, take the Bx4. Yes, she said, but Bx6.

I'll be able to find her. A family clunked up from the station arguing already, carrying protest signs and a megaphone. I asked her and I was yelling as she descended why she'd been following me and she paused and turned sniffling and clung to herself as she met me on the landing, and she answered that Kori Dienerowitz was trying to sabotage my friend, you, and that he had government resources behind him, because P had gotten involved with Thor Balk of b-Leaks, or his involvement was forced at the threat of disclosing his disease. But that at core P wasn't compelled by any of that and instead he was working on something beyond death, something spiritual. And that my friend, you, would never understand that, and that for all the chip and wisdom you cultivated you were just a nice guy out of your depth. Not nice but sad, she said. "Like Principal, he treats you like he's inventing you and knows that it's bad but still better than anything else," "you don't think he has a soul until you realize he just shares yours."

aar

://

10/14, FRANKFURT

Riding trains, in their impassive passing, in, their, speed, that, smoothes the tracks out, that straightens the rails and evens the ties—it feels like how you tour a museum. How you tour a busy museum on a weekend or holiday noon.

You streak by mindlessly, peeking over heads, pardon me, Entschuldigen Sie, until something stills you, something tries to keep you, but you can't be stilled, you can't be kept, you're bound to a schedule and hurried by, and the only impression you retain is one of resentment—not of the murmurous crowd, but of the artifacts in their cases, their stasis.

A city revolving its exhibitions by the neighborhood, the block, with the only explanatory labels the graffiti: *ZIZ* tagged along a quarter kilometer of trackfence in the chemical blue of the toilet in the trainstation's men's room, *ZiZiZiZiZ* bubbled in the neon pink of the powdered soap, then *Un train peut en cacher un auteur, fuck death, fuck debth, ¡mauerpower!* Drab Altbau progressing along the timeline into the new, the housingblock towers disinterred in tiers, archaeological strata of the future spilling onto balconies, hanging gardens of prams and bicycles, antennae, satellitedishes, and saggy feldgrau panties—all of it being left behind like a diorama display, as if Berlin were a museum of itself behind "glass."

Cranes guarded the route, imperious in their hover, monitoring progress, approving entry, denying entry, wreckingballs at the ready to prevent a touch, even a linger, enforcing a policy of No Eating, No Drinking, No Flash Photography.

~~The woman had emerged from behind a grate to ring in the next customer like an automaton skeleton in an astronomical clock of the Northern Renaissance, but with a Deutsche Bahn blazer, and without a scythe. Only after I'd managed to explain that I didn't want to go directly to Frankfurt but wanted to switch along the local routes instead, changing from train to train, each one smaller than the last, at the smallest and least convenient stations, accidental depots that were just collisions or breakdowns, and only after the woman had quoted me how that'd cost more than double than and take more than four times the time of the ICE, the InterCityExpress, I settled, but requested a ticket only oneway, which might've confused or even disappointed the customers behind me, who'd been convinced I was a criminal or escaped convict, but now realized that even if I were one, I was inept and beyond that, cheap.~~

~~Only a corpse would lay out for a oneway ticket. Frankfurt and the grave are the only two destinations to which the directest route is also the cheapest.~~

Have all the pensioned docenty dyejobbed perfume in their pits ladies of this continent shut all the ports and gates, bar all the entrances, barricade—screen—all the emergency exits, and it all becomes a museum, in which all us museumgoers become the exhibits, relics studying one another, studying ourselves.

This has been me just following a track, unable to stop and get off.

~~I hadn't slept. Just loitered, vagranced. Benched. No sleep now.~~

~~My suit still hadn't dried from showering in the sink. I felt clung to. The many things in my many pockets weighed on me. My rightleg had my keys, my leftleg had my wallet. Passports pinched my asscheeks. My Tetote, a pocket unto itself, was strapped left to right across my heart. All my possessions were pressuring me, hungrily, pressuring through my pockets, insatiably, until I myself was pocketed as a single speeding point, without volition, beating.~~

A couple of businesstypes toward the rear of my car had unpacked their tablets. Ereaders, which is a term that can indicate either the person reading or the thing that's read, but they were ereading. Any news that was newer would be prophecy, which the train enabled with wifi. To turn the page, to turn the screenpage of their tablet devices, they made a slight slash with the indexfinger, like how tyrants used to select their concubines and condemn their jesters to death. Stroke, off with her clothes. Stroke, off with his head.

And I was doing it too—dismissing my fellow passengers with their own gesture. I esat with my efinger in the iair and islashed it around. Then I went clicking on things, at least on the window between me and the thing, as if whatever I clicked would have to explain itself to me. As if I'd press on a village we passed and it'd surrender its name. Press on a town for population, demographic, economic realia. Press on a field we passed, press on the pane between me and field, and projected back through my whorled prints would be a history of its sowing, its reaping, the annals of who'd screwed between its sheaves.

We'd cross the Elbe (which the Soviets never did, though neither did the Americans), cross over its tributary the Saale, or I forget which one of the Saales, and how many Saales, and how many rivers we'd cross that weren't a Saale, but I'll never forget what redundancy feels like. Redundancy feels like doing this on my own.

Whatever lay in the path of the straightest standard gauge connection would be crossed and in that crossing, obliterated. We'd span every other river in the Reich and why not even the same river twice—we'd pass but not pass through the Harz, and we wouldn't cross the Rhine (my father the soldier did once, in the opposite direction).

A man who didn't strike me as a businesstype—rather he was closer to being into football, American, though his footballsized face was intelligent—settled across the aisle. What bothered me, initially as an affront to that intelligence, subsequently because it marked him as a danger, was that he wasn't doing anything, he wasn't reading or ereading anything that would've made his language public, he wasn't even playing a game.

I sat with head averted at my window, deep in a comp lit seminar with my and Principal's twin passports. As the strokers kept stroking screen-pages, and the fields blocked by like crosswordpuzzle blanks, like spot the differences between the photos teasers.

It wasn't obvious whether the man was weak fat or strong fat or even which seat he was sitting in besides the whole row, with the median armrest raised. He pivoted toward me, and his neckhair and wristhairs were so alert and bristling as though frequency tuning that I toted up, got away, over the metal tack, the bridles and saddles that coupled the cars, stopping midway between the caboose and the motive, the diningcar.

I needed a drink, to rid myself of my last coin.

The English/French/Spanish menu encouraged me to "Sample the Regional Wine," which was what I ordered by pointing.

No speech, just cork—no need to retail my own blushing terroir.

The waiter returned having linked his cuffs and buttoned his collar and clipped around it a redherring bowtie. He set down bread, which I refused with a headwag. He would've charged me if I'd touched it. Then he brought the grail of plastic goblets, already poured. Even the napkin had its price. It was a check that unfolded like linen, €4, a €1 tip rounding up, and that was all of it.

Prost, prosit—I took a sip. Trust nothing you read. Nothing about this wine was local. Motion has no local.

Just as I was rimming the sip the door autoslid. And behind it was another door, a wall, my aislemate. He was tall and wide as if he were quarried from the surrounding terrain, as if he were being quarried from the car itself, a raw rupestral growth who had to nick himself down just to fit into my fantasies. He boothed two booths away facing me and ordered a mineral water and was served that sparkling clarity in a glass anchored by a big crystal of ice with a big halfsliced citron floating atop like a buoy.

The English language is like a tunnel with endless clearance—an eye or ear too forgiving. Americans especially can usually get where someone's coming from. This has to do with being mediated, having seen and heard enough screenwise to know how Yugo gangsters inflect, when they plot amongst themselves without subtitles. How Russian assassins dress, when they're planning to explode a motorcade. We have every variation, not least the counterintuitive. But I can't say I can do the same offscreen and within another culture. I couldn't dig deep enough into his umlauts to judge them native. But I could still suspect some curry in his wurst. His skin was either racially tan or tanned. How he poured. How he drank. How he did absolutely nothing else. How he wouldn't leave my face. And so I slumped to show him his reflection in my baldspot—and then he finished—to repel him by his reflection—and then he left. Coins on the table, no tip. Just a cock of the head. Tongue out. Like he was aiming.

\

Probably just an overreaction. Probably he'd just never been around a Jew before.

In the next car another passenger sat reading another book. Not ereading an ebook. The passenger just closed the thing. And took a euro billsized card, an indexcard that spanned the indexfinger to the middle of the hand, and marked the page. No cornering, no folds. Cards. Reminders of the census. Cards were how censuses used to be conducted. Once, each city, each town, each village had an official going door to door, collecting information, marking each dwelling's data with pen or pencil on card. Each municipality collected its cards and summarized their stats in a report, and each bound report was put on a train and relayed to the capital. I'm wondering whether any of their couriering officials ever read them if bored on the journey. I'm just guessing that another book, containing and summarizing the stats of all the municipal books, would have to be compiled in the capital.

But then at the turn of the century—1890? 1880? I forget, my exactitudes are later—the census was automated, at least partially automated, first in America and only later in Europe. In 1933 the Nazis counted only in Germany, but in 1939 they counted in all the annexations too, counting Austria, Sudetenland, Memelland, counting Poland, the Generalgouvernement, at least in part. The censustakers distributed to each household a strip of paper, a survey whose filling was mandatory and whose findings the takers themselves coded onto a card by a system of punched holes, a punchcard. This citizen had blond hair, punch, this noncitizen had black hair, punch, cranial and facial type, nose type (straight or curved, weakly or strongly bent in which cardinality), tabulating religion (column 22 hole 1 was Protestant, hole 2 Catholic, hole 3 annihilated). Did he or she have one Jewish parent or two? even one Jewish grandparent? Any disabilities? and/or disfigurements? Glasses and/or hearing aid would help to complete the form—condemn. An accounting tallying poetically, still—all identities are voids.

The punchcard and its calculating machine—the storage/memory and processor of the earliest computing—were invented in 1890 by a German American from Buffalo, NY, named Hollerith, whose company became the company that became IBM, which, in turn, licensed the technology to the Nazis (but don't get all nitpicky angry if online contradicts me and says the year was 1889 and the city was Albany and the inventor's name was Höllerith and the licensing was done by an IBM subsidiary).

The technical execution of the punchcard's primitive programming was modeled on textiles, specifically on how looms used cards to separate threads into patterns for weaving, for embroidering things like swastika bands and yellow stars, though the inventor himself always maintained he'd initially been inspired to adapt the process by a train journey he'd taken through the American West—by the tickets required, their validation, their punching.

The conductor, a sturdy peasant in matching prussic pants and vest over boiled nasty sputumnal shirt, strapped his monkeycap and cowbelled into the car—weaved down the aisle and took your ticket and like a censustaker, with a small metal squeezer apparatus, punched it, put a hole in it, marking your fare and so marking your fate, your final destination. A flurry of chad, white discs of paper floating floorward like the Polish snow that greeted the steerage.

Genocide, like publishing, is 66.6% a problem of distribution—how to get the people/things you need to be killed where they need to be killed when they need to be killed, and at a minimum. How to get Halbwachs to Buchenwald to meet his dysentery. How to get the best Yiddish poets of Kiev all to Moscow, to the Lubyanka's basement, on the same summer night for mass execution. How to get Mandelstam to the Second River transit camp by Vladivostok in time for his official cause of death, which was frozen "unspecified."

Nowadays publishers just invest in writers, they have the writer's work edited, copyedited, proofed, but then they have to print it and make it public (murder). Nowadays writers are murdered mainly by their publishers, by being sent off to press and then to market.

American printers used to be the best in the world (the linotype, 1870–80? by Mergenthaler?), until for margin considerations too caustic to countenance, they merged with or were acquired by foreign companies, and so migrated abroad. Or else the companies uprooted themselves, keeping their corporate registries but moving their plants to Mexico, or China, the country that invented the book but bans books, and imprisons its authors—and in which, about two centuries before Christ, the Emperor I'd butcher his name erected a great firewall all around his Empire, buried its scholars alive, and then burned all their books, either to stifle their critique or standardize the writing system (the same Emperor whatever his name standardized his Empire's currency, busy man)—and in which, about two millennia after Christ, this book I'm not writing is scheduled to be printed, though it would still have to be approved by the censors before being translated, and before any of the workforce enslaved to its production, any of the billion other Chinese, would be able to read it.

If only they had time to read it—hordes of the desexualized toothless working alongside one another like stripped gears, loading and impressing by roll, gathering the signatures, by octavo, by quarto, for binding—12 hours/day, 6 days/week, roughly ¥12 or $2/day, approx $52/month, approx $624/year. I've read the same journalism as everyone else, and I'm still not sure what to fall for—either any job is a good job, any pay is good pay, or China has only one factory, is only one factory, and its only product is suicide.

After China the book—because only after China would my ms. be a book—would have to be loaded onto boats and shipped back to America, to my publisher's distributor in Delaware, or Maryland, or Virginia. The distributor would have to send the books out by truck and train, fraught stock freighted to whatever bookstores still existed, which would sell whatever inventory would sell and then return whatever wouldn't—returning it damaged unremainderable—and so again the trucks with their squalid cabs shrieking libertarian radio, and so again the trains chuggachuggachoochooing through backyards unmown and littered with stormwater kiddiepools, all the way back to the distributor again, only to be turned around again and redistributed, sent to that minor inferno of upstate NY, Buffalo, where they'd be pulped, where they'd be recycled, in a factory owned by Canadians.

And all this is set in motion once a year, with all of America's literary agents and editors and publishers flying off, business class, to Germany, "to network" with their international counterparts, to sell the books they agent and edit and publish to other agents and editors and publishers in other countries, to buy the books the other agents and editors and publishers in other countries agent and edit and publish—to stretch their expense accounts out to the desistive notch of the industry's debauched cardboard belt in lavish drinking and eating bingery and depressing indulgences in inroom krautporn—unsustainable.

It's all far less efficient than it was half a millennium ago, when that scum capitalist Gutenberg forced his underpaid, uninsured employees to pack a wagon or packhorses or perhaps only a single wormridden horse with communion fare and a few copies of the genesiac printed Bible—headed a full day on a pilgrimage that today can take all of half an hour, from Gutenberg's native Mainz following the river Main to Frankfurt, to the Messe, the Fair, where reading paraphernalia like tinderbox flints, tallow candles, and commodes were sold, where those first editions—literally the first printed editions of the word of God—were bought like any other commodity, by semiliterate merchants and papal emissaries, who haggled. The merchants went bust or were failed by heirs, the popes were divinely chosen by smokes and died, and likewise Frankfurt's Römer, or cityhall, the site of its medieval markets, was abandoned for a newer fairgrounds, equipped with the infrastructure required by car tradeshows and appliancemakers' expos.

The oldest extant building of the modern fairgrounds, though now only a performance venue, is the fin de siècle Festhalle, whose glass and steel were meant to reflect the design of Frankfurt's main trainstation. The square in front of the Römer hosted a famous Nazi "libricide," or "biblioclasm," in which fiction and poetry were burned only for having insufficiently imagined what followed. Kristallnacht. The owners of those libraries, Frankfurt's Jews, were herded into the Festhalle. From which they were droved to the trainstation, deported. It's incredible what can be compressed, confessed to, on paper. The stroll was calm, the hotel was not. It had a very useful library.

\

A History of Frankfurt was an oversized and useful book, which covered the city from its founding by tribal Franks to its destruction in the Allied aerial bombardments of 1944. This hotel was among the casualties. The photograph on its page was dated 1933, however, and showed the structure as grand, intact, staunch in tradition, ennobling in permanence, and indistinguishable from its incarnation today. *A History of Frankfurt* noted only that the hotel was subsequently rebuilt, but never addressed how or why it was rebuilt—though perhaps such questions are only for outsiders, or retrospect.

Because it seems to me that standing amid the rubble you have a choice.

You can rebuild, or you can not rebuild, and if you decide to rebuild then will you rebuild the thing exactly as it was or will you make it new. Either you can go get the exact same masonry and the exact same woods and the semblant rugs and the Aryan atlas figures that uphold the pediment with your name done up in vermeil, to make as faithful a replica as tenable of what you've lost, or else you can just hit reset and find an alternate design—other materials—and maybe not even a hotel.

I had this thought at and about the Frankfurter Hof, of course—this outstanding reproduction of a hotel, stolid in its blockbound prewar glory, truly the architectural embodiment of everything the city surrounding it has always aspired to, just acquired and spiffed by a consortium of Sunni hoteliers, apparently—but because I know the future will demand the explicit, let me also state: the questions of whether to make, or not to make, of whether to remake or make new, are just as germane to literature.

"Did Elisabeth Block check in yet?"

The Reception slab was a barricade protecting taste from the shabbiness of frequent flyers. The Hofmeister, Herr Portier, uniformed like a general, had a phone on hold over each shoulder like epaulets—"Are you Mr. Aaron?"

But then he raised a hand as if in salute, and, pressing extensions, transferred his calls to the garage, or wellness spa, or Ruritania.

"Again," he said, "my regrets. What is your name, sir?"

"Aaron Szlay?" It was a decent guess, and I even spelled it.

He nodded as if to indicate that he was going to vary this performance a bit from the way we'd done it in rehearsal, and then he went to charge my keycard.

The guy behind me reached around to tap his pda on the marble ledge—"What's the goddamned holdup?"

Herr Portier said, "Please, sir, we today are at the maximum." And then to me, "Ms. Block has taken care of everything."

I took the keycard, the luck, and repeated my room number just to have a line.

"Unfortunately we are not able to accommodate upgrade to executive."

"I understand."

Throughout this, I have to mention, Herr Portier had barely broken from his screen. I left, but the tapper didn't advance—not until he finished txting.

The room: I'm guessing we're already well past that posthistorical point at which it's still interesting to note that hotelrooms are like film sets—now I'm just assuming they're designed that way, and that thanks to film itself and to Frankfurt School theory classes the unconscious has once again become the deliberate (the tedious). Everything furniture to fabrics was squiggled and jotted as if all aesthetics were just a hedge against spills. Lamps giving off light to the circumferences of chipboard tables. The TV was atop the desk (the escritoire? secrétaire?), so that I won't be able to write—if I have to write another hotel sentence I'll die.

I sprayed myself wethot in my underthings and wrung them out hung, got into bed with the snackbasket. Crumbs. Sky News was doing the invasion of Libya and the occupation of Wall Street. Then *Germany's Next Top Model,* they hadn't translated the title, and then a show I didn't know, whose every voice was Ad's, and drooling into maybe, just maybe, sleep.

Until the phone rang, and it kept ringing, because I let it.

I was woken by a knock at the door—which nobody ever does on TV, they just bound in. Unexpected doorknocking is more a staple of the European novel, more ominous.

"Aaron Szlay?" The accent was abominable, even through oak.

The only thing worse than an Aussie or Kiwi intonation is its intermittent use. When it's Auckland talking, or Melbourne, fine. But when a snatch of downunder drawl erupts from the mouth of a Euro, it's like blood in your urine. Maleksen said, "I know you're in, mate."

"I'm in the bathroom," and I was flushing the toilet to stall. To stow my tote, hide my Tetbook.

But it wasn't fitting—not between tank and tile, not beneath the sink, and then, there on the floor and just as I'd left it, paged open to the spot I was in, it was *A History of Frankfurt,* which had the spatials and heft. I wedged my Tetbook and Principal's passport too in among the pages, and stashed the volume on the shelf with all the other volumes about life, war, and what to do in town.

Maleksen—he made a fist and put it to my pudge, fistbumped me back to bed until I sat, holding my towel's knot, pillowed at the headboard.

Then he was in the closet and hatching the roomsafe, at the window taking down the blackout shades. He straddled a clubchair and vented his crotch, dejacked the phone with a boot.

This was my thought, with him just across: this is what my children's children I'll never have will look like, will sound like, will be. From nowhere, from everywhere, edged up against crisp cropped skin in desert digifatigues whirring with muscle or device.

Not even his scars were humanizing: the 12 seared bars I counted just told other machines his price.

He unsnapped a pannier, dug out like a black snowglobe, set it on the table between us and dialed around until its northern antipode was palpitating red and on TV the contestants did the fizzle shimmy, dead.

"Gute nacht to you too," I said.

"You say that only to sleep," he said. "You must say instead guten abend."

"What fucking toy is that—an evil baseball?"

"We have here the yammer," he said. "It is yamming for us all wireless wave frequency and electromagnetic transmission. On multiband level to 1500 MHz for 30m radius. Including all remote neural dragnet spying on human brainwave."

"Here I was trying to keep my thoughts to myself. It's a jammer, by the way."

He tried to wrest a smile, from either of us. "It is very dumb that you left Berlin."

"Blame yourself," I said, "I left because I was broke. All you had to do was bring me my cash and still you fucked that up."

"How is that happening? Do you not get money?"

"Not from you. Not from Balk."

"I mean from Aaron Szlay, mate. That is why you come here. He gives you money you give to him files? But are they a copy on drive or your computer?"

"What's it to you? Haven't you fucked with enough of my technology?"

Maleksen juggled the dark globe, then repanniered it.

"Your trip to NY—breaking into my office? I was waiting for you to bring it up."

"They let me in, mate—you have no security. b-Leaks is only ensuring there is no copying of files."

"Why not just ask?"

"Because if we ask we have to trust. You know about this visit to your dumb office as you call it only because you go online, and you are ordered not to do that."

"I'm not in the Swiss Army, you fuck. I don't do orders."

"You must explain this to Thor. To me you must explain your addiction to Zionism. I like only the writings about your wife and the film script, because it is about space travel. The rest of the documents on that computer, no—I think your experiences are maybe not as important as you think they are."

"Maybe you weren't supposed to read them?"

"The videos," he said. "You must turn them over."

"What?"

"The videos of the interviews, mate."

"The interviews I did were audio."

"Any format is acceptable. Just turn them over."

"The recordings are only on my computer, and my computer's only in Berlin. Anyway, I don't do anything without authorization."

"Thor authoritates."

"I don't mean Balk—I mean the man whose life I'd be duping away. We have the same name, they're on the same contract."

"He is gridless. We have no coordinates."

"Writing himself barefoot in the dust of an interior Pradesh. That's convenient."

Maleksen stood—"But they are not secure, mate. The recordings. They can be wiped. Or corrupt."

"The plan was that I hold the recordings until deadline. If I fuck up the deadline and don't hand a book in, b-Leaks gets the recordings and goes live. Only then, though. And I have time."

Maleksen went over to the dresser. Pulled a drawer. The next drawer he pulled off its tracks. He capsized the table there's no name for.

"What the fuck? This isn't even my room."

He went for that shelf that ran opposite the bathroom. His hands under it, frisking. Pushing up on the bolts, shaking the snackbasket, mantelclock. *A History of Frankfurt.*

"Fuck, stop—will you? I didn't bring anything with me—the computer's in Berlin."

"No," and he turned, a hand lingering on the shelf. "In Berlin is a flat b-Leaks assigns you. In the flat are insects from the trash of shit hydrogenated cornsyrup America suppers, all over the antiques of senior b-Leaks allies. But in the flat there are no computers."

"You were there?"

"I am there at times you are not."

Neighbors, if people in adjacent hotelrooms can be neighbors, were smacking at the walls to quiet down.

I got up from the bed, it took me standing to realize how halfnaked I was. I had one hand to gesture with if I wanted to keep my modesty, or appendages.

I said, "I'll be back in Berlin—I don't need to tell you when—I'm sure you'll find out when before I do. Then we can arrange to talk this out with Balk."

Maleksen went for the door, but then aboutfaced, took my towel in hand and yanked it clear off. Then he left.

And there it was, my prick.

://

There was no way I was going back to dreamlessness after that—there was no Aar. It was 8:00 on the restored TV and the tickers scrummed the rugby scores. I went fisting my socks prolapsed, and my skidmarked tightywhities. By the time they'd dry frühstück would be over. Petit déjeuner, desayuno, breakfast. The Frankfurter Hof's laundry service takes 24 hours. I habilimented myself all stiff, retrieved my Tetbook. I left Sky News on for a ruse, left everything in the halogenic heated bathroom on, left the mirror on, left.

I elevatored down to the lobby, lined up behind my nose and became the garnish to a salad of Spanish, Italian, Greek, all propping menus I didn't have. Printer paper spiralized between clear covers, mss. I made the buffet, filled a plate with what was left of the healthies, fruitsnvegs, before staking out the carbohydrate troughs. Then it was all a matter of doing the school or employee cafeteria dance, whom to sit with, but none of the tables were empty enough, rather any that were just as I approached them were being whisked and stripped.

Some situations were meetings of four people reading and some situations weren't meetings but also four people reading. Still other business transpired, like the two bedheads blanking their faces above a twotop whose snidely gliding linens suggested footsie, legwork, crotching. Man with a hirsute Mediterranean goat vibe slumped low to gain traction, woman this pale Dutch scullery maid all gyral and shifting her sheath, neither of them speaking too good the English, the only language besides the shoelessness between them. They'd been adulterating everything. Their pdas mated vibrationally amid cutleries, their respective spouses calling—I had to resist picking up. I had to resist removing their footgear from the surrounding chairs and sitting to offer advice—it's always better to pick up, feign static.

Then toward the pastryside of the buffet in the middle of the room was this big burl of a guy by himself, tunic of a tshirt held together by electrical tape, baggy jeans from the nuclear winter collection, sneaks blatantly inspired by better sneaks, fingerless gloves he pounded into the pockets of a skanky nylon windbreaker. Wiccan roadkill hair parted sparsely in the middle hanging limp like two wimpy black anarchist flags. As I passed I noticed the catalog he was reading, the selfie, his, he was studying below his name, and I stopped without even proceeding into the accompanying bionote. There are no words, there is no word, for having translated my own translator.

"No family is intact," I said, and settled my plate. "No family is intact but the family of the dead."

"I am sorry," clipped, gruff, "but your meaning?"

"So you've forgotten the beginning of our book?"

He frowned, "That is the beginning?"

"Sure is."

Then he said, "Indefinitely," by which he must've meant "undoubtedly" or "indubitably."

"A pleasure, Dietmar Klug," I said.

He gripped me weakly, then throttled his neard, his neckbeard.

All the significance was already plated: just behind us were Anglo steamtrays of eggs, lipidinous wursts and rashers of bacon, puddings, hashbrowns, beans, mushrooms, tomato hemispheres, and behind that a jointly controlled French and German zone of what would've been a continental frühstück if consumed on another continent, the crepes and quark streusels preserved by marmalades and juice and milk selections from venturing into the Asian stations of noried rice, and yet all he'd hoarded was a, I'll traduce it for him, canapé.

As I chairbacked my tote and sat against it he picked up that plug of kornbrot and shook its mayosmeared hamfleck into his napkin, then took a dainty bite of the stale rusky round to chew over the coffee or tea question, before finally spitting crust in English, "I would have please a Heifeweizen," which compelled the server to ask not him but me, "Room number, sir?" Trust Aar to cover the cost.

Dietmar, Diet, had to wiggle his seat out and hunch just to face me. "OK, so first it is complete unjust," he said.

"What is?"

"OK, so first the amount, with schedule. To do the book by one month is two chapters every day, also Saturday, also Sunday, and that is 10 or 12 hours each and I have children. Second, the way it is that we must receive chapters from you each at a time is maybe how other translators work but not myself. To translate I require the complete text at all times to ensure the consistency and also the style. Consistent mood and style. I know you will say you have the editor to take care of that but you do not edit the same way because I do not have the agent to do this for me. I also have things to say about the contract. But wait."

"I'm waiting, but you're getting me mixed up."

"Ja, ja, you mix me up the worse. The title must not be in German the same. *Duskovites* means in German just nothing. *Dämmerung-Kinder* as Schmöker suggested is bad, however, very bad. I will think of the better title for you. I have thought potentials already but we will put in the contract extra if I do that and you use."

"Again, calm down, you're talking to the wrong guy."

"No, I requested to talk with the American publisher because Schmöker would not pass my worries and finally was vengeful of my influence. He said I was to go talk to you directly if I was sure I had a sense. I do, I have a sense. For pertinence this second volume must extend the plot of the twisted horn and to resolve also whether the unicorn can pass between the dimension zippers because in volume 3 it was no but in volumes 2 and 1 it was otherwise and between them nothing was explained about it."

"I understand."

"Also for the 10–16 year olds like for my children the erotic pretext of the frozen marquise is not appropriate."

"Finished?"

"Ja, ja."

"So you write yourself?" hoping to humor or just waylay his concerns halfway among the condiments, but his beer came.

He muzzled a toast and drank and dripped liberally from his neard, staining the lapels of his windie.

"So what are you translating now?"

He waried, "Truth?"

"Nothing but."

"Scheiße, other series. You test me that I do not tell but I have read the contracts."

"This isn't a test. Trust me to trust your discretion—just moneywork, then?"

"Ja, ja," he laughed, "translation is for money. Dress and feed two girls with only English."

"What would you choose to translate, if the money weren't an issue?"

"Truth again?"

"Try me."

"I like translating what I do, the Americans, romane, sachbücher, fiction like not fiction. It is not much, the work, you can even put it all into a computer the syntactics are so basic."

"American books are written by computer."

"The series we do is written for children but it is the same as the books for adult, the same identical differentiality, no?"

"Difficulty?"

"Quatsch, quatsch. It's not very much at all."

"So the dream is being lived?"

"Or once again if I retire and do not die I will write poesie," and then he was assessing all around us again, and the ceiling too, as if he were inspecting the sprinkler system.

I said to change it up, "What room are you in?"

"Gallus neighborhood."

"Do you come every year to the Messe?"

"Every month and every week and day it is like I go to this stumpfes Messe, because I live here."

Translation, by repetition, "You live here as in Frankfurt?"

"Ich bin ein Frankfurter. Sie sind ein Hamburger."

The beans and mushrooms were already ladled away, and the tomatoes followed. My mug was cold but the servers were disinclined to refill it, the frühstück hall was sparse with late and sluggard headaches, all the guests who'd make a differentiality today had gone, frühstück hours would be over in 10 or so minutes by the cheapo digiwatch my companion kept switching between his wrists and already even the occupied tables were being bussed.

Last chance, "*Keine Familie ist ganz*—you remember?"

"A book?"

"A book you did. About Jews, the Shoah. American. 2002, this would've been around."

"I did at that time but also before many books on Juden."

"Which was your favorite?"

But he was lost to me, "And now if not the books for children it is many books on Islam."

"This one was special. To me at least."

"The Juden books I don't know."

"Don't hold back."

"They are wrote to not be read I think."

"Just bought, you mean? Guilt purchases?"

"I mean—no, no," and he rubberbanded his hair back, "that they are wrote by writers who do not live today for readers who read who are not the people today with the problems," and picked his scalp, "totally not like life, or like nothing has happened between the war and date of publishing," and peeled a scab, "my English is not so good to conversate—identität ist nur rassismus, ein buch für juden ist kein buch für den menschen," and he reeled in his chair—definitively, undoubtedly, indubitably, perturbed.

"A shame you feel that way."

But he jumped up and backhanded smacked himself, his watch imprinting buttons.

He yelled, "My life is fuck—it fuck—scheiße, I am sorry fully, apologize fully, I never meant to do not," and he covered his mouth with his hands.

"Please."

"I hope I did not insult because this is a job I require and the series is wunderbar and Crown to me and Mrs. Janet Dofts at Crown Books has been wunderbar."

"Of course, of course."

"This is living money for me."

"Obviously, no offense."

But his jaw convulsed, "Two girls, one translator, Dietmar Klug."

He turned, I sat, as the waitstaff bared the table and plied its cloth.

\

As I slung my tote through the lobby and out, litzened doormen doffed their laureled caps.

Danke, guten tag.

It was a dank gutted tag, no sun toward noon. I wended around polygonous planters, barrier hollies unberried. Men adjusted wool blends, their tieknots the size of the Kaiser's scrotum. Women long and thin lightered long thin flavored cigs and exhaled into their phonecalls. Deathmasked Hungarians. Serbs or Croats, unplaceables or just Danes. Their scents were cloved smoke, buffet borborygmi, and olent Hofbrand unguents, and the languages they conferred in were all, or none—Euroenglish, Euronglish spraying like water not from the fountain, drained beyond the colonnade. And I was the only American among them—the only American to still be dawdling the day away with a fair on.

I followed the delegates from the smaller lesser nations of smaller lesser languages through the Platz der Republik, a dull hub of officespace like deserted barracks, bunkers exhumed. Every Mercedes M-Class 4X4 ever made rolled by, windows up. The access to the Messe was meshfenced and coned between signs indicating the airport, Lufthansa billboards vandalizing the orisont tethering inflatable jets. The forecast called for a 100% chance of flurried schedule sheets and complimentary bookmarks.

The newest structures formed a quad, or tetrad—four halls numbered consecutively, 1 and 2 projecting from a concession terminant in screeningroom, a massive A/V ark whose presence and purpose demonstrated the lack of confidence bookpeople have in their product—why read? why not just grab a seat in the theater and conk out?

Halls 3 and 4 were of architectural interest, roofed in gently sloping metal dunes. Impressions: each mirroring metal wave resembled an abdominal segment of a robotic roach, a cuttlefish's iridescent cuttlebone, or a toucan's beak cast in dental amalgam, an armoring scute of an armadillo, while the total effect was that of a multizeppelin crash, or a mashup of the Decepticon mothership Nemesis and the Autobot derelict planet Cybertron, from the animated TV series and liveaction movies, respectively, of *Transformers*.

Not just four halls—on the back of the backpage of the schedule was a map—everything was a mirroring. My fellow Americans were all in Hall 8, apparently.

Halls 5 through 8 inclusive reminded me of malls, best measured not in square meters but in parsecs. I walked through them and sidestepped their conveyors. I walked between them, and there was Frankfurt's skyline, like apocalypse does Dallas. Your friendly neighborhood global banking headquarters—Deutsche Bank's logo of a blue square slit diagonally has always read to me like the desolate vagina of a war widow.

She was being positioned, canted, bolted, this survivor of the gender wars, arm up, arm down, legs spread wide as if to imply a corresponding wideness of taste—a mannequin of Charlotte, whether her first name or last they'd only posted that, the first female printer in history. Paris, reign of Francis I. Alongside her pose was pasteboarded a polyglot factsheet about homosexuality and publishing. Friedrich Koenig, no umlaut for him, invented the first nonmanpowered, but steampowered, press, an unwieldy replica of which anchored the display. The Asians, despite all their advances, their innovation of paper and ink and styli before Europe, were underrepresented, inevitably. Theirs was just another but scanty polyglot boardtext noting all their innovation of paper and ink and styli before Europe. Clay and wood and bronze. Lead and tin and antimony. Samples. Gutenberg and his moneylenders were dummied prominently, don't doubt.

The translation's typography was blackletter Textura, Fraktur, the spelling unstable, incunabular: "Johanes." Mainz was referred to as "the once rival of Frankfurt." Once upon a time. Snobs. The installation featured animatronics, rather inside the cases were Poles and the murmurs reverberant from behind the plastic sheeting were in Polish responding to yelled German. They were running late. They were running with screwdrivers to tighten the screw on a press. It was the same as the oil principle, the crushing of seed, nut, olive. Smithing. Gemcutting. Platen. Windlass. Gutenberg's father, Friele Gensfleisch zur Laden, was employed by the ecclesiastical mint. My speculation, exactly. Chirography, typography, money mania. A coin is minted by mold, the metals are poured into it, and an image is stamped on the surface. Given that a nickel now is just a quarter nickel, it's strictly the image that coins the worth, glyphs of tetrarchs and portraits of feudal royalty, with time becoming kitschy graphics of livestock and wheat. Given that paper's still paper it's the scripting that authenticates the bill, the signatures of presidents or primeministers, treasurers, reserve chiefs. Pecuniary inscription being a residuum of the regent's seal or signet ring, the guarantor of authorship and so, of authority. Sphragides, sigilia, specie and fiat currencies, movable type, all systems of writing to date, in each instance an arbitrary materiality is forcibly impressed with transitory value. Proof of identity. Colophons of self. I told the registration guards my name was Aaron Szlay, and though I'd left my pass back in the room I could show them my swipecard in its sleeve with that name on it. They consulted their list, credentialed me, couldn't have been nicer.

I entered under scaffolding. Let history record that in my lifetime most major public spaces were being renovated and not many ever utilized their main entrances.

Stamping through literatures familiar and not. Books everyone in America who reads has already read, now finally new again in translation. Books that nanocosm of literate America will pretend to be familiar with, if given the opportunity. The same book in multiple editions, the memoirs of a writer, his wife, her lover, of some kidnapped juvenile who grew up to become the first democratically elected female CEO of Muslim Africa, each language's copy cut into the shape, the mapshape, of the land in which that language obtained, the books arranged to puzzle Europe. They were cutting the final books, the jigs and jags of Estonia, Latvia, Lithuania, with saws. Still on the schedule was when they'd gather the 10 thickest volumes published since last fair and toss knives at them or shoot them. As if to determine the densest. A banner tugged taut, into an expressionless mouth: this year, the fair's theme was either the Future of Books, or the Books of the Future—sometimes with German all I get are the nouns.

America, at last.

Stomping past my publisher, expecting Finn, his bosses. Other publishers had pavilions, mine had a breakaway republic. Hostile sovereign Midtown territory. I wouldn't have been surprised by a functional military. An intense assisterhood whose mufti concealed all variety of weaponry. The jaded. The coy. The derisive. I kept my head down to flatter myself. The intern of my enemy is not my friend, the extern of my enemy is, forget it.

Finn must've been elsewhere.

The agencies all had the same style of booth crowded clustered at center hall, foldingchairs but upholstered in oxblood, foldingtables but teak. Placards bearing agency name and Messe directory number propped atop. To be a truly venerable publisher you have to be European or owned by Europeans with a vast backcatalog of pogrom tracts or Nazi agitprop to rely on. To be a decent agent all you have to be is American and social. Convince, be competent. Smile.

"Seth," which wasn't my memory but his lanyarded tag, was skinny-suited with a skinny tie, a quiff. Hipbony, hipstery, novelty Masonic tieclip and links.

"I'm interested in making a bid for rights," I said. "I'm an editor at a discerning house in Sri Lanka."

But Seth's face was off wandering behind me, as if Sri Lanka were there.

"The new book by Caleb Krast, specifically. I'm told it's a novel. We'll bind it in coral. Dustjacket of leather, porpoise or whale. Targeted advertising and outreach to blogs. We're the best and only operation on the island—I'll translate it myself."

Even Seth's wince was forced, as he came around the table and said: "First off, Sri Lankans are a linguistically diverse people who tend to read Anglo-American writers of quality in the original. Second, Sri Lanka, as a former colony of Britain, is a member of the Commonwealth, and so its territory is typically covered under the terms of a UK agreement, which we've already concluded, prefair, in the case of Mr. Krast."

"Concluded lucratively?"

"With all respect, Mr. Cohen," but then she ran between us and cut him off.

She: Seth held her and shook her, and only then did I have her—it was Lisabeth Block. She was shaking crying and holding her nose, emulging. Seth let her go. He was diligent with a tissue.

Lisabeth was a bucktoothed and fawnish blonde braided by the better schools. Aar had hired high, and highstrung. She'd never needed this job, she'd only needed something to blame, to have some purpose to the days between breakdowns, ballets, Montauk, and Maine. She'd had a relative on the Mayflower but only Aar ever remembered his name. She was 22 years old, rather she'd been that age in my mind for over a decade. Not much more than a voicemail, the voice that put me through. I'd try to banter, I'd flirt with myself. She'd kept her distances, played close to the varsity vest, pencil skirt snug at the thighs.

But now she clung to me, and because I wasn't sure why, it was my fault—I read all of Rach's grievances graven across her cheeks, inconsolable.

"What's wrong?" I said. "Why don't you pick that up?"

Lisabeth stepped away and dabbed her lipfuzz, "What?"

I said, "A very small person's having a conniption inside your very small purse," and then Seth said, "That might be her."

By the time Lisabeth'd broken a nail to her Tetheld the ringtone had stopped. "I can't," she said, but went to ID what she'd missed and as she did the ringtone started again and with her crying the effect was of sirens.

"Achsa," she said to Seth, to me, and with a jagged thumb accepted the call.

"Achsa," she said, and heeled toward the exits, "Hello?—Frankfurt, in Frankfurt—hold on, I'm taking you with me."

"What's with the hysterics?"

Seth unfolded a chair, "Sit down."

"Where's Aar?"

"Joshua, please." He went back around the table and I sat tote in lap creaky across like I was begging for a temp job. "We've been setting up here since yesterday morning," he said. "Mr. Szlay was to have flown in last night."

"But?"

Seth fluffed his tietips, and his beltbuckle was a square and compass—"Why are you here?"

"You don't know?"

"No."

"Does Lisabeth?"

"We haven't had the chance to discuss it."

"So, what? Aar's missing and I'm the mystery?"

"What I'm telling you isn't public. But you're his friend?"

"Guilty, yes. But you know this."

"I know that when an agent takes such an interest in a client who isn't writing, he has to be a friend."

"So?"

"Mr. Szlay."

"Go on."

"Had a heartattack."

"Fuck? Where?"

"Up in the plane. Midflight."

"Is there a number where I can reach him?"

"He went, Josh, before they even landed."

"What—he went?"

"All agency travel lists Lisabeth as emergency contact—the airline notified her, and she's been trying ever since to contact Achsa."

"But where is he?"

"They diverted to Reykjavík, Iceland."

"Aar's where in Reykjavík, Iceland?"

"Understand me—he went, left, died. Before they even landed."

"Where?"

"What do you mean?"

"I mean, where fucking exactly did he die?"

"Up in the air. He died in midair."

"But above what where? Motherfucker, why won't you tell me?"

I both can and can't explain my focus. I needed something fixed, some fixed grounding at the time.

Aar died smack in the middle of the ocean. Aaron Szlay, in the middle of a cloud.

"I'm sorry," Seth said, "but why are you here again? I don't have his schedule—were you two supposed to meet?"

Now. I can't write this.

Can't. Cut.

://

a-bintel-b.tlog.tetrant.com/2011/30/06/thedumpydump1

if you go online you can find out a lot about mummies. fact: the oldest mummy ever recorded is actually of a south american child. two millennia older than anything egyptian. double fact: when the mummy of ramses ii was so deteriorated that the egyptians had to fly it from cairo to paris where it got modern preservation the mummy was issued an egyptian passport listing its occupation as king (deceased).
even if youre going to get more specific and tetrate "mummies in the department of egyptian art of the metropolitan museum of art on the upper east side of nyc" youll get too much to handle. fact: that actually the mummies arent the most important artifacts of the metropolitans egyptian collection but instead the small little wooden models of the thebian servants who were supposed to come to life to serve their pharaoh in the afterlife are. double fact: the big big temple building reconstructed at the tip of the wing wasnt looted from egypt as my x2b told me the many times we visited but instead was given by the egypt government to the met as a token of appreciation because it was going to be drowned by the construction of the aswani dam (the nile).
but despite any terms you tetrate one thing youll never get is that the associate curator of the department of egyptian art of the metropolitan museum of art on the upper east side of nyc is a whore. shes a mummy coordinator how perfect is that responsible for the linens or like the wrappings of the mummies that have like hieroglyphic or hieratic demotic writing on them that help if not identify them by name then at least by date region because of the materials and let me say also I got all this not from my x2b but

online. because j always lied. its like sites were invented just to call him on his bullshit.
at the met he was always into the fatties and this one wasnt any different she was chubbs chubbseroo like a sacrophagus. also dark enough that i prejudged from tetrating her that she was egyptian herself but the last names persian though im not sure jewish. on her cuny faculty homepage her titles listed along with a list of her publications on femininity and exhibitions curated like the one in washington dc last fall but im getting ahead of myself. i got her home addy too in excellent school district but trainless tribeca her parents def had paid for and her workphone and workemail at least but im getting ahead of myself no links.
id been prepping a new campaign for a sportswear client unmentionable in this context except it has all the cool hip eurosport feel of an adidas but also the vintage made in america brand identity of a converse despite it being neither so use your imagination and also unlike converse it doesnt just specialize in shoes. i was going around in their clothes for a while just to get a feel and remember thinking even a size or two bigger the clothes would be so comfortable i thought they would be kickass maternitywear. they were!! i wore them to work and that was acceptable because everyone else was wearing them like they wanted to be anywhere but at work like playing golf or tennis or taking couple strolls through the wetlands preserves or playing lacrosse with the 2.5s against the garage before refinishing. advertising is all about that aspiration and planning for the move you want to be when you grow up even though only grownups really have the real money to spend on the products and services especially advertised. like when you sit next on the bus where you can parse the ads and the cheaper the campaigns the cheaper this is evident. that chica doesnt actually want to go to that shitty profiteering technical college for an associates degree in underpaid midwifing as a second language what her pose communicates from the zoomy cleavage and the way her tush juts directly toward the older whiter professor photomanaged next to her is that she actually wants to marry up just like in the jewelry ads the men are always much older but

more tanned and rested and successfully physically heavier and thicker than the women because the ads are intended to communicate to men that if you take care of your woman and take the relationship honest into metals and gems this is what youll live to. But this is all kindergarten stuff and I worked on the larger accounts that had to be more subtle while being less subtle too and in every way larger but anyway the basics are the basics.
wed been having our appt sex with such regularity like they were fertility doc i or shrink doc m appts and maybe we got too regimented maybe we got too strict im an invertebrate scheduler. <u>but ive covered this extensively before</u>. to recap. it was gyms and no gyms diets and no diets mucus boosters ph levelers organic boli from the corsican homeo who said she worked at equinox but she worked behind the desk at equinox i guess also i got a bit freaky tossing out all the cleaning products convinced they were the problem and then stopped cleaning and hired a cleaninglady w referral but fired her before she came out of guilt then felt guilty about it and called around to get another referral but d picked up the phone while she was chasing her daughter trikeing down the hall i hung up i couldnt i couldnt take it. we made checklists and went to appointments and the problem was tubes or azoospermia zoospermia or motility tensions and stress and their effect on hormones and phobic overexpectancy in which failure to fertilize is attributed to failed desire like only feelings can fertilize like sperm and egg can only lambada when theres love and then he flipped when he researched that the potency boosters i had him on damiana and conium were versions of hemlock but everythings a version ok. the manuals with their clipart diagrams and advice motto slogans that were bad but also good routinize romance lust or bust porn is worn jerking for it isnt working for it getaway to get your way have only one reservation and thats at 8 practice worshipfulness cultivate a rapport with your mother or a member of the clergy. courtship. civalry. ovulation apps eggtimer apps basal thermometers next the precoital stretching the positions with the pillow under my tuchus and legs elevated wonder-

ing what color to do my nails in the air while he fantasizes about the anchors on ny1 on in the background liz viv or lew or lou the news guy with the moustache and john david the chief meteorologist with all the tides before the sports. or after the sports.
the appts he liked the least but if we canceled them even if we werent feeling well like i wasnt that day a year ago wed still have to pay (and if youre new here you can read why im tetranting all this as a therapy assignment here). parentheticly thats my suggestion ladies for a new anniversary not the birth of the baby but forty weeks or nine ten months before that the conception anniversary get your party on and kick me suggestions about how to name this holiday like a baby and the winner gets a surprise ill get it together.
so i came all nauseous out of the agency and toward time square taking anything but 40th street because i was feeling fat though he said i wasnt but he always said i wasnt avoiding the muffin place even though now they have raw and it was stifle hot and the ac on every bus and train id been on was busted and the sneaks were so comfortable and the striped tracksuit with the noticeably discreet logo placement was so light it was like i was wearing breezes that i decided fuck me with my metrocard im going to fucking schlep it like 50 blocks uptown and that would calm my tummy.
as i was schlepping i was calling him but he didnt pick up but i didnt leave a msg and instead checked my ical prsnl where i record my diets and gym and gyn routines to remind me he had that presentation at the met that hed finally gotten a job there even if it was freelance writing a handwriting on the wall text it was a job and that made me happy that he was happy enough to get out of the apartment and that goddamned office and bring in money doing something especially something more intelectualy stimulating than more housewives of bravo and matinees at film forum that he went to the pawnbroker four times and reading the covers and page 36s of books at the strand or getting ricepuddings from that ricepudding place on spring st that only nyu girls

dressed all in black with that one brightly colored scarf accessory
patronize except for him and his agent id find the receipts or the
$8.82 amex statement.
so i had the time to hike until taking a shower or better a bath at 7
before our sex appt at 9 both events dont make funny of me also
recorded. i hiked. it was still hot but breezier up by columbus circle after that time square jumbotron meshugas. i stopped in at
some stores and did some shopping but not too much because i
didnt want to have too much to carry so that id need to take the
123 or 104 up broadway. in the 60s i bought some soaps and bubblestuff no clothes for sure just some loofas and a cute pumice in
the shape of a foot from that cute independent sabon place i cant
recall its name and i keep confusing their stuff with sephoras and
not really having any thoughts really beyond thinking through
while applying samples this new responsibility the agency had
just given me of deciding which probono to do this year because
the agency did only one or two probonos a year like free campaigns for charities for kids with lead insult or like child bone
cancers important to the agencys rep and after checking out with
my purchases wondering also that even if this new green conditioner id bought was all eco it might still interact wacko with the
new shampoo id bought too just to try a different brand that
might not even be totes syntheticfree because the bottle label only
had no parabens phthalates sulfates or antibacterials. but somehow up toward the 80s on that big bright smoldering stretch between the ansonia and the apthorp thats very european
wondering about this other acct the agency had just landed some
home security alarm firm. but thats about the limit of my disclosure. i must seek mystique i must seek mystique i must
my tum i wasnt able to explain its just incredible how ignorant
you can be of yourself by missing the cues youve been waiting for
by ascribing them to just the strangest conditions such as passing
by this very precious adorable new american organic farm to
table bistro id read about on my chowblast app and decided the
rumbling meant i was hungry it would be nice to sit and deny
myself sangrias but treat myself to the ramps on special because i

didnt know what ramps were but was ready to know and scroll through some charity prospectuses and some of the alarm system factdoc hoping that would settle it all and keep the vomit from popping up out of my mouth like a chatbox.
so i went in and though it was 6oclock early the place was crowded or reserved to be crowded and the gwynethesque greeter girl said itd be a halfhour to 20 min to sit at the bar but though i dont like and always feel lonely and pandered to on stools at bars she took my name and number and listed me and i told her i was just going to run an errand and sweating.
so i walked up to the pharmacy the duane reade on 80something the one duane reade down from ours i like duane reade even though its a chain its a chain only in the city not like rite aid and so i think of it like an indie and heres a tip go down to city hall i got married there and before the park its duane street and reade street off broadway. but this was in the 80somethings and i was wanting a laxative or like the antilaxative whatever its called that calms the gut flora and fauna and i dont recall just what i was thinking dazed because the lights so spectacular from the hudson especially because it properly was nighttime the exact reverse of how early my period was i didnt need my ical to tell me either. but then there at the end of the aisles was the test. i had boxes of tests at the apt in the bathroom behind the mirror medicine chest but this was a different brand and if i could understand why i went with this one i could understand much more than marketing but myself. the box wasnt pink or that light red between reassuring the girl on her first menstruation and comforting the emergency bleeder but it wasnt overly serious paternalizing biblical either like it was a drug requiring prescription just an empowerinf strong shiny platinum with raised puffy pink and blue stripes because i the woman might be having a boy too or even a gay boy and its name wasnt too feminine or clinical but just something direct though ill conceal it too just to keep consistent the policy but something the name men might read as demanding and snippy though all women feel as reflex instinct like tell me true or i demand a response to this immediately. or maybe ill

invent one though i havent done that before and anyway that was his dept all lies and i suspect the book too but lets try it the test was bstraight with me no thats homophobe so maybe sincerity yes yes sincerit-e.
i forgot all about the cramp medication and like floated to the counter bought the box asked the old oprah who was selling it to me if i could use the bathroom but her reply was we dont have a bathroom only for the pharmacists even i have to go nextdoor. which was how i ended up nextdoor at the lingerie store pretending to rub the silk to examine a silk nightie for a moment so that the young oprah clerk approached to ask if she could help so that i answered by asking for the bathroom.
to which she said its for employees only but i told her i was preggers im not sure how to feel about any of this but she frowned and said ok and led me back past the fittingrooms into the last fittingroom with a fullsized locking door where I turned on the light sat on the toilet peed and peed all of works vitaminwaters waited and waited and then the two stripes came up not one but two and i really was preggers for real and screeching in the stall so that young oprah came back yelling you better come on out and not wreck anything but i was already pulling up panties and tracksuit pants while calling him but still he wasnt available leaving the stall pushing through the store and door and out to the street where we left a msg for him me and the yelling of young oprah so excited that only after I got home totes sweating the 10 blocks did i realize i still had a strand of toiletpaper hanging between my legs like mummy wrapping like the mummy was unraveling the spool inside me was unraveling out.
now i might be getting this wrong or just that its from j so dont trust it or do with grains of salt but after he came home and i told him we were pregs and we talked it out late into morning he excited but about which i couldnt tell insisted on telling me about his presentation. he said the curator liked his text actually liked it. fact: that in the egyptian embalming process not only are all the organs and glands removed through the nose and jarred and their cavities lined with resin and replaced with linens but by now the

ancient mummies have been replaced in full in that all that human flesh and bone has turned to like bitumen or like grains of natron salt. fact: whether it was a religious thing to satisfy the gods or the peoples expectations of their rulers or else just a practical consideration because a pyramid ramping up to the realm of the gods could take such effort and money and so many people and so much time regardless the first thing that all the pharaohs did upon ascending to power was to commission and break ground on their tombs.

://

I left Booth 8.S42 before doing anything dicey like A a Q, give or take advice, explain. I had to get away from that mortuary, Lisabeth when she returned, myself even. Szlay Literistic will have its pick of eulogists, obituarists, and apt quotation epitaphs—though for sheer eloquence none will surpass the silent punctuation of "Reykjavík, Iceland," that pause reassuring me that I had the same city/country combo in mind while also, condescending. "Reykjavík, Iceland"—that comma spoke—I heard that comma, I saw it on Seth's tongue before he spoke it, or didn't: Aar's bemused rectitude had become just a tic.

Seth, I'd been around that type before—back when I was new to a life I was better than, I'd been that type—too resentful to deal with anyone not me.

I'm imagining an airplane, planing through the air—a jet swooping through every cloud and so through everything swirling within the Cloud—all the Canadian maps, Greenland facts, and Frequently Asked Questions about water, average temperature of the Arctic (water, land, air temps), average surge of glaciers (time of year dependent), airline routes, ticket pricing, protocol for dealing with passengers deceased en route, which plane models have onboard morgues, or whether the attendants automatically upgrade corpses to first class. Aar's flight soaring through the omnibus nimbus, through all charts and graphs, all blogs and castings and torrential feeds, until the compressed uncompressed, the zipped unzipped, and stormed with every word, every letter, I've ever written, the .docs, the emails, every bit I've deigned to store—Aar passing through them all and though he wouldn't have had the time or life to read them, I'd like to imagine that he noticed them, and that he noticed what was missing from them—this.

LH403 (Lufthansa), Newark—Frankfurt, 18:05—Never, passenger Szlay, Aaron, losing life with altitude, losing life with speed, breasting the meridian untimely, to be descended with as a deceased body for burial under Iceland.

A corpse borne away winged to the lowerland, the iceland, that had the ring of saga to it—not a book to be written now, but a myth if written deep hesternal.

Break a hunk of ice off the land, crack off a chunk the same proportions as Manhattan Island, then slab Aar's emberous body on out, the winds floating a hyemal pyre melting toward the Pole. Now that's a way to pass.

Before simile rose like a star, before the star of metaphor rose, death was north, beyond Ultima Thule. This explains why the preeminent mourners are northerners, because they're already dead. In an unheated zone of the hall Slavs huddled together, in furs clipped with leaky pens like amulets, talismanic charms. All you can ever hope for is to expire peacefully among a people who deny Self-Help, and who refuse to countenance any genre distinctions between Religion and Spirituality. Their stalls repped books both origs and trans, appropriate for all ages, mortality being a market unto itself. On angels and demons, on thaumaturgy (thaumaturgia), eschatology (eschatologia), and Ragnarök (Рагнáрёк)—books that in this world have to toil in Polish or Ukrainian or Russian, but that in the next world will repose in print forever in that one language after this we'll all share—yes, ja, da. A drink? Why not?

To you, Aar. Prost, prosit, l'chaim.

I was drinking all the whites and reds on offer—free—and what appeared to be the Messe staple, prosecco, uncorked to toast Cal in German, Romanian, Bulgarian, Svorsk, fits of fizzy ebullience for whichever laureate just fell off a list and won the Booker, the sensation de rigueur of the rentrée littéraire, the finalists of the Prix Goncourt and Renaudot. But then I was sampling the clear harder stuff too, accepting shots like prizes, gripping bottles like they were the 108th Annual Stockholm Oslo Helsinki Awards. Members of the Royal Academy, thank you for the vodka. My ration aquavit, appreciated. I wouldn't be standing here with you today if it weren't for Aaron Szlay. Wouldn't, weren't, barely standing. A man who loved his sister, Miriam, his niece, Achsa, and the NY Knickerbockers, even through the post-Ewing/Isaiah Thomas Era. A man who also loved women he wasn't related to, and never engaged in oragenital stimulation without trying to make it mutual and simultaneous. He died above Iceland, which has nothing to do with Thor Balk, because I am sane. He is survived by a diner out on York Avenue, which, like him, would always refill an empty glass.

The Lapps clapped bookends stylized like sepulchral menhirs, condolence applause. I was about to lead everyone in a rousing kaddish. But the only editor who was also the only writer who was also the only reader in Greenland lit the cig in my mouth. A guard preempted with "Rauchen Verboten," but then used his body English.

"Alright, alright, I'll go immolate outside."

Wettish slate the sky. The satellites were wheeling.

Faces surrounded—from Midtown, the Flatiron, faces with whom I might've shared rides leaving parties in Park Slope or Astoria. Or with whom I might've had lifechanging convos about slipped my mind subjects stumbling south down the Bowery from a launch for a handsewn letterpressed poetry chapbook of two pages in a limited edition of 12.

They said they were going back to the hotel, so I went along, but it wasn't my hotel. It was too modern, too minimal as maximal luxe—it was this immense mercury raindrop, shaped like a tear.

Into, and through, the lobby—to throng the elevators, but I took the suspension stairs, which were mocked up into a bookcase holding coffinsized volumes.

I tried lifting the cover or lid of, I won't record which, but it was nailed.

Up on the mezzanine was this beton empyrean of ballroom, with a party on. And who wasn't there? I mean that literally. Who wasn't?

We clocked each other out in the vestibule—this lady and I—sciamachy by the cloakroom hung between the doorways. We clocked each other but let it go.

I studied the wall until she went inside. They were raffling off the wall. I took a ticket. I had one chance to win the wall. At the end of the night the DJ would draw the numbers. The wall was a series of screenbanks stacked like shelves that showed new books and if I liked any title flashing past all I had to do was doubleclick it open and stand amidst the clamor and read.

This lady, she was my successor—putative, emphasis on the first two syllables, because she was Spanish, barrio Spanish, Afro-Cuban NY.

I'm not trying to say she was my replacement, I'm not trying to say I was replaceable, only that I once worked for, and that she still worked for, the *Times*—our careers might've overlapped for a weekend edition. But while I'd written criticism and then quit, she'd been hired to cover the publishing beat, rather the media beat, whose "news" about how much culture was being bought or sold for, how much it grossed, and the business behind its production, was now unequivocally established as the apotheosis of culture and criticism both: the dramas and appraisals of boardroom and backstage, in one convenient package.

The *Times*'s local rovers, native floaters, chatted circles around her—they were Germans whose English was so competent that the paper had been able to discard its regular permanent foreign correspondents like second swizzlesticks. Laidoff, forgotten on a tray, as the budgets melted to water everything down. With ad revenue shrinking and so pagecounts shrinking it was better to downsize a single staff job with benefits into two dozen freelance gigs, relying on Germans to cover Germany, musicians to cover Music, artists to cover Art, dancers to terpsichore on the generalist's mass grave. Media being the last limit of our culture, this woman was one of the last culture staffers left, for the last major paper published in America's last major publishing city—or, to put it directly, like a journalist would, the *Times* put her on a plane from NY to write about NY people at the bookfair—they would've sent her to Abbottabad had wahhabi warlords bought fullpage ads for Allah.

Finn especially, I'm sure he's had to do with her—fill in a byline, whichever might be remembered from such filings as "Slicing, Dicing, Ebook Pricing," or else "Remote Revision: Amazon Alters Ebook Content Without Consent." Say Finn's ergosedentarily decumbent with feet propped atop the slushpile of a lazy day, pondering out the window whether that pigeon below him is crippled or just resting, and the phone rings, she has his directline, and he picks up, and she goes all Torquemada inquisitive.

I can't speak to anything about any layoff/reshuffling, he says. Regrettably. A Joshua Cohen memoir? Who? Hang up. Out amid that sixth floor catchment pool subroofed over Broadway, a pigeon either crippled or resting.

She extracted herself from the klatsch of Germans, taking appetizing nips out of every other server. Dipping crudités. Making cocktail napkin waves. Leaving her pda with a kebab skewer on a tray, turning, retrieving it.

She was big in her little black dress, lashed to it with lathered beads. Pageboyed, her complexion the result of mixed and matched 10 sites' cosmetic tips, glimmer, shimmer, comedogenic, an It girl who then had to earn It.

"Hey, Cohen, is that you?"

"This is me," I said, "and this is a vodka soda."

"Fuck, Cohen—are you alright?"

"Just fine."

"Seriously?"

"Allergies, it's an allergic reaction."

"To the vodka? Or small quiches?"

"Smalltalk."

LOL, "It's been since, what? *The New Yorker* holiday party, 2000s ago?"

"The Copper Age. Early Church."

"So?"

"What?"

"So who are you here for?"

I popped the quiche and chewed, which kept the expression straight and the tears in check and with a green mouth said, "On spec."

"Nope, no way."

"I'm a visiting scholar at the Institut für Sozialforschung," swallowing, frigid crusts and core.

"Legit?"

I wheezed, "I just happened to be in Frankfurt on assignment for a blog about Euro men's fashion."

"Fuck you."

"Negotiating the reorganization of IG Farben? Or attempting to overthrow the landtag of Hesse?"

"Fuck you limp," and she went to flip around my lanyard, but I put my hand over hers and prevented her, held her.

Then she withdrew and smoothed the stripe in her hair, puce until the roots, "Why don't you just promise you're not filing tonight?"

"Lots of plans tonight but none include filing. Swear on my totebag."

"Then you can be a source."

"I've been called worse, even nonanonymously."

"Mind if I ask you a question?"

She, Mary, Mariana (her own lanyard listing free from her breasts), was after the story—I'd better capitalize that, the Story—a tale that functioned like a sixth sense organ alive and proprioceptive, without which it didn't matter what'd happened in Frankfurt, it might as well have been that nothing had happened.

The Story wasn't everything, of course, but its telling had to convince editors that it was, or at least had to convince readers that it was—had to story its way into obliterating any intimations of alternative or individual experience. This was the worst of journalism—the realization that no matter how diligently you worked to be impartial, your presence alone was the slant, the tilt, and that even transcendence would have to become narrated, narratized, plotted.

The true story of the fair—she'd clutched for clickerpen, flippad—was that the world rights in every format to every fair's true story were determined beforehand. All the year's significant bookdeals were already arranged prior to Frankfurt, in emails, priority whispers. Frankfurt, then, was just where they were announced—when you brought a media property to market, you brought it presold to show it off, or show its price—though details such as the ebook royalty percentage on "copies" exceeding 100,000 might still have to be parsed by the carving stations, untangled on the dancefloor. What other industry has been so neuroticized that it needs a party as an excuse to do business? and needs a business as an excuse to party?

Everyone in this industry was a frustrated writer, which is like all Chairpeople of the Board being frustrated assemblyline workers or machinists, everyone had been a humanities grad with a dream—and that and that alone was the Story, perennially, a tale of people who'd bargained their ways into the business side of books and then once annually were given the opportunity to live their delusion of being crucial to a culture with a trip to a barbarian land conspicuously lacking in the one presence that depressed them at home: writers.

Mary, myself, and the other journalists gawking nonchalance as we sidled to the bar—awkward malcontents mentally annotating who I might've been—might've been the only writers around.

"The story is two writers discussing the story," I said, "two writers afraid of missing the story and so inventing the story, inventing whatever it would scare us to have missed, nicht wahr?"

"Off the record?"

"Off, on, background, foreground—we're doing Jäger shots in Germany."

"Are we? Why don't you have another kebab and then we'll consider?"

"The story's the same as it always was, what are the sums. The biggest advance is the biggest story, vice versa. It's how one print industry rewards another for paying out its confidence so recklessly. I'm fine, I'm fine—two Jägermeisters, bitte."

"You sure?"

"I'm saying the shareholders. Can't read. Do they even issue stock certificates on paper? Don't they just expect you to download and print nowadays?"

LOL again, and we cheersed and took the shots down.

I spilled and either she was indulging me by refusing to notice or her break was over and it was back to her job. She recounted which panels she'd attended before asking which were my faves—the oldest reporting trick in the—and I told her, inventing who spoke on what and what they said, she asked my opinion of the opening speech, and I gave it to her, and either she was fucking with me or fucking lying too because she agreed with me, then she went on to describe the Messe hall architecture so effectively that I've plagiarized her—all the roach/armadillo/*Transformers* comparisons were hers, above—and then a male Magyar bonobo swung over and said in a menthol dialect, "Congratulations, it is very [unintelligble], New Ink," or "News, Inc.," "Jew Kink," "Next Drink," crawled on.

"Congrats—to you?" she said, the pad open again.

"Can't imagine on what. He must've gotten me confused with someone else."

"Someone like Caleb Krast?" and she twitched her pen along my ribs.

"So we've finally gotten to the point of this flirtation."

"Don't you know him?"

"Guy with chronic stink breath from an oral hygiene aversion, the cashmere sweaters that cloy at the midriff, still trying to squeeze into slimfits, preshredded—Cal, I know."

"Have you two been in touch?"

"Not since he turned war hero. It's difficult to get an appointment."

"The new novel's been picked up in a dozen languages—care to give me a quote?"

"He's the novelist of our generation. Correction—he's the novelist our generation deserves."

She frowned, folded, capped, "You talk about all your friends this way?"

"You'd rather talk about the importation of Arab crime fiction to the American market? Or the enduring popularity of comix?"

She smiled, "Graphic novels."

"Graphic just used to mean you'd get a titty scene, after which a thug would get his legs blown off."

"Have you read any of the enhanced ebooks released for multisense ereaders? You hold the tablet and it shakes and you can manually feel the explosions?"

"Have I read them? Is that what you're supposed to do with them?"

"Tell me another story, then."

"Like a bedtime story?"

"You don't have it in you," and she smirked and then tugged my lanyard, me, close. "Who are you?—I mean, besides Aaron Szlay?"

The DJ spun up again and all around us glitter swirled like metal snowflakes. Laser tracerfire. Flashpot brisance. Strobes.

Our mouths were a tongue apart. But my teeth were too sharp and her lips were still moving.

"You have to help me out," she said. "My deadline was a drink ago. Lene Termin at Viking hasn't returned any of my msgs, I'm currently out of the office, no shit. The booths are all just assistants and so trained nowadays I get nothing but review copies, smiles. No one's in NY, but it's like no one's even in Frankfurt. Finally I called out to Iowa, but the students kept transferring me to extensions that might've been Caleb's but the voicemails weren't set up."

I put a fist at her back, "Why can't we just sleep next to each other, no touching?"

She flinched and dropped the credentials, "Why can't you do me one fucking favor?"

"Because you're dead."

"You're an asshole."

Then I was conjugating: "You're dead, I'm dead, they're dead, we're all dead."

"But you're still an asshole."

My reply was slurred toward the exit because—across the room past the median bar and splotched in ambers and clears amid appetizer molder—was Finn. Floridcheeked in grief carousal. He didn't notice me, he hadn't. This must've been his local lodging.

Finn's silk shirt was busted open to the butterflycrunches navel, and the suitjacket he held and danced with whipped and spun like a ghost. It was an unbuttoned black with white pinstripes ghost he dipped and twirled around, Sufi matador dancing on the ceiling of hell.

The vestibule was riled with revelers who weren't waiting for the elevators, or were, but swayingly, gropingly, humping one another up against the bookwall and the ballroom's sliding partitions, and suddenly it struck me as impossible that they were readers too, or claimed to be, impossible that they'd ever even once just sat still in a chair or lain in bed, alone, silently, one light, and read. Indirect light. Quiet, please. I went hushing the couples stairward. The partition walls were sliding apart, or the lidcovers had been pried off the bookcoffins along the stairs, and even as I had to tipsy around them to avoid tripping, craven Danish creatures were crawling out of the darkness and seizing me, tugging at my totestrap. "We take you to what room you stay," they said. "We are help you cannot stand." I can't say how or why, I just smelled it on them, through the herb liquor sulfur—they were Danish.

"I'm not a guest," I said, or intended to say. "Just get me a cab," like have it drive into the lobby and up to the landing at least.

Wheeliebags kept clunkaclunking past me downstairs, and all of them were mine, and I said to each, "You're mine," not because they were, because it entertained me. The railings were not to be trusted. I reached for them and they swatted me back, so I leaned against the cold-sweat porphyry, and sat. And assed myself between the steps.

By the time I got to the lobby it must've been midnight, because everyone was straight above me, shooting me: my attempts to rise, my sotted swipes at their devices, my pale hairy bellyflopping, staying on my belly so they wouldn't snap my face and tag it posthumous. #DrunkAmi. #LitSlob.

The carpet tasted bland. Because it was immaculate, unpatterned.

"Lass ihn," was said in a foreigner's German, but in a foreignness I recognized. "Er ist mein Arbeitskollege—mein Freund."

Such brute fancy watches on the hands that rolled me, on the hands that grasped the strap to drag my flab upright, even as I tried stuffing the tote under my shirt and pants at once, popping buttons. My waist tumbled out into handles. I was being lifted, taken by my handles and lifted and whatever I was yelling had to do with whether anybody was fucking aware of what this fucking suit cost? Anybody?

Maleksen—bulked albinic Maleksen—he was speaking with the stubblepated guards who had my arms pinned back and were twisting my wrists: "Er kotzt."

Sure enough if I kept protesting I'd puke.

Maleksen wagged a finger at me, before switching to the only sprache guards respect besides violence: "Bloke went bottle up on an empty stomach. But a good bloke. Good Arbeitskollege and Freund. We bunk at the Frankfurter Hof. I take him myself, no worries. Danke, mate."

I was basically shoved into him—"Macht Platz."

Maleksen staggered me into the doors like they were revolvingdoors, which they weren't, headfirst.

Outside. And shivering. But Maleksen still wouldn't let go, and no curbstumble I took or rut I forced myself into had him loosening his totehold. Whatever I was babbling went into the wind, beyond the kliegs of the hofzone and into the dimming. Au revoir, you logos. Adieu, you chains. It was too late in the day for late capitalism. Everything was closed. Maleksen jerked me back. "Wait." Then a boot to the calf. "Move, mate."

Because there were businessmen blundering inebriate. Because there was a crowd at the tramstop, though by the schedule of the night route a solitary kerchiefed pensioner huddling sackladen at the shelter was a crowd. Even just a cig would've been. Just a goddamned cig. We came to this intersection of shuttered bar, shuttered schnitzeleria/bar, vacant plaster atelier still affiched as a cybercafé, and as I hobbled along with the tracks Maleksen heaved me sharp by the strap into a turn, and now I was behind him, led, towed, like I was leashed. River gusts blew in through the gape in my fly. We crossed again, against the signal. Maleksen was scared of being followed, but also scared of not being—rather he was afraid of not having the correct followers.

He stopped again at the meridian, checked traffic—"What is the pass, mate?"

"The password?"

"It will be cracked," he said, "but it will be more gentle if you tell me—it is not fingerprint, no?"

"To my computer? None of my passwords have computers."

This was parkland now, grass swards scrawled over by the umbrage of bare branches. And my only witnesses, writers and the like more famous and for now more dead than I was, enpedestaled statues.

"Give it up, mate," Maleksen said.

"So we're going to visit Balk? He lives in a park?"

He was dragging me toward the willows. Behind that a road. Above us the stars. Plane weather.

"Give it to me."

"Stop talking porn to me."

He whirled around and as he spoke the scarred bars bent at his throat: "The computer. The laptop."

"Let's get clear on this—you're mugging me? For fucking recordings you'd be getting anyway? All because why? I violated terms? Because I left Berlin or went online like once at a welfare state library? Or is b-Leaks getting impatient with me and reneging?"

"Shut up. You will type and access for me."

"It's just suckmypenis, alloneword. The name of that twat teacher from Sydney who taught your accent, all CAPS. I should be mugging you, for all that cash you owe me. I should be tapping Balk's defense fund."

"Is it touch ID?"

"It's retinal. Or iris. I forget. It's lobal. Ears. You're going to have to cut off a nipple."

"I will hurt you if I must."

"With the blessings of Balk the utopian pacifist, I'm guessing?"

"Tetbook. Now, mate."

"I'm only trying to make sense of this, sort out your position."

"Toss it, mate."

"Wait, I've got it—you're striking out on your own. You're leaking the leaker, sticking it to Balk."

Maleksen scowled. "I count."

I said, "You're going rogue, like with a ransom thing. Going to publish the interviews yourself. Or sell them off for publication? Or sell them back to every last user they incriminate?"

Maleksen slashed out with his bootheel and knocked me to my knees and the tote swung around my neck and hung down in front of me.

"Fuck," I said, "just fucking hold up."

But he was whispering, "b-Leaks is become soft. In politics. Balk is also soft, sitting in Russian Iceland, cannot ever go outside. His intellect tells him he is persecuted because of advocacy and not because he is pederastic. I am only telling this now to you because you like him lie to yourself about your importance. I count."

"Four" went to "three," but then Maleksen's two was "dva" and one was "odin," and as I was fetching my glasses from the dirt I had to say, "You're Russian?"

There was a strangulated swan honk from beyond the willows.

Maleksen held a gun, and though all of it was camouflaged in flecktarn browns and greens, it gleamed, as if it were a plastic laser toy, with a black wire straggling through the tangle of roots back to a busted sniper game at a condemned arcade on the Jersey Shore. Then again, the way he was aiming it was real, like all my flesh wasn't real but pixel, to be shot to death infinitely, to be resurrected eternally—I had the hiccups.

"Why do this?" I said. "Who cares?"

But what I wanted to say was this: I'm only protecting myself. What I wanted to say was: You already know what's in it. Everybody knows. Within themselves.

There were contrails of light through the boughs. A gray Merc idled out in the raster.

I turned back from it and smack into the gun. Its butt to my jaw, my jaw to the grass.

I wasn't just wet but made of wetness, flowing along to the lowest ground, and then thrusting up from the matted blades. But when I put a hand to where it stung I fell again, flat, and breathed a puddle that felt like breathing a plasticbag. I wrenched off the plasticbag that had wrapped around me. It was from Kaufland, the hypermarket.

And that was morning.

I straightened my knees, slowly, achingly slowly straightened my grovel joints, patted myself down. No wallet, but Principal's passport was still there damp under a sock, gravel. The tag wound around my neck identified my corpse as Aaron Szlay's. What I didn't have was a tote, with all my lives inside. Each step sparked fire but I was cold, that back of the throat cold. Every swallow was mucous. Each step twinged up the spine, and shook me into coughing fits, croupy coughing, fuck. Sneezing stuff the consistency of gauze, as if to stanch the jawblood. I rubbed my shoulder, at the totemark, the strappage. The 2.4 lbs of my Tetbook, the 2.4 tons of the book it contained, gone. I'd backed nothing up. If posture be my judge I was fucked. I had no other younger version to reload. I had no other younger version of myself.

There was a construction site in my head and then farther along the street was a construction site, jackhammering, pointed pneumatics of kurwa, pizda, overalled gastarbeiters cursing in Polish while breaking asphalt, drilling at sewage with sexual fury.

I felt a car creep up, but it was just a cab, which once it'd crept alongside my condition veered away and soaked me. My suit had been made to order, not to get stretched—it had pleats now.

Here's the name of the street: Mainzer Landstraße. And here's another streetname: Taunusanlage. The air was a sodden drear like a frozen screen. A constant pane between me and the skyscraping curtainwalls of mirrored glass just ahead.

Observe, perceive, glean everything—it was as if I were compensating for the material I'd lost by collecting the trash around me. Piking it, staving it, to fill this pit in me. To heal the welts pulsing like stoplights at my temples. Gravel in my shoes like babyteeth.

Into the Messe again. A guard halted me, examined my blood against my tag—"What happens to you?"

"Nothing," I said. "I'm here for the panel on zombies."

He said, "There is that today?" As if everyone was in peril.

"It's on just now—zombie fiction, the undead."

He was giddy now, silly, "That is the book I please to read."

I went to the bathrooms and wet papertowels and pressed my face, spiffed up. Then slogged past the tropicalized Pacific Islander stalls, went unrecognized by the Czechs and Slovaks who just a diurnity ago had been my brothers.

Pod caffeine, strudel in a sleeve. And while I was at it, why not, grabbing the giveaway notebooks and ballpoints.

Lisabeth helmed the booth in mourningdress chic, channeling both the orphan and widow (typesetting jargon: an orphan the opening line of a paragraph stranded alone at the bottom of a page, a widow the closing line stranded alone at the top). It was as if she'd traveled prepared for a loss, a charcoal dress quivering to the knees. Her face was swollen from the crying or bouquets. Aaron would've appreciated that—he'd always been attracted to women allergic to flowers, and latex.

The foldingtable was shrouded in blueblack linens, furled roses and closelipped tulips, bonbons, sekt. Bereavement cards in soft and hardback, boxed sets. I lined behind the wild sprigs of a deliverer who turned around and cringed. My jaw must've been trickling again. Lisabeth signed for him, took another babysbreathed bouquet, set it among the aster strewings, doing her duty stalwart. Such rectitude, she wouldn't even avail herself of a chair, but stayed standing as if all the books the agency had ever represented were balanced on her head.

I was about to pay a visit emptyhanded.

But then a woman cut in front of me—Cal's editor, Lene Termin, Earth Mother. A batik peasant smock, a chunky butchness latebloomed with antidepressants.

Lene didn't even meet my sneer, only said, "Pardon, Entschuldigung."

She said to Lisabeth, "Pat Sagenhaft, my partner, just picked Seth up at Newark."

"So helpful," was all Lisabeth had.

"Pat's going to sit in with him and the lawyer—Rich?"

"Spence Rich."

"But just in an advisory capacity—make sure no one's getting shafted."

"Thanks."

"That meeting's for noon, NY noon. Meantime and with your OK I'll go personally make the followup calls, to reassure the clients, offer like second opinion, outsider perspective. The immediate goal is fending off the poachers."

"I understand. And thanks."

"Again I can't stress this enough, I'm here for you—Aaron meant a lot to me. If it makes sense to merge, you'll merge—I've already got a few names in mind and even just casually a couple of feelers."

"Already?"

"Too soon, but—interesting feelers."

"Your partner Pat's still with Riba Group, yes? Or Schwartzlist?"

"Then again it's never too soon—especially with our girl to take care of, the princess of Princeton."

"Achsa."

"Exactly—we'll be sure to involve her in all aspects of the process."

"Achsa," Lisabeth snuffed.

"I'm so proud of how you're holding up, Lisabeth—that won't go unnoticed. Now is there anything else I can do?"

There was nothing, and Lene lunged across the table to roll Lisabeth in her breast, then left, oblivious of me. Aar had loathed her—"Hel" he'd called her, "Helene, Queen of the Norse," senior editor at Viking.

Lisabeth, poor wealthy Lisabeth who'd never understood how to take advantage, forsaken by her lanky associate with the quiff and clip, her underling, but in terms of power dynamics, overling, Seth—I could write it out already, it could write itself out clearly even black on black: Seth would coordinate publicity, the funeral, any lunches he'd take with other agents from other agencies he'd explain away as merely convivial, or acculturating, but then by the time Lisabeth'd get back to NY Seth would've installed himself either in Aar's old corner niche, after having removed Miri's sexless bed and finally fumigated the closets of her mothballs, or in newer officing toward the top of a Flatiron vivarium repping the bottom half of the list, which, the bottom half quarter, would mean repping me. Clever boy. With any brains he'd eventually move into media, but still keep a bit of lit to keep the cred up. If he or his next partners had any class they'd offer Lisabeth a job, or wouldn't, that's the only point on which I'm undecided—I'm sure Lene'll be in touch.

To me, Lisabeth said, "The news just broke online."

"Seth?"

"He wrote the statement, but I—why do you deserve an explanation? And what happened to your cheek?"

"I don't. And Iceland happened."

"Another tragedy another excuse to drink? You're bleeding."

"Take it from me: Bleeding means I have a heart."

"Anyway," Lisabeth shrilled, "before he flew back he left this envelope for you," and she handed me a manila.

"Who? Seth did?" I gutted it for what, I'm not sure—a book already lost? already finished?

"It's Cal's, his manuscript. Seth said Cal was giving you a copy. For your thoughts. If you have any thoughts."

"Appreciated."

"You're not acting appreciative. What did you expect?"

"Forget it." The titlepage was inscribed: "With compliments and condolences—we have to be in touch—sethustings@szlayliteristic.com."

"Care to tell me what you're doing here, Josh?"

"What?"

"Here, in Frankfurt, why?"

"Aar never told you?"

"Told me what?"

"He never said anything about Switzerland? Our deal?"

"You have a deal or just a proposal, and didn't you just say Iceland?"

"He mentioned nothing whatsoever?"

"All I have is what I get from your wife."

"Exwife."

"Not yet. Don't worry, though—don't tell me where you're living and I can't tell her where to have you served."

"It's complicated, Lis."

"That's what her companion's always saying, the actor. Phoning twice a day about an Amex bill. He canceled the card. But he's wondering for next time whether it pays to get the extra identity theft protection. I'm like customer care with him. Member services."

"So you're just the person to talk to."

"What?"

"My money—can I have it?"

She stiffened, "Your money for what?"

"That's why I was meeting Aar."

"He was giving you a loan?"

"It was sort of like he owed me."

"So send a record or invoice, I'll have a check sent when I'm back."

"Not happening."

"If it's an address thing I can wire you online."

"Not that. Cash."

Lisabeth—let her be stunned by the gall of it all and not the truth of it. She tonguewriggled her toothgap, "Cash?"

"I need it bad."

"You need it badly."

"That's correct."

"But Seth has the agency Visa."

"You can't just stake me yourself?"

One inflamed white bud at tonguetip, "I make $40K a year."

"You make $60K."

"OK, $60."

"Just help me out, Lis. I promise I'm good for it."

She held her purse, both hands. That's it. Nothing else and no deeper meaning. Lisabeth held onto her purse with both hands. She pallbore toward the rear of the hall—heels icepicking past the newest electroflex displays and penputing and fingerink platforms, then wading sullen through crumpled snowballs of epaper—to a temporary slidewall set with fussy ATMs. As we waited our turn she went on a pillage for the appropriate card—tampon, aloe handsanitizer, lipstick, gums, cherry suckers—verlag businesscards origamized or anxiously twisted, laundryoom passkey, Tetheld, lists, personal debit, platinum Visa, its frosty hologram unmistakable.

"Just use that one," I said. "That has to be your parents'."

To be desperate is to live off what others let you have—I wonder if Aar ever met, and if so what his impressions were of, her parents.

She snorted and did the hairtuck behind the ears, what loyalty. Pathic girl, ticridden girl, who typed with nibbled nails and left voicemails with bruxism. She'd tolerated so much, so many clients reliant, and Aar, who'd insisted on salutations on email, phone honorifics, smoking indoors, rye in the drawer, regular drycleaning. He'd preferred the place 10 blocks south unless he'd needed the suit same day, in which case there was a place two blocks north, though he'd always leave it up to her to intuit which he'd needed. This was what I wanted to tell her, how grateful Aar'd been, how appreciative. How freeing but how guiltily freeing it was now that he wasn't around to stop me from deceit.

With our turn I hung back, pointlessly because Lisabeth faced fully machineward, screening me from the screen and the keypad, her mouth-breathing fogging the prompts but not her compliance. To both sides other patrons swiped, tapped, scifi luminance and blare, sci-nonfi. The units were teleporters, timemachines. This wasn't Frankfurt anymore, but Whitehall Street 2002. This was Miri's bookstore, but in its afterlife as bank, and not even a fullservice bank, just machined, a Chase, which anytime I visited Aar's office above it I took as command, chase the past forever. This was Achsa's first time back since the space's conversion. Aar, who had to work, and had no babysitter, and had to get cash anyway, had turned it into a lesson. Achsa knew what she stood in, tile, plateglass, she knew what'd happened to her mother's books, the same thing that'd happened to her mother. They'd gone away and been turned into money. She'd asked how the cash got into the machine and Aar'd asked her back, just guess. Achsa'd said maybe it was printed, like a printer was housed inside each unit. Try again. Maybe it was like a sewer, she'd said, or like with trees, the roots of trees, the money was always just flowing through tubes, which routed it to blossom at locations of customer request. Aar'd loved that explanation. On the way home they'd passed a produce stand, he'd said, and Achsa hadn't known what to make of an apple whose stem still had its leaf. It was news to her and shared delicious.

Choose English. I snagged the first two digits of Lisabeth's PIN. 8, 0. Choose the cash advance.

"How much?"

"How much's the max?"

Her $500/withdrawal limit rounded to €360, apparently, which we went for four times, and I even went in for scolding her, made her wait around for the last receipt to spit, while her Tetheld quaked with calls, msgs, txts, Momcell, Daddygreenwichwork, and fraud alert premonitions, and she ignored them.

What mystified, though, and heartened, was her holding out the bills and saying, "How are you going to convince me to expense this?"

"I'm a client, aren't I? Haven't we been discussing me?"

She shelled shut her wallet and pursed it. "Just don't lose it."

"All spending is losing, but sure."

She yelled, "I don't mean the money. Get drunk again, get a prostitute. You dick. I mean Cal's novel—we can't have it floating around."

The envelope, which I'd been carrying. "Confirmative."

A sigh. "Josh, tell me—why aren't writers invited to Frankfurt?"

"Why?"

"Because they can't deal with the fact that this is a business."

://

a-bintel-b.tlog.tetrant.com/2011/01/07/thedumpydump2

expectancy. life comes first in semesters for school second in quarters for career and third in trimesters after which life ends and no one hangs with friends. but when i got pregs all my friends had become mothers already and they hadnt had time for me in semesters quarters my first trimester where they finally surfaced because i was finally becoming their peer. babyclothes and cribs and strollers and just about every other type of castoff handmedown bottle bootie were arriving by mail or being dropped off and explained over wheatgrass juice and muffintop brownies. moom wanted to know how long i intended to nurse before she told me how long was recommended but her recommendation was shorter than anything in books or on weaner.org. its def a girl or boy i can tell moom was always telling me and "emi" said wed want to know before and that was the best decision and "tal" said we absolutely wouldnt want to know before and that was the best decision. hospital drugs and the nosocomical infections had to be weighed against the risk of homebirth and if homebirth a decision had to be made whether to purchase a tub or borrow a friends and disinfect it. like if you go to do what your parents did if you cursed as a kid you washed the kids mouth out but now that was considered abuse and if you did that you had to be concerned with whether what you washed with contained toxins. but $@#! it was $@#!ing exhilarating. i was glowing healthy and even smelled nice like a bakery of pearls j said i wasnt showing just yet. the fertility docs each recommended their own gynobstetrician so we went browsing and still to doc meanley who was encouraging. he said we were doing better than ever until he pressed

j to share and j who never liked being pressed said that he considered a child like a book like hed get to write a child but doc meanley dispproved and asked what happens if you get blocked dont books end up writing you and though j was peeved doc meanley pressured more by claiming that j was being "aversive." He asked why did you try for a baby if you dont actually want a baby to which j asked "why did i get married if i didnt actually want a marriage" and the doc said it was enough with the "aversives" but then j said "i got married and am having a baby with her so that no one else would [have to????] because i love her so much" what a schmuck if youre reading this having you in my life was already like having a child.
work was so great to me too that already just the moment i told my boss "ben itkowitz" (reread my pseudo/anonymity policy) he was jumping up and down with me saying bubele take all the leave you need. which in ben language meant you best square everything away before you pop one. which meant training my templacement just personable enough that s/he would get on as comfy as sportswear with the clients but also just shoddy and incompatent enough for dealing with coworkers officeside that s/hed get fired if they didnt consult me on every single detail throughout my maternity. that was the only move to make according to "emi" and "tal" for u&i to beg me back to acct mgmt and beyond that promote me. also i needed to prepare clientside transitions for all the open accts though i have to be careful what im typing "net bank of new england ii" "manic webisode" "hellacopter: da game" "pomegranate" "beverage" all while brainstorming a campaign for the alarm system thing and planning the probono.
the msgings always the difficultest but dealing with the city its doubled. the conceptual idea of it was about links between the local and nonlocal or between personal health and the environment. it was an initiative directed at minority communities that are come on in the majority if you ever get out of the cabs. now just lump general women and children in with the minorities and

you already have three quarters of the city and the rest are jewish males (the bulk of who are HANDICAPPED).
wed been working on the proposal copy/design for the promo material different versions for different schools and religious groups for community leaders and parents. it never made any sense that though the work was probono we still had to pitch but we did and so went downtown to the school like ps 188 that was interim headquarters until the office at the health dept got its hvac cleaned of mold.
a guard ushered us down the hall amid all the students leaving and told us to wait by the lockers and we obeyed like we ourselves were still in school and the guard became a teacher. i felt like that difficult to describe to anyone who hasnt felt it feeling of being elated but crap and feeling id rather be going with the students heading out from last class or extracurriculars to snuggle into carrot celery hummus and a nap. the students were so big in their bodies but their faces were small and they carried what i had high in front of me low on their backs huge enormous sagging backpacks. they were asian hispanic and every other race to justify my decision about bringing along "khan" who was pakistani and "rod" who was half brazilian half korean i think though this wasnt their acct. they were just relatively between accts at the agency and ive always known how to present. the rest of my team was "jim" and "jon" two guys (black) (and gay and jacked and impeccably tailored my bangers my banging creatives was our jk though they werent romantically involved with each other and me a preggers white girl rounding out her 20 lbs heavier filenes basement going out of business suit.
i wasnt sure what we were waiting for and then i was sure and getting queasy. i hadnt been told this was a cattle call the type in which prospective clients interview a number of agencies or i had been told and id forgotten but whichever i was flustered nauseated or nauseous j always corrected me. [501c3s and public agencies are worse than private corporations theyre the absolute worst to work with please forgive the digression. the money given to

them out of the goodness of hearts or from taxes doesnt go to the hungry children without healthcare but to midlevel professionals on disability and though i understand why a for profit has to try to get the best work for the best price the city likes to swing dick the same way and had already smacked u&i $20k in the hole on a campaign that ultimately lost its winner 4x that. well beyond any monies saved in the deductibles. still profile was enhanced.] i got that it was a cattle call and that i was the cow with the door letting out a team from an agency ill just call "the white agency." they all were hauling out their mockups i didnt have a chance to eval because of a pet the bulge reunion with this totes bitch wasp girl who shrieked that she hadnt known i was preggers as if we were friends and id neglected to tell her and she wrapped herself around me to exaggerate how burst i was but i only said i thought shed been laidoff and had gone into media admin or alumni affairs for like marymount or williams.

we went in after into not anything administrative but just this classroom all set up like a classroom just chilling. it made me think no way im going to send my kid to this or any other publicschool im just going to follow "tali" and move back to wykagyl or the north shore of the island or do like "emi" and straight from the hospital fill out an application for the 92nd st y anything but abuse my own kid like this. It was just this spare ugly dropceiling sheet tile flooring streaked like the dryerase board dented globe dump. At a table the color and greasy texture of fries and a seeded bun stool the size of a burger i eased down onto slow like i was at maximum capacity already.

now im already on thin ice writing about a client so im just going to composite with the assurance that unlike with j everything is true but the job must be protected. its really difficult to do that because i just have this urge to go ahead and type because there arent any consequences here in front of me besides my smoothie. in the future there will have to be this immunity. this immunization booster or whatevs that lets me both vent and erase lets me both tetrant and delete because i can say from experience from having been on the other end the receiving end that a spouse cant

be just a recipient or sender. there really have to be better ways than this or crumbling cookies and sneaking a scoop of yellow cakebatter icecream into my smoothie to cope with the pressure.
"verna smith" sat atop the teachers station across from us. she was the project mgr. an old but young mix of black mama poet laureate with dreadbraids twisted through cowry shells dangling peacock feathers and white dyke flannel over chinos. then maybe two maybe three other people inhouse. communications personnel at the health and education depts.
"verna" was talking forever about the project the expectations whatevs but always bringing it back around to her resume or core principles. it was difficult to pay attention especially by "in my socialwork days up in the Bronx" but also because of the cramping just severe excruciating cramping. though i dont mean to be so mean. its difficult because im making up "verna" from the combo of two people honestly the project comanagers and the one from health was tolerable enough because about to retire and haitian french but the other from education was middleaged an irish catholic phd cunt who said things like "advertising in schools can be justified only as a teachable moment for media literacy."
i was so out of it i could only could barely poke my bangers to represent. "jim" and "jon." big mistake. biiiig miiiistake. "jim" opened up with the tag "eat junk feel city" because he wrote it and was sure of its humor but the depts either didnt get it or did and just sat as he did the dumbest thing and tried to sell the sell or just neutralize by explaining that the agency didnt think the city was shitty or might be in any way associated with junkfood however we did think the msg would register with youth and i was feeling junky shitty myself. "jon" picked up with "get nutritionated" which was greeted similarly. neither of these were the tags to start with and i thought they knew that i mustve told them that with the city they had to start conservative and work up to the risquey or what the braindead would find risquey they had elected officials to please it was wet the stool. i got shaky up and ignoring the sense of having pissed myself had rod and khan hold the boards "eat and run—or walk—or bike" "eat the world (in

moderation)" my hand was trembling. but those only launched education "verna" into this on the rag rant about such "old played out dichotomies." though health "verna" had no issue with "edgy" the hope was to "get the best msg to the worst affected" education said "this has to be a quality of life initiative with a secondary benefit educational component delivered about or even through the very medium of ad culture inculcating critical reading techniques and consumer scepsis? skepsis? vital to differencing between exploitative msging and healthy mealplanning public service announcements." as comparables were being cited from like the american heart association and the presidents council on physical fitness i was dying literally physically dying. but just then "jon" and "jim" interrupted what was becoming another miracle of "verna" converting crackheads in tremont by recounting the modalities of the multiple intelligences. "the healthiest dinners have the shortest commutes" campaign featured an extension of the subway map extending the lines out of the boroughs into farm country to encourage consumers to relate to dutchess county and the mexicans who picked in jersey. "next bus: 2-10 minutes next local apple season: 1 year." and the "vernas" said "wed be very pleased to further this discussion" i was doubling over. and the "vernas" said "well be in touch" i was bent over my hands on the table slipping ketchup mustard picklewater blood slurping down my stockings and through the mesh a gob on the tip of a heel. now you and i mean you (but not you ladies. you. were supposed to be in dc. some archaeology conference. my memorys perfect. like a computers memory perfect. like a wrinkling going gray elephant computer. but let me check they dont have elephants in mesoamerica. it was supposed to have been some convention about mesoamerican archaeology four days three nights and this was just in the middle. youd been excited about it couldnt stop talking about it. i couldnt help but be excited for you. but then i was being squeezed toward the school lobby. "jim." "jon." hero friends. everything was a hero the hallways were heroes just for being halls and the lockers that stayed shut for me were heroes and the doors that were being opened for me were heroes and everyone was a hero except the education people and even the health people who did nothing but wait around houston street for the 911 "verna" called while even the guard was out yelling and hailing cabs though no cab would take us and 911 took forever. "verna" cradled me with womens room papertowels and told me about her two children who were grown architects in new orleans and how her daughter used to work much before my time and more in acct services at an agency ive forgotten. "verna" hung over me asking questions not to keep me with it but to accuse what did i eat did i drink enough was i on any drugs who remembered. my memorys as perfect as something i cant think about just now like how you j youd be writing your hackwork online and wouldnt know what analogy to use youd take a break and read some poetry and then return to work and write that whatever it was the experience of being in a hotel or motel or b&b inn was like poetry that was your default analogy. in the ambulance up 1st ave i had my bangers scrolling my contacts for you and calling but your phone was off and they were leaving msgs delirious. yo um j man your wifes going to where we going where. bellevue er. it was strange when they said your full name. which i never did because you dont deserve the vowels. through admissions before turning the corner i had enough mind presence to tell them how my mother was listed as moom and the bangers got her on the line and before they hung up she was already driving the triboro. then they kept calling you through the day through the night staying all that time until "ben" came too and kept moom company until d&c became dilation and curettage and she was let into my room and coming to all i said was that the day before the night before everytime id called youd picked up. i had moom call "tal" and "emi" and i talked to them while moom on her own initiative called your mother but i wouldve told her that was pointless you tell your mother nothing you hide and keep secrets from everyone and this is the repulsivity j how you keep them from yourself so who knows if she even knew i was preggers the bitch didnt even offer to drive up. then because i told moom you were in dc because you were writing walltxt for the met she called the met but they were closed and she got lost in the menus and transfers. she went to the apt and got the paper where you wrote down where you were staying but the numby and addy you gave were for two different dc hiltons and neither had a record of you as a guest and beyond that no record of archaeology either and moom came back to my room and immediately told me because j you have to respect and be open with the ones you love even if it slays them. because though what you dont know cant hurt you used to be legit now theres nothing that cant be known and so the greatest pain has become not the act itself but the thought of you trying to conceal it from me and how stupid that is and how pitiful the failure how petty. but at the time and it mightve been the anesthetic all my reaction was defending you to moom saying that you were always garbling logistics and that was accurate saying that you probably hadnt booked your own room and that was probably accurate too and reception clerks understand nothing about cuttingedge archaeology. also i was flipping because they gave me doxycycline a tetracycline or teratogen that causes birth defects as an antibiotic and not clindamycin with a shorter halflife so we wouldnt have to wait as long to try again. i wanted nothing i just wanted it out of my system now but though the nurses kept saying discharge and i kept saying discharge moom was just trying to get everyone talking about the same thing. also in the middle of that conversation j you called. you knew what was going on but pretended you didnt because you knew that if i found out youd checked your msgs before just calling me back the moment you turned your phone back on id be whacked youd be. i knew that you knew i was wasted because i didnt interrogate you on why youd turned your phone off or were pretending. we had levels between us deep with meaning to excavate. fuck you and fuck your mummy. you checked the amtrak schedule and said youd be back in four hours but that was a typical exaggeration because it took you all of six and moom who wouldnt leave the room to let me take the call alone had already gotten me back to the apt by then and wouldnt leave until you got there or here and even after discharge the discharge continued and like with this its still sour fresh.

i was out and apparently stayed out through a fight between you and moom who refused to leave until i came to but with all the pessaries and anesthetic and teratogen death agent ivs i was pumped with though wouldnt swallow as tablets and dropped behind the bed instead and later flushed it was all just a dream of you moom and emi and tal the four all the five of us in bed together dreaming. that was a week id say. week and a half. you were doing and even by past behavior overdoing everything and just by realizing that i was recovering. you even managed to impress moom and convice her to go to a show with emi and tal before heading back to wykagyl. jersey boys that was the show. then we were alone except for all the shiva trays and platters. so many of them so much ringing at the door you pried off the intercom and cut the wire but then all the ringing was phone. note how all the dormant instincts come out among the buddha jews and suddenly its tunafish and eggsalad and coldcuts and rye. the smell of meat i couldnt deal with. note the pareve cheesecake babkas and diet soda liters like a reflex from fairway. thankfully i couldnt keep anything down. the office called daily. “mia” my yoga instructor showed up with a healing asana a malasana variation to detox she said i had to do the moment i got up i had to squat down toes diagonal heels flat to pelvic width or wider abs or what was left of them to the front hands front elbows to the inner knee breathe shoulders to the inner knee breathe and hold imagining the vagina is a nostril and the anus a mouth or the other way around and drop them to suck the floor and she demonstrated and basically held her class for me on the unmatted floor of our room and you were admiring her ass her tits admit it but like me shes too fit shes not your type. you werent sleeping with me anymore. but that came out wrong because i dont mean sex i mean it would still be forever before id be able to use a goddamned tampon. instead we just stayed awake together and you gave me your story. the tale of the man whod garbled the hilton and the hyatt and how thatd caused you to miss the registration orientation. all through the calling youd been in different important sessions. also the topic wasnt pyramids but writing and curation. museumology and institutional critique. as you talked all i could think about was rabbi offen the friend of mooms you wouldnt let marry us whod said that even without a body we could have a funeral. but then i thought that a funeral after a shiva was meaningless. then i was out of bed. youd hired an inept cleaningperson or cleaned yourself we never discussed this. ill be straight with you id had enough of you being shut up together. all id wanted was tv but as always i felt judged when i switched on my reality crap even though when you were crapping out yourself with top chef i judged nothing and then you went and got movies but not my movies and be straight with me not even yours because theres no way you like or ever enjoyably or au fond thoroughly sat through godards vivre da vie or fastbinders berlin alexanderplatz. all id wanted was to be left to my workmails and tv. id gotten out of bed not because i was strong enough but because youd gone out for groceries. i had this urgent need for laundry to do laundry. you hadnt done it whether because you were "begging to be caught" or giving "a cry for help" or just suffering from a passive aggressive s&m complex or guilt resulting in reversal (selfsabotage or sad cingulate gyrus selfhandicapping) according to doc meanley. the suitcase youd taken was in the closet and i emptied it all into the machine that roller suitcase the friedmans got us for our wedding. by the time the load was ready for the dryer id read through the conference convention schedule a map of the smithsonian. from the map fell this limpdick amtrak ticket to dc. faded but also oneway. folded into the schedule were printouts. hertz rental car reservations from dc. your name. receipt for the mainstay inn cape may nj the night that night your name vowels intact. payment type was cash. depraved. you were two hours from ny but only an hour from your mother and didnt visit. i got out my work laptop and put it atop the lap that had just held our child of fingers toes eyes and ears but not yet sexed. or barely. or i resisted asking but asking would never have occurred to you and i took your lack of curiosity as trauma and then as gender equality because we were mourning ourselves and not just genitals and then i realized what it was and realized that id always known what it was selfishness all along id known and been lied to and so lied to myself to banish from my mind that shadow like the sagittal sign on the ultrasonogram the cranial notch that says penis and the caudal notch that says not vagina but clitoris the penis pointing up to the empty head because in utero its in perpetual erection but the clit pointing down out of shame because with women even our own bodies are against us. i tetrated every name in the schedules list of panelists every name. small versions of photos on paper bigger ones online. the curator of the whore collection at the met gave a presentation about the fate of possessions in the afterlife. whether they were believed to actually incarnate into use or were just purely symbolic. whether a clay slave was believed to have represented a flesh slave or to become one. interesting. it was the middle of the second trimester we miscarried you did. how am i doing check back with me in october. i was all over the computer ignoring my backmail and well wishes and you came through the door. you were carrying groceries. youd actually gone to get groceries.

://

10/16

There's something different about writing by hand again (something ~~rebooting, refreshing, restoring,~~ restorative), using pen and notebook, for the first time since I'm not sure, school. Writing with the whole hand, writing with the entirety of my handedness, not just with the fingers. Get a grip, a hold, let the punctuation loosen, let the ligatures slack, shed the remanence, degauss the ghost, release, breathe. Do whatever.

Writing by hand, it's not just the foreign words that get italics, every word gets italics. Capitalization becomes a negligence. Letters in the middle of words are capitAlized. Or at the end, like seX. Bold is pressure exerted. Underline, a bump.

The pen—not a dippable nib but a disposable ballpoint. Ink through a tube like marrow in the bones, which lubricates a ball as it's rolled over a page—I can't help but be reminded of heads, of decapitation. Cut off my own, dripping its fresh indigo, and roll me over all that blankness outside. Me, rolling over the fields, punctuating with my nose.

The paper—like the traintracks laid straight out below me, ruling Europe, lining mind—I'm wondering, what year did lined or ruled paper first appear? And which is it—lined or ruled? German goes for Liniert. In school the marble swirl notebooks were Wide-Ruled, like a Homeric epithet. My gut's telling me that this longitude first emerged before the war—but which war? But then the gut gets all unsettled again and says—maybe the 1840s? That feels more like it. 1642, in London or Paris. Venice. Amsterdam. Make it up. Feel more. At the time, the writers must've been thinking, just another pointless novelty! The grid's too cramping!

Too controlling! Once again, technology's depriving our thoughts of freedom! (I haven't used an exclamation in a while! Feels great!) ~~Bear with me hairs, plant fibers, horse hooves! Bear me nut galls and berries, resins, tannins!~~

Computers keep total records, but not of effort, and the pages inked out by their printers leave none. Screens preserve no blemishes or failures. Screens preserve nothing human. Save in the fossiliferous prints left behind by a touch.

But a page—only a page can register the sorrows of the crossings, bad word choice, good word choice gone bad, the gradual dulling of pencil lead, which is graphite. A draft by hand resembles the mechanism of computational processing. A semiconductor, an integrated circuit or in plaintxt, a chip. Think of the paper as the silicon substrate, and think of the multicolored scribble piled atop as having been fabricated in layers, in strata dug from the earth—it's like an archaeology in which the artifact you're seeking is the earth itself, which is mining, I guess, like drilling for mineral deposits, metals, copper, aluminum, gold, silver, nickel, tin, zinc.

On second thought, on 40th thought, forget the analogy. Rub it out, don't rub it. Semiconductor levels ("the wafers") are smaller than particles of dust, semiparticulate small, and if even one of them from the solder on down to the boarded substrate becomes compromised in any way, at any point in the fabrication, the entire circuit's fucked, and the computer might be too, fucked integrally. That's why they're manufactured in spotlessly white compartments kept airlocked and ionized, seismically stabilized, fascistically regulated for temperature and humidity, and free of contact with contaminants like sweat and dust ("the human"). That's why they're increasingly being manufactured by robots. Just like prose is.

A notebook is the only place you can write about shit like this and not give a shit, like this. Cheap and tattered, a forgiving space, dizzyingly spiralbound, coiled helical.

\

Enough tetricity—I left Frankfurt, but never went back to Berlin.

You could line a triangle, you could triangulate, among Berlin, Frankfurt, and where I am, or was, moving. 10:18 with no timechange.

At least the windows always change. The tracks are always on time.

Switch trains at Nürnberg, 12:30. Just across the platform.

Field, house, church, house, field—and they've stopped checking passports when you cross the Inn (the river) (tributary of the Danube). In a pleather banquette, passing cows—cudding huddled stupey cows grazing at grass fenced just off the trackbed—meatcows the color of rancid butter, fenced separately from milkcows whose piebald inkblots remind me of roundbordered countries I'd rather be in.

Memory, that roundbordered country.

Vienna, terminus was the Westbahnhof, which I'd never been through before—on my last visit to Vienna, to research my book, 12 years ago now, I'd driven in from the east, taking the route of my mother's war through what'd only recently been called Czechoslovakia, from Poland. I admit, I was momentarily perplexed: I'd expected an Austro-Hungarian railroad shed of clichéd fin de siècle grandeur, not this stagnant dingy penal colony advertising telecoms, art exhibitions, operas, and comp-generated architectural renderings of the unfinished Hauptbahnhof—slated to replace this facility in a ludicrously futuristic 2014—gummed with dotmatrix printouts of the take a tab variety.

I took a tab—no decent hostel was ever very far from trains. The city was turning its back on the sun and getting slapped with darkness.

At the hostel I was assigned a drywall cell fitted with foldout bunks that every time I counted them I got a different sum, but at least they were empty.

And to think—on my last visit I'd stayed at the goddamned Bristol. On my mother's dime, but still. The Bristol. Only to sink to this.

Don't think.

Read.

I fell asleep but at some point was woken by the nightmares—Dutch and some Gabonaise, and the former were saffronrobed backpacker Christian hippie maybe gay but maybe not gyrovagues, while the latter might've been involved in the logging industry and crashed around our cell like drunken trees, and the drywall was wet from the stalled bathrooms above and the bathrooms were showers too or rather just total wetrooms each with a sprinkler system showerhead above a rank Turkish squat toilet that slanted toward a drain.

But I didn't mind—I'm not letting myself mind even the blanketlessness, the starchy sheet that required a deposit or the towel that had to be renewed daily, no exceptions and no discounts for extended stays, because privacy had become loneliness again (nothing to do but submit to conditions if the cost of privacy becomes loneliness)—except, the no smoking policy bothered (always going up and down).

\

A quarter moon after the looting, [PFC. CHRISTOPHER] Bringdom's unit was assigned to secure the Museum and monitor its cleanup. They had to make sure its fabled collection sustained no further losses. Bringdom found it funny to be soldiering among all these Arab men doing what was supposed to be women's work, all these misogynistic Arab men who seemed not to mind doing it. Sure, men were good for hauling gear, or those priceless hunks of busted Mesopotamian vases, but the Army had convinced him that men were pretty damn bad at sweeping and mopping.

Bringdom's patrol brought him up to a large gallery with a small dune of glass on the floor. He broke away to kick at the sharp jagged shards, scattering them into reds and whites and blues, depending on the light. He was awestruck, but also confused. No windows had blown here. All the glass above was intact. Bringdom bent over his rifle and scooped a handful of the fragments into his flakvest pocket.

It was desert glass, created by a lone renegade comet. As the comet entered our atmosphere, it exploded like a celestial bomb. The heat of the blast fused the sand directly below it into a pane, which, just a moment later, was shattered by the impact of the nucleus. What resulted was this glistening mess.

Bringdom didn't know this, though, he never would know any of this. The glass just reminded him of a girl.

—Caleb Krast, *Bringdom's War*

\

10/17

Iz, I've walked—coiling myself into circles, into rings. Bunions, corns, and a bathfungus developing. All the natives or the Viennese I'm taking for natives are old and women, their men must die before them, and they all have tiny little plasticbags under their chins that fill and empty with air. The women, even as I resisted the suggestion, I saw as Moms. I heard my name, but only in reference to coal. Kohle.

The morning was paved with pigeons. You can never wake up earlier than pigeons—you can never wake up earlier than streets.

I'm not sure how or even if you're going to respond to whatever crisis comes out of this, Rach, what sort of pathos is still in you or whether

Vienna—of course this is where you ended up, Iz. This is where I sent you packing. Away from your husband, into your brother's house. Bankrupting myself in the process, bankrupting my soul's accounts too. Is the fact that you have family in this city a sign or just a coincidence? Which would you rather it be?

or whether, Rach, you'd regard whatever transpires—yes, transpires—as just another example of my fucking up—my fucking everything up—but

I'm trying to figure out how to find you, Iz. I'm trying to engineer a coincidence, but maybe you didn't go out today, maybe you don't go out ever, or just not in the citycenter. I'm assuming that you're allowed to, that you've received or don't require your brother's permission. Being a glass scientist, or at least a laboratory rat, must make him strict but liberal. He wouldn't have slaughtered you to preserve the family honor, so I'm fairly confident he won't stab me. He might even speak my language, if only a specialized technical dialect. I'm judging all this based on having tetrated him once. Yasir.

Is he married? To a Muslim? Have they reproduced? Do you cook or babysit to defray what you cost in room & board?

I have my fantasies. Like you're not getting along with the wife, she resents your beauty, your youth, her husband's affection for you, the way you have with the baby.

Like on the Karlsplatz, this woman passed me by in an abaya or whatever her culture calls it—the first abaya I've been around since yours—a cape unfurling out behind her as if to umbrella her girls, two of them, clinging. It's been raining off and on.

A caricaturist blandished pastels at a canvas. An accordionist busked out a wheedly waltz. A Gypsy laid down a swatch of velvet and laid a coin at its center to assure me that others had found him deserving. But I was a beggar too, crouched on the floor of the ÖBV Buchhandlung, copying out my appeal into German with the help of a phrasebook.

Is this the office Ist dies das Büro of the glassworks/glass manufacturer der Glaswerke/Glasfabrik Birefringen AG? May I with an employee Darf/Kann ich mit einem Mitarbeiter/Arbeitnehmer named namens Yasir Almaribi speak sprechen?
I would like a message to leave. Ich möchte eine Nachricht ver/hinterlassen.
It concerns his sister. Es betrifft/konzern this phrasebook doesn't differentiate between the verb senses of "is about" and "worrying to" and the noun senses of "personal problems" and "business interests" seine Schwester. I will for him outside wait. Ich werde für ihn draußen warten. Ich bin aus Amerika. Danke.

\

I read my own name at a news kiosk and went to open to an article, which the kioskist said I'd have to purchase, but I didn't because it was just a belated photospread of Principal's birthday party. Happy 40th. Exklusiv! Tetraten sie sich selbst?

Bankside flat plasmas updated the stocks and scores, and the name Balk was whipping around a ticker in red LED, though what followed was too densely rapid and German and I tried to keep still until the relevancy scrolled my way again, but it never did.

and if there's any fallout for you let me apologize in advance, Rach, please, you have to understand that my intention was merely to

Which street is yours, Iz? Which building? Which floor? Which window? Nothing in this neighborhood, I'm guessing. The district of guided package tours. Schoolgroups younger than online. Retirees snapping selfies in Napoleon poses backed by fake French Habsburg landscaping. Queues of airport shuttles. Taxis debating lanes with hansom cabs, whose horses hoofed so serenely haughty it's as if they were proud of having been tamed, and disdained the wildness of their Balkan drivers.

though I'd appreciate that in the event of any fallout you'd refrain from making any comment whether on or off the record to journalists about anything, Rach, but particularly about our life together, which is or was after all

Iz, have you returned to your parents? Or been returned to your husband? To Oman or Yemen? To France? Didn't make your connection in Cairo? Stayed in Cairo why? If you're in Vienna, just bump into me. Just there, under the porte cochère. I'll take you to a café, and pay. And in return you'll take me back with you and shelter me and read my drafts, you'll learn this language and read my drafts, slake me with urchins de la mer Rouge and schnapps.

I walked around the Ring, that broad treed boulevard that's just the raised footprint of the ancient walls that'd protected the city against the Turks and Slavs but that, as the city grew, became dangerous, entrapping, and so were razed to make room for tourists to take their leisure in a setting both pleasant and surveillable.

Today the fallen walls of Vienna—but also of Frankfurt and Berlin—are held by Turks and Slavs peddling souvenirs, bringing history a crooked full circle.

Are you Sind sie Yasir al-Maribi? Speak you English
Sprechen sie Englisch?

I am a Ich bin (ein) friend of your sister Freund (von) deine/ihrer Schwester.
I am not sure Ich bin nicht sicher what Izdihar has war Izdihar hat about our RELATIONSHIP said über unsere RELATIONSHIP gesagt.
This might be die letzte Chance the last chance ich habe zu sprechen I have to speak mit Iz wegen durch because of future events das sein was sein wird in den Nachrichten which will be in the news (which is the same as "message" just plural?) (shookrun?).

\

A soldier has that last night of sex before deployment that's never quite as great as later claimed. And then after a tour spent getting mortared by rounds of Iranian 60s and Soviet 82s and emails from Texas, from the pregnancy announcement to photo and video attachments of the birth, he rotates home and meets the kid. Immediately, the doubts set in. This was just what the sergeant had warned him about in Fallujah.

Bringdom would be holding the kid, and her nose would remind him of Dexter's, or Malcolm's, or her expressions would recall Groin Plate Dave's, or Tibb's, or Narvaez's, or even What Did You Sayyid's, and they were dead. It was as if all of Bringdom's unit had fathered his child, sneaking out of their outposts silent, invisible, like Paiute Indians in a ghostdance, going all the way with Rachel-Anne and back before rollcall. He imagined his girl at 8, or 12, 16, or at his age of 22. Suddenly, after beating him in H-O-R-S-E, or correcting him after he called it The HBO, she'd get that smirk, and it'd be like the sergeant's latrine smirk.

Once, after Rachel-Anne had put their daughter down for a nap, Bringdom confessed all this, but Rachel-Anne just laughed it off. 'Stupid ain't sexy, hero.'

He brought it up again a day later after Rachel-Anne had returned from working a double at the Kmart pharm to find their daughter still awake and bawling. And Rachel-Anne bawled too, this time. 'Don't matter what you think, Daddy. What matters is what she thinks of you.'

—Caleb Krast, *Bringdom's War*

\

Vienna's Mater, its uberous mothering Venus—among the world's oldest and most perfectly preserved fertility figures—is not to be found among all the Rubens and Bruegel and Roman and Greek and Egyptian antiquities at the Kunsthistorisches Museum, but rather just across the park, with the mammoth taxidermy and Diplodocus and tektites and diamonds and ores, at the Naturhistorisches Museum—as if the Venus hadn't merely been dug from the Danubian loess, but had been created by it. As if She were Nature Herself. Too divine to have been made by mortals. Too fundamental to be grappled with as art. Her limestone is oolitic, meaning its sediment is compounded of ovular grains that tend to crack and crumble and leave behind dimples, one of which serves ingeniously as Her navel. Loads of that stone are found throughout Europe, but never in the Alps of Lower Austria. Also, not only is the Venus's tint not native to lime, but that Martian red ochre can't even be derived from local materials. Note that while the figure's steats and teats and utter facelessness are on display, the head is concealed under a crowning spiral. Some interpret this as plaited hair, concentric braiding. Others, as some sort of pious covering. Regardless, any creator expert enough to have carved a fully sprouted scalp or raveled scarf would certainly have been capable of carving eyes and ears and mouth features too, it's just that he—most scholars, being male, have assumed a male—for whatever reasons chose not to. And so it would seem that everything about the Venus's appearance is equally intentional and inexplicable. She, being faceless, was never an individual, and any tribe that might've idealized Her is gone now. She's outlived herself both as a goddess possessing and an idol possessed, as a deity to be appeased and an apotropaic symbol. The only identity of Hers that still survives is that of immigrant. Of foreigner.

(SOURCES: a docent who conducted a tour in English. *The Birth of Fertility: Artifacts, Geofacts, and the Male Imagination,* Alana Hampur, PhD.)

10/18

Glass. What do I know about glass?

The problem with the most effective glass treatments, the coatings and such that protect the best from abrasions and deflect the most harmful waves and rays, is that with age they muddle the glass, and if reapplied will only muddle it further. Here's how I know that problem, Iz—from being a husband and son and writer and liar.

Facts are of a similar solution. Facts protect and deflect until they cloud over and dirty our wonder.

What else, Iz? Pane sizes are measured in "generations." The larger the pane, the higher its "gen," as the abbrev goes. But the scale has never been globally standardized.

I was on the wrong side of the Danube—in the Floridsdorf district, which had no flowers. Just stunted trees screening the properties of hypermarkets and malls.

I sped through the cold along either Birefringenstraße or Birefringengasse or Birefringenstrasse or Birefringengaße—I'm forgetting whether it's the "ß" or "ss" after a long or short vowel. Anyway, all the intersecting roads were numbered, as unimaginative as their paving bricks.

I paused at the pylons marking the Zulieferung/Livraisons/Deliveries entrance for the glassworks, taking in the grounds—evened hedges, an azimuth of lawn mowed level, and a monumental vitreous gridshell that enclosed a mirrored cube. The Personal/Personnel/Staff entrance was up a grated ramp suspended through a tube. It all reeked of resiliency tests, ductility and tensility trials, research and tech development. A facility as transparent as this would only be into pane design—the manufacturing itself would be confined to that mythically silicic slave island called Off-site, floating through a minor sea of the Indies.

I paced the parkinglot, and counted the cars. No one bothered me. No one had to. The spyquip swiveled noiselessly. It would've been insane to charge inside all American slovenly, demanding an audience with an employee, the brother of an ersatz lover. I might as well have thrown a brick, a cobblestone, a rock.

I counted the clouds in the car windows, but none had the reflection I was after. I stood at the curb shivering that face to mind—Yasir's.

But my only memory was of that blemish, a red nevus like a crescent curving left in the middle of his dark bulb head—or, because the site thumbnail I'd tetrated at the Staatsbibliothek would've reversed it, curving right. He'd been scarred in the lab, an experiment with acids gone awry, or else back in an Arab Nationalist phase, which I'm also inventing, Allah was still God but Marx and Lenin had become His prophets, and Yasir had been in an accident while smuggling dynamite to Aden from Sana'a.

If I found him, offline flesh found him, I wouldn't introduce myself. I'd just follow him until he led me to Iz, who'd know how to introduce me. Because she knew me. I was a savior, a suitor, a bum—the fallen sharer of her airmattress, his floor.

I kept a vigil for his crescent as employees ramped down to the grass, shrugging lodens over labcoats, slinging IDs.

I stepped to the pave and wavered there between a Fiat and what wasn't a Fiat.

The sun fell to a beheading, dusk was bleeding out.

A dozen middleaged Arabs were lugging rugs rolled like blueprints. They headed toward what had to be the hedge closest to Mecca and spread them on the green.

They reached under their paunches for beltclipped pdas—not even, half of them still had flipphones—and flipping them agape held them up to the sky, as if seeking reception, a signal from a tower or heaven itself, approving of the time. Then they fussed up their belts and assumed the knees, the fourth prayer of the day.

White men, inured to the fervor, hurried to their VWs and Opels and Škodas. A lot of them drove Škoda hatchbacks in Alpine white, and I couldn't tell them apart, the cars, I mean—it was amazing they could all tell their cars apart.

The Arabs finished with their worship, rugged up, and lined for the mustering buses. Drivers were reversing the placards in their windshields, from indicating Birefringen and Schott and Siemens and Strabag AGs, to indicating the districts. About half the worshippers, about six or so, were lining up for the bus to Josefstadt-Neubau-Mariahilf, and I hustled over to get behind them, as a man up front turned to chat—Yasir. It was brother Yasir—I'd lay my hand on an ereader loading the Koran and swear to Mohammed about all of this.

Yasir was friendly with the Arabs, and even religious in his way—not enough to have prostrated with them, but enough to have waited for the concluding rakat. All his lapsed coworkers and even the driver had stood without complaint, as if it were a sin to depart before the As-Salaamu Alaykum. Toward the right and left. Toward Mecca again. The busdoors sighed out, for boarding. I was hoping the seats outnumbered the crowd.

I drudged the aisle past drowsing, txting, calling—my presence was the least of their cares. I was lost, or had lost my license to booze or drugs, or my Audi or Saab to a divorce, or else I was reconnoitering the commute as a consultant, for ways to reduce its costs. Whichever it was, they rebuffed me. Yasir and his seatmate were engaged, not in whispers, but also not in German, and though he didn't even raise his mad scientist dome as I went by, I felt his forehead measure me, that stain like a voracious sensor.

I settled into the nosebleed row of empties, alone on the aisle. I had only the backs of their heads, carpet bunches of skin, treadless tires. Bridge congestion. Stops.

Yasir got off with a few coworkers who'd kept the faith and a few who hadn't, and an unemployed Jew in a straightjacket suit—I crossed the street and down the block. They peeled off in all directions. Petting unripe melons at the markets, laying dominoes for khat, or just sitting by the TV in the movie of their lives, for me, their only standingroom audience. Yasir slipped into a joint booming ghetto lute music and tacked with kebab posters in lieu of menus, its Biohalal Geöffnet sign drooping its plug onto the polyvinyl, dim.

I dawdled catercorner in front of a clothingmart, until its proprietor leaned out to spit a husk of sunflower seed. I moved nextdoor, the other nextdoor. Bazaars of adhan chronometers, qibla compasses, digi misbahas, that collapsible thing you rest your book on, a rehal. Another prop wielded a pikstik to beat the rainwater off his awning.

Yasir stepped out through the flap of the plastic tarp tent for sidewalk dining, holding a brownbag flat because its bottom was spotting greasy.

We went on until we came to what Vienna calls a Trafik, apparently, a boxy phoneboothesque kiosk, a newsagent. The sign atop it, Maribi.

The clerk, who must've been late or just impatient for a bathroom, bowed under the counter, removed his apron and embraced it around Yasir, and Yasir, who wouldn't bow, but lifted the counter, became the clerk—next shift.

What Yasir did was: took a razorblade and slit the brownbag into a placemat, chewed at a tangle of red drumsticks shaped like Austria. Then he folded the placemat over the bones, wedged the parcel behind the racks. He cracked the beverage cooler for a bucket and squeegee. Then it was lifting the counter and out again to swipe at the plexiplastered ads on the side (the lotto), the rear (budget airfare), the side (the lotto), and the sliding partition (between the automat pennants).

What else: he sold some papers and magazines, some stamps, candies and tickets for the bahn or tram, Almdudlers, Red Bulls, and diapers. Individual diapers. A customer brought in a blender and he repaired it. Atop the coingrimed counter. Yasir fixed a watch, toolless. But it might've been his watch.

He batched the papers and mags now a day deceased and bound them in twine and stacked them tidy for curbside burial.

But only after he'd hopped up on them, for the height to lower the Trafik's shutter—he strained. And I would've helped. If I hadn't been his size, or strange to him. The lock he used was like the U-type, for bicycles.

Yasir zipped his jacket, and turned the corner, so I did too, turned it for blocks. His apron flared out behind him. I kept up, kept studying him, and tried to adopt his shambles of a stride so as not to alarm the night. The engine misfiring was inside me, my heart.

He stopped at a middle house. A flypaper façade of swatted windows. This was a man who didn't bring his glass home with him. I stomped for warmth, and for a light that wasn't the moon's, which wasn't at crescent, or full, but half.

I went up to the door and read the slapdash stickered buzzers. Their names were twinned, written in this script and then repeated below in a script resembling my testing this pen, licking its tip then testing again. Maribi. All pens at the very end of their ink begin to write in Arabic.

At a middle floor a light went on. No shadow child. No revenant wife. And then curtains were drawn like how Moms lets down her hair.

\

The oldest representations of the human: that their physiques remain consistent throughout the Upper Paleolithic augurs for a religious explanation, while the fact that their materials, sizes, postures, and adornments vary considerably within that period augurs for an artistic inspiration as well. Still, yet another theory is more practical. They're maps, itineraries, schedules, lessons in that most primitive school, the body. A culture might've chipped the softness of the human form from out of hardness as a lesson for its children or even for posterity, to show what it too will inevitably suffer, the swell of pregnancy, starvation, dehydration, disease, all burst at once in the selfsame corpus. If this were true, however, there would've been a tale that interpreted all the massed tragic layers, the strata. There would've been an encryption key, to enable the deciphering of the intricate systems of nicks and knaps since lost to hydraulics, aeolian processes, and time. Which brings us to the issue of value. Given that all pebbles are primordial, age can't determine worth, rather it's the hand, the presence of the human hand, which cuts from red tuff the stuff that merits enshrining. It's this intentionality or, better, mindful guidance, which distinguishes nature from both religion and art. A sedimentary hunk cleaved by wind or water tells nothing, while a hunk cleaved by a human who'd lived with the imperative to make tells all. But then there are still a handful of rocks that might go either way—rocks that some "read" as anthropomorphic, undoubtedly purposefully shaped ("artifacts"), and that others "read" as the result of tectonic accidents, of convergences of erosion, spall, and aberrant psychologies ("geofacts"). What some regard as an intentional slice or whittle—a woman's waist or limb—others regard as the wishful incidents of weather, tidal salinities, volcanic spews, ground mineral grinding mineral. See what you want to see, hear what you want to hear, whatever you search for, you find. And the more controversial specimens have been found in Israel, mostly by Arab children.

(SOURCES: *The Birth of Fertility: Artifacts, Geofacts, and the Male Imagination,* Alana Hampur, PhD. My mother, my loneliness, winter.)

10/19–10/20–

Museum hours remain the same, but prayer hours are subject to change. Gods don't take a day off, the sun just leaves earlier. The clouds. The clouds weigh gravid.

Out of my hostel the Trafik was a right and a left and between the turns, a bridge like a gangrenous rainbow over the Wienfluss.

A minority cleft, a migrant clave, posteverywar buildings to accommodate any ethnicity. In the yards weeding intervenient to the units of whatever the German term is, Socialistcommunistworkerhousingthebalconiesarefalling, the laundry was being taken in, colorless veils and shawls like photos hung dripping but not yet developed.

All of this neighborhood might as well have been downtown Jewish NY at the turn of last century—here was the same stage of nascent assimilation—just translate the Yiddish, switch around the referents, and update the technologies. Easier times, simpler times, tenements, peddler carts—what's the Arabic for "egg creams"? the Persian for "spaldeens"? Bundled boys were choosing sides for a game that involved kicking a punctured tire. Then they were kicking each other. Scarves waved. Penalties.

Yasir wasn't at the Trafik. Only one of us was early or late, for an appointment only one of us had made. The other clerk was working. The clerk from earlier. Describe him later. Describe how all day he was on the headset phone talking bluetoothed Arabic that no foreigner would ever be able to tell whether he was delighted or enraged.

Was he Yasir's nephew? And so Iz's cousin? Yasir's son? How old? Still plenty young to busy with the future. He was too consumed with not becoming his father or uncle or cousin to be troubled by me—he wouldn't still be moonlighting at our age.

I stroked the glossies, rubbed the ink from the print. The Trafik carried only a few German/Austrian titles: *Kronen Zeitung, Kurier, Die Presse, Die Standard, Wiener Zeitung, Der Spiegel, Vogue, Glamour,* a few copies each.

The rest of the papers were folded into racks as if in the alphabetical order of my incomprehension, from tabloids in Turkish to broadsheets of abjad, and in that emoticonese I think is Sinhalese, and in that zodiac handicap signage I think is Amharic. Papers in languages left to right and right to left. And verticalized until continued, next page. They must've published out of London or Paris or Berlin, because boxed above their prices in both euros and pounds were weathermaps of London and Paris and Berlin and it was raining.

And that was the good news, which readers never trusted or skipped. The bad news was that elections were rigged, bribery scandals were sanctioned, and schools and social services had been suspended in cities that readers would never return to. Something happened to 16 somewhere somewhen, something happened to 30,000. Also, Israel.

I was pleased to find the classifieds healthy, and the backgammon column still thrives.

I wasn't going to leave this Trafik until the work I'd done with Principal was public—until I recognized the headline of every frontpage as my own writing, and my outdated groomed promo bookphoto made the cover of every periodical in stock.

And then he'd recognize me, and nod, and I'd nod back—not him, Yasir.

The clerk was talking, but some to me, some to his headset: "Heast, Oida—du Penner—wos wüst?"

I said, "Ich spreche kein Arabisch. Nicht Arabisch?"

He chewed at his cheek and gestured my putting down the mag he'd doubted I could afford and now was sure I couldn't read—another issue with a centerfold on Principal's birthday.

I reracked it and showed him my empty pack of Camel Lights. Put money in the dish. Change came back in the dish, along with a fresh pack of, I'll live, Camel Regulars. I reached into the cooler for a beer, an Ottakringer. Put money in the dish. Change came back in the dish. He popped the cap with a countermounted popper like a rusty torture chamber contraption. Worst thing about Europe is that you have to pay for matches.

Around the block again, a two cig walk. I would've liked to dump that sour warm beer over the cold, be done with it.

I went and stood outside Yasir's building in another window's light as all the desires I'd been feeling constellated into the desire just to stand there, within them, under that haloing light, to prove that I could, that I could be faithful—to anything, to myself.

According to the Muslim press it was 1432. And by the Jews it'd just turned 5772.

It's as if, simultaneous with the invention of printing, the last uninhabited planet in the Tau Ceti system was being colonized by cyborgs.

I tried to explain Yasir's absence, but I didn't have his schedule. Anyway—the next night, he was there.

He seemed fit, at ease. Disinterested in me. I stood by the Alawwam Obst + Gemüse produce market, holding this notebook like a shopping-list, and watched, and wrote, and watched. The streaks of blood to the right and left of this sentence, this paragraph, are from the grapes I snuck, and crushed.

Because you were there, Iz. Without warning, you were across the street from me and swaying toward the Trafik. Though I wasn't certain it was you initially. And my rationale for it not being you was that I saw your face. If it was recognizably your face, then it wasn't yours, or it wasn't only yours anymore. Unmasked. Healed. Keen. Breathing. You seemed happy.

Your skirt just touched the knee. It was a black skirt riding up at the rear and crimped twisted at the waist, and you leaned by a bugswarmed lamppost to adjust it. Black wool pointelle sweater, I'd bought that too. Zara, The Gap.

The heels, haute heels for an evening errand, were opentoed. Your raintoes, Iz. Your head covered in a red wetcolored scarf. Because a freezing rain will make anyone pious.

You weren't wearing a coat, though. You never did like that coat.

You carried a tray of brass, clung around with foil. You set it down in front of your brother on the snackclogged counter you barely reached.

You exchanged a word. And then he leaned over and tied your headscarf. Cinching it tighter, pinching your cheek. Then you brought yourself to the corner and crossed away from me.

Iz, I didn't chase you—rather I'd already chased you, but now that I was seeing you wet to the skin I realized it wasn't you that I'd been after. It was a dream. It was another life. It was forgiveness—it was to be forgiven.

I approached your brother, and crowded him under his canopy. He was hunched over a calculator, fluttering receipts.

"I'm Joshua," I said.

Before this, only his stain had addressed me, but now I had the man. Bewildered.

“So let me have a paper,” I said. “A newspaper.”

Yasir pointed, his mouth exhuming a relict tongue. “But all are German.”

“Not all of them. But that’s not what I mean. Just give me one. It’s not for me.”

“What one?” Yasir said. “Who?”

I went with a *Wiener Zeitung*, thick as a blanket. Put two coins in the dish, or atop the dish you’d brought still wrapped and steaming, Iz, and let any change due back to me be his.

My blessings.

://

Dear Cal,

I might not be the best person to caution you against dreaming. Or to give any writing advice. Or even to be reading you. Particularly now. And anyway I'd rather get paid to do this up as a critical essay, review the living shit out of you for—what's that paper the homeless sell, *Street News*? Or does *Beaver Hunt* still publish? Cal. It's not like either of us have finished every single book we've ever reviewed. All dreams in books are typeset in italics, that handwriting that during the Renaissance (15th to 17th centuries, also M&W 10:35–11:50 612 Philosophy Hall, Dr. Gerds) developed into the earliest fonts for the earliest books from the Latin and Greek, and so Antiquity was a dream, that's all I've got to offer. Truth is, I've never actually cared about dreams, and anytime I get to them in a book I feel cheated, even worse than I feel cheated by flashbacks, because at least in flashback the present revisits the past to further nuance itself into future (like we'd slum out to the Bowery today not to meet new friends but to toast the friends we wouldn't meet who are out in Westchester and sad), while dreams just float or unfloat as timeless spaceless inconsequentials, meaning everything, meaning nothing, not beholden, never beholden, the fuckers (everyone dreams in Westchester). But hey, this oneiric somnic verbigerage can't be of interest to anyone I'm not sleeping with. And I'm not sleeping.

Cal, this is not an email I'm ever going to send—this isn't even a letter, Dear—and anyway I can't send anything.

Aaron's kids passed on your ms., and I've read it—on trains and then in this "youth pension" I'm in—night after night gutting the manila (postseason joke: the Mets moved to the Philippines and changed their name to the Manila Folders), getting that glue smell and unclipping, unrubberbanding, tracing each line with the clipedge, wrapping the bands around my typing injury wrists nervously because I want it to be brilliant, I want it to be terrible—my competitiveness competing with a weak need to be transported, even entertained.

~~It's all I have with me is why, that and a passport that both is and isn't mine—bookmarking your book by my side, under my head as a pillow—reading it in cafés, museums~~

~~The night before, I came back late and the pension was closed—I'd never had the key to the front. I rung the bell labeled HAUSBESORGER, and this ogre Hungarian opened the door a gibbous swing like he'd been standing just behind it polishing the phrase "No One Will Admit Between Hour of Two and Six." He was stubborn, it must've been that hour. So, given that I was already carrying all my possessions in this nifty, recently acquired, green in every sense Amazon.com totebag—because everyone's a thief—I left,~~

It's like my standards are gone with Aar, and I'm not sure what he's told you, or whether you even wanted me to read your novel—you never asked, and you used to ask, directly—or Aar's kids just wanted to keep me amused and out of their hair (meaning Lisabeth), or flatter me and so keep me as a client (meaning Seth, who has a nose on him).

But in the event that *Bringdom* came from you, I've been giving it my all. Thorough notes will have to wait, but here:

1. you shouldn't have a sex scene longer than a page that's a dream (pp. 99–101),

2. you shouldn't have a death scene shorter than a page that's a flashback (p. 250),

3. the war theatricals have all obviously been informed by reporting, but they're too much in the fact department, the military lingo is too much especially for the abstracted Kafka or like Camus in the Sunni Triangle mood you're aiming for (let the Weinsteins or The HBO tang up the slang for the next generation of soldiers),

4. because once I was out of Chapter 2—and this is my main point—once Bringdom's PTSD and debt and failed marriage and failure to engage with his child have been effectively established in "the present," by which I mean "the topical," and the novel's deployed on this death mission account of his past, his enlistment and training, all his ballsdeep macho martyrdom antics (you'll get a Purple Heart for nonpurple prose under fire), I was doing that guiltily-flip-ahead-to-gauge-how-many-

pages-are-left-in-the-chapter thing, the guess-how-many-desert-boring-pages-are-wasted-on-this-already-wasteful-war thing, and was disappointed to find that all of them were (about war), except for the jerking-it-to-the-Kurd-girl-who-turns-into-his-mother-in-the-middle-of-a-soyfield dream, and the maybe-suicide-maybe-not-of-his-father flashback I mentioned above, which though I realize I just warned you not to use flashbacks and dreams, I meant only contextually, because in terms of content this is your truest territory: Home.

~~(And Rachel-Anne, nice touch—as perduring as the Plains, and as open as the Kmart pharmacy.~~

~~I know, I know, she's not my Rach—she's your authorial prerogative.)~~

Anyway, onto your concluding scenes. Rachel-Anne getting that call, and fainting, with all the customers just waiting. That you've written it so that readers can only suppose they know what the call's about, but can never know for sure: it'll play better with the soundtrack behind it, unison cellos and solo muted horn. That the concerned customer who pats her hand and gives her a plastic poppy is black but is never described that way and it's only made relevant by her coworker's racist comment: it's like I'm reading you sweat. This restraining tendency feels especially unfair with the decision to withhold the baby's name. Just name the baby, Cal—for me.

There's more, of course. And more about style. But then you always doubted that, style. Next time, if time and I get squared.

"With compliments and condolences—we have to be in touch" (about how to market what's basically a male violence novel to females ages 18 to 80 who together are responsible for approx 68% of all new book buying and approx 64% of all public library book borrowing in America today) (my stats are reliable),

j

\

P.S. Read this postscript first.

The way I was raised, Cal, from the earliest, was that my mother's was the only war. That what she experienced (her Yiddish would be *vos mikh hot getrofn,* "what has befallen me"), being stowed away in that Carmelite convent in southern Poland on the Czechoslovak border and beaten and enslaved, essentially, was worse than anything any other human had ever experienced, but what occurs to me now was that Moms had never insisted on this, Dad had. Only Dad would attempt to exploit her trauma in explanations of her insomnia and bedsoilings and health issues, including, of course, her infertility, or in rationalizing her lateness in picking me up from baseball practice, or in leaving the laundry in the hamper and the pantry bare. This is all to establish that from the very start of planning my book (Moms had agreed to let me interview her, but only after I'd threatened to write about her regardless), I had no impression of my father's pathologizing as anything other than an expression of his devotion to my mother, a duty that required both uxory and coddling. I'd failed to recognize his denial—abnegation, sublimation, displacement mechanism (I'm the first in my family to ever talk to a shrink) (about anything)—how my father had developed this smothering veneration in order to avoid discussing his own war. It was how he avoided anything even remotely to do with himself.

But the time to return to is 12 years ago, Cal, the research, the writing, Tel Aviv. I sat with my Tante Idit, not my aunt but my mother's first cousin, interrogating her in the parched garden of the white duplex she shared with her seething companion, a retired Maghrebi army general who resembled King Hussein of Jordan and never once said shalom to me. He blamed me for the crying—Idit was crying all the time. And her brother Menashe was crying, and he was calling his crying sister by her birthname, Yetta, and they were calling Moms by her birthname, Yocha. They answered all my questions sincerely, shamelessly, but with rivalry too—after finding out how selective of an account Moms had given me. 12 goddamned years ago.

And then it was fall already, and I was off like a thief to Poland—to Warsaw. Renting that Daewoo on Moms's MasterCard and driving it to Sobibór and Majdanek, or what Communist memorials remained of them, to Bełżec, or what Communist memorials remained of it, past the lot that'd been my mother's house in Kraków, and the convent at Chyżne that'd abused and saved her thanks to luck and her parents' money and their influence with the Kraków Judenrat, and finally across the cankered karsts of the Tatras in what'd lately been Czechoslovakia, to Vienna—from which I flew back to the States.

I stayed in NY and wrote, and went down to Jersey only to present Moms with my transcripts to confirm or deny, as the intelligencers say—but she just set down the pot she was glazing and made me promise never to print anything the cousins told me, and I agreed, or she said I agreed, and that she trusted me.

So then I went ahead and printed all of it, Cal, because that's just what we do—I'm not going to pretend it was ever a choice, but neither am I going to pretend it wasn't difficult. 9/11 pubdate, Miri pulverized, Aar gnashing out in the wilderness beyond all assuagement and phone reception, you and your fame, Cal—and then in the midst of all that, Finn came through, or Kimi! did (and what the hell ever became of Kimi!?), either one of them or just a distributor's order fulfillment robot sent Moms a finished copy. I hadn't let her read any earlier version (I'm not about to lecture you, Cal, on how agonizing it is letting others read your drafts, doubly so if they're the subject and are bound to be troubled). Moms wasn't just troubled, she was furious, but she didn't call me, she called Israel. She'd gotten online at the house around then, and she and her cousins were emailing too. She was never "raped" by the Soviet starshina, she said, because after the first time, he paid her in food, and after the last time, he paid her in a map and outlined a tentative route to where her brothers lived, where they had lived and operated branches of their family's lumber firm, in Žilina (or Sillein in German) and Brno (or Brünn). Anyway, she said, the soldier wasn't a starshina, but a podpolkovnik. Moms and Tante Idit and Onkel Menashe feuded back and forth over whether "rape" meant the same thing in Yiddish, Polish, and Russian. Whether the Red Army rank of the soldier corresponded to the Israeli Army rank of seren or segen—lieutenant colonel? full colonel? And it wasn't like I was trying to stay out of it, Cal—Moms kept me out of it, and the only way I knew anything was that the Israelis would fwd: me the emails. That's how I knew that Moms otherwise enjoyed the book, or just wouldn't admit to her cousins that she hadn't—all her emails began "Dear Yetta and Menashele," and ended with her signing herself, not Yocha, but "Love, Gloria."

I also got a letter then—through the mail, through the fanmail, Cal—forwarded from Random House, October or November, 2001. I responded, and it led to a lunch. Which led to another. Retirees transited in from the Five Towns on the Island and from Main Line Philly to have lunch with me and then go gawk at the pit downtown.

They were readers, they were my only readers—if I didn't snare the women I at least had a corner table with the only consolation demographic, geriatric Jews—but they didn't want to talk about my book. They wanted to talk about my father.

You know, I'm sure you do, Cal, how you expend all this effort writing something and thinking through the detail of every decision (do I name the restaurants we met at? or just describe them? do I mention what was ordered? who took care of the bill?), but then you finish, or you delude yourself into finishing, and realize—too late, with the book already a classic of the bargain bin—that you'd missed something, a scene or even just a line that would've brought everything together, that would've resolved all the fogs—a gesture just as crucial to your life, but also as easily forgotten in daily life, as a person you'd loved who's now dead.

My father. I'd hardly mentioned him in all my pages. Because Moms's account of their meeting had demoted him into a handsome uniform that acted swiftly. My father was like a new character introduced at the end of a book, as the end of a book—a Daddy ex machina, maybe. And it's been on my mind ever since, or—I'm trying for honesty—what'd then been a guilty notion I was in no psychological state to pursue is recurring only now, the notion that if there were to be any reissue or updated edition I would write an afterword to it, an afterword about him. And hey, a girl can dream, can't she? a girl can flashback????

David Cohen, Private First Class, US First Army, had liberated Buchenwald, where the Yiddish competency he demonstrated so impressed the OSS officers he debriefed that they took him along to interrogations at Dachau, Mauthausen, and after V-E Day, here, to Vienna, where he was attached to command—according to the oldsters I was meeting with, my father's former colleagues.

To be totally accurate, Cal, the guy who'd read my book and initially contacted me was this decorous epitomist Connecticut WASP, from rep tie to bucks with the blueblood suit between, and it was only after he'd vetted me over lunch at the Union Club that he sent the other guys my way, his octogenarian Jewish subordinates who claimed they recalled me coming up to their knees, their knees since replaced, at my father's funeral—there was a Prussian yecca type with spoon up his ass posture who as a policy refused to eat and talk or even be talked to at the same time, and then two widowers who resembled Dad biographically, being the sons of Jewish immigrants from Warsaw who grew up south of Delancey speaking Yiddish. That language had bound them together, and brought them to the captain—the WASP had retired from the OSS as a captain—for whom they interpreted interrogations of, and translated testimonies by, survivors of concentration and labor camps, which were cited extensively in the subsequent war crimes tribunals.

Cal, they were filling in a man I had never known. A man my mother, reciting the shameless sanitized version of this story, the Story, had never known either—or had forgotten with her arrival in Jersey, her renaming as Gloria, her infirmities (avitaminosis) (stomatitis), and lack of baby, her spats with my father's parents, attempts to master cooking and English by reading *Ladies' Home Journal* recipes and cooking through the irreconcilable fascinations of *The Honeymooners* and *Bonanza*.

Vienna, 1945, the latter winter of a year that'd felt all winter—my father left US Army HQ, the former Hotel Bristol, located on the Ring (after the war it became a hotel again, and now its rooms cost north of €308/night). In one direction was the recently unnamed Adolf-Hitler-Platz, in the other the recently renamed Josef-Stalin-Platz—Vienna, like Berlin, was divided into zones. But my father headed for neither. Nor did he stop at his lodgings off Kärntner Straße. Instead, he went on toward the river—Why? The downtown Jews said, Why? Because word had come in that the Danube had just frozen over, and my father wanted to check. The downtown Jews told me this as if it was unimpeachably logical, and it was, because that's who Dad was: the type of man who if you told him the river's frozen was going to want to check. There by the riverbank he met a woman—a woman who'd just walked in gaiters taken off a Wehrmacht soldier, which meant off a Wehrmacht corpse, from Poland to Žilina to Brno to Vienna (I'm in no position to record the numbers just now, Cal, but consult the book or imagine around 600 kilometers or 400 miles), and was starving and feverish and out in the incipient snow begging—Moms would never admit to begging—and who called out to him in Yiddish, *Zeit moychel,* because Dad had a face like one of her brothers, who'd died in Theresienstadt, or Auschwitz. Dad gave her chewinggum, took her for a sawdusty schnitzel at a basement café. And then maybe to his room, the downtown Jews said. Then again, maybe not. Because she was icicle skinny like a Muselmann, they said. That's what they called the people in the camps not gas exterminated but exterminated by hunger, Muselmänner. My mother was named Yocha then—did I mention that? Is this what senility is like? It was illegal to marry her. The downtown Jews said the Army might've courtmartialed my father under the GI ban on fraternization, which tended to treat brides unable to provide evidence of their identities as enemy nationals until proven innocent. But the captain said they wouldn't have dared. The yecca, that scooped asshole Prussian, who just before I closed our tab at French Roast ordered fries for takeout, said that he was the one who'd forged her papers—though, he noted, it might not have been forgery because it was done on the captain's orders—and not a Nansen Displaced Persons document either but a straight Shipley US passport that characterized the bearer as a secretarial assistant in the office of the special advisor on Austrian affairs, and falsified her age. My father was 21 and had an honorable discharge pending, Moms was—she guessed she was—16. They married, 4/16/1946, in the synagogue on Seitenstettengasse, the sole shul to survive in Vienna, in a ceremony officiated by Chaplain Rabbi Daniel S. Daniels of Worcester, MA, who died in a car wreck on I-95 in the late 1980s, on Shabbos. Back in civilian life, Dad studied actuarial science at Newark Technical School. In the gaps between assignments and a Bamberger's shift he set about tracking down Moms's relatives. Yetta had become the Hebraicized Idit, after Birkenau, but Menashe, who'd fled to Argentina, was still just Menashe—did I mention that? Am I confusing you, Cal? Moms and Dad visited them regularly in Israel—because, Moms liked to say, the Tel Avivniks were always too poor to visit us—and after I was born they brought me with them, though they went less and less, until we moved from Newark out to Shoregirt and they got up the confidence to fly without me maybe twice, because Shoregirt had a yard and picket fence and Jewish neighbors in the insurance business for me to stay by, the Tannenbaums. The last time my parents made the trip I wasn't yet 12, and I'd worked out this compromise by which I was able to spend the afterschool day at my own house all alone, but had to report to the Tannenbaums' house at dinnertime each night, for boiled chicken "cacciatore," kugel "moussaka," a dessert review of my bar mitzvah portion, and bed. Then my parents returned, and the back muscle that Dad had strained—from having lifted their suitcases loaded with a copy of Walt Whitman's *Bletlekh groz* for Menashe and bras for Idit and cameras and camcorders for all their children and grandchildren—was diagnosed as a lung sarcoma, and all the traveling they did after that was to Sloan Kettering. My father refused to die only because it meant leaving my mother, but what was truly remarkable was that he'd lived that way too, which was why he'd never attended the reunions, and only met his army friends on worktrips to NY, and at his funeral—he had to be there anyway.

\

You can't fly anywhere, anywhen, from Vienna.

Or you can, but it's never cheap. To JFK, Washington-Dulles, Chicago-O'Hare. Connections in Amsterdam, Brussels, or Frankfurt knock a schilling off the price. There was also a layover option via Budapest. Layovernight. Tuesdays were the most affordable days to fly. Still, I was barely able to afford London on a Tuesday, noon. Vienna–London–Toronto–LaGuardia, more than 20 hours, eight procedurals, six sitcoms, four films with their plane fatalities edited out, four meals (or "snackboxes").

I wasn't checking luggage but if the clerk found that suspicious she didn't say.

Let her just try and check this prose, let everyone.

Vienna—I slotted Principal's passport into an aperture fit for transacting with an ulcerous deli clerk out on a drug corner. The guard took it and swiped it and flipped his interest through, in a way that convinced me of his scrutiny, so I said, "I get that all the time," and either he didn't find that hilarious or it wasn't hilarious or he was just keeping busy for the surveillance scrutinizing him, then waved me through.

On the other side, in the immigration zigzag in NY—CNNing all around with Afghan dronestrikes, and then as a teaser before commercial break, which realityshow celeb really and showily got tossed out of a Manhattan Gopal store for cutting in line?

But then it was my turn to passport the officer, so I said, "I get that all the time," which got a grin. "You must be the 10th guy who's said that today."

Just then I recalled how I always used to like having my passport stamped. It fixed my persona. Nailed my being down. So I asked the officer for a stamp.

And he answered by saying, "I'd love to, friend, but they're phasing out that ink stuff."

Customs was/were: spit thrice over your shoulder when anyone praises you, knock wood twice when praising yourself. Another line, another form handed over, smudged with Moms's addy, permanent addy.

I went out into the chill, cab exhaust.

I joined the queue, waited, though I guess I could've called the agency, collect, could've had Lisabeth or Seth spring for a livery out of pity, shave and a haircut, suite at the Plaza, a sandwich. But I wanted to continue on my own—wanted Jersey, mother, buffer.

The expediter was a deadringer for La Guardia, the mayor, but with cornrows—"Where you going?"

"Jersey," I said.

She sneered borough cred, directed me with her middlefinger down the idlers.

Aar, leaving a client's afterafterparty, a launch, or reading—he'd get into a cab and say to the driver, "Take me to work with you," or "Take me somewhere we can be alone," and I miss that something wretched.

I, with my no balls, just told the driver how to drive but he demanded the addy and knucked it into his GPS, which calculated the same distance and time and directions that I had, and then he said how much, off meter, and that was as much as he said.

Nasty habit. It used to be that every time I'd take a cab there would come this moment, this intersection, and Rach hated it—when I couldn't help but talk, couldn't help but engage the driver, and some of that is a Jew thing, but some certainly was all that white baggage, which won't fit in any trunk—wanting to show the driver that I held by what that Berber slave playwright once wrote, nothing human was alien to me, nothing was strange, or rattling, wanting to show respect by talking politics domestic and foreign, I'd be honored by his opinions, because they came from a land in which opinions were criminal, a land I'd never get any closer to than now—a mangled divider between us.

But for whatever reason, this trip—for two hours in gutimpacting traffic—I didn't.

After the negotiation only the GPS talked, voicing my welcome homescape in Arabic. Every lanechange or so a familiarity would surface, Semitic fricatives, faucal honkings of phlegm, and then "I-95, NJ Turnpike." The rusting midtide marsh, dead fish methane waft, an egret balanced onefooted out in that muck like it'd have to be crazy to step full in. A Canaanite hairball, then "Garden State Parkway."

Through the Pinebarrens saying nothing and with nothing said unmechanical—maybe that, just that, was dignity.

Or I did say something, once we got to the house.

Some things like "I got your money inside," OK, "Come in and use the bathroom, if you have to," no thanks.

Which spared him having to witness me begging my mother for money (the hug, the kiss, the beg). I was embarrassed, sure, but only because she was embarrassed for me, and disapproved, and disapproved of what I was being charged, went for her clutch, and that earthenware bowl for tzedakah I'd forgotten, and finally outside to beat down the price. I collapsed. Never even got the driver's face.

11/15 or 16, everything broke. The *Post* headline was punny enough, "Balk-Mail!" The *Daily News* went with "Tetraitors!" You know the rest—everyone knows.

Moms paid for my two Heinekens and Camels. The only thought I had I thought daily, twice—what a beautiful name for a convenience store, Wawa.

\

Basically at that point it ends.

And then the phone rang.

Moms said it hadn't rung like that since September. I had mail from back then too and I signed the enclosed papers and got an envelope and stamp from Moms and included a note to Rach asking what I owed her, and promising her that whatever else had to be done, she'd be able to find me. I walked over to the postoffice. And by the time I'd walked back they were outside, CNN, Fox News, MSNBC, ABC, CBS, NY1, and our porch was on the TV in the livingroom and Moms was having a fit about how the stoop was chipped and leaves were clogging the gutters. Leaksmen—the organization that claimed responsibility for releasing the recording files, my transcriptions of them, my attempts at shaping them into Principal's life, and the diary I kept of my own life in the Emirates—was headed by a dual Australian Swiss citizen by the name of Anders Maleksen. Descramble Maleksen—get Leaksmen.

An anonymous source of the senior American intelligence official type stated that the organization was a Russian front, and that Maleksen was the field alias of FSB agent Daniil Kalemov, who'd been assigned to infiltrate b-Leaks by providing documents regarding Israeli nuclear capability that now appear to be Kremlin forgeries. Whether he entrapped Balk in the rape charges or not, he certainly arranged for the flight from Copenhagen and asylum in the Russian embassy in Reykjavík. No comment from b-Leaks. Which is to say, no comment from Balk.

People kept knocking at the door asking to help or be helped, to share their findings about how the C band electromagnetic range used for wifi transmissions stimulated the growth of or even implanted parasitic worms called "cestodians," which track our movements, diets, cyberchondria. Moms said that a person in a Jersey Central Power & Light uniform who'd resembled Kalemov or Maleksen but was maybe shorter and with a bit of a stomach and very polite and so maybe it wasn't him, had stopped by about two weeks or even a month ago now "to read the meter."

She wouldn't trust any news that would trust me as a source.

A body was hauled out of the river Ganges, Varanasi, India, 11/19 or 20, apparently. This was just downstream from the Manikarnika Ghat, the main crematorium ghat, a perpetual stream of burning bodies plunging down the stairs but not plashing at bottom because by the bottom all was ash, a cloud of flies scattering across the waters.

I can only assume that the Indian authorities wouldn't ordinarily bother with a floater, but he was white, or what was left of him was white, apparently. Other or the same Indian authorities, evincing impressive operational prerogative, ordered an autopsy that determined the COD as accidental/suicide, ordered a DNA test and copied both the results and report to the US State Department, which matched the genetic markers as being Principal's. Sari Apt Le Vay petitioned for the body's return, but it was in such a bitten crocodilian or ultimately imaginary condition that it was cremated, not at the Manikarnika but in a facility. No pics or vids of the body exist or have—like a missing pancreas—leaked yet.

It was Moe all over again—but because I switched off the TV after PBS had on Seth without Lisabeth, I can only piece this together from scrap bits of the *Asbury Park Press,* the *NJ Jewish News,* and whatever general interest nonpotting rags Moms still subscribes to, though delivery's been iffy. And the house modem, which has been broken since I got here—Moms doesn't even remember it breaking.

I couldn't go to Wawa and couldn't have Moms go for me, so I quit drinking, quit smoking, I guess. I made myself useful in the attic department, heirloom rearrangements. Suddenly everything heavy in the house had to be moved. The coverage didn't leave the lawn until purdah season's winter storm advisory.

Cal called and left a msg, and I still haven't gotten back to him. Finn called and left a msg saying he'd consider a reprint of my book, be sure to be in touch.

I haven't been. I never made a statement—I wrote.

Consider this: A dozen Moes crashed Principal's "medimorial" (meditation memorial) held at the Tetplex, four of them legally named Vishnu, and one even named Vishnu Fernandes. Cullen de Groeve and Owmar O'Quinn read a selection from the Tibetan Book of the Dead: "Void cannot injure void, the qualityless cannot injure the qualityless."

Kori Dienerowitz did not attend due to a prior commitment in Bermuda, a premature retirement with prosecutorial immunity.

A Pew Research poll, of around this date, queried a responsible sampling of Americans as to whether their government's online surveillance initiatives were justified (62%)? or unjustified (28%)? with only 10% undecided.

Into December, another whitish body washed up in a drainage culvert at the Verna Industrial Estate, Goa, and the boy who found it, shockingly recognizing his find, posted the pics and vids online, which were reasonably convincing, according to the convinced: Principal, already decaying. Anyway, something happened next like the boy's father without contacting anyone, perhaps without even being privy to his son's exploits, tried selling the body. But he was caught. Or the guy who'd bought it from him and contacted Sari Apt Le Vay was caught, the body taken into custody or whatever, but lost before tests, according to the tabloids. Subsequent corpses turned up in Cairo, Lisbon, Kifl Haris outside Nablus (Palestinian Territories). The great wheel turned and memed. Live in the flesh spottings in Brazil were a thing. Principal was a wayfarer in a Finnish disco. The wheel was turning me 40. A child was born in Kanazawa, Ishikawa, whose soul was recognized as his.

://